ROYAL FLUSH
&
SLEEPING CRUELTY

ALSO BY LYNDA LA PLANTE

The Legacy
The Talisman
Bella Mafia
Entwined
Cold Shoulder
Cold Blood
Cold Heart

Prime Suspect
Seekers
She's Out
The Governor
The Governor II
Trial and Retribution
Trial and Retribution II
Trial and Retribution III
Trial and Retribution IV
Trial and Retribution V

Lynda La Plante was born in Liverpool. She trained for the stage at RADA and worked with the National Theatre and the RSC, before becoming a television actress. She then turned to writing – and made her breakthrough with the phenomenally successful TV series *Widows*.

She has written eight subsequent bestselling novels, *The Legacy*, *The Talisman*, *Bella Mafia*, *Entwined*, *Cold Shoulder*, *Cold Blood*, *Cold Heart* and *Sleeping Cruelty*. Her original script for the much-acclaimed *Prime Suspect* won awards from BAFTA, British Broadcasting and the Royal Television Society, as well as the 1993 Edgar Allan Poe Writer's award.

Lynda La Plante also received the Contribution to the Media award by Women in Film, a BAFTA and an Emmy for the drama series *Prime Suspect 3*. She has been made an honorary fellow of the British Film Institute and was given the BAFTA Dennis Potter Writer's Award 2000.

LYNDA LA PLANTE

ROYAL FLUSH & SLEEPING CRUELTY

PAN BOOKS

Royal Flush first published 2002 by Macmillan.
First published by Pan Books 2003
Sleeping Cruelty first published 2000 by Macmillan.
First published by Pan Books 2003

This omnibus edition published 2004 by Pan Books
an imprint of Pan Macmillan Ltd
Pan Macmillan, 20 New Wharf Road, London N1 9RR
Basingstoke and Oxford
Associated companies throughout the world
www.panmacmillan.com

ISBN 0 330 43925 1

1 3 5 7 9 8 6 4 2

A CIP catalogue record for this book is available from
the British Library.

Typeset by SetSystems Ltd, Saffron Walden, Essex
Printed and bound in Great Britain by
Mackays of Chatham plc, Chatham, Kent

ROYAL FLUSH

I dedicate *Royal Flush* to my two racing partners, Stephen Ross and Duncan Heath. We are: Action Bloodstock. We've had some lucky and exhilarating times as well as a few bad days but overall the sheer joy our racehorses have brought us has been worth every hard-earned cent. I wish my partners good fortune, good health and may the three of us one day have a Derby winner.

ACKNOWLEDGEMENTS

I would like to thank the many people who helped research and authenticate much of the action in *Royal Flush*. Very special thanks go to John Gosden, my own trainer, and to Annette and Andy Dive, Emmanuel Coste, Peter Middleton, Clive Driver, Jessica Cobham, Ann Duggan, Dr Ian Hill, Stephen Ross and Andrew Bennett-Smith, Matthew Tucker and Steve Nicholls.

I would also like to thank my steadfast team at La Plante Productions, especially Lucy Hillard who runs the research department and had the job of coordinating all of the research contacts for me to meet. I would also like to thank Kate Fletcher, Kerry Appleyard and Jocelyn Cornforth.

As always, a thank you to my wonderful agent Gill Coleridge and all at Rogers, Coleridge and White and my thanks also to Philippa McEwan, Imogen Taylor and the terrific backup at Pan Macmillan, as well as my steadfast editor of many years, Hazel Orme.

PROLOGUE

THE INFAMOUS Krays and Richardsons dominated London's gangland during the 1950s and 1960s, but now, with a modern police force, the crime lords' empires have crumbled. The king pins have all been banged up for twenty to thirty years, their exploits fodder now for TV documentaries, movies and memoirs written from their cells or on their deathbeds. Their territories have been taken over by the Triads, the Yardies, and the Russian and Italian Mafia. Drug-related crime undermines every major city in England.

But did the police really break the old underworld? Are all of the true perpetrators languishing in prison or at peace in cemeteries? Were those who escaped arrest by fleeing to sunny Spain or Brazil as important to their plots as they continue to tell the press? The proceeds of many robberies have never been recovered. Gold bullion worth millions has disappeared without trace. Where is this bounty? Will the answer to the mystery remain shrouded for ever in secrecy?

The police crime squads of the 1960s maintained that a 'Mr Big' was behind the great criminal operations of that time, and rumours about his hidden fortune were rife. No one arrested, either in England, Spain or Brazil, has ever disclosed any information about him, so if he existed, he must have had the power and the shrewdness to protect his anonymity. He would have had to surround himself with an élite group of trusted 'soldiers', men trained to instil such fear in others that those who knew him kept their silence, even when facing lifelong prison sentences.

Those who believed that one man alone was responsible for these robberies nicknamed this shadow figure the 'Colonel'. Some said he owed his title to the military precision with which he executed his crimes. Others whispered that he had once been in the Army.

Forty years on, the officers of the old robbery squads have retired, and the mystery of the Colonel is no longer of any interest. No movie or biography of any famous villain, from Freddie Foreman to Reggie Kray, has ever referred to him. It is indeed as if he never existed. But what if he did?

CHAPTER 1

JUNE 2001, and Royal Ascot was into its third day, the crowds enjoying the unusually warm sunny weather. The ladies, in extravagant hats and escorted by men in morning suits, were a sea of colour, and the champagne was flowing as the affluent headed for the private boxes or to the Royal Enclosure. The atmosphere was almost of carnival, intensified by clowns on stilts and booths selling racing memorabilia. On the central bandstand a brass band was warming up, and the aroma of fish and chips hung on the air. Ascot week brought out racing enthusiasts from every walk of life and today Her Majesty the Queen was present: one of her own horses was running.

Outside the racetrack Rolls-Royces, Bentleys and Mercedes queued with buses, coaches and family saloons for the car parks. The one closest to the main entrance gates was for owners and trainers, and rows of attendants examined the passes displayed on car windscreens. Police and racecourse stewards were directing pedestrians over a crossing that led to the gates and turnstiles, the stewards in old-fashioned bowler hats, smart black suits, white shirts and, as requested by the track officials, sober ties.

Christina de Jersey, in her husband's navy Corniche

3

with her two teenage daughters and two of their friends, pulled into the owners' and trainers' car park. The girls all wore large straw hats bedecked with flowers, but Christina's, which had been designed especially for the day, was in the boot. She and her husband had invited several guests to lunch in their box and she had overseen the menu with the usual meticulous care. It was not twelve o'clock yet, but she had set off early to avoid the even greater crush that would ensue nearer to the start of the first race. She had wanted time to check the table and, of course, to greet her guests.

A couple of hours earlier Edward de Jersey had piloted his jockey Mickey Rowland and trainer Donald Fleming to the track in his helicopter. In his morning suit he cut a striking figure at almost six feet three with broad strong shoulders. At fifty-seven he was still athletic and exceptionally fit from his daily exercising of his vast stable of racehorses. De Jersey did not wear a grey top hat, but a black silk one with a slightly curved Victorian-style brim. From the helicopter pad, where numerous others had already landed, he made his way towards the racing stables on the far side of the track. He had a tight sensation in the pit of his stomach, even though he had kept in constant touch with his stable lads, who had travelled by road from his stud farm. He would not be satisfied until he had seen his entry, Royal Flush, for himself.

'What stall is he in?' he bellowed to the diminutive Mickey who, with Fleming, trailed behind him.

'Number four,' said Fleming, out of breath as he

caught up with de Jersey. 'They've been walking him around the back field since breakfast.'

Like de Jersey, Fleming had spoken frequently to the lads, making sure that their prize colt had not suffered any adverse effect from the journey. Royal Flush could be difficult and moody: a horse as volatile as he was might injure himself on the way in or out of the horse-box. He was to race in the three o'clock seven-furlong Chesham Stakes for two-year-olds with a £37,000 prize fund. However, de Jersey was principally interested in whether his precious colt could pull off another triumph. He had won his maiden race at Lingfield by over a furlong, a spectacular result. Royal Flush had cost a fortune but de Jersey was convinced that he was special enough to win the Derby the following year. But Royal Flush still had to prove he wasn't a one-race wonder.

Already numerous owners and trainers were checking their horses as de Jersey approached the stables. Royal Flush was draped in his blanket and appeared calm and unruffled by the hubbub around him. His two lads were on hand, and de Jersey greeted them. 'How's my boy?'

'He's been a right bugger, sir. We cladded the sides of the box but you know what he's like, tried to bite me hand off earlier – and he's been kicking and bucking. We gave him a good walkabout, though, so he's calmer now.'

De Jersey moved forward and bent close to kiss the horse's soft velvet muzzle.

'You be a good fella now.' Then he checked virtually every inch of the horse and the knot in his belly tightened. As he ran his hand over the muscular glossy flanks of his 'boy' he felt breathless with anticipation. At last, satisfied that all was in order, he went off alone to walk the track. He and Fleming knew Royal Flush's potential, but there was big competition against him for the Chesham: the Queen's horse was the favourite and the Sheikh had a runner worth over a million.

De Jersey strode along the famous racetrack, which he knew by now was perfect for his colt. It was well watered, and with the forecast of a hot summer day, he couldn't have asked for better. Royal Flush did not run well on soft ground; he liked the going to be firm.

As de Jersey headed towards the starting gates, he turned to look back down the track to the finishing post then at the stands and boxes. He half wished they had not invited so many guests to join them. If his boy wasn't placed he would be hard pushed to remain the genial host.

'Good day for it, sir.'

De Jersey turned but didn't recognize the wizened little man in his suit and bowler hat.

'Harry Smedley, sir,' the man added. 'Your lad came up earlier. Says to be sure Royal Flush goes into the starting gate last. Apparently he's got a bit of a temper on him.'

'Yes, it's imperative,' de Jersey replied. 'He doesn't like being stalled and with so many young colts there'll be a delay getting them in.'

Smedley nodded. 'I'll make sure of it. The men aren't due up here yet, not until just before the first race, but I'll warn 'em. Your lad said the ground's perfect for him too.'

'Yes, it is,' de Jersey agreed, and felt for his wallet.

'No need, sir, but let's hope he runs a good race. Certainly ran a blisterer on his maiden.'

De Jersey was eager now to make his way back down the track.

'Your dad would have been proud,' Smedley added, and gave a knowing wink. 'Right old character he was.'

Smedley reminded de Jersey of a garden gnome, with his bulbous nose and flushed cheeks.

'You knew him?' he queried.

Smedley looked baffled. 'Don't you remember? I'm Maureen Smedley's son. My family used to run the dairy at the end of your street and we was at school together. Mind you, that was before you got into the grammar school. Long while ago now, but my mother knew yours.'

De Jersey still had no recollection of the man but he nodded and smiled anyway.

Smedley moved closer to him.

'You know the corner shop just up from the dairy, two doors down from your old fella's bettin' shop? Gawd almighty, she was in and out like a ferret, my mother, never could resist a bet and with it being on her doorstep . . .' Smedley chuckled. 'You was always held up as an example to me. First, the only lad from round our way to get into the grammar school, then you went off to that officers' training place, didn't you?'

'Sandhurst.' Still de Jersey couldn't place the man.

'Your dad, he used to show us your picture in your uniform, proud as punch he was of you. Mind you, it's only 'cos I knew you way back that I've followed your career. I'd never have recognized you now, but being a

7

racing man meself, I wondered if you was him. Then I spotted you at Epsom a few years back. Your dad was a card, wasn't he?'

'He died a long time ago.'

'I know, I know, but those were the days, eh? We was at his funeral. Didn't he want his ashes sprinkled over the Epsom racetrack? I remember that, great character he was. Did you do it?'

'I'm sorry?'

'Do like he wanted, with his ashes?'

'No, they wouldn't give me permission. Well, it's been nice talking to you, Mr Smedley,' said de Jersey shortly, and half turned to walk away, only to be stopped again when the man tapped his arm.

'Harry, it's Harry, sir, eh? Funny old life, isn't it? I heard you had to leave that military college. Hurt yourself, didn't you?'

By now de Jersey was anxious to get on but Smedley had made it difficult. 'Yes, I injured my knee.'

'Fell off a horse, was it?'

'Playing polo.' Despite himself, de Jersey laughed at Smedley's persistence.

'Right, but let's face it, it must have been fate. I mean, look at you now, eh? I hadda do National Service. Life's full of surprises, isn't it?'

'It certainly is, Harry,' replied de Jersey.

'No one would ever believe it, you and I was at school together in the East End.'

'Well, not many people know,' said de Jersey. This time he withdrew his wallet and took out two fifty-pound notes. 'Have a flutter on Royal Flush for old time's sake,' he said, tucking the notes into Smedley's top pocket and, before the man could say any more, he walked off.

'Good luck today, sir,' Smedley said, and tipped his bowler hat.

De Jersey was not upset by Smedley's recall of the childhood he had left so far behind him. At any other time he might have been irritated but not today. As he walked back down the track he thought of his dapper little father, Ronnie Jersey. The 'de' had been acquired many years after his father's death: de Jersey thought it gave his name more of an upper-class ring, almost like a title, and it was hard now to detect any sign of the East End in his speech – he had acquired the deep, rather plummy tones of an aristocrat.

The injury to which Smedley had referred had destroyed any hope of a career in the Army and *perhaps* in retrospect it *had* been fate, although at the time it had almost broken de Jersey's heart. The fall had damaged his kneecap so severely he still limped and was often in pain, but he had never allowed it to interfere with his gruelling daily rides.

Down the track, Smedley was regaling one of the other stewards about his 'school pal' Edward de Jersey.

'His father ran a bookies' – in fact, he had two of 'em. Nice earners they were, but back in the fifties he had a lot of aggravation from the villains. Word was, he was forced out of business and his son took 'em over but he soon sold out. Hard to believe, isn't it? Looks a real toff now, talks like one too, but we was at school together. I tell you one thing, I'd like a share of his life. He's worth bloody millions!' Smedley would have continued but the time was drawing near for the stewards to start monitoring the track: the first horses would soon be led into the parade ring.

De Jersey headed past the winner's enclosure and through the famous hole-in-the-wall archway towards the boxes. He got into the lift to go to the third floor then walked to his double box. He paused to look over the railing at the throng below, milling around the bandstand. By now, the crowds were almost shoulder-to-shoulder and the atmosphere was good humoured, enhanced by the brass band playing a medley of old-time music-hall songs. The crowd joined in with the chorus: 'Ohhhhh, there ain't a lady living in the world that I'd swap for my dear old dutch.' As he listened, de Jersey felt the past sweep over him, and remembered his dad standing at the piano in the pub close to their terraced house. He still could not recall Smedley or the dairy, but he could picture the pub and his dad singing at the top of his voice. His dad only had the bottle to get up and sing when he'd downed several pints, his button eyes focused on his beloved wife, Florence. De Jersey laughed softly to himself as, across the years, he heard his mother say, 'Eddy, finish your chips an' get your dad's hat. We're goin' home!'

Someone brushed against his shoulder and he turned to find Lord Wilby standing next to him.

'Hello, Edward, wonderful day for it.' Wilby offered his hand and introduced his wife.

'Charming as ever,' de Jersey said to her, gave a small bow and tipped his top hat.

'How do you rate your colt's chances?' Wilby asked. He himself had two runners that day.

'Rather good, as long as he keeps his head.'

'Is Mickey Rowland on him?' Wilby checked his race card. 'Ah, yes, he's a good jockey. Saw him handle well at Lingfield.' Before they could continue their conversation, more owners were acknowledging de Jersey, and he moved on to his box.

Christina had decorated it with his racing colours, navy and white, and comfortable cushioned chairs stood around a table laid for twelve. Beyond it, on the balcony were rows of seats overlooking the track for his guests to watch the races. De Jersey's double box faced the large screen that would televise the races and was opposite the winning post. There were also television screens inside the box, where some preferred to watch the action, especially if the weather was bad. Today though, it was perfect.

At first Christina did not see her husband enter the box, as she was arranging the flowers on the table. She wore little makeup and, like her husband, was lightly tanned. No matter how many years they were together de Jersey never ceased to be amazed by how attractive he found her. She was tall, almost five ten, with long naturally platinum blonde hair, which she wore loose or caught up in a wide-toothed butterfly clip. De Jersey loved the delicate wisps that fell down to frame her perfect face, chiselled cheekbones and full mouth. However, Christina's eyes, a strikingly deep blue, were her best feature. She was de Jersey's second wife, but his first was no more now than a distant memory. He and Christina had been married for twenty years and had two children, yet she still had the body of a young woman, with a wonderfully voluptuous figure that de Jersey adored. She was Swedish and still retained the lilt of her original accent.

She was wearing a white, wide-brimmed hat, with a black band and a large bow draped down one side, a tailored white jacket, tight black pencil skirt and high-heeled black sling-back shoes. She looked cool and sophisticated. It was easy to tell that she had once been a model.

De Jersey slipped his arms around her waist and kissed her neck.

'Mind my hat,' she said, laughing.

'You look stunning,' he said. She cocked her head to one side. 'Quite tasty yourself, Mr de Jersey. Now, go and welcome your guests, there's champagne open.'

'In a moment. I was watching you and thinking what a lucky man I am. I do love you.'

She stood on tiptoe to kiss his cheek. 'Did he travel well?'

'He did, and he's behaving himself, but he's got serious competition. I'll be happy if he just gets placed.'

'He's going to win,' Christina said with certainty. Unlike her husband, however, she did not share his passion for this horse. She enjoyed riding, though, and was always encouraging at whatever race meeting they attended. Although they had been married for so long, she knew little of de Jersey's past and would have been astonished to learn that he had come from the East End. He had been in property development when they had first met and was already a very rich man, the cultured voice honed to perfection. Christina had been at his side throughout his career in racing and had watched with

12

pride as the stud farm grew to be one of the biggest in England. She was predominantly a homemaker, and took no part in the running of the racing yard, but she played an important role in de Jersey's life. Not only did he adore her, she gave him a stability he had never previously believed possible.

She poured him a glass of champagne and prompted him to join his guests. It was her turn now to watch him. She was nineteen years younger than her husband but the age difference had never been an issue between them. Christina was a happy woman and, above all, a contented one. Unlike de Jersey she was socially at ease, and enjoyed entertaining and smoothing the way for him. She knew that behind his extrovert image her husband was a private man and, at times, inadequate at small-talk. They made a good team.

'Well, we have a beautiful day for it,' she heard him say as he shook hands and checked glasses, then opened another bottle of Krug. She knew he would touch hardly any alcohol, preferring to drink water until Royal Flush's race was over. She had chosen her guests carefully, aware that her husband would be focused on his horse. Apart from the four girls, Donald Fleming's wife was there, and their local Vicar, who had leapt at the chance of going to the races, with his wife, a shy, retiring woman. After the racing they could spend time box-hopping with the Sangsters and the Henry Cecils.

Their daughters, Leonie and Natasha, stood close by their father as he sat down to discuss the racing form with the over-eager Vicar. 'Now, then, here's my tip: first race I'd say an each-way bet on Cold Stream and maybe a tenner on the outsider, Charcoal.' Before he could continue, however, Christina called to him. David Lyons, his business and financial adviser, had arrived with his wife Helen.

De Jersey dwarfed David Lyons, who was no more than five feet seven, and gave him a bear hug. David's hired morning suit was a trifle large and his prominent ears held up his top hat.

'David, how nice to see you. And Helen, what a wonderful creation,' he said, referring to her elaborate hat, a bright pink ensemble of huge roses that made her pinched, nervous face seem paler than ever.

'Thank you, Edward. David said it was awful.' Helen had never been to Royal Ascot before, and had spent weeks shopping for her outfit. She had been really upset when her husband had criticized her hat.

'It's stunning,' Christina enthused, and kissed Helen's cheek, then passed her a glass of champagne.

De Jersey laughed and tapped David's topper, which sank low on his red, sweaty face.

'I'd say your husband has some cheek,' de Jersey said. 'What happened, David? No suits in your size left at Moss Bros?'

David smiled but obviously felt self-conscious. Like his wife, he had never attended Royal Ascot before. He had been so busy with work that he had left it until the last moment to hire his suit. Normally he was fastidious in his dress.

'I think you look splendid,' Christina said to him, smoothing things over and handing him a glass of champagne.

'Now, if you need any help placing bets, Natasha will guide you through the procedure. Edward's already suggested a possible winner for the first race, but I never pay any attention to him. I bet on the horse whose name I like best.'

As quickly as he could, David removed his hat and went to sit on the far side of the box where he lit a cigar. De Jersey joined him. 'Glad you could make it, David. We've not met up for weeks – no months – and I certainly have a lot to thank you for. You've made me a wealthy man.'

'I've been caught up with work, but I have tried calling you,' David said, and drained his glass, which de Jersey refilled. They had known each other for twenty-five years but rarely, if ever, socialized. David's latest business venture on de Jersey's behalf, financing an Internet company, had proved a goldmine and de Jersey had invited him today by way of thanks. However, he had originally been unsure about inviting him along with the Vicar there since David was a great one for telling risqué jokes. Christina, however, felt that instead of the Vicar being in anyway compromised by David's dirty jokes he would more than likely chip in a few of his own! As de Jersey rarely, if ever, set foot in their local church, he didn't know that the Vicar was a great humorist and could probably drink them all under the table. Indeed, when de Jersey left David to join Christina, David and the Vicar were in deep discussions about the upcoming first race. A moment later, David, with his cigar clamped in his teeth, called over to de Jersey.

'Come on now, you've got to have insider information, Edward. What do you say is going to be a sure-fire bet?'

'There never is one,' de Jersey called back. He hesitated, David's words had reminded him eerily of the past.

15

His father always used to say the same thing. Whether or not his father was foremost in his mind because of meeting Smedley, he couldn't tell, but he suddenly felt the need to talk about his past but he knew he couldn't. David knew nothing of de Jersey's roots and he would have heart failure if he knew of some of the things de Jersey had done. David was straight and honest, the very reason de Jersey placed so much trust in him.

'You know, David, I am really pleased you and Helen could join us today. It gives me a chance to thank you.'

David smiled. He had whiter than white teeth and always appeared suntanned. His balding head and big ears were often a source of amusement but he was, in actual fact, a very confident man. David had his own style and was usually immaculately dressed, if not in the style of suits de Jersey favoured. It wasn't therefore until he was flushed with champagne, that David's discomfort at wearing an oversized morning suit began to lessen.

'Edward, lemme tell you. What with Helen and that ruddy flower garden hat and me in this suit, I was of two minds about whether or not to come today. I said to this bloke at Moss Bros, can't you take the trousers up? No, he said, then puts the jacket on me and the sleeves covered my hand. I said you gotta take the sleeves up. I mean I can't go to Royal Ascot looking like a chump. So I says to him, can't you recommend someone that's got one more my size and you know what he said? No one will notice! I said they will when I do a pratfall in front of the Queen. And then I get the manager and he starts kneeling down with these pins in his mouth. He says to me, can you stand on the stool and I says, that's not gonna help. I can't carry that around the race track!' David chortled with laughter and showed the wide hem on his trousers as Helen blushed with embarrassment. Like her husband however, she was also feeling more at ease after two glasses of champagne.

By the time Christina suggested they all sit down for lunch, everyone appeared to be enjoying themselves. The Vicar had accompanied David to the Tote and appeared to have backed every horse in the first race. It was one thirty. More champagne was offered, along with chilled white Chablis, as the oysters were served. They were to be followed by wild salmon in aspic with new potatoes and salad. As they ate, conversation centred on the forthcoming racing. The first race would begin half-way through the luncheon, and they would break between courses to watch from the balcony.

Just as they finished the oysters the crowds below cheered wildly and everyone left the table to watch the Royal procession pass along the track just beneath the balcony. A few moments later the first runners were under starter's orders, and they were off. Christina smiled as her guests, led by David, cheered on the winner. The Vicar and he celebrated Charcoal's triumph at twelve to one, and rushed out to collect their winnings.

De Jersey felt the knot in his stomach tighten. Two more races to go before he would go down to the stables.

Before the second race, David made his way to the Tote on the floor below de Jersey's box. Natasha had already placed her bet when she saw him join the line, so she waited for him and they returned to the box together. David hurried straight to the balcony but Natasha joined her father.

17

'Daddy, David put on an enormous amount of money. I've never seen so many banknotes!'

'Shush, don't speak so loudly,' Christina admonished her.

'He can afford it, and it's not your business, sweetheart,' de Jersey said, then grinned at her. 'What's he backed?'

'Classy Lady,' Natasha said, and giggled. 'Maybe because of his wife's rose-garden hat. Isn't it awful?'

Christina frowned at her and said sternly, 'That will do, Natty and, Edward, don't encourage her. They're your guests.'

De Jersey pulled a po-face. 'Me? I never said a word.'

Natasha stood on tiptoe to kiss him. 'I'm on Blue Babushka, the outsider, a fiver on the nose.'

'Then go and join the others or you'll miss the race,' Christina said, and glanced at the table, now freshly laid for the next course. As Natasha left, de Jersey sat down to watch the television screen as the horses cantered past, heading for the starting gate. 'Royal Flush will go in last,' he said. 'He travelled well but he gets so frisky. I might have to go and have another look at him.'

'Not before we finish lunch, darling. You've got almost two hours yet . . . Darling?'

He was staring into space, then turned to her. 'He stands a good chance, Christina, and next year it'll be the Derby. That's my dream, to have a Derby winner.' He lapsed into silence as she came and sat beside him. Sometimes he wanted to tell her about his father, about his childhood, but so much of his past was buried beneath the person he had become that the less she knew the safer he felt. There was always a chance that something might rear its head. Something or someone far more dangerous than the harmless Harry Smedley.

They had just finished the main course when Donald Fleming came into the box. 'Mickey's in the weighing room,' he said, then waved to his wife.

'I won the last race!' she called to him.

Fleming blew her a kiss then turned to Christina. 'Thank you for inviting my wife. She's been planning that outfit for weeks. To be honest, I never thought she'd leave the house.'

Christina patted his arm. 'She looks wonderful.'

'That's thanks to you, all those dresses you sent over – she was like a little girl at Christmas. And you can't tell me they were just ones you didn't wear any more because a couple had the price tag still on them.'

Christina looked concerned. 'You didn't mind, did you? But I knew she hadn't been well enough to go shopping.'

'Mind? Course I didn't. Just to have her here makes it even more of a special day for me. Cream'll be if Royal Flush wins.'

Fleming crossed to his wife, who had been sitting with Helen Lyons talking about her recent mastectomy operation. Helen found operations fascinating.

De Jersey checked his watch. Impatient to go to the stables, he turned to Christina. 'What was that about his wife?'

'Oh, I sent over some dresses for her to choose something to wear. She's been very poorly.'

'I thought the operation was a success,' he said, again looking at his watch.

'Oh, it was, but she's lost all her self-confidence.' Christina touched the emerald-and-diamond brooch on her lapel, checking it was secure. 'Can you see if the safety catch is on?' she asked her husband, who bent to look. 'I don't know why you wanted me to wear it. I'm always afraid of losing it and with these crowds I'd hate to get jostled. Is it safe?'

'Looks okay. It suits that jacket.'

Christina laughed and nuzzled his neck. 'Darling, this would suit any woman, any jacket. It's magnificent.'

He gave a boyish grin. He adored buying her expensive gifts but the brooch had been an especially costly one for her last birthday. He had the matching earrings in his pocket. He'd had them for a few weeks now and had intended to give them to her to wear before he had left that morning but had then decided that if Royal Flush won they would make it a memorable day for her too.

The next race was ready for the off. Fleming beckoned to de Jersey: it was time to leave the box and get Royal Flush saddled up. De Jersey turned to Christina and asked her to take the girls to the parade ring: he would join them there. He leaned close to her. 'Just you and the girls, darling. You know I don't like too many people around when we saddle up.' She nodded and then joined the guests on the balcony as de Jersey and Fleming left. Christina explained to her guests that they would not be long and that she would return after the race. David was very put out that he could not come into the parade ring and Christina explained that Edward was very nervous about too many people being around Royal Flush. If he wanted, he could make his way to the stands around the parade ring and watch the saddling from there.

'Will the Queen be with her horse?' he asked like a kid.

'Yes I believe so, she has a runner in the same race.'

'Bloody hell, I wouldn't miss that. We'll go over to the stands then as soon as the next race is over. Where is it? I mean, which way do we go?' Christina gave him directions and then signalled to her daughters, and eventually agreed to let their friends go with them. The five left the box as the waiters opened more champagne.

Christina and the girls passed under the archway then headed along the grass path towards the arena where the horses would be brought in to their owners and trainers. There, the jockeys would receive last-minute instructions, mount and ride down the track to the starting gate. Crowds lined the fenced walkway to watch the Queen as she, too, made her way towards the parade ring.

De Jersey arrived at the stables as the horses were being walked around outside by their lads. They were unsaddled but draped in their owners' colours with their numbers attached to their reins. The sun was blazing and some were already starting to sweat. Royal Flush was number seven and playing up, tossing his head, and a couple of others were walking sideways, some kicking out. The crowds were now growing quite dense as Her Majesty was making her way slowly towards the ring. She was accompanied by her own trainer and surrounded by discreet bodyguards and security officers who walked six feet in front and behind her. Although they had walkie-talkies and monitored the crowds, there was a wonderful atmosphere of wellbeing. Here at Royal Ascot the Queen was relaxed and enjoying her favourite pastime. She acknowledged the cheers but was also deeply engrossed in talking to her trainer.

Way behind her, Christina and her daughters strolled towards the ring, her girls and their friends agog at the show of such glamorous people. They spotted with excitement the actors and stars they recognized from the movies and television and they kept taking secret glances ahead to the Queen's party.

Royal Flush was led into a stable still playing up as Fleming and de Jersey saddled him. De Jersey dipped a sponge into a bucket of water and squeezed it into the horse's mouth past the bit, talking to him all the time, but he was becoming increasingly hard to control. Finally, the saddle was on and they led him out, but he reared and bucked, his ears flattened.

'He's in a right mood,' muttered Fleming.

De Jersey looked on, concerned.

'It's bloody hot for him,' he said.

The stable lad took the reins and de Jersey tapped his shoulder. 'See you in the ring.'

'Yes, sir. He'll calm down. He's just desperate to get on to that track.'

De Jersey straightened his grey silk cravat, replaced his topper and turned to Fleming. 'Let's go.'

The two men walked side by side towards the parade ring. By the time they reached the centre the crowds were pressing against the railings and the green was full of owners and trainers. The Sheikh was there, waiting for his runner to appear, and de Jersey could see Christina and the girls chatting to friends. He made his way towards them and as he did he had to pass the Queen, standing with her trainer. De Jersey tipped his top hat as he passed and was astonished when she acknowledged him. He had seen her on several occasions but never before had she spoken to him.

'Do you play cards, Mr de Jersey?' the Queen asked, smiling.

'Infrequently, ma'am.' De Jersey bowed.

'I wondered how your horse came about his name.'

De Jersey flushed to the roots of his hair: the 'royal flush' was an unbeatable poker hand. 'Whether or not it will prove to be his rightful name remains to be seen, ma'am,' he replied.

The Queen inclined her head and the conversation was over.

De Jersey replaced his top hat as he continued to cross the green, his heart leaping out of his chest. He could hardly believe that Her Majesty had known his name. He had to stop a moment to get his breath.

'You all right, Edward?' Fleming asked.

'I'm fine, just . . . She knew who I was, Donald!'

Fleming laughed. 'She doesn't miss a trick. You bet your sweet life she knows who you are. She's got a stable of horses on a par with yours and I bet she knows just what the competition is from our boy. That's her horse being led into the ring now.'

De Jersey turned to see a magnificent bay draped in the Royal colours. He was bigger than Royal Flush but much calmer. Royal Flush, a deep, almost burned chestnut, was still tossing his head and there was a white film of sweat on his neck.

'Bloody hot for his second time out,' he said to Fleming. Then he greeted Christina, slipped an arm around her waist and watched as his lad walked Royal Flush round the ring.

Mickey Rowland was adjusting his chinstrap, his whip

under his arm, and looking around for his governor. When he spotted de Jersey he came over to him. 'Hot out here isn't it?' he murmured, and nodded to Christina.

'You've met my daughters and these two young ladies are . . .' He couldn't remember their names so Christina stepped in. At that moment de Jersey suddenly saw that Leonie was about to take a photograph. 'Not now,' he snapped.

'But, Daddy—'

'No! Christina, take the camera off her *now*!'

Leonie looked frightened and lowered it but Christina moved forward, took it from her, and explained, 'It's supposed to be unlucky, sweetheart. You can take as many as you like after the race, just never before.'

By now de Jersey, Fleming and Mickey were deep in conversation, the incident forgotten. 'I think it's best to give him his head. With this ground it's going to be fast. Let's see what he can do, maybe give him a tap half-way, keep him off the rails, centre of the course. It's already been churned up, so if it's too rough move him across.'

Mickey's face was expressionless. Royal Flush was ready and waiting: he and de Jersey walked towards him.

De Jersey bent low to speak to him privately: 'You know him better than anyone, Mickey. Do what you have to do. Let's see how good he is.'

'Will do, sir.' He smiled. 'See you in the winner's enclosure, then, shall I?'

De Jersey laughed, then gave his jockey a leg up. Mickey tightened his gloves, tapped his helmet with his whip and urged Royal Flush to walk out of the ring. The horses would take a good easy stride up to the starting

24

gate as the crowd headed back for their stands to watch the race.

De Jersey strode ahead, his fists clenched, leaving Fleming to guide Christina and the girls towards the owners' and trainers' stand, from which de Jersey preferred to watch the race. He didn't see David and Helen Lyons waving from behind the barrier, but they had seen him pause by the Queen and David had the photograph to prove it.

By the time they were in the stand, they were all very hot. Christina was fanning herself with her race card as they headed up the steps to the front row. She knew not to speak to her husband, but Fleming was more relaxed. De Jersey was training his binoculars on Royal Flush cantering up to the starting gate. He lifted them, lowered them, looked to the wide screen, then went back to the binoculars.

'He'll start his shuffle in a minute,' whispered Fleming to Christina, and they both smiled. Whenever de Jersey watched one of his horses race, he shifted from one foot to the other as if he was standing on hot coals.

They could hear the commentator now, saying that all the horses were in the gates except Royal Flush. Then he was in, and the next second they were off. Now Fleming was standing close to de Jersey. 'Came out well, but he's boxed in,' de Jersey muttered. 'Move him up, Mickey, that's it – good, he's in a nice position.'

Christina squinted at the screen and Natalie leaned closer, asking where Royal Flush was.

'I think he's fourth, no fifth – he's right in the centre. See the star on Mickey's cap?'

De Jersey yelped, and everyone turned to look at him: he was hopping up and down. 'He's dropped back! What the hell is he doing?' De Jersey yelled, his face like thunder. 'Come on, come on, Mickey! *Ride him. That's it! That's it.*' De Jersey nudged Fleming so hard that he almost knocked him off his feet. 'He's moving up, sitting in a lovely position, see him?'

But the Queen's bay was breaking away from the pack. He was almost a length in front of the rest of the field.

'He's not going to do it,' de Jersey said softly, and lowered the binoculars. Now they could see the horses thundering down the track towards the finish. Royal Flush was still in fourth but looked as if he was tiring. He was boxed in on both sides, struggling to hold his position, neck and neck with a horse either side of him. Then, suddenly, he began to draw ahead.

'He's picking up,' Fleming yelled, and Christina turned to see her husband standing, as if frozen, his hands at his side. He didn't even appear to be watching, but then Christina was shouting at the top of her voice: 'Come on . . . COME ON. YES, YES. COME ON!'

Suddenly Royal Flush seemed to get a second wind. The horse started to take the race, and flew, his stride never faltering as he moved up from fourth to third and then he was unstoppable. He crossed the winning line two lengths ahead of the field. Mickey, high in the saddle, turned to look behind as he raised his whip in victory.

Fleming turned to de Jersey. The two men looked at each other, unable for a moment to speak. 'He's done it, just like you knew he would,' gasped Fleming.

De Jersey was blinking back tears, and then Christina

was in his arms, his girls were hugging him and from all around he was congratulated. But he could hear nothing. His heart was pounding as if it would burst through his chest.

They all had to hurry to reach the winner's enclosure to be there for the horses coming off the track. Mickey rode in to cheers and de Jersey and Fleming took the sweating horse's reins. He slid off Royal Flush and wrapped his arms around the horse's neck. Then he removed the saddle and prepared to move off to the weighing room. As he loosened his chinstrap, he said to de Jersey, 'He's got a lot more under the bonnet. I've never felt anything like it. I hardly had to touch him.'

De Jersey moved close and held the horse's head. 'Next year it's the Derby, my boy.'

Fleming laughed. 'Give him a break! He's just won the Chesham. That's good enough for now.'

The prize-giving was a blur for de Jersey who had to force himself to keep calm. He wanted to shout from the rooftops, he wanted to hurl his hat in the air. He knew now that he had a champion of champions. To possess such a horse is every trainer's and owner's dream, and this was the fulfilment of twenty years' hard work. Moments later, Fleming was interviewed by the television sports team, but de Jersey sidestepped fast. He loathed the camera and hardly ever gave any interviews, either for the racing channels or the racing post. He always left that to Fleming.

After he had seen that Royal Flush was hosed down and made ready to be driven home, de Jersey returned jubilantly to his box. Royal Flush was the talk of the track and the guests had all bet on him. David was standing on a chair waving a fistful of fifty-pound notes, singing, 'We're in the money!' They all continued to celebrate well into the afternoon and David and Helen Lyons were the last to leave de Jersey's box. Helen assured Christina that David was sober enough to drive after monitoring him drinking numerous cups of black coffee.

'Don't you worry, it'll take us a good hour to get out of the car park,' David said and then clasped de Jersey's hand.

'This has been one of the best days of my life. Delicious food, the best champagne and . . . and . . . I'm going to get that photograph of you with the Queen framed. I'll have it on my desk!'

'It was a special day for me, David, and I am glad you were here to share it. If it wasn't for you I probably wouldn't have been able to afford it!' de Jersey said, shaking David's hand. David's mood suddenly deflated as he held on to de Jersey's hand for a moment, looking up into his face. He seemed to want to say something more but decided against it turning rather briskly to his wife.

'Let's go, Helen, we don't want to overstay our welcome or we won't be invited next year.' Then dropping his voice he soberly said to de Jersey, 'Everything is going to be all right.' Then he ushered Helen out before a bemused de Jersey could reply.

Much later de Jersey sat down, exhausted. Christina was marshalling the girls, making sure they had everything ready to leave. 'Will you be all right to fly the helicopter?' she asked.

De Jersey made no reply and she repeated her ques-

28

tion. He reached out, caught her hand and brought it to his lips. 'I'm going for a walk so don't worry, I'll see you at home. Thank you for today,' he said. 'It was a good idea to invite David and Helen. I think it meant a great deal to them.'

She laughed softly. 'I don't know if it was such a good idea to invite the Vicar. Donald's had to drive him home. He could hardly stand up.'

De Jersey turned to his daughters, who were now sitting on the balcony with their friends. He blew them a kiss and stood up, then said to his wife, 'Drive carefully. I won't be too late.' He picked up his top hat and walked to the door. 'There's something for you on the table,' he said over his shoulder. Then he left.

De Jersey walked towards the winner's enclosure, recalling the events of the afternoon. It was cooler now and thousands of racegoers were streaming out of the gates. He went to the number-one post and stood there for a minute – it had felt so good to lead Royal Flush into the winner's position. Then he headed on to the course, and walked towards the helicopter pad. By now his was the only one left. He took his time, breathing in the scent of the grass, which reminded him again of his father, who had opened his betting shop with his own winnings. He had won on an outsider, then never laid another bet. 'It's a fool's game, but sometimes the fool wins. And luck runs out, so I'm not takin' any chances,' he had said.

Ronnie Jersey's luck had run out months after he had opened his second betting shop when cancer was diagnosed. Shortly before he died he had said to his son, 'Eddy, take care of your mother and you run those shops for me. I know it's not what you wanted but you can earn a good living, an' there's a good kid that works for me. You know Tony Driscoll.' He was the illegitimate son of a woman Ronnie employed to clean the shops. Tony had been a toddler when Ronnie took Mrs Driscoll and her child under his wing, and they owed everything to him, even Tony's first suit. Now de Jersey tried to remember Mrs Driscoll's name but it escaped him. What he did remember was how they had both wept at his father's funeral. In a way Ronnie had been a surrogate dad to Tony and had even left him a few hundred pounds.

'I was hopin' I'd see you.'

De Jersey was surprised to see Smedley again. By the tilt of him he'd had more than a few beers.

'What a win, eh? Clean as a whistle! And I didn't think he was gonna do it! I nearly had heart failure – I'd put those two fifties you give me on him!'

'Really?' De Jersey moved away, not wanting to get into conversation with him again.

'All the lads was on him, I tipped them off.' Smedley bumped against the fence then ducked beneath it. There was no getting away from him. 'You got anythin' running tomorrow?'

'No.'

'Ah, well, maybe not push your luck too far, eh? You goin' down the track? I'll walk wiv you. I need to sober up. Been in the stewards' lounge.'

De Jersey made no reply but strode off leaving Smedley, swaying slightly, to look after him, a hurt expression on his red face. 'I'm sorry if I bothered you,' he said loudly.

De Jersey stopped. 'Sorry, I don't mean to be rude. I have to get a move on – don't like flying at night.'

'Oh, understandable,' Smedley said, and trotted after him.

As they approached the helicopter pad, de Jersey could hear Smedley wheezing. 'You'd never get me up in one of them,' he gasped. Then he watched as de Jersey opened the cockpit door and climbed aboard. He was beginning to find the man unbearably irritating.

'I'd like to shake your hand, sir.' Smedley held up his square rough hand, and de Jersey bent down to grasp it. 'I'll tell my grandson about it, me and you being at the same school. You got any?'

Jersey looked down into the upturned gnome-like face. 'Just two daughters.'

'Ah, well, we can't all be blessed. I got four lads, three grandsons and . . .'

The engine started up and de Jersey slid the door shut. He waited for Smedley to scuttle away to a safe distance as the blades began to turn. As the helicopter lifted into the air, de Jersey saw the man grow smaller and felt an odd mixture of emotions. He had spent most of his life escaping his past but even now, with his massive wealth, the Smedleys of the world proved to him that he could never let down his guard. He had far too much to lose to allow that to happen. He had, by various means, acquired what he had always wanted in life. However, Smedley did have something he coveted, a son. In fact, the funny little fellow had four of them. De Jersey's good humour returned. He laughed out loud. He had Royal Flush and today had been the beginning of fulfilling a dream to win the Derby. If he did, he would kiss the track like his dad.

The light was fading as de Jersey flew over his home. He couldn't help smiling as he saw, way below, his vast estate. It comprised a racing stables, just twenty-five miles from Newmarket and its famous racetrack, and close to the famous Tattersalls bloodstock auctions. The stud farm was located at a separate holding, ten miles from the stables. He had vast tracts of land for training, with separate yards and paddocks for the brood mares. The electronically controlled gates led to a three-mile drive at the end of which was his mansion with a lake in front of it. At the house the drive branched off towards the stables. The garages were set back from the house and the chauffeur lived above them. De Jersey owned a Silver Cloud Rolls-Royce, a convertible Mercedes, a Range Rover, two Aston Martins, three motorbikes and four golf carts, all in the same dark navy as the stable colours. His personal favourite was his Mercedes, whose registration plate read 'Champion'.

Some of the stable lads in the yard looked up and shaded their eyes when they saw de Jersey circling the farm. They yelled and waved their caps as he flew over the neat row of outhouses that had been converted into living-quarters for them. Beyond was a complex of cottages for the jockeys, a sauna, swimming-pool and gymnasium. The estate and its occupants were valued at over a hundred million pounds. De Jersey employed head lads, yardmen, work riders, two assistant trainers, a head trainer, stable lads, travelling head lads and contracted two top jockeys as well as Mickey Rowland. There were three large stableyards and Donald Fleming's house was on the northern side of the old yard. The office, in the newest yard, was manned by a PA, a racing secretary and two managers.

De Jersey landed and jumped down from the helicopter to cheers from his staff. 'Champagne all round!' de Jersey shouted.

Although de Jersey appeared at this moment to be very genial and easy-going, he was not an easy man to work for. He had naturally a rather off-putting steely manner but if you got to know him it was soon dissipated when he gave one of his sweet smiles, and the trust, admiration and respect he demanded was returned by his employees threefold. He was, as his wife knew, a very reserved, almost shy man. He had never raised his voice to anyone at the stables. He had never needed to. With the adroit management and competent secretaries successfully running the business and overseeing the loyal employees, there was little to criticize. De Jersey actually detested losing his temper because to him it was a sign of weakness. He had a studied and tight control of his emotions but his charm made his employees guard his privacy with a ferocious loyalty. There was not a single member of staff's wife, husband, child or grandchild whose name he couldn't recall and now, surrounded by them all as the champagne corks popped, he toasted his success and was blissfully happy. He raised his glass.

'To Royal Flush and to next year – the Derby!'

There were cheers all round, made even greater by the arrival of the horsebox, with the Champion himself aboard. As Royal Flush was led down from his box they grouped around him and de Jersey cupped some champagne into his hand and patted his head with it. After everyone had a chance to congratulate Royal Flush, de Jersey led him back to his stable and watched over him like a doting father. He waited for the travelling stable lads to bring his feed and was pleased when Royal Flush couldn't wait to get at it. It was always a good sign after a race when a young horse was not put off his feed.

The oak-panelled drawing room was comfortable, with polished pine floors and exquisite Persian rugs. Soft throws and cushions covered the sofa and a fire blazed in the grate.

'You'll wear it out,' Christina said, putting down a tray of sandwiches and tea, but de Jersey rewound the tape of the race and pressed play to glory once more in Royal Flush's great victory.

'I'm going to keep him under wraps for the rest of the season. Just some light training before he rests for the winter.' He ate the sandwiches hungrily.

'Thank you for my beautiful earrings,' she whispered, and drew back her hair to show him she was wearing them.

'I'd give you the world if I could.' He kissed her neck but his eyes strayed back to the TV screen, and the moment when Royal Flush passed the winning post.

Christina took the remote control from his hand and switched off the television. 'Can we go to bed so I can thank you properly?' she asked provocatively, and then she had all his attention. He scooped her into his arms and they kissed passionately. They didn't make it to the bedroom, and as she nestled beside him in front of the fire, wearing nothing but the earrings, de Jersey sighed. 'I'm a lucky man,' he murmured.

CHAPTER 2

DURING THE months after the flat season ended, Royal Flush enjoyed the rest he deserved. De Jersey, however, was still busy at his yard. He entered many horses in international races, and there were frequent trips to Dubai and Hong Kong during the winter. It was December now and Royal Flush's training was low-key. From November his programme had consisted of walking and trotting but after Christmas it would build up for a couple of preparation races. If all went according to plan, he would run the Thresher Trial at Sandown in April and then the Lingfield Derby trial.

De Jersey, driving a golf cart, buzzed into the yard. He wore a checked cap, jodhpurs and a yellow cashmere polo-neck sweater beneath his Harris tweed jacket. His hand-stitched, brown leather riding boots were highly polished. As usual he acknowledged everyone, then paid his first call of the day to Royal Flush. He was still a moody horse, with a bullyboy streak to him, and lashed out at every opportunity. He'd given a couple of the lads nasty bites too. De Jersey had been worried that if he remained a stallion Royal Flush would be too much to handle and a danger to the other horses – he had already attacked a couple in the yard. It would have been heartbreaking to geld him, but Royal Flush, perhaps sensing what was at stake, was finally settling down.

After a while de Jersey returned to his golf cart and drove over to the east wing of the yard to inspect a new filly he had purchased from Ireland. As he started the engine, his mobile rang. It was his wife, and it was unusual for her to disrupt his morning schedule. 'What's up?' he asked.

'It's David. Helen called.' Her Swedish accent was always more pronounced on the telephone. 'She was very distressed. I could not make out what she was saying, but I think David is sick. You'd better call.'

De Jersey made his way back to the house, and scraped his boots outside the kitchen door. 'Christina,' he called. When she answered, he said, 'Did Helen say what was wrong with David?'

'No.'

De Jersey walked into the kitchen. Recently he and David had discussed liquidating some of his investments: he needed to cut costs. The running of the stables was astronomical, and the foot-and-mouth outbreak had meant the adjoining farm had made a hefty loss. De Jersey was not unduly worried, but since he had invested most of his liquid funds his cash resources were stretched to the limit.

De Jersey picked up the phone and called David, but the number was engaged so he decided to have breakfast before trying again. The table was already set for him with grapefruit juice, black coffee, two slices of Christina's homemade rye bread and a lightly boiled egg. De Jersey had not seen David since Royal Ascot, preferring to leave the financial side of his business to his adviser.

Christina came in, her arms filled with holly and fir

branches for the hall. The tree would not arrive until a few days before the girls returned from boarding-school. 'Did Helen say what was wrong?' she asked, as she dropped her burden on the floor.

'The line was engaged. I'll try again after I've had a look at the papers.'

Christina spread some old newspaper on the floor, and began to spray the branches silver.

'She sounded upset. She was crying. It's very early, so something must be wrong.'

He sighed. 'OK, I'll try again now. I hope to God I don't have to go over there. I've got a hectic day ahead.'

A few moments later de Jersey ordered the helicopter to stand by and arranged to land at the small airport close to David's house in Radcliff.

'What's the matter?' Christina asked.

'Not sure. I spoke to Helen's sister. I'll be back as soon as possible, but I'll call to tell you when to expect me.' He kissed her cheek and was gone before she could question him further.

David Lyons' house was set back from the road with large electronically controlled gates, which were open; the taxi de Jersey had taken after landing his helicopter drove straight through. The white stucco house had fake Georgian pillars and latticed lead windows with Swiss style shutters and a green slate roof. The front door was open.

'Hello,' de Jersey called, as he stepped into the hall and made for the lounge, a dreary sea of beige. It was eerily empty. 'Helen?' he called, but there was no reply.

Frustrated, de Jersey headed towards the ornate

indoor swimming-pool, and found no one. He returned to the hall just as a small, pale-faced woman appeared. 'Hello, I'm Edward de Jersey. The front door was open. Helen doesn't seem to be at home?'

'I'm her sister, Sylvia Hewitt. I spoke to you earlier. I didn't think you'd get here so quickly.'

'Helicopter,' de Jersey explained.

'Helen's upstairs. Shall I get her for you?'

'I'd be grateful if you could tell me what's going on. You didn't say much, just that Helen had to see me. Is David all right?'

'No – no, he isn't.' She started to cry.

'What's happened? Has there been an accident?' De Jersey was worried now.

'I'll get Helen. Please go and sit in the lounge.'

De Jersey sat on one of the over-plump sofas and waited over fifteen minutes before Helen came in. Her face was drawn and her eyes red-rimmed. 'Helen.' He rose to his feet.

'Edward.' She closed the door.

'Helen, what on earth is wrong? Has David had an accident?'

She took out a tissue. 'He's dead,' she said sadly, and burst into tears.

De Jersey was stunned. 'I'm so very sorry.'

She crossed to perch on the end of the sofa, blowing her nose. 'I found him this morning. He must have done it in the middle of the night. He was still wearing his pyjamas.'

'Found him?'

She nodded. 'In the garage.'

De Jersey had to sit down.

'He was in the car with the engine running. It was full

38

of fumes. The doctor said he'd also taken some sleeping tablets. He'd left me a note on the kitchen table, said for me to call you and not go into the garage. But I did.'

'Oh God.'

'I found another letter in the car, on the dashboard, addressed to you.' Helen dug into her pocket and took out a blue envelope, which she passed to him. 'The police took my letter, but I didn't give them this one. I'd forgotten about it.'

De Jersey took the envelope and slipped it into his pocket. 'Helen, is there anything I can do?'

She shook her head, then broke down again into shuddering sobs.

Twenty minutes later de Jersey walked to the waiting taxi and headed back to the local airport. David and Helen had had no children and had been a loving couple for thirty years. What on earth had possessed him to kill himself? De Jersey found little to enlighten him on the single sheet inside the blue envelope: 'My dear Edward, I am so sorry. It ran out of control and I was unable to do anything about it. You will find all the documentation in the second drawer of my office desk. Yours, David.'

De Jersey arranged for the helicopter to land in London, at the Battersea heliport, then took another taxi to David's office in the City where he was met by two shocked, weepy secretaries and David's long-time assistant, Daniel Gatley. Gatley was white-faced and his hands were trembling.

'This is all so dreadful, and just before Christmas too,' he whispered.

David's oval desk bore a bank of telephones, a computer and a large silver-framed photo of de Jersey talking to the Queen. 'This was taken at Royal Ascot, the day my horse won the Chesham Stakes,' he said quietly.

'David was so proud to have been there. He talked of nothing else for weeks after,' Gatley said.

De Jersey replaced the photograph on the desk. 'He said something about the second drawer and some documents?'

Gatley took out a bunch of keys and opened it. It contained a thin file and a small square box. De Jersey's name was printed on both. Gatley passed them to him. 'That's all. The box contains disks and these are contracts that I believe you have copies of anyway.'

De Jersey flipped open the file. 'What's all this about, Daniel?' he enquired.

'I believe David lost a lot of money – he has been here most nights for the past few months. He didn't tell me much but I knew he was in big trouble.'

'Financial?' asked de Jersey crisply.

'Two days ago he gave everyone here a month's notice.'

'Embezzlement, or what?'

'Good heavens, no. David was one of the most honest men I've ever met.'

De Jersey opened the box, which contained four unlabelled disks. 'What are these?'

'I don't know. His drawer was always locked.'

'But you have a key.'

'Only since this morning and I hadn't opened the drawer until now. I've been calling his clients and his friends.'

'So, you have no idea what is on these?' De Jersey asked, holding up the disks.

'No, but I can open them for you and print them out.'

'I can just about manage that.' De Jersey laughed, in an attempt to make light of the situation, but he knew that something was very wrong. All he wanted to do was leave so that he could find out what it was.

Christina was as stunned as her husband had been. David was dependable, always in control. For him to have committed suicide was unthinkable. 'Was there another woman?' she asked.

'No, he worshipped Helen, and I don't know why he did it, but I've got to go over some disks he left me. They may give me the answer.'

'What time would you like dinner?' she asked. 'I'm cooking shank of lamb the way you like it.'

'What?'

She put her arms around him. 'I'm sorry, it's ridiculous, isn't it, me thinking of what to cook for dinner and—'

'Eight thirty will be about right,' he said.

'Eight thirty it is, then,' Christine said eagerly. 'Had you seen David since Royal Ascot?'

'The last time we spoke was a few months back,' he told her. 'I wanted to sell off some shares.'

'How did he sound then?' she asked.

'I don't know. He was . . .' De Jersey frowned.

'He was what?'

'I don't know . . . a bit short with me.' And with that he walked out.

In his office, de Jersey poured himself a small whisky, added soda and ice, then sat down at his computer. He decided to start with the documents and tackle the disks later. He perched his half-moon glasses on his nose and peered at the first wad of papers. It was six thirty-five.

Two hours later he was still flicking through the documents. His wife popped her head round the door. 'You almost done, darling?'

He swivelled round in his leather chair. 'Almost.'

'Dinner's ready and I've lit a fire.'

'Good. Just let me close down my computer.'

'Did you find out what David's problems were?'

'I think so. He'd got himself into rather deep financial trouble – not worth topping himself for, though.'

'Too late to do anything about it now,' she said sadly.

'I'll be right with you.'

David had actually been in deeper water than de Jersey had told his wife, and it looked as if de Jersey was about to plunge into it too. An Internet company, in which they had both invested, had gone bankrupt and David had lost his life's savings. All he had ever implied to de Jersey was that there were 'problems' with the website, but he had given no indication of their extent. As ever he had said, 'Just leave it to me,' and, foolishly, that was exactly what de Jersey had done.

David's suggestion to invest in the Internet company had come at the right time. The stables and stud were in trouble, and with just over two million left in various accounts, de Jersey had taken a risk and released it to David to invest. Within six months de Jersey had been worth thirty-two million on paper. His shares had continued to rise faster in value than either man had anticipated so, eager to make more, de Jersey had remortgaged the stud farm and invested another forty million, using the farm as collateral. Now he was about to lose everything, the millions he had invested for the future of his stud farm, the millions he had saved for retirement. No wonder David had attached the garden hose to his new Mercedes exhaust pipe and rammed it through the window. De Jersey gave a short, mirthless laugh. David had loved his Mercedes, a high-tech car with voice recognition locks and satellite route maps. De Jersey wondered if the mechanical voice had alerted him, 'You are killing yourself. Turn off the engine,' before he died.

Christina carried a large oval platter of crisp lamb and placed it on the candlelit table. The air was permeated with the scent of rosemary. De Jersey sat down and smiled as she poured him a glass of Californian red wine. He sipped and let it roll around his mouth before he swallowed. 'Oh, it's so good.'

'Especially with the lamb,' Christina said, and handed him his plate. He leaned back to flip his starched white napkin across his knee.

Christina sat back and raised her glass. 'I want to make a toast,' she said. 'To David.'

He lifted his glass. 'To David, God rest him.'

There was a moment's silence as they began to eat.

'Is everything all right?' she asked.

'Perfect,' he replied, and he felt the warmth of the log fire on his back as he broke off a piece of bread and buttered it.

'I wasn't referring to the dinner. Tell me about David's financial troubles.'

43

'He's made some foolish investments. Not quite sure exactly how much he's frittered away of mine.'

'Yours? I don't understand – what do you mean?' Christina asked anxiously.

'Oh, nothing I can't take care of. Don't worry about it.'

'But is it going to be a worry for you? Did Helen know anything about this?'

'I don't think so.'

'Was he already in trouble when he came to Ascot?' Christina persisted.

'I don't know. I haven't had time to review all the records yet.' He gave nothing away. It was as though he were two people: one quietly enjoying his meal with his beloved wife, the other white with rage. He was not prepared to lose all of this, but he had never felt so impotent in his life. He had trusted David and his judgement.

When dinner was over and Christina was clearing the table, he sat preoccupied, tapping a dessert spoon.

'Should I call her, do you think?' asked Christina.

'Up to you,' de Jersey said offhandedly, standing up and tossing aside the spoon.

'Well, do you think it would be appropriate?'

'How should I know?'

'I hate it when you behave like this,' she said and pulled off the tablecloth.

'How am I behaving?' he snapped.

She glared at him. 'Like that! Shutting me out and snapping at me. I'm only trying to find out what's happened. David has killed himself, for God's sake, and then you say he frittered money away. Well, I would just like to know—'

'Sweetheart, I don't know the full extent of what

44

David has or hasn't done,' de Jersey interrupted her, softening his tone. 'It's difficult. Twenty-five years is a long time to know and trust someone. Now I'm sorry I've been abrupt, but I really must go back to try to sort out the facts.'

Back in his office de Jersey was forced to accept the reality of what had occurred. But someone would pay for it. He realized that David's suicide was just the beginning: he had a terrible feeling that the gamble he had taken with David might now cause him to lose everything. He also knew he would not be the only loser: he had drawn in two more investors, Wilcox and Driscoll, his two oldest friends, who would also lose out as a result of the website bankruptcy. Earlier in the year, when the website had been booming and de Jersey's share had trebled in value, he had contacted them both and advised them to invest. Now he feared that their unwavering trust in him had been misguided. He knew that he should contact them but couldn't bring himself to make the calls.

An hour later, de Jersey opened his desk drawer to take out the disks. Christina had lit the log fire and left a bottle of port with some cheese and crackers on the table. In the dark, womb-like room, with its heavy oak furniture and dark red velvet curtains, de Jersey sucked at a cigar as he slotted a disk into the computer. His chest was tight with anger. Why had he been so foolish as to invest so much money in the Internet company? 'Never get involved in anything you don't understand,' his father always told him, but he had done exactly what his father had warned him against.

De Jersey closed his eyes. Harry Smedley the funny

little man in the bowler hat at the races had said how proud de Jersey's father would have been to see him now, the successful stable owner, doffing his hat to the Queen and leading his champion into the winner's enclosure at Royal Ascot. He repeated his father's saying over and over in his mind – he had not just got into something he didn't understand, he had walked blindly into a nightmare like a mug. Then he had become greedy and poured in more, and, even worse had encouraged the other two to do the same.

They were the only living souls who knew where and how de Jersey had acquired his original wealth. Together the three men had staged some of the greatest robberies in British history and had never been caught. After their last heist they had agreed to a strict set of rules, which included not contacting each other again. But when David Lyons had started the investment bonanza, de Jersey couldn't resist breaking the rules to encourage his old friends to jump onto the gravy train. Now it had well and truly stopped and he just hoped they had not acted as rashly as he had.

Several days later, Christina was in the kitchen cooking up a storm for Christmas.

'I'm going to get some air,' de Jersey said, pulling on his coat.

She turned to him, her hands covered in flour. 'You want company?'

'No, I just need to clear my head.'

'You sure? You've been holed up in the study for days on end.'

'That's why I need to walk. I won't be long.' He walked out and Christina sighed. He had been unapproachable ever since David's suicide. Every time she tried to find out more about what had happened he dismissed her worries. As long as he was troubled, however, she couldn't let it rest. She washed her hands, took off her apron and put on an overcoat and boots. She walked across the yard to Donald Fleming's house and knocked at the door.

'Christina,' he said, surprised.

'May I come in?' she asked, and he stepped aside. His wife was in the kitchen, preparing for Christmas as Christina had been doing. 'Could I speak to you in private?' she asked tentatively.

'Of course, come on into the lounge.'

She refused sherry and didn't take off her coat. 'I don't know if you've heard but David – you met him at Ascot with his wife Helen . . .'

Donald nodded, pouring himself a beer.

'He committed suicide recently. I think he had been involved in some bad investments and as he was our business adviser there is a possible connection to us. I think we've lost money and . . .' she hesitated '. . . I am sorry to ask you this, and if it compromises you in any way then please don't feel you have to answer, but I am worried about Edward. Do you know if we are in financial trouble?'

Fleming frowned. 'Not that I'm aware of. I mean, it's been a bad year with the foot-and-mouth epidemic but everyone else in our business has been hit and we've looked into cutting costs. I'd be the first to know if there was a major problem.'

Somewhat relieved, Christina stayed a few minutes longer then went home.

It was a cold night and already the frost was forming on the ground but the snow that had been forecast was not yet falling. De Jersey walked for miles, his hands deep in his coat pockets, his breath steaming out in front of him. Christmas was always financially draining and without liquid funds de Jersey knew he was in dire trouble.

He lit a cigar, and leaned against the white fence round the paddock. He began to contemplate a return to the life he had left behind. The thought of losing the estate was more than he could bear. If he did not come up with a lucrative solution he would soon be forced to start selling off his horses. He had to find a way of recouping his losses – fast. What on earth could he do to get himself out of trouble? He tossed the cigar to the ground and ground it out with his heel. He knew he was going to have to contact Driscoll and Wilcox, and it wouldn't be to wish them a Happy New Year.

'I'm going to see a specialist, maybe try this Viagra stuff,' Tony Driscoll said, in a depressed tone as he switched off the bedside lamp.

'Don't worry about it.' Liz tried to pretend it wasn't important.

'Of course I worry about it. That's the fifth time this month. Something's *got* to be wrong – I've never not been able to get it up.'

Liz sighed.

'I've put on weight too.' Tony rubbed his hairy chest

then let his hand slip further down to the rolls of his belly. 'You think it's something to do with my liver?' he asked.

'More likely it's just the travelling or the heat.'

'It's never bothered me before. We've been to Florida five times so why should it suddenly affect me? I'm going to cut down on my drinking.'

Liz sat up and bashed her pillow: he was not going to let her sleep. She snapped on the bedside lamp, got out of bed and slipped a silk robe around her shoulders. At forty-seven she was in good shape, much better than her husband. But, then, the only thing she had to fill her time was exercise.

'Do you want a cup of tea or something?'

'Maybe a glass of water,' he muttered.

Liz padded to the fridge across the wide expanse of oyster pink carpet and poured some Perrier water into a tumbler. 'I'll have to call down for some ice.'

'Don't bother.' Tony leaned back on the pillows. The hair on his chest was now flecked with grey, as was the thick, bushy thatch on his head. At least there were no signs of baldness.

Liz returned to his side of the bed with the water. 'I think I might spend the day at the hotel spa tomorrow.' She yawned. 'Have you got anything arranged?'

'Golf,' he muttered.

'Shall I meet you at the clubhouse when I'm through?'

'Yeah, we'll have a drive around, then book somewhere nice for dinner. What do you think of the restaurant here?'

'I don't know. I've not even looked at it, just read the leaflets. After that long plane trip, I could do with a

49

stretch and a massage. I might have my hair and nails done too. Shall we meet up at about five?'

'I'm not playing golf all bloody day.'

'Well, why don't you meet me back here, then? And don't get so shirty. It's not my fault you're impotent.'

'I'm not fucking impotent,' he snapped.

Her smirk turned into a laugh, and he knew she was teasing him. She tickled him.

'Get off,' he said, but couldn't help smiling. She cuddled him, and kissed his chest.

'I think I'll go to sleep now,' he said, and turned away before she could make a second attempt. He couldn't stand the thought of failure twice in the same night.

Liz got up, walked over to the dressing-table and gave her long blonde tresses a flick.

She admired herself for a moment, then leaned closer to the mirror to check her face. 'I hate this light,' she muttered, tracing the lines at the side of her mouth. They seemed deeper than ever, even though they had been injected recently. She pursed her lips: they too had been 'fluffed up' with collagen injections.

'Are you coming back to bed?' Tony said.

Liz was studying the lines between her eyes. She was not supposed to be able to frown: her brow should have been frozen. 'I don't think these Botox injections work, Tony.'

'Well, I think you're crazy to have anything done, let alone stick poison into your face. You must be nuts.'

Liz pouted. At least her new lips looked great. It was just the lines she was worried about. She went into the bathroom.

'What are you doing?' he shouted.

'Having a tiddle. Is that all right with you?' She shut

the door and, in the privacy of her own bathroom, gave herself the satisfaction her husband had been unable to provide.

Liz and Tony were both in deep sleep when the phone rang. Tony sat up like a shot. 'What the hell . . . What time is it?'

Liz moaned. 'It might be one of the kids.'

'If it is I'll give 'em a mouthful. It's only four o'clock.'

The phone kept ringing as he wrapped a robe around himself.

'Well, answer it, then,' Liz said, worried now.

'All right, all right.' He snatched up the phone. 'Hello?'

'It's the Colonel,' came the soft voice at the other end of the line. Tony pressed hold and put down the receiver. He glanced at Liz and said, 'It's okay, business. I'll take it in the lounge.' He walked out.

'Business?' she said angrily, and flopped back, relieved that her children were not in trouble. They were in the South of France, staying with friends. She missed them but they had grown out of accompanying their parents on holiday, even to Florida for Christmas. She wondered if they liked their gifts – they wouldn't have waited until Christmas Day to open them. Michelle had a gold neck-lace with her name picked out in diamonds, a matching bracelet and her own credit card with five thousand pounds' spending money; she was seventeen years old and stunningly pretty, thankfully taking after her mother. Michael was the spitting image of his father, stocky, with dark eyes and thick curly hair; he had been given the keys to a Lotus in a gold box, while the car had been delivered to their home. He was nineteen and a first-year student of business studies at Liverpool University. He was very intelligent and Liz doubted that a Lotus was the right kind of car for him: unlike his sister, he was quiet and studious. She worried about him much more than she did about the outgoing Michelle, whose only real ambition was to be at the forefront of fashion and was almost as obsessive about clothes as her mother. She could spend money just as fast too. Liz knew that Michelle was spoiled, and especially by her father, who doted on her. A good marriage with a nice respectable boy was what they both wanted for her. At the moment, Michelle had a constant stream of boyfriends, all from wealthy families. Liz was determined, though, that her daughter wasn't going to get pregnant and ensured that she took sensible precautions. This was their mother–daughter secret: she knew Tony would not approve of his princess being on the pill. She yawned and looked at the bedside clock. The red light on the phone was still blinking and Tony was supposed to be semi-retired.

'Tony? What's going on? Tony?'

'With you in a minute, sweetheart,' he called.

Driscoll sat on the plush six-seater sofa, the phone pressed to his ear. He hardly said a word, just listened to the soft, clipped tone of de Jersey's voice. He had known it was him the moment he introduced himself as the Colonel. It was the nickname he and Wilcox had given him and only they used it. Driscoll's heart was beating rapidly and he had broken out in a sweat. His mouth was dry. He did not interrupt, just gave the occasional grunt to let de Jersey know he was still on the line.

'There's nothing to be done before the Christmas break is over but we'll meet up after you get back,' said de Jersey. 'The usual place, at the Ritz, but I'll call again as soon as I have more details. Tony?'

'We're due back mid-January.'

'Fine. I'll contact James and pass on the news.'

'He's in Aspen.'

'I know.'

Driscoll paused. 'There couldn't have been some fuck-up, could there? I mean, are you sure?'

'Afraid so. David killed himself, that's proof enough. It's bad. I'll need time to sort through everything. I am truly sorry, Tony. I feel it's down to me, and I'll try to think of some way to make good our losses.'

'I put all my eggs in.' Driscoll closed his eyes.

'I think we all did but, like I said, I feel responsible.'

'Hell, we're all grown men. You never twisted my arm, but I would like to know exactly what's gone down. We're talking millions.'

'I know, and I don't suppose my saying happy Christmas will help, but I mean it. Try not to think about it. I'll work this one out for us, and that's a promise.'

The phone went dead, and Driscoll sat cradling the receiver in his hands. He was still unable to take it in. If what de Jersey had said was true, he had just lost his life savings.

Tony Driscoll had started out as a runner in Ronnie Jersey's betting shops, but he was clever with his money. With the initial pay-off from the Colonel after they had turned to crime, he had moved into the rubbish-collection industry, opening up big waste-disposal dumps and buying a fleet of trucks. In the mid-seventies he had married Liz, his secretary, and in the early eighties they had had their children, and moved from Cobham into a massive mock Tudor mansion just outside Guildford. Driscoll had begun to play a big part in the local Labour Party, donating funds and attending functions. But thinking about the life of crime he used to lead exhilarated him and made the adrenaline pump into his tired veins. He returned to the bedroom.

Liz was fast asleep. She woke as Tony stroked her breasts and suddenly he was on top of her, like a man possessed. She didn't try to stop him as he went for her with a hunger and a passion that made her climax with a scream.

'Well, that must have been some phone call,' she said, giggling. 'Whoever it was, you get him to call you just once a week 'cos I couldn't take this every night. Tony? Was it good news?'

He closed his eyes. 'Yes. And now I'm knackered.' He turned over and fell almost immediately into a deep sleep, leaving her wide awake and smiling.

Liz had no notion of what her husband's life had been before he had married her. None of his business associates had given any hint that they were not one hundred per cent legitimate. In fact, Tony had a fixation with honesty: he'd even had arguments with his accountant over a few offshore tax-dodging schemes the man had suggested.

If anyone had hinted to Liz that her husband had been involved with some of the most daring robberies ever committed in England she would have laughed in their faces. Not her Tony. He was paranoid if they were late paying the milkman. She loved and trusted him totally and had never been unfaithful to him in all their years of marriage, though recently she'd fantasized about it, especially since she'd hired a personal trainer. In many ways Tony treated Liz as de Jersey treated Christina: she was cosseted and adored but kept in ignorance of her husband's past activities. It was one of de Jersey's rules. She had never heard her husband mention Edward de Jersey, just as Christina did not know about Tony Driscoll or James Wilcox. The three men had drawn up the 'freedom' rules, their survival tactics. The less anyone knew about their past, the safer they would be. So their secrets were buried deep and covered with well-rehearsed lies. De Jersey had been wise to insist that they tell no one of their past.

When Driscoll woke he wondered if he should call Wilcox, but he decided against it. The Colonel's primary rule was that the three should avoid contact unless it was absolutely necessary. Driscoll remained sitting alone, wondering how much Wilcox had lost and glanced to the closed bedroom door. He felt numb, hardly able to take it all in. There was fear too, exacerbated by his agreement to meet up with the others. He knew he couldn't take part in another caper, not now, not after all these years. His hand was shaking as he poured another shot of whisky. Whatever the Colonel suggested to get them out of trouble, he would refuse. But he kept looking at the bedroom door, wondering how he could explain his predicament to Liz. He'd have to get rid of his girlfriend – he'd need to sell the flat she was living in. That was another secret he kept from Liz. He started to calculate just how much he would be left with and reckoned he'd have to sell off property fast, including his villa in Spain. Yet again his thoughts returned to Wilcox. He knew that his losses would be worse. He'd never been careful with his money and he had four ex-wives to maintain, never mind his brood of kids.

The snow-capped mountains, with the mellow light of sunrise streaming across their peaks, were a wonderful sight. Aspen was great skiing country and offered a fantastic social life, which was why James Wilcox and his present girlfriend, Rika, had booked their Christmas break there for two years in a row. Wilcox was not as wealthy as Driscoll or de Jersey, but through wise deals in the car trade he had turned his earnings from the robberies into a lucrative business. At one time he had owned restaurants and garages, but had recently liquidated the majority of his holdings in favour of a semi-retirement plan. He planned to pack up and live abroad. He had only stayed on in England all these years to educate his six kids. All of the older teenagers either boarded at school or were heading for university and only the twins were still at school. It would be simple now to move to Geneva, keep a small house in England and send the boys to boarding-school.

Rika had been their nanny. When she had first arrived at his home from the Ukraine she had hardly been able to speak two words of English. She was a raw-boned, handsome blonde, with a curvaceous figure, and after six months she had moved into the master bedroom. Wilcox knew that this relationship would be hard to leave even if he wanted to: Rika knew a good catch when she saw one and, born into poverty, she was determined to become Wilcox's wife number five.

At fifty-nine, Wilcox was still slender and muscular from his daily workouts. He ran about fifty miles every week, cycled and played tennis in the summer. He was still handsome and had only recently taken on the slight puffiness associated with age and high living. Rika was only twenty-eight and they often joked that he couldn't keep up with her. He could hardly ever understand what she said as her English was still appalling but the arrangement suited him: he had no desire for meaningful conversations and she was a great fuck, kept the kids in order and his homes clean. And he still had time to screw around. He could never resist a pretty girl.

In fact, Wilcox had stupendous energy, and required only five hours' sleep a night. He practically rattled with the vitamin pills he swallowed in handfuls every morning. He ate sparingly, drank little, and smoked only the occasional cigar. His one vice was cocaine: he snorted mountains of it, and depended on it to kick him into gear every day.

Wilcox had met de Jersey at Sandhurst and they had left at around the same time. Wilcox, though, had been thrown out for punching an officer. It was through de Jersey that Wilcox had made his fortune, but he had maintained it himself and become a wealthy man. Wilcox's past forays to the altar had always been disastrous and he often thanked the Lord that de Jersey had made him promise never to discuss his past with his wives. He was sure that if he had, they would have squeezed him dry for maintenance money, and he would certainly have been arrested by now. He was enjoying his semi-retirement, content to buy and sell expensive cars; what had been a hobby had become a lucrative sideline. Like his hero de Jersey, Wilcox too was legitimate now, but over the past few years he had overstretched his finances, unable to resist women and top-of-the-range motors. Despite his extravagance, though, he still had considerable funds. The last robbery the three had pulled off had set him up for life. He had not, however, accumulated as much as either of his ex-partners so when de Jersey had suggested the Internet venture he had agreed to join in. As he'd headed to the Ritz hotel, their usual meeting place, Wilcox had been uneasy about what de Jersey was going to propose. He soon discovered, however, that he was not alone in his concerns. Driscoll too was loath to get involved in any further criminal activity. Why take any further risks, especially at their age? But when they met with de Jersey, he soon eased their worries. In fact he had laughed at them. He wasn't in any way going to suggest another robbery, far from it.

'The Colonel's retired my friends,' de Jersey had said. 'I'm putting him to rest. I am about to offer you the chance to double your savings, no risk, nothing illegal.'

De Jersey had gone on to explain in detail. The investment was a new Internet company with its main base in the US. He had inside information that within six months, if they invested now, they would become billionaires. De Jersey had already invested and seen his investment treble. So the other two joined in and the three of them had become the main investors in leadingleisurewear.com. They all released millions and watched their shares double, then treble, then skyrocket. The company's website became one of the most popular sites in the country and the press heralded the company as a major success. Wilcox had even re-mortgaged his house to enable him to invest more. Like Driscoll, he had truly believed his retirement was more than safe and secure. He had no reason to believe otherwise. David Lyons had continued to hype the company and send details of the immense turnover and expected returns. He was therefore as unprepared for the next contact from de Jersey as Driscoll had been.

He was leaning back in the chalet sauna, drenched in sweat, when Rika opened the door. She was wearing a silk wrap, and her long blonde hair was in a plait down her back, but judging from her expression, she was not a happy woman. She was holding a ring box, and her face was taut with anger. 'I fund dis inda luggage!' she snapped.

'What?' He wrapped a small towel round his waist.

'I'm nut stupid, Jimmy,' she shouted. 'I bring ta Aspen da Christmas presents you give me, the ones from you to me and to da children. So who is diss for?' She wafted the box in front of his nose.

He sighed and stood up, towering over her, then walked out.

'Don't turn da back on me. I hate you!' she screamed.

He took the box from her and flicked it open. 'Have you had a good look at this, Rika? Don't you recognize it?'

'No, I do not.'

'Well, you should. Go back to last Christmas, to that charity dinner we went to. Sylvester Stallone was there. We were on the same table as Goldie Hawn.'

'Vat about it?' she said, her hands on her hips.

'Well, this ring is identical to the one Goldie Hawn was wearing and you admired it and she said it was from a local jeweller. So I ordered one for you last year but it wasn't ready in time. I paid for it, and asked them to keep it for me. Yesterday when I went out skiing I picked it up for you. It's three diamonds on platinum and yellow gold. You don't want it? Fine, I'll chuck it out of the goddamned window!'

He strode to the window and she ran after him. 'No, don't!'

'You want it now, do you?'

'I am sorry.'

'Yeah, well, you ruined the surprise. I'm getting sick of this, Rika.'

She started to cry and he wrapped his arms around her. They kissed and she slipped on the ring.

'Can I finish my sauna now?' he asked.

'Yes, I make breakfast. I so sorry. I just love you so much.'

He walked into the sauna and closed the door. It was all a lie, of course. He'd bought it for Cameron, his mistress in England, and had meant to give it to her when he returned. He had just poured pine essence over the coals when the door opened again. 'A call for you.'

'Who?' he snapped.

'I not know. You want me to bring it in here?'

'Yeah.'

She shut the door, and returned a minute later with his mobile, which she passed to him, then backed out and closed the door again.

Wilcox spoke into his phone. 'Wilcox.'

'Hello, Jimmy,' came the soft reply. 'It's the Colonel.'

'Oh.' He was surprised to hear de Jersey's voice, and his stomach lurched.

'Listen, I'll cut to the chase. This isn't a social call, it's bad news, so I'll give it to you straight.'

Wilcox listened, not interrupting as de Jersey outlined the Internet crash. 'But I don't understand. Can't Lyons sort this out?'

''Fraid not, Jimmy. He's dead. He topped himself.'

Rika had set out breakfast. Wilcox was meticulous about how his food should be served and she had it down to a fine art. Fresh white linen napkins lay next to the fine bone-china plates and coffee cups. She had changed into a navy ski suit with a white sweatshirt. 'I'm meeting da boys on da slopes. Will you see later?'

'Nope, not this morning. I have a few things to do. Maybe we could meet for lunch, take the boys to the hamburger joint.'

'But you no like dat place.'

'I know, but they love it. Tonight I'll arrange a nice place for us to go and eat, maybe dance. What do you think?'

She curled her arms around him. 'Good.'

'We need to arrange for the tree to be delivered, buy some more decorations and do some last-minute shopping, which I know you'll hate.' He handed her a roll of notes.

'Vatever you vant. I love you,' she said.

'I love you too.'

He gave her no indication that he'd just been hit with a bombshell. But somehow Rika knew something was wrong. She cupped his chin in her hands. 'You vould tell Rika somethink happen if it's not good, yes?' she asked.

'Of course. Go on, now, see you later.'

She paused at the door to look back at him with a puzzled expression. She knew all his moods, his cocaine-wired energy, his short temper, his loving side, but she was seeing something in Wilcox that she had never seen before. He was quiet and appeared tired. Something was weighing him down. 'I take care of you good,' she said softly.

Wilcox smiled. 'Yeah. Now, go on, go meet the kids.'

This time she left and he sighed, closing his eyes. His entire fortune, bar a few hundred thousand, had gone. David Lyons had topped himself and, as he sliced the top off his egg, Wilcox wished he had done it for him. Like Driscoll, he did not blame de Jersey: he knew it had been his own decision to bankroll the Internet company. And even after all this time he still trusted de Jersey to get them out of the mess. Deep down though, he was afraid. He wondered if de Jersey would have to resurrect the Colonel.

CHAPTER 3

DE JERSEY sat at his computer, slotting in disk after disk and jotting notes on the pad beside him. A newspaper, open on the desk, had an article ringed in red. It was about the fall in prices of stocks in Internet companies. Some compared it to the Wall Street Crash, but it did not help de Jersey to know he was in good company. The headline screamed, 'Tycoons Who Lost a Billion Overnight' and 'The Stars Who Saw Their Internet Fortunes Crash'. Five British investors had lost a billion in less than a year; five others had lost more than half a billion. The only compensation for de Jersey was that his name was not mentioned in any of the press reports.

Leadingleisurewear.com, the company into which de Jersey, Wilcox and Driscoll had poured their savings, was one of Europe's leading Internet retailers and it had now been confirmed that they had brought in liquidators. The company had spent nearly £230 million since its inception eighteen months previously. Staff at its headquarters learned that the fledgling enterprise had collapsed, taking with it the entire backing of its investors. The founder, Alex Moreno, admitted that perhaps the company had been too visionary and had failed to control costs.

De Jersey wrote and underlined the man's name on his pad and continued scrolling through the reports drawn up for him by David, detailing previous companies started by Moreno. This was by no means his first enterprise. He had successfully launched four companies on the Internet over the past six years, but admitted to 'living the high life' and 'overstretching his ability and resources'. Then de Jersey read a lengthy article in which Moreno expressed his deep regret but said he still believed the company had been on the right track. Their aim had been to become the biggest retail Internet business worldwide. He admitted they had spent money too freely on offices in London, New York, Stockholm, Germany and Sweden, and on advertising and 'perks'.

De Jersey almost bit through his cigar as he read about the outrageous lifestyle of the young entrepreneurs: they had purchased fleets of cars, and enjoyed first-class hotel accommodation, luxurious apartments and houses. The article identified the big losers in leading-leisurewear as 'an English aristocrat and two other British businessmen'. As the controlling shareholder de Jersey had suffered the biggest loss: nearly a hundred million pounds.

It was almost five o'clock in the morning when de Jersey finished assessing all the documentation David had compiled for him and shut down his computer. His losses were far greater than he had at first anticipated and it was more than likely that the same would apply to Wilcox and Driscoll. All he had left was his offshore account in the Caymans. The three million he had stashed there was now all he had left and, with David gone, he would now have to gain access to this money personally.

He unlocked a drawer and slipped into it his notepad

with the names of the founders of leadingleisurewear, their last-known addresses and details of their attempts to sell off what was left of the company. Moreno had already formed another company in a different name. This meant he could be traced and de Jersey had every intention of doing just that.

It snowed heavily during the night and on Christmas Day de Jersey's home resembled a picture postcard of idyllic country life. The house was decorated with bunting and Christina's arrangements of silver holly and fir branches. The tree, positioned in the hall, reached the ceiling and was decorated with silver ribbons and baubles. The gifts at its foot were all wrapped in silver paper with silver ribbons and holly leaves. Christina adored Christmas. She had baked and cooked for days beforehand and made up baskets of Christmas puddings, cakes and mince pies as gifts for the staff and the local church. She loved the smells that wafted through the house, and most of all she loved her family being together. Natasha and Leonie had arrived home yesterday. They had spent a few nights with some classmates in their chalet in Switzerland and had enjoyed some skiing before heading home. At seventeen and fifteen the girls had their mother's crystal blue eyes and long blonde hair and looked stunning. Although de Jersey spoiled his daughters he was quite a strict father and liked the rules of the house to be adhered to. Their friends were always welcome to stay, as long as plenty of notice had been given. He never encouraged people to drop in: he valued his privacy too much, and his family understood that.

Now the usual Christmas Day drinks party was in full

swing, and all de Jersey's staff had come. Christina had chosen gifts for each employee and their families, and there was a white envelope from the Boss, which contained a bonus. No one was overlooked. De Jersey stood at the front door looking out with a lump in his throat. Royal Flush was walking sedately through the snow carrying two baskets loaded with gifts from the staff to their employer. The horse was draped in a red velvet blanket, with a sprig of holly in his forelock, and his breath steamed out in front of him. They surrounded de Jersey and sang 'For He's a Jolly Good Fellow'. He approached his champion and stroked his nose. He was not about to lose all this, he thought. This was everything he had dreamed of possessing.

In the celebrations that followed de Jersey slipped away and was not missed for some time. Eventually, Christina sought him out in their bedroom and was surprised to find him changing into his jodhpurs.

'Darling, what are you doing?'

'I need a ride. I won't be long.'

'But lunch is soon. You said you wanted to sit down at four.'

'I'll be back by then. Please, I'm sorry, I just need some air.'

He saddled up Royal Flush himself and rode towards the snow-covered track on the outskirts of the farm. Only the footprints of foxes and birds marked the snow as he cantered ahead. As his lungs filled with the icy air, his thoughts turned with greater clarity to the problems he faced. By the time he returned he had decided to leave first thing the following morning. He'd have his pilot arrange permission to fly into Heathrow's private heliport and would then take a flight to New York. In the US the Christmas holiday was over by Boxing Day and he felt sure that Alex Moreno would be at work. He planned to pay him a surprise visit.

Christmas lunch culminated with the pudding which blazed with blue flames and was carried in to great applause. Christina wore the delicate diamond bracelet that had been her husband's present. He had given both of his daughters a special piece of jewellery too, as tasteful as their mother's. He hated anything ostentatious. He had received cigars, socks and a flamboyant embroidered waistcoat from the girls.

They had coffee in the dining room and played word games in front of the roaring log fire. At seven Natasha and Leonie went to change to go to a party. The mantelpiece was crowded with invitations, not only for the girls but for Christina and de Jersey too, though de Jersey rarely accepted. Christina curled up beside him, her arms loosely wrapped round his knees.

'I have to go to London tomorrow,' he told her. 'I shouldn't be more than a couple of days. I'm sorry, it's business.'

'But it's Boxing Day,' Christina exclaimed.

'I know, but I have to go. I'll make it up to you.'

She looked up into his face. 'It's to do with David, isn't it?'

'No. Why do you ask?'

'Oh, don't do this to me.' Christina sighed. 'Since David's death you've been acting so strangely . . . understandably, I suppose. Please talk to me. Is it to do with him?'

'Yes,' he admitted. 'He's left a few loose ends that I need to deal with right away. I'm meeting a banker who's going to help me unravel the mess.'

'Okay, but don't be more than a night or two – do you want me to come with you?'

'You stay with the girls. The sooner I leave the sooner I can come home, but it might be three or four days. If it's any longer I'll call you.'

Christina stood up and threw another log on to the fire, then glanced at the mantelpiece: a Christmas card from the Queen was in pride of place. Her husband had been so proud when he saw the crest on the envelope. She knew he coveted acceptance in high-society circles but did not understand why. But, then, she knew little of his past – not long before he had met her, his last relative, his mother Florence, had died. Sometimes she wished she knew more about the complex man she had married.

'Penny for them,' he said, and kissed her neck.

'I was admiring the Queen's Christmas card.'

De Jersey laughed, and she smiled contentedly. When he was close to her, she felt she needed nothing more. 'Why do you never talk about your family?' she asked suddenly. 'You are so good with mine when they come to stay but I know no more about yours than I did when we were first married.'

'What brought this on?'

'I don't know. Well, actually I do. You go away sometimes – inside yourself, I mean. I know this David business is on your mind but you told me it's not that serious. Then you have to go to see a banker on Boxing Day. It doesn't make sense to me. If it *is* serious why don't you tell me, let me share it with you?'

De Jersey had to control his temper.

'This is the only time the banker's available to meet me. My parents died a long time ago and I don't know

68

why you're suddenly interested in them. You know all there is to know.'

'No, I don't,' Christina persisted.

'Yes, you do,' de Jersey snapped. 'And you've had too much champagne.'

'No, I haven't.' She hesitated, then tried to lighten the mood. 'The Vicar had too much to drink at the party, though.' She leaned against the mantelpiece watching her husband. 'What was your home like, Edward?' she asked tentatively.

He blinked rapidly, then sat down and rested his head in his hands. 'Clean, neat and tidy. My mother always said you could eat your dinner off her kitchen floor. We always had a tree in the front-room window and paper chains all over the hall. There was usually a big fire – well, it seemed big but the fireplace was small. It had pinkish tiles and two brass animals on either side.'

Christina stared at him. 'You make it sound . . .'

'Clean, neat and tidy,' he said.

'No, friendly,' she said.

'It was. Everyone loved my father and mother.' He changed the topic. 'Now, as I'm leaving tomorrow, I thought maybe we could retire early,' he said, cupping her breasts with his hands. She turned to face him and they kissed passionately, until he picked her up in his arms and carried her towards the stairs.

As Christina lay sleeping beside him de Jersey stared up at the ceiling, then at her peaceful face. He moved a wisp of hair from her cheek. His marriage to Christina had been so happy; his previous one seemed like another lifetime. He had met his first wife, Gail Raynor, at a nightclub. Her father was a wealthy real estate agent who had offices all over London and she was the worst kind of spoilt 'daddy's girl'. She had been educated at Roedean, one of Britain's top private schools, and attended finishing school in Switzerland. Her early twenties had entailed nothing but a constant round of parties and clubs. She had an annoying nasal twang and haughty manner worse than that of her aristocratic 'debby' friends. Gail was waif-like with long auburn hair that reached down to her waist. She wore miniskirts that showed off her beautiful legs and high, white Courrèges boots. Her long delicate fingers had perfect oval shaped nails. When he first saw her in the dim lights of the Piccadilly Blue Elephant Club she had looked like a tempting angel as she danced in a provocative manner. The Blue Elephant club was the 'in' place to be and be seen at, always full of celebrities and famous socialites. De Jersey had been there with Wilcox. De Jersey was not a man who frequented nightclubs on a regular basis, even when he was young. Wilcox, who was a regular at every club in the West End, had cajoled him into going. They had not as yet pulled their last robbery and agreed to go their separate ways for their own security, a decision that de Jersey made partly for his own protection. Wilcox was always a daredevil and seemed to have an endless string of women. In fact it was he who had first known Gail Raynor and introduced them.

'Can't you sleep?' Christina murmured, interrupting his thoughts.

'No, just thinking.'

'About what?' She sat up and leaned on her elbow.

'My life before you came into it.'

70

'You mean the time when you were married to, what was her name?'

'Gail,' he said not wishing to discuss it.

'Do you think about her often?'

'No, not usually. Maybe it's David's death. My mind's been all over the place. I've been reflecting about a lot of things.'

'Like what?'

'Like how strange it was that I ever got involved with Gail. To be honest, I think I was more impressed by her successful father than her.'

'Why?'

He sighed, wishing he had not even begun the conversation. 'Maybe because my own father was dead and he was very encouraging. I was not sure what I wanted to do with my life and he gave me a direction.'

'By marrying his daughter,' Christina said yawning.

'Could say that. Whatever, she was a mistake but my friendship with her father wasn't. He was a good man.'

She snuggled close to him. 'You hate talking about her, don't you?'

'I'd say hate was a bit harsh. I just don't like wasting any time thinking of her. She isn't worth it and that part of my life is over. Hate has nothing to do with it. It was my mistake and I got out of the marriage as fast as I could.' He made no mention of the fact that he had divorced Gail as soon as her father had died and left him to run the business. It had also been Gail's father who had suggested, for appearance sake, that if he was selling property to top level clients he maybe should think about dropping the use of the over familiar 'Eddie'. He felt that Eddie Jersey wasn't classy enough. It was at this

71

time that he decided always to refer to himself as 'Edward', then he went one better and inserted the 'de' in his name. So it was due to his first wife's father that he eventually became Edward de Jersey. Gail's father would never know how many other names his son-in-law would, by the end of his criminal career, have used.

'What happened to her?' Christina asked.

He shrugged his shoulders. 'I don't know. When the firm went bust I sold up and . . .' he sighed. He was moving into dangerous territory now because after the company fell apart he started planning his final robbery.

'I never saw her again,' he said. He leaned on his elbow and smiled. 'I met a woman who made up for all the tedious years I'd been with Gail. This woman, well she was just a young slip of a thing and I saw her photograph in a magazine and . . .'

Christina giggled. She always loved to hear him tell her how he had cut out her picture and traced her through the model agency. He had even travelled to Sweden to try to find her when she was already living in London.

'And this slip of a girl is now my wife and the mother of my daughters and . . .' he kissed her, cutting his story short, not wanting to let Christina return to the subject of his ex-wife or more importantly get close to the time in his life when he, Wilcox and Driscoll had pulled off their last robbery: the robbery that had been the foundation of their wealthy lifestyles.

Gail was no comparison to his second loving wife. Christina was everything Gail had not been. What troubled de Jersey deeply was that when he met Christina he was immensely rich, using his wealth to court her obsessively. At first she had thought he was too old for her.

'Do you regret anything?' he asked stroking her cheek.

'No, well, yes there is one thing,' she said softly.

'What's that?' he asked kissing her neck.

'I would like to have given you a son.'

He eased away from her and rested back on the pillows. After a moment he raised his arm and drew her close to him.

'I do not have a second of regret, not one second,' he said. 'We have two perfect daughters and . . .' he looked down into her face, 'Royal Flush.'

'I know,' Christina said, 'but it's not the same.'

He gripped her tightly, his voice hoarse. 'I don't want anything to change.' The manner in which he said this frightened her a little but then he tucked the pillow beneath his head and closed his eyes.

'Goodnight sweetheart,' he murmured.

'Goodnight,' she replied, remaining curled by his side, still lying in the crook of his arm.

'Happy Christmas,' she whispered.

De Jersey kissed her head. 'Happy Christmas, sweetheart.' He knew he would not allow anything to harm their idyllic life.

Christmas in Florida was different from what it was in England. The Driscolls ordered turkey and the trimmings but it wasn't the same in eighty-degree heat. On Christmas Day Driscoll lay by the pool. He was deeply tanned, and reading yesterday's *Sunday Times*, a cigar burning in the ashtray and a large Pimm's on the glass-topped table beside him. His recent impotence was a thing of the past. It was strange that whenever he remembered his lost millions he got an erection. For most men it would have been the reverse. Folding his paper, he mulled over the reasons why his financial disaster had sexually aroused him. Perhaps it was the fact that it cut through the complacency his semi-retirement had brought on. Dropping his paper to the floor, he stood up and dived into the pool.

Driscoll did a few lengths, then rested at the side in the shallow end. He was surrounded by elegant young women and ageing, tanned men. It was an expensive hotel and there were few families or children. All of the guests were extremely wealthy. You could almost smell the money. The diamonds on the women's Rolex and Cartier watches, necklaces and earrings caught in the sunlight, and like Driscoll, the men wore expensive watches and rings. Driscoll got out of the water, returned to his sun bed and reached again for the financial section. There were numerous articles about the Internet crash but it didn't help to know that he wasn't the only one who'd lost millions.

At six the Driscolls were sitting in a booth in the main restaurant for Christmas dinner. Driscoll had already ordered Krug champagne as, he noticed, had most of the other guests. By the end of the meal, he had to undo the button on his trousers. He had drunk more than usual but he felt stone cold sober.

'Do you like this colour?' Liz asked, showing him her pearly false nails.

'Yes, very nice.'

'It's oyster pink shimmer,' she said. 'It's a perfect match for the dress I bought for New Year's Eve. I was just testing the colours out to see which one I should wear. Do you remember me telling you about the dress? It's from Chanel in Knightsbridge.' Driscoll recalled the floating chiffon with an embroidered vest top and ribbon straps. It had looked like a nightdress but he'd told her he loved it – he loved anything that made her happy. Suddenly he turned away, overcome by emotion.

'Tone, what's the matter?' she asked, alarmed.

Driscoll was crying now, tears trickling down his face. How could he tell her he was broke? That he'd been a bloody idiot and lost his life savings. A few thousand here or there wasn't going to keep this pretty little soul in the manner to which she was accustomed. 'I've had too much to drink,' he muttered.

She reached over and caught his hand. 'Let's go up to the room, order some more champagne, get into the Jacuzzi and have dirty sex.' She giggled. 'They've got the porno channel if we want it, I checked in the TV guide in our rooms.'

Dear God, he thought, how am I going to keep this up until New Year's Eve? All he wanted was to get back to London, meet de Jersey and hear his plan. As he thought about it he got another erection. 'Yes, darling,' he said. 'Let's go up to the suite.'

They didn't make it into the Jacuzzi and he didn't need to watch any porno film. To Liz's delight, Driscoll didn't even take off his dinner jacket, he was so desperate. They screwed against the bathroom wall, in the bedroom on the carpet and then in their bed until he passed out. She wished their sex-life was always this good. On this holiday Driscoll had been more rampant than he'd been in a long time.

Unlike Driscoll, Wilcox had never been money-conscious. He was living life on the edge in Aspen, keeping his mind off his financial crisis with excessive amounts of cocaine. But Rika was worried by his recklessness and his eagerness to ski at all hours of the day and night. Wilcox was more like de Jersey in personality than Driscoll, but although he had more innate class than de Jersey, he lacked prudence. He was a man who liked taking risks. Over and over again Rika questioned him and tried to stop him going out late at night, but she always backed down at the first hint of anger. Fury lay dormant in Wilcox and she did not want to provoke it against herself. So, when Wilcox left the house on Christmas night she didn't try to stop him.

Wilcox knew that the loss of his fortune had left him balancing on a precipice. When he got off the ski lift at a level for experienced skiers, he positioned himself, checked his skis, adjusted his goggles then eased forward and down the slope. In the five-minute descent, he made a near-perfect run. When he reached the lower slopes, however, he felt a tightening in his chest. He gasped for breath and by the time he was at a standstill he had to bend almost double. The pains in his chest had been recurring more frequently of late. Added to this, he'd been experiencing dizzy spells and a couple of times during this holiday his nose had bled profusely. As he pulled off his goggles and tossed aside his gloves, he saw spots of blood dripping on to the snow.

He removed his skis and carried them to his truck. Once inside, he leaned back in his seat until the dizziness subsided. Then he adjusted the rear-view mirror to look at himself. His nostrils were encrusted with dried blood. He took a tissue, wiped it away, then drove back to the chalet. Every light in the house was on: the kids would be listening to music, playing table tennis or watching videos, and Rika was probably waiting to have another go at him for disappearing. He told himself he was too old to be burning the candle at both ends and indulging a serious drug habit – if he caught any of his kids using the same substance he'd thrash them. Yet even as he berated himself he could feel the itch starting, the need for a hit. He dumped the skis on the ground by Rika's car and hurried up the stairs.

He locked the bathroom door, unfolded the wrap, chopped three lines of cocaine, rolled a dollar bill and snorted. He had just rubbed the residue on his gums when the door handle turned. 'James, are you all right?'

He unlocked the door, smiling. 'I'm great. Just got caught short coming up the drive.'

'I vas vorried vhen I saw you just throw your skis inside the garage. You haven't viped dem clean.'

'Yeah, yeah, I'll do it later.'

'You do it now, James. You shout at the kids for doing just the same thing.'

'Get off my back, Rika.'

'I'm not on it.' She stormed out and Wilcox sat on the toilet. He'd have just one more hit, he thought, then he'd go and dry off his skis. He snorted two lines, then reached for the phone. He knew it was against the rules but he couldn't stop himself. A little later, he went into the bedroom, packed a bag and went downstairs to Rika. 'I've got to go away for a day. I'll be back tomorrow.'

She gripped his arm. 'Vhere you going?'

He pushed her aside and headed out. 'I've got a business problem. Just leave me alone!'

'I von't be 'ere ven you get back,' she screamed after him.

Wilcox drove erratically down the drive then reversed back up, almost skidding into the garage. Rika ran from the house and banged on the windscreen with her fist but her anger turned to worry when she saw the look on his face.

'I'm sorry,' he said, and she opened the car door and got in beside him. 'I've got big problems.'

She put an arm around him and he rested his head against her. 'Maybe I'll go tomorrow,' he said, and then she helped him out of the jeep and into the house. He told her only that he had lost some money and needed to talk to someone about it. The following morning she drove him to the airport.

Wilcox flew to Florida. He knew it was against the rules but he had to talk to someone and it could only be Driscoll. Now he was sitting at a booth. In front of him was a massive aquarium with exotic fish diving around elaborate fake rocks. He'd had two diet Cokes and had calmed down since the previous night but he was cold – the air-conditioning made him feel as if he was still on the ski run.

Driscoll, in a white golfing cap, white T-shirt and shorts, entered the bar. He looked around then saw Wilcox slouched over the table at the booth. He headed towards him. 'How did you find me?' he asked, sitting down.

'Phoned all the top-notch hotels and asked for you. Simple. Got to the tenth and they said you were there.' Wilcox turned a bleary eye on his friend. 'Christ, Tony, you look like a right arsehole! It's the shorts and what have you got on your feet?'

'Gucci sandals. You look as if you've had a night on the tiles. If you must know, these are Lacoste shorts.'

'Still a label man, are you?' Wilcox asked.

'Yeah,' Driscoll responded. 'The wife buys it all. I don't give a shit but if it doesn't carry a designer name she won't buy it.'

Wilcox slurped his Coke and Driscoll ordered a decaffeinated coffee from a waitress in a pink uniform. They didn't speak until she had returned with the coffee and gone away again. It was hard to know where to begin but eventually Driscoll said quietly, 'How much did you lose?'

'My shirt,' Wilcox said flatly.

'Me too. I mean, I've still got a few thousand here and there, some property, but . . . he called you, did he?'

'Yeah.' Wilcox leaned back and rubbed his arms. 'Bloody cold in here.'

'Yeah, the hotel dining room's like a fridge, gotta wear a jumper to breakfast.' They were unable, it seemed, to discuss the reason why they had met up.

'What are we gonna do?' Wilcox finally asked in a depressed tone.

'I dunno. The Colonel said he was trying to sort it all but not to hold out much hope. The company's gone belly up. We may be able to salvage something.'

'No way. That prick David Lyons didn't top himself

for nothing, and if you've read the financial papers, we're in a long line of losers. The Internet bonanza's screwed thousands like us for millions.' Wilcox twisted his glass. 'Gonna meet us at the Ritz again, right?'

'Yeah, that's what he said. He's arranged the meeting for when I get back from here, mid-January.' Driscoll was staring at the fish.

'What do you think he's doing in the meantime?'

'I dunno, what do you think?' One tiny fish was swimming around so fast it was like quicksilver.

'I'd say he's up to his old tricks again. He must be nosing out some hit. Said he was gonna try and track down this son-of-a-bitch Moreno but what if he suggests we get involved in something? Are we up for it?'

Driscoll burped. 'Thing is, Jimmy, I owe him. His dad Ronnie took care of my mother. If it hadn't been for him she'd have been in a right mess. Always looked out for us. Paid for my school uniform. Like a surrogate father to me was Ronnie.'

'I know.'

Driscoll closed his eyes. 'He used to look after a lot of people, did Ronnie, but when the shit hit the fan . . .'

Wilcox leaned back against the booth, staring at the fish in the tank.

'Those villains, Jimmy, were something else. They came in the bookies with fucking sledgehammers, terrified the lot of us. I mean, I didn't know Eddy that well. Seen him around but he was at the grammar school so we didn't mix. And when he got into Sandhurst I hardly ever saw him. It was hard to believe they were father and son. I mean Ronnie wasn't a big fella and Eddy was always head and shoulders above him. My mother said it was from Florence's side he got the height. She was a big woman. Always knitting. She got him elocution lessons so's he wouldn't feel out of place at Sandhurst. But when I saw him at Ronnie's funeral limping on a crutch after he'd busted his knee, I said to myself, "He's not gonna be able to deal with these villains coming into the shop, extortin' cash, smashing the place up." I said to him that as much as I respected his dad, I wasn't gonna stay around to get my head kicked in. And do you know what he said?' Driscoll answered his own question. ' "They've offered to buy me out," he said, and I said to him, "Sell. If you don't, they'll go after your mother." With bastards like the Krays and the Richardsons fighting it out between them, I told him to sell up and get out, but he said he was going to the police.'

'I know.' Wilcox was looking around the bar, bored. He'd heard the story a thousand times, albeit many years ago.

'Offered him peanuts, the bastards did,' Driscoll continued, 'and those two betting shops were goldmines. Cops were no help. I said to him, "Eddy, they're probably getting back-handers," and I'll never forget his face. When they came back, pushing and shoving him around, he just stood there like a wimp. They threw the money at him and made him pick it up off the floor.'

'I was there, Tony.'

'I mean, if you'd told me then what he'd go on to do, I'd have laughed in your face,' said Driscoll.

Suddenly Wilcox got up. Driscoll looked up at him. 'Where you going?'

'To take a leak, then I want out of this place. We can go back to my hotel, have a sandwich.'

'Oh, okay, I'll settle this.' Driscoll took the check.

Wilcox gave a soft laugh. 'That's generous.'

They walked out into the brilliant Florida sunshine and made their way to Wilcox's hotel. It was evidently not a five-star establishment and Driscoll balked at going in. 'Gawd almighty, Jimmy, why did you book into a place like this?'

'Anonymity,' Wilcox snapped, and they went into the threadbare foyer then up to his room. Once there, Wilcox opened a miniature vodka from the mini bar.

'I was just thinking back there about you moving in with Eddy after Sandhurst,' Driscoll remarked. 'I bet his old mother didn't like it.'

Wilcox flopped back on to the bed. 'You know, Tony, you sound like a record that's got stuck. I dunno how many times I've heard you rapping on about Ronnie and Florence Jersey. You don't owe Eddy. If you hadn't helped us out we'd never have got away with robbing the shops.'

'I know,' said Driscoll.

Wilcox chuckled as he recalled the way de Jersey had laid the plans to rob his father's old betting shops. They hit them on every big race meeting, de Jersey working out the details like a military manoeuvre. They wore balaclavas and carried shotguns as they systematically cleaned out the takings. As a result of their robberies, the two big rival East End gangs started a war that eventually saw the shops fire-bombed and burned to the ground. That was when de Jersey became the Colonel, because of the way he barked out orders when they rehearsed their attack on the shops.

82

'How much do you reckon in today's money we got away with?' Driscoll asked.

Wilcox shrugged. 'Maybe a quarter of a million, not a lot.'

'To me it was. When he shared it out three ways I couldn't believe it. I thought I'd get a cut but not that much. You see, that's another reason I owe him. I was able to set my mum up for the rest of her life, God rest her soul.'

Driscoll called room service and ordered two hamburgers and french fries.

'You ever think, Tony, that he owes us?' Wilcox asked quietly as Driscoll hung up.

'No way. He even split it three ways for the train robbery. He didn't have to do that.'

'Why not? He couldn't have robbed his dad's shops without our help, and on the train job, all he did was suss out how to stop the train.'

'And I was the only one with a car. Remember that Morris Minor? You two were havin' to schlep all over the place to check out the trains. You guys were catching trains to stop one!'

'Yeah, and we spent hours up at that railway bridge too. And it wasn't Eddy's idea about fixing the signals, it was mine.' Wilcox lit a cigarette.

'But he worked out how to move the mail train into a siding,' Driscoll said.

This annoyed Wilcox. 'Look, you just did the route for that, you were never part of it, and I don't call twenty grand in cash a big deal or any reason to feel you owe him for the rest of your life. You owe me just as much. I agreed to split that cash three ways as well.'

'Well, thanks a lot, but all I am saying is, he didn't always have to cut it three ways.'

'Just think about his reasons. The others got thirty years apiece, right? And when they questioned us we could have put him in the frame with them. We were lucky they just thought we were dumb kids.'

'Not that dumb. We got away with it.'

'Yeah, yeah, yeah. And here you are, Christ knows how many years later, bleating on about how much you owe him. That's why he always did a three-way cut.'

'What do you mean?'

'So we'd feel indebted to him,' Wilcox snapped.

'So you do feel you owe him, then?' Driscoll asked, surprised.

Wilcox sighed with exasperation. 'No, I don't. We all took the risks. It was only fair to cut three ways.'

Driscoll opened a bottle of gin from the mini-bar and yanked out the ice tray. 'Not the same on the last caper, though, was it?' he asked quietly, watching Wilcox's face.

Wilcox had tensed and was opening another bottle from the mini-bar. 'I was up for it,' he snapped.

'Yeah, but the last time it was a big number. Not like running up and down a railway track timing the trains or smashing up his own betting shops.'

'All right, I hear you.'

'Yeah, stealing fucking gold bullion, Jimmy, I don't call that small fry. If we'd been copped that would have been thirty years. Without Eddy we'd never have got away with it. But we did, Jimmy,' Driscoll said. 'And it wasn't you or me that found out how to launder the cash but Eddy.'

'Right, and it was almost a fuck-up. He didn't have any idea just how much of it there was.'

Driscoll started to laugh. 'Three tonnes of gold. Worth around twenty-five million pounds. And we split the profits equally between us. Too damn right we owe him.'

Wilcox lay back again, his eyes on the ceiling. Most of the gold had had to be melted down and moved abroad fast. De Jersey's friend's helicopter and yacht had ensured that this happened relatively easily. The robbery had gone almost without a hitch but the sheer volume of gold was a nightmare to move around. De Jersey had deployed everyone he could think of to melt down, move, carry and shift the bars. Some were melted in a private kiln at the bottom of a jeweller's garden. Others were buried around London, carried out to Spain in suitcases, even left in safety-deposit boxes. De Jersey shipped some to Africa, then brought it back into England after altering the hallmarks at a smelting plant he had purchased. Then he sold it on the open market. The largest amount, however, had been stored in a small jeweller's workshop in France.

There was a rap at the door and Wilcox got up to take in the hamburgers. He handed one to Wilcox, and unwrapped the other. 'He moved those gold bars around and turned them into cash,' Driscoll said, as he tried to open his tomato ketchup sachet.

'I don't know how he bloody did it,' Wilcox said.

'Well, I do. Or some of it anyway. He used assumed names and identities. He told me he'd worked out a system of depositing vast amounts of cash into high-street banks, sums as large as eight hundred grand. It wasn't just us he took care of.'

Wilcox unwrapped his hamburger.

'Those "soldiers" who were picked up, he looked after them as well. They never put any of us in the frame.'

Still Wilcox refused to acknowledge there was any debt owed to de Jersey. 'Well, they wanted their pay-off when they came out of the nick.' Driscoll swore as the ketchup spurted over his T-shirt. 'You know Scotland Yard officers recovered eleven melted-down bars in 1985. None of the remaining stolen ingots has ever been found.' Driscoll peered at his hamburger. 'Have you got a raw one? This is like old leather.' Wilcox passed over his hamburger untouched and opened another miniature from the bar.

The two men fell silent. Wilcox drinking, Driscoll chewing huge mouthfuls and stuffing French fries into his mouth with a studied concentration.

After the bullion raid, under de Jersey's orders, Wilcox and Driscoll had split up and moved to Canada then to Los Angeles. They had instructions to make no contact with each other and especially not with de Jersey, who had covered their tracks: he had given them fake passports, and they made sure they were constantly on the move until all was quiet. They had not received the big pay-off for another few years. It was a long time later that Edward de Jersey had emerged as a racehorse and stud-farm owner and by then Driscoll and Wilcox were living in luxury with their own flourishing businesses and growing families.

'Why did you come here, Jimmy?' Driscoll asked suddenly.

'Thinking of writing my memoirs,' Wilcox replied.

'Come on! You're here because you're worried about what he's gonna suggest, right?'

'Well, you keep saying how much you're in debt to him so I guess whatever he suggested you'd be up for it.'

'And you don't feel like you owe him?'

'Like fuck I do. It was his idea to back that Internet company.' Wilcox opened yet another miniature.

Driscoll opened a half-bottle of white wine. He had finished his hamburger and was munching Wilcox's.

'Okay, let's be honest with each other,' he said, and sat back.

'Reason I'm here is just to talk it through,' Wilcox snapped.

'Come on, Jimmy. Reason you're here is that you're scared shitless.'

'Listen, you fat bastard, I'm not scared of anything but I *am* being realistic. I don't want to do a caper. This time we could fail and no way do I want to spend the rest of my life in some nick.'

'Well, why didn't you come out with it before? I feel the same way.'

'You do?'

'Yeah. I've got a wife and two kids. I can get by, like I said, but I'll have to sell off everything. Liz will go bananas but, hell, I ain't gonna starve.'

'But you go on about being in debt to him. And when we meet what are you gonna say? We should get it worked out between us.'

'I know.'

'So, are we agreed? Whatever he suggests we both walk away from and we don't let him wear us down. You know what he's like. If we stand up to him together . . . Tony?'

Driscoll took a gulp of wine, then another, draining the bottle. 'I hear you,' he said. 'And I agree. I hope they serve better stuff than this at the Ritz because when he gets going the way I know he can I'm gonna need a few drinks to look him in the face.'

'Yeah, it's not gonna be easy facing him out but if we do it together it'll be better.'

'It's agreed, then?'

'Yeah.' They shook hands but neither could meet the other's eyes. They felt as if they were somehow betraying de Jersey.

Liz was buffing her nails, surrounded by boutique bags, when her husband reeled in. 'Do you know what time it is?' she asked.

'I do, my love. I've been out on the golf course.'

'No, you have not. I called them and, anyway, your golfing shoes are still in the wardrobe.'

'Well, I lied. I've been at the Pink Flamingo bar.'

'Who with?'

'Brad Pitt, and if you think I'm plastered you should see him.'

'Tony!' she yelled, as he tottered off to their bathroom and slammed the door behind him.

Whatever Driscoll had agreed to with Wilcox he knew he still owed the Colonel. It was going to be very hard to say no. It would be even harder for Wilcox, despite what he had said. He remembered the look on Wilcox's face when de Jersey had made them all agree all those years ago to having no contact with each other. Since leaving Sandhurst they had hardly been apart and although it was for their own safety, Wilcox had not really believed that de Jersey had meant it. He had joked that maybe they could, for old times sake at least, have a drink sometime.

'No, Jimmy,' de Jersey had said. 'When I walk away, that is it. You don't know me, we never meet up again, it's the only way we will protect each other.'

Although he had shook Driscoll's hand, de Jersey had hugged Jimmy tightly and after he had gone Jimmy was in tears. 'I feel like I just lost my brother,' he had said.

Driscoll felt sorry for him and almost as emotional. 'He's just looking out for us, Jimmy, like he's always done. So we do like he said, okay?'

'Yeah, yeah, goodbye, then.'

'Goodbye, Jimmy. You take care now. The Colonel's set us up for life so have a good one!'

So they had all gone their separate ways and with great success and above all there hadn't been so much as a whisper of their involvement in any of the robberies. They had each been lucky and enjoyed a good life.

He sighed and sat on the toilet looking down at his feet and his leather sandals. They reminded him of the ones he had worn when he was a kid, the ones Ronnie Jersey had paid for. Outside the bathroom his wife was dripping with diamonds and she had no doubt spent a fortune at the boutiques and it was all thanks to Edward de Jersey. It would be hard for Wilcox, but Driscoll knew in his heart it would be just as hard for him. But the good life had softened them both and he was sure Wilcox was as afraid as he was of being drawn into another robbery. They would have to say no.

CHAPTER 4

D E JERSEY needed a big injection of cash, not only to keep his estate afloat but to fund whatever he decided to do as a follow-up to the bullion robbery. It had taken careful planning to survive and remain undetected. There had not been a single whisper of his involvement in any of the robberies he'd masterminded. His first target now was Alex Moreno and he had already set the wheels in motion to track him down: he had hired a private investigator from an advert in the *New York Times*. The man had a lead on Moreno and de Jersey was flying to New York to confront him.

In his study, as his wife slept, de Jersey removed the top right-hand drawer of his antique desk, then reached over to the side of the desk, pulled a section of the edge towards him and a hidden compartment slid open. He got up, walked round the desk to the front false drawers and opened a four-shelved cupboard. First, he removed an envelope and put it on the desk. Next came a large square makeup box, and lastly a plastic bag containing two wigs, a false moustache and eyebrows. He sat in his chair and shook out four passports from the envelope, all in different names. He laid them out side by side, then shredded one that carried an out-of-date photograph of him which he could never match. The other three, which he was glad now he had diligently kept up to date, were in the names of Philip Simmons, Edward Cummings and Michael Shaughnessy. He returned Michael Shaughnessy, an Irish passport, to the envelope and put the other two into his briefcase. He had bank accounts and credit cards in all three names. None of them held a substantial amount of money, just enough for emergencies.

De Jersey opened the makeup box, and selected a few items then placed them in a wooden pencil box. He checked the wigs: they smelt musty but were in good condition. The glue and cleaning fluids were usable and the wig meshing clean. These he placed in his packed suitcase. He locked it then closed the secret compartment in his desk. He'd always travelled in disguise using his aliases with confidence, but now he'd have to be extra careful. Since the 11 September terrorist attacks in the United States, security at the airports, especially in and out of New York, had been stringent.

On 26 December, de Jersey left home and booked into a small hotel close to Heathrow airport as Edward Cummings, an English art dealer. The following day, using his Cummings passport, he travelled with Virgin, in economy class, to New York. He landed at JFK and booked into the Carlisle hotel, looking nothing like Edward de Jersey. The wig for Cummings was dark and curly with flecks of grey, and de Jersey winced when he eased it off. He used a Pan Stik makeup base to lighten his face and hands, then switched his own watch, which had belonged to his father, for a flashy Rolex. He slipped on a thick gold chain, a large diamond ring and a gold bracelet. His suit was expensive but a shiny, light grey silk. The shirt was white with a pearl grey tie under the stiff collar. Adjusting the pale blue silk handkerchief in the top pocket, he stared at his reflection. It had been a while since he had worn the suit and it was a little tight but it added to the persona he wanted to create. Lastly he took out the other wig: it was a reddish colour with a matching moustache and eyebrows and had been made for him many years ago by a theatrical costumier. Then he trimmed the sides of his own hair so it would fit tightly and show no gauze. He had arrived as Edward Cummings; now he was Philip Simmons and he called the Ritz Carlton hotel to arrange his first meeting.

'I'd like to speak to a Mr Donny Baron, please,' de Jersey said.

'One moment, sir. Who shall I say is calling?'

'Philip Simmons.'

There was a short wait before he was connected then Baron was on the line. 'Mr Simmons, did you have a good flight?' he asked.

'I did – came in on the red-eye from Los Angeles. Can we meet up?'

'Sure thing. Come on over for breakfast. I think I have what you need.'

'Good. How will I recognize you?'

'I'll be in a back booth of the Jockey restaurant. Just look for a short, bald guy.'

'Be there in about fifteen.'

De Jersey hung up and stared at himself in the mirror over the small telephone table. The game had begun.

De Jersey left by the side entrance to the hotel and hailed a taxi. Shortly afterwards he entered the Jockey restaurant at the Ritz Carlton and approached the only short balding man in the room. Most of the diners were young and rowdy, dressed in an odd assortment of designer clothes – the hotel was a known haunt of rock stars and their managers. Donny Baron was a security guard for a middle-of-the-road band that usually supported bigger names. As de Jersey approached, he tried to stand, wipe his mouth and hail the waiter at the same time, but de Jersey gestured for him to remain seated. 'I've had breakfast but, please, carry on eating.'

Ex-detective Baron had spoken to de Jersey numerous times over the past week. 'Mr Simmons' had seen the advert he'd placed in the *New York Times* after leaving the NYPD. But PI work had not provided a steady income so he had recently taken on the job with the rock group and hated it.

De Jersey took an envelope from his breast pocket and placed it on the table. 'You trace him?'

'It wasn't hard. I've got a few pals still in the game, you know, guys I was in uniform with. These days, with computers, tracing's a whole new game, a hell of a lot simpler.'

De Jersey glanced around covertly but no one seemed interested in them.

'He's here in New York,' Baron said, as he chewed a mouthful of omelette.

De Jersey patted the envelope again, impatient to get his five hundred dollars' worth. Baron reached into the breast pocket of his crumpled, navy blue suit and took out a slip of paper. 'A phone number, and an address just up from here. Apartment block facing the park. Lovely old building. He's on the second floor. Must have cost a couple of mill. He's got another place out in the Hamptons, being renovated, new pool, guest-house. Place is like a building site but he goes out there most weekends to see how it's coming along. Stays at a hotel called the Maidstone Arms.' Baron handed de Jersey the slip of paper. 'I've got a few extra expenses from tailing him out there and back. You've got my gas receipts, phone and a couple o' meal tabs and this is a snapshot of the guy. Moreno's a snazzy dresser.' He passed a photograph.

De Jersey glanced at the photograph and slipped the paper into his wallet. He smiled. 'I think you'll find that'll cover anything extra,' he said, and pushed the envelope across to Baron. 'I'm glad you were available.'

'Yeah, well, the band I take care of has been doing a recording here before we go on a twenty-city tour.' He smiled ruefully.

'Nice to meet you, Donny. Thanks.' And with that de Jersey stood up and left him.

De Jersey walked to Moreno's apartment, which over-looked Central Park. He stood in the shadows cast by the trees on the park side, watching the comings and goings at the entrance to the old-fashioned block. A uniformed doorman stood outside, leaping to the kerb-side when any of the tenants or their guests drew up. He tipped his cap and held open the glass-fronted door. De Jersey's eyes narrowed as Alex Moreno walked out. He was rather small, about five eight, wearing a navy blue ankle-length overcoat. A yellow scarf hung loosely around his neck and he smiled at the doorman, who walked with him to where a gleaming black Lexus sedan was parked. The doorman opened the driver's door,

Moreno got in and drove off. De Jersey checked his watch: it was ten fifteen. At ten thirty a white stretched limo pulled up. The doorman was kept busy carrying parcels and luggage back and forth as two women and a small child entered the block. De Jersey moved fast: he crossed the road behind the doorman, entered the block unseen and headed up the stairs.

Moreno's apartment was on the second floor. De Jersey rang the bell and waited, in case a housekeeper or someone else was at home, but no one answered.

At the end of the corridor there was a large window with heavy curtains, which opened on to a narrow ledge, no more than a foot and a half wide. De Jersey looked down on the small square garden below, then noticed that the ledge ran the length of the building and that a window in Moreno's apartment was open. He climbed out and, his back pressed to the wall, moved sideways along the ledge until he reached the window and slipped through it.

He turned to face the reception room in which he was standing. It was a high-tech space with high ceilings and a minimalist feel. The floors were of stripped pine and the brown leather furniture resembled the kind seen in art galleries or dentists' waiting rooms. Leather and chrome reclining chairs were placed around a large plate-glass table with the obligatory stack of artistic coffee-table books. There was a wide-screen TV set and Bang and Olufsen stereo units with chrome cases holding hundreds of CDs, plus a couple of huge oil paintings, both depicting a full-frontal nude man. The once old-fashioned fireplace had been sand-blasted and treated to resemble rough red stone, and fake logs were stacked in the grate. De Jersey took it all in. Moreno was a man of undeniable wealth but questionable taste. He moved cautiously into the hallway. More paintings and large photographs, all of handsome men, adorned the walls. He located a shining state-of-the-art kitchen, with a black-and-white chequered marble floor, a central hob and a restaurant-sized sink unit and fridge-freezer. It looked as if it had never been used.

De Jersey moved into the office. A bank of computers lined one wall and massive television screens hung from the ceiling. The leather swivel chair was well worn, the wastebins were overflowing and a large shredder basket was full. The desk, which ran the length of the room, was stacked with documents, loose papers, notebooks, dirty ashtrays and used coffee cups. It was the only room in the apartment that looked lived-in.

De Jersey began to go through the filing cabinets and looked over the items on the desk. He attempted to open the computer files but they were protected by a personal password. He continued his search and gathered as much information about Moreno as possible. He had set his wristwatch alarm to go off at twelve, hoping that Moreno would not return before then.

By one fifteen de Jersey was back in his suite at the Carlisle. He showered, then sat down at the small antique desk and began to work through the hurried notes he had made. He now felt that he had a pretty good assessment of Alex Moreno's personal life but he had yet to familiarize himself with his business activities. From Moreno's bank statements he discovered the soaring costs of his property development in the Hamptons but could not see where he was going to get the money to pay for it.

By eleven the following morning Edward Cummings had checked out of the hotel by phone. At ten past he slipped out as Philip Simmons and caught the twelve o'clock Jitney bus to the Hamptons. He sat at the back, spoke to no one and read the *New York Times*. He arrived in East Hampton two and a half hours later. He hired a car as Philip Simmons from Pam's Autos and booked into a bed-and-breakfast called The Huntting Inn, also under the name of Simmons. From his room he contacted the contractor who was running Moreno's building project and made an appointment to see him at the site at five that afternoon. He said he was acting as business adviser to Moreno and needed to oversee the progress of the renovations. He now knew that Moreno had an outstanding invoice for a hundred and fifty-five thousand dollars; he also knew that Moreno did not have the funds to cover it.

De Jersey drove to Moreno's property, which stood on a plot of land off the Montauk highway towards the luxurious and most sought-after district of Georgica. He was looking for Hedges Lane. He eventually found it off Baiting Hollow Road.

The guesthouse, which de Jersey passed as he drove in, was near completion. The roof was on and the windows installed. A line of trucks stood beside the partially built main house. Massive plumbing pipes and air-conditioning vents were stacked beside the skeleton building and on the far side a digger was removing earth for the swimming-pool. All the workers were wearing white hard-hats and the winter sun didn't even begin to warm the air. It was freezing cold and ice covered the pools of water left by the rain that had fallen that morning.

De Jersey parked the car, and no one paid much attention to him. He knew that the pool alone was costing a hundred thousand dollars and the guesthouse two million. The budget for the finished estate had to be around seven or eight million. De Jersey's anger grew inside him. He would claw back his losses from Moreno. By the time he returned to London the property would belong to him.

'Mr Simmons?'

De Jersey turned and was confronted by a muscular, rather stocky man in his late thirties. 'I'm Brett Donnelly.' They shook hands. 'This is my team. The architect was around earlier. Did you want to see him? He's tough to pin down. They're all running from one deal to the next. It's like a property bonanza. You live out here? Know the area?' Donnelly fired off questions seemingly without wanting an answer. He pointed to various precarious areas of potholes and planks as they made their way to his trailer. He banged his boots clean at the door and entered, de Jersey close behind him. The heat in the cabin was overpowering. Donnelly took off his padded jacket and hard-hat and put a coffee pot on one of the rings of his gas burner. 'With or without cream?' he asked, fetching mugs.

'Just milk, if you have it,' replied de Jersey.

Donnelly unhooked his phone, put down the coffee then sat in his office chair, rocking back and forth. 'So how is Mr Moreno?'

'He's fine,' de Jersey said coolly. 'I think it all looks very impressive here,' he added.

'Yeah, it's been a big job. The East Hampton Village Zoning Board has been driving us crazy. We've been waiting three months due to a variance with the land on the west side, a further two weeks for the pool permits and then another eight weeks for delivery of the timber. There are so many properties being built and it all means delays.'

De Jersey sipped the bitter coffee as Donnelly talked. It was fifteen minutes before the man finally fell silent, leaning back in his chair with a blue cloud of cigar smoke above his head.

'When do you fill the pool?' de Jersey asked.

'Any day now, it's almost dug. There was a pool there before so it's not taken too much excavation.' Donnelly gave de Jersey a quizzical look. 'Are you Canadian?' he asked.

De Jersey smiled. He had never thought of the accent he was using as Canadian but he nodded.

'How can I help you?' Donnelly asked.

De Jersey opened his wallet and proffered a card; he'd had it printed at a stationery store. 'As I said, I'm Mr Moreno's business adviser.'

'I see. Nothing wrong, is there?'

'I think we need to discuss my client's financial situation.'

Donnelly opened a drawer. 'You know we have an interim payment due?'

'Yes. It's why I'm here.'

'That's good. I'm just a local contractor and I can't afford to keep all these men on without the payments

99

being met on schedule. I've got a few other projects but this is the most substantial.'

'Mr Moreno is broke.'

'What?' Donnelly was stunned.

'I said, Mr Moreno is broke. I have to tell you to halt the rebuilding until we have released certain funds. At the moment, Mr Moreno cannot pay your last invoice.'

'What?' Donnelly repeated.

'I'll see that it is paid, eventually, but you must stop work until further notice. In fact, you might want to call a meeting with my client to discuss how we are to proceed. He should be here on site for a review of the situation.'

'Jesus, God, I've got twenty-four men on this contract. It'll bankrupt me. I've gotta pay them a weekly wage. What am I gonna do? I mean, are you saying the guy's *totally broke*?'

'I am saying that there will be difficulties in meeting your last invoice. However, we could probably sell the property as a work in progress, at a substantial loss, of course, but you will be paid eventually. Another buyer might even retain you to complete the work.'

'Oh, my God, I don't believe this!'

'I'm sorry. This is an excellent piece of land, though, in a prime position and with building permits already in place. I'm confident this is just a short-term situation, but you'll want to get Mr Moreno down here fast to sort it all out as amicably and as quickly as possible.'

Donnelly hesitated and swivelled in his chair. 'Am I missing something here? You say you're Mr Moreno's business adviser but you don't sound like you're employed by him, more like you're . . .'

'Handling a tricky situation. When I refer to myself as

his business adviser, it's rather more complicated than that. I'm taking over his business because of his mounting debts, some of which are owed to me. This is simply my way of making sure this development is completed, so I also get what is owed to me.'

Donnelly reached for the phone. 'You want me to get Moreno here?'

'Correct, and I suggest you do not mention I'm here. We don't want to make him feel like he's being ganged up on.'

Donnelly punched the buttons on his phone, and spoke briefly to Moreno, who said he would be at the site the next morning at nine a.m., then hung up. He told de Jersey what had been said.

Then de Jersey shook his hand and returned to his car. He watched Donnelly instruct the workers to quit for the day.

De Jersey dined at a sushi bar in Sag Harbor. It was almost seven when he returned to his room and placed a call to the Maidstone Arms, which was virtually opposite his hotel. He knew from Baron that Moreno stayed there but wanted to check that they were expecting him. He was told that they were but that Moreno would not be arriving until after ten. He didn't leave a message.

It was near to eleven when de Jersey called the Maidstone Arms again and was told that Mr Moreno had now checked in. He said that he was Mr Donnelly and left a message asking if the meeting could take place earlier, at seven a.m. This would give him two hours alone with Moreno.

De Jersey slept well, woke at five and checked out at six fifteen. He arrived on the site at six thirty and used a crow-bar to open Donnelly's Portakabin where he brewed a pot of coffee. He was confident that no workers would show up now that Donnelly knew Moreno's money had run dry. At seven on the dot the Lexus turned into the drive and the immaculate Alex Moreno stepped out. He walked towards the cabin, stepping gingerly over the debris, afraid for his Gucci loafers. He entered and was surprised to see de Jersey. 'I'm looking for Mr Donnelly,' he said.

'He's not here. Sit down, Alex, we need to talk.'

'Excuse me, do I know you?'

'No, you don't, but I know you.'

Moreno was going to refuse but something about de Jersey's manner, his strangely soft voice and steely eyes, made him hesitate. He sat down in front of the desk. 'What's this all about?' he asked.

'How many people did you take down when the company liquidated?' de Jersey asked.

Moreno shrugged. 'Oh, so this is about leadingleisure-wear. I don't know. Investors are investors. Sometimes they win and sometimes they lose.'

'Not everyone is a good loser, Alex,' de Jersey said quietly.

Moreno leaned forward. 'If this is some kind of scam then screw you! I don't know you and whatever you lost is not my problem.'

Without warning, de Jersey reached out and gripped the collar of Moreno's cashmere coat with both hands. 'It *is* your problem and I won't go away until you solve it.'

'I dunno what you're talking about,' Moreno stammered.

'I work for someone who invested millions in your

company and he is not a happy man. He wants compensation.'

Moreno pushed away de Jersey's hands. 'I'm clean out. We went into liquidation and there's nothing I can do.'

'Wrong. My friend wants this house, plus the lease on the Central Park apartment.'

'*What?*' Moreno asked.

'You heard. Now, I have some agreements here that will transfer your rights in those properties to my friend. Just sign here.'

'Fuck you,' Moreno said belligerently.

De Jersey got up and walked to the door where he stood, blocking Moreno's exit. 'It's you that will be fucked, my friend, if you don't agree. Sign the papers and you walk out of here intact.'

Moreno hesitated, then drew them towards him. He glanced over them.

'My, my, you've done your homework,' he said.

De Jersey moved away from the door, picked up a pen and handed it to Moreno. 'Just sign and no one will get hurt.'

Moreno's hand was shaking. 'I don't understand all this,' he said, like a child.

'It merely instructs funds to go into the necessary numbered accounts.'

Moreno glanced at him. 'You work for this guy with these accounts?'

'Yeah.'

Moreno bit his lip, then smiled. 'Why don't you and me do some private business? I can cut you in. When this place is finished I'm gonna ask fifteen million. Nice

103

profit! You'd get a nice bonus and walk away from . . .' he glanced at the document '. . . this guy, whoever he is. Who is he anyway?'

'My client,' de Jersey said.

'Well, screw him and you'll be a rich man. It's up to you. You just say you never found me. Who's to know?'

'Sign the papers,' de Jersey said.

'He pays you that well, huh?' The smirk remained in place as Moreno tapped the desktop with the pen.

'Sign the papers,' de Jersey snapped.

Moreno took a deep breath, still toying with the pen.

'Sign the papers,' de Jersey repeated. 'Now.'

Moreno dropped the pen, his smirk wavering. 'This is fraud,' he said.

'No, it's called paying off your debts.'

'Bullshit! I don't have to pay a fucking dime. I dunno who this guy is. There were a lot of investors. It was a new business. The investors knew the risks yet they ploughed in more funds. All they wanted was to see them double – treble, even. They were just plain greedy and that's not my fault.'

De Jersey dived for Moreno, gripped him by the hair and pushed his face roughly into the desk. 'Sign the papers!' he thundered.

'All right, all right, I'll sign them. No need to get nasty. I'll do it, okay? I'll do it,' Moreno said. De Jersey released his grip and Moreno put up his hands in a gesture of defeat. 'You've won, okay? You get this place and the apartment. I got nothing else, man.'

De Jersey placed one document after another in front of Moreno, who duly signed each one, flicking glances at him.

'Okay? All signed. Is that all? You wanna try on my suit for size?' he asked sarcastically.

De Jersey inspected each signature calmly then folded the documents and placed them in an envelope.

Seeing his way clear to the door, Moreno sprang up and crossed to leave. He yanked it open, turned and laughed. 'Listen to me, you son-of-a-bitch, if you think those papers would stand up in any court of law, you're wrong. My attorney will have them laughed out of court and I'll have you fucked over for kidnap and extortion.'

Despite his bravado, Moreno was so eager to make a run for it that his sleeve caught on the door handle as he turned to leave. He tripped out of the door and fell headlong down the iron steps. His head cracked against the side of the railing and he rolled on to the ground. His body jerked for a few seconds, then lay ominously still. De Jersey came down the steps and felt for a pulse but there wasn't one. He straightened up. This wasn't the outcome he had intended. His mind raced.

He dragged Moreno back into the cabin and felt again for a pulse but there wasn't so much as a flicker. He unbuttoned his coat, rolled up his shirtsleeves and walked outside. He picked up a spade and jumped down into the half-finished swimming-pool. He worked feverishly, digging in what would become the deep end of the pool until he had a hole big enough for the body. Then he returned to the Portakabin, emptied Moreno's pockets and found a wad of cash in an envelope addressed to Donnelly. De Jersey quickly counted the money and discovered that it was enough to cover Donnelly's outstanding invoice. Moreno had found the money somewhere. De Jersey removed Moreno's watch and anything else that would identify him, dragged him from the cabin and rolled him into the pool. He jumped down after him and pushed his body into the newly dug grave. He was filling it in when his watch alarm sounded. Time was running out. He climbed out of the pool, jumped into Moreno's Lexus and drove it into a nearby lane out of sight. He returned to the pool then and, to be extra careful no one discovered the body, used the compressor machine to level off the ground. He had just finished cleaning himself up, double checking that the gauze of the wig was in place, when Donnelly drove up and de Jersey crossed to his car, smiling as if nothing had happened. 'I want to take you to breakfast,' he said. 'There have been some new developments. Moreno isn't coming. Where do you suggest?'

The two men sat opposite each other in Marty's Diner. Donnelly had eggs over easy and a side portion of pancakes, while de Jersey sipped black coffee. First he handed over the envelope containing the wad of cash. 'That should cover your last invoice. You'll find it's all there. Count it. You can trust me. As you will see, there's a bonus for the problems you've had to deal with.' Donnelly's face showed his relief.

'As of now,' de Jersey went on, 'I am monitoring the project and controlling the payments. I have here post-dated cheques to cover work for the next two months and I assure you that I have funds to cover them. You are to complete the house, and I want the gardens landscaped. You know a good company?'

'Yes, I do. I've worked with them before.'

'Good. So I can leave that with you to arrange?'

'Sure.'

'We want the estate finished, if possible, by early summer.'

'We were scheduled for completion by June.'

'Good. I'll have someone, if not myself, come to the site at various times, but I've also hired a solicitor to take care of all payments due. It's a local firm called Edward and Maybury. They will deal directly with you and liaise with me. I require photographs and reports of work in progress to be sent to the solicitors, who will subsequently pass them on to me.'

'So what's happened to Moreno? Is he coming round as well?' Donnelly asked, confused.

'He's gone to South America – keep that to yourself – and he's handed over the running of his finances to me. I will also be handling the sale of the property. As I mentioned to you yesterday, Mr Moreno owes me a substantial amount and this way we both suffer no adverse loss.'

'Isn't he going to live here?'

'He can't afford it so he has agreed to sell, and I will arrange a real-estate agent to view the property when it is near completion.'

Donnelly drained his coffee then put out his hand to shake de Jersey's. 'Thank God. I didn't sleep last night with worry. I'll get the men back working today.'

De Jersey signalled for the bill, then opened his wallet. 'I saw they had begun work on the pool. When do they pour in the cement?'

'Well, we were set to do it when you called a halt to the work but now it's all back on they'll probably finish it today.'

'That's good.' De Jersey stood up to pay for breakfast,

and left. He went into East Hampton to discuss the value of the property with a real-estate agent. They were eager to please: a property in such a prime position would sell quickly. After the estate was completed they would, they felt sure, be able to ask up to fifteen million for it. That, plus the money from the sale of Moreno's apartment, meant that a small part of de Jersey's, Wilcox's and Driscoll's fortunes had been salvaged.

De Jersey returned his rental car to Pam's Autos and ordered a taxi to drive him back to where he'd left the Lexus, which he drove into Manhattan. Now in possession of Moreno's keys, he let himself into the apartment. He worked quickly, packing most of Moreno's clothes into suitcases and making appointments with three real-estate agents for that morning to discuss selling the lease of the fully furnished property. Then he called for the doorman to take the bags down to the Lexus. When the first agent arrived, de Jersey explained that he was asking a price below the market value to ensure the property sold fast. By the afternoon, using the legally binding letters and the reverse of the lease, all of which Moreno had signed, a cash deal had been struck. Before leaving the apartment, de Jersey unscrewed the back of Moreno's computer and, with an electric drill he'd found in a cupboard, made several holes through the hard drive. Unable to gain access to the files without the password, he didn't want anyone else to do so.

By seven that evening, de Jersey had parked the Lexus in the long-stay car park at JFK. He left the car unlocked with Moreno's suitcases on display. He wondered how long they would remain intact. De Jersey went to the Virgin Atlantic desk to catch his flight back to London, this time using his Philip Simmons passport. He also paid for an upgrade into upper class. He dined in the lounge, then boarded the plane and changed into the courtesy tracksuit to sleep for the entire flight. He spoke to no one and was woken for breakfast shortly before landing. After clearing customs, he went into the men's toilets, removed his wig and moustache, placed them in his case, combed his hair, and left the airport as Edward de Jersey.

He was home in time for the New Year celebrations. He knew it would be a considerable time before anyone became suspicious of Moreno's disappearance and he was certain that his body would never be discovered. His car would be found, but it would be hard to detect that there had been any foul play, just as it would be hard to trace his own movements in and out of the US. Once his finances had been investigated, it would probably be surmised that Moreno had done a runner.

De Jersey calculated that the money from Moreno's properties was a drop in the ocean compared to the losses the trio had suffered. However, his share of the cash from the sale of the apartment would be enough to keep his estate running for the time being. It was just short of a week since he'd left for New York. In that time he had felt the adrenaline pumping, the old excitement at being on the wrong side of the law. It was different from the enjoyment his horses brought: a thrill that made him feel as if he was walking on a tightrope. He liked being forced to use his wits and cunning, and felt no remorse for Moreno's death. It hadn't been his fault, but he was happy to use it to his advantage. The Colonel was back in business.

CHAPTER 5

THE NEW YEAR celebrations were over, and Wilcox and Driscoll were due to return from Aspen and Florida, but de Jersey had still not formed a plan. He had spent much of his time learning about the Internet: a vast world of which he knew so little.

After a few hours' surfing the web, he realized that his criminal expertise and methods were outdated in today's cyber-world. A successful modern criminal needed only a computer and a modem to carry out a lucrative heist, no breaking and entering, no weapons, no getaway car. And the more he surfed, the more he realized that nothing was secure in cyberspace. Aside from Internet-based crime, de Jersey was intrigued by the way information could be appropriated by criminal organizations internationally. The May Day riots, which gathered protesters and support worldwide, had been almost exclusively organized on the Internet. Even the Mafia carried out cyber-meetings these days. Crime was committed behind a hidden web of corruption and orchestrated from a simple keyboard. An eighteen-year-old hacker had broken into the US defence system and another into the

Bank of England. It astonished de Jersey that US institutions were so vulnerable. In the aftermath of the recent terrorist attacks, more security had been initiated around the world but the dangers in cyberspace continued unabated.

Restricted information was accessed all the time through password-sniffing programs. Hackers posed as authorized users, disguising their computers rather than themselves to acquire sensitive information. Computer credit-card fraud was big business, costing consumers billions of dollars per year. But successful hacking required high-level expertise. De Jersey was concentrating so hard on his screen that he didn't hear Christina walk in. She was carrying a shirt. 'What on earth is this on your cuffs?' she asked. 'It's on the collar too.' She held up the shirt he had used as Philip Simmons and he couldn't think what to say.

'It looks like makeup to me,' she said suspiciously.

'You've caught me out,' he said.

'What do you mean?'

He grinned sheepishly. 'It's fake tan.'

'What?' she said, taken aback.

'Well, I looked so bloody pale I tried it out, but it turned me orange so I washed it off.'

'Well, it's ruined the shirt.'

'Chuck it out, then.'

She flicked it towards him.

'You silly old sod – wait till I tell the girls how you were trying to impress this banker. No, don't tell me, he was a woman!'

'No, but he was twenty years younger than me.' He laughed, and made a grab for her but she dodged him and headed for the door.

'You *will* be pale and feeble if you keep yourself holed up in here,' she said. 'What on earth are you doing?'

'Moving into the high-tech world. It'll cut down on all that paperwork and it'll be cost-effective.'

'Will it? But you don't know what you're doing, do you?'

'I'm learning,' he said.

'You should get Tom to help you, he's doing a computer course.'

'Tom who?'

'The Vicar's son – Tom Knowles. He's been mooning around after Natasha but she's more interested in the horses.'

'I'll think about it – but if he's anything like his father . . . Did he recover from the state he was in on Christmas Day?'

'Well his midnight service was certainly something to behold.'

De Jersey looked at his computer. 'Maybe you should get his son to come over – sooner rather than later.'

'I'll do it now, then,' she said and left the room. De Jersey tapped the desk agitatedly. The shirt had been a foolish mistake. He should have dumped it before he came home. He would never have made a mistake like that in the past.

A few moments later Christina was back. 'Tom is ready, willing and able. I said you'd pay him per hour.'

The lessons began. Tom Knowles was training as an information-technology tutor at a local college. He looked similar to his father but was smaller, skinny and wore thick-rimmed glasses. He always arrived promptly at nine o'clock and stayed for two hours, three times a week.

One morning he opened his laptop as usual and said to de Jersey, 'Right, sir, last session you wanted to look into web privacy. The best way to keep your personal data personal is by not giving it out in the first place. So, if I wanted total electronic privacy I'd start with a made-up name or nickname for my email account, using Hotmail or Yahoo, for example. They'll ask you for personal information but there is nothing to say that you have to tell them the truth. Always skip any optional fields. If, however, you want to order things off the Net, you'll have to give your address. If this is a concern, you can get a post-office box.'

De Jersey nodded.

'You may think that surfing the Net is an anonymous activity but every website you contact keeps a record of your computer IP address. Combine that with your computer's ISP logs and you're right in the spotlight.'

De Jersey pursed his lips. 'Are there ways to cover your tracks when you're online?' he asked, staring at Tom's small screen.

'There are ways to hide behind someone else's IP address but I don't know much about that. You'd have to talk to someone who's more knowledgeable in that area.'

'And what about these ISP logs? Can't you just delete those from your computer?'

'Yes, but it's not as simple as using your delete key. Many people think that when they send documents to the recycle bin they're deleted but they're not. And even if you take the next step and delete the contents of your recycle bin they're still on your database. Private detectives and police investigators could still use programs such as EnCase and FRED to recover evidence from parts of your drive.'

'So you're telling me that if I, for example, had something sensitive, let's say illegal, and pressed delete, or put it in the recycling bin, it's always going to be on the hard drive?'

Tom nodded. 'Exactly. Which is why the police have been able to arrest so many paedophiles. The evidence of their illegal activities has been retained on their hard drives, even when they thought they had deleted it.'

'Is there anything you can do to remove something completely from your computer?'

'There's something called Evidence Eliminator. It's the equivalent to a government-level wipe that people say can deep-clean your computer of sensitive material. I have never used the program myself, though, so I don't really know how efficient it is.'

'Interesting,' de Jersey said. 'What about email?'

'Well, when you send an email it travels through several servers on its way to its destination. This means it can be intercepted and read. You never know who might be reading your email. At the moment, with the war going on in Afghanistan, police are monitoring the Net for terrorist communications. Numerous people have been arrested here that way.'

De Jersey's mind was racing with ways to use the new technology to his advantage. 'I read an article about hacking recently. How does that work?'

'What do you want to know?'

'Well, if someone wanted to hack into a company's files, how would they do it?'

Tom shrugged his shoulders. 'I have a basic under-standing of what's involved but I've never done it myself so I couldn't tell you. Some of the things hackers have done are pretty funny, though.'

'Like what?' De Jersey asked, not very interested.

'A few years back, two hackers rigged a radio station's phone system during a phone-in show to let only their calls through.' He laughed. 'They won two cars, trips all round the world and twenty thousand pounds! Very funny, really.' Tom noticed that his pupil's attention was wandering.

'You know what, Mr de Jersey, the best place to get hold of this information is the Net itself. You should start using the chat rooms, get online with some guys who know what they're talking about.' Tom checked his watch.

'Could you show me again how to get into the chat rooms? Then we'll call it quits for the day,' de Jersey said. 'Why don't we use your computer?'

Tom began tapping away. De Jersey was learning fast: he didn't want to take any risk, however small, that someone might trace anything back to his computer. Although it might seem overly paranoid at this stage it was obvious from what Tom had told him that you couldn't be too careful. De Jersey thought it prudent from then on to use Tom's laptop exclusively.

'Okey-dokey,' Tom said. 'Anything in particular you'd like to chat about or discuss?'

De Jersey gave it a second's thought. 'Yeah, how about something like those kids that hacked into the radio show?'

Tom tapped away for a few seconds. 'If we get

someone online who doesn't have the information we want, he can direct us to a more specialized chat room. Here we go.'

Tom typed away in search of information about hacking, then asked what de Jersey wanted to call himself.

'Erm, how about Bill Haley?' he said. Tom did not react – he was probably too young to remember the old rock-and-roller. He simply typed in the name. Then they watched the screen. Within moments they had received a message. 'Good God, that was quick,' de Jersey said, fascinated.

'Well, some of these guys spend all day on there.'

A short message on the screen told them that its author didn't know anything about hacking but that he had lost the password to his Toshiba and did anyone know the break-in starter password for this computer?

Tom tapped the screen with his pencil.

'Get out of this one. I'd say this guy has a stolen computer, that's why he doesn't have the password.'

'My God, I've got a lot to learn,' de Jersey said, intrigued.

Just then they heard Natalie return from riding, her voice calling to Christina. De Jersey glanced at Tom, who looked flustered.

'Excuse me,' he said, 'may I use your toilet?'

De Jersey nodded. 'Say hello to Natasha before you come back,' he teased. It had amused him that every morning during their lesson when his daughter returned from riding, the boy needed to use the bathroom.

Tom slipped out of the room so he missed the next message that flashed across the screen.

It was from someone calling himself 'Elvis' and suggested that Bill Haley attend a public course on the

116

Internet and thoughtfully listed numerous lectures taking place in colleges across London.

De Jersey asked which 'Elvis' thought would be best.

'I hear St Catherine's Church Hall, Lisson Grove, Notting Hill, Tuesday, eight fifteen p.m. is pretty good,' came the response.

'Thank you,' de Jersey replied.

Tom returned just as his watch alarm rang to herald the end of the session. He watched as de Jersey closed down his laptop for him, and then delved into his rucksack. 'I got you this. It's a novel by a guy called Douglas Coupland. It's a terrific read.' He passed it to de Jersey.

'*Microserfs.*' De Jersey read the title.

He walked Tom to the door, thanked him for the book and then, as an afterthought, said he would have to curtail his lessons for a few weeks as he had to go abroad on business. Tom looked disappointed but perked up when de Jersey handed him an envelope containing two hundred and fifty pounds. 'That's for all your help. I'll get in touch when I need you again.'

De Jersey had no intention of seeing Tom again: he had enough knowledge now to go on to the next stage. It was imperative that he went beyond what Tom could teach him and got to grips with identity protection. If he was going to plan a robbery utilizing the Internet, he had to know how to avoid being traced. Either he needed to find someone who could help him or work it out for himself. He would prefer not to involve anyone else, so he'd start by attending the lecture 'Elvis' had recommended.

De Jersey spent the rest of the day moving in and out

of chat rooms. He used various different names – on the Internet he could be whoever he wanted to be without the need for a disguise. Physical attributes, age and gender were irrelevant when de Jersey entered a world of make-believe, where the only truth was what he chose to write on the electronic page.

De Jersey was amazed at the ease with which he could contact other criminals on the web. Many even had their own websites, paying homage to their crimes. He looked up the Metropolitan Police's list of 'Most Wanted' criminals and allowed himself a satisfied smile at how successful his life of crime had been: none of his many pseudonyms were mentioned. It was de Jersey's sharp mind and ruthlessness, however, that had ensured the past robberies' success. De Jersey had planned each one. He had become the natural leader but he never forgot the debt he owed Driscoll and Wilcox, a debt he felt stronger than ever now that they had lost their fortunes on his investment advice. They'd been there for him in the past and he was comforted by the fact that he was sure he wasn't in this mess alone. They would be there for him again, whatever he decided to do.

As de Jersey dived into this new ocean of knowledge, a seed was sown in his mind. He had not yet formed a plan but was storing away information to use later. As he became more proficient he ordered a higher-powered computer over the Net, and arranged for it to be delivered and installed in his office. As he completed the order form on line, he noted with interest how many personal details he was asked to provide. Edward de Jersey was now a known entity in cyberspace.

Christina became increasingly frustrated as her husband continued to work all day at the stables then shut himself away in his study after dinner. His new hobby worried her. She had always been understanding about her husband's obsession with his horses but found this new development tiresome. She decided that enough was enough, and she was not going to take any more.

The next morning as she served breakfast, she asked him what had happened in London just after Christmas.

'Why do you ask?' de Jersey said. He was reading the Internet novel Tom had left with him.

'Since you came back, you've been in front of a computer morning, noon and night. You've stopped talking to me, you pay no attention to the girls, and you've hardly been near the stables.'

He shut the book and sighed. 'I'm sorry.'

'That's not good enough, and I won't have my parents to stay if you're going to continue to behave in this way.'

'What?'

'Don't you remember? They're coming for a week's holiday. But if you're going to continue to live in your office, they might as well stay at a hotel. They only come once a year and they want to see the girls before they go back to school.'

De Jersey was upset to see Christina so angry. 'I'm sorry. Why don't we go for a walk?'

'No, I'm going to do some baking.'

'I really am sorry. I guess I just got caught up in my new toys and I've been working a lot too.' He slipped his arms around her. 'Let me make it up to you.'

But she moved away. 'They'll want to do all the touristy things. I know you hate anything like that but it

119

means a lot to them to be here with me and I want to make it special.'

'I'll drive them, fly them and entertain them twenty-four hours a day, I promise,' de Jersey said.

'You don't have to go that far, but they look forward to coming every year.'

'Fine, then I'll make it a trip for them to remember. I'll arrange tickets for shows, guided tours, Windsor Castle, you name it.'

'They went to Windsor Castle last year,' she said. 'They said they'd like to go to the Tower of London this time and maybe see London Zoo. Perhaps we can go by barge up the Regent's Canal.'

'Done.' He slipped his arms around her again. 'When do they arrive?'

'In a week's time.'

'That gives me time to get it all sorted out. You sure you don't want to come for a walk?'

'Okay, then,' she said, turned in his arms and kissed him.

Later that afternoon de Jersey made his presence felt in the yard, talking, as he always had in the past, to each member of staff in turn. Then he leaned against Royal Flush's stable door as the sweating horse was hosed down after his exercise, and wrapped in a thick blanket.

De Jersey left the horse to his feed, satisfied that he was in good condition. He walked from stable to stable, examining the condition and performance of all the working horses, the progress of the brood mares, the growth and development of the foals and yearlings with the trainers and lads. Then he went back to the house, pausing to look back at the row of groomed, glossy heads protruding from the immaculate stables. It had taken twenty-five years to build up a stable of such calibre and Moreno's money would not last long. He needed a vast injection of hard cash to keep going and de Jersey was not prepared to fire one employee or send one horse to auction. This was his life, the life he had coveted and created, and no one was going to take it from him.

Christina was cooking dinner when he entered the kitchen from the yard. As he passed her she caught his arm. 'Are you going into your study again?' she said.

'I am, but only to arrange theatre seats and tickets for tourist attractions. I'll join you for dinner the moment you call me.'

In his study he lit a cigar and logged on to the Internet. He started searching for West End shows. When he had bought more theatre tickets than he had evenings to fill, he started to book tours of London, ending up at the Tower of London's website. He was not really paying attention as he printed off the information but articles about the spectacular jewels on display captured his interest. The gems included the Second Star of Africa, part of the Cullinan diamond, the Koh-i-noor diamond, St Edward's Sapphire and the Black Prince's Ruby. He leaned closer to the screen as the page went on to describe the magnificent pearls worn by Elizabeth I, and the Stuart Sapphire from the time of Charles II. It was fascinating to read that, over the years, the regalia had been altered to suit various coronations.

Queen Victoria's hand had been too small for the coronation ring so a copy had been made. Edward VII had not worn the St Edward's Crown as he was ill at the time and it was deemed too heavy. Likewise, the arches on the Imperial State Crown had been lowered for Queen Elizabeth II's coronation as she was so tiny and the crown such a weight.

De Jersey became immersed in the Crown Jewels. He printed off some photographs. The St Edward's Crown was magnificent and the article stated that the gold might have come from the Confessor's crown. It was set with 444 semi-precious stones. The breathtaking Imperial State Crown was set with over three thousand precious stones. Then he stared at the Koh-i-noor, set in the Queen Mother's platinum crown. Lastly he looked at the little crown made for Queen Victoria, studded with over 1,500 diamonds. A response to a letter in the web page's mailbox stated that the last attempted robbery of the Crown Jewels had been foiled in 1671. These closely guarded gems were kept in the Tower of London and were seen by millions of tourists every year. A crown jeweller was responsible for their maintenance and cleaning. The Queen had last seen them in 1994 when the new jewel house was opened.

De Jersey was deep in thought and Christina had to call him numerous times for dinner. When he appeared, he smiled, kissed her and presented her with the printed information about shows and attractions, assuring her that he would be available to come with them.

'Oh, darling, that won't be necessary,' said Christina. 'Perhaps just a few dinners. I know how you hate the theatre.'

'Well, I'll make a bargain with you. You let me out of

the theatre dates and I will personally take them to the Tower of London to see the Crown Jewels.'

De Jersey waited until Christina had fallen asleep before he returned to his study and accessed more sites about the spectacular jewels. Their history was fascinating. He learned that the foiled attempt to steal the gems had been instigated by a Colonel Blood, who had almost got away with his booty but was trapped at the East Gate of the Tower. Edward the Confessor and his successors had accumulated most of the regalia but much had been sold off or melted down by Oliver Cromwell between 1649 and 1660. The current hoard dated from Charles II's coronation in 1661. De Jersey remained in his study until dawn. By the time he returned to bed, he was tired but elated.

He woke feeling well rested, then showered and changed into riding clothes. He rode hard for a good hour, then brought the horse to a halt. He was riding an old favourite, a big eighteen-hand grey called Cute Queenie. At fourteen she was no longer racing, but had produced some good colts and was kept for de Jersey's personal use. She snorted and tossed her head as they stood looking out across the downs.

'Good girl,' he whispered affectionately, and pushed her to trot on, then canter, and finally he coaxed her into a full gallop. It was like opening the throttle of a fine old racing car. The big grey tore up the wet morning grass, her breath steaming. He had not felt so alive for years. The adrenaline buzz was indescribable: it stimulated every part of his body – but confronting danger had always been his preferred drug and the Moreno business had given him a taste of it. Now he craved it. The next audacious heist was forming in his mind, and he felt as he had when he'd received the tip-off about the gold bullion at Heathrow. This time he was contemplating stealing the Crown Jewels. But contemplating it and pulling it off were worlds apart.

CHAPTER 6

TONY DRISCOLL arrived home from his holiday, tanned and with three extra suitcases full of his wife's purchases. Jet-lagged and exhausted, he contacted David Lyons' office straight away. He spent two hours on the phone, then sat in a stupor staring at the walls.

'Tony, have you unpacked?' Liz asked, as she barged in.

'You know I haven't,' he snapped.

'Well, you can't skive in here. You have to put out your dirty laundry for Mrs Fuller. I'm not going to do it.'

'I'll be with you in a minute. I've got a few business problems to take care of.'

'Can't they wait? We only just got home.'

'I guess they can,' he said, and stood up, but sat down again when she left the room. Throughout the holiday he had maintained a positive attitude, sure that some of his money could be salvaged. Now, having been told bluntly by Lyons' assistant that he had lost all his savings and there was no hope of recouping a cent, he felt sick.

James Wilcox had also discovered the extent of his losses and that there was no hope of any return. He had arrived home in Henley with all the kids and Rika only to discover that his basement was flooded. He stared at the mounting bills. His numerous maintenance cheques to his ex-wives were months overdue. Rika was irritable from the long journey home and kept asking him to arrange a grocery delivery from Tesco but he couldn't think straight. One minute he had been worth millions, the next peanuts. He had not anticipated it would be this bad. He had almost forgotten how much he had foolishly liquidated to invest in the Internet company.

Rika slapped the grocery list down in front of him. He looked at it, then flew into a rage.

'This is gonna cost a fucking fortune, Rika. We've got eight different types of cereal here!'

'Vell, that is vat they eat!'

'From now on they're all gonna eat the same one.'

Rika glared at him and slammed out of the room. He looked at the list again, then screwed it up. What the fuck difference was a packet of cereal going to make?

He was in real trouble. He had even remortgaged the house to throw more money into leadingleisurewear. He wanted to talk to Driscoll again and, what's more, he wanted to talk to de Jersey but he resisted picking up the phone. He knew the Colonel wouldn't like it that he and Driscoll had met in Florida. He began to contemplate how he would react if de Jersey suggested another heist. It had been easy to agree with Driscoll to walk away but now, faced with his situation – six kids, four ex-wives, a Ukrainian mistress and only a garage full of vintage cars as collateral – he knew was heading for bankruptcy. If things got any worse, he would be hard pressed to say no to anything de Jersey suggested.

De Jersey told his wife he would be away for a couple of days on business, staying at his club. He flew by helicopter to London and by mid-morning he was seated in a student lecture hall attending a computer-programming seminar. He knew that he would have to make his plans from a new location: it was too dangerous to do it at home. Afterwards he approached the young lecturer and asked him to list some books that would assist in his training.

Later, armed with two bulging carrier-bags, de Jersey went to the St James's club and sat in the lounge reading. As he pored over the complex manuals, it became clear that he still needed assistance. He hurried off to St Catherine's Church for the lecture suggested by 'Elvis' in the chat room.

The hall was small and freezing, and a clutch of nerdy figures with plastic coffee cups and cling-wrapped sandwiches gave him the impression that it would be a long session. They all had tiny laptops. A plump blonde girl munched a Mars Bar on the door as she collected five pounds from each member of the audience. As de Jersey paid her, she handed him a computer printout of the evening's agenda; the session was to be conducted by someone called Raymond Marsh. 'You been here before?' the blonde asked.

'No.'

'You got a contact who got you here?'

'Yes.'

'The name? I've got to fill in the attendance list.'

'Elvis,' De Jersey said, feeling rather foolish.

'Oh, that's okay, then. Go in and sit down. He won't be long – babysitter didn't show up. What's your name?' She was ready with her pen.

'Philip Simmons,' he said, and headed towards the rows of plastic chairs.

By eight thirty sixteen people were hunched in thick coats over their laptops as they waited. De Jersey wondered when the lecture would start. As he glanced to the rear of the hall he saw a strange apparition entering. It turned out to be Raymond Marsh, but from the look of him, he had to be known otherwise as Elvis. De Jersey deduced that the blonde was his wife and he watched as Marsh counted out the cash from the cardboard box and pocketed it.

De Jersey tried not to stare at Marsh too much but it was hard not to. His face was thin and pointed, his chin protruded and his cheeks slanted. His hair was combed in from both sides to form a quiff, held in place by thick layers of lacquer. He was wearing a worn black leather jacket, skin-tight drainpipe trousers and winkle-pickers. He went to the small table and checked that the computer was running correctly through the overhead projector. 'Right. We're all set. I've done some printouts that should answer yer queries from last week right? I gorra bit worried about last session, so any questions needin' going over like, now's the time to do it.' He had a thick Liverpudlian accent.

A tall thin man in the front row put up his hand. 'We were talking last week about hacking techniques being employed to protect computer systems rather than for criminal purposes. Could viruses ever be used for protection?'

Raymond licked his hand and swept it over one side of his head. 'Well, there has been talk of creating good viruses in the future that, as with human diseases, will increase the host's immune system. Are you with me? This can happen theoretically but hasn't yet, as far as I know.' Marsh paced up and down.

A large jolly-looking woman asked a question about the approaching Defcon conference in America. Marsh was in his element as he launched into an enthusiastic description of the underground hacking convention. De Jersey listened and watched. Much of what was being discussed was alien to him and he was rather lost. He paid close attention to Marsh: he obviously had a high IQ, but his manner of speaking and delivery seemed to suggest low social skills. He wondered if the man worked in the information-technology industry.

Raymond Marsh actually worked as a telephone engineer but hacked and explored the Internet in his spare time, so de Jersey hadn't been too far off the mark. He was so deeply immersed in his own analysis of the man that he jumped when he heard another audience member asking about identity protection and creating fake identities on the Net.

'Of course, mate, it's stupid to use your own details,' said Marsh. 'Depending on what you wanna do you can build up all kinds of identities in loads of different countries and create plausible histories for all of 'em. Right, one of my own Net IDs is an Australian schoolboy. He gets up to all sorts! This morning I hacked into a school in Adelaide, registered him and created school reports for him. Gave him straight As in every subject. I've travelled all around the world under dozens of different names but I've never even left the country. I'm a grandmother of five in Russia, an S&M enthusiast in Ireland and a fish farmer in Alaska. And there's no way they can catch me because I have a satellite link-up courtesy of work, which I use whenever I'm on the Net so I can easily break the link. Working for a telecommunications company comes in handy when you've got this hobby!'

Everyone in the audience chuckled, but de Jersey was mesmerized. All this was perfect for what he needed to do. He knew he had to draft in Raymond Marsh to help. The question was could he trust him?

As the meeting ended, de Jersey slipped out, his mind reeling. Rain was pouring down, and he caught a taxi back to the club. Once there, he sat in the reading room going over the literature he had taken away from the meeting, which included Marsh's email address, home phone number and address. The next morning he dialled and a rather laconic female voice at the end of the phone replied, 'He's at work.'

'It's important. Is there a number I can contact him on?'

'Yeah, but his work don't like him taking personal calls. If you gimme your number I'll get him to call you, or he'll be home about six.'

'I'll call later, thanks.'

It was almost six o'clock when de Jersey took the tube to Marsh's home in Clapham. It was a small semi-detached house with a bright pink Cortina, sporting two large fluffy dice in the windscreen, parked outside. De Jersey walked up the path and rang the doorbell. A woman answered. As he'd guessed, the blonde from St Catherine's Church was Raymond's wife.

'Is he back yet?'

'You the bloke what called earlier?' she asked, glancing back over her shoulder to where a baby was screeching.

'Yes. I'm sorry if this is inconvenient.'

'Well, it is a bit, he's not home yet.' Suddenly she looked past de Jersey and waved. 'Tell a lie, he's behind you.'

De Jersey turned as Marsh, wearing an overall under a thick tweed coat, walked up the path. 'Who's this?' he asked, as he kissed his wife.

'Dunno, come to see you.'

De Jersey passed him one of his Philip Simmons 'Computer Electronics Inc' business cards.

'What's this about then?' he asked de Jersey, as his wife ran to the baby.

'A job you may be interested in.'

'Already got one, mate.'

'I need some information and some help with a project I'm working on.'

'Well, I've got plenty of that. My mind's full of it, but it depends if it's the stuff you're looking for.'

'It would be helpful to know your experience,' de Jersey said.

Marsh was obviously not going to invite him in: he seemed to settle himself on the doorstep. 'I work as a phone engineer now. Got into phone hacking in the early eighties, you know, before computers took off, phoning everywhere long distance for free. That's how I found my vocation and progressed on to computers. I

131

worked for a company who hired me to local firms to set up their networks but it bored me rigid. So me and my wife packed up, came to London and I went back to phones – all legit now, of course. It's all computerized these days anyhow. Like to keep the computer hacking for my spare time.' He cocked his head to one side. 'Is this the kind of stuff you want to know?'

'Yes. Go on.'

Still Marsh made no effort to go inside the house. 'You wanna sit with me in me car?' he asked.

De Jersey was glad to get out of the full view of the neighbours and they got into the old Cortina. Marsh leaned back in his seat, stroking the white leather steering-wheel. The more he talked about himself, the more arrogant he became. An undercurrent of danger hung about him, anger, whose source de Jersey couldn't determine.

'So, Mr Simmons, what is it you're after, then?' he asked.

'You,' de Jersey said.

'Oh, right. Well, I don't come cheap.'

'I didn't think you would.'

Marsh took another look at the business card.

'I was at your talk at St Catherine's. I'd like you to help me build a fake identity and make it seem as real as possible.'

'Anything's possible, mate.'

Later that afternoon, acting on Marsh's detailed instructions, de Jersey withdrew a hundred and thirty thousand pounds from his depleted accounts. He set up a post-office box and topped up the account in the name of

Philip Simmons. From now on he would carry out all his financial transactions online. De Jersey waited while the bank assessed his details, and when everything was cleared, he rented a flat in Kilburn online. The company sent his keys to his post-office box and de Jersey arranged for the domestic bills to be paid via the Net.

Two days later he returned to London, collected the keys and travelled by bus, an experience he hadn't had in years, to Philip Simmons' new abode. The flat was two flights up and as seedy as he had expected for the price he was paying. It had that stale-food smell and orange-coloured foam-filled furniture. At least the bathroom and kitchen were clean and in working order. He had purchased two mobile phones in the name of Simmons, via the Internet, and another computer. The deliveries arrived within half an hour of each other. Now all de Jersey needed was a link to his own computer that could be destroyed at a moment's notice. For this he would need more help from Raymond Marsh.

By the time de Jersey returned home that night Christina was already in bed. He got in beside her and nuzzled her neck. 'Sorry I'm so late. It's been another day of meetings. David Lyons certainly left me in a mess.'

She turned towards him sleepily. 'Tell me about it in the morning.'

'I love you,' he whispered, and fell straight into a deep, dreamless sleep.

The next morning at breakfast de Jersey noted the date. His meeting with Wilcox and Driscoll at the Ritz was four days away, but in the meantime he had in-laws to entertain. He was amused to realize that the 'Three Musketeers' would meet on the same day as he had arranged to visit the Tower of London with his wife's parents. He had time therefore to begin to formulate his plans. He hoped that Raymond Marsh would not prove a liability.

Christina was taking down the Christmas decorations and stacking the cards in a cardboard box. She cut off the senders' names and kept the rest for a local prison charity. De Jersey joined her and she pointed to the mantelpiece. 'I thought you'd like to keep that one,' she said.

De Jersey picked up the Queen's card and smiled. 'You know me too well. I'm going to keep it on my desk. You think it'll impress your parents?'

'I'm sure it will, but you impress them too. Sometimes I think Daddy's frightened of you.'

'Well, he's never approved of me. He's always thought I was too old for you – I'm almost his age.'

'That is not true and you know it.'

'Well, I hope they enjoy the Tower of London and Buckingham Palace. How's that for a tourist's day out?'

'Thank you, but you don't need to go.'

'I'm sure I'll enjoy myself. I've lived in or near London all my life, yet I've never seen the Crown Jewels. Now I can't wait.'

CHAPTER 7

DE JERSEY was as good as his word and played the perfect host. At the Tower of London, they followed the guide into the main chamber where the jewels were on display. De Jersey was so eager to hear the guide's description that he kept stepping on the man's heels. Then, he stopped dead in his tracks. There, in all its glory, was the Queen Mother's platinum crown with the dazzling Koh-i-noor diamond. As he moved on, he noticed an empty case in which a small plaque stated 'In Use'. De Jersey wondered what the occasion was. Then a thought struck him: the jewels were occasionally taken out of the Tower and he had to find out when. He hurried to ask the guide.

'The empty display back there, what's the crown being used for?' he asked.

'The Queen has gone to Norway and will be wearing some of the jewels.'

'What would happen if there was an occasion when they were all in use?'

'Well, they never are, but there'll be a few cases empty for the Golden Jubilee celebrations. If there's not a good enough selection on display, we offer reductions.'

'What crown will she be wearing for the Jubilee?' de Jersey asked.

The guide shuffled impatiently. 'I believe Her Majesty is to wear one of the smaller ones. That one,' he pointed to the crown with the Koh-i-noor diamond, 'weighs a ton. There's over a hundred carats' worth of diamond in that one big stone alone. Would you mind moving on now, sir? We've the next guided tour coming through.' He moved away to stand closer to the first display case. De Jersey glanced again at the sumptuous crown.

James Wilcox arrived at the Ritz early. He was wearing a new suit he'd ordered from his tailor before his investments had crashed. Over the years he had become fastidious about his clothes and accessories. He ordered a vodka martini at the bar and sat down. De Jersey had booked a suite on the first floor under the name of Simmons, as usual. Wilcox ate the cashew nuts provided and unwrapped a cigar. As he searched for his lighter, Driscoll lit it for him.

'How you doing, my old son?' Driscoll said, plonking himself down on a stool next to him.

'I've been better. Just when you think you can sit back and relax for the rest of your life, everything disappears down the plughole. I've been over it all with that assistant at Lyons' office.'

'Tell me about it. In a couple of days he's shutting up shop, closing down.' Driscoll ordered a chilled glass of Chablis. 'Right mushroom this deal was,' he muttered.

'What was that?'

'You know, kept us in the dark and then that little

bastard shovelled shit over us.' He sipped his wine as Wilcox laughed.

'Very funny, always the joker.'

'Yeah well, this has set me back too many years, more than I care to mention.'

'Tell me about it,' Wilcox said looking around. He checked the clock behind the bar and continued. 'I'm skint. You able to salvage anything?'

'I've got a few thousand here and there, own some property but . . . yeah, bulk went into the leading fucking leisurewear.'

'We should keep stumm about us meeting in Florida,' Wilcox added.

'Right,' Driscoll said. 'I can't sleep. Every night I crash out about ten then wake up again, you know, thinking it all over. I can't believe it. I remember Ronnie Jersey saying to me once, "Tony, learn from these punters coming in day after day. You might get lucky once, but you'll have ten non-runners and it's not worth throwing hard-earned money away." Fuck me. Pair of us must have been crazy. I kept on pouring everything I had into that damn company.'

'Yeah, but as the investments doubled then trebled, we got greedy, right? Schmucks, the pair of us.' Wilcox drained his Martini and then sucked on the olive.

'I remember one day at Ronnie's, we'd got a sure-fire winner. You know, in those early days there was none of the TV sets in the betting shops and we listened to it over the radio.'

'Please don't start the Ronnie Jersey stories again,' Wilcox moaned. 'I couldn't take it.'

'I'm not, I'm not, I am just saying . . .'

'I've heard it all before and I'm not in the mood.'

'Oh, excuse me for living.'

They sat in silence a moment and then Driscoll looked at Wilcox's suit.

'What's with the bright satin lining?'

'I like it.'

'Bit poncey, isn't it? That suit's a good cut. Pity to ruin it with the cuffs turned back like that.'

'I ordered the cuffs that way!' Wilcox snapped.

'How much did that suit set you back, then? Go on, how much?'

'I had thirty odd million. You think I quibbled over how much a friggin' suit was going to set me back? Just change the subject, will you?'

Driscoll sipped his drink then placed it down on the Ritz mat and took out a slim cigar.

'You want one of these?'

'No. You want another drink?'

Driscoll hesitated and then nodded as Wilcox signalled to the barman.

'You see that race, then . . .'

'I said, Tony, I don't wanna hear about fucking Ronnie and the betting shops.'

'I'm not talking about the old days. I'm talking about Ascot; the Colonel's horse romped home. Liked to have had a flutter on that Royal Flush. It's called Royal Flush.'

'You know something that you do,' Wilcox said. 'You've always done it. You repeat things twice.'

'I do not. I don't.'

'Yes, you do, you just did it then.'

'I didn't. No, I did not.'

'You just did it again!'

Driscoll looked past Wilcox, then leaned in close.

'He's here. Shit, he's looking fit. See him talking to the doorman?'

Wilcox swivelled round. De Jersey stood head and shoulders above anyone else in the hotel lobby. He was a hard man to miss, wearing a brown trilby and a brown tweed suit. He looked very much the racing gentleman, right down to his checked shirt and brown brogues. He made his way to the restaurant and disappeared.

'What's he doing? Isn't he goin' up to the suite?'

'Looks like he's gonna have lunch.'

They both looked towards the entrance of the Ritz restaurant where de Jersey could just be seen now chatting with the maître d'. Then he walked back towards the lobby as if to leave the hotel. Instead of going towards the entrance, however, he took a sharp turn and headed for the stairs.

'He's going up now,' said Wilcox.

'He's putting himself about a bit, isn't he?' Driscoll said softly.

'Nipped up the stairs sharpish, though, so I reckon it's time we made a move. Split up as usual, okay?'

The spacious suite was furnished with elegant, Regency-style furniture and thick gold curtains. A polished mahogany table displayed salmon, cheese, and a large bowl of fruit salad with cream. De Jersey was opening a bottle of champagne when Wilcox tapped on the door and entered.

'Tony's coming up via the stairs,' he said, as he closed the door. 'You look good – all that riding, I suppose.'

'You look in shape yourself,' de Jersey said. 'I'm sorry this has happened.'

'So am I.'

There was a pause, then de Jersey popped the cork and set the bottle in the ice bucket. He crossed the room and hugged Wilcox. 'Good to see you, Jimmy.'

'Yeah, go back a long way, huh?'

De Jersey broke the emotional moment by pouring the champagne. Wilcox accepted a glass as Driscoll came into the room.

'Christ, my knees – I tell you, I'm falling apart. I got to the second floor and thought I was having a heart-attack.' He shook hands with de Jersey. 'Still the same fine specimen. How do you think the years have treated me, then?' Of the three, Driscoll showed his age the most.

De Jersey passed him a glass of champagne, then raised his own. 'I wish we were meeting under better circumstances.'

They drank, and when de Jersey sat down, they followed suit. They chatted in the relaxed atmosphere of the suite, about wives and children, then ate the meal, enjoying their reunion. Driscoll congratulated de Jersey on his win at Royal Ascot.

'Next one will be the Derby,' de Jersey enthused. 'He's going to do it. He's the best colt I've ever had.' Suddenly he turned to Driscoll. 'Did you ever know someone called Harry Smedley? He was at the racetrack and came up to me, said we were at school together but I can't for the life of me remember him.'

Driscoll wiped his mouth with his napkin. 'Harry Smedley. Yeah, I remember him. He was at the comprehensive with us – well, with me. I dunno if you knew him. He'd have been in the class below me. Little kid with a big head.'

'I still don't remember him,' de Jersey said.

'Well, maybe you wouldn't. You might remember his mother, Maureen, though. Gawd, she was a case. Your dad, he tried to talk sense into her. She'd go an' collect her social dosh in the morning and lose it by the afternoon. Ronnie tried to stop her gambling. Every day she'd be in the shop, soon as the doors opened, shilling each way. She knew the form, though, did Maureen. She was a tough old boiler.' Driscoll waved his fork. 'She was at the counter when those heavies came in with the sledgehammer.'

Wilcox sighed impatiently.

'Maureen was under a table when it was all going down. As soon as they left the shop, up she pops and all the while it was going down the racing commentary was coming out over the Tannoy.'

'God help us, Tony, does this have a point?' Wilcox enquired testily.

'Yeah. She says to Ronnie he's got to pay out on the bet she was just about putting on. She says it was a pound on the nose, a twenty-to-one outsider called Danny Daly and then Ronnie says to her—'

Wilcox got up. 'Which is the bathroom?'

De Jersey pointed to a door close to the entrance of the suite. 'There's one, or there's another off the bedroom. Take your pick.'

Wilcox went into the bedroom and closed the door.

'Go on, Tony, what did my father say?'

'He says to her, "Maureen Smedley, you haven't put paper on a runner in here ever but just for your bottle, I'll pay out," and he did. He was some fella, your old man.'

De Jersey still had no recollection of Harry Smedley or his mother.

Wilcox came out of the bathroom. 'Has he finished,' he asked, 'or is he just drawing breath?'

Driscoll gave him the finger.

Wilcox poured more champagne and returned to his seat as de Jersey passed the cheese board. They continued to chat about old times until at last they fell silent and Driscoll pushed aside his plate. 'Our luck just ran out, though. This Internet crash has done me in good.'

De Jersey started to clear the dishes off the table and the others knew it was time to talk.

'Let me explain how we lost our cash.' De Jersey pinched the bridge of his nose. 'You must know by now that the Internet crash has affected a lot of people. Believe it or not, a lot of people came out worse than us.'

'In leadingleisurewear?' Driscoll asked.

'No, lots of companies have gone down. Ours was just one of many.'

'What chance do we have of getting it back?' asked Driscoll. 'I spoke to that bloke at Lyons' office and he said that if we could contact this fella Alex Moreno he might be able to salvage something.'

'Not a hope in hell,' de Jersey replied. 'Leadingleisurewear has been liquidated and Alex Moreno, the MD, has disappeared.'

Driscoll closed his eyes. Then he banged the table with the flat of his hand. 'I'd like to get him by his scrawny neck and throttle him. Has he just walked into a new job?'

'He's been trying to form another company.'

'The little shit,' Wilcox blurted out.

De Jersey opened yet another bottle of champagne. 'I've done what I could.'

'You've been over there and seen this Moreno guy?' Wilcox asked, surprised. De Jersey remained silent, and Wilcox continued, 'I'm not bleating, Colonel, but I'm only just keeping my head above water right now. I'm going to have to sell my homes, my cars . . . I've got six kids, four bloody ex-wives . . .'

'I know.' De Jersey lit a cigar.

'I'd like some kind of retribution from this arrogant son-of-a-bitch.' Wilcox was getting worked up.

De Jersey blew a smoke-ring above his head. 'Moreno is taken care of. He had property in East Hampton. We should get at least twelve million for it, hopefully more, and he also had a lease on an apartment worth a couple of million. I'll split it three ways as usual, but it can't be touched until we're sure it can't be traced. Like I said, we'll each get something out of the mess but not yet, maybe in six to eight months' time. Moreno is not a factor any more.' De Jersey gave each man a cold-eyed stare. 'He's out of the loop. I've taken care of him. Understand me?'

Wilcox and Driscoll fell silent. They knew that Moreno was dead, and not to press for details. There was a strange, depressed silence. Wilcox got up to use the bathroom again.

When Wilcox returned de Jersey entered the bathroom to wash and comb his hair. He checked the time. He would have to leave shortly to collect his in-laws from their shopping expedition at Harrods. It was only a short distance away, but he needed at least another hour with Wilcox and Driscoll.

When he came out, he said, 'I've been thinking of something we could do.'

Driscoll leaned forward to interrupt. 'Eddy, listen, I

143

don't want to hear about anything. I'm too old. I've got responsibilities. I can't go back to what I was like in the old days. I almost didn't show up here this afternoon, because I reckoned you'd have arranged some kind of business to get us out of this mess – but nothing illegal, not for me. I can't, I'm sorry.'

'That's okay.' De Jersey reached out and touched his hand, then looked at Wilcox, who was staring at the table. 'What about you, Jimmy?'

'I'm glad he got it in first, Edward, because the same goes for me. I reckon I've lost my nerve. I just don't have the bottle for it any more and if, like you said, we're in line for a few mill from the sale of the Moreno property, that's . . . that's enough for me.'

'You're right. I forget how old I am sometimes and it was a crazy idea anyway,' de Jersey said. 'Everything is paid for, so we leave our separate ways and maybe see each other again when we're on walking frames.'

De Jersey started to count. He reckoned that when he got to ten Wilcox would want to know more, but he was wrong: it was Driscoll.

'So come on, then, don't leave us in suspense. Just 'cause we're not players any more doesn't mean we're not curious. What caper were you gonna line up for us?' he asked.

De Jersey faced them. 'No, you're right. Better if we just walk away now.'

Wilcox couldn't meet his eyes.

'No hard feelings, eh?' said Driscoll.

'No hard feelings, Tony,' de Jersey said. 'There never will be. You are two of a kind and they broke the mould when they made you.'

'Ah, stop it,' Driscoll said. 'If we don't come in will you go it alone, whatever it is?'

'Maybe, I don't know. But now I have to leave and collect my in-laws.'

'Why don't you just run it by us?' Driscoll said again, stubbornly. 'It's not as if you can't trust us. You know whatever you say to us won't go any further.'

De Jersey put on his hat. 'Not this time.'

'Come on, you can't bullshit a bullshitter,' Driscoll said, smiling.

'There's a first time for everything, Tony,' de Jersey said.

Wilcox had said nothing, just stared at the table. Now he glanced at Driscoll and their eyes met. They both wanted to know what deal they had just turned down.

'You let us decide, Colonel, that's fair, isn't it?' Driscoll looked at Wilcox.

There was a long pause and de Jersey returned to the table. He took off his hat. 'You forced my hand.'

Both men waited and de Jersey seemed to relish the moment. Then he leaned forward. 'I want to steal the Crown Jewels.'

'Not the ones in the Tower of London?' Driscoll asked, incredulously.

'The very same.'

'The fucking Crown Jewels!' Wilcox let out a loud laugh.

'He's having us on,' Driscoll said, with a grin.

De Jersey picked up his hat again and twisted it around on his hand. 'It'll take months of preparation and I'll need a big team. I've not formulated the details as yet, or picked out the people I'll need.'

'You're gonna break into the Tower of London?' Wilcox said.

De Jersey put on his hat and pulled the rim to the angle he liked. He walked to the door and unlocked it. 'I can't say I'm not disappointed you weren't interested in hearing me out, considering our past connections. Take care. See you some time.'

'Edward!' Wilcox flew to the door. 'Don't do this. I've been grateful to you more times than I can remember, but this ... You can't expect us to take you seriously! This isn't a serious gig, is it?'

Driscoll joined them at the door. 'Like James just said, I owe you for everything and I won't ever forget what you or your old man did for me, but no way am I going to feel guilty for turning this caper down. So come clean. Admit it's a big joke.'

'No joke,' de Jersey said. 'When I get the money from Moreno's properties you'll get your cut. Don't depend on it, though. A lot could go wrong before the cash is freed up.' He gave them a long cold stare. They moved away from the door and he opened it again.

'I have to go – I'm taking the in-laws for dinner at San Lorenzo. They'll be waiting for me outside Harrods.' He closed the door silently behind him and walked down the thickly carpeted corridor. He passed the elevator and headed down the stairs. He didn't feel let down, just foolish for believing that the three could pick up where they had left off. That was his mistake. Too many years had passed.

Still in the hotel room Wilcox chopped a line on the table. He offered one to Driscoll.

146

'Not for me. Gives me a runny nose.'

Wilcox sniffed and wiped his nose then tapped the rolled banknote on the table. 'Well, it was good to see him anyway.'

'You feel as bad as me?'

'Yeah.'

'But we agreed, right? I mean, no way. Not at our age.'

'Yeah.'

'You think he was serious?'

'The Crown Jewels – it's insanity, isn't it?'

They looked at each other.

'What do you think he meant about taking care of that bastard Moreno?'

'I don't want to discuss it,' said Driscoll.

'You're right. Less we know the better.'

Driscoll's stomach churned. 'Whatever he gets he said he'll split it three ways, like he always did, so maybe we won't be too badly off. I mean, that estate he's got has to be worth millions. So right now he may be hurting for a bit of cash-flow, but maybe he handled his money better than us. He's the one with the brains, right? And I'd say he's got more than the two of us put together.'

Wilcox nodded, as though he wasn't so sure. 'Yeah, no way is he hurting for cash in a big way like me. Maybe he didn't put all his eggs in one basket.'

'We just gotta take our losses on the chin.'

De Jersey made his way to Walton Street where he had arranged for Christina and her parents to meet him. The entrance was busy as Harrods was holding its January sale. The Rolls-Royce was waiting, his chauffeur inside, and once he was seated in the car, de Jersey closed his eyes and tilted his hat over his face. Thirty minutes later Christina came out with her parents and they drove towards Beauchamp Place where they had booked a table at San Lorenzo for an early dinner. He did not allow himself to think of Driscoll or Wilcox as he became the charming host and made polite conversation about their visit to the Tower of London. De Jersey had purchased a video of the tour and all the books on sale at the kiosk, maps and numerous large colour photographs of the crowns.

Wilcox left the Ritz feeling depressed. He doubted he would ever see de Jersey again. He made his way to Bond Street, irritated that he could not get a taxi. He passed Asprey & Garrard's, and paused to stare in at the window. He felt jaded. The cocaine was wearing off, and he was cold. It was raining and his suit was damp. His knees were now a constant source of pain after so many skiing accidents. He wondered if de Jersey still suffered from his knee injury. Memories of his past came flooding back. In the beginning it had not been de Jersey's idea to rob his father's shops and take back what was rightly his. It had been Wilcox's: he was all for going in with shooters and using the same tactics as the villains had, but de Jersey refused to do that. A few weeks later, de Jersey had contacted him: he had conceived a plan. Wilcox gazed into the window. The diamonds on display were just a blur as he pictured the three of them as young bloods, daring robbers. Those had been thrilling times and they had taken care of each other. But even de Jersey couldn't steal the Crown Jewels. Or could he?

Driscoll walked towards Piccadilly Circus and his new Jaguar, which was parked in the Brewer Street car park. He drove out and was dismayed to hit gridlocked traffic in Soho, then grew increasingly frustrated as he inched along towards Haymarket. As he turned into the Mall, the magnificent sight of Buckingham Palace confronted him. He thought of de Jersey and his insane suggestion of stealing the Crown Jewels. As he drove past the Palace he remembered the crazy guy who had broken in and had made it into the Queen's bedroom. Even with all those guards on duty, the alarms and security devices, he had slipped through and sat on the Queen's bed! It just goes to show, he thought, that anything is possible.

Liz was waiting outside Victoria Station's bus depot, soaked to the skin and loaded with bargains. She shot into the road when she spotted the car. Driscoll loaded the bags into the boot.

'Why are you so late? I said seven fifteen. I've been standing there for over three-quarters of an hour. What have you been doing? Did you buy the golf clubs you wanted? I went to Harvey Nicks . . .'

He never listened to her monologues. Liz didn't need answers to her questions or his views on her purchases, which seemed to include an entire new wardrobe. He felt tired, old and bored.

'You're very quiet,' she said. 'How's your stomach?'

'Fine.'

'You take your antacid tablets?'

'Yeah.' He sighed as they came to yet another traffic jam at Vauxhall Bridge.

'If you'd gone over Chelsea Bridge it'd have been better or you could have gone over Wandsworth Bridge.'

'Shut it, Liz.'

'I don't know what the hell's the matter with you lately, Tony. All you do is moan. Half the holiday in Florida was ruined by you and your bad moods.'

Tony didn't reply. How was he going to tell her that forty-five million pounds had gone missing in cyberspace?

De Jersey felt drained when he got home, but he maintained his good humour for the rest of the evening, and even the following morning as he walked round the estate with his in-laws. However, his mind was only half there. He wanted to get rid of them and Christina for a while so that he could concentrate on planning the heist. He was determined now to go ahead, even without Wilcox and Driscoll, but he needed time on his own. Their refusal to join him had not dampened his spirits: it had made him even more determined to go ahead.

CHAPTER 8

THE FOLLOWING Wednesday de Jersey's helicopter landed at the heliport beside Heathrow airport. The pilot's orders were to refuel and return to the estate within the hour. Christina and her parents had been delighted with the surprise gift of a trip on the Orient Express. Planning robberies had been easier when he hadn't had the commitments of marriage to hinder him. He needed the space and freedom to work on it and to gather a new team of people familiar with the modern world.

De Jersey travelled by bus to Kilburn. It was almost twelve when he arrived at the flat. He spent some time arranging the orange nightmare into what looked like a lived-in home, with newspapers and magazines on the coffee table, books on the shelf and some clothes in the wardrobe.

Raymond Marsh had called to arrange a meeting time and arrived promptly at two thirty. He spoke little as he set up the computer de Jersey had bought. He had brought with him various virus programs and other systems he said would protect de Jersey's files. He also brought with him a satellite dish. This, he explained, would enable de Jersey to use the Internet by connecting

151

through a satellite rather than a phone line. The beauty of the system, in hacking terms, was that it was much more difficult to trace and the link could be broken in seconds. When he had finished he accepted a cup of coffee and sat down on the orange settee. 'Fire hazard, these, you know,' he said, tapping the cushion and slurping his coffee. 'Against the law to sell them, catch light faster than a match. My missus won't have anything flammable around.'

'It serves its purpose,' de Jersey said, then brought out cash to pay Marsh. He peeled off the notes from a thick wad then set the remainder on the arm of the chair he was sitting in. Marsh stashed them in a zip-up wallet, which he tucked into his overalls. He glanced at the remaining wad of money. 'Anything else you need from me?'

De Jersey nodded.

'What?'

'Show me how it all works.' He smiled and Raymond stood up to check his watch.

'Not got long.'

'How about we arrange some private lessons, maybe a few evenings or when it's convenient? I need to get more familiar with chat rooms and how to retrieve information from the Net.'

Marsh cocked his head to one side. 'I'm not cheap. One on one will cost you a hundred an hour.' He walked over to the computer and sat down. 'Let's open her up and play,' he said. His fingers flashed over the keyboard. 'You gotta remember that if you want to be a player in this community you got to earn respect from them. So familiarize yourself with the geek-speak. There's a lot of goodwill around the community. Hackers don't work for money, they work for intelligence. The value system of a hacker, pirate or cracker, the good or the bad, is different from normal consumer society. If you want to be recognized as a good citizen in the Net community you've got to contribute and that means sharing material or information for free. In this case, if I'm getting paid I won't ask any questions about what you're up to.' Marsh laughed.

De Jersey hated to be at his mercy like this. 'Get me up something on anyone who's worked in the Royal household recently. Someone who was on security,' de Jersey said.

Marsh gave no indication that he was surprised by the request. Instead he gestured for de Jersey to sit beside him. They worked together, pulling down newspaper reports, logging into various different sites until Marsh had printed off sheets of articles from numerous newspapers dating back about eight months. Exactly an hour later he checked his watch and said he had to leave. He put out his hand for his payment and they arranged for the next session.

When Marsh had gone, de Jersey returned to the computer and sat down to read the news articles. One man's case stood out from the others. His name was Gregory Jones and he had been convicted of murdering his wife and was presently serving life at Franklyn Prison. He was a former palace security guard and had discovered his wife in bed with another member of the Queen's household. De Jersey knew it was imperative to find out about the security set-up at the Palace and the procedures surrounding the Royals when they appeared in public, how many security men were on duty and how many ladies-in-waiting would accompany Her Majesty. Perhaps Gregory Jones could provide this information.

He began to log on to websites that gave information about the Royal Family. At one point he was sidetracked into reading about the Queen's love of horses. There were pictures of her in the winner's enclosure at Epsom when her horse, Enharmonic, had won the Diamond Stakes. The jockey Frankie Dettori stood beside her, wearing her racing colours. Then de Jersey scrolled through pictures of the Crown Jewels and paused when the screen filled with the Queen Mother's crown. This was the only one mounted in platinum and there, set in the front, was the magnificent Koh-i-noor diamond. It drew him like a magnet. He touched the screen with his hand and sighed. Right now, it was so far out of his reach.

While Christina was abroad de Jersey planned to fabricate a plausible reason for him to stay in London from time to time when she returned. Raymond Marsh became a frequent visitor, guiding and encouraging him to experiment. The more de Jersey got to know the odd man, the more he admired him. Marsh openly admitted that he was not only a top 'cracker' but a 'phacker' because of his ability to gain unauthorized access to phone systems. He was adept at disrupting and illegally tapping into phone systems via his computer. De Jersey felt sure all his experience would come in handy at a later date. When he left, either to go to work or to return home, de Jersey would set timers on the lights in the flat to make

154

it appear that it was constantly occupied, then travel to his estate to carry on his work there.

Slowly he began to formulate a plan for the robbery. In order to visit the disgraced ex-security guard in Franklyn Prison, he had to acquire fake documents. He researched the firm of solicitors who had dealt with Jones's case and printed out an imitation of their headed notepaper, then wrote to the prison requesting a visitor's pass for the solicitor handling the man's appeal.

Next he had to hunt down another ex-employee of the Royal household, someone who could provide inside information on protocol, and placed a message on various electronic bulletin boards: 'UK novelist wishes to contact any employees (or recent ex-employees) of Royal household for confidential information.' He was astonished at the number of replies. He knew that a vast percentage would be from idiots messing around, but after a while it became easy to assess them and he made lists of those he would contact. It was time-consuming work, though, and the pressure was on.

De Jersey had been occupied with the running of the stables virtually all morning. He had to discuss forthcoming racing events with his trainers, the twelve mares in foal, and various veterinary matters. A three-year-old colt that had cost him almost three-quarters of a million dollars had not been fit enough to race yet, and the strangles virus had struck a wing of the yard that stabled eighteen horses, most of which had been affected. Veterinary bills were always high but this winter they were astronomical. And foot-and-mouth restrictions still held up travelling. The good news, however, was that his pride and joy, Royal Flush, was in fine health and training for the season, which would hopefully place him on track for the Derby.

De Jersey returned to his office and had only just sat down when he received a call from David Lyons' widow, Helen. She asked if he would be kind enough to see her. It was a personal matter and she would prefer not to discuss it over the phone, that afternoon if possible. De Jersey agreed.

Helen was waiting outside her house for him. She looked terrible: her face was white and drawn and she was not wearing any makeup. Usually she was immaculately dressed, but today she was wrapped in a drab brown coat with a fur hat pulled down roughly over her hair. 'Thank you for coming, Edward. I had no one else to turn to,' she said, her eyes brimming with tears. She led him inside the house, offered coffee, which he accepted, and they sat down at the kitchen table. She began to fiddle with a teaspoon. Her eyes had the lost look of the recently bereaved. 'I don't know where to begin. I didn't have anyone else to ask.' She paused. 'It's to do with David's death.' She reached for a tissue and blew her nose. 'He left everything to me and I'd always believed we were comfortably off, but . . .' She stopped.

'Go on, Helen,' he prompted quietly.

'David borrowed on the house. He liquidated almost everything we possessed and I don't know what trouble he had got himself into, but the savings accounts . . .' She took a deep breath. 'In the past few months before he died, David withdrew every penny we had. According to my sister, who's been overseeing everything for me, he took out almost two million pounds, and it's all gone.' De Jersey said nothing. 'I'm not asking you for money, please don't think that. I've still got a few thousand in my own account. I'll be all right.' She twisted the sodden tissue. 'I don't know what he was doing, I really don't. His assistant is devastated and they're closing the office. My sister took a week off work to help sort everything out. None of us can understand what he was doing – or we didn't until a few days ago.' De Jersey was beginning to feel edgy but he gave nothing away.

'My sister is also an accountant. In fact, David and I met through her. She began going through all of David's business accounts and it seems he had invested in an Internet company based in New York, leadingleisure-wear, something or other. Anyway, he and many of his clients had invested in this company.' She glanced towards de Jersey, evidently knowing that he too had backed it. Although he didn't show it, de Jersey was furious at David's indiscretion. 'My sister was stunned at the amount of money you and David put in and those others, a man called Wilcox, and I think Driscoll was the other.'

De Jersey's mind was racing. This was probably the only time in their career together that their names had been linked. 'Really?' He smiled. 'I had presumed I was the only unfortunate gambler.'

'I am so very sorry,' she said, and patted his hand. 'The reason I asked to see you was because my sister . . .'

'The accountant?'

'Yes. Sylvia. She works for an international invest-ment company. This company had invested in a similar venture to the one you and David invested in and lost a

157

considerable amount as well. So she did some checking for me.'

'Into what exactly?'

'Into the company you and David invested in and she discovered it was started by a young man called Alex Moreno. Apparently he and another leadingleisurewear ex-employee have been trying to set up another Internet deal. Sylvia couldn't believe their audacity, having lost all your money and David's and those others'.'

'So?'

'So, I said to Sylvia that, if I told you this you'd want to do something about it. You've lost millions! I know I'm not supposed to know anything about David's trans-actions but I couldn't help finding out. Sylvia said if there was a possibility of getting some of the money back then I or you or the other men should contact this Alex Moreno and find out what's going on.'

De Jersey leaned forward. 'My new financial adviser has told me there is no possible recourse to take and that I simply have to accept I made a poor judgement.'

'But you can't just accept it!' she exclaimed.

'I am afraid, Helen, that that is what I have to do. I don't know about the other investors. We are a part of a worldwide Internet collapse. There are not just a few losers but thousands. Many Internet companies have gone bust.'

'You could find Moreno.'

'I dare say I could but I've accepted my losses and, as I said, I've been advised that I have little or no hope of recouping them.'

'You're just going to walk away?' she asked, aghast.

'Yes, unless my adviser suggests otherwise.'

She looked at her hands. 'Sylvia has consulted a private investigator in New York to try to trace Moreno.'

De Jersey sat back and felt his gut tighten. 'Has she succeeded in finding him?'

'No, this is why she thinks he has probably stolen a lot of the funds. She found a letter from the auditor contracted by leadingleisurewear shortly before they collapsed, questioning the figures of the annual audit. And now it would seem he's disappeared.'

'Really? No one knows where he is?'

She shook her head. 'No, but Sylvia found out that he sold his apartment in New York. A doorman from his block said it went to a German, but that Moreno had a house in the Hamptons too.'

De Jersey was seething inside but reached across the table for Helen's hand. She gripped his, and the tears started again. 'I feel so bad about what happened,' she said. 'Do you think I should try to trace the other men involved?'

He released her hand. 'I don't know what to advise you to do, Helen. The investors have never publicly admitted their losses, as I have not. It is highly confidential information.'

'Oh, I realize that, Edward, but don't you think they would want to know what my sister has discovered?'

'I can't speak for them,' he said quietly.

'But don't *you* want to find out about Alex Moreno?'

He chose his words carefully. 'To be honest, hiring an investigator in another country is not something I have considered doing. I am sure if David believed he could retrieve any of the money he would not have taken such a drastic way out.'

159

'Would you look over some of the documents I have found?'

'Of course, but I doubt I can be of any assistance. I want my involvement with this company kept from the press. This could all blow up if the investigator's discoveries were ever made public.'

'I thought perhaps you'd help me.'

'I'm afraid not, Helen. And I'm confused as to how you gained access to my personal files.'

'They were in the safe in his study upstairs.'

'Are the other investors' details there too?'

'Yes.'

'Then I would like mine returned and I advise you to return the others.'

'I'll tell my sister,' she said, and flushed.

David Lyons' study was in disarray. Boxes and files were stacked against the wall and mounds of papers were heaped on every available surface. Helen gestured to the paperwork. 'I've been sent these from his office.' She crossed to the fireplace and lit the fake-coal gas fire. 'It's cold in here. I've not had the heating on.' She looked at the mound of files. 'David kept all his files on his computer but always made hard copies for reference. I think he had started to shred most of them but these are quite old. They're the most recent ones I found.' She looked around the study with a puzzled expression, trying to recall where she had put de Jersey's account details. 'Oh, I think I took your files to the kitchen,' she said, and hurried out, leaving de Jersey alone. A few moments later, she returned with a large square box. She handed it to him and moved aside some papers for him to place it on the desk.

De Jersey spent almost an hour in the study. Helen hovered for a while then left him when she went to answer the door. It was the removal men, who carried out items of furniture and ornaments she had earmarked to sell. She was flustered as she directed them around the house, and made frequent appearances in the study to apologize to de Jersey. Eventually he walked into the hall. 'I'm taking all my personal papers and details of transactions relating to me and my business, Helen.'

'Oh, yes, yes, of course.'

De Jersey ordered a local minicab and returned to the study to await its arrival. He double-checked the room to make sure he had not missed anything. As he was going through the desk drawers one last time he found an extra set of house keys, which he slipped into his pocket. He would have to warn both Driscoll and Wilcox about the new developments and ask them to refuse any request they received to trace Moreno.

As soon as he arrived home, de Jersey started to thumb through a stack of documents with his name underlined at the top and a thick wedge of accounting ledgers that he'd retrieved from David's study. His head started to throb. David had systematically plundered all of de Jersey's accounts to meet Moreno's requests for more funds. In a desperate attempt to salvage leadingleisurewear, he had thrown good money after bad. Had de Jersey just lost his original investment, he would have had enough to keep running the stables but this was far worse: his estate was seriously threatened and he was heading for bankruptcy.

Although he welcomed her home warmly, Christina knew something was wrong with her husband. He was deeply distracted and hardly said two words to her before he retreated to his study. She unpacked and went down to join him but, as usual, he dismissed her concerns.

'Please, darling, don't fend me off as if I was a child,' she said angrily. 'I know something has happened. Stop hiding things from me. What is it?'

He sighed and poured another glass of wine. Now that Helen and her interfering sister had details of his private affairs he could no longer keep it from Christina.

'David Lyons lost millions of my money. He invested badly, then tried to salvage the initial investment by throwing more money at it and it snowballed out of control. He lost his own savings too and a few other people's.'

'Oh, my God, that's dreadful. Can you do anything about it?'

'No, it's all gone.'

'Is that why Helen wanted to see you?'

'Yes. She and her dizzy sister have hired a private investigator to try to retrieve some of her losses.'

'What can an investigator do?'

He shrugged. 'I doubt he can do anything. The money has gone. The Internet company went bankrupt.'

'What is this investigator looking for?' Christina asked.

'Some Internet whiz kid.'

'If they find him, will they arrest him?'

'Even if they did they couldn't prove embezzlement.

162

He kept the money he made from selling the company's software, but as he designed it, he owned it. The investment stank and David was a fool. I have only myself to blame . . . and him, of course.'

'But what about that banker you met up with? Can he help?'

'I hoped he might but he can't.'

'Are we going to be okay?' she asked.

'Oh, we'll manage. I just don't like the idea of Helen nosing around in my affairs.'

'Well, maybe she has reason to. David did kill himself.'

He stood up and tossed his pen on to the table. 'Good job too. He saved me the trouble.'

Christina looked shocked. 'How bad is it, Edward? Tell me.'

'Nothing I can't fix.' He forced himself to give her a reassuring, warm smile.

'Oh, thank goodness,' she said, putting her arms round him and holding him tightly. 'I know how much you love this place.'

'We're not going to lose this. I may have to attend some meetings in the City but nothing will take me away from home for too long.' He kissed her and walked to the door. 'Just need to check something in the yard, then I'll be done.'

'Promise? I've only just got home and I've missed you.'

'Promise. I won't be long.'

Across the yard he let himself into the office and shut the door behind him. He used the mobile phone he'd bought in Simmons's name to call Driscoll and Wilcox and tell them about Helen's intervention. Then he locked away the phone and returned to the house and

Christina. She was curled up in bed watching TV, and as he entered she was laughing.

'What are you watching?'

'An advert,' she said, pointing to the TV. 'It's for Royal Jelly and she's so like her it's unbelievable. For a moment I looked and I thought, it can't be, surely she wouldn't, but it's . . . Look, she's identical!'

De Jersey stared at the TV. A lookalike playing the Queen was sitting on a throne wearing a fake diamond crown and holding up a pot of Royal Jelly. On the screen she mimicked Her Majesty's voice to perfection.

De Jersey pulled his tie loose, laughing. Another piece of the jigsaw had just fallen into place. It was the first piece of good news he'd had all day and he relaxed.

The following morning de Jersey was up earlier than his stable staff and went riding alone. He did his rounds at seven then returned to the house for breakfast. He suggested to Christina that she might have lunch with Helen Lyons to show her there were no hard feelings. He said he felt guilty for being so brisk with Helen yesterday and for not attending David's funeral, even though he'd been with Moreno in New York and couldn't have got there. Christina was not keen on the idea, but she slipped her arms around her husband's neck. 'I'll call her if it's what you want but I hardly know what to say to her, considering how David has treated us.'

'Thank you, my love. Can you ring her now?' he asked.

'But it's too early.'

'No, it isn't.' He continued with his breakfast as he

heard Christina call Helen and arrange lunch for the
following day.

De Jersey watched Christina leave in the chauffeur-driven
car to collect Helen from the station. Then he flew
himself in the helicopter to the small airport close to the
Lyons' house. He hoped the house would be empty. He
had presumed that Helen lived alone now but called
ahead twice to make sure no one picked up the phone.
He let himself in with the keys he had taken from David's
desk, waited for the sound of an alarm, then when
nothing happened, he went through the house into the
study, where he turned on the fake-coal fire. He kicked
some files closer to the grate, then gathered as many
documents as he could find relating to Wilcox and
Driscoll and left.

De Jersey landed the helicopter and went directly to the
stables. He had received an urgent call. He was joined by
one of the girls who worked in the stable, who was
waiting for him by the fence in his golf cart, and they
drove towards the east wing.

'How in God's name did it happen?'

'We don't know. He just stumbled on the way to the
gallops and when he returned, we noticed he was lame,'
she said. 'It's quite badly swollen but we don't think
there's any bone damage.'

Royal Flush was standing in the centre of the yard, his
trainer and a couple of lads hovering around. The vet
asked for him to be walked about, and Royal Flush
dropped his shoulder, showing a pronounced limp. De

Jersey was on his knees beside the vet when Christina and Helen walked across the yard.

'We'd given up on you,' Christina said, then fell silent as her husband looked up at her.

'We don't think anything's broken, but it's badly swollen,' he said. 'Helen, I'm sorry but as you can see this is a bit of an emergency.'

'Will you be joining us for lunch?' Christina asked.

'Yes, yes. Start without me, darling. I won't be too long, I hope.'

In the end, to Christina's annoyance, de Jersey never made it to lunch, so concerned was he about Royal Flush. After a rather tedious lunch which involved many tears from Helen, Christina saw Helen on her way with promises to stay in touch. When Helen arrived home her house was blazing and the fire brigade was struggling for control. The study, hall and part of the staircase had been gutted. David Lyons' papers had fed the fire and charred documents fluttered in the chilly afternoon air. Already devastated by her husband's suicide, Helen now faced the destruction of her home. She became so hysterical that her doctor sedated her.

'Who was that?' de Jersey asked Christina, as she put down the phone.

'You won't believe this,' Christina was stunned. 'It was Helen. She didn't say much, just thanked me for lunch then burst into tears and said that the house was on fire when she got home. All of David's papers were destroyed, apparently. Does that matter to you?'

166

'Oh . . . well I don't suppose so. Whatever documents he had I'll have copies of.'

'She asked me if I knew a man called Driscoll and another called Wilcox.'

'What about them?' he asked.

'She just wanted to know if I knew them because they were the other investors.'

'She asked me the same thing. But I've never heard of them. I wish she'd just leave it alone.'

Sylvia helped Helen into her car. 'You can move in with me until it's all sorted out. The estate agents aren't worried – you could repair the house to sell, or sell it as it is.'

'I'm never going back into it, Sylvia.'

'You won't have to. I'll get all your clothes and anything you want to put into storage.'

They reversed out of the drive and set off for London. A couple of hours later, they were at Sylvia's large flat in St John's Wood, overlooking Regent's Park. Eight years Helen's junior, she had never married. The apartment was spacious, with three bedrooms, and tastefully furnished. Sylvia hurried around, making up a bed, then setting a tray with tea, scrambled egg and smoked salmon for Helen.

Helen got into the bed and leaned back on her pillows. Her head was throbbing and she was simply too devastated to talk.

'Eat up, Helen. You're going to fall down a crack in the pavement you're so thin,' Sylvia said, puffing on a cigarette as she wandered restlessly around the bedroom. She hung her sister's discarded clothes in the empty wardrobe. 'Bit odd that the fire started in David's office,' she remarked.

'I think the window was open and I must have left the fire on and some papers blew on to it.'

Sylvia stubbed out her cigarette. 'Suppose there was information in David's files that someone wanted to keep secret?'

'What do you mean?'

Sylvia folded her arms. 'This Alex Moreno guy seems very dodgy. My detective, Matheson, can't find him anywhere. All that money poured into leadingleisurewear and he's just disappeared. Matheson thinks something smells about the whole thing.'

Helen sighed. 'I really don't know about this, Sylvia. I'm so tired.'

Sylvia got up and removed the tray. Helen had hardly touched the food.

'You'll feel differently when you can get your head together. I won't let it go. You've lost a lot of money.'

'I know but it wasn't just me, as you know. Edward de Jersey lost millions too, but when I spoke to him he wasn't interested in doing anything about it. Didn't want to hear about the private detective you'd hired.'

'Maybe he can afford to lose the odd million.'

Helen sat up. 'Sylvia, he lost a lot more than a few million and it was mostly David's fault. He could have advised them to get out when he knew it was heading for a fall. Instead he encouraged them to put up more money and . . .' She hesitated. 'He and Edward had been friends for twenty-odd years and they trusted each other implicitly. Well, I think David made some illegal transactions. I found correspondence between David and this man Moreno and some documents from a private account. I think David took some of that money as well as encouraging Edward to keep investing more and—'

'You told me. Helen, what if Alex Moreno didn't want those papers floating around? What if he started the fire? I think we should contact all the people who lost their fortunes and see what they think. I mean, maybe de Jersey has so much money he doesn't need what he lost but the others might.'

'Oh, I don't know.'

'Try and get some sleep. Don't think about any of this – leave it to me. Daniel from David's office is coming round to talk over a few things.'

Sylvia left the room and called Victor Matheson, the private investigator. She told him what had happened at Helen's house and of her suspicions.

'You might be right, Miss Hewitt. I've still got no trace of Alex Moreno but he left the hotel in the Hamptons early on the morning after his arrival in his Lexus, which I'm also trying to trace. According to the building contractors, Moreno's business adviser was a Philip Simmons. Have you heard of him?'

'I don't think so.'

'He's a Canadian, tall, well over six foot, red hair and a moustache.'

'Still no. My sister had a meeting with one of the investors who lost millions, Edward de Jersey. You have his details in the file I sent you. He didn't seem interested in discovering Moreno's whereabouts.'

'He must be stinking rich if he doesn't give a shit about finding this bastard and where all the money's disappeared to.'

'Continue your enquiries for now,' Sylvia said. 'I'll be in touch again shortly. Tomorrow I'm going to contact the other investors. If Mr de Jersey isn't interested in taking this matter further maybe one of them will be. I'm determined to salvage my brother-in-law's savings, which now belong to my poor sister.' She hung up.

The doorbell rang almost immediately and she hurried to let in Daniel Gatley, David's assistant.

'I have all the information you asked for.' He put down his briefcase.

'Daniel,' she said, 'Helen doesn't know I've lost money on this company as well. It may not seem like a lot to the other investors but it was my life savings – two hundred and fifty thousand.'

'Yes, I know. I'm sorry.'

'Not as sorry as I am, and I don't believe that fire was an accident. It's odd that it started in David's study and that his papers fuelled it. Helen says she might have left the fire on and a window open but that doesn't make sense to me.'

Daniel shuffled uncomfortably. 'I've brought round all I could find on the main investors but I shouldn't allow these documents out of the office. They're confidential.'

'Oh, for goodness' sake, Daniel, there *is* no office now but if anyone asks I'll say David left them here.'

Daniel opened his briefcase and took out the files. He placed them on the table. 'Does Helen know?' he asked.

She pursed her lips and shook her head. 'Of course not. Nobody does, apart from you,' she said. There was a long pause and she covered her face with her hands. 'I've had to look after Helen when all I wanted to do was curl up and cry. I miss him so much.' She patted her pocket for a tissue. 'She hasn't the slightest idea about

David and me. I don't know what it would do to her if she did find out. But it's hard, Daniel.'

'I know he cared deeply for you,' Daniel said awkwardly.

'Yes, I know he did too. But he also lost my life savings and I'm going to do something about it. Do you think Moreno could have had anything to do with the fire at the house? I mean, it's all very convenient, isn't it?'

'Well,' Daniel said, 'I've got the files here for the other investors, apart from Edward de Jersey. After David's death, he came and took everything out of the office. David had put everything on disk for him.'

Sylvia got up and opened a drawer. 'I have some disks too, which David left here, so I know just how much de Jersey lost.'

Daniel nodded to the files he had brought. 'Details of the small investors plus the other two main ones.'

She snatched the top sheet of notes from him. 'Driscoll and Wilcox,' she read. 'I'll concentrate on them.'

Daniel stood up to leave. He pulled a Jiffy-bag out of his briefcase and handed it to her. 'Just a few personal items from David's desk that I thought Helen or you might like to keep.'

'Thank you for coming over. I hope you'll keep my secret. If it got out it would only cause poor Helen more pain.'

He nodded, and moved to the door, where he paused and turned. 'Sylvia, I don't think I would bring this arson thing to anyone's attention. The police will no doubt be looking into the fire because of David's suicide and if there is any hint that it wasn't an accident the insurance won't pay out. As you said, Helen has been through enough already.'

CHAPTER 9

SYLVIA HEWITT contacted James Wilcox first – his ex-directory telephone number had been in David's file. 'I'm David Lyons' sister-in-law,' she told him. 'My sister Helen has asked me to help her sort out David's financial problems in connection with the Internet company leadingleisurewear. I believe you were one of the main investors and suffered considerable losses.'

'That is correct,' Wilcox said. 'My own business adviser is looking into the matter on my behalf.'

'I have hired a private investigator to try to trace Alex Moreno.'

'Well, my advisers are handling my interests and I am loath to confuse the issue by becoming involved with any other backers. I have also been told that it is unlikely any funds will be returned to me. Thanks for contacting me, but I would appreciate it if you did not press this matter further on my behalf or call again.'

'But you lost a fortune!'

'That's my business.' Wilcox sounded annoyed.

'Do you know Edward de Jersey?'

'No.'

'Mr de Jersey was the largest investor and will lose everything he has—' But that was as far as Sylvia got:

Wilcox had hung up. Sylvia was astonished that he didn't want to know any more.

Undeterred she called Anthony Driscoll, and told him of her connection to David Lyons. He was not as brusque as Wilcox had been, but he made it clear that his own advisers were looking into the company's downfall. 'Please feel free to call again if you acquire any information you think I would be interested in,' Driscoll said.

'I am contacting all the investors,' Sylvia persisted. 'Are you aware that a Mr Edward de Jersey lost nearly a hundred million pounds?'

Driscoll was taken aback momentarily. 'No, I am not. Listen, are you asking for me to assist this investigator?'

'Only if you wish to do so. I am quite happy to continue paying him until I get results.'

'Well, I admire your tenacity, Miss Hewitt, and I don't want to put you off in any way but I am quite perturbed that you have called an ex-directory number and that you seem to have access to very personal details.'

'I explained who I was,' Sylvia replied rather petulantly.

'Perhaps you did but that still does not give you or anyone else close to Mr Lyons the right to access my private and highly confidential transactions. I want my losses to remain my own business.'

'Well, I apologize,' she said, embarrassed. 'I am really doing this for my sister.'

'Frankly, Miss Hewitt, I am not interested in who you are doing this for. I did not know David Lyons's wife and, although his suicide was certainly tragic, he made some extremely ill-advised business moves. I hold no one to blame but myself for making the investments, nevertheless they were made under Mr Lyons's guidance. That these have proved to be a disastrous loss for me is my business and I would appreciate it if you did not call again or use my name with reference to any private investigation you may have instigated.'

Sylvia interrupted, afraid he would hang up on her as Wilcox had done. 'May I just ask if you know any of the other investors? A Mr James Wilcox.'

'No, I've never met him or any of the others.'

'Did you ever meet the man who ran leadingleisure-wear, a man called Alex Moreno?'

'No, I did not and I have no interest whatsoever in meeting him. I wish you success in your endeavours but I really have no time to discuss this further. Goodbye.' He hung up abruptly.

Sylvia did not find their reaction suspicious: big investors did not like their losses made known. However, she was infuriated that these three men were so wealthy that they could accept losing millions. She had lost a pittance in comparison but it had been her life savings. She had no intention of letting the matter be swept under the carpet. Sylvia had unwittingly put the cat among the pigeons by calling both Driscoll's and Wilcox's homes. As Driscoll's wife had answered the call, she was monitoring her husband's reactions for some time after he had hung up.

'So who is this Sylvia woman then?' she asked eventually, when it looked as if he wasn't prepared to explain the call.

'She is the sister of an old business adviser's wife.'

'So what's she calling you for?'

'He topped himself,' he said irritably.

'Who did?'

'David Lyons, the former business adviser.'

'Do I know him?'

'No, but he handled an investment of mine.'

'Oh I see,' she said, pouring some power juice ingredients into the mixer.

'Do you?' he snapped as the mixer whirred noisily.

'Yes, anything concerning money is a mood swinger with you. Bad news was it?'

'Yeah, but nothing I can't take care of.'

'Nobody said you couldn't, darling, but what's she doing calling you at home? You never take business calls here. Was it an emergency?'

'No.'

'So was it about this guy topping himself?'

'Yes,' he hissed.

'Why did he do it?'

He hesitated, then decided now was as good a time as any. He rested both hands on the marble worktop and faced the music. 'I just lost a bundle on what I was told was a sure-fire investment.'

'Oh Tony,' she said sipping her drink.

'Yeah, oh Tony,' he sighed.

'Did you lose a lot then?' Tony simply shrugged and couldn't make eye-contact. Suddenly she was a little worried. 'Tony, answer me. How much did you lose?'

'I don't want to talk about it.'

'Why not?'

'Cos I hate fucking losing, all right?'

'Don't you swear at me. I knew something was up. I just knew it. And I know it started in Florida. It did, didn't it? You were told about this then, weren't you?' He nodded. 'Why don't you talk to me, Tony? Here I am, worrying myself sick, asking myself, is it me? Isn't he

175

enjoying his holiday or is something up with the kids? Tony, all these things go through my mind when you get this way. I was worried all holiday. Look at me. Do you know what I'm talking about?'

'Yeah, yeah.' He walked out of the room and she followed.

'Tony, tell me. What is going on? I mean have you got yourself into real financial difficulty with this? I need to know, especially now.'

'What do you mean especially now?'

'I was going to tell you tonight.'

'Tell me what?'

'It's Michelle. She wants to marry that Hamilton boy, you know the one who plays polo with Prince Charles? Him.'

'What?'

'She's been keen on him for months. Blond with nice blue eyes. He's been around here, Tony, loads of times. They met at the Dunhill polo match at Windsor last summer and she was with him over Christmas in France.'

'She's only seventeen!' he blustered.

'So? I was only eighteen when we married.'

'I know, but this is different. She's my daughter.'

'He and his family are coming for dinner Thursday to discuss it all.'

'Thursday? I might have to go into town to get this stuff ironed out.'

'What stuff?'

'I told you. I done a bad investment, got to catch up on the finances.' Under pressure he always lost his grasp of grammar, even his old accent returned.

'How much have you lost then?' she asked, frightened. The wedding was going to be very costly. What they lacked in class she had intended to make up for in cash expenditure. She had planned a sumptuous event.

'Not enough for you to worry about.'

'I hope not. If they want a wedding it's up to us to provide it. He's a sweetheart you know and his family are all titled. It'll take me three months to plan and prepare and they want to do it as soon as possible. Where are we going to hold the reception? What about her dress? I was going to see about getting Stella McCartney to do it, you know, have a real fairy-tale wedding like I never had.'

'Sweetheart, if my baby wants to get married in a palace I'll arrange it, you know that. She'll have the wedding of her dreams, that's a promise. But why the rush? She's not up the spout is she?'

'No, she bloody isn't! Oh Tony, you've got me all worried now.'

'Don't be. When have I ever let you down?' He kissed her.

'Never. I love you, Tony,' she said, returning to the kitchen for her power drink.

Tony plodded up to the bedroom and fell flat on the bed. 'Oh Jesus Christ,' he muttered, a fucking wedding was all he needed and it didn't help his stomach pains. He stuffed two antacid tablets in his mouth and chewed them like peppermints. He then thought about the call from Sylvia Hewitt. It worried him. The three had never been linked together before and he didn't like it one bit. But it was de Jersey's financial situation he was really concerned about. In all the years he had known him, he could never recall a time when he had felt sorry for de

Jersey. Although Driscoll had lost most of his own savings he could still lay his hands on nearly a quarter of a million but, if Sylvia was correct, de Jersey had lost everything. Driscoll knew, probably more than anyone, what the stud farm meant to de Jersey. He remembered old Ronnie Jersey's words: 'I once owned a leg in a horse. I cried when he won a little race at Plumpton. After that he cost me an arm and a leg just to keep but I couldn't send him off to the glue factory. He was like a pet. I loved that horse, Tony,' he told him. He remembered Ronnie getting carried away and fantasizing about owning his own racing stables. 'It's a mugs' game for the rich nobs, though,' he'd said. 'You can't win. It's all payout. Gotta have more money than sense,' he would mutter. His son Edward had achieved all Ronnie had ever dreamed of and Driscoll was sad that the old man had died, never knowing of his son's success. He knew Ronnie would have been overawed at Edward talking to the Queen at Ascot. Truth be told, he'd been a bit overawed by it himself. In many ways he was more like Ronnie than Ronnie's own son. Driscoll had certainly loved Ronnie as much, if not more.

The wind eased in his belly but Driscoll didn't feel better. He took a slow wander around the vast upstairs part of his home, from his children's bedrooms to the gym where his wife was working out with a butch young instructor in tight Lycra shorts. Making his way down the wide staircase he stood in the baronial-sized hall with its antique side tables and oil paintings of God knows who that decorated the circular, oak-panelled reception. The spacious drawing room had been copied from a

Homes and Garden picture his wife had liked. Sitting at the grand piano that no one ever played, he lifted the lid, revealing the ivory keys in perfect condition. He looked over the array of large, silver-framed photographs of his family and their various dogs, his daughter's horse and his son's aviary. He reflected once again, that this good life had come courtesy of the Colonel. Admittedly he had spent his money wisely, invested well and run his own business, but the reality was, without de Jersey he would have remained a nobody.

He loved his wife and he loved his family. He was proud of his own achievements, even if they were built from the proceeds of armed robberies. He also reckoned that he was a good man. He'd certainly given enough to charities over the years. He had never been a violent person. He'd seen it at close quarters but he had never taken up a gun or taken a life. He drummed his fingers on the polished lid of the piano, wondering. If he had refused de Jersey all those years ago, how much of this good life would he now have? He looked at the photographs of his daughter, now engaged to a titled bloke. Michelle's wedding would have to take a backseat to his efforts to sort out his finances. The villa would have to go plus the Chelsea Wharf apartment. All the trappings of wealth he had acquired would need to be sold off and all this just as he had a massive tax bill coming in. Right now he did not have the means to cover everything. He wondered if de Jersey really was planning another caper, even if this Crown Jewels thing was a joke. Though he didn't know what de Jersey's plan was he knew that, whatever it was, it would be planned down to the last detail. He slapped the piano lid hard with the flat of his hand and swore out loud at David Lyons. He should have refused to invest, refused because he was almost bloody well retired. He shook his head at his own stupidity and his indigestion started to rumble again in the pit of his stomach.

Wilcox was leaning over the Ferrari Testarossa in his eight-car garage, wearing an oil-stained overall. His young mechanic was sitting inside the old car, revving it up. Wilcox spent hours tinkering with his vintage sports cars. They were much-beloved toys. He had built his own small racetrack in his grounds and he would race round and round, testing and reworking the engines for the sheer joy of it. Sometimes he felt as if these were the only times he was totally content. His domestic life was clouded with various ex-wives and mistresses, his six children and their assorted pets. He had always searched for the perfect union but the reality was he had found it and it had four wheels. No woman had ever held such fascination for him or warranted so much loving care and attention. Today, however, he was unable to concentrate. The call from Sylvia Hewitt had unnerved him. It was nagging him like a mangy dog hungry for food. He hated the fact that she knew so much about him and had connected him to Driscoll and de Jersey and knew instinctively that she could be trouble. He was also rattled by the fact that de Jersey had not brought him or Driscoll into his plans to get rid of Moreno. It was, after all, very much their business. They had both suffered massive losses and had a right to confront the man themselves. It was also very unlike de Jersey. He had never advocated violence, so why had he murdered him?

It should not have been his decision alone and might have been the wrong one to make.

Wilcox let the mechanic go for a spin on the track and sat wiping the oil from his hands, perched on the bumper of a Silver Cloud Rolls-Royce. He had been running through his financial situation all morning and it was even worse than he had at first anticipated. Having liquidated funds for the investment, he had left himself short and his outgoing costs were substantial. It was not just the kids and all the maintenance payments. He had various other outstanding debts that needed to be paid. His drug dealer for one was screaming for his due. Wilcox had been shocked at how much he owed – two hundred thousand pounds to be exact. He was shocked by how much he was using. He had planned to cut down but under this recent pressure he'd needed more. He was afraid that de Jersey would find out and consider him a security risk.

Wilcox tossed the oily rag into the bin. He'd wondered about trashing the entire garage and hangar and claiming on the cars' insurance but he just couldn't bring himself to do it. The premiums were another vast expense. His days of running twenty garages were long gone. Later on in his life he had blithely and irrationally continued buying vintage vehicles, hardly ever reselling them as he had done for a living in the past. He'd begun buying and selling cars at the age of forty when he was flush with the proceeds of the gold bullion robbery. But now he was tired with the business side and just wanted to race and enjoy life more fully. He truthfully did not want to be drawn back into crime. Whether or not de Jersey was serious about the Crown Jewels, he knew enough to know that the Colonel was brewing something up. He also knew that he would feel obliged to go along with it, especially with the severity of his own financial troubles. The prospect scared and excited him, both emotions causing him to take more cocaine. That was more worrying than anything else. He needed cocaine from the moment he opened his eyes in the morning and used all day, even though he kidded himself that he wasn't addicted. What had started out as a release from boredom had slowly taken over his life and eroded his once sharp judgement.

'I've got to kick the habit,' he muttered, but just thinking about it made him want a couple of lines. He chopped four lines up in the back of the garage. He wondered how Driscoll felt about it all and after snorting all four lines he called him.

'It's me.'

'Yeah, I recognized your voice. You heard from the Colonel?'

'Only to warn me about that woman.'

'Oh right, well that's why I'm calling you.'

'It had better wait, you know, we're not supposed to make contact.'

'Yeah, well, I just did, all right? An' we're not doing anything fucking illegal, right? Not any more, okay? But I am really worried about this woman, Tony,' Wilcox said.

'She called me at the house.'

'Yeah, me too.'

'I didn't like it,' Driscoll said. 'And why are you

182

calling? We're not supposed to know each other, remember? We've both got pasts that we don't want catching up with us, for Chrissakes. Are you on something?' Driscoll could tell Wilcox was unusually wired.

'No, I'm fucking not. I'm just looking out for us. Is that a bad thing? What's got into you?'

Driscoll cut across the potential argument. 'He's lost the lot. Did she tell you? Reckons his stud will go down the tubes.'

Wilcox let out a long sigh, 'Yeah, she said he'd lost his shirt. You know what that means, don't you?'

'Yeah, he's more broke than we reckoned.'

There was a pause and then Wilcox's voice came back over the line sounding slightly muffled. 'No, Tony, it means whatever he wants from me, he's got.'

There was a long silence on the line. 'Me, too, I suppose,' Driscoll finally said, nodding in resigned agreement. Wilcox slapped the mobile off and turned to see the young mechanic standing close by, close enough to have overheard every word.

'What's with you?' Wilcox snapped.

'Sorry, James. We broke down on the S bend, pouring smoke and oil. You wanna take a look?'

'Don't go sneaking up on me like that,' Wilcox said angrily.

'Sorry, but I did knock.' Wilcox stared at the kid's young, concerned face. He relaxed and smiled.

'That's okay, Dan, no problem. Let's go check out the car.'

Rika was looking for Wilcox because she needed him to pick up the twins from school. She headed into the garage and, finding it empty, walked into James's back room, where she found the mirror. She licked her finger and tasted the cocaine. She shook her head. It was bad enough him using it but to leave it out in the open for the children to find was something she would not tolerate. Rika found him with his mechanic, leaning over the open bonnet of the smoking Ferrari on the track. She didn't waste any time with smalltalk but marched straight up to Wilcox and pushed him away from the car.

'Ve got to talk.'

'Not right now, I'm busy.'

'Vight now, James, I mean it. You have to collect the twins from school. I told you diz morning, you are late for them now.'

'Why can't you do it?'

'Because I have an appointment wid my dentist. I tell you diz.'

'Okay, okay, I'll get them.'

'No you von't.'

'What?'

She faced him, hands on her hips. 'You look at yourself in the mirror you leave in ze garage?' she asked. She threw the mirror at his feet. 'I'll get them but tonight ve talk because I von't have diz near to de kids. You should be ashamed of yourself, a man of your age. Vat you think you are playing at? And vipe your nose, it's running. You sicken me.'

Wilcox gripped her arm tightly and frog-marched her to the side of the track. 'You never speak to me that way, you hear me? Especially not in front of someone like Dan.'

'Why? Because he'd lose respect for you? Don't kid yourself, James. Everyone around you knows vat you are

184

doing; ve can't miss it! You vant to kill yourself, I no watch you do it! I am leaving you and your kids.'

Rika, not even his kids' mother, stormed back across the field and Wilcox wiped his nose with the sleeve of his overall. If he had felt shame before he now felt it doubly and he could not meet the eyes of the young mechanic, who tried hard to appear as if nothing had happened. Wilcox went back and patted the boy's shoulder.

'Can I leave you to finish up here?'

'Yes, sir,' he replied shyly.

Wilcox headed back to the house. He let himself in via the kitchen entrance, which was cluttered with kids' skates, Wellington boots, fishing rods, and skateboards. He passed the racks of kids' clothes hung up in various sizes and lengths: overcoats, raincoats, riding hats. Wilcox kicked off his muddy shoes and stripped off his overall, adding it to the pile of kids' clothes discarded in a corner. The phone rang as he passed the big pine table already set for tea. Four of the six kids were expected and usually more of their friends. His house was always jammed with kids of every shape and size. They ran wild, wrecking the place, even though they had an entire floor to themselves with a big games room full of equipment, computers and computer games.

He stormed up to the bathroom to snort another couple of lines, then lay down on the quilted bedspread. Deep down he knew the cause of his anguish; with de Jersey losing so much money, his plans to regain it would be illegal, whatever they were. He knew he would end up getting involved. Despite how he had protested otherwise to Driscoll in Florida, his loyalty to the man ran too deep. How could he say no?

De Jersey was with Fleming in his office discussing forthcoming race meetings. The going would be difficult, the ground frozen. Some of the horses loved this but others, like his precious Royal Flush, hated it. However, the big-money races didn't get under way until the weather warmed up.

The vet was with Royal Flush again. The swelling had gone down but he was still lame. They led him into the indoor exercise arena so that the vet could observe him. Even at a walk his lameness bothered him.

'What the hell is the matter with him?' De Jersey was beside himself with anxiety.

'I've X-rayed him, checked and double-checked, but I can find nothing that would stop him putting weight on that leg.' The vet was at a loss. 'It might be psychosomatic – he avoids using the leg because he remembers the pain it caused.'

'So what do we do?'

'Encourage him until he forgets. Next time he does a good run make a fuss of him. He'll soon stop limping.'

De Jersey went up to Royal Flush and stroked his head.

'You old so-and-so. Need a bit of love, do you?'

The horse pushed his head into de Jersey's chest. He was after peppermints and de Jersey slipped him one. He loved Royal Flush and still dreamed of the day he would see him cross the Derby finish line in front.

By the time de Jersey went back to Fleming's office, his mood had darkened. The vet had made an apologetic request for him to cover his quarterly bill: the usual cheque had bounced. De Jersey was shocked that his bank had not contacted him before refusing payment. He tried to recall which account it had been drawn on.

When de Jersey enquired of the bank manager why he had not been contacted about the refusal of payment to the vet, the man suggested a discussion in his office. De Jersey was horrified when he was told just how far his account was into the red. Of course it was only one of many: all he had to do was transfer funds from his other major account but the incident demonstrated just how quickly money was draining away.

When Fleming came in, de Jersey dropped a bombshell. 'Sell off the east wing,' he said. 'Contact Tattersalls and add our entries to the next catalogue. You might also want to contact some bloodstock agents about selling privately. I made a bad investment, but I should recoup my losses shortly,' he said, with a confidence he did not feel. He still had his offshore account in the Caymans and he calculated that he could keep the yard running, with a few cost-cutting exercises like this, for another six to eight months, but he would have to prepare for the money running dry altogether. He was so deep in thought that at first he didn't hear Fleming speak.

'What?'

'When you said to sell off the east wing,' Fleming repeated, 'you didn't mean that Cute Queenie should go too, did you?'

He was referring to the old grey mare de Jersey always rode himself.

'Yes, let her go. Get whatever you can for her.' He clenched his fist, wanting to punch something, anything.

'Is there anything I can do?' Fleming asked tentatively. 'I've got a few thousand saved and if it's just a short-term problem . . .'

De Jersey put his arm around him. 'It is, but I want to be careful. I don't want to get into real financial difficulties. We just have to ease the strain for a few months until I can release some more investments.'

'Whatever you say. You still sure Cute Queenie has to go?'

'Yes.'

Christina had hardly seen her husband recently. He'd been spending more and more time in the City. She was happy therefore when he suggested they spend a week in Monaco. What she didn't know was that the trip served many purposes for de Jersey. It meant they would be away when Fleming sold off the east wing. To see the horses led away would have cut de Jersey to the quick. It also meant that Christina would not be privy to what was going on and he didn't want to worry her. And also while they were in Monaco he could attend a race meeting, check on the state of his off-shore accounts and touch base with an important contact: Paul Dulay, alias Philip Christian, alias Gérard Laroque, alias Jay Marriot, alias Fredrik Marceau. Dulay had not seen Philip Simmons for twenty years, not since the gold bullion robbery. De Jersey, as Philip Simmons, had acquired his services when Dulay had become a French citizen fifteen years previously, using a false birth certificate and passport. Dulay had trained at the London Guildhall and become an apprentice for Cartier. He remained with the firm for five years until there had been an unfortunate incident concerning a Royal customer's brooch. The diamonds had apparently been replaced with mosonite. Dulay insisted there had been no diamonds to start with but he lost his job although no other action was taken against him. He turned the scandal to his advantage: capitalizing on the profile he had acquired during the affair, he became a freelance jewellery designer for the top Paris designers. However, although they commissioned his work and paid him well, they eventually ripped off his designs, as did the smaller stores and retailers. It was around then that Dulay had met up with Philip Simmons. Like Driscoll and Wilcox, Dulay had played a leading role in the bullion robbery and, also like the other three, he'd been lucky. There had not been so much as a whisper then or now of his involvement in the heist and for that he owed Philip Simmons his freedom. He was unprepared, therefore, for Simmons to re-establish contact. He was even less prepared to participate in another dangerous robbery.

De Jersey and Christina flew to Monaco in a private plane. A suite at the Hôtel de Paris had been booked and was prepared for their arrival. De Jersey had been a regular customer over the years and champagne, caviar, fresh fruit and large bowls of glorious flowers welcomed them.

Christina adored Monaco but she'd only ever been there when the Grand Prix races were on so this was her first proper trip. They hoped the weather would be mild but it was almost as cold and wet as London. Christina had first to unpack. They were going to the casinos that evening so she needed to press her evening-wear. She had also booked hair and manicure appointments and a massage, so her afternoon was full. She felt like being cosseted and, far from complaining, de Jersey encouraged her to enjoy herself.

He told her he had decided to take a walk, and headed straight for the exclusive shopping malls not a hundred yards from the hotel. He carried an umbrella and, in his immaculate grey pinstripe suit and brogues, looked every inch the wealthy Englishman. He paused by Paul Dulay's small, elegant jewellery shop, located on a corner of the arcade. The main window displayed a diamond tiara and matching necklace. A smaller display at the side boasted an array of emerald rings and earrings.

The entrance to the shop was covered by a small camera, positioned to allow whoever was inside to observe each customer as they arrived. De Jersey pressed the small bell once and the door buzzed open. The sales assistant asked if she could help him.

'Is Paul Dulay here?'

'*Oui*, Monsieur. May I ask who wishes to see him?'

'Philip Simmons.'

The assistant had disappeared through a mahogany-panelled door. Dulay knew him only as Philip Simmons. De Jersey wandered around the reception area. A few display cases were visible, exhibiting even more opulent jewels than were in the window. A velvet-covered chair stood close to an antique Louis XIV table on which lay a black leather visitors' book, a white telephone and a credit-card machine. De Jersey took note of the security cameras swivelling to keep him in focus.

In the back room, Dulay was selecting diamonds laid out on a black velvet cloth. He was using a jeweller's magnifying glass and a pair of long, delicate tweezers.

'Monsieur, there is a gentleman to see you.'

He looked up, irritated at being interrupted.

'A Mr Philip Simmons.'

Dulay removed the eyeglass and his breath caught in his chest. 'Show him . . .' He could hardly speak. Sweat had broken out over his entire body. He found his voice and told her to take Mr Simmons into the private showroom.

He needed a few moments to regain his composure. He packed away the stones he'd been examining, then gritted his teeth and left the room. He was so on edge that he could not stop shaking. As he approached the small inner door, he looked through the two-way glass and saw that it was indeed Simmons. His heart rate increased. Dulay took a deep breath and went in.

CHAPTER 10

PAUL DULAY was no more than five foot nine but was broad-shouldered and had a large face. He had aged considerably since de Jersey had last seen him. They had met in South Africa while Dulay was buying stones for a top French jewellery design company. He had been at De Beers to negotiate for them. They had stayed at the same hotel in Pretoria. De Jersey was there to find a contact to move the stock of gold bullion he intended to steal. He was already using the name Philip Simmons and travelling on a fake passport. They had formed a loose friendship over a misunderstanding about their rooms. The confusion, however, benefited de Jersey.

Dulay had been in the hotel bar quite drunk: he had just been fired by his Paris-based company. He refused to divulge the reasons for this but ranted against the bastards who had 'shopped him' – they would steal his designs, he said angrily. He rambled on about his prowess with gold, but eventually fell silent and looked morosely into his glass. Then he said that, with a bad reputation, it would be hard for him to get into another legitimate company.

A few days later de Jersey had broached the subject of

setting up Dulay with a store of gold that would make him a wealthy man. By this time de Jersey knew that Dulay had been sacked for switching real diamonds with fakes and pocketing the proceeds. Dulay had maintained that most people wouldn't know a real diamond from a zircon then, in the same breath, protested his innocence.

Their meeting all those years ago in South Africa had been fortuitous. They had both made a fortune and had agreed never to make contact again. Until now. Dulay's face showed clearly that he was very wary, if not afraid, to see Philip Simmons again.

He closed the door behind him and ran his stubby fingers through his thinning hair, which fell to the shoulders of his collarless black shirt. He wore well-fitting black trousers and black shoes with white socks. 'Well, Philip, it's been a long time,' he said.

De Jersey shook his hand and smiled. 'Maybe fifteen years.'

'More. Please sit down. Can I offer you a glass of champagne?'

'No, thank you. Can we be overheard here?'

'No. Do you mind if I do?' Dulay bent down behind the desk and opened a small fridge that was hidden behind it. He took out a half-bottle of champagne, then, replaced it and brought out some vodka. As he poured, his hands shook. The glass rattled against the bottle and de Jersey knew that Dulay was unnerved by his presence. The Frenchman gulped down the vodka in one and immediately poured himself more. 'To . . . old times,' he said softly. 'Why are you here?'

'Possible business deal,' de Jersey said.

'I am legitimate now, Philip. It would not be worth my while to consider other avenues. I have a good business and a good life here, and I don't want to lose it.'

De Jersey shifted his weight. 'You married?'

'You mean again? Yes, I am, and I have three kids. We live on the outskirts of town, a wonderful old farmhouse. We've spent years renovating. And you?'

'No, but I have my lady-friends.'

'Well, it's certainly been a long time since we first met.' Dulay cocked his head to one side. 'Apart from the other business, you were in real estate then.'

'You have a good memory.'

'Well, I am not likely to forget you, am I?' Dulay unscrewed the top of the vodka bottle again. He was feeling faint with nerves, his stomach knotted. 'As your trusted old colleague, please don't draw me into any-thing,' he begged.

'I have never forced anyone into doing anything. You should know that,' de Jersey said.

Dulay opened a leather cigar box and proffered it to de Jersey, who refused, and watched Dulay's hands shake as they picked up a long panatella, cut off the end and lit it. The blue haze of smoke circled his head like a halo.

'Have you ever seen the Koh-i-noor diamond?' de Jersey asked.

'Yes.'

'What do you know about it?'

'It's the biggest in the world.'

De Jersey indicated the size of the diamond with his hands. 'When it arrived in England it weighed 186.1 carats and was set in a kind of armlet. It was recut in Prince Albert's time. I'm talking about Queen Victoria's Albert, not Monaco's!' He laughed softly, then continued, 'At that point it went down in weight to 105.6 carats.'

'I didn't know that,' Dulay said quietly.

'You ever seen the Imperial State Crown?' de Jersey continued. 'It contains over three thousand precious stones – sapphires and rubies that would make your display cabinet a joke. Costs a fortune nowadays even to get in to see them, almost twelve quid. I've been there quite a few times over the past few weeks.'

'Time on your hands, then?' Dulay asked, smiling weakly.

'You could say that.'

There was a short pause. De Jersey stared at Dulay then leaned forward. 'It can be done, I'm sure of it. It's a massive operation but I know it's possible.'

'You're insane!' Dulay said hoarsely.

'Yes, I suppose so. But you would not be involved in the insane part, just the aftermath.'

'I don't understand.'

'Yes, you do. And just thinking about having access to those stones must excite you.'

'It scares the living daylights out of me. I mean it. Even to contemplate stealing the Crown Jewels is insanity and I won't get involved. No matter what you say about me being at the so-called safe end, it took me years of careful planning and dealing and living on a knife's edge to melt down that gold bullion and distribute it.'

'And you were fucking brilliant. Some of those pieces you designed were spectacular, all in eighteen-carat gold – bracelets, necklaces, earrings, rings.'

Dulay nodded, sweat pouring off his brow.

'Course, then there were the larger items: hubcaps

and other motor vehicle accessories. And you were never found out. But you were expert with gems too, and cutting is your speciality.'

Dulay had spent many months in South Africa before he had met Philip Simmons, and had been taught by the old De Beers masters.

De Jersey made an expansive gesture. 'I look around, Paul, and see that you are doing very well. I'd say with all that excess of gold and your knowledge of diamonds you've produced some of the finest exhibitions in Europe and now this chic little shop right next to the Ritz. Great location. You're doing well. I congratulate you.'

'Thank you. But it's taken hard graft, Philip. My name—'

'I know your name, Paul. For the last fifteen years your name has been synonymous with class and beauty. Your work has been featured in *Vogue* and *Elle*. Your jewels are worn by the rich and famous. I have followed your career over the years with interest, my friend.'

'I've opened a Paris shop, in the Avenue des Beaux-Arts.'

'Ah, yes, close to Chanel, YSL, Christian Dior and Cartier. Very good position again. Is it going well?'

'The usual teething problems, as with any new business.'

De Jersey plucked at the crease in his trouser leg. 'Any way you look at it, though, Paul, the gold bullion, used sparingly over the years, has made all of this possible.'

'I am legitimate now, Philip. I've been straight ever since and I want to stay that way.'

'But you weren't always so straight, were you? You laundered tons of gold bullion for me,' de Jersey said.

'Yes, and it aged me ten years. If I get involved in this jewel heist it would kill me.'

De Jersey collected his thoughts. 'Maybe it aged you then but you're looking good now and you have a great lifestyle. This place is classy.'

'Yeah, but I don't need any more, Philip. I'm looking to retire in a few years and I've got responsibilities.'

'Fine, no hard feelings.' De Jersey stood up abruptly and offered Dulay his hand. 'You would have nothing if the Colonel hadn't taken care of you. I protected you. You never needed to live your life looking over your shoulder because there was never so much as a hint of your involvement in the bullion robbery. But that is what the Colonel promised you. That was his deal.'

'Philip, I know that and I have always appreciated it. I mean, I would do anything within reason for you, but what you are asking is—'

'Just a possibility at the moment,' de Jersey interrupted. 'Until I have more details I won't know how secure the plans are but, as in the old days, I like to be prepared and you were top of my list. Don't for a second think that you were the only fence for the gold bullion. Don't think you are the only craftsman I'd trust with gems of this size and of such value, but as we had a good relationship I came to you first, to give you the chance to be part of this.'

'Thank you. It goes without saying you can trust me.'

'I always have.'

'Good. No hard feelings, then?'

'No hard feelings.'

Dulay was still sweating. 'Do you want me to put out some feelers?'

De Jersey shook his head. 'No, do nothing.'

Dulay crossed to buzz open the security lock on the side door.

'Do you have a work room here?'

'Yes, at the back. You want to look around it?'

'I think I would, thank you.'

Now that the pressure was off, Dulay became quite animated as he led de Jersey down a narrow corridor into a large back room. Inside there were two steel vaults, which held all of the gems, and a long trestle table on which equipment for cutting the stones was laid out. At the rear of the room was a small kiln for melting down gold, silver and platinum. A white-coated lapidary was hard at work shaping a magnificent pink diamond to be set in a necklace.

'This is my pride and joy. It's a piece that's been commissioned by Prince Rainier.' Dulay crossed to the table. 'It's a tiara that has been in their family for generations but the band has been bent and the stones loosened, so we're resetting and replacing a few missing ones. It's not as easy at it sounds.' He held up the work in progress. 'It's a beautiful piece but intricate work. The filigree between the stones is so old and fine it's very delicate and easily broken off. To match the design and make it sturdier is complicated. I'm making platinum bars first then coating them in eighteen-carat gold so it'll have more strength and durability. The fire in the diamond is astounding.'

De Jersey bent over the table to examine it. 'Never ceases to amaze me that a man with such big hands can do such fiddly work.'

Dulay nudged him in an over-familiar way. 'You know what they say about big hands?'

'Ah, yes.' De Jersey laughed. 'But earlier you were

shaking badly. Shaping these tiny stones into settings must take a steady hand.'

Dulay blushed. 'I admit I was nervous to see you again.'

'But you're not now.' De Jersey looked at his watch. 'I'd better go. You can call me on this number, should you change your mind.'

'Thank you. You must come to dinner and meet my family,' he said.

'Another time perhaps.'

Dulay watched Simmons exit the building on the surveillance camera monitors. He saw him pause a moment outside to glance at the window. The way Simmons suddenly looked up, virtually into the eye of the camera, unnerved him.

'Who was that?' the shop assistant enquired.

'Just a buyer. Wanted a birthday gift for his wife.'

'What did he buy?'

'Nothing.'

'Will he be coming back?'

'No.' He hoped to God that he would never see Philip Simmons again.

The bank manager laid a thick file in front of de Jersey and uncapped his fountain pen. 'A deposit was made recently from a US bank account for one point five million dollars,' the man told him. 'The transaction was cleared two days ago.' He passed the documents to de Jersey, who studied them. This was the money from the sale of the lease of Moreno's apartment.

'I will need to make a substantial withdrawal,' he said.

'No problem. We can have the money transferred within the hour.'

De Jersey looked up. 'Good. Could you now give me the details of my discretionary trust?'

The manager turned to the relevant pages and de Jersey was stunned to see that the balance of the offshore account in the Caymans stood only at a few hundred pounds. He flicked back through the pages, checking the transactions and the truth dawned on him. David Lyons had abused his position as a named trustee in the discretionary trust to withdraw nearly every penny from the account. All de Jersey had now was the money from Alex Moreno. 'That seems to be in order,' he said, without emotion, as he stood up and shook the bank manager's hand. 'Thank you very much.'

De Jersey tilted up his head to feel the jets of ice-cold water from the shower pummel his face. He was angry that he had misjudged David Lyons to such an extent; angry that he had not retained more control over his finances. His whole fortune was gone. He had nothing to support the estate. Worst of all, he was unable to do anything about it. But he refused to allow himself to dwell on the disastrous events. Instead he made himself focus on his meeting with Dulay. He had presumed that any man with such a passion for the profession would be unable to resist the lure of the Koh-i-noor diamond but Dulay had turned him down.

Wilcox and Driscoll had turned him down too.

De Jersey dried himself then lay down on the bed. He

200

closed his eyes. He adored Christina and his daughters. He loved his life and his champion Royal Flush.

He opened his eyes and stared at the ceiling. 'All or nothing,' he whispered, and knew that that was what made him different from the others. He would take the risk, with or without them.

Dulay parked his Jeep outside his villa and hurried inside. The kids were playing in the sprawling back garden. His wife, Ulrika, was gardening, wearing old jeans and a sweater. The extensive gardens were lined with olive trees that forged avenues lined with thick borders of lavender. Tall, pointed conifers reached like slim sentries to the sky, towering above the old stone walls. The large vine-covered terraces were winter bare. Dulay paused a moment, relishing the peace and tranquillity.

'Hi, you're home early,' Ulrika said, stretching her arms wide for a hug. Even at forty she had a taut body and was naturally beautiful without a trace of makeup. Her silky black hair was twisted into a thick braid down her back. 'I've had a really lazy day. The kids and I just hung out here all afternoon. Then when it rained we watched TV. We have that big party tonight,' she reminded him. She was six inches taller than her husband and hooked her arm around his square, solid shoulders. 'You want me to fix you a sandwich or something?'

'No, I need a shower. I'll eat later. Do we have to go?'

'Yes, we do. A lot of your customers will be there and it'll be good for business.' She ruffled his hair.

'Don't do that.'

'You're in a nasty mood.'

But Dulay had already started to walk to the house, stepping over the steel straps of the pool cover. All he could think of was the visit from Philip Simmons. Your past always catches up with you, no matter how many years go by, he thought.

Christina and de Jersey dined at the hotel then decided to have a quick flutter at the tables. They didn't do well so they returned to the hotel. The following morning they went shopping, but de Jersey could muster little enthusiasm and eventually returned to the hotel alone. By the time they met for lunch she was carrying several boxes and two suit-carriers.

'Did you enjoy yourself?' he asked, smiling.

'We're going to a big charity function this evening,' she told him. 'So I decided to buy something new to wear. I met a girlfriend I haven't seen for years, not since I was a model, and she lives here with her husband and young family.'

'I thought we might go to Longchamps,' he said. 'I wanted to meet up with a breeder who's been recommended to me and see his yard.'

'We can go another day,' she said. 'Ulrika's lovely and she's very up in high society here. All the Monaco Royals will be at the ball and I think it might be fun.'

'In that case we'll go to the stables another time. We're here for a few more days.' But he felt frustrated: he had to plan his next move and he did not have the time for frivolous charity events.

'It's just that we haven't seen each other in so long and, besides, I'd like to meet Ulrika's husband. They have three children. She said I could borrow some jewellery from her as I've brought so little with me, and as her husband is Paul Dulay I'll have quite a choice.'

The waiter interrupted them to take their order and de Jersey went on automatic pilot, hardly aware of what he ordered. What a coincidence.

'So it'll be a stuffy dinner-jacket evening?' he asked eventually.

'Yes, darling, but Ulrika is so looking forward to meeting you. We didn't have much time to catch up. They have this farmhouse they've converted and a huge yacht in the harbour. Maybe we should think about it for summer.'

De Jersey's mind was turning somersaults: this was a potentially dangerous situation. Paul Dulay knew him only as Philip Simmons.

On returning to their suite, Christina promptly called Ulrika to arrange a meeting to choose her jewellery. De Jersey watched her become almost girlish as she discussed what she might wear and arranged to meet up later at Ulrika's husband's shop. Then she unwrapped her purchases, showing de Jersey a sleek emerald green silk dress, and another in ice blue chiffon with a tight bodice and multi-layered skirt.

'I feel very hot,' De Jersey said quietly. 'It's warm in here. I think I'll take a shower.'

When he returned, he lay down on the bed. 'My head hurts,' he murmured.

Christina walked over to him. 'You should never order oysters out of season. I'm always telling you this. Let me feel your head.'

She laid a hand across his brow. He was hot – he had showered in almost boiling water. 'Darling, I think you have a temperature.'

He got up and hurried to the bathroom. 'I'm going to throw up.' He remained in the bathroom, making retching sounds and flushing the toilet, then came out and slumped on to the bed. 'It must be those oysters.' He moaned as if in agony.

Christina wanted to call the hotel doctor but he wouldn't hear of it, insisting she leave him to sleep so that he would feel better by the evening and, although she didn't want to, she eventually agreed to go to meet Ulrika as she had arranged.

When she had gone, he threw back the sheets and began to pace the suite, mulling over the situation with Paul Dulay. He seemed to be losing his touch. This would never have happened in the old days. Then again, he was a bit out of practice. He sat at the writing desk, picked up a pen and began to doodle on the hotel notepaper. The present situation would not have occurred years ago because he would not have risked meeting up with Paul Dulay without being certain he would bite. He should not have mentioned the Koh-i-noor diamond. When the time came for the robbery and it hit the press, Dulay would know the identity of the thief. The Colonel was losing hands down and he had to do something about it fast.

CHAPTER 11

SYLVIA HEWITT received the call in her office at twelve. Victor Matheson had some news. A car owned by Alex Moreno had been discovered in the long-stay car park at JFK airport. A police informant friend of Matheson's had tipped him off. Moreno, however, was not listed on any flight leaving or arriving at the airport at around the time the car had been parked there. The Lexus was discovered unlocked and empty, the stereo missing, wires hanging loose.

Matheson had also made enquiries at the Maidstone Arms, East Hampton, and gained another possible lead. Moreno had indeed arrived at the hotel. He had gone out after dining there and not returned until late in the evening. He had gone straight to his room and left early the following morning after settling his account. He had received one call on his arrival and had made a call himself. Matheson had tracked down the call to a local gay club called the Swamp. Unfortunately it had since been sold and was closed for refurbishing.

'Did you trace anyone who talked to Moreno that night?' Sylvia asked.

'Not yet, but I can go back and see who was running the place at the time. I might be able to find someone he spoke to at the club.' Matheson had also talked to Brett Donnelly, a local contractor who was working on Moreno's property in the Hamptons. Matheson had found Donnelly still at work on the property, which had now progressed considerably since de Jersey's visit. Donnelly was evasive at first, not wishing to be questioned about his business matters, but after Matheson told him he was investigating a fraud for a client Donnelly became more helpful; he discussed Moreno freely and told the investigator about the man, Philip Simmons, who had shown up on the site. 'From what I could make out,' Matheson said, 'this guy Simmons was owed cash by Moreno and somehow or other made a deal with him. Anyway, it looks like this Simmons is running the show now 'cos he's arranged for the renovations to continue. When it's completed, he told Donnelly that the property would be sold.'

'Do you have a contact number for Simmons?'

'Donnelly's got a box number for him but no other details. Perhaps when he invoices Simmons he'll get further information.'

'I hope so. In the meantime, I'll check out if he was one of the investors. I don't recall his name, though. Did he say he was English?'

'I didn't ask.'

'Doesn't matter.' But Sylvia was disappointed that she did not have anything more concrete to go on.

Matheson cleared his throat. 'If I'm going to keep looking for Moreno, I'm going to need an additional retainer.'

'I wonder if there's anything more to discover,' Sylvia mused.

'Well,' Matheson said, 'finding that car abandoned at

206

the airport is suspicious. I still haven't taken a look at Moreno's apartment in New York. Who knows what I might find there.'

'Do you think he's just upped and done a runner with my money?'

'Could be. Or maybe one of the other investors got to him first. You gonna check if one was called Simmons?' Matheson asked.

'Sure – but even if it was one of the investors, he might have been using a false name.' Sylvia was starting to get into this detective work.

'You're right. Are the other investors Brits?'

'The main ones are. There are others scattered all over the world but their losses were not as great.'

'Well, let me see what I can come up with. If Simmons comes into the US, maybe I can track him down. I've got a lot of contacts at the airport.'

Sylvia decided she should discuss the latest developments with de Jersey, maybe Wilcox and Driscoll too, before she went ahead. 'Don't do anything yet. Let me get back to you,' she said.

'Whatever you say – but somebody has just got themselves a valuable property, maybe as a pay-off,' Matheson said.

'How much is the property worth?' she asked.

'I'd say up to fifteen million,' Matheson replied.

Sylvia thought for a moment. 'Okay. Keep on trying to track down this Simmons man. I'll discuss your findings with the other main investors and get back to you.'

'You're the boss. I'll send on my accounts and carry on the work.'

'Keep in touch.'

Sylvia hung up and dialled de Jersey's number. The

housekeeper informed her that both Mr and Mrs de Jersey were in Monte Carlo. Sylvia hung up and called James Wilcox, but he refused to speak to her. She hung up, frustrated, then called Tony Driscoll. At first he was rather short with her, but became intrigued by her discoveries.

'So this private investigator believes that someone received a nice pay-off, right?'

'Moreno signed over the property and it was all organized by a business adviser named Philip Simmons. Do you know him?'

'No, I don't.'

'All I have is a box number for him in New York and so far Moreno seems to have disappeared without trace.'

'I see.'

'What I was wondering, Mr Driscoll, is if we couldn't, all four of us, pay Matheson's accounts. You see, if Simmons is taking over Moreno's property, by rights we should benefit too.'

'Let me think about it,' Driscoll said, and promised to get back to her.

A few minutes later, Driscoll was talking to Wilcox.

'Whatever he's done, we don't want to know. The less we know the better. But he's got careless. The stakes are higher for him and he's not handling it well,' Wilcox snapped.

'He's never been violent before.'

'And I hope he's covered his tracks well because it's not going to be too hard to figure out who he is.'

'Yeah. How're your finances?' Driscoll asked.

'Fucked, but I'm not getting involved in murder.'

'Same here. But we should be careful. You know what

he's like. If he finds out we've been talking behind his
back—'

'But we haven't really known him for a long time,
Tony,' Wilcox interrupted. 'We can't keep harking back
to the old days. A lot of water's run under the bridge
since then. Sometimes I wonder if we ever really knew
him at all.'

Wilcox's words hit a nerve in Driscoll. 'We shouldn't
be talking like this.'

There was a pause and they hung up, as uneasy as they
had been before their conversation.

De Jersey had only just got back into bed when Christina
returned. She had obviously been shopping again and a
porter was struggling with her purchases.

'How are you feeling darling?' she whispered, and sat
on the edge of the bed.

'Not too good. Did you have a happy reunion with
your friend?'

'I went to her husband's little jewellery store. I just
looked, but Ulrika was choosing a diamond necklace to
wear tonight with matching earrings. It must have been
worth at least half a million pounds but I'd be afraid to
wear anything so valuable. She told me she likes to
advertise his work! She showed me the most unbelievable
Russian tiara. The owner's grandfather got out of the
country with the diamonds sewn into the hem of his
coat.'

De Jersey leaned back on the pillows. No wonder
Dulay wasn't interested in working for him – he was
hobnobbing with high-society Euro-trash.

Christina yawned. 'You are coming tonight, aren't you?'

'I'm not sure. I still feel as if I have a temperature.'

She touched his head. 'No, you don't. You can't get out of it either. I decided your old dinner jacket wasn't smart enough so I've got a new one for you, plus shoes, a shirt and a tie. You have no excuse, darling.' She gave him a wonderfully seductive smile. 'Anyway, I want to show you off. I can't wait to see her face when you tell them who you are. I didn't mention the estate or the stud.'

He sighed, as if he was still feeling unwell. Maybe he should rob Dulay's shop and not bother with the Crown Jewels.

De Jersey admired himself in the full-length mirror. The white tuxedo was a perfect fit, as were the shoes and the shirt. Christina wore a pale pink beaded dress that fish-tailed out in a slight train behind her.

'I returned the other dresses and replaced them with this. You know, for a man who was at death's door only hours ago you have improved vastly.' She smiled at him in the mirror. They made a handsome couple.

De Jersey's mood had lifted because Ulrika had called to say that her husband was ill and had taken to his bed. Instead she was bringing her close friend Julian, a family friend who owned a restaurant and had shares in their yacht. She suggested that they might walk down to the harbour to see the *Hortensia Princess*.

'What *did* you tell her about me?' de Jersey asked.

'I could hardly get a word in edgeways. She never

210

stops talking, especially about the yacht. Never even got a chance to tell her your name.'

'Did you tell her I was almost as old as your father?'

'All I said was that you were rich and handsome and I loved you.' She kissed him, then held him at arm's length. 'Because you are the best thing that ever happened to me.'

'Thank you,' he said.

'We're having a glass of champagne in the bar before the car takes us to the palace,' Christina told him.

'You make me feel old,' he whispered.

'You are the reason I stay young,' she said, and slipped into his arms to kiss his lips. Then she gently traced his mouth with her little finger to remove signs of her lipstick before she took his hand and drew him towards the door.

He'd forced all thoughts of his dire financial situation out of his mind and now he was looking forward to their evening out.

Ulrika approached them with a handsome, swarthy companion. De Jersey kissed her on both cheeks then shook Julian's hand. Ulrika was wearing a black sequinned bias-cut dress that showed off her perfectly toned body. She had a full-length sable coat draped over one arm and clutched a tiny gold lamé purse. They went into the hotel bar for a drink and, as de Jersey ordered a bottle of champagne, the two women chatted about fashion shows they had worked on together. De Jersey called over the waiter and chose a small Havana for himself. As he puffed on the cigar, he watched Julian and wondered why he looked so on edge. He gestured towards Ulrika's diamonds. 'They are very beautiful,' he said.

Ulrika paused for breath. She touched the necklace then drew back her hair to show off the large drop earrings. 'Aren't they gorgeous? And look . . .' She held out her slender wrist to show off the matching bracelet, two diamond-encrusted bands linked by emeralds in the style of a daisy chain.

'Oh, that is just *beautiful*,' Christina said.

De Jersey glanced at his wife, who wore only a wedding ring and a thin gold chain with a pear-shaped five-carat diamond. It was simple but had cost fifty-five thousand pounds. The diamond was a yellow stone and had been auctioned at Sotheby's. It had been his first gift to her after they had met.

When they had drunk the champagne their car arrived to take them to the palace.

'I hope you've brought a lot of money,' Ulrika whispered to de Jersey. 'It's a charity ball Princess Caroline throws annually. Everyone always feels obliged to buy raffle tickets and bid for silly things in the auction after dinner. It's all in aid of a children's charity. In the past a number of guests bought items in the auction and their cheques bounced! So now it's cash only.'

The venue for the ball was the Salle des Étoiles, a vast space with a roof that slid back in summer. There were wondrous views across the bay and it was often used as a concert hall by stars such as Whitney Houston or Barry White. Tonight, however, the room was a sea of white tables and waiters. Anyone who was anyone from the glittering world of Euro-trash was there and at the head table sat Prince Albert, surrounded by an array of models and raffish young men. Everywhere the eye fell there were glorious gowns, sparkling jewels and the high-pitched babble of women greeting each other in various languages: French, German or Italian.

Among the four other guests on their table de Jersey saw, to his surprise, a well-known British financier who owned twenty-five racehorses stabled in France. De Jersey had met him once fleetingly at an auction. Michael Maloney was a City whizz-kid turned tax exile and still only thirty-eight. He was accompanied by a nubile blonde who had drunk too much champagne and kept falling off the seat next to him. There was also an Italian prince and his fourth wife, an American heiress. Her facelift made her look about the same age as Christina but de Jersey thought she was closer to his. She had recently had cheek and chin implants and, as she gaily informed everyone at the table, more implants in her lips and a full laser treatment on her skin. She was very amusing as she described the extent of her operations including how many surgeons she had checked out and she was totally unconcerned about everyone knowing. Her husband, however, visibly cringed with embarrassment as she loudly gave the name of her surgeon to Ulrika and passed a card to Christina with a flourish.

'If you want the best lip line, lady, you gotta visit this woman in Paris. She is just the best!'

De Jersey attempted to talk to Maloney but it proved difficult because the tittering blonde demanded Maloney's complete attention. Julian hardly spoke a word during dinner and looked constantly at his watch as if he was impatient to leave. De Jersey leaned across to ask him if he was expecting someone.

213

'No, I just hate these balls. Same people. Same food. I don't drink much and the smoke gets in my eyes.' He shrugged and turned away.

Two hours later, it was time for the raffle, the prize-giving and the charity auction. De Jersey excused himself and kissed his wife. 'I'm going for a breath of air,' he whispered to Christina. 'I'm still feeling a bit fuzzy.'

He walked out to the balcony and threaded his way through palms and flowerbeds to look out at the sea and sat on a thickly cushioned chair. There he lit a cigar and watched the blue smoke drift into the night air.

A voice startled him. 'You mind if I join you?' It was Norma, the American woman, carrying a tumbler of Scotch and her cigarettes.

'Please do,' he said, hoping she would not start to talk about her facelifts again.

'I hate these charity balls. They expect you to throw thousands around but I leave that to my husband. He's gay, you know.'

'Really?' de Jersey said, amused.

'I only married him for his title and he married me for my dough. I like being a princess. Here they're two a penny but in the States it sure gets you the right table!' She gave a throaty laugh and perched beside him. In the soft candlelight she was rather beautiful, her cheek implants giving her a Marlene Dietrich look.

'Your wife is exquisite,' she said, sipping her drink.

'I think so too.'

'Nice stone round her neck,' she said, leaning forward as he lit her cigarette. 'Bet that didn't come from the creepy Paul Dulay. His wife has a lump of mosonite round her neck.'

He laughed. 'I think you're mistaken.'

214

'Honey, I have one of the finest jewel collections in the States. I bought up a lot of the Duchess of Windsor's pieces. Now *there* was some high-class junk, but with her name attached it retains its value.'

'Are you in the jewellery business?' he enquired.

'Only the business of buying it. I don't invest in anything else. My daddy was a Russian Jew who arrived in the States with a couple of roubles to his name and opened a hardware store. When Wall Street crashed he made his fortune because he had hard cash. Lesson in life, that. He made himself a fortune but he was always paranoid that he would lose it all so he put his money into things like this.' She lifted her thin, freckled hand with its red-painted nails. The solitaire diamond ring was not of breathtaking size, but was set in an almost flat base surrounded by rose diamonds. De Jersey leaned forward to admire it but she waved her hand dismissively. 'Not the ring, honey, this.' She withdrew a fine platinum chain from beneath her gown. Attached to it was a pendant with a single, stunning diamond. 'Liz Taylor owns one just like it. What do you think?'

'I'm awestruck,' he said softly. 'Aren't you taking a risk wearing it?'

'Nope, I've got my protection.' She turned and pointed to a small square-chested man in an ill-fitting evening suit. 'He's never far from me. He'd spring into action if you tried to rip it from my neck.' She opened her top to let the stone drop back between her silicon-enhanced breasts, and laughed. 'I had them lifted so they could carry the weight of it.' She picked up her tumbler and sipped. 'That's why I can spot a fake. Ulrika's is mosonite. It might glitter like the real McCoy but it wouldn't pass a double refractive test.'

215

'What's that?' De Jersey asked.

'Well, honey, when you look at a diamond, tilt it. Look for the light that's refracted through it and if it's a real diamond it'll shine in one straight line. Now, with a fake or a mosonite you tilt it and it's got two lines. It's something every gem dealer does without thinking. Ulrika is saying to me that this necklace she's wearing is worth a fortune so she hands it to me in the ladies' room!' She laughed. 'That necklace ain't no girl's best friend! The bracelet she's wearing is a nice piece, but I've never been an emerald woman.' Norma downed her drink and stood up. 'She's working the room trying to sell her husband's wares. She took that necklace off faster than a whippet the minute I showed some interest, but I won't buy it.'

Her bodyguard swayed in her direction.

'Nice talking to you, Edgar,' she said, and strolled away, her minder following her like a dog.

De Jersey didn't care that she had forgotten his name. What she had said was swirling around in his brain and he frowned. Could Dulay still be replacing diamonds with fakes?

De Jersey surprised Christina by insisting on staying to dance, although he didn't spend much time on the floor with her. He chose instead to partner Norma and listened intently to her as they danced. She was witty and delighted that she amused the handsome man who partnered her so she leaned closer to him. When she started to discuss Paul Dulay de Jersey listened even more intently.

'Dulay's the darling of society out here but I wouldn't trust him as far as I could throw him. My sister, God rest her soul, was in Paris where he's got another shop. He tried to sell her a diamond and black pearl ring that wasn't out of any oyster. But he does beautiful settings. That wife of his, she's a pretty little thing. Costs him a lot to keep but not as much as that floating gin palace she talked him into buying. Believe you me that thing costs!' Norma didn't seem to need to draw breath, and De Jersey didn't try to stop the flow.

'You were getting on well with that awful American woman,' Christina said, as she cleansed her face.

'She was delightfully crude,' De Jersey said.

'What on earth did you two have so much to talk about?'

'Horses,' he said flippantly.

'She looked like one,' Christina replied testily.

De Jersey washed his face.

'I had to listen to Ulrika for hours. I never knew her all that well and I'd forgotten how self-centred she is. Her guest hardly said a word. Then you danced more than I've ever known you to dance before with that raddled old woman.'

'She's not that old, sweetheart. She's probably my age.'

'She's seventy-two!' Christina exclaimed.

De Jersey laughed.

'What are you laughing at now?' she snapped.

'That she's seventy-two and, if I didn't know you better, I'd say you were jealous!'

'No, darling, I am not jealous. But I hate to be left sitting like a fool.'

'You wanted to go, not me.'

'Yes, I know. Maybe I'm just fed up because you had

217

such a good time and I didn't. I didn't win anything and I paid a fortune for the tickets. I noticed, however, that Ulrika and Julian never opened their wallets. I just don't understand her. They're obviously not short of cash. And even if we aren't, I don't like people taking advantage.'

'What's a few raffle tickets?' he said.

'It's more. When we went shopping Ulrika said she'd lost her card and I ended up putting all the things she bought on my credit card.'

'Christ, not that sable coat?'

'No, that's her friend's, but she bought the dress, shoes and some other things, and tonight when I asked her if she'd found her card she sidestepped it. I told her we're leaving in the morning.'

'You think they're in financial difficulty?'

'It seems like it.'

He put his arm around her and drew her close. 'I can drop in at the shop in the morning and sort it out. How's that?'

'I'm sorry – I do hate being used. It was nice to see her but she did get a lot of money out of me. I don't like feeling a fool.' He laughed softly and she nuzzled his neck. 'And with you chatting up a seventy-two-year-old crone with a plastic face and her dreadful prince touching my thigh all night, it's no wonder I'm in a bad mood.'

Her foot stroked his and he turned to face her. 'I'm exhausted. The last tango did me in.'

She giggled and de Jersey felt her warm body slither down his and she started to kiss his thighs. Thoughts of mosonite diamonds and Paul Dulay's scams left him as he concentrated on making love to his wife.

Dulay was having a heated conversation on the phone with Ulrika. She had returned late after the ball and he had left for work the next morning before she had woken. She had called him about repaying Christina. He had been happy to do so until she told him how much was owing.

'You've got to be kidding! How could you do that when we just had a discussion about cutting back?'

'Because I wanted to make an impression. They're leaving this morning so I should go—'

'Just forget it. You said they were loaded.'

'But they might become good customers. I'll have to go to the bank and get some cash out. Which account should I use?'

Dulay pinched the bridge of his nose. 'The mortgage one. I'll sort it out later. But this has got to stop, sweetheart. Ulrika? Hello?'

She'd already hung up and he slammed down his receiver just as the door buzzer sounded. Dulay pressed the entry release without looking at who it was.

'Trouble?' de Jersey enquired.

Dulay looked up and paled. He began to busy himself with his selections for the window display and tried to avoid de Jersey's eyes. 'My assistants don't come in until ten thirty. Is there anything you wanted to see?'

'Cut the bullshit,' de Jersey said softly.

Dulay's lips tightened as he crossed to unlock the display window. 'You won't get me to change my mind.' He switched on the low lights for both the displays then locked the window and turned back to de Jersey. De Jersey flicked the switch to lock the front entrance.

'What do you think you're doing?' Dulay stuttered.

'Ensuring some privacy.' De Jersey strolled past the counter to the door of the small showroom where he had met Dulay the day before and went in. Dulay followed him.

'Listen, if you're worried about me opening my mouth to anyone, then you must know you can trust me one hundred per cent. I mean, I wouldn't be so foolish as to drop you in it, not after all you've done for me in the past.' Dulay was nervous now.

De Jersey sat down and seemed to change tack. 'I'm interested in a bracelet for my girlfriend. Something special. She likes emeralds.'

Dulay began to relax. 'I've got a beauty. It's expensive, but high-quality stones, matching diamonds, beautiful emerald links. I designed it myself. Or there's a ruby link with sapphires and pearls.'

'Can I see the first?'

Dulay left the room and returned shortly with a large flat leather case. He laid it on the desk.

De Jersey opened it and looked at the bracelet, then lifted it out. Dulay passed him a jeweller's eyeglass and turned on a high-beam spotlight. De Jersey studied it and nodded. 'Very nice.' He glanced at the necklace and earrings also in the leather case.

'What about the necklace?'

'That's not for sale. It belongs to an Italian couple, ditto the earrings. The pieces are in for an evaluation. Only the bracelet's for sale.'

'They're fakes, aren't they? Unlike this piece,' said de Jersey.

'You are mistaken!'

De Jersey sat down. 'I met someone last night who is on to you. I know you're switching stones and all I wanted to do was tip you off to be careful.'

Dulay rubbed his head.

'By the look of things you don't need to be doing that kind of shit. Why are you getting so greedy? And I'm looking out for myself here too. I mean, they pick you up on one thing and they might dig backwards.'

Dulay opened a pack of Gauloise cigarettes. 'I just did it a couple of times. Some of these rich bitches don't know what they've got. But you're right, it's stupid to take that kind of risk.'

'Must be easy pickings,' de Jersey said. 'Come on, though, it's not just the odd one, is it, Paul? Is that how you work your business? You value the piece and replace a stone or two. Then, because of your reputation, the owner is unlikely to have it revalued and is therefore none the wiser. Correct?'

'Listen to me,' Dulay said, 'I run a legitimate business. Like I said, it's just the odd stone here and there.'

'You must have built up a lot of trust to be so popular. But that's what it's all about, isn't it? Trust.'

Dulay remained silent, as de Jersey continued, 'I won't meddle in your private deals but I could cause you a lot of trouble.'

'And I could do the same for you,' Dulay said angrily. He had found the courage to stand up to the man he still knew only as Philip Simmons.

De Jersey sighed. 'How?' he said coolly.

'You know damned well so stop this bullshit. I will not be pressured into working on this robbery. It's insane and I refuse to be drawn into it by your threats because, although you may have something on me, I've got just as much on you. The gold bullion is only the beginning.'

De Jersey sat back in the swivel chair. 'Are you threatening me?'

'No more than you are me.'

'Don't take me on. You'll lose. I'll make sure of it.'

'Try it and see,' Dulay said, blustering now.

'No, but you have to straighten out, Paul. I'm not pressuring you to do anything. All I am doing is making sure I feel one hundred per cent certain you'll keep your mouth shut. Stop what you're doing with these fake jewels because I can't afford any worries where you're concerned.'

'My financial difficulties are not going to make me blab about your criminal activities.'

'Oh, so it's money problems, not just greed?'

'Things are a bit tight,' Dulay said, 'and I don't want to lose this buyer I've got, a billionaire Japanese gem dealer. He's too big and lucrative a fish not to provide the goods for.'

'Asks no questions, huh?'

'Precisely.' Dulay sucked on his cigarette. 'Don't get me wrong, though, I'm still not interested in your proposal. I've just got into a bit of difficulty, that's all. It's called divorce and my new wife, the one I'm crazy about, spends money like it grows on trees. She also talked me into buying that fucking boat with that French twat Julian. It's the size of Versailles and it took every franc I had to refurbish it. Now we can't sell it 'cos we still owe the shipbuilders and nobody wants to charter it.' He sighed, then shrugged his wide shoulders and stood up. 'Maybe things will pick up in the summer. I hope to God they do.' He was pacing up and down.

'Sit down, Paul.'

Flushed with anger, Dulay reminded himself that he was not going to be cajoled into something as risky as Simmons was proposing. He remained silent as de Jersey toyed with a gold Cartier pen that was lying on the desk.

Then he twirled the bracelet on his index finger and slipped it into his top pocket. 'I'll take this in lieu of all the worry you've caused me,' he said. 'No hard feelings. And don't worry, your secret's safe with me. Like you said, we're bound to each other in many ways. Love me or hate me, we're shackled together for life.'

Dulay didn't say anything about the bracelet. 'Why are you attempting this robbery? It's insane.'

'Because, like you, I'm hurting for cash, and after years of legitimate work I'm not prepared to go under. It goes without saying that I won't take any foolish risks. And since I do not intend to be caught, I will take every precaution to ensure the safety of everyone involved.'

Dulay interlocked his fingers. 'You always did take great care. You using the same team again?'

'Yes. No one will take any undue risks and everyone will be paid handsomely. After all, the Colonel has always been fair.'

'I know all that,' Dulay said, flushing. 'I didn't mean some of the stuff I just said. You know I'd never put you or Driscoll—' Dulay stopped.

De Jersey leaned forward, so close that Dulay flinched. 'You had better forget that name, Paul, but you can give me one. Who's this Japanese buyer? Tell me more about him.'

'No way.'

'If he's buying anything you throw his way maybe he'd be interested in what I might have to offer.'

'I don't want to risk getting on the wrong side of him. I don't ask him too many questions and he isn't interested in the finer details of what I sell. If I start passing his name around he's not gonna like it and I don't want to end up in the river with my hands cut off.'

De Jersey raised an eyebrow.

'I mean it,' Dulay said. 'He comes to Paris a couple of times a year, that's it.'

'What about London?'

'I don't know.' Dulay closed his eyes and his voice dropped to a low, hoarse whisper. 'Don't do this to me. Please don't draw me in.' Beads of sweat were forming at the edge of his receding hairline. Then he licked his lips. 'Look, I can't promise but when I see him next—'

'Not good enough,' De Jersey said. 'I need his name and a contact number.'

Dulay sighed. He opened his desk drawer and took out a crocodile leather box edged in gold. He pulled out a card and passed it over. 'He's a computer giant. His company's worth billions.'

'He buy any of your gold items?' de Jersey asked softly.

Dulay flushed, then nodded. 'That's his box number and email address. I don't have a direct phone number.'

De Jersey glanced at the card. He slipped it into his wallet and took out one of his own before he stood up. 'Good. Now I know I can trust you. And I'm sure you don't have to worry about Mr Kitamo. You've been dealing with him for long enough. Did he approach you or the other way round?'

'He came into my shop as a straight customer but over the years after I'd built up his trust, he would ask if I could get this or that for him.'

'Legitimate stuff?'

'Some of it, and once he had some gems he needed me to disguise.'

'Disguise?'

'Cheap settings, a few glass beads mixed in with the

emeralds and diamonds. After that he started buying the gold items.'

'I see.'

'I hope you do, Philip. This guy has been my lifeline and I wouldn't want anything to jeopardize my relationship with him.'

'Not with that boat round your neck.' De Jersey smiled. 'If you need me, you can always contact me on this mobile number and also my email address.' He placed Philip Simmons's card on the desk.

'You really believe it can be done?'

'I wouldn't be here if I didn't. Nor would I approach anyone I couldn't trust to do his part. It's been good to see you again. No hard feelings?'

'No hard feelings,' Dulay said, and de Jersey shook his hand.

Dulay watched him walk away from his shop with a diamond and emerald bracelet worth thousands but no way did he feel like stopping him. After all, he owed him. The bullion had got him started. Dulay picked up the small white card with 'Philip Simmons, Consultant' printed on it. He didn't rip it up, just stared at it then went into the rear office. He opened the small fridge and took out the vodka bottle, poured himself half a tumbler and gulped it down as if it was water. He placed the glass on top of Philip Simmons's card.

'The Koh-i-noor diamond,' he whispered. Now, there was a stone he'd like to get his hands on.

Christina loved the bracelet, and told de Jersey that Ulrika had contacted her at the hotel and returned the money. During the helicopter flight back from the

225

airport he said little. When his phone rang he turned to see if Christina was paying any attention. She wasn't, so he checked the message screen and saw, to his amusement, that Paul Dulay was calling. His pilot glanced at him – it was always foolish to use mobile phones in flight.

'Two minutes and I'll turn it off,' de Jersey reassured him.

'That's okay, sir. More of a risk when landing and taking off.'

De Jersey answered the phone and listened to Dulay. He arranged to meet the jeweller in London in a week's time. He smiled. Dulay had bitten faster than he'd thought he would.

CHAPTER 12

THE NEXT morning de Jersey left the farm to go to London. Once inside the Kilburn flat he began work on his files. He had already made lists of the names and backgrounds of the men he wished to interview. When he opened up his email he was surprised at how many messages had accumulated. He printed them all out and sifted through the answers to his Net enquiries. He put one message in particular to one side. This was from a Lord Westbrook who had, he said, in-depth knowledge of the Royals and the running of their households. He had been a page and later an equerry. He added that he had also recently been a 'guest of Her Majesty' for seven years. This interested de Jersey.

De Jersey had also printed out a series of questions he had sent to an infamous computer hacker with their answers. In responding to one query the hacker had written that all companies should be far more worried about an insider than an outsider. An insider had easy access and would be much more capable of infiltrating the company's systems. Nine times out of ten, security breaches in big companies were caused by an employee and rarely reported. De Jersey made himself a cup of coffee. He would need someone on the inside to deal with the aspects of this robbery that related to the Royal Family. He was sure the Royal household's security would be difficult to crack but he needed access to Her Majesty's diary and, most importantly, to the security that surrounded her.

The coffee tasted rancid – he'd forgotten to buy fresh milk. He threw it away and concentrated on the message he had put aside. From 1984 to 1986 Lord Henry Westbrook had been an equerry to the Queen. Soon after his employment was terminated he had been sentenced to seven years for 'taxation fraud', a rather neat way to describe setting fire to his ancestral home then claiming the insurance for art treasures he had already sold. Now, eight years later, he was still stony broke, living in a small studio apartment in Mayfair that belonged to an elderly relative, he was constantly searching for a way to make a living. It seemed to de Jersey that he would be perfect for what he had in mind.

Despite his debts and his chequered past, Lord Westbrook was still sought after socially and not just for his title. At fifty-four he was still a handsome, charming escort and a sharp, witty character. Since his release from prison he had been the life and soul of every dinner party to which he had wheedled an invitation. Of course his title helped: some woman was always eager to be seen on his arm, even if it meant taking on his mounting debts. Lord Westbrook was no fool, he knew that his next bride had to be wealthy. He was an outrageous flirt and adored pretty young girls as much as they adored him but securing one as a bride was proving difficult. All the eligible society girls had been warned about his reputation and kept well away so middle-aged widows or divorcees were his best bet.

De Jersey remembered seeing Westbrook at various

228

charity events but they had never met. Now he made phone calls to various exclusive gentlemen's clubs, then tried restaurants and the Jockey Club. Finally he resorted to calling what had been Westbrook's estate, aware that his lordship no longer lived there. Eventually he was put through to a manager. He said that he had arranged to lunch with Westbrook but was unable to keep the appointment and had lost his telephone number. He was given Westbrook's address and number.

At long last he got hold of Lord Westbrook. He had deliberately chosen to telephone him rather than emailing. He still preferred to speak to people, especially on such an important matter.

Westbrook answered the phone abruptly. His drawling voice had the husky quality of a chain smoker.

'My name is Philip Simmons,' de Jersey said. 'I'm a novelist and you replied to the query I posted on the Net—' He didn't get a chance to finish the sentence.

'Oh, yes. How did you get my number?'

'I asked around. It wasn't that difficult.'

'Right. Well then, how can I help you? In your query you said you wanted some research done?'

'Yes, I wondered if we could meet to discuss it. I have a deadline so I would appreciate it if we could get together as soon as possible.'

'Of course. Where do you suggest?'

A cigarette dangled from Westbrook's lips as he strolled into the bar at Brown's Hotel. De Jersey had chosen the venue because it was dark and in Kensington rather than the West End. He was loath to risk running into anyone he knew.

'Lord Westbrook?' de Jersey asked softly, as the man gave a cursory glance around the almost empty bar.

'Yes,' he said bluntly.

'I'm Philip Simmons. Please sit down. What will you drink?'

'Vodka martini.' He drew up a high stool and sat beside de Jersey, flicked ash in the direction of a cut-glass ashtray, then stubbed out his cigarette and immediately lit a fresh one. The Silk Cut packet was almost empty.

'Vodka martini, twenty Silk Cut and a Bloody Mary,' de Jersey said. The barman nodded and placed two small bowls of peanuts on the bar in front of them. De Jersey had no intention of remaining where they could be overheard and beckoned Westbrook across to a small table in the darkest recess of the room.

'Well, this is all very cloak and daggerish,' Westbrook said, with a lopsided smile. The waiter put down their drinks and more peanuts. 'Cheers!' Westbrook sipped his drink. 'You never know with this Internet stuff if it's for real or not. I'm not very adept at it. A pal recommended that I hunt around on it to try to get some work. I was in one of those Internet cafes, awful places.' Westbrook's dark eyes roamed the bar. 'Not been here for years. Odd place.'

'That's why I chose it.'

'Perhaps you could enlighten me about your project. You said it was a novel? Not another on the Princess of Wales, I hope.'

'No, it's not, but it will be worth your while.'

'Right, but if you're hoping to use me as a social come-on I'm afraid my name won't do you much good. It did for a while, when I was first released from the nick, but now I don't generate much excitement. I'm probably talking myself out of a gig, aren't I?'

'Not at all.'

'Well, as I said, my glory days are over.'

De Jersey smiled. His lordship was very self-effacing and it was amusing to hear him run himself down. After two more martinis, Westbrook's tongue was looser. He talked endlessly about his days in prison and the cons with whom he'd been banged up. Eventually he wound down and said, 'So, let's cut the small-talk, shall we? What you up for? I've got a feeling it's not kosher, that it's a tickle of some kind.'

De Jersey liked Westbrook. 'You could say that.'

'What do you want?'

'You.'

Westbrook looked perplexed.

'I want you, and your past experiences in particular.'

'In the nick?'

'No, before that.'

'Oh, really? What for?'

'The book I'm writing.'

'Oh. "Aristo gets arrested for fraud and ends up in the nick", that kind of thing?'

'No, your connection to the Royal Family. To be more specific, your knowledge of the Royal household and the Queen's routines. Protocol. For example, I need to know more about Her Majesty's ladies-in-waiting: where they stand, how they dress, how they address her. Also, how many security men travel with a Royal cavalcade, what they wear, how many to each vehicle and so on.'

Westbrook frowned into his empty martini glass. 'You'd pay me, of course.'

'Obviously.'

'What kind of money are we talking about?'

'That would depend. I need to be able to trust you. The more details you are prepared to give to me, the higher the bonus. I am prepared to pay a high price for the information. Can I get you another drink?'

'I don't think I should have any more. Coffee, maybe.'

De Jersey patted Westbrook's arm. 'Good. I'd hate to work with a drunk. Excuse me.' He left the table, ordered coffee and sandwiches, then went to the men's cloakroom. He wanted to give his lordship time to think, to get hungry for the money he was dangling in front of him, hungry to become a part of the team.

The sandwiches were consumed rapidly but when de Jersey ordered a second pot of coffee, Westbrook's manner changed. He had sobered up. He sat back, lit his sixth cigarette and sucked in the smoke.

'Now, let's put some cards on the table. The first one is, who the fuck are you? You come on like some James Bond figure. I can't fathom you and I'm usually pretty good at it. This novel doesn't ring true to me.'

De Jersey coughed, hesitated, then began. 'Okay, my name is Philip Simmons and I'm a nobody. I have lived mostly in the US for the past decade, got a nice little nest egg and was about to retire when I lost it on some bloody useless Internet company that was supposed to make me more than secure for the rest of my life. It bankrupted me.'

'I know the feeling,' said Westbrook, with a detectable undercurrent of anger.

'I need to make a quick kill,' de Jersey said.

'I gather that, but from what you've just said how are you going to pay me for what you want to know?'

'There's bankrupt and there's bankrupt. I can still lay my hands on a few bob.'

'I see, but this information isn't for some coffee-table book, is it? So, get a bit clearer, Mr Simmons, and stop wasting my time.'

'It's a nice earner.'

'How much of a nice earner?'

'Enough.'

'So the sum is just what size?'

'If you produce the goods, your cut will be in the region of five or six million.'

There was a long pause. His lordship lit another cigarette. 'So it's certainly not legal. Let me think. You want my information regarding the Royals and their household. What are you going to do? Break into Kensington Palace? If that's the idea, forget it. Christ, they've been broken into more times than I can count and everyone always gets caught.'

'It's not that.'

'Pity. I know the place like the back of my hand.'

De Jersey watched him like a hawk.

'You going to tell me?'

'Not yet.'

'If it's the Crown Jewels, old boy, you don't stand a hope in hell. Waste of time. Only one chap ever broke in, sixteen something. He failed – but he was such a charming fellow he didn't lose his head.'

'I know.'

'Ah, so it could be the Crown Jewels, or something similar.' There was another long pause. 'They do come

233

out now and again, for the State Opening of Parliament, coronations. Ma'am's Golden Jubilee is this year. She'll need a fitting – Royal heads have swelled a bit since Edward the Confessor's time . . .'

They left the hotel together and picked up a taxi to drive the short distance to Westbrook's home where they continued their discussion.

De Jersey grew more confident that Westbrook would agree to help when he saw the wretched apartment. The single room in Pimlico was shabby. The once good-quality Persian carpets were beyond threadbare and the single bed was draped with a tatty Paisley throw. There were a few elegant oil paintings, but even those were damaged. The small kitchen was filthy and Westbrook opened cupboard doors that were falling off their hinges to look for some instant coffee. 'I just use this pad to doss down in. It's not even mine – belongs to an old and distant cousin. Ah! What about a chilled vodka?'

They drank from chipped glasses as Westbrook showed off his most prized possessions, probably the only ones he had left: a row of silver-framed photographs of his children. He had a son and twin daughters. The pictures also showed an austere blonde woman. 'She was my wife,' he said sourly. 'She got custody. They all live in South Africa now. I could see them but the plane fare is a problem. The bitch wouldn't give me a tissue if my nose ran! Not that she's that flush herself.' He sat down cross-legged on the couch and gulped his vodka. De Jersey did not touch his.

'You are now aware of my circumstances,' his lordship

said flatly. He lit a cigarette. 'There's an added problem.' He sighed.

De Jersey remained silent.

'I have cancer.'

'I'm sorry,' de Jersey said, with sincerity.

'So am I sometimes. I look at the photos and I remember such happy days but the old man left me with a nightmare of death duties. I couldn't get out of it. But I loved that place with a passion. It's my heritage and by right my son's. Before I die I'd like to own it again, pass it on to William.'

He got up, picked up one of the silver frames and passed it to de Jersey. 'My ancestors have lived there since seventeen eighty. Now it's owned by a group of bloody salesmen in grey suits. Tragic. All my family looking down the baronial staircase while the imbeciles ruin the place. I can't even visit.' He replaced the photograph and rested his hands on the marble mantelpiece. 'Now you know all there is to know about me.'

De Jersey remained silent.

'I have told you all this for one reason only and that is to make you understand that this little . . . "flutter", shall we call it, could not have come at a better time for me and I'm up for it *if* there's enough lolly in it for me. If there isn't I can't take the risk. It's got to be all or nothing, especially as I'm going to snuff it.'

De Jersey drained his vodka and put down the glass. 'You were on to it,' he said softly.

'What?'

'You almost gave me heart failure, but you were on to what I have in mind,' De Jersey said.

'Not the bloody Crown Jewels?'

De Jersey laughed. 'Yes.'

'You must be out of your mind.'

'Not really. What do you know about these jewel fittings, the one for the Queen's Golden Jubilee?'

Lord Westbrook poured himself some more vodka and gulped a mouthful. 'My God, are you serious?'

'Yes.'

'I see. Well, my cut would certainly buy my old pile back. How many will be in on it?'

De Jersey hesitated, then went for it. 'Eight, I think, including you. I may need a few more heavies. Not everyone will get the same amount. It all depends on how important they are to the heist.'

'I see.'

'Do you?' de Jersey asked seriously.

'I spent seven years in the nick so I can see quite clearly that it's a hare-brained idea. Why decide to trust me?' Westbrook asked.

'I like you.'

'Bollocks. What else?'

De Jersey gestured to the squalid room. 'To die in this place isn't what you want, is it?'

Westbrook drained his glass. The bottle was empty.

'I'd say you are an embittered man. You've lost your self-respect, your children and your home. Spending years in prison gave you plenty of time to review your future and reflect on your past. That is why I'm willing to pay you, starting this week, to work for me. I can't say at this stage if it will go ahead. And it won't until I'm satisfied we can do it with the least risk to all concerned.'

'What's the down-side?'

'There isn't one. If I think it's impossible and call it

off then it's just been an experience. However, if I think it's a viable project, the only down-side would be if one of us opened his mouth because that would ruin any chance of our survival.'

De Jersey stood up straight, like a colonel, his massive frame dominating the small studio. 'So I demand total loyalty.'

'Demand?' Westbrook smiled.

'Yep. We cannot afford a weak link and if one did arise it would be erased.'

'How would you know?'

'I would know, and I would see personally that it was taken care of. You come on board, you obey the rules.' De Jersey picked up the empty vodka bottle and tossed it into the fireplace. It smashed to pieces on the empty grate. 'No boozing, no drugs, and this . . .' He moved close to Westbrook, took his jaw in one hand and ran his fingers over the man's mouth with the other. 'One word leaked and everyone goes down.' He released his hold and picked up one of the photographs of Westbrook's children. 'Every man involved is hungry. They have families, children. So if a blabbing mouth hurts them they will want retribution. Do you understand?' He set down the photograph carefully.

'I do, and I resent the threats.'

'I hope you do, Harry. That *is* what your friends call you isn't it?'

'And we're friends now, are we?' Westbrook asked.

'No. But I will be more of a friend to you than any other man you know. If this is going to work you will have to trust me one hundred per cent, and trust is what makes a friendship.'

Westbrook watched as de Jersey picked up his cashmere overcoat. 'If you decide not to go ahead, will you still pay me?'

'Of course, per week for however long it takes to accomplish your part of the heist.'

'How much?'

'One thousand cash every week and a cut of the jewels once they've been broken up.'

Westbrook lit another cigarette.

This time de Jersey struck the match to light it. Their eyes met. 'You should get enough to leave your son and heir his rightful inheritance.'

Westbrook stared into de Jersey's cold blue eyes. He did not flinch and de Jersey was impressed.

'Thank you,' Westbrook said. 'I put my trust in you, God only knows why – it's a gut feeling. I don't know how long I have to live and this morning I really didn't care, but now I do. I want to live long enough to pull this bloody thing off and if I die in the process it doesn't matter. But if we do it, you'll have given me the chance to leave my son more than an empty title. I'd like that.'

Back at the flat in Kilburn, de Jersey could hardly wait to sit down at the computer. He logged on and began to search. 'The Golden Jubilee Programme Pages' came up and he scanned them for details of the Royal calendar. The festivities would begin in early May and continue through June and July. He was sure now that the crown and the jewels to be used during the celebrations would have to be removed from the Tower some time before the event. Then they would have to be held in safekeeping – but where? Perhaps with the jeweller appointed to the Queen. A plan was finally forming. He closed down his computer and leaned back in his chair, smiling. Just then his mobile rang.

'It's me, Eddy,' Driscoll said. 'Me and Jimmy. We want to meet up again, the sooner the better.'

'Sure,' de Jersey said calmly. 'Tomorrow. Not at the Ritz, though. There's a pub by Robin Hood Gate in Richmond Park. See you both there at twelve.' He hung up. At last he felt confident that he could pull this off. His team was coming together.

CHAPTER 13

THE LARGE public house chosen by de Jersey for the meeting was actually in Kingston. It was far enough away from their homes for them not to be recognized and full enough for them not to stand out. It had a large family dining room attached to the bar. The pub meals were home cooked and cheap, the atmosphere friendly. Driscoll's dog had accompanied the threesome.

They ordered beer and sandwiches and sat in a booth. They exchanged pleasantries as the drinks and food were put before them, then got down to business.

'It's this fucking Sylvia Hewitt,' Wilcox said.

'She's called us both at home,' Driscoll said, and peered at his sandwich. He'd had his usual stomach trouble for days now and was scared to eat.

De Jersey sipped his pint. 'What's she on about now?' he asked. She hadn't called him.

'Well, for one thing, I don't like her having my private number,' Driscoll said.

'Goes for me too,' Wilcox said. 'She's getting Rika on edge. She thinks I'm having an affair with any woman who calls the house.' He gestured to de Jersey's untouched plate. 'You want yours?'

'No.' He pushed his plate forward. 'Change your numbers.'

'We're in the middle of organizing my daughter's wedding and my wife'd go ape-shit if we changed the number now. And her knowing my phone number is the least of our worries. She's on to Philip Simmons,' Driscoll said.

This caught de Jersey off guard. 'What?'

'Yeah, she's on to you as Simmons.'

De Jersey placed his beer on the mat. 'Shit.'

Wilcox took over from Driscoll. 'You need to be careful she doesn't work it all out. I mean, what if she discovers you went to New York? Security in every airport's tighter than my arse. Do you think you can be identified?'

'Well, she's certainly been playing the detective, hasn't she? I think I'm okay, though. Philip Simmons is only the facilitator of the house sale. When she can't get hold of him, she'll start pursuing other avenues to try to track down Moreno. All anyone over there knows is that Simmons is a red-headed Canadian business adviser.' De Jersey tried to make light of the situation but he knew this was a major spanner in the works.

'Listen,' Wilcox interjected, 'Tony and I still have some collateral. I don't mean to be rude but this Hewitt woman also told us how much you lost and we know how much cash those horses of yours eat up. Why don't you get shot of the Hampton property and use the money from that until you get something worked out?'

'You can pay us later,' Driscoll chipped in.

'I have something worked out.'

There was a pause. Wilcox wouldn't look up from the beer mat and Driscoll chewed a nail.

'So, you do have a caper in mind?' Driscoll said at last.

Wilcox wiped his mouth. 'Just so long as you're not still on about the Crown Jewels. I mean, that was just a gag, right?'

'It wasn't. It still isn't.'

'Sweet Jesus, he's serious!' Driscoll said incredulously.

'Yep, and I know it can work. It'll take a lot of time and preparation, though, because we can't afford to make any mistakes.'

'Oh, *we* can't huh? Well, in that case—'

'Just listen to me. The items we're going to take will not be in the Tower. It's going to be the jewels the Queen wears for the Golden Jubilee. They'll be taken somewhere else for preparation and that's where we'll pick them up.'

'Where will they go?' asked Driscoll.

'I'm not sure yet, possibly one of the jewellers in Hatton Garden,' de Jersey replied, 'but I'll find out soon enough. I've been gathering the people we'll need to help us. I've hooked in an equerry who's been close to the Royal Family for years and knows the protocol. We need a substitute for the Queen, some motors, a lady-in-waiting, and two heavies apart from ourselves.'

Driscoll and Wilcox were speechless.

De Jersey continued, 'We'll also need to get into the Royal household's diary of events to get an understanding of the security measures and I'm going to look into finding a computer hacker.'

The three sat hunched around the table. Driscoll's dog yawned and shifted position under the table.

Wilcox broke the silence. 'So, say you get this organized and pull it off. How much do you think we're looking at?' he asked.

'The Koh-i-noor diamond should fetch us millions. Then there's diamonds, rubies, pearls . . .'

'Fuck me,' Wilcox said.

'It's got to be firmed up, and until then it's just a work in progress.'

Driscoll drained his beer. 'What do you want from me?' he asked quietly, glancing at Wilcox, who was frowning, his head bowed.

'I need the name and address of the actress who does the advert for Royal Jelly on TV.'

'What?' Wilcox was convinced he hadn't heard correctly.

'I can do that,' Driscoll said. 'It'll just mean a few phone calls.'

'You have to line up the vehicles,' de Jersey said to Wilcox. 'We need two Daimlers done up. Copy the badges, Royal coat-of-arms. But tread carefully. Spread it out. The cars must never be connected to any of us.' De Jersey drained his glass. 'Another drink?' he asked nonchalantly, as if he was discussing nothing more serious than a golf tournament.

Driscoll asked for tonic water: the pain in his gut was worse.

Wilcox got up. 'I'll get this round, you paid for the last.' He headed for the bar.

'You feeling all right?' de Jersey asked Driscoll.

'What do you think? You've got my nerves run ragged. I can't take it all in. I didn't come here to discuss the fucking heist, Eddy. I told you I wasn't up for it and neither's he.' Driscoll jerked his head towards the bar.

De Jersey ignored what he had said. 'Watch the advert. When you see it you'll understand why I want the actress.'

'Fine, right, I'll check it out. Watching TV's about all I'm good for with this indigestion.'

Wilcox returned with the drinks.

Driscoll leaned in close to de Jersey. 'What time span are we looking at here?'

'It'll be May. According to my contact they always do the crown fittings four or five weeks before the event and the Jubilee celebrations take place on the 4th of June,' de Jersey said, lighting a cigar. 'I'll have the exact dates soon but it looks like early May. From now on, contact me only on my mobile – no calls to the house.'

'Hang on!' Wilcox said. 'I only went to get a round and now you're talking as if this is all agreed to. Good job I didn't go for a slash too or I'd have really missed the plot.'

De Jersey gave him a half-smile. 'It's a work in progress, that's all. Decision time is still way off. Right now I just need the pair of you to help me set it up. That's all.'

Wilcox paused, looked at de Jersey, then raised his glass. 'Early May it is, then,' he said.

De Jersey glanced at them both. 'So, it's agreed. You'll help me set it up?'

They nodded and de Jersey raised his glass too.

Wilcox had left de Jersey and Driscoll, who had walked into the park with the dog towards Driscoll's wife's Toyota estate. Driscoll opened the door and the dog hopped in. De Jersey watched him swing the door back and forth. He sensed that Driscoll wanted to say something. 'What's worrying you?' he asked.

'Well, for starters, you're not on the balls of your feet

like you used to be. And that's not a good thing 'cause I think this Hewitt woman could be trouble.' Driscoll closed the door and stared at de Jersey. 'And Jimmy's another worry. I think he's doing too much coke for his own good. I don't like ratting on him behind his back but I've already told him to his face that I think he's got a problem.'

De Jersey put his arm around Driscoll's shoulders. 'I've never taken undue risks with you or James and I'm not about to start now. If this caper looks like a no-go or if one of you isn't fit to do the job, I'll be the first to put my hands up. Until I'm sure, just do as we've planned.'

Driscoll nodded, unconvinced.

'I also want to thank you,' de Jersey went on. 'It means a lot to me that you've both offered to help.'

Driscoll sighed. 'You're worth it.'

'I'll talk to James,' de Jersey said. 'He won't know it came from you. It's obvious to me, too, when he's high.'

De Jersey watched Driscoll drive away, his dog staring out of the rear window. He had suspected Wilcox of doing coke, although he had never witnessed it. He would have to monitor him. He wasn't unduly worried about him, though. He'd always been a bit of a livewire, but he delivered too. And this time he delivered even faster than de Jersey had hoped. Later that afternoon he got a call from Wilcox saying he might have found the cars. He'd seen an advert in *Motor News* and he was going to check it out.

The following morning, Wilcox walked along the cobbled mews a few back-streets away from Leicester city centre and paused outside a double garage. The 'Hudson's Weddings and Funerals' plaque on the garage door was peeling and hung precariously from a rusty nail. He had parked his Ferrari a good distance away down the street outside a large petrol station. He'd asked the proprietor to check the oil and fuel, telling him he would return shortly.

Hudson's appeared locked and Wilcox stepped away, pissed off. Then he gave a really hard knock and, to his relief, heard footsteps inside. The door creaked open and a short, wiry little man with bifocal glasses peered out. He had iron-grey hair in a spiky crew-cut and was wearing filthy, oil-stained overalls. Ken Hudson was seventy and suffered from glaucoma. He gestured for Wilcox to follow him into the gloomy garage.

It was larger than it had appeared from the outside, with four covered vehicles parked in a square. Hudson switched on a yellowish light and launched into a monologue on his now defunct wedding and funeral business. He was selling everything, including the tools, the paint-spraying and car-cleaning equipment, the four vehicles. Wilcox poked around the small back office, which was home to a kettle and a small camping stove.

Hudson squinted at him through his thick glasses. 'You wanna look at the vehicles?'

Wilcox smiled and shrugged. 'Eh, Pops, I can shift the hearses, but they're not what I'm after. I want to make this a paint shop, respray cars, stuff like that. I'll take 'em, but it's the premises I'm primarily interested in. What's your asking price? It'll be cash, so don't play silly buggers.' Wilcox lifted a tarpaulin and discovered a Daimler.

'Ten thousand,' Hudson said.

'I'll give you eight, cash.'

Hudson paused. 'All right, but that's a damn good price.'

The deal done, Hudson brought out the grubby documents, signed everything over to 'Tom Hall' and gave him a receipt for the cash. After another fifteen minutes of small-talk, the old boy handed over the keys and left. When he was alone Wilcox dragged the tarpaulin off each of the Daimlers. They were exactly what de Jersey had requested. Two were hearses and two had been used for weddings, but not for some time. Mildew and cobwebs threaded across the seats. Wilcox inspected each vehicle's engine. He would use two for parts, and it would take a lot of elbow grease to get that bodywork gleaming again.

Before driving back to London he purchased a book on the Royals and, using a magnifying glass, checked out their Daimlers. He would need to make a copy of the mascot fitted to the Queen's car. He also had to match the seat colours. It would take time, but he was in no hurry. It was still early days. In some ways it was good to have something to take his mind off his financial problems and, as the Colonel had said, if it didn't work out and he wanted to walk away, he could. He was just carrying out orders as he had in the past.

Later that day de Jersey arrived outside Sylvia Hewitt's apartment block in St John's Wood. He telephoned her from a small cafe along the high street. Helen answered, and told him Sylvia was not at home but that she expected her at any moment.

'I wondered if I could see her.'

'Oh, I'm sure. Would you like her to call you at home?'

'No, I'm in London. In fact, I'm not far from St John's Wood. May I come round tonight?'

'Of course,' Helen gushed.

'Good. I'll see you shortly then.'

He snapped his mobile shut and sat with his cappuccino, wondering how to approach the matter with Sylvia. He had to find out the private investigator's name and, most importantly, if the man had discovered anything that would lead Sylvia to him.

Helen opened the front door. She looked dreadful, even thinner than before. 'I didn't expect you so soon but Sylvia's on her way. I called her office and she was just leaving.' She gestured for him to follow her into the drawing room. 'Would you like some tea?'

'That would be nice,' he said. 'I've had a long day.'

Helen clasped her hands. 'I'll just slip out to the high street. There's a very good deli, wonderful cakes, unless . . .'

'I don't want to put you to any trouble but I'm a sucker for chocolate éclairs.'

Helen tucked a wisp of hair behind her ear. 'I'll be two minutes. Would you like the television on?'

'No, thanks. It'll be nice to sit here and relax.'

As soon as he heard the front door close de Jersey was on his feet. He searched the room, then looked over the rest of the apartment, walking past the immaculate kitchen and bathroom to reach Sylvia's room. He was fast and careful, first her wardrobe, then her dressing-table. Lastly he searched her bedside table and in one of the drawers he discovered a photograph of her with David Lyons, several letters and personal documents, such as Sylvia's birth certificate and driving licence. He hurried from the bedroom into a small adjoining room that served as her office and discovered the mail from Matheson in New York, his carefully listed expenses and updates of his investigation. Then he heard the front door open and was caught near the bedroom door. He smiled apologetically. 'I'm sorry, where's the bathroom?'

Helen pointed to a door opposite as she made her way into the kitchen.

He went in and closed the door. Then he opened and read one of the letters he'd taken from the bedroom. It was a love letter from David Lyons to Sylvia.

Christina had just boiled the kettle when Donald Fleming tapped on the back door and peered in.

'Hi there,' said Christina. 'I've just made tea. Do you want to join me?'

'No, thank you. I just wondered if you could contact Mr de Jersey. The vet's been out again to Royal Flush. I need to speak to him.'

'I'll try to reach him. He's in London on business but he's due home shortly. Is it serious?'

Fleming looked glum. 'I don't think so, but I just didn't like the sound of him this morning when he came back after a bit of training. I'll be out in the yard if you get in touch with the governor. 'Bye now.'

Christina called de Jersey on his mobile but it was

turned off. She left a message and carried a tray of tea into the sitting room to her daughters; they had just arrived home from boarding-school for the weekend.

'There's something wrong with Royal Flush,' Christina told them, as she put down the tray. 'I've called your Dad but his mobile is turned off.'

'What's up with him?' asked Leonie, who was the image of her mother, with fine blonde hair almost down to her waist.

'He's not well after training.' She poured the tea.

'Did they say what was wrong with him exactly?' asked Natasha. She was so different from her younger sister with a thick mop of unruly dark hair and blue eyes. She'd only been home for an hour but she'd already changed into her jodhpurs.

'No, just that he seemed a bit off after his training run. Do you want a mince pie?' But Natasha was already walking out.

'Tash, where are you going?' Christina asked.

'Over to the stables.'

Two minutes later she was back. 'Daddy's sold off the east wing! All the horses there were sent to auction – even Cute Queenie!'

Christina bit her lip. She had been as shocked as her daughter. It had been Fleming who had told her about the auction. She had also been surprised that her husband would even consider letting Cute Queenie go. 'He had to do it, darling – he has a few business problems, but I don't think we need to worry.'

'How could he do that, Mum? Cute Queenie was always here. I thought he loved her.'

'He did, but it costs to feed them all and, well, she

was getting on. He'll explain it all to you when he gets home.'

Natasha pursed her lips and ran out again.

Fleming turned as Natasha strode into the yard. He was with the vet and two lads and they were all grouped around Royal Flush's stable door.

'Daddy's not answering his mobile,' Natasha said as she joined the men. 'What's up with him?' The vet told her it might just be phlegm. He'd done tests and they would have a result by the morning.

'God, I hope you're right,' Natasha said, as she opened Royal Flush's stall door. She had to move away fast as Royal Flush went for her.

'I'd stay away from him for a while, Miss,' one of the lads said. 'He's got a hell of a temper on him.'

'He doesn't look sick to me.'

'He doesn't until he's had a run. Then his chest rattles like an old drainpipe.' The vet and Fleming had already moved off, and the lad went on, 'I noticed it a few times even before his leg injury, but then it cleared up. He ran like hell last year at the race at Epsom. Did you see it?'

'No, I was at school, but I read the *Racing News*. I'm not supposed to but we've a porter there who asks me for tips – not that I ever have any but he knows I'm Daddy's daughter.' Natasha stood looking at Royal Flush for a while. 'If he's sick now, will he be ready for the Derby?' she asked.

'I should reckon so, but we've not got into the racing season training schedule yet.'

She could think of nothing further to say so she left

251

Royal Flush and wandered down the immaculate stalls looking at the rest of her father's prized horses, their heads peering over their stable doors. Then she glanced towards the east wing and the rows of empty stalls. She returned to speak to the lad.

'When were all the horses from the east wing sold?'

'A few weeks back.'

'And even Daddy's horse went?'

He nodded and flushed. 'Cutting back on the finances, I was told.'

'But he loved her. Do you know who bought her?'

'I don't, Miss, but it's never a good thing to get too fond of them.'

'Tell that to Daddy. He worships Royal Flush.'

'Ah, well, maybe the boy's different.'

As an ex-racehorse, no riding school could take Cute Queenie and they'd been unable to find a buyer for her. She'd gone the sad route of hundreds of magnificent animals – the glue factory. De Jersey had not asked about her fate. He had put her out of his mind. As the lad had suggested to Natasha, it was best not to get too fond of them. She'd been correct, though, when she had said her father cared for Royal Flush. It was obvious to everyone. That was why they were surprised that he hadn't come out to the stables for the past few days. Rumours were spreading that he was in deep financial trouble.

It was almost five thirty when Sylvia finally arrived and de Jersey stood up to shake her hand.

Helen seemed as relieved as he was to see her. 'If you two will excuse me, I think I'll just go and have a lie-down. I hardly sleep at all these days.'

252

'I'll wake you for dinner,' Sylvia said.

Sylvia took off her coat and gestured for de Jersey to sit down. 'I suppose you've heard all about her depression. I have to listen to it day and night and it's becoming a strain.' She tossed her coat over a chair and sat primly opposite him. 'After everything is settled I think she'll have enough to buy a small place of her own. These things take so much time, though. We've sold the house, or what was left of it after the fire, but poor David was in a dreadful mess. The house was in both their names but he'd even remortgaged that. Helen just signed whatever he put in front of her.' She sipped her tea. 'For a while the police and the fire specialist were suspicious of the way the fire had started but in the end they couldn't find anything so the insurance company was forced to pay up. At least Helen has salvaged something from this mess.'

'Unlike you,' he said quietly.

'What?'

'I understand that you also invested money in the Internet company.'

'How did you find that out?' Sylvia asked, surprised.

'You aren't the only one with access to information, Miss Hewitt.'

'Helen still doesn't know I was one of the unlucky investors,' she said. 'I'd prefer to keep it that way, at least for now. It has been a very sad business all round.' She took another sip of tea. 'I have contacted the two other main investors and they are surprisingly reticent about discussing the matter with me. But although I haven't lost as much as them or you, I'm not prepared to sit back and accept it.'

De Jersey shrugged. He was angry. 'So, contrary to

my request that you keep my financial documents confidential it seems you have been using them.'

'Well, David often stopped off with me to do some homework. He left a few files and I looked through them,' she admitted.

'Homework?' de Jersey asked, feigning surprise.

'It was such a long journey home that he often waited here until the rush hour was over.'

'You should tread carefully. If you are privy to my private transactions—'

'Not all of them,' she interjected.

'That is beside the point. As I have told you, I am distressed to think that my financial documents are being discussed without my permission. It is highly irregular, not to mention illegal.'

'I am aware of that. But under the circumstances with his suicide—'

'The manner of his death has little to do with me, Miss Hewitt. If you continue to search through my private papers I will be forced to consult a lawyer to—'

'I haven't shown them to anyone else. In fact, I'd have thought you'd be pleased that I'm making progress in trying to trace the man responsible for the losses you have incurred.'

'I am here to request again that you cease doing this.'

'But why? You have lost a substantial fortune, Mr de Jersey. Don't you want it back?'

'I am more than aware of what I have lost—'

'But I have some information. My private investigator has discovered that a man called Philip Simmons has been acting on Alex Moreno's behalf in financial matters and I am determined to track him down. I think they have made some kind of deal that enables Moreno to benefit from the sale of his property without having to worry about creditors seizing the funds.'

De Jersey clenched his teeth.

'I'll get the details for you.' Sylvia scurried from the room and returned with a bulging file. She sat down at the table and began to take out documents. She handed them to de Jersey with a flourish. 'I think you'll find those intriguing. The same man, Philip Simmons, organized the continued refurbishment of the East Hampton property and apparently intends selling it as soon as it is completed. He also sold Moreno's apartment. I have searched through file after file and I can find no one of that name in David's records. I've asked his assistant Daniel Gatley and he cannot recall meeting him, although they had dealings with Moreno and his colleagues. So who is he? Is he in partnership with Moreno? At the very least this Mr Simmons must know how to contact him. Or maybe it's something more sinister.'

'Sinister?' de Jersey repeated.

'Moreno has disappeared without trace. Maybe Simmons is using an assumed name. I'm sure we're on to something because Mr Matheson has confirmed via some contact he has in Immigration that no one by that name ever arrived in the US from Canada. In fact, they have no record of him entering the US at all.'

De Jersey thanked God he had used his Cummings passport to enter the US. 'Is Simmons among the investors?' he asked.

'No, he isn't. He might be Canadian but I assume he lives in the States because why would Alex Moreno use a Canada-based financial adviser? It doesn't make sense. I have a list of the other investors if you would like to see it. None suffered the losses you, Mr Driscoll or Mr Wilcox did.'

Every time she mentioned their names together he cringed inwardly.

'I have paid this detective a substantial amount already, so to just let it go would be silly,' she went on. 'I have therefore asked him to continue. I think it would be sensible to pool our resources, split the cost of hiring Mr Matheson. I'm sure he will get us results.'

'How much do you believe the house and the apartment in America are worth?' de Jersey asked.

'You mean, what has Simmons got away with?' she asked.

'Didn't you say he was just a business adviser that Moreno employed?'

'Yes, but even if he isn't profiting himself from the sale, he will know who the money goes to when it's sold, won't he?'

'And if you trace that person do you think they will just hand over the money?'

'Well, whether it's Simmons, Moreno or someone else, they should be forced to split it with us. If we can't make them, we'll get the police and the courts involved.'

De Jersey remained silent for a moment as she began to collect the papers. Then he asked, 'These two other major investors, have you their permission to act on their behalf?'

'No, as I said earlier, they're rather dismissive. All the other investors I've spoken to are eager for results. I've also discovered David began to communicate with Moreno six months before the crash. He was emailing him on a daily basis to discover how serious the situation was. Would you like to see copies of the emails?' She passed the printouts to de Jersey. 'As you can see, around five months ago Moreno wasn't giving David any hint of the company's financial troubles and instead was suggesting that he bring in more financial backers. And he did. You yourself remortgaged your property, as did Mr Wilcox.'

De Jersey became very still. 'It seems suspicious to me that you have access to such sensitive information,' he remarked, in a cold but even tone.

'What do you mean?' Sylvia said, unnerved.

'I'm not sure if you want me to discuss this here,' de Jersey said, and glanced towards Helen's bedroom.

'Is it to do with Helen?'

'Yes. You see, David was an old and trusted friend. He often confided in me.'

'Really?' Now it was her turn to tense.

'I have said that my business with your brother-in-law was highly confidential. The fact that he embezzled substantial amounts of my money is shocking and I was not prepared when my solicitors informed me of another perplexing and deeply worrying discovery.'

Her face took on a puzzled expression.

'Perhaps David had a partner assisting him in the fraud. Someone with access to his papers, to his clients, someone to whom he was very close.'

Sylvia sat back nervously. 'I don't follow.'

'I think I should make it clear, then. I'm presently taking legal advice and we have been discussing taking action against you, as we believe you assisted David in embezzling money from my accounts, which I had not authorized to be invested.'

Sylvia sat in shocked silence.

'There is also a trust fund that David stole from me and we believe he must have had an accomplice.'

'That is ridiculous.' Sylvia bristled.

'Is it? Well, then, perhaps you should know that we are aware that you and David were involved sexually. We have photographs taken of the two of you together in—'

'That isn't true!'

'I'm afraid it is.' He knew he'd got her. 'I know that you were his mistress.'

Sylvia stood up, her face drained of colour.

'I'm sure poor Helen has no idea that you and David had been having an affair for years. You may have hired a private investigator, Miss Hewitt, but so did I. I can assure you that my information regarding your connections to David could have you charged with conspiracy.'

'No, no! I swear before God it's not true.'

'Isn't it? Maybe you're pretending to pay for a detective when what you're really doing is attempting to squeeze even more money out of the investors.'

'You're wrong.'

De Jersey stood up and stared at her. 'I'm warning you, Miss Hewitt. You will return my financial documents and everything else in your possession that concerns me or I shall proceed with legal action.'

Sylvia began to weep. 'I admit that David and I were lovers and that I had access to his files but I did nothing illegal. Nothing.'

'Well, I would like to believe you, but my solicitors do not agree. I came here today to warn you. I care for Helen and don't want to see her hurt any more than she already is.'

'Please don't tell her this, she'll have a breakdown.'

De Jersey ran his fingers through his hair. 'Then you had better call off this chap in America. My financial situation is not your problem. My people do my research on my behalf. If they prove to me without a doubt you had no involvement—'

'But I didn't!' She started to sob. 'I loved him but whatever I say won't help. I know how it must look but I had no idea he was involved in such terrible frauds. I'm sure most of it was unintentional. He always spoke so highly of you.'

'Miss Hewitt, I am not interested in hearing sad stories about David,' he snapped, and this time he moved very close to her. 'I will not hesitate to make sure your sister knows the truth, and I won't be sorry to drag you through the courts if that's what it takes to stop you invading my privacy. Do you understand?'

Fifteen minutes later de Jersey left the St John's Wood apartment, carrying disks and papers he had taken from Sylvia. She had called Matheson in New York and, in front of de Jersey, taken him off the case. She also signed a confidentiality agreement, promising not to divulge anything she had learned about his private affairs. She wept as he promised that he would reimburse her losses at some time in the future if she kept her word. He warned her against making any further calls to Wilcox or Driscoll or making his losses known to other investors.

It was after eleven when de Jersey arrived home. He went straight to his study and had just filed away the papers he had taken from Sylvia when Natasha walked in. 'Daddy, we've been trying to contact you all day.'

He whipped round, startled. 'What's wrong?'

'It's Royal Flush. The vet's taken swabs from his throat. He's had a bad chest after his training session.'

De Jersey kissed her. 'Thanks for telling me. I'll go

and have a look at him.' He threw on an overcoat and walked out into the yard. He let himself into the manager's office and read the vet's reports with a sinking heart. After tests it had been surmised that Royal Flush had nothing more than a cold, but it was worrying. The mere fact that the horse had been off colour worried him. First the leg injury, now the chest infection. If Royal Flush had trouble with his breathing it was a sure sign of problems to come. As soon as the weather cleared the horse would begin training for the Derby but thankfully there was still considerable time before June. He put the documents back in their place. He had noted that one of his best fillies was coming into season. De Jersey had big plans for her and needed to discuss them with his manager, but having to travel back and forth to Kilburn so much had exhausted him. For the first time he wondered if he was up to everything.

He was so deeply in thought it startled him to find his daughter Natasha standing over him. She had on an overcoat over her nightdress, and wellington boots.

'Is he all right, Daddy?'

He reached out his arm to draw her to his side. 'He's doing fine.' Then he stood up and ruffled her hair. She buried her face in his chest and he chuckled. 'Still my little girl. But you should be in bed.'

'I was worried about Royal Flush.'

'So am I, but the vet says he's just got a chest cold and there's plenty of time for him to recover before the season starts.'

He turned out the lights and they walked out of the office past the back room. This was where the racing colours of his stable were kept. He switched the lights on and stood breathing in the smells that he loved and touching the colours displayed on the wall alongside all the plaques and pictures of past champions. So many races, so much of his life was here in this tack room. Next to his knee boots and weight cloth hung Royal Flush's bridle. Laid out on the table was the grooming kit that the lads used with such care to maintain his beautiful coat. 'I love it in here,' he said softly. Natasha slipped her arm through his as he touched Royal Flush's bridle. She wanted to ask him why he had sold Cute Queenie but she didn't want to spoil the moment.

'Your grandad, he would have been so proud. You missed a lot not knowing him and my mother. You'd have liked her. In fact, she looked a lot like you: tall, strong, knitting. Always knitting. Do you?'

'Do I knit?' she asked surprised by his question. 'No, no, I don't.'

'Well, your grandma was always click clicking away. For me, for my father, for the kids in the street. Click click. We didn't have TV for the longest time and when we did, she never watched it. And when I was a little boy she'd read to me. She could read and knit at the same time. Click click. She had a soft, warm voice. She read me all the classics. Sometimes I think she knew whole passages of them by heart. I owe her a lot.'

His daughter had hardly ever heard him talk about her grandparents and she cherished this moment, looking at him as he stared around the tack room. He was unaware of her adoration though. 'Shall we go and say goodnight to my boy, then?' he asked.

They went into the yard and he opened the stable door. Royal Flush kicked out then stared at de Jersey angrily.

261

'What's up with you, my old son?' he said quietly, and approached him.

The magnificent horse snorted and allowed de Jersey to stroke his neck. From his glossy coat and impressive presence it was hard to believe there was anything wrong with the stallion.

De Jersey rested his head against the big beast's neck and closed his eyes. Here was the jewel in his crown. Never before had he placed so much expectation in a horse. 'Don't let me down,' he whispered. He felt so close to Royal Flush that it was hard to drag himself away. As he shut the stable door he took one last look.

'What is it, Daddy?'

He had almost forgotten Natasha was there. 'Well, darling, I've never before put my dreams on the line like this. Sometimes at night I close my eyes and I see him winning the Derby. I truly see every moment and I feel the most extraordinary pride. That's my boy coming out of the starting gate and I know he's going to win for me. Then, when he passes that winning post, I'm cheering and waving my hat in the air . . . But then I wake up and realize it was only a dream.'

She slipped her hand into his and they walked back to the house in silence.

He had been thinking that he should come up with some kind of insurance in case the robbery was unsuccessful, whereupon he would not only lose Royal Flush but the estate. If he lined up a buyer for the yard, whoever it was, they would want Royal Flush. In the past, he had always had a backup plan in case a robbery failed and he was caught. Now was the time to put in place a safety-net.

CHAPTER 14

THE PROBLEMS with Royal Flush continued and it was decided that his throat should be scraped. Any inflammation caused by mucus might have repercussions. The next morning, de Jersey gave the go-ahead for the operation to be carried out and watched sadly as the horse was driven from the yard. It was not yet seven o'clock and the girls were still asleep, so he called his personal fitness trainer and had a lengthy workout in his gym. He pushed himself, first on the treadmill, then the rowing-machine before moving on to the weights. By the time he was showered and changed he felt clear-headed and hungry. Christina cooked him scrambled eggs and bacon. He buttered his toast thickly.

'You'll give yourself heart failure,' she murmured.

'Nonsense, I've just worked out.' He stood up and stretched, then reached for her hand. 'Got some business to do in London. If I have to stay over I'll call you.'

'Then say goodbye to the girls,' she said. 'They have to be back at school today.'

'Right.' He drained his coffee cup just as Natasha and Leonie came in. He hugged and kissed them both and was just wishing them a safe journey back to school when the phone rang. His body went rigid. It might be the vet. He nodded for Christina to answer it, which she did, then held out the receiver to him.

'Darling, it's the vet.'

De Jersey took the phone with trepidation. Then his face broke into a wide smile. 'You're kidding? Are you sure?' His prayers had been answered.

'We're certain,' the vet reassured him. 'We don't think the operation's necessary after all. It was just a bit of a cold. His chest is clear and although his throat is a bit rough he's in terrific shape compared to when we last examined him. It must have been the antibiotics.'

'Are you bringing him home?'

'We are. Give him a day or so, and then he can go back into training.'

It was just what de Jersey needed. He rushed to Christina and lifted her off her feet. 'My boy's coming home. They don't need to operate!' He kissed her lips and bounded out of the back door without a backward glance. Now he could get on with preparing for the robbery without worry about his 'boy'. Everything was back on track and he knew he had to get moving. It was already late January.

De Jersey checked his emails as soon as he walked through the door of the Kilburn flat. There was a message from 'Elvis' enquiring when de Jersey wanted his next tutoring session. In the post he found the letter for which he had been waiting: a reply from Gregory Jones in response to his fake solicitor's letter. The blue notepaper was stamped 'Franklyn Prison'.

Gregory Jones's handwriting was looped and slanted backwards but the letter was well constructed and worded. It said little but that a visitor's pass would be allocated shortly and he was looking forward to discussing the possibility of appeal. De Jersey wrote back to confirm he would see Jones then, signing himself Philip Simmons.

Later that day he took a call from Dulay. He had an appointment in London and they arranged to meet. Nothing was said with regard to the robbery but both men knew the reason for the meeting. Things were starting to pick up pace. The team was forming.

De Jersey, as Philip Simmons, Solicitor, pinned a visitor's pass to his jacket. His briefcase was searched but only contained documents from the firm of solicitors Hunting and Letheby. He was ushered into a booth next to the main visiting hall. The security cameras monitored his every move.

He was alone for ten minutes before the door opened and Gregory Jones, wearing a yellow striped bib, was led in. Two officers accompanied him and stood by the door as he sat down in front of de Jersey. Then the officers moved outside.

As soon as the door was closed Jones, a surly-faced man with wide shoulders and an athletic build, took out his tobacco and cigarette papers. His face was pock-marked, with two fresh scars down one cheek, like thin tramlines, where he had been cut with a razor. It was a typical prison injury, probably caused by two razor blades stuck into a nailbrush so close together the wound they caused was difficult to stitch. Neither man spoke as Jones rolled a thin cigarette, took a box of matches from his pocket and placed it on the table. Eventually Jones broke the silence. 'You had no trouble getting in, then?'

'None. Thank you for agreeing to see me.'

'You intrigued me.' His voice was coarse with a trace of the West Country. His teeth were stained. 'I've got no hope of an appeal so I know you aren't from my solicitors.'

'Do they tape these meetings?' de Jersey asked.

'Not allowed to, invasion of privacy, pal.' Jones leaned back in the chair, folding his hands on top of each other on the table. 'They're supposed to monitor the odd phone call, though, but they don't bother. Too much aggravation. Imagine how many fucking hours of gibberish they'd have to wade through.'

De Jersey nodded, then looked down at the papers. 'Your two daughters are living with a relative in America?'

'California. One wrote for a while, then stopped. No one visits me. This is a break in the routine. Why do you mention my girls?'

'You must want to see them again.'

'They'll be married with kids of their own by the time I get out, if I ever do.' He turned away and sighed. 'I'd like to see them. It'd be a light at the end of the tunnel.'

'How are your finances?'

'The savings I had disappeared with the legal costs. The wife spent anything she could lay her hands on. Turns out she was spending it on another bloke, my mate.' He sucked in his breath. De Jersey could feel the man's pent-up bitterness. 'So, let's get to the point, Mr Simmons. You got the visitor's pass. I'm here. What do you want?'

'Information.'

'I thought as much. Who are you?'

De Jersey glanced at his watch. 'I have a proposition for you.'

266

Jones was staring at the ceiling. 'Well, I'm all ears.'

De Jersey took out a file and glanced through it. 'I need certain information, and it is imperative to me that the details I acquire are legit.' De Jersey passed him a sheet of typed questions.

Jones took a long time to read it. He flicked ash from his roll-up a couple of times but did not look up. Eventually he slid it back to de Jersey. 'What's the deal?'

'Fifty thousand. Any bank account, any name, any country.'

'Oh, yeah, but I'm in here and you're out there so how can I trust you to do what you say you will?'

De Jersey leaned forward. 'You can't, but I'm going to give you my word. How about putting faith in the old saying, "My word is my bond"?'

'I suppose I've not got much to lose,' Jones said.

De Jersey began to pack his briefcase. 'You interested?'

'Maybe.'

'Do you have the information?'

'You know I do. That was my job. But I've got to trust you. I mean, you could be setting me up.'

'Not much point in that. As you said, you're in here already.'

'I need to know more.'

'Well, you won't. The less you know the better – but I mean no harm to the Royal Family.'

Jones rolled another cigarette as de Jersey clicked his briefcase shut.

'You want me to phone you with the info or what?'

'Too risky, even if they're too bored to tape calls. I think the best way is for me to visit you again. Before then you can phone me with the details of the account you want the money to go to ... I gather you *are* interested?'

Jones lit up. 'Bet your arse I am – and I'll tell you something for nothing. I know a lot more than what's on that page. The security there is archaic.'

A bell rang to indicate that time was up. De Jersey looked coldly at Jones. 'I have no intention of breaking in. As I said, I have no desire to harm the Royals or put them in jeopardy.'

Jones lowered his head. His voice was hardly above a whisper. 'You're not the fucking IRA, then? 'Cos I draw the line there, pal, draw it fast.'

'I can assure you I am not connected to them.' De Jersey leaned close, his voice hardly audible. 'I can give you the light at the end of the tunnel but no more questions. I just need answers to the questions on the list, understand me?'

Jones nodded. Their eyes locked for a moment before the door opened.

Jones stood up. 'Mr Simmons, can we shake on it?'

De Jersey smiled and grasped the prisoner's hand. He felt Jones grip tightly.

'I'll call you just to arrange payment, all right?' Jones said softly.

'Absolutely, but say nothing with regard to my queries. I'll wait to hear from you and then we'll organize another visit.'

Jones was led out and de Jersey waited for an officer to take him back to the gates. At his next visit Prisoner 445A Jones should have all the answers he needed. He was confident that the man would come through.

Raymond Marsh seemed even more odd-looking than previously, if that was possible. His hair seemed to shimmer as if it was sprayed with crystallized sugar. 'Can't stay long. Taking the wife out. There's an Elvis at a pub that's shit-hot. He's Chinese but I've been told he's got an amazing voice.'

He sat in the chair next to de Jersey's computer and swivelled towards him. 'You've been spreading a lot of messages around the chat rooms. You're getting quite good but I was miffed you were checking out other hackers. I'm the best.'

De Jersey smiled. 'Prove it. See if you can get me some information I need.'

'Yeah, and what's it for this time?' De Jersey didn't reply and Marsh gave him a sideways glance. 'I read your messages. Novel, right? What do you want for it?'

'I need to know the Queen's diary movements. It may sound odd, but I am writing about the Golden Jubilee and I want to get ahead of my rivals. Can you do that?'

'Do what exactly?'

'Gain access to the Royal household's computer and check out the Queen's diary dates, especially for a fitting of the Crown Jewels. I know it should be in May some time but I want the exact date and time she's expected for that fitting. It should be listed.'

Marsh chewed his lip. 'That's a bit dodgy, mate.'

'I am aware of that, but I'll pay you well.'

Marsh nodded. 'A grand?'

'Five hundred, cash.'

'Okay, I'll have a go. It might not be that easy. You could always read it in *The Times*. They list her comings and goings next to the births, deaths and marriages.'

'Yes, but by the time it's public it'll be too late for what I have in mind.'

'Yeah? You said you were writing a book.' Marsh gave him a sidelong glance and grinned. 'I believe you. Thousands wouldn't.'

De Jersey went into the kitchen and put the kettle on. He could hear the click of the keyboard as Marsh moved through cyberspace, inching closer to his destination. After about half an hour he laughed. 'I'm in! I'm fucking in!'

De Jersey leaned against the table.

'You're in luck, pal,' Marsh said.

De Jersey looked over his shoulder as he printed out some lists that had appeared on the screen. He passed the pages to de Jersey with a flourish. 'Her Majesty's diary.'

De Jersey glanced down the list of all the Royal Family's current engagements. He flicked to the May/June dates: 1 June, Princess Royal takes salute at the Centenary Parade; 3 June, the Duke of Kent to open the Montgomery Exhibition; 4 June, Duke of Edinburgh as Master of the Corporation of Trinity House attends the Outward Bound Charity Golf match; 5 June, the Queen holds an Investiture at Buckingham Palace. There was no mention of the jewels fitting, no mention of the Jubilee celebrations at all. He sighed with frustration.

'This isn't any good. This is just from the Royal website. I could have got it myself,' he said dismissively.

Marsh dangled two more sheets of paper in front of him. 'Not these, though. Gimme an extra two hundred and you get them.'

'One hundred. And let me see them first.'

Marsh threw the pages to him.

De Jersey studied them. This was quite different from

the engagements site to which the public had access: it was different because of the alterations, queries and question marks. 'TBC' was written beside numerous appointments. His heart jumped. There, the week starting 2 May, was the word 'Fitting'. Beside it was the name of the jewellers, D'Ancona, and the time, 10.30 a.m. De Jersey cleared his throat and folded the pages.

'Is that what you wanted?' Marsh asked. 'I couldn't come up with anything else.'

'It's not really,' De Jersey lied. 'I was hoping to find out about her sittings for a portrait but this'll still be of use.' He walked into the bedroom, opened his wallet, withdrew six hundred pounds and returned to the kitchen. He handed it to Marsh.

'Ta. I'm gonna put it towards a holiday I've promised the wife. She's not seen her sister for eight years. They live in New Zealand.'

As the door shut behind Marsh, de Jersey breathed a sigh of relief, partly because the man had left but also because he had found not only the date and time of the fitting, but also the location. He reread the printout and laughed. He had seen another piece of vital information on a previous page for February: a D'Ancona representative was flying in from Antwerp in a few days days' time and had an appointment at the Palace. D'Ancona was a jeweller by Appointment to the Queen, so the alterations must already be under way. Could he discover the location of the 'safe house' where the jewels were being kept by tailing the D'Ancona agent from the airport? He needed Marsh again: he'd be able to find the list of passengers travelling on the nine fifteen from Antwerp to Heathrow.

The Daimlers had been stripped down and Wilcox was checking the engines before moving them to London in one of his own trailers. He didn't want them to be seen driving through London. He had spent hours in the dank mews garage respraying and fixing them. As he had originally thought, buffing up the bodywork to gleaming Royal standard took time, but fitting the new carpets and replacing the leather seats would take even longer. He had already made the Royal mascot, which would be attached to the front, a silver St George on a horse, poised victoriously over a slain dragon.

He was using an electric polisher when de Jersey made an unscheduled visit.

'Any problems with your neighbours?' he asked.

'Empty on one side and the other's just some antique shop's storage. I get here early and leave late. I see no one.'

'Good. How's it going?'

'The engines are all tuned up but the bodywork's a problem.'

De Jersey inspected the cars. 'Travel in style, don't they?'

'I guess so, but they don't make them like this any more. We were lucky to find them. You wanna hear the engine?' He turned it on and they listened to it purr.

'You here alone?'

'What do you think?'

'Just checking. Got a place to brew up?'

'Sure, out the back,' Wilcox said, and wiped his hands on a rag.

As the two men sat with mugs of tea in the grimy back room, de Jersey updated Wilcox on the plan. Wilcox said little, smoking one cigarette after another.

'We've also got a date, May the second. Can you have the cars ready by then?'

'Hell, yes. I'll get them to London and work on the upholstery, but we need a place to store them and for me to work.'

'I'll find somewhere,' de Jersey said. 'Gregory Jones is putting together what we need to know. I can proceed with the Palace security research once I get his answers. And with luck the D'Ancona rep will lead us straight to where the jewels are being kept.'

'You hope. What arrangements have you made for moving them on?' Wilcox asked.

De Jersey sipped his tea and Wilcox repeated his question.

'You know, Jimmy, I still don't have it direct from you that you're not going to get cold feet – or Tony for that matter. Asking me about what I intend to do with the jewels is taking a liberty.'

'Come on, don't do this to me,' Wilcox said.

'What am I doing, Jimmy?'

'My head in. Because you gotta know that I wouldn't be schleppin' up and down the motorway fixing up these motors if I wasn't in.'

'But you haven't said it to me directly.'

'I'm saying it now, all right? And I reckon Tony's in too but I'm only speaking for myself.'

De Jersey continued drinking his tea.

'Did you hear what I said?'

'Course I did.'

'So why no reaction?'

De Jersey looked into his eyes. 'Cut out the coke, James. I mean it. You can't work hyped up like this. Doesn't do you any good and it worries me.'

'I'm clean, Eddy,' Wilcox protested. 'I'm not using any more.'

'Keep it that way because I need you beside me.'

Wilcox gave de Jersey a look and then his face broke into a smile.

'If you'd backed out,' de Jersey told him, 'I dunno what I would have done, Jimmy.'

They shook hands, and for the first time since de Jersey had arrived Wilcox relaxed. He asked again about the movement of the jewels.

'Got to tread carefully there but I think I've got a buyer, a Japanese guy.'

'What about Dulay?'

De Jersey nodded. 'The contact came from him. Dulay's not firmed up yet. He was a bit iffy at first.'

'Well, so were we, Eddy. We've all been out of the game a long time, and he was always jittery, wasn't he?'

'He's coming for a meeting in three days' time but I reckon he's on board. I don't want him meeting you or Tony. Less he sees of any of us the better.'

'All right by me. I never met him anyway. Tony did, though, said he looks like that French actor Gerard somethin'. You went over to Monaco to see him, did you?'

'Yep, as Simmons. He still doesn't know who I am and he never will. But if he produces a buyer, he'll be up for a big cut.'

'Well, do whatever you need to do.' Wilcox stubbed out his cigarette. 'Have you found out where the jewels are being held?'

De Jersey glanced at him. 'I told you, the D'Ancona rep's flying in. He'll go to wherever the jewels are.

They'll be in a safe house somewhere, being prepared for the fitting.' He stood up, preparing to leave.

Wilcox walked with him to the garage door and de Jersey patted his shoulder. 'I'm getting there. Don't worry. Just a lot of strings need knitting together.' With that he stepped through the doorway and left.

Wilcox locked the door behind him. He was shaking and the palms of his hands felt clammy and cold. He walked back to the annexe and drained his mug of tea, then opened a silver snuffbox and performed his regular ritual. He went back to work, still shaky but with a clearer head. It did not occur to him that he had lied to de Jersey about his drug use. He was confident that de Jersey would never find out he was still using.

De Jersey called Christina to say he would be going to Dublin for a few days, then spoke to Fleming about Royal Flush. He was informed that the horse had been able to start training again with no problems. They were pacing him with other horses and he'd passed them with ease on the gallops that morning. Fleming asked about the filly coming into season and which stallion he should put her to but de Jersey said he would give it thought. He was calm and had noticed that the date for the Derby was almost a perfect month to the day after the heist. After it was over he would have more than enough cash to keep the estate going for the rest of his life.

A few days later he received a call from Jones and arranged for his second visit to Franklyn Prison. He had

275

deposited the money in Jones's account and Jones was now ready to give him the information he wanted. In fact, he was able to provide more information than de Jersey could have hoped for. He knew how many and which vehicles would be required per Royal, how many motorbike cavalcades would be allocated by the Metropolitan Police, the number of police cars, and how many of their own security guards would act as bodyguards.

'Her Majesty, of course, gets the full treatment. The numbers of guards and security officers go down according to the rank of the Royal. There is a complete department at Scotland Yard allocated to the Royals, so get your pencil out.'

De Jersey wrote fast. Jones knew the contact numbers of every police officer attached to the Royals working out of Scotland Yard. He also knew the police and security procedures that were in place before the Royals even stepped into their cars.

'Every vehicle is inspected for bombs and engine faults, as is the route they'll follow. That means every inch of it – every doorway, any possible sniper location – is checked and cleared. Ditto any conceivable danger to the family. They'll be thoroughly checked out before their departure. You getting all this?' he asked.

'Carry on.' De Jersey's pen flew across the page.

Jones leaned back in his chair. 'Right. The Scotland Yard unit that only takes care of the Royals is called the Royalty and Diplomatic Protection Department. These guys maintain twenty-four-hour protection for high risk and politically sensitive premises. All the men attached to it are skilled motorcyclists and car drivers. They are recruited from the ranks of police officers with some years of operational street-duty experience. I was part of this group for five years, that's why I know what I'm talking about. There's nothing I don't know about all areas of Royal protection.'

He struck a match and lit a roll-up, heaving the smoke deep into his lungs, then let it drift from his nose. He divulged that the head of Palace security was given a special codeword by Scotland Yard each day, which the Yard would use to let Palace security know if an IRA threat had been made. Then any Royal visits planned for that day would halt until Scotland Yard gave the all-clear.

'Can you just go over that one more time?' de Jersey asked.

'Only the head of Palace security and Scotland Yard officials know these codewords. And, of course, the IRA.'

'Wait a second. The codeword comes from the IRA?'

'Yeah, they set it up every morning. The IRA gives Scotland Yard a codeword that the IRA will use that day if they want to alert Scotland Yard to an impending terrorist attack.'

The warning bell rang to say that visiting time was up. De Jersey began to collect his papers and put them into his briefcase. Jones's information was invaluable. He had also filled in all the answers on de Jersey's questionnaire. As de Jersey put the last papers into his briefcase, Jones pushed back his chair but remained seated. The door opened and two prison officers walked in. 'Thank you, Mr Simmons. I appreciate you comin' to see me. Good luck, then,' he said.

De Jersey clicked his briefcase shut and shook Jones's hand. The officers stood aside to allow him to pass and he walked into the corridor then left the prison.

Armed with the information from Jones, de Jersey plotted his next major step forward. He needed Marsh again but was beginning to worry about his involvement. He could not proceed without the man but he wondered if he had the expertise to carry out the work he required. Marsh had only dabbled in amateur hacking. De Jersey knew he would now have to divulge the entire plan to him to get the job done.

CHAPTER 15

MARSH ARRIVED at the Kilburn flat reeking of hairspray as usual. His pointed winklepickers tripped him as he headed up the narrow staircase to the flat. He and de Jersey headed straight for the computer. 'Not got long. I've got another of my lectures tonight. Gotta make a few bob, know what I mean?'

'What if I was to offer you something that might make you millions?' de Jersey asked softly.

'I'd go down on you for millions,' Marsh said, and gave a high-pitched laugh.

'You wouldn't have to go that far.' De Jersey smiled, then continued, 'What I'm suggesting would be illegal and dangerous. Not necessarily physically dangerous but risky.'

Marsh crossed his skinny legs. 'Wanna tell me about it?'

'First I need to know how you would feel about doing something that would mean a long prison sentence *if* you were caught.'

'My job already feels like one!' Marsh joked, but he didn't laugh this time. Instead, his eyes were steady, beady and direct. 'I reckoned you were up to something. It's no novel, is it?'

279

'It's a robbery.'

'Oh. Daylight, is it?'

'You could say that.'

Marsh pointed to the window and the satellite dish. 'That got something to do with it?'

'Yes.'

'So I'm involved already, aren't I?'

'No, you can walk out right now, no hard feelings.' De Jersey sat back. 'You would not be involved in the physical part. You'll never even get to meet any of those who are.'

'Apart from you,' Marsh said softly.

'Correct.'

Marsh got up and squeezed his hands into his tight leather trouser pockets. 'Well?' he asked.

'Well what?' asked de Jersey.

'What do you need from me?'

'I need you to use your position as a telephone engineer and your computer expertise to get me information relating to communications between the Royalty and Diplomatic Protection Department at Scotland Yard and Buckingham Palace. I'll also need you to identify the line on which IRA threats are made into Scotland Yard. I know they use a codeword so you'll need to identify that too. I'm looking for the one that will alert Scotland Yard to a possible terrorist attack that in turn will halt any movement of Royals from the palace.'

Marsh thought for a moment. 'That'll be tough. The Protection Department is bound to have more than one line. I'd have to monitor them all to find out which one receives calls from the IRA. It's risky but there's no one in a better position to do it than me.'

'I know,' de Jersey said.

'But you're not IRA, right?'

'Correct.'

'So why do you need this information?'

'Because I want to steal the Crown Jewels.'

Marsh's reaction threw him. He collapsed on the floor in a heap and rolled around laughing. Eventually he lay flat out, his arms outstretched. 'The fuckin' Crown Jewels? Oh, man, you're something else!'

'You'll get a thousand pounds cash every week until we make the hit, then you'll wait for the pay-off.'

'What sort of pay-off?'

'We don't know exactly how much yet but it's going to be well into the millions. You'll have to wait, though. It could be weeks or months. In the end it's about trust. You and I have to trust each other.'

'When's the job?' Marsh asked, and sat up.

'May the second. You should have plenty of time to monitor the calls.'

Marsh sprang up and stretched out his hand to de Jersey. 'You're on pal. I can start tomorrow.'

'Good, but tonight you're not finished. I need a little hacking job. There's a flight coming in from Antwerp the day after tomorrow. I need the passenger list. Can you do that?'

'Is the Pope Catholic? You gimme the flight number, the time and date and I'll have it.'

By the time Marsh left, de Jersey had the passenger list of the Antwerp flight bringing in the D'Ancona representative. What he did not know was who, out of the twenty-two names, was their man. Marsh suggested they call D'Ancona and ask for him but de Jersey had already decided that Dulay, due in at the same airport shortly before the Antwerp flight, would perhaps be able to identify the man; he had once worked for the company. Also, on the day of his arrival the representative was likely to be carrying gems with him and would have a briefcase chained to his wrist. He would probably be accompanied by a security man, and should be fairly easy to identify.

Even if de Jersey located the safe house, he still did not know what kind of security to expect inside it, but it had to be high tech. He needed to know more about modern security techniques, particularly those used by D'Ancona. He went on to the Net, surfing the sites that dealt specifically with high-tech security. Eventually he came across one for a company called Interlace Security, which proudly listed D'Ancona among its clients. De Jersey made a note of the name, then saw that Interlace would be attending a security trade fair in Birmingham the next day.

Early the next day de Jersey set off for Birmingham in a hire car. He was used to luxurious cars and this was a small, cheap vehicle. The seat hurt his back, the gears kept jumping and he was none too sure about the brakes.

When he arrived the vast hall was crowded, and he was astonished to see so many gadgets on display. Electronic alarms for cars, houses and businesses were predominant. Some stands were selling high-tech surveillance equipment. Security guard companies were also represented and some gave martial-arts and self-defence demonstrations. He wandered the aisles, sometimes stopping to look over the goods for sale and watch demonstrations. The section in which he was most interested displayed large safes and alarm systems. He checked out three stands before he spotted Interlace Security. He crossed the thick red carpet to pick up their brochure and was approached by a sales representative. 'Can I be of assistance, sir?'

'Possibly. This is all very impressive.'

'Thank you. We are one of the top security consultants in England – indeed, worldwide. We provide a complete range of services for business, and we provide real, workable solutions for risk management. It is our job to relieve you of worry.'

'Do you concentrate specifically on large companies?'

'No, not at all. Did you have something in mind?'

'I'm about to open a jeweller's. It'll be close to Theo Fennell's shop in London, Fulham, actually. It's a central location, three floors. I had a shop close to Harrods and we had two robberies within months of each other.'

De Jersey continued lying, knowing that the young man had probably never visited the places he mentioned. The assistant showed him a steady stream of brochures, proving that the company had a list of top clients including British Aerospace, the National Criminal Intelligence Services, Oracle, the Post Office, Railtrack and, of course . . .

'Good heavens, you do the D'Ancona security. What security do they have?'

'Well, sir, we provide a virtually impenetrable surround with active infra-red beams and digital door locking devices. Panic buttons and strips are placed at strategic positions around the location and are linked to an Alarm Receiving Centre, which is in direct contact with the police. We work closely with all customers at all

283

times to ensure one hundred per cent security. The grilles on the vault act automatically if an infra-red beam is broken or a panic button is pressed.'

'Expensive?' de Jersey mused.

'Yes. For D'Ancona we shipped in specially reinforced steel from Germany, which was fire- and bomb-proof, and have subsequently been requested to use similar materials for Asprey and Garrard's.'

De Jersey let the young man gabble through a few more sales pitches, noting his cheap suit and his tatty lace-up shoes. He spoke with a public-school accent. 'Would you oversee the installation?' he asked.

'Oh no, sir. I'm in Sales.'

'I see. How long have you worked for the company?'

'Six months, sir. My father is one of their top consultants, though. He's been with them for eighteen years.'

De Jersey accepted the card passed to him. He glanced at the name: 'Malcolm Gridley, Junior Sales Executive'. 'Thank you Mr Gridley. I'll certainly know who to contact when I've made up my mind.'

De Jersey left with his arms full of brochures and Malcolm Gridley's mobile number. He also had the firm's London, Birmingham and factory addresses.

Gridley had twice asked his name but on both occasions de Jersey had distracted him with more questions and requests for leaflets. His inexperience showed, and when de Jersey glanced back he was being grilled by one of the older salesmen.

De Jersey spent a few more hours in the hall, waiting until he saw his young salesman heading towards a hamburger stall on the outer circuit of the exhibition. He waited while Gridley ordered a cheeseburger and chips before he went over and ordered coffee. Just as de Jersey was about to join him, Gridley headed for a bar on the far side of the exhibition. He was unaware that he was being followed and de Jersey watched him order a pint then sit smoking at the bar. After a moment he walked over to him. 'Hello again,' he said. 'On your lunch-break?'

'Yes,' Gridley said, surprised to see him.

'Can I get you another drink?'

'No, thank you. I've got to get back. Erm, I didn't get your name when you were at the stand. It's sort of company policy and—'

'I meant to ask you if it would be possible for you to arrange a private showing of the D'Ancona installation. I've gone over all the data you gave me and it's far superior to any other.' De Jersey reached into his pocket and withdrew his wallet. 'I don't think I gave you my card.'

'Thank you,' said Gridley, 'but I'm afraid it won't be possible to give you any details of the D'Ancona facility as no one is allowed to view any of our clients' locations after the contract has been completed and the security measures installed. In fact, D'Ancona hired its own contractors to install the equipment.'

De Jersey signalled to the barman. He was about to remove one of his Philip Simmons cards from his wallet and order a glass of wine for himself when Gridley swore under his breath. 'Oh, Christ!'

De Jersey saw a portly man in a navy pinstripe suit striding towards them. He sat down next to Gridley. Instinctively de Jersey moved off. The man was speaking sternly to Gridley, wagging his finger then pointing at

285

the half-drunk beer. After a moment Gridley got up, his face tight with anger. 'It was just one drink, for God's sake!' he said, and walked away.

'One too many, Malcolm. I warned you – Malcolm?'

But Gridley had gone and the portly man took off after him. De Jersey decided to call it quits but he had earmarked young Gridley as possibly useful to him.

Driscoll sat in an Italian restaurant for half an hour. He had eaten the roll and was of half a mind to take the other from the place opposite him when de Jersey walked in. They ordered minestrone and cannelloni, with a bottle of house wine. 'How are we doing?' de Jersey asked.

'I got a list of numbers for agencies that represent lookalikes and rang round until I found her. They said she was booked up, so I gave a lot of bull about needing to speak to her about a personal appearance. Anyway, I got her home address and phone number. She lives in Esher.'

'Family?'

'She's married, husband's retired. She makes a fortune doing special appearances.'

'Any children?'

'Nope. It's freaky. She's the Queen's absolute double.'

'Good. Have you checked out her home?'

'Not yet.'

Their first course arrived and they ate in silence.

'I went up to have a few words with Jimmy,' de Jersey said.

'Oh, yeah? How was he?'

'On good form. I mentioned his problem but he

assured me he wasn't using. The vehicles are looking in great shape. We need to find a London base soon though, for him to do the final adjustments.'

Driscoll nodded. 'He say anything else?'

'Like what?'

'Come on, Eddy, stop footsying around. Is he in or out?'

'In.'

'I see. Well, I expected he would be.'

'What about you? I mean, you've never come clean. Are you up for it?'

Driscoll licked his lips.

'I need to know, Tony. You're doing all this legwork for me, and I appreciate it, but is it going to end?'

'What do you think?'

'I'm asking you, on the level. You in with us or not?'

'Course I am. I'm in. God help me.'

'I couldn't go without you. It'll be the three of us again, right?'

'We must be out of our bloody minds. So, we still going for May the second?'

'Yes. It's proving tough but I'm working on the safe house location. Dulay is flying in and so is a D'Ancona representative. Anything's possible.'

'I don't follow.'

'We have to follow him to wherever they have the goods. Then I've got to work out how to get past the security system. It's very high tech and they installed it themselves.'

'How do you know if you've never been there?'

'Trust me. I've checked out the company that did the security. It sounds like a bloody big walk-in vault with lasers and panic buttons like you wouldn't believe.'

287

Driscoll dribbled soup down his chin.

'But the vault doors are going to be open for the Queen,' de Jersey assured him.

By the time they were on the cheese and the wine had been consumed Driscoll was less worried but still edgy. 'You'll be keeping your eye on Wilcox, then?' he asked.

'Yeah. But he said he was clean.'

'Maybe he is, but he was shoving a lot of snow up his nose not too long ago. He's got to be monitored. He's not the way he was, you know.'

'None of us are, Tony. But we'll keep an eye on him. We're all a lot older now. That's why I am taking it slowly. We can't afford any mistakes, and if it's too risky we pull out, simple as that.'

Driscoll changed the subject. 'What about the Hewitt woman?'

'She's sorted. We may have to bung her a few thousand but not until we've done the job.'

Driscoll wiped his mouth. Sometimes de Jersey frightened the hell out of him. He was keeping the plans for this one close to his chest. It was not the way they had worked in the past and it made him very uneasy.

'I need to know our progress, Eddy,' he said, folding his napkin.

'You will,' de Jersey said, 'as soon as I've moved on to the next stage.' He sounded annoyed. 'You've got to trust me, Tony, like we all trusted each other in the past. Now, give me the photographs of our lady and the contact address. I'll get Wilcox to check it out.'

Driscoll passed him a manila envelope and signalled for the bill.

De Jersey pushed back his chair. 'I'll be in touch. You know the number to call if you need to speak to me,' he said. 'Maybe in three weeks' time I'll be ready for preliminary talks. You have your instructions until then.' He handed him an envelope.

Driscoll put it into his inside pocket.

Then, as if they had been talking about nothing more than a golfing match de Jersey asked, 'When's the wedding?'

'Two weeks,' Driscoll said, as the waiter gave him the bill.

'Enjoy it.' He turned and left.

Driscoll looked at the bill. Dinner for two, three courses and a bottle of house red, had come to forty pounds. His wife was using caterers who were asking fifty-five per head and that didn't include wine.

De Jersey knew he needed another person on the team. A lady-in-waiting would surely accompany the Queen on her visit to the safe house. He sighed. He had never used women in the past and he had no idea whom he could trust. She would have to be right in on the action, perhaps even armed.

Tomorrow would be another busy day. He was to meet Dulay and hoped they would identify the D'Ancona representative and follow him to the safe house. A lot depended on them picking him out.

CHAPTER 16

DULAY WAS wearing a navy cashmere coat and an Armani suit. He carried only a holdall and a briefcase. De Jersey was waiting for him at the arrivals barrier in Terminal Four. They had over an hour to kill before the flight from Antwerp was due in. Dulay agreed to identify the man but he would not accompany de Jersey when he followed him. He'd booked into the Grosvenor House Hotel on Park Lane and the two would meet up again later that day. De Jersey would sit in his car in the car park and Dulay would call him on his mobile as soon as he had picked out the target.

The Antwerp flight landed and Dulay called to warn de Jersey, who drove out of the car park and into position outside Arrivals. Dulay called a second time. The passengers were through Customs and coming on to the concourse but the flight had coincided with two others. The departure lanes were full of trolleys and passengers and he had not spotted the D'Ancona representative. Then Dulay said, 'I've got him. It's got to be him. He's carrying a brown leather briefcase, raincoat over his arm and *yes*! A tall blond man is right on his heels. That's his guard. I can just see the chain on the guy's briefcase – it's handcuffed to him.'

'Describe him,' de Jersey snapped.

Dulay spoke rapidly. 'He's moving fast, heading for the middle exit. He's balding, wearing rimless glasses, a navy suit, white shirt and tie, about five ten, slim build, and he's using a mobile. He's heading out now!'

De Jersey inched his car closer to the doors, but he couldn't see the man. Suddenly a black Range Rover passed him with a uniformed driver at the wheel and then de Jersey spotted the D'Ancona man. He and his bodyguard came out together. The driver was quickly out of the Range Rover and had the passenger and rear doors open. Both men got into the vehicle and closed the doors. Neither had any luggage and they moved off quickly. De Jersey followed, right on their tail.

He was able to keep the Range Rover within easy viewing distance due to the heavy traffic moving out of Heathrow. It was still backed up even when they hit the A4 and moved at a snail's pace. Twice, when the traffic thinned out and they came closer to London, he almost lost them but roadworks saved him and he was able to watch their progress four cars ahead. He was still a good distance behind them as they drove into Cromwell Road, heading for Knightsbridge, but traffic was heavy again. Suddenly they turned off and headed towards Earls Court. He was still following as they crossed the Fulham Road, then King's Road. They appeared to be headed for Battersea Bridge but the Range Rover did not turn off and continued towards the Victoria Embankment. Then it was driving towards Blackfriars Bridge and from there to Newgate Street, passing St Paul's. De Jersey sensed they were taking a very roundabout route. They were passing Montague Place when the Range Rover slowed down and took a sharp left. Now it was impossible for de Jersey to stay on their tail without being spotted so he drove on and made the next left. He drove into Smithfield but there was no sign of them. He had lost them! Frustrated, he circled the roundabout in West Smithfield and branched off down a narrow side-street leading into Bartholomew Close, which came out at King Horn Street where he slowed down. The Range Rover was parked on the corner of Newbury Street. He was just in time to see the two men from D'Ancona enter a building together. A moment later, the Range Rover drove off.

De Jersey turned into a side-street, parked, and walked back to Newbury Street. The safe house was on the corner. A narrow road ran alongside the four-storey building. Rubbish bins had been placed on the pavement at the side. The safe house was unimpressive, painted black, and gave no indication of its function. There was no plaque outside, no bell, no letterbox, and the double door leading into the property was made of reinforced steel. Glancing upwards he could see that, although the upper windows looked innocent, they were not windows at all. The casements were built over shuttered protectors, with tinted black glass. De Jersey could not risk spending any more time in the area and walked on.

He had gone less than a hundred yards when the road curved to the right and led into Aldersgate Street. He went a little further then paused outside a large two-storey flat-roofed warehouse for lease. It would be perfect, de Jersey thought, for their purposes. It even appeared to back on to the street where the safe house was. He couldn't believe his luck. By the time he got back to his car he had called the estate agents and arranged to view the property the following morning. Then he went back to the West End to meet Dulay at the Grosvenor House Hotel.

Dulay had a pleasant room overlooking Hyde Park on the fourth floor. De Jersey and he sat opposite each other at a small table by the window.

'Pigeon went home to roost. It's a building in the Barbican, small back-street, not far from Smithfield market, and it's smack on a corner. Getting into it won't be the problem. It's knowing what we'll be confronted with once we're inside,' de Jersey said, and drew the safe house on a square of paper from his notebook. He passed it to Dulay, who glanced at the drawing, then jabbed it with his stubby finger.

'D'Ancona will have it secured like Fort Knox. They'll have cameras on the outside. How the hell do you think you're gonna get in without being seen, especially with it being on a corner?'

De Jersey repeated that there would be no problem about getting in. It was the layout inside the house that he needed to know. 'What would you say I'm up against?' he asked Dulay.

'Well, there are usually two reinforced doors as an external entry system, then another door leading into the foyer. I've been to a couple of their locations and there were always several inches of bulletproof glass. They will have a sophisticated phone system to link the safes and selection rooms and even the fitting rooms. There may also be another set of doors, maybe three or four, to get into the inner sanctum. They have panic buttons dotted around like Smarties. I doubt they'll have a walk-in safe but I could be wrong. I've never seen one before in a safe house.'

De Jersey ripped up the drawing and sat back. 'I take it by this you're in.'

Dulay nodded, 'Yeah, I'm in.'

'Okay then, what about your Japanese buyer?'

'I've contacted him. All I said was that I might get my hands on one of the most famous and largest diamonds in existence. I said I'd be looking for around a million a carat.'

De Jersey smiled. The Koh-i-noor was 105.6 carats so the figures were enticing.

'He said he'd be in the market for something of that price. He was interested in any other stones. I could get the Koh-i-noor cut by my lapidary, but if we sell to my Japanese buyer I'd say we wouldn't need to touch it. He'd want it uncut. It's the stone's size and history that's of interest to buyers like him.'

'Can you trust the lapidary? Maybe we don't touch the Koh-i-noor but we're going to have other stones of immense size and value and our buyer isn't going to take the lot, is he?'

'No. But you don't need to worry about my man. I'd trust him with my life. We've worked together for twenty years. That said, to move the stuff fast he'll have to work day and night to alter the stones and put them into new settings so they'll be untraceable. I need a nice cash incentive for him.'

'How much are we looking at?'

'Well, maybe a quarter of a million, and if we do have to cut the Koh-i-noor, he's the man to do it. If the buyer wants it cut it'll take weeks to do and we'd have to pay him extra. We can transform it into a pear shape from an oval by tapering it at the back, to disguise it without dropping its value. I've listed gem dealers worldwide where we can spread the other stones. I've got contacts in New York, Antwerp and India.'

De Jersey listened as Dulay talked. Occasionally the Frenchman would run his finger round the collar of his shirt. He sensed that Dulay was leading up to discussing his cut of the proceeds.

'How honest are the D'Ancona employees?' de Jersey asked.

Dulay shrugged.

'I think we might need an insider and wondered if it was a possibility.'

'Well, I was one.' Dulay laughed. 'I'd say the top brass would be unbribable – you only get to the top at D'Ancona by being above suspicion. But there are always the underlings. There's always someone ready for a pay-off if it's big enough, but it's all in the choosing. You get the wrong type and they'll blab.'

'Could anyone in the safe house be skimming?' asked de Jersey.

Dulay looked doubtful. 'If they're dealing with such top-quality gear there's no way they could skim so much as a tissue. These guys are working by appointment to the Queen, and I'd say that that rep you followed had to be carrying in some heavy-duty stones, with his briefcase chained to his wrist.'

'Right.' De Jersey sighed. It wasn't what he wanted to hear so he changed the subject. 'How's the boat?'

'The fucking money pit?' Dulay said angrily. 'That's partly why I'm here. It's costing me a fortune. I wish to God I'd never agreed to it.'

'If I needed to use it would you be up for it?'

'If the price is right.'

'Not for charter, for the pick-up.'

Dulay sucked in his breath. 'Woooooh! This is drawing me in closer than I want to be.'

'Not if it's, say, chartered to a company. We can use your crew. Can you trust them?'

'Sure, but it depends what they have to do – and they'll cost.'

'They won't know what they're doing. You and I will.'

Dulay tapped the table with his knuckle. 'When would this company charter the floating palace?'

'I'll need it ready for the first week in May.'

Dulay got up and crossed to the mini fridge. Suddenly he was not quite so confident. 'So it's May, is it?'

'I haven't got the exact dates, nor have I worked out how I want to use the boat, but make sure it's crewed up and ready.'

Dulay scooped a handful of ice into his vodka, then returned to the table. 'I want a heavy slice, Philip. If I'm going in this deep, I want to be paid big bucks. I've brought you the buyer and now you want me to get the boat ready. So how do we work the pay-off?'

'You'll get a split. Not a pay-off, a split. We can't do it without you. How does that sound?'

Dulay drank thirstily. 'Good, but I need cash upfront to start getting the shop prepared for the work we'll have to do. Extra furnaces, a smelting kiln for the gold. It all costs.'

De Jersey agreed to pay him ten thousand. 'I'll also need some assurance from the buyer. All I have is your word that he's interested. Don't take this the wrong way because I do trust you.'

'That's big of you, considering how far I've gone already.'

'Calm down. It makes sense, though, doesn't it? We need our buyer to put himself on the line with us. If he wants the Koh-i-noor, we want a cash incentive from him to know he's trustworthy.'

'We can trust him. He's worth billions and I'm vouching for him, for Chrissakes.'

'Not good enough. We want a million per carat and we want a million in cash upfront as a down payment or we might sell to someone else.'

'He's not gonna go for it.' Dulay drained his glass.

'If he wants it he's rich enough to make sure he gets it,' de Jersey said.

Dulay was pulling at his thinning hair. 'Okay, I'll put it to him but you can't mess him around. Like I told you before, I don't wanna turn up as chopped liver.'

De Jersey stood up to stretch his legs. 'Put it to him, or if you don't want to, I will.'

Dulay hesitated. 'Okay, let's see what he says.'

'Is he still in Paris?'

'Yes. I'll fly out this afternoon.'

As soon as Dulay was in his car de Jersey called Wilcox. He wanted to check out Dulay and, more importantly, his buyer: so he needed Wilcox to tail him from the London hotel to Paris.

'Paris?'

'This afternoon. You've never met Dulay, have you?'

'Tony did once but I never have. What time have I got to be there?'

'Go straight to the airport and wait.'

Wilcox sighed. 'I've only just got in from Leicester, Eddy.'

'So, make a trip of it. Take your woman.'

De Jersey viewed the warehouse, took it for a year and paid six months' rent in advance in the name of Philip Simmons. Also through the agents, he gained, with some financial persuasion, access to the drawings of the D'Ancona building. For security reasons, no single party ever held a complete layout of a safe house, so all he found out was the size of the building, the rear door area and small backyard. The drawings showed that it had four floors and a basement. He could not discover anything about the work they had had done inside. He noted that four years previously, the owners had applied for planning permission, which had been granted by the council, for the installation of undisclosed security measures. D'Ancona had certainly covered their tracks: anyone attempting to find out the details of these 'undisclosed security measures' would alert the company to a possible security problem. De Jersey knew he had to find another way of gaining an overall plan of the interior of the safe house.

As he drove back through Aldgate into the East End he called Driscoll and told him he wanted the D'Ancona safe house monitored. He had spied the perfect place to watch from. The warehouse had a flat roof and Driscoll could watch the safe house from there without being seen.

'I got a lot going on right now,' Driscoll said, sounding tired.

'And I haven't?' snapped de Jersey.

298

'Why can't Jimmy do it?'

'He's tailing Dulay, who's meeting up with our buyer. I just want to make sure he's on the level.'

'The buyer or Dulay?'

'Both.'

'So I got to schlep over to this warehouse now? The wife is gonna have a fit.'

De Jersey was impatient to get on. He told Driscoll where he would find the keys to the warehouse and hung up.

When he got home de Jersey was unprepared for Christina's reaction. She had become worried when she had contacted the horse breeders in Ireland and been told they were not expecting him. When he showed up her concern turned to anger: she felt it irresponsible of him to go off without leaving any contact number. Every time she had tried his mobile phone it was turned off. She told him that her mother was ill and she had to go to Sweden.

'You should have just gone, darling,' he said.

'*You* should have called home.'

'I didn't think.'

'No, you didn't, and I want to know why you lied about going to Dublin.'

'I didn't.'

'You did. Freddy said you weren't even expected.'

'I wasn't with him.'

'I don't understand.'

'I don't buy all my horses from Freddy. Sometimes I want it kept under wraps exactly what I'm thinking of buying. But I'm sorry. It won't happen again.'

She sighed. 'You've always got such good excuses for disappearing but I've been worried about my mother. You've not been fair.' Christina hesitated to voice her suspicions, but she couldn't help blurting out, 'Are you seeing someone?'

De Jersey was genuinely shocked that she could even consider it a possibility. 'Of course not! No woman could ever—'

'Well, why have you been taking so many clothes from your wardrobe then? You take them each trip and they never come back with you. I checked because I wondered if anything needed to go to the cleaners. Two suits are missing and several shirts.' She folded her arms.

De Jersey had left the clothes at his Kilburn flat but came up with an excuse fast. 'I gave them to a couple of the trainers. Ask them if you want proof, but this is so unlike you, Christina. I've never given you any reason to think I might be having an affair.'

She burst into tears. He took her in his arms and held her close. 'Listen, I think you should pack your things and catch the first plane out to see your family. There's not another woman in the world I would so much look at.'

He helped her pack and arranged for his pilot to fly her to the airport. It was unlike her to be so anxious but he knew he must take greater precautions from now on: he would need to spend more and more time away from the estate. It was already early February and if they were to go ahead on the 2nd of May they had to work fast. They still had no notion of how they were going to deal with the alarms at the safe house. They would be able to walk in, but getting out safely was another matter.

It was just after four o'clock when Wilcox called from Paris. He and Rika had caught the same plane as Dulay and had followed him to the Ritz.

'I had to book in, Eddy, just for a night. And it got Rika out of my hair anyway. Dulay didn't book a room. He went straight to the desk. They handed him the house phone, he had a few words, then went into the coffee bar. About ten minutes later this huge guy appeared. Looked like Oddjob in the James Bond movie. He had a few words with Dulay then they went out to the foyer.' Wilcox explained how he had followed Dulay out of the hotel where he had had a conversation inside a parked Mercedes with another man, presumably their buyer.

'He's tall for a Jap,' Wilcox said. ''Bout five eleven, well-built, snappy dresser. Odd Job was hovering around so he's got to be the bodyguard.'

De Jersey was heading towards the yard, listening to Wilcox on his mobile. He stopped. 'Jimmy did you get his address? Who the fuck is this guy?'

'Yeah, I got it from the porter. He's a regular guest. Comes over five or six times a year. He's a computer giant. His company's worth billions and he's based in Tokyo. His name is Mr Kitamo—'

'Okay. That's all I need to know right now. Why don't you—'

'That's what we should have put our money into, computer software.'

'Well, we didn't, did we? I'll talk to you when you—'

'He'll probably have a website—'

'Jimmy, get off the phone and have a nice night.'

'You're into this computer stuff. Try searching for Kitamo triple K computer software and—'

'Jimmy, go and screw your girlfriend!' de Jersey snapped, ending the call.

De Jersey spent the rest of the day with his jockeys, trainers and managers. Money was so tight and covering the costs of the heist was taking its toll of his limited resources. He knew it would be paid back by the Moreno property, but that was still not liquid. He gave instructions for two more horses to be sold. His decision hurt him and perplexed the managers and trainers. They said nothing but they had not seen him so concerned about the running costs before. Later, when he sat looking over the accounts, he saw that he could not keep the estate going for more than four months – and that took into account the sale of another eight racehorses and two brood mares. It was imperative that he pulled off the heist or everything would have to be sold before Royal Flush got his chance at the Derby.

That afternoon Fleming took Royal Flush out on the gallops for de Jersey to watch him, and he was in stunning form. However, that night, de Jersey couldn't sleep. He was overtired and his head was filled with plans. He got up, went to his study and sipped some brandy. Eventually he decided to go for a walk.

It was a clear, cold night and his breath steamed as he walked. He was jolted out of his dark reverie by Fleming.

'Can't sleep?'

De Jersey turned. His faithful trainer was hunched in his overcoat. De Jersey shook his head.

'Me neither,' Fleming said.

They walked in silence for a while, then stood against the fence that surrounded the grazing paddock.

'You have problems, haven't you?'

De Jersey nodded.

'It's obvious with the pick of your crop being sold off. It's breaking my heart.'

'Mine too, but I'm in a deep hole. Sometimes I don't think I'm going to be able to get out of it.' He paused. 'I have a friend in Ireland, Michael Shaughnessy, not a big breeder but a good man.'

'I don't think I know him,' said Fleming.

'He keeps a low profile,' de Jersey said. He wondered how Fleming would react to what he was about to suggest. He guessed that he'd have to make it worth his while with cash. It usually came down to that.

When he quietly suggested to the trainer what he had in mind, Fleming was so shocked he could hardly speak.

'We'd get a nice kickback – in fact, a blinding one. She's the best filly I've ever had.'

'Sweet Jesus! He's the best too. You know what this could do, sir. Illegally covering a mare is a terrible risk to take.'

'We keep him separated directly afterwards, then push his training up.'

'I don't know. It could be disastrous.'

De Jersey kicked at the ground. 'You're right, forget it.'

But Fleming put his hand on de Jersey's arm. 'We'll need three of us. My son'll help, but we have to keep this quiet. We'll do it at night when the yard's silent. If it ever got out . . .'

De Jersey put his arm round Fleming's shoulders. 'Well, we hope something will come out, and I guarantee Shaughnessy will most definitely want something out of it.'

It was almost one in the morning. The two men talked for another half-hour, then shook hands. Fleming would receive ten thousand in cash but the mare had to be in foal or there was no deal. They would ship the filly out to Dublin for Shaughnessy to collect and stable, de Jersey said. No one would know. They shook hands a second time. Both men knew that what they were doing might spoil the chances of the greatest horse de Jersey had ever possessed. They returned to their beds, depressed.

Driscoll and Wilcox were now taking turns to monitor the safe house. Wilcox found it tedious, irritating work but Driscoll didn't mind it: it gave him something other than the escalating wedding costs to think about.

When Wilcox was not on surveillance he had been scouting out other locations for the vehicles to be parked. They would not be placed in the Aldersgate warehouse until the day before the heist. He eventually found a disused barn in the Surrey countryside and the Daimlers were moved there. This was also where the team would gather to complete preparations for the raid.

Wilcox had also discovered various costumiers around the country where he could hire authentic police-motorcyclist uniforms. He would pretend to be employed by a film-company when he needed them. He had also acquired two motorbikes, which he was respraying to match the Metropolitan Police ones. Driscoll was assigned to find two shotguns and several small handguns. As he had an arsenal of his own, he decided he'd alter some of his own licensed guns by removing the numbers so that they could not be traced back to him.

Driscoll's daughter's wedding costs were soaring out of control and if de Jersey's wife bemoaned his disappearances, Liz Driscoll was beside herself.

'Where do you keep charging off to, day in and day out? I've no idea where you are and I can't get you on your mobile. Why don't you leave the damned thing turned on?'

'I've been busy.'

'YOU'VE been busy? Well, try arranging invitations for three hundred people, the marquee, the band, the caterers, the wedding cake, and the bridesmaids' dresses, not to mention your own daughter's gown. I'm having to organize everything myself.'

'Well, you wanted a big show-off wedding, not me!'

'She's your daughter, for Christ's sake. Don't you want this to be a special day?'

'Of course I do, but where did you get fucking three hundred people from all of a sudden? The last count was a hundred and fifty.'

'The groom's got his family too!' she yelled and burst into tears. 'I just can't cope and she won't make a decision about her dress. You talk to her.'

'I don't know anything about frocks, for crying out loud.'

'Well, go and see the designs. She can't make up her mind.'

'You help her. How can I decide which frock she's going to wear? I've got business to sort out to pay for this lot.'

'I thought you were retired,' she sniffled.

'I am, at least I was until this fucking wedding. How much are you shelling out now?'

She thrust a bundle of books and papers at him. 'See for yourself.'

He sighed, took them to the table and sat down. He looked up a moment later, his jaw dropped.

'Fifteen grand for bridesmaids' dresses? FIFTEEN GRAND?' He estimated the cost of the wedding would be three hundred thousand, possibly more. It was beyond belief to him. There was an endless list of requirements. 'Jesus Christ, why do you need the best champagne?'

'Because I am not spending this much money for it all to be ruined by cheap plonk!' she snapped, grabbing back her notes and receipts. 'Why are you being such a tight arse about it? You told me everything was okay money-wise.'

'I am not being fucking tight, I am just pointing out that this is my daughter's wedding. She's not frigging Madonna. Why does she need all these bridesmaids and pageboys?'

'Because it's what she wants, that's why, and you are going to give it to her whether you like it or not.'

He sighed. He needed this aggravation right now like a hole in the head and he got up to walk out of the room.

'Where you going now?'

He didn't answer but went into the hallway and headed for the stairs.

'Tony, where are you going?'

'I am going to have a shower, if that's all right with you?'

She followed him up the stairs. 'Will you go in and talk to her then?'

'Yes,' he hissed and plodded up the stairs.

Michelle Driscoll was lying on her bed with a face mask on, wearing a white towelling dressing robe. She was very petite, with a pretty doll-like face, and looked far too naive and unworldly to be getting married.

'Hi there. Your mother says you can't make a decision about your wedding frock.'

'Gown,' she corrected, her lips pursed, not wanting to crack her face mask.

'Well, let's have a look and see what you have come up with.'

'I haven't come up with anything, Daddy. It's the designer. The drawings are on the dressing table.'

He sat down on her frilled silk stool and opened a velvet-covered file. The designer's name was printed in gold on the front.

'Nice layout,' he muttered to himself.

He turned page after page of pictures of long slim gowns: full flounced ones, ones with trains, and ones without. He flicked through to the back page to see if there were any prices listed. There weren't.

'Which one do you like?'

'I don't know. I've got to lose some weight,' she said.

'You're as thin as a rake now.' He took the book to the bed and sat beside her.

Michelle carried on mumbling. 'I thought I wanted Stella McCartney but I didn't like Madonna's dress.'

'How much are these going to set me back?'

'Ask Mum, she's been talking to them. I can't think straight she asks me so many questions.'

'Why so many bridesmaids?'

'Ask Mum.'

'Well, I will, but it's your wedding, not hers.'

'Tell me about it!'

Michelle sat up and leaned against his chest. 'I'm getting fed up with it, I really am. I know she means well but sometimes I wish I'd run off to a register office.'

'You wish? With these costs it's me that's wishing! But you can't back out of it now, it'll break her heart. So why don't you make a decision and have done with it? Have the one with the big train. That looks nice.'

'The one with the seed-pearl bodice?' she asked, leaning close to turn the pages.

'Yeah, have that one.'

She sighed and took the book from him. 'What about the Grecian-type one? Do you like that one?'

'Look, anything you want is fine by me. You'd look beautiful in a dishcloth.'

She laughed and kissed him, cracking her face mask.

He chuckled. 'I hope your fella doesn't see you with that crap on your face, he'd run a mile. Have that seed-pearl job, that looked the best to me.'

'Okay. Yeah, I'll have that one.'

He left her sitting cross-legged, looking at swatches of silks and the separate veil designs.

Undressed and looking forward to a relaxing sauna, Driscoll was about to pour the pine essence on the coals when his wife returned.

'Well, thank you. One minute you're telling me to cut costs, now you tell her to have the seed-pearl gown. I've been trying to persuade her against that one, it's twenty-five thousand quid.'

'What?'

'You heard me, twenty-five grand. Then she's going

to have to have the tiara and the veil, that's another fortune. I just don't understand you, Tony, I really don't.'

'Listen, have whatever you want, sugar, have a diamond tiara, have thirty bridesmaids, anything to make you happy. Just don't keep on at me, I've got a headache.'

'You've got to have a fitting for your suit. You can't wear that old one you've got. When can you get to the tailors?'

He opened the sauna door and the heat blasted him in the face. 'Next week, all right? I'll go next week.'

'That's cutting it a bit fine, isn't it?'

'I'll go next week. I'll have a fitting, I'll bloody wear a tutu if that's what you want, just stop the aggro, will you? I've had enough.' He slammed the sauna door shut. He was still financially okay for the wedding but it was draining his remaining resources. His wife did not know the full extent of how bad things were.

Rika wore the silk negligee Wilcox had bought her in Paris. She lay on the bed in a sexy pose. Like de Jersey and Driscoll, Wilcox had been doing a disappearing act, but unlike Christina or Liz she had been to Paris and spent a fortune.

'Come to bed,' she said, opening her arms, and he sighed, flopping face down. He closed his eyes. She started kissing and trying to undress him. Driving up and down to Leicester was taking its toll. Working in the freezing garage had given him a cold and he felt rotten. He was tired out and sex was the last thing he had on his mind.

'Leave it out, Rika, I've got flu or something.'

'I don't care vat you got, I love you.'

'Yeah, I love you too, darling, but . . .'

'I massage you.'

'No, just let me go to sleep for a bit. I've been working hard and I'm knackered.'

'Vorking? On vhat? You supposed to be retired so just vhat you vorking on that's making you not like me?'

He sighed and took out a tissue from the box beside the bed to blow his nose.

'That's not cold you got, that's runny nose from cocaine.'

He glared at her and she started to unbutton his shirt. 'Don't, Rika. I don't feel like it.'

'Ven then? You don't feel like it for veeks. Ve got to Paris for sexy weekend, vone night, then you make me come back.'

'Christ! I don't feel well. I've got a headache.'

He staggered to his feet and she pushed him back onto the bed, climbing on top of him.

'You don't vant Rika no more.'

'I do, I do. Just not right now.'

He took a deep breath and gripped hold of her. 'Listen to me. I've got some business problems, understand? I made some very bad moves on the Stock Exchange and I've lost most of my savings. I'm short of cash, Rika, almost broke.'

'Vhat?'

'Oh yeah, that shut you up, didn't it, but it's the fucking truth. I'm having to sell off the remaining garages, the cars. That's what I have been trying to do, salvage what cash I can for you and the kids.'

310

'Vhy didn't you tell me?' she asked, cradling him in her arms like a baby.

'I didn't want to worry you.'

Rika was disappointed. She knew he wasn't lying this time. He was almost in tears.

'You should have told me, Jimmy, explain things to me more.'

'Like I said, I didn't want to worry you with the kids being at school and stuff. I'm hoping we won't lose this place, but I need to sell the other properties. I won't know for a while exactly how bad it is, but it's not looking good.'

She sighed, still holding him in her arms. 'But you had millions, didn't you? You had millions and millions.'

'No, I had quite a few quid, but look, I reckon I can get my head back above water. It's just going to take time and that means putting in the hours at the garage.' He sneezed and she reached for a tissue for him to blow his nose.

'Poor baby. You vant Rika to make you some soup?'

'Yeah and do we have any medicine? I don't want it to go onto my chest. You know how bad I get.'

She drew aside the duvet and fluffed up the pillows.

'I'm sorry, baby, you go to bed and Rika bring up a tray for her poor sick boy. Come on, get into beddy now, there's a good boy.'

He flopped back on the pillows sniffing. He felt terrible. She removed his shirt and helped him into his pyjama top as if he was ten years old. She even undid his pants and pulled them off him, then tucked him into bed, kissing his forehead, mothering him. As she tucked him in her big breasts swung in front of him in her frilly

311

silk negligee but he couldn't get aroused. All he wanted was to be left alone.

Moments later he could hear Rika singing and moving around downstairs. He curled up on his side, waiting for his soup, thinking about the mess he was in. Any time soon they would have a meeting to discuss the heist and it made him nervous. He wished he had not agreed to it, wished he had not listened to de Jersey or got involved with him again but it was too late to back out now.

Raymond Marsh arrived at the Scotland Yard telephone exchange at eight forty-five, as he had every morning that week. He had arranged to do the regular maintenance check on the exchange's telephone lines. He would spend the next two weeks there every day, checking the main systems, and return at regular intervals to do spot-checks. Scotland Yard's telephone exchange handled the lines for the Yard exclusively. Marsh had been provided with the password, security code and an electronic card to allow him access to all areas of the building.

The basement held the batteries and the equipment, the middle floor housed the computer systems, and the administration was on the top floor. The day after his last meeting with de Jersey, Marsh had gained access to the master computer and had quickly located the twenty-four lines responsible for all incoming and outgoing calls to Royalty and Diplomatic Protection. Today would be the first opportunity for him to set up a tail on these lines: all calls made and received by the Royalty and

Diplomatic Protection Department would be logged, with incoming and outgoing numbers.

Once he had set up the tail, Marsh began to monitor and record the calls. If he was caught he would be fired, or worse. By the start of his second week at the exchange, Marsh had worked out who was responsible for liaising with the Palace and confirming that security measures were in place.

When de Jersey received an email from Marsh informing him of his progress, he had an adrenaline rush. They were a step closer to executing the robbery and it was time for his second meeting with Lord Westbrook. His lordship answered the phone and gave an audible sigh of relief. 'Thank God. I was beginning to think you'd got cold feet.'

'You received payment, though, didn't you?'

'Yes. Thank you.'

'We need to meet. Do you know Shepperton?'

'Yes.'

'Go to Church Square. There's a bench in front of a small waterfront mooring. We'll meet there, then go to the pub for lunch.'

'Fine. When?'

'Tomorrow, midday.'

When de Jersey called, Wilcox was in bed with a bad cold. 'I've got something I need checked out.'

'I'm sick.'

De Jersey continued as if he hadn't heard him. 'I want

313

you to check out an address in Esher but don't approach the property, just monitor who's coming and going. Mark it out, front and back, and ascertain if only the woman and her husband are living there. Then report back to me.'

'You want it done tonight, then?'

'Yes.' He gave the address.

'I've got a terrible cold. I'm in bed.'

'Then wrap up,' de Jersey snapped. Both Driscoll and Wilcox worried him but he said no more and hung up. Then he went over his meticulous lists of everything still to be done, ticking off each item he had dealt with. They still had no lady-in-waiting.

Wilcox was freezing. Number twenty-three was a neat house with a large pond in the front garden. A garage stood to one side with a clean red Toyota parked on the pink-and-white squared drive. Wilcox walked past on the far side of the road first, making it look as if he was searching for a specific address. As he crossed the road to make his way back, the door opened at number twenty-three. A bald man was wrapping a scarf around his neck, shrugging on a camel coat, his car keys in his hand. Then a small woman, wearing a blue coat and a woollen hat, came out.

'Eric, did you lock the back door?' she called.

'Yes.'

She shut the front door and headed for the passenger door of the Toyota, which her husband held open for her. 'I don't want to stay too long,' she said. As she got into the car, her face was lit clearly by the streetlights. Wilcox's jaw dropped but he did not stop.

Eric started the engine and they drove out past him. The woman was talking, looking ahead. He could hardly believe it: she was the Queen's exact double.

Now, with the occupants gone, Wilcox was able to have a good look round. He headed up the path and rang the front doorbell, peering inside as if he expected someone to be at home. He even called, 'Eric?' Then he went round to the back and did the same, checking the path, the kitchen and the windows. He saw no one so he returned to his car and called de Jersey.

De Jersey was alone, smoking, when his mobile vibrated. He answered it. He knew it was Wilcox from his hacking cough.

'It's easy access both back and front, and I had a good look as the occupants left. Only the two of them live there. The back door's hidden from the other houses by a big hedgerow. The front is visible to the neighbours.'

'Mmm, good. You still there?'

'On my way home.'

'You see her, then?'

Wilcox sneezed. 'It's freaky. She's the image of her, identical.'

'She makes her living as her double.'

'We kidnap her, then?' Wilcox asked.

'No. We offer her a job first,' de Jersey said.

'I don't understand.' Wilcox sniffed.

'She's our way in, Jimmy, that's all you need to know right now.'

De Jersey was exhausted but before he went to bed he called Christina. She told him she'd have to remain in Sweden for some time as her mother had been diagnosed with a severe form of cancer and was undergoing chemo-therapy. De Jersey offered to join her but she refused. Although he wasn't glad her mother was sick, his wife's absence would leave him free to focus on the robbery.

CHAPTER 17

LORD WESTBROOK was already waiting in Church Square by the riverbank at Shepperton. De Jersey was taken aback by the change in him: he was grey with fatigue. He sat on the iron bench, hunched in his coat, a cigarette dangling from his bluish lips.

'You all right?' de Jersey asked, and sat next to him.

'On some new medication. Been burning the candle at both ends,' Westbrook joked, but his eyes betrayed him. They were dull with exhaustion.

'I have a list of queries,' de Jersey said crisply.

Westbrook reached beneath the bench for his brief-case. 'I have tried to ascertain all that you want to know.'

'Look, why don't we go over to the George? They've a comfortable lounge there. We can order coffee.'

'Thank God, I'm freezing.' Westbrook stood up and dropped his case. De Jersey scooped it up. 'Thank you,' he said. They walked into the pub. 'Shall I order some coffee, something to eat?' Westbrook asked, as de Jersey chose a window-seat away from the bar.

'I'll just have a coffee.'

De Jersey spread out Westbrook's notes and began to study them as Westbrook ordered coffee, cigarettes and chicken sandwiches from the friendly bar staff. De Jersey watched him out of the corner of his eye as he went into the men's cloakroom. When he returned, his eyes were red-rimmed and he sat down heavily. 'Fire away,' he said laconically, his face shiny from sweat. He lit a cigarette and had a coughing fit as their order was brought to the table. De Jersey poured coffee for them both and passed a cup to Westbrook, who grabbed a sandwich and ate hungrily, still holding his cigarette.

'Right, let's get started,' de Jersey said.

'Ready when you are.' Westbrook swung his legs on to the cushioned window-seat. He continued to eat at an alarming rate. He then gulped at his coffee and lit another cigarette, although the last was still smouldering in the ashtray. 'We do have a deal, correct?' he asked.

'Yes, of course.'

'I've been thinking. I'm sick and I'd hate to snuff it and not get what's due to me if you pull it off. I was wondering if you could draw up something for me in the name of my son. We are talking about big money here, aren't we?'

'Yes, but as you so rightly pointed out, it all depends on whether we pull it off. If we fail, none of us gets a penny, so making out a contract is impossible. All I can do is give you the agreed amount while we are in preparation. If we're successful, you will get your cut.'

'Mmmm, asking a lot on the old trust market, aren't you?'

'Not really. We're all dependent on each other to protect our identities, so we're not likely to swindle you out of your share.'

'Oh, I see that. But if I snuff it, who will make sure my son gets my share?'

'I will.' De Jersey stared hard at him.

'Okay.' Westbrook swung down his feet.

De Jersey drew his pages of questions towards him and unscrewed the top of his gold Cartier pen. 'Who would accompany the Queen on such a visit?'

'She'd have an equerry. He supports HM in her official duties and private life. He's a member of the small but select team responsible for the detailed planning and execution of the daily programme.'

'You can carry that off, be this equerry?'

'Oh, yes, that's my background entirely. Good family connections and all that tosh. They are seconded from the armed forces after three years. They wear a uniform during HM's daytime engagements when they're in personal attendance. I still have my uniform so no worries there. But often it's not necessary. HM will say, "No medals today," that sort of thing, so then it's just a smart suit. Did I mention I was based in the Royal Mews at Buck House? I co-ordinated transport for HM. Now, if it's a state occasion, the ponies and traps are out, but for something like this, a fitting, it'll just be her in a Daimler and another following.'

'And she would use a Daimler. You're sure?'

'Oh, yes.'

'The mascot—' de Jersey began.

Westbrook slapped the table with the flat of his hand. 'Very important. The Queen's vehicle has to have her silver St George and the dragon on it.'

'I believe one of my team has already copied it. Who else besides the equerry would be with her?'

'Well, she'd have a lady-in-waiting, who deals with the handbag and flowers and acts as a part-time secretary, answering letters and so on.'

'Would she be around the same age as the Queen?'

319

'Usually. She'll be well-dressed, pleasant, nothing that sticks out. A fade-into-the-background type.'

They continued discussing the line-up, which was tedious as Westbrook went off on irrelevant tangents, but de Jersey needed him to act as the Queen's equerry. Sick or not, he was an integral part of the team.

Shortly after his meeting with Westbrook de Jersey called Christina to see how her mother was. The news was not good. She had not responded well to the treatment.

'She's dying. I'm going to talk to my father about stopping the treatment altogether. She's in such pain and, as the doctors don't hold out much hope, it seems wrong to subject her to it.'

'It must be terrible for you. I miss you and I wish I could do something to help.' At the end of the call he felt depressed, and his thoughts switched to Lord Westbrook. Just how sick was he? He hadn't looked good that morning. His condition worried de Jersey: the equerry had to be fit and well to be convincing. He headed into town, stopped the car outside a public telephone kiosk and rang Raymond Marsh. His wife answered and after a moment Marsh was on the line.

'Who is this? Mr Simmons, right? About time. We gonna meet?'

'I hope so. You free tonight?'

'Yep, and have I got news for you! Can you come to my place?'

Marsh opened the door and de Jersey followed him into a hallway with such thick carpet that he felt as if he was wading through soft mud. Marsh was wearing skin-tight drainpipe trousers with thick-soled suede shoes in a shocking pink. They matched his shirt, which he wore with a skinny strip of leather as a tie. The walls bore rows of pictures and posters of Elvis Presley. 'My hero,' said Marsh. 'Come upstairs.' He led the way up the stairs past posters from all of Elvis's films. Marsh opened a door at the end of the landing, stood back and gestured for de Jersey to walk in. Inside there were banks of computers, a mass of cables, overflowing ashtrays and pizza boxes.

'Sit down,' Marsh said. 'This is my office. As you can see, it's all state-of-the-art equipment, worth thousands.'

'How have you been getting on at the exchange?'

Marsh bent down and brought out a cheap canvas bag. He dumped it on his desk. 'Good. I've made printouts for you to take away, plus tape recordings. The IRA call in every morning at a designated time. They have ten lines, which they use in a certain pattern. They call the first line one day, the second the next and when they get up to the tenth they go into reverse. I think I've predicted which line will be used on the day of the heist as long as they don't change their pattern – but we've got plenty of time to see if they do.'

'Great work. What about the link between Scotland Yard and the safe house? What conversations have already taken place? Who has placed calls and to whom?'

'Well, they've had no contact yet concerning security for the fitting but we're still a long way off the date. I expect something soon.'

De Jersey was impressed. Marsh was coming up with aces at every meeting, but he wouldn't let go of the canvas bag. He looked at de Jersey in a very determined manner. 'It looks to me like I've got a pretty hefty role in this and I'm not doing it for the joy of hacking. We need to talk about what my cut is going to be.'

'Okay. We now know that the main piece we'll get our hands on will be sold for close to sixty million and we'll get more for the rest of the jewels,' de Jersey lied, knowing it would be considerably more.

Hearing this, Marsh wanted to be assured of at least ten million, plus the thousand a week. De Jersey agreed to this, and Marsh tossed over the canvas bag and said, 'When you get closer to the day of the fitting, the Commander of the RDPD will liaise with D'Ancona about security procedures. I can identify the line to the safe house and I'll intercept it to receive the call that will notify them that the Queen's visit has been cancelled.'

The two continued working through the plan. As soon as Marsh had secured the codeword for the 2nd of May, he would call de Jersey with it. De Jersey would then pose as an IRA informant and call the police giving the codeword and making a bomb threat that would be deemed genuine. Scotland Yard would call the Palace and all Royal proceedings would be brought to a stand-still. As Marsh had already explained, he would wait for the Commander to call the safe house to cancel the visit. When the call was placed, he would break into the line and answer it himself. The head of security at the safe house would still expect the Queen, unaware that a different convoy would arrive.

'So I'll be in the exchange from before six a.m. and I'll stay until about ten thirty when you'll be doing the business,' Marsh said. 'I'll keep a check on the lines to see if anyone has noticed anything dodgy.' He sucked in his breath. 'Get out of the safe house as fast as you can 'cos they won't take long to suss this out you know.

Palace security are gonna keep checking for clearance.' De Jersey knew Marsh's physical presence in the exchange would be risky. 'You'll have ten to fifteen minutes to pull this off.'

'We'll be as quick as possible,' de Jersey said. 'Straight in and out, hopefully. Is there any way you can get a layout of inside the safe house?'

'Are you telling me you're making all these plans and you don't know what the inside of the place is like? It's fucking nuts! It's imperative you know what the layout is.'

'It's not necessary. We're going in through the front door and I'm sure it's not going to be a problem. We just need to know where the vault is.'

Marsh pointed a finger at de Jersey. 'This is an amateur's night out, mate.' He was angry.

De Jersey's mouth tightened. 'Not necessarily,' he said. But Marsh's remark had hit home.

'I just hope to God your other guys know what the fuck they're doing. You can't seriously contemplate busting into this place if you don't know what's gonna be waiting for you. Can't you get to someone on the inside?' Marsh paused. Then he said, 'Listen, I might be able to help but I can't promise anything. Maybe I'll be able to find something that shows their security system layout. If it's on a computer somewhere, I can get to it. Any place with a telephone or a computer is vulnerable to somebody of my ability.'

'How long do you need?' de Jersey asked.

Marsh grinned. 'Question is, how much are you prepared to pay?'

323

De Jersey didn't feel any better after a good night's rest as he sat pondering the plans. His interaction with Marsh had unnerved him and the word 'amateur' stung. His wallet was also hurting from his further payment to the man. He just hoped he'd come up with the goods. De Jersey still had to find a suitable woman to take part in the scheme, persuade the lookalike to take part, and he was minus the two bikers. Perhaps he should use the Internet again. He sighed. He was tired with all the plotting and dealing with the ever-increasing cash drain.

De Jersey caught a train back to his estate. He needed to unwind: his mind was scrambled and his body ached. Alone in the house, the tranquillity soothed him as he wandered from room to room. Later he rode with the jockeys, spent time with Fleming, and inspected Royal Flush, who was coming on even better than they had hoped.

He was sitting at his desk when Christina called. Her mother had died that afternoon. She wept and tried to be coherent but constantly broke down. Her mother had been only sixty-two and her poor father was bereft. De Jersey was gentle and understanding. After he hung up he contacted Driscoll to say the plans would be halted for a few days. Driscoll was relieved to hear that the funeral would take place over the same weekend as his daughter's wedding. Wilcox was now really sick with flu and was in bed, unable to move. Like Driscoll, he was relieved that de Jersey was taking time out. It would give them all a breather. De Jersey noticed that neither man mentioned the heist and he wondered if they were still having doubts.

The truth was, after his meeting with Marsh, he had lost confidence that they would be able to pull this off. All he could see now were the holes, and his team members were a motley crew: cocaine addict Wilcox, wide-boy Driscoll, cancer-riddled Lord Westbrook, pockmarked Gregory Jones, egotistical Raymond Marsh and nervous Paul Dulay. He calculated the cost to date and felt sick.

The following day, de Jersey left for Sweden. Throughout the flight he sat with his eyes closed, going over the details that were now so familiar to him it was like turning the pages of a book he knew by heart. He was woken from his daydream by the stewardess offering refreshments and the newspapers. He asked for coffee and took *The Times*, the *Express* and the *Daily Mail*. In the *Express*, an article caught his eye. Two elderly spinsters had conned the equestrian circuit out of thousands of pounds. A picture showed them beaming into the camera holding a winner's cup and rosette. It triggered a memory. He frowned as he tried to calculate how old Pamela Kenworthy-Wright must be now. They had met in the seventies through a mutual friend. Pamela had been an actress, and had trained at RADA. She was moderately well connected and had married a wealthy stockbroker, whom she had later divorced for his infidelity with a manservant. Afterwards she had tried to continue her theatrical career, appearing in a couple of TV series, but in the late eighties had been arrested for shoplifting in Harrods. In fact, she had spent a few months in Holloway for credit-card fraud. He smiled to himself. Pamela might be just the woman he needed for the heist, but he had to find her first.

The funeral was a small family affair with just Christina's father, her siblings and their children. The service was short and the luncheon rather heavy but it was a well-organized occasion. Though Christina was pale, she managed to maintain her composure apart from shedding a few tears at the funeral. She was so pleased her husband was there for her. De Jersey was very attentive and caring and her father was grateful for his support. When de Jersey suggested that his daughter stay on to deal with her mother's belongings and to help settle her father in a smaller house, it was deemed a caring, thoughtful suggestion. He gave no indication that he wanted Christina to stay away for as long as possible. He made his suggestion seem even more caring by offering to remain with her but she knew he had business to attend to and, as de Jersey had hoped, refused his offer. The fact that he had no intention of spending any more time there and would have engineered a call that forced him to leave if she had taken him up on his offer, was an indication of just how much he was able to coldly divorce himself from his emotions. He loved Christina but his present predicament took priority. Time was moving on. It was already into March and his team was still incomplete. Most importantly, he still did not have the layout for the safe house.

It was after midnight and Driscoll's daughter was safely on her way to her honeymoon while her father sat by one of the specially installed outdoor heaters near his lily pond. It was full of streamers, confetti and cigarette stubs but he couldn't have cared less. His head throbbed – he'd had too much to drink, but didn't feel drunk – and his gut was on fire.

'It's Tony, isn't it?'

Driscoll looked up at the burly figure in the green security uniform.

'Do I know you?'

'In a way. Been twenty years, maybe more. I'm Brian Hall.'

Driscoll didn't recognize the guy.

'Used to work for you, long time ago, when you had that waste-disposal company. You did me a big favour. I was on parole, needed work, and was just starting to get back into a spot of bother when you gave me the job, even though you knew I had a criminal record.'

'Oh, right. So, how're things going?' Driscoll asked, not really caring.

'I get a bit of work here and there. Been with this company for a few years, but I'm a reserve. They pull me in when they need extra hands, like for this kind of gig.' He gestured to the wedding remnants around him.

'Did you stay clean?' Driscoll asked.

Hall shook his head, laughing softly. 'Hell, no. I tried for a while but when you've got a wife and three kids you've gotta do what you've gotta do for 'em, know what I mean? I got my fingers burnt a few times more. In fact, I've only been out ten months.'

Driscoll was waiting for the hit. He even put his hand into his pocket for his wallet but Hall laid a hand on his arm. 'Oh, no, I'm not looking for a hand-out. I just wanted to thank you.'

'Fancy a drink?' Driscoll asked.

'Not while I'm on duty.'

'Who's to see you? Besides, I hired you.'

They made their way back to the bar in the marquee. Driscoll found a half-full bottle of brandy, picked up two glasses and made his way to the corner of the patio. 'Brandy suit you?'

'Yeah.'

Driscoll divided the bottle between them, then proffered a cigar and they lit up, sitting in the darkness with the music still banging away.

'I don't suppose you've got any work going?' Hall asked.

'Not really. I'm semi-retired,' Driscoll said, then gestured to the gardens and the house. 'But don't think all this is safe and secure. I'm skint. I made a bad business deal and got screwed out of all my savings.'

'I'm sorry,' Hall said. 'I've got a little sideline, though, if you need any heavy work – know what I mean? If these people that screwed you on this business deal need sorting, me and my pal Kenny Short, we do contracts. Not the really heavy stuff, but we certainly put some pressure on.'

Driscoll remained silent.

'Hope you don't mind me asking. It was just a thought.'

An idea slipped into Driscoll's mind. It sat there for a while before he said quietly, 'You know, I just might have a nice earner for you. Can this Kenny geezer be trusted?'

'With my life!' Hall said.

'Gimme a contact number and maybe I'll be in touch. I'll have to talk it over with a pal first, all right?'

As soon as he was back in England after the funeral, de Jersey turned his attention to tracing Pamela Kenworthy-Wright. He quickly established that she was no longer a member of Equity, then checked the telephone directory and discovered that three people had the same last name and initials. He rang the first. The phone was answered by an upper-crust military type, 'This is Peter Kenworthy-Wright speaking,' and de Jersey hung up. The second time the phone rang twice.

'Hello?'

'Miss Pamela Kenworthy-Wright?'

'For my sins, yes, it is. Who is this?'

'I'm doing a census enquiry for the government with regard to people living in your area and claiming unemployment benefits.'

'Oh, God, this really is an invasion of one's privacy.'

'Do you own a computer?'

'Yes, I do. I also vote Conservative, I smoke and I'm divorced. Now piss off.'

'Were you an actress?'

'I still am.'

'Thank you very much.'

He hung up before she could say anything else, sure that he had found the right Pamela but he called the third number just in case. This time he spoke to an elderly lady, who said Miss Petal Kenworthy-Wright was out walking her dog.

De Jersey thought his own rented flat in Kilburn was rundown but compared to Pamela's place it was a palace. She had a bedsit in an old converted fort in Plymouth. To gain access to the apartments you had to cross a drawbridge before entering the main courtyard, which was filled with boarded-up huts. Stray dogs and cats scuttled around stinking rubbish bags outside the building. Broken sinks, lavatories and fridges littered the corridors, which were cold and damp. The stench of urine pervaded the stairs and the second-floor corridor leading to bedsit number twenty. There was a sign on the door that read, 'Do not disturb before eleven a.m., thank you.' De Jersey smiled and rapped on the door.

'Who is it?' demanded an authoritative, aristocratic voice.

'Philip Simmons.' De Jersey heard the lock slide back and the door was edged open.

'Are you from Social Services?'

'No.'

'So what do you want?'

'To talk to you. I met you a long time ago.' He smiled pleasantly.

'Well, I don't recognize you and I'm very busy right now.'

'Please, Miss Kenworthy-Wright, I really do need to speak to you about something that may prove very lucrative.'

'Do you have identification?'

He produced his driving licence in his fictional name.

'Oh, come in. I'll need my reading glasses.'

She disappeared into the flat and he followed. It was better furnished than he had expected, with a good-quality rug on the floor and comfortable leather armchairs. She also had a computer, a large TV set, and the gas fire made it very warm. A few large oil paintings of gentlemen in wigs and a dour-faced woman dominated the walls. A sofa bed with an orange duvet took up the rest of the room, dangerously close to the fire.

Pamela was wearing a velvet dressing-gown over her skinny frame with rabbit-fur slippers. She delved into a cloth bag and brought out her glasses, held them to her nose, glanced at his driving licence and passed it back to him. 'What do you want?'

'May I sit down?'

She shrugged. Her face was heavily wrinkled and lipstick rivulets ran from her thin lips in rows of tiny red lines. Only her eyes retained a spark of brightness. They were a wonderful china blue enhanced by the dark shadows of old mascara. Her hair was dyed, probably by herself, in various shades of dark auburn tinged with grey.

'Do you want some coffee?'

'Thank you.'

'It's good Columbian. I suggest you take it black.' The cup was chipped but clean.

Pamela sat in the chair opposite him. 'You must be after something but I can't for the life of me think what I could have that would be of any interest to a nice strapping man like you. I like your shoes.'

'You're a technological lady?'

'Yes. I had computer training in prison,' she said, without embarrassment. 'I'm quite proficient. I'm writing a book about my life. It would be so nice if you were here about that. I did send off a first chapter to all and sundry but I've not heard a squeak back.' She lit a cigarette.

'I'm not here about your book.'

'Pity, that was really why I let you in but we all

have these fantasies, don't we? You know, dreams of overnight success. Couple of small parts in *The Avengers* wasn't going to take me to Hollywood but at the time I believed it might. I was in it with Honor Blackman. Lovely-looking woman. She's kept her figure and her looks – but I suppose she never married a scumbag. That was my undoing.' She got up to fetch an ashtray.

'I met you with Victor Markham, back in the seventies,' de Jersey said.

'Did you? He's been dead for years. Of course, after my problems I lost touch with a lot of the old crowd. Do you play bridge?'

'No.'

'You said something about . . . lucrative – was that the word you used? I'm running out of pleasantries, Mr Simmons. I'm waiting with bated breath to hear why you've come to the fort.'

'I may have a proposition for you.'

She laughed a smoker's throaty laugh, revealing coffee-stained teeth. 'Well, talk, dear boy. You've come to the right person. I'm in need of anything that'll make me a bob or two.' She looked at him with a sly smile. 'It's not legal, though, is it?'

'No.'

'Anything or anyone who knew Victor Markham was bent.' She lit another cigarette as he sipped his coffee. 'So why are you here, Philip Simmons?'

'I need you to impersonate someone.'

'And what would it be worth to me?'

'More than you would get from any publishing deal. I'll need you to stay in London. I have a place – it's not very comfortable but it would only be for a short time.'

'Mmmm. I think I'd rather like a gin. Can I offer you one?'

De Jersey was feeling better. On his return to Kilburn, he rented a small studio in Maida Vale and arranged for the keys to be sent to his Kilburn address. His mobile rang and he picked it up. It was Driscoll.

'How are you doing?' de Jersey asked.

'Not bad. I think I've got your motorbike riders,' Driscoll said thickly.

'You don't sound like yourself,' de Jersey said warily.

'Got a hangover, but I'd say these guys are the business. You wanna check them out?'

'Yes.'

'I'll arrange a meet. Tomorrow morning?'

'Fine, what time?'

'Lemme get back to you.' De Jersey switched off the phone.

It rang again straight away. This time it was Wilcox. 'How we doing, my old son?' he asked, sounding perky.

'I'm fine, and you sound a lot better.'

'I am. Few days in bed sorted me out. I think we should meet at the barn so I can show you what I've been up to.'

'Fine. Tomorrow?'

'Let's say seven, make it really early. It's quite a schlep in from Henley, you know.'

'Seven it is. See you there.'

The two calls had made de Jersey feel good. Driscoll

and Wilcox were both moving things forward just as they had in the old days. He liked that. It meant they were starting to be more of a team.

Just after seven the next morning, de Jersey met with Wilcox. He parked by a thick hedgerow and walked towards the large barn, which had huge double doors. Wilcox opened them and came out. 'I saw you drawing up. It's freezing in here, but we're pretty secure.'

De Jersey followed him in and closed the door. The vehicles, shrouded in big white sheets, were parked in the centre of the barn. Beside them were the two bikes, also draped in sheets. Next to them was a trestle table with stacks of items they would require: the weapons, the mascot for the Queen's car and so on.

'This looks good. And the nearest farm is, what? Two miles north?' de Jersey queried.

'The two houses at the top of the drive are empty so we can come and go. Nobody's gonna be around.'

Wilcox pulled the sheet off one of the Daimlers, which gleamed. 'I'm almost finished with the upholstery. I've got a guy making up the seats. He has no idea what they're for and I can collect them in a couple of weeks. The colour is close enough. Dark maroon, right?'

De Jersey walked around the car. 'Tony says he thinks he's got the bike riders. I'm going to meet them this morning.'

They went to a small back-room area, screened off from the main barn. Wilcox had collected together a few chairs, a kettle and coffee mugs.

'We'll need some heaters in here,' de Jersey said.

'I'll get one of those big ones they use on film sets.'
Wilcox sniffed. His nose was running.

De Jersey wondered if this newfound energy was not
a return to health but, in fact, chemically fuelled.

'You want the surveillance details me and Tony have
been working on?' Wilcox asked.

'Fire away.'

'We've been taking turns monitoring the safe house
and we've got the following regular workers and visitors.
Two females, one about twenty-five, the other middle-
aged. Three males, mid-thirties, and two white-haired
men. Four security guards. Two come on early morning,
two at night. Four other men turned up but they weren't
regulars.' Wilcox laid out photographs of each one. Even
if he was still doing coke, de Jersey could not fault his
preparations. If anything, he himself was lagging. He felt
uneasy when Wilcox pressed him for details about the
interior of the safe house.

'We'll discuss all that at the first big meet. I need a
few days. Good work, James.'

'Not got it together yet, then?'

'Almost but it's taking more time than I thought. I'm
getting there, though.'

'I sincerely hope so, old chap. Time's moving on.'
They gave each other a brotherly hug. 'So, what's next
for me?' Wilcox asked.

'Just get the vehicles ready.'

'We're on course, are we?'

De Jersey hesitated a beat before he answered. 'Yeah,
we're on course, James.'

Later that morning, de Jersey met with Driscoll and the possible bike riders, Brian Hall and Kenny Short. De Jersey suggested they take a ride on an open-top bus and the four men were the only occupants of the top deck. As they stared out at the sights of London, de Jersey – as Simmons – questioned Hall, then Short. As they parted, he tapped Driscoll's arm and said softly, 'Nice work. They seem steady guys.'

Driscoll nodded. 'I reckon we'll have no problems. They agreed to the fee and I trust them. I have to, 'cos Hall knows where I live.'

'Right,' de Jersey said. In the old days, Tony Driscoll would have moved house. Thankfully de Jersey did not have to. No one new coming into the team had the slightest notion who he was.

When de Jersey called to say he was arranging a meeting for the following week, Westbrook had been having migraines that left him so weak he could hardly lift a cigarette to his lips. The pain was so violent it made him retch until he lay exhausted on the cold tiled floor of the bathroom, crying like a baby. De Jersey's call lifted the pain and cleared his head abruptly. He didn't know if it was terror or having something else to think about. He wasn't scared: there was nothing to be scared of. He was dying anyway.

Pamela Kenworthy-Wright agreed to travel to London. She didn't ask questions except where she would find the keys to the apartment she'd be staying in.

Just as de Jersey was beginning to feel he was making good progress, Raymond Marsh called and dropped a bombshell.

'This is hot off the Buck House telephone wires. She's snuffed it.'

De Jersey took a deep breath. 'What are you talking about?'

'She was rushed to hospital last night and died early this morning. It'll be front-page news by tonight, so they'll be lowering the flags.'

De Jersey clenched his teeth. 'She's dead?'

'Yeah. Be big funerals and stuff going down.'

'Dear God, I don't believe it. Are you sure?'

'I'm certain. My Gran always said she should have been allowed to marry that Peter Townsend. Lord Snowdon didn't do her any favours.'

'Wait, you're talking about Princess Margaret?'

'Yeah. Who did you think I was talking about? But it means that HM might not be keeping to her diary, know what I mean?'

De Jersey's heart rate dropped a fraction. For a moment he had truly thought the Queen was dead.

'How soon can you find out if this will affect the date of the fitting?'

'Well, all I can do is keep you posted. I just thought you'd want to know.'

'Yes, thank you.'

De Jersey replaced the receiver and sat in stunned silence. This could throw a major spanner in the works. A few days later, however, after the media had run the coverage of the Princess's death virtually into the ground, Raymond called again. He said he needed to talk to de Jersey urgently.

'Is this about the funeral?'

'Nope. As far as I can tell that'll all be over soon. The diary hasn't changed for May. Busy this month, though. Not sure I'd fancy being cremated myself, but . . .'

'What did you call to talk about then?' de Jersey asked, cutting Raymond off.

Raymond refused to say, however, over the phone, so they arranged to meet in a coffee shop a stone's throw from the entrance to Buckingham Palace. It was Marsh's morning break and a long line of tourists was waiting for the Changing of the Guard, their umbrellas up against the cold March drizzle and their coats buffeted by the brisk wind.

'You've got real problems,' Marsh told him. 'I did some rooting around at work 'cos I figured the D'Ancona alarm system might work through their phone lines.'

'And what did you find out?'

'They've got serious panic buttons – fifty-two of them – all wired up individually to the phone system with a direct link to an Alarm Receiving Centre, which contacts the police. I suspect they'll be set up so that if you deactivate one line the others will go off.'

De Jersey's heart sank.

Marsh continued. 'They'll be dotted around all over the place. I tried to get more information using the web but there's nothing on D'Ancona that we don't already know and, besides, they ain't gonna give details on the web about their security. But it's logic that they'll have 'em on the walls and under the carpet so you won't even be able to tell if one's been set off until it's too late. Step on one an' you'll trigger the rest.'

'So you got nothing on their security layout?'

Marsh shook his head. 'The plans aren't stored on any computer network that I've dipped into. They're gonna protect themselves an' gotta be wise to hackers. One more thing I did find out, though. There's activity on those lines at precisely nine a.m. every morning. I assume that's when they check their system so if you deactivate the phone lines connected to the panic buttons, it'll need to be done after that. But it's not all bad news.'

'Go on.'

Marsh wiped his mouth on a paper napkin. 'I hacked into the Royal diary page again. Been keeping my eye on it for you, especially since the princess died. The fitting's been confirmed. It's Thursday the 2nd of May, ten thirty.'

De Jersey stared at him. If the fitting was now confirmed so was the date of the robbery.

'See? I said it wasn't all bad news. The party they've got listed for the fitting includes Her Majesty, a lady-in-waiting – Lady Camilla Harvey, the equerry plus a detective, two bike riders, the chauffeurs and some security geezers.'

De Jersey gave Marsh a guarded smile and patted his arm. Then he got up and walked out. Marsh pocketed the fiver de Jersey had left for the waiter, and substituted two pound coins.

Two steps forward and a bad one back. It was disappointing if not catastrophic not to know the layout of the security at the safe house. De Jersey knew how many people worked there, what time they came in and out. He knew how many telephones there were but he did not know on which floor the main vault was and, most importantly, the location of the panic buttons and security alarms. He put up his umbrella and walked towards Victoria station where he caught a bus to Kilburn. He sat upstairs in a front seat, deep in thought, watching the rain pelting down. He calculated that, apart from the obvious, they were in good shape all round with more than six weeks to go. He stared out of the window at the traffic snarled up alongside Hyde Park. Just as the bus drew up by the Park Lane underground garage, he noticed the Eye Spy security company housed in an elegant corner shop across from the old Playboy club. It was not the shop, however, that had caught de Jersey's interest but the figure of a young man leaving it. It was the young salesman from the security exhibition in Birmingham. The bus jolted forward and de Jersey watched him walk down Park Lane towards the Dorchester Hotel.

De Jersey jumped off the bus as it idled and made it safely to the pavement, just a few yards up from the Grosvenor House Hotel. He put up his umbrella and walked back briskly in the direction of the Dorchester.

'I am so sorry,' he exclaimed, as he caught the young man with the edge of his umbrella.

'It's okay.'

He was about to walk on when de Jersey said, 'Wait a minute, we've met before, haven't we?'

'I don't think so.'

'No, I never forget a face. You were on the Interlace Security stand at the Birmingham exhibition.'

'You're right.' But the puzzled expression on his face meant that he didn't recall de Jersey.

'Philip Simmons,' he said.

'Oh, yes.' He obviously still had no recollection.

'Are you working in London now?'

'Erm, not as yet.'

He seemed eager to continue down Park Lane and was obviously uneasy as de Jersey walked alongside him.

'Is there an exhibition on? I still haven't contracted a security company for my new business.'

'I'm just here for the day, going back on the four o'clock train.'

'I'm going to have a bite to eat at the Grosvenor House's coffee shop. Do you have time to join me? We could perhaps continue our discussion.'

The young man hesitated and glanced at his wrist-watch. 'No, thank you. I should get to the station.'

'Nonsense. You have plenty of time. Join me, please. As I said, I really would like to continue our conversation.'

Gridley looked at de Jersey. 'Are you picking me up or something? If you are you've got it wrong. Excuse me.'

'Dear God! I've never been accused of that before.' De Jersey laughed. 'I assure you, I simply wish to talk to you about my business and I'm sure you have plenty of time to catch your train. We could have a glass of wine or coffee, whichever you prefer.'

'Thank you,' Gridley said. 'I'm sorry if I seem crass but . . . oh, why not? My train isn't until four.'

They sat at a window table and de Jersey took charge, ordering a bottle of Merlot. The young man seemed awkward in the elegant surroundings. They had both removed their wet coats and the cloakroom attendant had taken de Jersey's umbrella. Gridley was wearing the same cheap suit he had had on the last time de Jersey had met him.

'Mr Simmons,' he said, 'I think I had better tell you that I'm not going to be working for the company for much longer. My father retired last week. After he'd gone they gave me a month's notice. I think they only kept me on because of him so I came up here to look for work.'

'Any success?'

'Not as yet. At the end of this week when my notice is up I'll come back and have a really good scout around.'

'Well, I wish you every success. We never did get to finish the conversation we started in the bar at the exhibition. That man who interrupted us, he seemed to be giving you a bit of a dressing-down.'

Gridley sipped his wine. 'I don't remember. It's been a daily occurrence, the dressing-downs.' He drained his glass and de Jersey refilled it. 'Thank you. This is part of my problem,' he said, tapping the glass. 'I have been a bit hung over a few times but . . .' He tailed off and stared into his glass. De Jersey could feel the adrenaline pumping. He knew he had to take this opportunity very carefully. First he intended to lull Gridley into a false sense of security. He would then dangle a carrot the young man would be unable to refuse. He suggested they order lunch, his treat, and Gridley agreed.

They finished lunch, having discussed the progress of the building works on his fictional jewellery-shop premises. By this time Gridley had consumed most of the wine and de Jersey had ordered another bottle. Then he went for it. 'You know they had another robbery in Bond

Street, and Gucci's warehouse was also done over? Did you read about it?'

'Yes.' Gridley nodded. 'They should have used Interlace. It would never have happened. I mean, although they're making me redundant, I reckon they really are the best company. You don't get contracts like we have for not being top of the ladder.'

'Exactly, which is why I am so pleased to bump into you this morning.'

'But I'll be an official job seeker next week so if you decide to go with our security system, I won't get the salesman's bonus.'

De Jersey topped up his own glass. 'I don't think that's fair. You sold the company to me. I shall insist you get it. How's that?'

'Well, I obviously appreciate it but as I won't be employed there I doubt if it could be arranged.'

'Well, then, I'll do it on a personal basis. How about that?'

There ensued another fifteen minutes of discussion on how de Jersey could pay the bonus to Gridley directly. Then he went for the kill. 'I would pay you more than the bonus if you could let me see how the D'Ancona security works. I don't think that company has ever been robbed. I know they lost a diamond recently but that was just one stone.'

'It was worth a couple of million, though.' Gridley glanced at his watch.

'But their safe houses have never been breached and it would be a major plus for me to have an insight into how they have been so successful. And since your company, or your ex-company, drew up their plans . . .'

'That would be impossible,' Malcolm said.

'But not if they didn't know. Just make me a copy. Could you do that?'

'I really couldn't. Besides, they'd probably know it was me.'

'All I want is to be sure my business is as well protected as possible and Interlace would get the work. I could pay you five thousand for your trouble. I'd also make sure you got the bonus. I don't think they could possibly have any ill feelings towards you. On the contrary, they should offer you a better position instead of firing you.'

He still had not bitten and was now checking for his train ticket. He had consumed almost the entire second bottle of wine.

'I might even be able to help you get another position. Are you planning to continue working for—'

'Mr Simmons, I have to be honest with you. The type of work I was doing bored the pants off me. I was only working there because of my father and I have no idea what I want to do next. I'm sort of looking around but . . . I've recently split up with my girlfriend. She's gone to live in Sydney, Australia, and it's really cut me up. And when I said to you before that I had been rather hung over occasionally, that was putting it mildly. A couple of times I was three sheets to the wind so I can't really blame them for firing me. I was probably a bit sozzled when you came to the exhibition.'

He looked morose and fished in his suit pocket for a packet of cigarettes. 'Can we smoke in here?'

'Go ahead, unless you'd prefer a cigar.'

'I'll stick to these.'

De Jersey ordered a brandy for himself, and Gridley

344

flicked nervously at his cigarette ash. 'I've had a series of job interviews. The old man has virtually given up on me but I can't seem to find anything that, you know, interests me, and with Francesca leaving . . .'

'Why not go out to Australia? Maybe that's the place for you.'

'I only had just enough dosh for the ticket to London, but I have thought about it.'

'That bonus I spoke of would come at the right time, then, wouldn't it? Why don't I take you round my shop? I really do need some advice. We can be there in half an hour, and you could look over the premises.' De Jersey had seen Gridley glancing at his watch. He knew he was on safe ground inviting Gridley to his non-existent shop as Gridley had said he was catching the four o'clock train. It was already five past three.

'I'm afraid I can't. I have to get to the station.'

De Jersey wasn't sure his fish was on the line but he had gone quiet, which was a good sign. De Jersey paid the bill and they collected their coats and de Jersey his umbrella. Malcolm remained silent as he watched de Jersey give the cloakroom attendant a heavy tip. They walked into Park Lane together. De Jersey was getting worried: perhaps he had overestimated his powers of persuasion. He wondered if he should have offered more money but that would have made Gridley suspicious.

'They have me in the office working out my notice,' Gridley said suddenly. 'I'm not a salesman any more. They have me doing menial tasks around the office.' He hesitated. 'It means I have access to the files but, while I would really like to help you out and obviously the bonus you mentioned would come in handy, I don't think . . .' He was flushing.

345

'Really? Well, that makes it even easier for you.' He'd got him. Relieved, de Jersey put up his umbrella, sheltering them both from the rain. 'But I don't want this to get you into any trouble. It would help me cut corners but if it's at all risky then I understand if you feel you can't help me.'

Gridley looked relieved. 'Thank you. And I'd like to help you out, but it's impossible and I'm afraid you're rather out of touch.'

'I'm sorry?' De Jersey was stunned by the young man's change of heart.

'I doubt that any reputable security company retains easily accessible blueprints of their customers' premises. Everything is computerized and it's virtually impossible to gain access to them without permission. If you open up a file on the computer, you need the password, and the date and time will be recorded. So, even if I attempted to do it for you, I'd be caught red-handed. I suppose that's why Interlace is such a good company and why D'Ancona employed us.' De Jersey was struggling to contain his anger. 'But thank you so much for lunch,' Gridley said. 'It was really nice to meet you again. Now I should jump into a taxi or I'll miss my train.'

De Jersey forced a smile. 'Good luck. And here's some advice,' he said, gritting his teeth. 'You only live once. If you don't go after what you want you'll watch it slip from your grasp.' Then he turned and walked away, his face taut with anger. He had certainly misjudged the young man. In fact, he would have liked to ram his umbrella down his throat.

The meeting when all the team would get together for the first time was set for two thirty at the barn on the following Monday. It was imperative that de Jersey showed one hundred per cent confidence in his plan to ensure that they all followed his orders to the letter. But it would be difficult: so much still depended on him being able to secure the layout of the D'Ancona safe house. Once again he contacted Marsh. To date he had only attempted to gain access to D'Ancona records but what if he could tap into the Interlace computer files? Marsh promised to 'give it a whirl' but he warned de Jersey that they risked tipping off Interlace that someone was sniffing around.

'I need the layout,' de Jersey said stubbornly.

'Listen, mate, it's not you that's doing the dodgy stuff. I got to watch my back. Like I said to you, I'll give it a go but these top-notch companies have got all kinds of hidden traps an' I don't want nothing zapping back to my gaff.'

'Will you do it?'

'I'll see if I can break in tonight but this is their business – they're a security company and a damn good one. All I'm saying is, it's a risk.'

'Take it,' de Jersey snapped, then took a deep breath. 'It's very important.'

'I know, pal. Without it, you're walking into a mine-field. Like I said, I'll do what I can.'

De Jersey had a restless night waiting to hear back from Marsh, but when he opened his email the next morning it was not good news.

'Problems,' the message said. 'Attempted to do as requested. Gained password, entered and then all hell broke loose. Pulled out fast but the company will have been tipped off. Sorry! Elvis.'

De Jersey stared at the screen with no idea of what his next move should be. As Marsh had so succinctly put it, entering the D'Ancona safe house without a floor plan would be like walking into a minefield.

CHAPTER 18

As THE meeting grew closer, de Jersey had still not overcome the heist's major problem. Five days had passed since he'd spoken to Marsh and all he had was a guide plan of the building itself before the security had been put in place with over fifty panic buttons. Then he received a small padded envelope in the mail, postmarked Birmingham. He did not recognize the handwriting. He opened it, and caught his breath. It contained a single CD and a typewritten note from Malcolm Gridley:

Dear Mr Simmons, We recently had an electronic security alert and all our computer files had to be checked as it was first presumed to be some kind of virus that would corrupt all the data. As I was working in the office part of my duties was to assist the IT department to verify whether any of the data had been corrupted. I therefore had access to the enclosed. I am leaving for Australia to join my girlfriend but if you do decide to use Interlace and perhaps see your way to paying me the bonus we spoke of, my address will be Apartment 4B West Street, North Sydney, NSW 2060. If, however, you decide otherwise, perhaps you would destroy the CD. Thank you for lunch. Yours sincerely, Malcolm Gridley.

De Jersey could not believe his luck. He kept staring at the CD and rereading the letter. He sat at his computer and his jaw dropped when he saw what was on the disk. Then he started to laugh. It contained everything he could possibly have hoped for – and all for the price of a cheap lunch.

The Interlace CD contained an interactive floor plan of every section of the D'Ancona safe house. It indicated where Interlace had recommended the panic buttons to be placed. It also showed the security cameras, the grilles and electronic pulses required for each door and the costing for the equipment. One incredibly useful feature was a virtual tour of the entire safe house, and de Jersey was able to visualize the route from the front door down to the basement where the vast vault was located. If one panic button was pressed the Alarm Receiving Centre would alert the police almost immediately and a fast-action team would be dispatched with an estimated response time of two minutes. Once the alert was given, all access to the building would be secured.

De Jersey was aware that D'Ancona might have made changes from what was on the CD but even so he now felt prepared for the first meeting with his key team members.

In a pinstripe suit, brown brogues and a blue shirt, de Jersey sat at the back of the Surrey barn. Wilcox had sectioned off the area with screens and four calor-gas heaters were blasting out warmth. There were a few folding chairs, a picnic table and an easy chair he'd found in a skip. A camping stove stood in the makeshift kitchen to brew tea and coffee.

The team had been instructed to leave their cars in the yard at the back of the barn, which was protected from view by the overgrown hedge. As soon as de Jersey heard the first car arrive he stood at the door with a box of surgical gloves and handed a pair to each team member as they entered. A large drawing-board had been set up for his use and he had brought his laptop.

Driscoll was the first to arrive and snapped on the gloves without a word. He was closely followed by Pamela and Lord Westbrook. The bike riders would not be privy to these early meetings. As de Jersey bolted the door behind them, Pamela complained about the rubber gloves. 'Wear them at all times,' de Jersey told her. 'This box will be placed by the back door.'

'Are we expected to do some kind of cleaning?' Pamela enquired.

De Jersey showed her that he, too, was wearing them. 'You know how they identified Ronnie Biggs? He put a dish of milk out for a cat. One thumb-print, that's all it takes. When we move out of here to the second base we must leave no record of any one of us ever having been here. Is that understood?'

The team all nodded in agreement, and Pamela made tea and coffee before taking her seat in the row of plastic chairs facing the drawing-board.

The team sat in awkward silence, avoiding each other's eyes. De Jersey leaned against the table. 'From now on you refer to me only as the Colonel and you will refer to each other by Christian names only. First, Pamela.'

She raised her beaker.

'James. That's Tony, and Henry.' He nodded to each as he said their name. 'From now on we protect each other's identities. The less we know about each other the better. I have put my utmost trust in each of you.'

They remained silent as he picked up a black felt-tipped marker, crossed to the drawing-board and listed roles beside the names: the Colonel, main bodyguard; Henry, equerry; James, driver; Her Majesty the Queen, not present; Pamela, lady-in-waiting; Tony, private secretary; two bike riders, not present.

Everyone listened as he gave the date and time they would be moving base to get ready for the hit. He detailed their jobs and explained the complex method by which he and Marsh would stop the Royal convoy and how they would arrive at the safe house in place of the authentic party. By the time he told them how they would accomplish entry to the safe house, they were all ready for another round of tea and coffee. Everyone seemed tense: they had been listening to the Colonel for over an hour and it was a lot to take in.

After the short break, de Jersey moved on to the last phase of the plan. 'So far so good, but the most important element for all of us is getting away with it. I will use four helicopters to act as decoys. They will be ordered from various companies in the South-East to pick up a passenger or package from various points in London. When they arrive and their passenger is not there, the helicopters will leave London to return to their bases, which will coincide with the time of the getaway. It will be mayhem after the hit and the police will monitor the air traffic so we want as much organized chaos and as many distractions as possible. We will all split up and move across London separately. First, two boats will be taken from a mooring at Tower Bridge Marina and driven across the river by the two bike riders. They will both motor to Putney Bridge, put the boats in the boat-house and take the tube home from there.'

'That all seems very . . . well, not what I expected,' interrupted Westbrook.

'You expected fast cars, speedboats and getaway drivers?'

Westbrook gave a shrug. 'Well I don't know about boats. That big diamond heist that fell foul of the Dome, they were going to make their getaway by the river.'

De Jersey pinched his nose in irritation. The police, he pointed out, were already on to them and, they were not making their getaway via the river. 'Anonymity is our best disguise. Just blend in with the commuters.'

De Jersey pointed to Pamela and Westbrook. 'The City Thameslink station is a five-minute walk from the safe house. You two will jump in a cab to the station. There's always a stream of them near the Barbican. You'll travel from there to Brighton. There's a train at just gone eleven, which, if all goes to plan, you will make easily. The next one is fifteen minutes later. From Brighton you are to separate. Pamela will go by train to Plymouth. Henry will return to his studio in Pimlico. De Jersey knew that the only one of them that could possibly be recognized by his high profile was Westbrook but his life expectancy was so short, De Jersey didn't feel the risk of his discovery would endanger any of them as long as Westbrook and Pamela separated.

De Jersey then pointed to Driscoll and Wilcox. 'Tony, James and I will work out the best way to get the jewels to my helicopter for the drop.' De Jersey flipped the pages on the board back to the beginning. 'Any questions?'

No one said a word. Now de Jersey turned to an enlarged copy of the safe-house layout, which he had obtained from the warehouse's estate agents. He gestured to the warehouse, which was to be their second base. 'So, we move out from here on 2 May and drive round the block. Now you all know the fundamentals and I want us to begin to break it down into sections and allocate specific roles.' De Jersey nodded to Westbrook and gestured for him to come to his side.

'Henry here will detail the line-up of the Royal party, how they behave, protocol, et cetera.'

Westbrook opened a bottle of water and drank thirstily. His pale face shone with sweat. 'The lady-in-waiting must, at all times, adhere to the Royal protocol. She will always be to the left side of the Queen, two or three paces behind, a small enough gap for Her Majesty to pass her her handbag or flowers without stretching. Seated in the car, she must sit well back and not in any way hamper the view of Her Majesty. In public, she will speak only when spoken to.'

Pamela asked a few questions about her dress, her demeanour, and whether or not she should also carry a handbag. De Jersey held up his hand. 'As we all have a lot of work to do, I suggest Henry works with Pamela, and we can get on with other things.'

Pamela and Westbrook disappeared into the main area of the barn. De Jersey took out a cigar and lit it. 'So, what do you think?'

Wilcox glanced at Driscoll then back to de Jersey. 'What about the security measures in the safe house?'

Wilcox pointed to the basic layout of the house. 'This doesn't give any information about what we're going to be facing once we're in there.'

De Jersey dismissed his concern. 'We know there'll be top-of-the-line security measures. I'd say we can handle it, though.'

'Yeah, well, saying and knowing are two different things. Christ only knows what could go wrong.'

When Westbrook had finished with Pamela, he took Driscoll through his paces as the private secretary: where he would stand and how he would behave at each step of the way. By now, Wilcox was seated in the car acting as the chauffeur. The grey uniform was slightly too large, but this would not be noticed from his position behind the wheel. Westbrook instructed him to stare ahead, never look back at the passengers and never remove his cap.

De Jersey, playing a front-line role for the first time since the early raids on his father's shops, was the bodyguard. Although the Queen usually had more than one, Westbrook agreed that as this was not a public event, they would be fine with just de Jersey. The two bikers would pose as Special Branch police officers. De Jersey would be the first to leave the safe house and it was imperative that he moved fast.

The meeting went on for four hours and by the end the strain showed in them all, apart from de Jersey, who remained energetic and alert. Westbrook looked grey, almost matching the chauffeur's uniform. He took pain-killers continually throughout the session. Eventually de Jersey called a halt and arranged a time for the next meeting. By then they should have done all the necessary shopping and any further research. He doled out cash to Pamela and Westbrook for their purchases. He agreed that Westbrook would assist Pamela in selecting the most suitable outfits for herself and for their Queen, including the correct type of handbag.

After the others had left, Wilcox and Driscoll remained behind with de Jersey and a dissection of the meeting commenced. Wilcox asked about the validity of their security information.

'For Christ's sake, James, we have the safe-house plans and they're authentic.'

'That's not good enough, Edward. I want to know *how* it's going to be done. We're risking a fucking lot out there.'

De Jersey lit another cigar. 'We walk in through the front door, James. We've discussed this.'

'Yeah, okay, so what about this other unknown quantity? This guy that's gonna give us the IRA codeword and intercept the call. We are dependent on him but we've not even met him. How can you be so sure of him and that he'll be okay on the day?'

'Marsh is an expert, not only in computers but in telephone engineering. He's done fantastic work so far, and if it weren't for him, I'd never have worked out a way to stop the Royal party without the safe house knowing. He's handling the whole technical side of the operation and it was at his request that he has no involvement in the physical side of the heist. I respect that because it's not necessary for him to take part.'

This satisfied Wilcox and Driscoll to some extent, but not completely.

'Look, Eddy,' Wilcox said, 'we've come this far and it's just odd for us not to know the full details. I dunno how Tony feels but we're putting a lot of responsibility on Marsh and also on Dulay. I think we should have had them here for a face-to-face. I mean, how much are we paying these guys?'

'I hear what you're saying but look at it from my point of view,' de Jersey said. 'I've been laying out the cash for this. I haven't asked you two for anything. If you want to know what I'm shelling out, then get out your chequebooks and we'll split it three ways and you can take over.' De Jersey picked up his black marker pen and began to write on the board. 'Right now I'm paying Westbrook, Pamela and Marsh full-time, plus a one-off to Gregory Jones and the security guy.' He listed the payments, even down to the money he intended paying Malcolm Gridley. Next he listed the fees for the helicopters and the money put aside for them to secure the speedboats. 'You calculating all this, Tony? Both of you start figuring it out 'cos I'm the one who's thousands out of pocket. Then there's the costumes, the rent for this place and for the warehouse. Too damned right I've kept quiet about a lot of things, especially what it's costing me to set up this fucking robbery! So far you two have contributed a few grand between you. You hear me complaining? *No!* You don't hear me asking for the major slice when, as you can see, I've been working morning, noon and night on this. But don't fucking thank me. Sit there and moan your arses off. The pair of you make me sick.'

Driscoll and Wilcox were stunned by the ferocity of de Jersey's anger, and by the size of the sum he had invested in the heist. An equal contribution would make a deep hole in the funds they'd salvaged from their ruined fortunes.

'You got something to say, Tony?' de Jersey asked, as he started putting away the drawing-board. He ripped up the big sheets of paper with the lists of payments and folded up the safe-house plans. He put the plans into his briefcase and tossed the other papers into a dustbin.

'You could say that.' Driscoll was agitated.

'Well, say it,' de Jersey snapped, struck a match and lit the paper.

'I'm getting serious cold feet about the whole fucking thing.'

De Jersey sat down, flicked the ash from his cigar and stared at Driscoll. 'Spit it all out now.'

'Look, Eddy, we go back a long way, but we've never had such a big core team. This Westbrook character, he was stuffing himself with pills all bleeding afternoon. Come four o'clock he was spaced out of his head and this was only the first meeting. What's he gonna be like on the day? Neither of us has met Marsh so how do we know we can trust him? How do we know he's going to pull it off?'

De Jersey turned to Wilcox. 'What about you?'

Wilcox shuffled his feet with embarrassment. 'Well, what Tony's saying is true. That Pamela woman's a flake too. Thinks she's auditioning for the National Theatre the way she's carrying on. If we come in on the expenses you're paying out, we'll be paying her a grand a week like the others, more than she's ever earned in her life I reckon.'

'She's worth it. She's going to be right in the thick of it,' de Jersey snapped.

'You say so, but how do we know she won't cave in?'

'She's as tough as they come, plus she knows the consequences if we fail. She's worth her price.'

'But, again, we only have your word and you only have the trust you've placed in them. Then you say we've got two speedboats and you've ordered four helicopters as decoys. Have you got all these extras lined up or are you just making out lists of things you're thinking about doing but haven't got round to yet? Where are we gonna get these two boats from? Then there's got to be river moorings organized. It's still all up in the air.'

De Jersey bit off the end of his cigar and spat it out.

Wilcox continued. 'We've got to be tooled up and I wouldn't trust that Westbrook character to carry a water pistol let alone a shooter. We've never used so many amateurs for a gig before.' He took a deep breath. 'It could all fall apart and then I'll be in an even worse situation than when we started. You say you've laid out for everything and you have, I can see that. But I've paid for the cars and Tony sorted out the weapons. I can't pay out any more.'

Driscoll started again. 'I'm broke from this wedding. I mean, we've been lucky in the past, we all know that, but this is stretching it to the limit. We've not even got into how we're getting the gems into France. How the hell do we do that?'

De Jersey blew a smoke ring above his head as Wilcox took over where Driscoll left off.

'And this Dulay character. You say we can trust him, but you've had to squeeze his balls to get him to agree to be part of this, and that's always dodgy. Carrying that gear out of the country is impossible. The scream will be up so loud that every airport and dock will be surrounded. I know you've worked out decoys, and I'm sorry to sound so negative, but I just don't buy it.'

'Dulay has a big yacht. I was planning to use it unless you want to use yours,' de Jersey said to Wilcox.

He was taken aback when Wilcox shouted, 'I bloody can't use mine! I had to sell it months ago. You see what I'm talking about? We're up Shit Creek on this one and you are gonna have to admit it.'

De Jersey was finding it hard to maintain his calm. 'Things will go wrong if you don't keep your cool. Dulay is picking up the jewels from the south coast. It's all taken care of.'

Wilcox bowed his head. 'All taken care of! I hope bloody Sylvia Hewitt's also taken care of. That's more cash you'll likely have to pay out to keep her quiet. So, if you've got it all planned, why the fuck don't you tell us about it and take care of our worries?'

Driscoll put up his hand, like a schoolkid. 'There's another thing, Eddy. I see what you've paid out and I know I've not come in with much, but you've never discussed what you expect to get from the sale of the jewels. Can you give us an idea?'

Wilcox interrupted: 'Hang on a minute. We're depending on Dulay for this Japanese buyer. Dulay says he's got him, but that's just his word. If he doesn't pull off the sale we're gonna be left with the hottest gear around. Nobody'll touch it, no matter what it's worth. We'll all be left with fuck all. And another thing—'

Driscoll put up his hand again. 'Have you met the buyer?'

'No,' de Jersey said, and he flushed with anger because he knew they were right. He was not being as pro-

360

fessional as he had been in the past and he was depending on Dulay and Marsh to a major extent.

'Shit, this is a mess. Admit it, Edward, it's just not working.' Wilcox heaved himself out of the worn, old armchair.

'It is, and it will work. I trust Dulay. If he says this Japanese guy is good for it, he is, and you checked him out in Paris.'

'I don't call that checking out,' snapped Wilcox. He was pacing up and down now in fury. 'All I did was tail Dulay to the Ritz and see him meet up with the guy. What they said and how far we can trust them is another matter.'

'He's agreed to pay an excellent price for the Koh-i-noor diamond alone,' de Jersey said, opening his briefcase.

'How much?' asked Driscoll.

'One million per carat. It's over a hundred carats,' de Jersey said, tight-lipped. He took out his notebook.

Driscoll's jaw dropped.

'He wants the Koh-i-noor for starters but selling the other gems will be no problem.'

'But who is this guy?' Driscoll asked.

'He's a contact of Dulay,' said de Jersey defensively.

Wilcox looked at Driscoll. 'But how can we trust Dulay? How do we know he's not going to just disappear? And now you tell us this buyer *knows* about the diamond already. Jesus Christ! We're leaving ourselves wide open. What if this fucking Jap raps to someone?'

Now it was back to Driscoll. 'He's right, Eddy. And, thinking about it, I have big worries. If the worst comes to the worst, I can sell my properties and go back to work full time. At least I'd still have something. I'm getting too old to take such risks. I'm really sorry to sound off at you this way but—'

'You want out?' de Jersey asked coldly.

'The way things are right now, yes, 'cos I just don't think we can do it. It all depends on people trusting one another and with so many parties involved we could get screwed from any angle. Right, Jimmy?'

Wilcox nodded.

'I've never let you down before.' De Jersey sounded bitter.

Wilcox gave an impatient sigh. 'We both know that. But the plan isn't right yet and all this farting around today wasn't good enough. We've not got that much time to get it together.'

De Jersey flicked the ash from his cigar. 'Fine. Walk away. I won't hold you to anything. I never did before and I won't now. That's not to say I'm not disappointed. Of course I am because I'm down a lot of cash already. You two don't want to come in and help me out, fine. But I've always made sure that whoever worked alongside me got a fair share and I'm not about to change that. The fair share is the reason we can trust the people I've brought in. It is that element of the deal that binds us all together. It worked for us in the past and it will work for us this time.'

'Come on, Eddy, we know that,' Driscoll said. 'And don't think I'm not grateful for our past deals but they were a long time ago. We were younger then, more prepared for the risks.'

Wilcox nodded. 'Yeah, I've got six kids.'

'And a habit to feed,' de Jersey snapped.

'I'm clean,' Wilcox said defensively.

'So you say.' De Jersey knew he had to steer them back on course and, worse, that without them he could never pull it off. He pointed to Driscoll. 'You think you and Wilcox here are the best I could get for this? I brought you in on this to ease my guilt for the bad investment advice I gave you. I'm not prepared to lose what I've spent the best part of my life building up. Neither do I want to lose my wife or my daughters by spending the rest of my life banged up in prison. I will ensure there's as little risk as possible for all of us. I've taken on board what you've said but when in the past did you ever know all the details and every member of the team? Never! You trusted my judgement. If you no longer trust me then get the hell out.'

Driscoll put his hands up. 'Come on now, no need for this. You said it yourself, Eddy. You said if it didn't look kosher you'd call it quits and there'd be no hard feelings.'

'What do you say, James?' de Jersey asked.

'I am not doing drugs! I've worked my arse off getting these two cars and the bikes ready. I just think the plan's not up to your usual standard, that's all. Maybe if we thrash out the details a bit more, know exactly what you've planned, we'll feel happier.'

'Come on, we've all done a good share,' Driscoll said, angrily.

'Yeah, us three have, but the computer geek is getting a grand a week and a big cut!' Wilcox was still in a rage.

De Jersey stood up, his military bearing intimidating. 'You two are getting greedy. Raymond Marsh is not going to betray us. He's already in too deep. He's hacked into the private Royal diaries, intercepted Scotland Yard calls and made sure there won't be any links between him and me when this is all over.'

Wilcox sucked in his breath. 'Leaving yourself out in the open, aren't you? You may be using Philip Simmons as a cover but something this big will have every cop in the UK after you.'

'It's more than a cover,' de Jersey interjected brusquely. 'In cyberspace, Philip Simmons is almost as good as flesh and blood. As soon as this is over he disappears into thin air and all the leads and clues disappear with him. There is no connection back to me because Philip Simmons organized the whole thing.'

Neither man understood what he was talking about, but his confidence in the alias was a bonus. After all, de Jersey himself was a direct link to both of them.

De Jersey continued, 'Marsh is worth every cent we pay him because we couldn't pull this off without him. He's a genius.'

Wilcox and Driscoll fell silent. Then De Jersey's bravado slipped. He gave a long sigh. 'All I can say is this, I'm not just protecting myself. I have to look out for all of you. I've been working on how all of us move out when the scream goes up, just as I always did in the past. It takes time and planning down to the last second. If there are loopholes then we have to rethink, or I do. So, ask me what you need to know.' He picked up the black marker pen and crossed to the board. 'List every loophole. We'll go through them one at a time.'

Driscoll rested his head in his hands. Wilcox slumped into the old chair. 'I can't fucking think straight now.'

De Jersey looked from one to the other. He tossed aside the marker pen. 'Sleep on it, then, but I need to know what the two of you decide by tomorrow.' He picked up his briefcase, took out the CD and opened his laptop.

'Take a look at this. When you're through close it down and remove the CD. Don't let it out of your sight. This is for our eyes only.' He snapped his briefcase shut and collected his coat. 'Goodnight.' A moment later they heard the side-door slam shut.

Both men remained silent for quite a while. Eventually Wilcox stood up. 'Did you tell him I had a drug problem?'

'No way!'

'Did you understand any of that stuff about the alias?'

'Nope, but he seemed to and that's what counts.'

Wilcox got up to look at de Jersey's laptop. Driscoll followed him and pushed in the CD.

'Fuck me!' he exclaimed. 'Look at the screen, Jimmy.' He pointed to the interactive floor plan of the D'Ancona safe house that had come up.

They sat close to the small screen, taking the virtual tour through the safe-house rooms. When it ended Driscoll pressed eject and took out the CD. 'Jesus Christ, do you know what we just watched?' They looked at each other and knew without saying it that they were back on board for the heist.

'Let's go for it! All or nothing!' Wilcox said.

'Yeah, give it our best shot. If we go down at least we'll be famous. This is gonna be the biggest robbery in history, right?' Driscoll was now determined to see the positive side.

Wilcox laughed. 'Just one thing. You don't have any sort of moral issue over this, do you? I mean, they are the Crown Jewels and breaking them up is sort of—'

'Unpatriotic?' Driscoll laughed. 'Fuck 'em! The Royals have had 'em long enough.' He clapped Wilcox on the shoulder and the two of them packed up and left.

In the darkness, inside the main part of the barn, de Jersey moved silently from behind the screens. Neither man had seen or heard him return to listen to their conversation. He sat down in the armchair and went through every second of the meeting, listing every gripe that had been raised. Each was valid; they were still a long way off. Could he trust Marsh? So much depended on him. He sighed. Bottom line, he could trust no one involved completely, but that was the risk in this game. He must check out the Japanese buyer for himself and contact Sylvia Hewitt to make sure she was behaving. It irritated him that he had promised to pay her off but it would be worth his while to keep her silent.

David Lyons was still in Sylvia's thoughts and her sister was still living with her. Helen had recovered somewhat from the trauma of losing her husband but she wanted to talk about David all the time. Some nights Sylvia didn't want to return home, and wished Helen would find her own place to live, but she had to respect her sister's grief and need for companionship.

On the day de Jersey had brought together the key team, Sylvia had just got home, later than usual as she had dined with a client.

'I'm in here,' came Helen's high-pitched voice. She sounded angry.

Sylvia felt annoyed that her sister would undoubtedly ask her where she had been until so late. 'Give me a minute,' she called back, and took off her coat. She hadn't had time to hang it up before Helen marched out of the drawing room carrying a bundle of photographs. 'I wasn't prying. I was looking for a needle. I knew you used to keep a sewing kit in your bedside-table drawer. Explain.' Helen thrust the pictures at her. One photograph showed Sylvia and David kissing.

'Oh, it was some office party,' Sylvia said lamely.

'No, it wasn't. How do you explain the beach and palm trees? What was going on between you and my husband?'

'He's dead, Helen. What does it matter now?'

'It matters to me. I want to know the truth. Look at me, Sylvia. Tell me what was going on.'

'Oh, for God's sake Helen, it's obvious, isn't it?'

'No, it isn't. I want you to tell me.'

Sylvia sighed. 'I never wanted to hurt you.'

'Tell me what was going on between you and my husband!' Helen shrieked.

'We were lovers,' Sylvia said at last. It all came out: how long it had gone on, all the times they had been together. She felt wretched as she blurted it out, and so sorry for Helen that she burst into tears.

'Sylvia, you disgust me. My own sister!'

Helen walked into her bedroom and shut the door.

The following morning Sylvia tried to speak to Helen again, but she remained in her locked room. When she returned that evening, two suitcases stood in the hall and Helen's coat lay over them. She was waiting, her face drawn and chalk white. 'I'm leaving. I can't talk about it. I don't know if I ever want to speak to you again. I trusted you, and you went behind my back and took the only thing in my life I have ever felt proud of. My marriage is now just some terrible sham, and you are despicable for letting me stay here with you. I was pleased to have you at my side at his funeral and now I discover that all the time you've been lying to me.'

'Did you really want me to tell you the truth? How would it have made a difference, you knowing once he was dead? You certainly never suspected when he was alive. And I let him use all my savings and he lost the lot! So much for good, dependable, honest David. He was a fool!'

'I don't believe you.'

'I'm telling you the truth. I've lost over two hundred thousand, all my savings. That's something else I didn't tell you because I didn't want you to worry. Whatever happened between me and David is history now and—'

Helen didn't wait to hear any more. She picked up her coat and her suitcases and made for the door. She glanced back at her sister and delivered a parting shot. 'That explains the real reason why he went with you. He was using you for your money.' With that, Helen slammed the door.

Sylvia was incensed by Helen's insult, which also reminded her of Edward de Jersey's accusation. How dare de Jersey suggest she had been involved with David's frauds? She walked around the flat kicking the furniture, feeling impotent and lonely. Her bedroom was littered with torn photographs of her and David together. She picked them up, then let them fall from her hands like confetti and started to cry. She had loved David and now she had lost everything, lover, money, sister. She wondered what had happened to de Jersey, whether or not he had held on to his estate. It had been weeks since she had spoken to him.

The phone rang and she picked it up. 'Hello.'

'Is this Sylvia Hewitt?'

'Speaking.'

'This is Victor Matheson, Miss Hewitt, the private detective you hired. Remember me?'

'Yes, of course.' She was puzzled: she'd told him his services were no longer required.

'A strange coincidence has just happened. I think it would be worth us meeting up.'

Sylvia listened as Matheson explained that he had met another private investigator and discovered that he had been hired to trace Alex Moreno by Philip Simmons. 'I have to arrange time off from work,' she told him, 'but it shouldn't be a problem. I'll fly out as soon as I can and meet you in New York.'

'Good.' He hung up.

She gave no thought to the fact that she had promised de Jersey she would not take her enquiries any further. In fact, she was determined to prove that David Lyons did not commit any fraud. She called her boss and told him that urgent family business had cropped up and that she needed to take the week off work.

De Jersey outlined 'rehearsal' days for the team to meet at the barn. They had moved another step closer to the plans being completed. Driscoll had booked 'the Queen' for the morning of the heist. She was to be collected at eight a.m. for a day's commercial shoot. The agent did not query the name of the TV company but seemed more interested in the fee their client would receive, which was substantially more than usual.

Far from being a big risk, Westbrook proved invaluable. He was sick and getting worse by the day but he remained in good humour and the team admired his determination. Pamela was highly professional and a constant source of humorous stories during coffee-breaks. She provided cakes and biscuits for the team, too, which they always devoured hungrily. She was having a wonderful time. She had always enjoyed the company of men and it was a long time since she had been surrounded by so many. She adored Westbrook, and they swapped stories about their time in the nick while smoking their way through packets of cigarettes, their conversation interspersed with coughing fits and shrieks of laughter.

De Jersey rarely joined in the banter. He was constantly checking his notes and plans. Dulay's boat was now set to anchor six miles off the south coast, near Brighton. The diversion helicopters were booked and false pick-up points agreed. De Jersey had arranged for one of his horses to be at the Brighton racetrack on the day of the raid. He had also marked in blue crosses on the floor of the barn the positions of the panic buttons in the safe house, taken from information on the CD. Every one of the team was made to learn their exact locations.

'Darling, just a small point,' Pamela said one day, cigarette dangling out of her mouth. 'We know where these thingies are, and we need eyes in the back of our heads, but what if one of the D'Ancona employees throws caution to the wind and stamps on one? Will we get out fast enough before the police show up?'

'What?'

'Well, darling, do we know how long we've got if

someone inadvertently or deliberately steps on one? There's going to be an awful lot of anxiety and . . .' she hopped from one blue cross to another . . . 'they're all over the place.'

De Jersey gave her a dismissive glance. 'Hopefully we'll have discovered a way to deactivate them. In the meantime, however, we should know exactly where they're located.'

'Yes, but do you know how long it takes for the boys in blue to arrive if one goes off?'

'Pamela, why don't you put the kettle on?' De Jersey crossed to Wilcox.

He kept his voice low. 'We hit one and the lot of us will be in trouble. Steel trap-doors come down like a guillotine.'

Wilcox turned away. 'So, we've got to deactivate the buggers.'

'I'll work on it.'

The two bikers were scheduled to arrive that afternoon and de Jersey wanted everyone out of the way except Driscoll, who knew them. Brian Hall arrived first. He parked his motorbike as instructed in the yard at the back of the barn. Kenny Short turned up in an old Mini five minutes later.

De Jersey had watched them arrive and was ready for them. He opened the door almost immediately and handed them pairs of surgical gloves. The two men followed him towards the table and he gestured for them to sit. Driscoll sat to one side. De Jersey took the two men through their duties and the getaway details. They listened attentively, asking relevant questions to which de

Jersey always had answers. They knew the risks they were taking, but the authoritative manner of the Colonel eased their fears and after the instructions were clarified both men tried on their uniforms and tested the bikes. If they had any doubts they did not voice them. They knew that they were joining a well-schooled team.

De Jersey took pains to ensure that the two men realized their importance. They were all dependent on each other to pull it off, he told them. Every one of them was an essential part of the heist and one mistake could bring the rest down. When the two men left, de Jersey turned to Driscoll. 'What do you think?'

'They'll do the business. It's just his lordship we've got to watch out for. He's very jittery and well drugged up.'

'I know. If he gets to be too much of a liability we might have to lose him.'

Driscoll licked his lips and changed the subject. 'What about deactivating those panic buttons?'

'Working on it.'

'Want to look over the guns?'

They had been under pressure for a considerable time now so de Jersey suggested they all take a few days' break. Christina was expected back from Sweden, and he was worn out, but they all needed time to recharge their batteries. Then they could stand back and review the plan for any weak spots they had missed.

De Jersey returned to the estate but although he needed a rest he didn't take one. Work at the estate needed his supervision for although his staff worked diligently when he was absent, some issues had to be solved by the Boss. There was a stack of paperwork that needed his attention, but the financial pressure was uppermost. He wondered if he could sell the Moreno house yet. He was still in the office after midnight when Fleming tapped and entered.

'Brandy?' de Jersey asked.

Fleming shook his head. 'You owe me the cash we agreed on,' he said softly, not meeting de Jersey's eyes.

There was a long pause. De Jersey unscrewed the top from the brandy bottle, opened a drawer and took out a glass.

'My son and an old lad helped me out. They're both trustworthy. My son won't say anything and if the lad had a notion of what we were up to he didn't let on. I gave him a couple hundred quid.'

De Jersey gulped the brandy. 'How did my boy do?'

'Fine. So now we wait. I've put him in the far stall. We'll push his training up and see how he behaves, but we've risked a hell of a lot.'

'I know.' De Jersey was hardly able to speak.

Fleming changed his mind about the brandy and the two men sat drinking quietly. They were both ashamed of the subterfuge and were worried that they might have damaged Royal Flush's concentration and thus his chance of winning the biggest race of his life. Eventually Fleming stood up and buttoned his coat. He nodded to the racing diary displayed on the office wall. 'We'll see what effect it's had when he races at Lingfield.'

Two days later Christina arrived home and he took her in his arms. 'I've missed you so much,' she said, as they hugged.

'I've missed you, too, darling. Let me carry your cases upstairs.'

'No, they can wait but I can't. Let's just go upstairs,' she said coyly.

He smiled. 'Whatever you say.'

'How's everything been?' she asked.

'Not too bad. I've had to sell a few more horses but Royal Flush is in great shape. It's been very quiet here without you,' he said.

'It's such a comfort to be back here with you. This place is so precious to me,' Christina said. If he pulled off the heist they would continue to live at the estate. If he failed, he would spend the rest of his life in jail.

De Jersey didn't reply as he followed her up the stairs. So much was riding on him pulling off the heist.

CHAPTER 19

SYLVIA HAD taken a taxi straight from JFK airport to the Intercontinental Hotel because of its close proximity to Central Park and easy walking distance to Moreno's apartment block. She had decided that since she had time to kill before her appointment with Matheson, she would do some research of her own. She'd taken Matheson off the case before he had had a chance to check out Moreno's apartment. Maybe she could discover something there that might help them. She had slept badly on the plane so she decided to have a nap until midday, but she was still sound asleep when the chambermaid woke her at three. She showered and changed and eventually left the hotel at four.

The doorman at Moreno's apartment was none too friendly until Sylvia slipped him twenty dollars. Then he told her he remembered Moreno well, a pleasant enough man, but he'd kept to himself.

'Did he warn you that he was leaving?'

'No. One minute he lived here, the next he didn't.'

'But did you see him leave?'

'No. He might have gone when I wasn't on duty. All I know is, the apartment changed hands. You need to talk to the agents. They handle the leases. The guy living there now is German but I don't see much of him either.'

'Is he at home?'

'No. Leaves early, comes back late. Days can go by and I don't see him but he uses a limo company.' He passed her a card. 'They're good. I know one of the drivers. Mr Goldberg is a regular customer, like I said.'

'You've been most helpful but I really did need to speak to Mr Moreno. It looks like I'm out of luck, though.'

'Afraid so.'

'Thank you.'

'Have a nice evening.' He hovered for another twenty dollars but she drew her collar up around her face and walked off.

She had gone no more than twenty yards when she saw a limousine draw up. An immaculate gentleman climbed out of the back seat. He was wearing dark glasses and carried a slim briefcase. As he headed into the apartments she hurried after him. 'Mr Goldberg! Excuse me.' He turned and stared at her. 'I wonder if I could possibly have a few moments of your time?'

'Do I know you?'

'I'm trying to trace Mr Moreno. He lived in your apartment before you.'

'I'm sorry I cannot help. I did not know him. He has nothing to do with me. Excuse me.'

'Please – if I could just ask you a few things?' she persisted.

'I did not know Mr Moreno. If you want any details about him I suggest you contact the agents for the property. Excuse me.'

She stood helplessly as the door swung closed after

him and the doorman took up his position outside again. 'If you want the agents, they've got an office in the next block up across 86th Street. Dugdale and Martin. Mr Dugdale handles this place.' Sylvia handed him another twenty-dollar bill, and headed for the Gothic-style block he had indicated.

Dugdale and Martin had a small office on the ground floor of the plush apartment block. The thickset doorman said he thought she might be too late: their office closed at four thirty. He hovered at her side as she tapped on the door and waited. She was about to walk away when it opened.

'Good evening, my name is Sylvia Hewitt. I wondered if I could speak to someone concerning Mr Moreno's apartment?'

'He's no longer a tenant there,' said a stern, grey-haired man.

'Yes, I know, but perhaps I could tell you my reasons for contacting you. I've come all the way from England.'

'Come in.' He opened the door wider. He was already wearing his overcoat. 'I'm off home, Jacob. Can I leave this with you?' he said to another man, then walked out and closed the door.

Sylvia took out one of her business cards as the man at the window turned. 'Sylvia Hewitt. I'm an accountant. I'm enquiring about a Mr Moreno who lived in—'

'Come in and sit down. I'm Jacob Martin. So, you are Mr Moreno's accountant?' he asked.

'No,' she said. 'He had various interests in London but I've not been able to contact him since before Christmas.'

'Well, he just disappeared, and we have no forwarding address.'

'But you must have arranged the change-over of his apartment. There's a new owner, a German gentleman.'

'Yes, he purchased the lease.'

'From you?'

'Yes, we handle the property, but we did the transaction with a solicitor acting on behalf of Mr Moreno. All the documents were in order so we had no reason to query the sale.'

'So Mr Moreno never discussed leaving the apartment with you?'

'No. He left without notice but that's not unusual. The only thing unusual was . . .' He hesitated. Sylvia waited. 'He left a lot of personal items, which we removed before the next tenant moved in. He seemed to have departed in quite a hurry.'

'Can you tell me what he left?'

'Clothing, stuff like that. We kept it weeks in storage. The new owner bought all the furniture and fittings.'

'He just bought everything?'

'Well, not everything. There were items like videos, books. He didn't want those.'

'Who took all that?'

Martin gave an embarrassed shrug. There had actually been a hell of a lot that Mr Goldberg had not purchased: the paintings, mirrors, ornaments and so on. But after keeping them in storage for a short while Martin and Dugdale had done a little filching for themselves. In fact, they had stripped the place of anything remotely valuable. Sylvia suspected this but that was not why she was there. 'Do you have the name of the solicitor who handled the transactions?' she asked.

Martin walked to a cabinet, flicked through a row of files and withdrew the one with Moreno's apartment number written on the front. 'Mr Philip Simmons. We have a phone number and . . .' he turned a page . . . 'just a box number, which is unusual, and a further contact number for an address in the Hamptons.'

'Could you give me the number? I really would like to speak to him.'

Martin took one of his cards, copied down the number and passed it to Sylvia. Then he walked back to the cabinet, still reading the file. He paused, frowning and turning pages. 'I doubt you'll have much luck. Seems we've attempted to contact him as various maintenance charges were left unpaid and we wanted to get the accounts settled. It was not a large amount but our letters went unanswered.' He rested his elbow on top of the filing cabinet.

'Did you meet the solicitor?'

'No, I didn't. This was all handled by the boss, Mr Dugdale. You saw him as you left . . . Ah, forgive me, I did meet him just once, when he came to sign over the lease to Mr Goldberg. He went into Mr Dugdale's office.'

'Could you describe him?'

'He was well dressed, elegant, I'd say, and tall. A big man, much taller than me and I'm almost six feet. He had reddish hair, and a moustache.'

Sylvia stood up and shook his hand. 'Thank you so much for your time. I really do appreciate it.'

After he had shown Sylvia out, Martin returned to the filing cabinet and sifted through all the papers they had acquired since Moreno's departure. There had been a visit from the New York State Police, who had found Moreno's car at JFK. They surmised he had skipped the country after getting into financial straits in his business. The outer door opened and Dugdale walked in. 'Left some papers I need. Everything okay?' he asked.

'I think so. That woman was trying to trace Moreno.'

'Well, she'll have a hard time. We couldn't.'

'So I notice. And his solicitor's a bit odd. You know we only have a box number for him?'

'There was nothing illegal about the transaction.'

'Sure, but what did you make of the guy? Was he working for Moreno?'

'I guess so. We got him a good price and Mr Goldberg paid in cash.'

'Did he?' Martin whistled.

Dugdale walked into his office and Martin followed. 'What was he like?'

'Pleasant enough. Eager to leave New York. Probably carrying out the cash for Mr Moreno. Said he was Canadian.' Dugdale put an envelope into his briefcase, closed it and headed out of his office.

Martin trailed behind him. 'The doorman at the apartment still gets mail addressed to Moreno.'

Dugdale sighed, irritated. 'Look, Jacob, I have enough to do without worrying about the whereabouts of one of our former tenants. He is no longer our problem. I suggest we toss his file and get rid of anything still left in storage. That's the end of it. Goodnight.'

Martin collected the keys to lock up and turned off the lights. He was annoyed. He knew Dugdale had arranged the cash deal between Goldberg and this Simmons guy and he had a good idea that Dugdale had got a nice bonus out of the transaction. He wondered how much. It would have been substantial and he hadn't had his usual cut.

Sylvia returned to her hotel and called the number for Simmons. As she expected, it was no longer in use. Later she called Matheson, who agreed to meet her in the hotel bar at nine. She asked what he looked like.

'I'm small, nothing special. I'll have a big red and black scarf round my neck, glasses and thinning hair.'

'I'm dark-haired and I'm wearing a tweed suit with a white blouse and pearls,' she said primly.

Sylvia entered the reasonably full bar, and peered around until she spotted the investigator. Then she threaded her way through the low tables to join him. 'How do you do?'

'Miss Hewitt, it's nice to put a face to the voice. Can I get you a drink?'

'White wine, please.'

He signalled to a waiter as she sat down on one of the low seats opposite him. The man came over and he ordered a beer for himself and a chilled Chablis for her.

'It's so noisy here,' Sylvia said. 'They even have music in the lifts.'

'You get used to it,' he said, and drew his chair closer to her. 'Can I just get something straight? I mean, I don't wanna sound pushy, but this is my livelihood and I'll charge my hourly rate for tonight's meeting. How's that suit you?'

She nodded. 'Fine.'

He sat back as the waiter put down a bowl of nuts and their drinks. She raised her glass and sipped the chilled wine. 'Well, I'm here, Mr Matheson. You did say you had some developments and I've come a long way to hear them in person, as you suggested.'

'Like I said on the phone, I met up with an old friend. I want you to know straight up, I wasn't being unethical in discussing your business with him. It just came up in conversation. I never mentioned your name.'

'Who is he?'

'An ex-cop, like me, from way back. He's about the same age, works mostly on security now. Been on tour with this rock group. In fact, he's with them now.'

'What's his name?'

'Donny Baron. Nice guy. He says to me that he's fed up with schlepping all over the country. I ask him if he's doing any private work and he says he had an interesting gig a few months ago. He ran an ad in the *New York Times* and this guy made contact, wanted him to do a bit of ducking and diving around town, checking out a guy that had done a little Internet fraud and I said to him, "That's a coincidence. Guy's not called Moreno, is he?" So he looks at me and he laughs and says he is. Said he'd been checking out Moreno's apartment for his client.'

'When was this?'

'Just after Christmas. So I ask him about his client and he tells me he was a Canadian, flew from Los Angeles on the red-eye. Paid him a nice whack and that was it.'

'Did he say what this man's name was?'

'Well, he was a bit edgy about that but in the end he said it was Philip Simmons. Same guy we discovered. Donny's met him.'

'So he was an investor?'

'Could have been. He's obviously more than just Moreno's financial adviser. I mean, if he was Moreno's financial adviser why did he need to hire Donny to find him? He would have known where to find him, right?'

Sylvia sipped her wine again then placed it carefully on the table. 'He's been posing as his solicitor too.'

'Really? Well, Donny told me that this guy's accent was strange, said he sounded more like a Brit, so that was why I contacted you. The contractor in the Hamptons, he said he thought he was Canadian. There's obviously something dodgy going on with this guy.'

Sylvia sighed. 'I was a small investor in Moreno's company. I was told not to interfere by someone who had lost a considerable amount more than myself. In fact, three people I know of lost millions and they all said they were handling it. They also refused to help me pay your wages. I thought that when I told them about your investigation they would have been eager for you to continue, but they weren't.'

'Maybe they're getting a cut from Simmons. Who knows what's going on? I just reckoned you'd want to know about him cropping up again.' He toyed with his empty beer glass. 'I reckon you should go out to the Hamptons, like I said when I called, and check it out.'

'How far is it?'

'Train would be about two hours. If you drive it's around the same, but out of season there won't be much traffic. I can go out there with you if you want me to.' Matheson was pushing to be rehired, but Sylvia was not prepared to pay out any more than she had to.

'I'll go alone tomorrow.'

Matheson had reckoned she would want him along and he needed the money. 'You mind if I say something?

This Philip Simmons is, by my reckoning, somebody you should tread carefully with. If, as you say, that property in the Hamptons is worth millions, he might just have . . .' He took a deep breath.

'What?'

'Murdered for it.'

She was not taken aback. Quite the contrary, she was very calm. She leaned forward and conspiratorially lowered her voice. 'I thought about that, even more so if he lost his savings. It's a strong motive.' The wine was making her feel giddy. 'I feel like throttling him myself,' she said.

'Yeah, well, feeling like doing something and actually doing it are two different things. This guy, whoever he is, feels like a real pro to me. He's covered his tracks too well not to be.'

She beamed and gripped his shoulder. 'But he *has* made mistakes. We can report this to the police and they can look for him. Or perhaps we can find this man, put pressure on him, and then I'm sure he'll pay us off. That's all I am interested in now, Mr Matheson. I want my money back.'

'You lost a lot, huh?'

'Yes, I lost my lover because Moreno used him. He took his own life because he couldn't face what he had done. Moreno lost my life savings and I intend on getting them or part of them back. And after what you have told me, I think there's a possibility of doing so.' She hesitated. 'I've not been able to discover if Philip Simmons was an investor. His name isn't on any of the documents I have, but he may have been investing in Moreno's company through someone else. There's something else I need to ask you, Mr Matheson.

384

During your enquiries, did you ever come across a David Lyons?'

'I don't think so. Was he in on this Internet deal? Did he lose out too?'

'He lost out completely. He committed suicide. He was very dear to me.'

'He couldn't take the loss, huh?'

'No, he couldn't, but he was also responsible for encouraging people to invest with Moreno. He lost his own savings and a lot of other people's as well.'

'I see,' Matheson said.

'He was my sister's husband.' She had tears in her eyes.

'Oh dear. Tragic all round,' he said.

'It was implied that he might have been involved in some kind of fraud with Moreno but I know he wasn't.' She took out a tissue and blew her nose. 'I'm sorry.' She picked up her handbag, took out a wad of cash and paid what she owed him.

'I've got one final invoice for you covering some miscellaneous expenses, but I forgot to bring it with me,' he said.

'Send it to me in London.'

'Good luck, Ms Hewitt. I hope you find him.'

'I will,' she said softly, and left the bar.

When she got back to her room, Sylvia was exhausted but she sat down at the desk and added up how much she had paid Matheson. At least she had made progress. It was looking more and more as if Simmons, whether acting for Moreno or one of the investors, was collecting a lot of money, and she felt that at least some of it should be hers. Could it be possible that Simmons had killed Moreno for the money invested in his properties? Certainly Simmons was not all he seemed. He had asked Donny Baron to check out Moreno's apartment: why would a financial adviser use a PI to keep tabs on his own client? It didn't make sense.

Sylvia sighed and gathered her papers together. She opened her briefcase to put them away and saw inside a photo of herself and David at a Christmas party. She pulled it out. 'It was you who got me into this mess,' she said to David's smiling face. It was a group shot, but it was the only one she had of her lover now, Helen had destroyed all the others. As she looked at it, something caught her eye. One man in the shot stood head and shoulders above the rest. Edward de Jersey. The estate agent's and Matheson's words suddenly flooded back to her. 'A big man . . . sounded more like a Brit . . .' Now if one man had lost out in the fall of leadingleisurewear, thought Sylvia, it was Edward de Jersey. Could he and Philip Simmons be the same person? The more she thought about it the more convinced she became. She felt like a cat with the cream. She had to think carefully about how to handle Mr Big Cheese de Jersey. She could go one of two ways: either expose him, or push him for a very large pay-off, a lot more than she had lost in her investment. But first she needed proof.

Early the following morning Sylvia checked out and caught the Jitney bus to East Hampton where she checked in to the elegant Maidstone Arms. This was where Moreno had stayed and she could see why: it was a charming, elegant hotel with blazing log fires in the stylish public rooms.

After unpacking, she went down to the desk and asked to speak to the manager. He was charming too but not very helpful. Moreno had been there numerous times, he said, but he had no idea of his present whereabouts. Sylvia had coffee in a long room overlooking the street, and located Moreno's property on the hotel's street map. Later she hired a taxi and asked to be driven around Georgica. To her annoyance she'd lost the piece of paper with the exact address on it that Matheson had given her the night before. All she knew was that it was a large piece of land not far from the ponds and under construction. The taxi driver was chatty, but Sylvia lost interest in what he was saying when they passed a large fenced property with construction in progress. 'Could we drive in there?' she asked.

He reversed and they passed the open drive, still not paved and muddy with tracks from the construction vehicles. They splashed and jolted along until the path widened and she could see the substantial house. It was almost as large as the Maidstone Arms with a porch, gables and massive pillars positioned at intervals along what would become a wide south-facing veranda. It was raised high on the crest of a hill, overlooking a pond with willow trees trailing on the banks. There was an Olympic-sized swimming pool, covered with a dark green tarpaulin to protect it from the debris that littered the site, and a newly constructed pool-house with a white stone patio. Then she saw the large Portakabin with the construction company's name written across it. 'I won't be a moment,' she said, and got out.

'Excuse me. Could I see the person in charge?' she called, as she approached the open Portakabin door.

A burly man carrying a hard-hat filled the small doorway. 'Who do you want?'

'Whoever's in charge,' she said sweetly.

'Can I ask what it's about? He's busy.'

'I'm a friend of the owner and I just wondered, as I'm here, if I could be shown over the house. I'm from England,' she added.

He disappeared, then returned and beckoned her inside.

'I'm the foreman,' said a ruddy-faced man, who was sitting behind a desk.

'I'm Sylvia Hewitt, and I wondered if I could speak to whoever is in charge.'

Sylvia waited in the cramped office as the men cleared up plans and went outside. The foreman said he would see if Mr Donnelly was around. Ten minutes later Donnelly came in. 'You wanted to see me?'

'I would really appreciate it if you could answer some questions for me.'

'What about?'

Sylvia took a deep breath. 'I believe a Mr Moreno owns this property and I'm eager to speak to him.'

'Well, I can't help you. We never see him now. Our only dealings with him are through his financial adviser.'

'Oh. I'll be honest with you,' she said, 'Mr Moreno owes me a substantial amount of money. I was told he might be here. I've been trying to make contact with him.'

'Aha,' he said slowly, eyeing her up and down.

'I even hired a private detective. I think he might have spoken to you, a Mr Matheson.'

'Yeah, but I told him what I'm telling you. I don't know where he is. He almost left me in a real hole, too. He couldn't make the payments, but it was settled in the end by his financial adviser.'

'Philip Simmons?' she asked.

'That's right. He's running the show. I get his orders from his architect and designers. They come down and check everything's to their specifications.'

'Do you have a contact number for Mr Simmons?'

The number he passed over was a local one for a firm of solicitors in East Hampton. When she asked to be shown around he said it was not possible.

'Did you ever meet someone called David Lyons?'

'Who?'

'David Lyons was a business associate of Alex Moreno's and I wondered if you had ever met him here. Small, dark-haired, balding.'

'I don't think so.'

'If I showed you a photograph perhaps that would help. Would you mind? It will only take a minute.'

She took it out and passed it to Donnelly. She pointed to David Lyons. 'That's him.'

He stared at the photograph, shook his head, and was about to pass it back when Sylvia stopped him. 'Is that Philip Simmons with him? Just to the right of the picture.' She pointed to de Jersey.

Donnelly stared at the picture. 'It sort of looks like him. I dunno. Could be him.'

'But you're not certain? Please, look at it closely. Is that Philip Simmons?' Her heart was pounding.

Donnelly stared at the photograph, then handed it back. 'Like I said, it could be but it's hard to tell. Mr Simmons has a moustache and red hair.'

389

'But you do think it looks like him?'

'Yes, sort of. What is all this about? Why are you here?'

She stood up, rather flustered. 'I'm trying to trace Mr Simmons.'

'Then I suggest you talk to his solicitors. I gave you their number.' He was obviously impatient for her to leave.

Sylvia walked out of the Portakabin, then decided to take matters into her own hands. She wanted to check out the property and if anyone asked she would say she was just another English tourist. She inched back over the wooden planks then on to the path to walk up to the house. She made her way to the pool-house and peered inside. A white marble floor had already been laid and ornate light fittings were being hung. A boy with paint-stained dungarees passed her. 'Hi there,' he said affably.

'This is going to be very nice.'

'Yeah, it sure is. That marble was shipped in from Italy and one of those lights cost more than my year's salary.' He grinned.

'It's a very large swimming-pool,' she said.

'Yeah, it's one of the first things that was done out here. One end's more than ten feet. Diving-board's gonna go at that end and over there they're gonna lay a tennis court.'

Sylvia thanked him and headed for the guesthouse. She peered inside. It looked fit for Royalty. Then she returned to the cab.

She had lunch in the hotel dining room. Her waiter was a young, rather handsome boy with dark slanting eyes.

He suggested the eggs Benedict, which were a speciality of the house and served with home-cured ham. They were wonderful and after she had finished he asked if she had enjoyed it. 'Delicious, thank you.'

She decided to take a chance. 'I wonder if you can help me. I'm trying to find someone who used to stay at this hotel, a friend. I'm desperate to get in touch with him. His name is Alex Moreno.' She looked at him directly. 'Did you ever meet him?'

'I met him,' he said softly.

Sylvia flushed. Could she have struck lucky? 'Oh, great! I can see you're busy now but could we talk later?'

'I'm off duty at two thirty, unless we get busy.' He stepped back.

'I'm in room—'

He shook his head. 'Staff are not allowed to go into guests' rooms, invited or not. House rules. I'll be in the hotel parking lot at two thirty.'

'What's your name?' she asked.

'Ricky.' He walked away but turned back briefly and gave her a dazzling smile.

Sylvia went to the coffee area where she ordered a cappuccino, disappointed that Donnelly had not identified Simmons and de Jersey as the same man. She wondered if she was being foolish. Then from the window, at two fifteen she saw Ricky leave the hotel and meet a blond man on the pavement. They talked for a few moments, then walked out of sight. Promptly at two thirty she went into the hotel car park. It was almost empty, with no more than seven parked vehicles. A black soft-topped jeep headed towards her. The blond she had seen talking to Ricky was driving and Ricky was sitting in the small back seat.

'Hi, you want to hop in?' he said. 'We can drive to the beach.' He was tanned with white teeth, bluer than blue eyes and a whiter than white cap-sleeved T-shirt.

Sylvia climbed into the passenger seat.

'I'm Brian,' said the driver. 'What's your name?'

'Sylvia,' she said, wondering if this was a wise move. 'Where are we going?' she asked nervously.

'Just to the beach. You want to talk, right?' All the way there, Brian chatted like a tour guide while Ricky remained silent in the back seat.

When they arrived, Brian helped her out and suggested they take a walk. Sylvia looked at Ricky, who remained in the back seat. 'Aren't you coming?' she asked.

'It's not me you need to talk to.' He nodded to Brian, who was putting on a leather jacket.

Sylvia walked beside him. The wind was bitingly cold so she pushed her hands into her coat pockets.

'So, is there some cash in this for me?' he asked, staring ahead, not looking at her.

'Well, I hadn't anticipated paying anyone but I can go a couple of hundred. I don't know what you know that might help me.'

'Maybe something, maybe nothing.' He hunched his shoulders against the wind.

'You met Moreno?'

He nodded, and they walked in silence. After a moment she said she needed to know what he could tell her before she agreed to pay him.

He stopped. 'Say five hundred?'

Sylvia sighed. She was really cold now. 'Okay, but it's got to be worth it.'

'Cash?'

'Yes,' she said sharply.

They walked on, and he turned towards some sand dunes. She followed him, and as they reached them he ducked down and jumped into a hollow. 'Out of the wind here,' he said, and sat down.

Sylvia joined him. 'So, what do you know about Alex Moreno?'

Brian held out his hand. She opened her purse and counted out five hundred dollars. He pocketed them. 'He was a real sharp dresser, designer labels, down to his socks. Never wore anything but the purest cashmere sweaters.' She had not paid out five hundred bucks for a clothing catalogue but she said nothing. 'I used to meet him when he came down looking for property over the summer. He always ended up at a place called the Swamp, real late, always alone. Sometimes he'd have way too much to drink. He liked the odd joint too, always asking around if anyone had any grass. I guess he was down there maybe four or five times over a few months and then one night, it would be about the sixth time I'd seen him, he said he was celebrating and did I want to have a drink with him. I said yeah. We both worked there, you see, me and Ricky. That's how we met. Anyway, Moreno was sitting up at the bar and he'd had a few already. He said he wanted to get blown so after we closed he was waiting with his flash new Lexus. We went back to his hotel. He was drunk and he told me he'd done this great deal, bought some property and got all the building permits agreed. He said it had taken months.'

'When was this?'

'Oh, around July, maybe mid-August. Next time I met up with him would have been around mid-November. Ricky tipped me off that he was in town. He was staying at the Maidstone. I got a call from him. He wanted to see me so I met up with him at the Blue Parrot – it's a bar on Main Street. We had a few drinks and went back to his hotel room. We were on the bed when he starts crying. He tells me he's got into real trouble financially. He rambled on and on, blubbering like a kid about how it was all falling apart. Then he passed out. I took my money and left. I could have taken a lot more but I reckoned he was the type to cause trouble.'

'When was the last time you saw him?'

'Okay, this would be just after Christmas and he came in real late. We met up again in the bar. He looked beat, needed a shave, but was all cashmered-up as usual.'

'December?'

'Yeah, said he'd come to sort out his property. He was having a hard time meeting payments. I thought he was just trying it on again, you know, not wanting to pay me, but then he says he's real serious about me, wants me to come to New York. He was drinking heavily, said he was staying at the Maidstone as usual but he was meeting someone real early the following morning. Said he was gonna check out of the hotel before breakfast. He said he'd take me to New York and told me to get a taxi to his place for eight. I live way out in Montauk, right? So, anyway, this time he was real edgy, like nervous all the time. Kept on about how much trouble he was in and that he was having a lot of pressure from some guy.'

'Did he tell you his name?'

'Just that it was some builder.'

'Donnelly?' she asked.

'I can't remember. I was real buzzy about him offering to take me to New York and to travel with him. He was making me big promises and, you know, come winter out here, it's hard to make a living. Summer's when I make the dough.'

'You get paid for sex?'

Brian's face tightened. 'Moreno offered me a trip, lady. Whatever I get paid for is my own goddamned business.'

'I'm sorry. Please go on. You agreed to accompany him to New York and then what?'

'That I'd see him after this meeting he had was over.'

'Did he say who he was meeting?'

'No, but it was at his property. It's a huge place over in Georgica Ponds. I was to get there and we'd drive to New York together.' Brian yawned and ruffled his hair. 'So I'm packed and ready at seven. This guy was always going on about the place he had in New York just across from Central Park. He sort of made out that he was getting out of his problems, said something about his company crashing but that he might be doing some big deal and his finances would be in better shape and if I wanted we could go to Bermuda.' He was staring at the ocean. 'So one of my mates gives me a ride in to the gas station on the corner. I just had to walk across to Georgica Road, and over to where Moreno's house was.'

'Did you meet up with him?'

Brian shook his head. 'No. There were trucks and stuff around, big diggers, so I reckoned it had to be the right place. It was still quite dark and there were lights on but I couldn't see him or his car, so I took a walk around and a few streets away I saw his Lexus parked, which I thought was odd. I hung around it for a while, maybe ten, fifteen minutes, then started walking back along the lane. I could hear machines turning over so I reckoned the builders had got to be starting work. I headed into the drive and the noise was really loud. Then it stopped, so I kept walking and what had been making all the noise was a machine to flatten down the earth in the bottom of the swimming-pool.'

'So work *had* started?'

'I dunno. There was just this one guy working the big compressor machine. There was no one else around. I wondered if maybe I'd got the wrong place. Like I said, Alex's car was some distance from the site.'

'Did you go in?'

'No. I stood watching for a while, then I left to go back to the Lexus.'

'Could you describe the man you say was using this machine?'

'Er, not really, he was a good distance away from me but it wasn't Moreno. Too big for him.'

Sylvia licked her lips. She opened her bag to look for the photograph. 'What did you do next?'

'I hung around at the car, maybe another ten minutes or so, then I went back to the garage 'cos I had Moreno's mobile number. There's a pay-phone there so I reckoned I'd better call him and find out what was going on.'

'Did you get hold of him?' she asked impatiently.

'No, I tried but it just rang then clicked into his message service. I wasn't sure what to do and I was hungry now so I grabbed some breakfast. I was thinking of giving up then decided I'd check one last time to see if Moreno's car was still there. Then, just as I was heading back across the road, I saw it turning left on to the highway. He had to drive right past me almost. I waved and yelled but it just drove on.'

'With Moreno driving?'

'No, it was the guy I'd seen by the pool. I never got a good look at him. All I could see were wide shoulders – he was hunched over the wheel and in profile to me.'

'Then what?'

'So now I go back again to the building site. Figured maybe this guy was getting coffee or somethin' for Moreno. It was quite a walk and I had a big bag to carry. All the guys were starting work. They were concreting over the bottom of the swimming-pool for the lining.'

'Did you see Moreno?'

'I asked if anyone knew where he was but nobody had seen him. I finally gave up and went home.'

'Did he contact you again?'

'No. I called his mobile a few times but it was dead.' He shrugged. 'That's it.'

Sylvia was chilled to the bone but she wasn't through, not after paying out five hundred dollars. She brought out the photograph of herself and David at the Christmas party. Her hand shook, partly from the cold and partly because she knew this might be the confirmation she had been looking for.

'Was this the man you saw at the building site?'

Brian looked at the photograph intently. There was a short pause and Sylvia held her breath.

'I think so. Can't be sure, though. Now I think of it, the guy I saw had reddish hair and this guy's blond, right?' He tapped Edward de Jersey's image.

She sat tensely. 'Is this the man who was at the building site?'

Brian took a deep breath. 'I'm pretty sure it is. But, like I said, it was dark and when he drove past me I only got a profile – but it could be him.'

'Could be isn't good enough,' she said. 'Please, really look at the photograph. It's very, very important.'

Brian sighed. 'It was a while back now, four months.' He stared hard at the photograph. 'Yes, it's him.'

Sylvia replaced the photograph in her handbag and smiled. Her lips were almost blue it was so cold. No wonder de Jersey hadn't wanted to help her trace Philip Simmons. He'd threatened her and now she was pretty sure that those threats had been designed to throw her off the scent, but she'd show him! Edward de Jersey, alias Philip Simmons, was going to pay her handsomely for what she had discovered.

CHAPTER 20

RAYMOND MARSH wove through the busy market towards a small sandwich bar on the corner of Portobello Road. He stopped for a minute to look over the stalls selling vintage 78s and rock-and-roll memorabilia. He was well known to the stallholders as a valued customer. Today, however, he saw nothing of great interest. He knew that most of the autographed photographs of his hero were fakes. He was so familiar with Elvis's signature, he could have written it in his sleep.

The seedy coffee bar was a fog of steam, and the small plastic-covered tables were mostly occupied by street-vendors having their morning bacon butties with large mugs of strong tea. Seated at the far end of the cafe was a skinny youth with hair the same colour as his yellowish complexion.

Marsh bought tea and a jam doughnut at the counter and walked over to sit across from the nervous, chain-smoking youth. 'You got it?'

'Yeah, in my pocket. But it's gonna cost and I want cash.'

Marsh gazed nonchalantly around the squalid cafe. The object the youth had acquired for him was a tiny electronic device that could steal information from credit cards in seconds. It was already a headache to the police as it posed a massive threat to the retail industry. The ultra-high-tech contraptions were known as 'skimmers' and were often used by waiters to skim their customers' platinum and gold credit cards. All it took was one swipe. Marsh couldn't wait to get his hands on it. The youth offered him a cigarette. He nodded and took the packet of Silk Cut, opening it casually, the cuff of his coat hiding his actions. 'Bet this was made in Germany,' he muttered.

The youth leaned forward. 'The mate that got it for me says it can carry about a hundred credit cards. Ray, it's blinding.'

'So you say, but how come you want to sell it?'

'Well, after you've scanned the cards, you need to link it up to a computer to read the information or something. But you can't do it in Windows, you have to have a special program. I don't know much about computers. Nor does my mate. He nicked it off this waiter, an Italian geezer. That's who's bringing them into the country. One of his pals got six months for bringing them in.'

'Don't you ever clean your teeth?' Marsh asked. 'Your breath stinks.'

The youth sat back. 'I'm homeless. What do you expect? Look, if you ain't interested I know someone else who would be. I'm not hanging about here. I know what that's worth.'

'How much?' Marsh asked, closing the cigarette packet.

'Fifteen grand, and that's cheap.'

'Go fuck yourself. In a year they'll be putting microchips on every card to beat this thing. I'll give you five. Take it or leave it.'

'Fifteen or nothing.'

'Okay, thanks for asking.' Marsh lifted his butt off the seat.

'All right, five it is, but you got a real bargain.'

Marsh pocketed the skimmer and reached inside his coat. He took out an envelope, one of three he had stashed in his pocket. 'If you want to count it, do it in the toilet. It's all there, in nice crisp fifties.'

The boy pocketed it fast, with a furtive look around the cafe. 'I trust you.'

Marsh got up, leaving his doughnut untouched, and drained his tea. 'Tarra. Don't go spending it on drugs. You should get yourself together.' He buttoned his coat and walked out, well pleased, as the yellow-haired boy scoffed the doughnut.

After the scare over Princess Margaret's unexpected death and the possible change to Her Majesty's Jubilee celebrations, de Jersey was in for a further shock when, only two months later, he was watching the racing channel on television and the programme was interrupted to bring the nation the news that the Queen Mother had died peacefully in her sleep at Sandringham.

Her Majesty had been a constant supporter of racing, owning many horses herself, and her death affected de Jersey more than he would have believed. All his employees at the stables wore black armbands and the jockeys even rode races with them attached to their colours, but it was Fleming who broke down and wept.

The Queen Mother's death was the end of an era and, as sad as de Jersey felt, his main concern was that this would surely mean a change of plans in the Royal diary.

He contacted Marsh to ask him to check the official diary as soon as possible.

'I was waitin' for you to call,' Raymond said. 'Give me a bit of a turn. The wife says that Queen Elizabeth's snuffed it. I thought she meant you know who and I know what that would have meant. Thing is they always come in threes, don't they. With her daughter going as well, I mean, who do you think is gonna be next?'

'How soon can you check out the diary?' de Jersey interrupted impatiently.

'Well, I read she's gonna be lying in state at Westminster Abbey for three days. I mean, they don't hang about, so I reckon she'll be under the turf in less than a week. It won't be worth checking anything out until after the state funeral.'

'Okay. As soon as you know, get back to me.'

'Right you are. Sad though. She was a grand old bird. Nation's Granny. But she was a ripe old age. My gran snuffed it at seventy-two but it was a good thing. She'd lost her marbles by then and . . .'

Raymond would have prattled on if de Jersey hadn't cut him off. De Jersey need to get off the phone and contact the rest of the team, to instruct them that they were to continue as planned until further notice. That said, he knew he had to face the possibility that the day of the heist might change – the Royal Family was in mourning. As he waited for Marsh to get back to him, he, like the rest of the nation, was inundated by coverage in the newspapers and television of the Queen Mother's life and times.

Five days later, however, Raymond called to report that, despite the Queen Mother's death, there had been no change to the Royal diary. They were still on course.

Only appointments close to the death and burial had been cancelled. De Jersey gave a sigh of relief. The waiting was now over, he returned to planning the heist with a vengence, even more so after Marsh had told him that he had seen the infamous Koh-i-noor diamond.

'How did you see it?' de Jersey had asked, concerned.

'On the old lady's coffin during the ceremonial procession,' Marsh replied. Marsh had gone on to describe the sumptuous crown and how shafts of light had blazed from the diamond as if it had captured the sun. He had also asked nervously if de Jersey knew what they said about the diamond.

'About its value?' de Jersey had snapped, irritated.

'No the curse, man. You know: "He who owns this diamond will own . . ."'

'" . . . the world",' de Jersey had finished, quickly ending the call. De Jersey hadn't wanted to dwell on the curse any further, especially with Marsh, but after hanging up, he had recalled the entire curse from the Hindu text: 'He who owns this diamond will own the world, but will also know its misfortunes. Only God or a woman can wear it with impunity.' The curse didn't concern de Jersey. He had no intention of wearing or owning the Koh-i-noor diamond. It would be for sale.

Over lunch, the following day, Christina told de Jersey that she was planning a dinner party.

'Who do you want to invite?' de Jersey asked, as he unfolded his napkin.

'I don't know. Maybe some of the jockeys and trainers, make it a fun evening.' She ladled out the spinach soup. 'What do you think?'

'Sounds good to me. We've not had a staff get-together for a long time.' He broke up his bread and dipped it into the soup.

'Shall I organize it, then?'

'Sure.'

He looked up in surprise as her roll hit his head. 'What was that for?'

She glared at him. 'Do you think I'm blind, stupid or what? I want you to stop treating me like a child and start telling me the truth. The yard is like a morgue. The entire east wing is empty and half of the staff are missing. We're in dire financial trouble, aren't we?'

'Ten points.'

'Don't use that sarcastic tone with me.'

'I wasn't aware that I was using any specific tone.'

'God, I hate you when you're like this. It's like I'm sitting opposite a stranger. If things are bad then we should discuss it like adults.'

'And what could you do about it, my darling? Did your mother leave you a vast legacy?'

She stood up, walked round to him, removed his soup plate, went into the kitchen and threw it into the sink. She returned with a large bowl of salad and banged it down on the table. 'Help yourself.'

'Thank you,' he said. She returned to the kitchen and came back with a roasted chicken. She banged that down too, jabbed it with a carving knife, then returned to her seat.

'Throwing a tantrum, Christina, is not going to help. Pass me your plate and I'll serve.'

It whizzed past his head and crashed against the wall. 'I'm waiting for you to tell me what is going on,'

Christina said. 'Or, do you want me to go out into the yard and ask Donald Fleming?'

She poured herself a glass of wine as he carved the chicken breast. Eventually he said 'It's those investments I lost out on. The situation is worse than I initially thought. A lot worse.'

'How long have you known?'

'Quite a while. I just didn't want to bother you with it. With your mother's illness, I felt you had enough to worry about without me adding to it.'

'How bad is it, then?' she asked.

'Well, I've had to sell off a lot of the horses and I'll probably have to sell more. Now is the time to do it. I shouldn't be away too long. Couple of days.'

'Where are you going?' she snapped.

'To look at some auctions, maybe Dublin. I'm not sure.'

'I'll come with you.'

'If you want.'

'What I want, Edward, is for you to be honest with me. If you're saying we're in financial trouble, why buy more horses?'

'I'm more than likely going to try to find buyers for the ones I have to let go. Does that answer your question?'

'Why are you being like this?'

He pushed away his plate and sighed. 'Because it's breaking my heart.'

'So you have to hurt me too?'

'Not intentionally. But I have a lot to think about and—'

'Maybe if you shared it, it wouldn't be so bad.'

She was shocked when he met her eyes. His were brimming with tears.

'Oh, Edward,' she said softly.

'Christina . . .' He turned away from her and she got up to put her arms around him. 'I'm sorry,' he said.

'Darling, whatever happens, no matter how bad, if we see it through together we'll be okay. That's what's important, sharing it together.'

He drew her down to sit on his knee. 'This is what happens when you marry someone old enough to be your father,' he told her. 'I should be taking care of you and the girls and here I am getting tearful because it's all crumbling about my ears.'

Christina hugged him tightly. 'So, from the beginning. I know it started with David Lyons' suicide. I want you to tell me everything.'

He sighed. 'David Lyons got me into this mess. He stiffed me rigid. He delved into every account and proved to me how dumb I was to place such trust in him. He had *carte blanche* . . .' He rocked her. 'Let's continue this in more comfort. I need a brandy.'

De Jersey walked with his wife into the drawing room. The fire was blazing and she drew the curtains as he poured himself the brandy. He was working out in his mind how much to tell her. He lit a cigar and sat in the centre of the sofa. He patted the cushion beside him and she curled up next to him, more like one of his daughters than his wife. She seemed so young and he felt so very old.

'I forgot to tell you. You must promise me that you'll be free on the second of May.'

'What?'

'We have a school open day. They're doing *The*

Taming of the Shrew and Natasha's got the lead part. We have to be there at about six.'

He took a deep breath. 'I wouldn't miss it for the world.'

'So, now that you have your brandy and your cigar and I'm sitting comfortably beside you, start with David Lyons' suicide.'

He blew a smoke-ring, then closed his eyes. 'I can't believe you threw a roll at my head.'

'Don't change the subject.'

'Followed by a dinner plate.' He laughed but stopped when he saw her expression. 'I love you so much,' he said quietly.

'Don't cut me out, Edward. Please. How bad is it?'

The lies began. 'Well, for me to lose one horse hurts like hell, so to lose an entire wing was a catastrophe. But I made enough from the sales to cover a substantial part of my losses. The estate is worth millions – the land alone is worth a fortune and I can sell some if I need an infusion of cash.' He talked on, embroidering the lies for his wife, wishing they were true.

That following afternoon, de Jersey went out into the yard with Fleming to look at the horses, particularly Royal Flush who was being saddled for a training session. De Jersey stroked his neck. 'How you doing, my son, eh?'

'He's a special one, isn't he?' Mickey Rowland, de Jersey's top jockey, had joined them. He was fixing the strap beneath his riding helmet. 'He's been a bugger the last few days. If he gets downwind of the stud he's a right handful. Couple of mares are in season and you know what the young colts are like, randy sods.'

De Jersey nodded. It was rare to have a racing stable and a stud in the same vicinity – a colt could smell a mare in season from a good distance away. This was why racing stallions did not go to stud until they had won enough races to make it worth the stud fees. Once they had mounted a mare, they became wilful.

Mickey took the reins and could not resist kissing the horse's velvety nose. 'I love him, he's a real character,' he said.

De Jersey helped him into the saddle. 'Yes, he's special, Mickey, and he's going to win the Derby.'

'That's every racehorse owner's dream,' Mickey said, as he slipped his feet into the stirrups. 'It's my dream too, Boss. I'd give a lot to ride him in the Derby.'

'It's your ride, Mickey, but first you've got to bring him in first at Lingfield, yeah?'

'Thank you, sir. I'll do my best.'

De Jersey watched as his beloved Royal Flush walked out of the yard, Mickey talking to him as he tossed his head, eager to get to the gallops.

'Tony. *Tony*!'

Driscoll sat up in bed, his heart beating fast.

'What?' he yelled back.

Liz walked in with an invoice in her hand. 'You've not paid the florist and they're saying that if we don't settle up they'll take legal action.'

He flopped back on to the pillows. 'Shit, is that all? I thought there was a bleeding fire.'

'I'd like to throw you in one,' she snapped. 'The caterers are screaming too – and don't you hide under the duvet 'cos I've not finished. I had Michelle on the phone this morning. She tells me an estate agent's been walking in and out of the villa showing buyers around. They're on their honeymoon, for God's sake!'

Driscoll closed his eyes. She sat on the edge of the bed and prodded him. 'You'd better come clean with me, Tony. What the hell is going on?'

Driscoll burped, and she threw his antacid tablets at him. 'I'm waiting. Have you not told me the full story about these bad investments?'

'I lost everything I invested.'

'And how much was that?'

'A lot. We're in trouble now but I'm gonna sort things out. In the meantime, though—'

'In the meantime you've got to pay these bills. It was your daughter's wedding and you know how people round here talk.'

'I don't give a fuck.'

'Well, I do!' She paused. 'Do you need the money from the villa to pay for the wedding?'

'Yeah. Soon as it's sold I'll sort out the florist.'

'But it might not sell for ages – and what about all my stuff there?'

'I'm selling it furnished.'

'But I worked my butt off doing that place up! I could have a real go at you, Tony. I really could.'

'Oh, go and work it off with your muscle man. I can't take any more of your yelling.'

'I'm not yelling. But I think we're gonna have to sit down and talk this out. I need to know just how badly off we are. We don't have to sell this place, do we?'

'Not yet.'

409

'*Not yet*! I've got a garden party arranged for this summer. We *can't* sell. Please don't tell me we're in that deep.'

He sat up and rubbed his head. 'Can you just leave me alone? I've got a headache.'

'You've had one for months,' she said and stormed off.

Kevin was warming up when Liz came in. She was about to join him when she burst into tears.

'I've just about had my fill of him,' she sniffled. 'He's selling the villa without even asking me.' Kevin handed her a tissue. 'He's got into some terrible financial difficulty. It's just unbelievable that he's not said a word to me,' she added.

Kevin hovered. 'Perhaps he didn't want to worry you.'

'Worry me? He can't pay for his daughter's wedding. I'm worried all right.'

Kevin took another tissue and handed it to her as she blew her nose. 'I'm sorry. Do you want to leave the work-out this morning?'

'No, no I don't. I want to work this out of my system. I want you to really push me this morning, Kevin. Take my mind off that husband of mine.'

'I can think of a number of ways I can do that,' Kevin said, taking her in his arms. They went into a passionate embrace as he tried to peel off her red leotard.

'No, Kevin, we can't. He's in the house.'

'So? He's been in and around before. It never bothered you then.'

'Well, it does now. I'm just not in the mood. I'm sorry.'

'That's okay, but you know sometimes? You should think about the way you treat me, like I'm just a hired stud.'

'You know that's not true.'

'Isn't it? You pay for me to train that body. How long's it gonna be before you start asking me how much I charge for a fuck?'

'Ah stop it. You know I care about you.'

'So you say.'

'I do. But I've got a lot on my mind.'

'You said that about the wedding, so you didn't see me. Now it's something else, but I'm not taking it, Liz. This has been going on for almost a year now.'

'Kevin, don't do this to me please.'

'It's my doing it to you that you said kept you sane. Your old man can't get it up so is that all I am? Sex therapy because he's impotent? You said you two don't do it anymore. Well, what's going on, Liz? I care about you, you know that.'

'Kevin, it's not the way it looks. I really care about you, I do. But he's my husband, impotent or not. He has been a real pain for the past six months. You know that. He's never home. I dunno what he's doing. He's hardly said two words to me.'

Kevin flexed his muscles and stared at his reflection in the gym mirror. She came to his side and touched his muscular arm, resting her head against his back, staring at their reflections. Kevin was lean, his body honed to perfection. His hair was just starting to recede at the front but he was handsome and he noticed her. If she had a new hair cut, he noticed. When she had her nails done, he noticed. He'd even recommended the doctor who'd pumped her lips up and noticed when she'd had

411

it done. Tony had asked if she'd got a cold sore because her lips looked puffy! Lately Tony seemed to be in a perpetual bad temper, burping and complaining about his stomach and snoring beside her every night, usually without so much as a goodnight kiss. As she thought about her husband, Kevin gently eased her around to face him and began kissing her neck and stroking her breasts. He lifted her off her feet and laid her down on the bench press, stripping off her leotard and sucking at her nipples. If Tony tried to lift her in his arms, he'd put his back out! They became more passionate.

'Not here, Kevin. Take me into the sauna,' she sighed and hugged him close.

The pair were having such a good time that neither heard Driscoll calling her name, nor the sound of him opening the sauna door. He only opened it a fraction but he saw enough: his wife naked with her legs over Kevin's shoulders and her face flushed in ecstatic pleasure as she screamed in delight. He shut the door, saying nothing. He went and took off the shorts he'd been planning to work out in and left the house fifteen minutes later. His initial anger was gone and in its place there was a cold, seething calmness. He was going to be risking his neck in a few days' time, and in many ways he had been risking it for her because he had not wanted to let her down. Now he didn't care if he ever saw her again. Win or lose, he would do this last one for himself, alone.

Driscoll drove to Chelsea and parked in the underground car park at Chelsea Harbour. He went into the apartments and up to number 204. The apartment was now on the market but he'd not yet had time to tell Nikki, his patient long-time girlfriend. Nikki opened the door and immediately wrapped her arms around his portly little body.

'I've missed you. I've not heard from you in weeks.'

'I know darling but I've had big troubles.'

She brewed coffee the way he liked it with hot milk and then heated up some ginger biscuits. He also liked them hot. Driscoll, for all his fury against his wife and the trainer, never considered that having a mistress was in any way a fault. In the good old days when he had been flush with money, Liz had shopped 'til she dropped and he had screwed until he dropped. He had seen nothing wrong in it.

'Nikki, I've got financial problems. I'm gonna have to sell this place. I'm sorry. There's no way round it. But if you go and live with your mum for a while, maybe . . . I can't say why or how, but I think I might be free and you and me can go off abroad to live together.'

'Live with my mum?' Her pale face clouded and she started to cry.

Nikki was twenty-nine years old. He'd met her in the perfumery department at Harrods several years ago. For a while his wife received more gifts of perfume and cosmetics than most women would need in a lifetime. Three months later Nikki agreed to move into the apartment. They had been lovers ever since, on and off. He knew she probably dated other guys but if Nikki had other men, he never saw any sign of them and she never mentioned any other person being in her life. She simply focused on him when he arranged to see her. He paid money into a bank account for her every month but now he had to tell her that he couldn't do that any longer either.

Driscoll managed to make love to Nikki. It was not a majestic performance by any standard but, as always, she made him feel as if he was the greatest stud in the world. They had some lunch together and a bottle of champagne and, with a few more tears, she showed him out, promising that she would leave the apartment by the end of the month. She also promised she would show any potential buyers round whenever they called. They kissed passionately at the door and then he left.

As the door closed behind him, she swore under her breath and went to the phone. She dialled her brother first, telling him to get a van round ASAP. She wasn't going to leave a single stick of furniture behind. She then called her boyfriend and asked him whether she could move in with him. Driscoll had been a 'nice little earner' for Nikki, nothing more. She was just angry that she hadn't persuaded him to put the apartment in her name! She had a good mind to call his wife and give her an earful but she didn't bother. Besides she didn't want to tip the idiot off that she was doing a moonlight flit.

Driscoll met up with Wilcox at Kingston boat yard for some 'shopping' required for the heist. Wilcox was checking over a second-hand two-seater speedboat for sale. It had seen better days and smelt of mildew as he hauled the tarpaulin off the trailer.

'It's been knocked around a bit. It's had a shoddy repaint job. How much are they asking?' Wilcox asked, looking at the 'For Sale' card stuck on the windscreen. 'I suppose we won't do better for this price,' he said but Driscoll was miles away, still deep in thought about Nikki.

'I mean, I couldn't say anything,' Driscoll said to Wilcox. 'But you know, if we pull this off, I'm gonna make sure Nikki does all right, take her abroad with me.'

'What, leave the wife?' Wilcox asked, still more interested in the boat and looking over the controls.

'Yeah, she nags all day. Caught her with her legs akimbo in the sauna today with her one-on-one trainer!' Driscoll said.

'How long have you had her?' Wilcox asked.

'Who, the wife?'

'No, the little girlfriend,' Wilcox said as he bent down to check out all the rust. 'This hasn't been under cover for a few years, never mind in the water,' he said.

'She's been a fixture for four or five years,' Driscoll said. 'She's a lovely redhead. Tall, lovely long legs. You know, she's always there for me, makes me feel good and she's great in the sack. Used to work in Harrods.'

'You've been keeping her then?'

'Yeah, nice pad she arranged. Very tasteful. I used to love going to see her when I could. Needed her, know what I mean?'

'Yep, this is a real old boat. We do the business then torch it.'

'Okay, what about you? You got any little dollies stashed away? You always used to.'

'Nope. I had but they've been elbowed. Rika and I are on a good thing right now and I don't want her to get her knickers in a twist just when I need to be chilled out.'

'Right, yeah right. I don't want any aggro either. I'm

just sorry I've got to sell the apartment. And me and Nikki'll get back together. She's gonna move in with her mother.'

Wilcox nodded, not really interested. He fished in his pocket to bring out some readies to deal with the boat owner. The bulbous nosed elderly mechanic, wearing oil-streaked dungarees, had been hovering unobtrusively in the background, tinkering with another boat. Wilcox gestured for him to come over and together they eased the boat off the trailer and down the few yards of slip road into the water. Wilcox started up the outboard and he was surprised when it turned over quickly and appeared sound. He climbed out again as the old boy kept hold of the rope.

'Five hundred,' Wilcox said, counting the fifty-pound notes.

'Nah, no way. Thousand quid pal,' the old boy insisted, winding the rope round a post, then wiping his filthy hands on an equally filthy rag.

'Six is my final offer,' repeated Wilcox, still counting.

'Na, I'll go nine fifty and I'm doing myself an injury.'

'Six hundred, take it or leave it,' Wilcox said again. By this time he had the money stacked in a neat tight wad.

'I can't do that. I'm giving you a good price. This is a fast boat. I worked on it myself. Nice seats too.'

'You don't drive the seats, though, do you? And with the amount of rust it's got I'll be lucky if it stays afloat.'

'Look, I'll come down to seven fifty but that's it, that's my final price.'

'Okay, thanks. Sorry not to be able to do business with you.'

Wilcox opened his wallet, about to replace the money when the dirty hand made a grab for it.

'Six hundred, you bastards. Go on, take it!'

Wilcox climbed into the boat followed by Driscoll, who almost overbalanced and fell into the water. He then started the outboard and they set off up the river towards Richmond.

'We got moorings for this?' Driscoll yelled, above the noise of the engine, his hair standing on end.

'Yeah, the Colonel's arranged it. Plus we've got another speedboat to check over. It's already at the boat-house.'

It was blisteringly cold as they sped past Bucklands Wharf, then on towards Chiswick. Just past Teddington Lock the outboard coughed and spluttered, then cut out. Wilcox managed to get it going again and they turned round, back up the river towards Putney.

'What a piece of fucking junk,' Wilcox said, as they made it past the Putney rowing club and puttered-on towards a boat-house a quarter of a mile away.

'We only need it for a few hours and, besides, it won't be us using it,' Driscoll said, rubbing his hands.

'Right, but if it screws up they're fucked.'

They passed beneath a willow tree. Wilcox manoeuvred the boat into the boat-house, then switched off the engine. The boat-house was at the end of a garden. The house was up for lease and the owners had let the boat-house and their speedboat for six months to a Mr Philip Simmons. They had advertised it in the property pages on the agent's Internet site. The other boat was moored inside, covered with a tarpaulin. Driscoll stepped out on to some broken steps then climbed up on to the garden path. 'I'll see you later,' he said. 'I'm going to get us some food – I'm starving.'

The boat-house was in need of renovation. There were gaps between the floorboards and holes in the roof. The water was murky and clogged with weeds and debris. Wilcox eased the doors shut and put on an overall to start work on the old boat.

When Driscoll returned he was carrying two takeaway hamburgers, two cartons of soup and coffee.

'You took your bloody time. This other one's rusted to hell and back too,' Wilcox muttered, as he scraped then peered under the speedboat's steering column.

'I got you a cheeseburger,' Driscoll said, handing him one, then sitting on an old orange box.

'This engine's been hammered into the ground but I'm tuning it and it's sounding better.' Wilcox opened his cheeseburger box and then looked at Driscoll slumped on the crate.

'You okay? Tony?'

Driscoll shook his head.

'What's happened? You get bad news?'

'No more than five hours; no six. I only told her six fucking hours ago. It's unbelievable. She's even taken the fucking toilet-roll holder. The kitchen's like a war zone, all these fucking wires hanging out. I was selling it fucking furnished!'

'What are you talking about?' Wilcox asked as he stuffed the food into his mouth.

'Nikki. I went back by the apartment. I just wanted to make sure she was okay. She must have got a bloody furniture removal van there before I got the bleeding front door shut. She's cleaned the place out, the bitch!'

Wilcox couldn't help grinning and Driscoll became irate.

'What's so funny?'

'Well, you going on about this lovely redhead and now she's a bitch. Maybe she's gone with it all to her mother's.'

'What? With a whole furniture van full of gear?'

Wilcox made his face straight and went over and patted Driscoll's shoulder.

'Good riddance and better you find out now. If she had been around when you get the cut from this little job, she'd have screwed you over even worse, right? Best it happened now.'

Driscoll sighed. He felt wretched, foolish and totally humiliated. It had been bad enough finding his wife with her fitness trainer, now Nikki had betrayed him too.

'I tell you something, next woman I get is gonna be one hundred per cent special.'

'Hello?' Pamela's throaty, theatrical voice floated in to them and she appeared at the door. In an oatmeal-coloured coat, low-heeled fawn shoes and a white silk shirt she was looking much smarter than usual.

'What are you doing here?' Driscoll asked.

'Bringing you the mooring permits from our lord and master.' She tossed over a large manila envelope.

'You look different,' Wilcox said, as he sipped his soup.

'I've been buying my wardrobe for the opening per-formance. I'm the perfect lady-in-waiting.'

'Apart from the fag hanging out of your mouth,' Wilcox joked, and she laughed, turning to leave.

'See you later, I suspect. Have a lovely day out on the river, boys!'

Driscoll checked his watch. 'We should be going to the barn soon. How long you gonna be?'

'As long as it takes to fix the engine and see what gears it'll need. You go on ahead. I'll see you there.'

When Driscoll entered the barn, he was still chilled from the river and blew into his hands. 'Will somebody get those bloody heaters on?'

'You're in a pleasant mood,' Pamela said, opening a bottle of water to fill the kettle.

'Yeah, well, I've had a bad day.'

'Let's have a cup of tea and maybe you'll feel better.' She opened the box of teabags and looked around. 'Have you heard from his lordship? He was supposed to be here before me.' She lit a cigarette.

On cue the door opened and Westbrook entered. He smiled wanly, began to unbutton his coat then keeled over on to the ground.

Driscoll stood over him. 'Christ, is he pissed?'

'No, he's sick. Help him up. He gets these awful headaches that make him faint.'

They assisted Westbrook to a chair. He sat down, shaking, and gripped his head. 'I'm so sorry. Feel rather poorly today. Be okay in a while.'

Driscoll turned away. It was fucking ridiculous. What a choice for the heist!

Pamela fussed over Westbrook, fetching him water, searching his pockets for his pills, and standing over him as he sipped, holding the glass for him. Then she helped him to the back of the barn where he lay down on some sacking. 'Will you marry me?' His voice was racked with pain.

Pamela stroked his head, which was glistening with perspiration. 'I would have done like a shot, dear, once, but I'm too old for all that now. The best thing for me now would be retirement in the Bahamas. You could always be my house guest.'

'I'd like that,' he said, hardly audible. Pamela watched over him until he drifted off to sleep. He didn't stir when Wilcox came in and banged the door. He was dishevelled and freezing cold, and went straight to the heater to rub his numb hands.

Driscoll passed him his rubber gloves and nodded to Westbrook. 'He fainted, flat on his face.'

'Is he gonna be all right?'

'He's sleeping,' Pamela said, as she put the kettle on the burner.

'Oh, that's brilliant,' Wilcox said. 'He's a fucking liability.'

'Don't you swear at me, Jimmy, because I won't take it,' Pamela said. 'Tony is popping antacid tablets like mad, and you're not exactly a choirboy, so the pot's calling the kettle black, isn't it?'

Wilcox became irate. 'I'm clean. What about *you*? Top yourself up with gin before you came, did you?'

'Stop it,' Driscoll snapped at Wilcox. 'Just shut the fuck up! Any problems we've got we put before the Colonel and let him sort them out. Bickering's a waste of time and energy.'

De Jersey stood motionless outside the door, listening, choosing his moment. Eventually, he stepped forward and they saw him. 'Problems?'

Wilcox pointed to where Lord Westbrook was sleeping.

'Did a pratfall when he came in. Couldn't stand upright.'

De Jersey went to the back of the barn, sat back on his heels and looked at the sleeping man. Westbrook's eyes opened. 'I will not let you down,' he said. 'I'll make sure of it. I'll take the tablets before I go, not wait as I did today. It's just that I have to test how long I can go between these wretched attacks.'

'What do they feel like?' de Jersey asked.

'Excruciating migraine, dizzy, sick. But my pills sort me out, really they do.'

De Jersey patted his shoulder. 'Okay, old chap, I believe you. Just rest here a while and when you feel up to it, come and join us.'

'Thank you.'

De Jersey began to confer with Wilcox and Driscoll about the lookalike. 'We take her straight to the Aldersgate warehouse. Try to keep her calm, maybe even let her think that that's where we'll be filming. Not until we have her secure inside do we give her the details. We need her standing by earlier to be sure, I'm thinking now maybe six o'clock, seven at the latest, so we can prime her. Meanwhile we need to get to her husband fast. There'll be no need for any rough stuff.'

Pamela broke in, 'If the Queen becomes troublesome, what should I do?'

'She won't if we're threatening her husband.'

Driscoll snorted. 'If it was me and you had my wife, I'd tell you to keep her!'

Later that evening, when everyone except Wilcox, Driscoll and de Jersey had left, de Jersey asked them for their

422

opinion on a problem he'd been mulling over. He believed he had come up with a solution to the panic alarms. He opened the diagrams he'd printed off from the CD. 'The power source for the alarms is located here in what would have been the old coal chute.' He pointed to a spot on the diagram. 'The on-street chute access has been cemented over so the only way into it is from inside the house.' De Jersey marked it on the diagrams as he spoke.

'How the hell do we get in there?' Driscoll asked.

De Jersey opened his cigar case and offered it to Driscoll and Wilcox, who shook their heads.

'Have another look at the information on the CD,' he said. 'The warehouse where we'll be is just a hundred yards from the safe house but its cellar extends beyond the actual warehouse space. Look at where the cellar extends to – it's almost next to theirs. All these properties were supplied with coal using the same chute. If we enlarge the small chute door in our warehouse's cellar, we'll have access to the room at the bottom of the chute. At the other side there should be a similar door leading into the safe house's cellar. We open up our side and gain access to their cellar through this coal chute. We can't do it any other way. Marsh tells me they test the alarms every day at nine. After that we disconnect the lines. We will have only a short time because we're moving out the convoy at ten twenty-five, but at least we'll know that anyone pressing a panic button is not going to worry us because there'll be no help on the way. What do you think?'

'It might be the only way,' said Wilcox.

Heartened, de Jersey outlined how long it would take and what equipment they would need, and both men agreed the idea was workable. They would use a high-powered laser gun to cut soundlessly through the cement, but as they would have to go brick by brick, their nights from now on would be busy. All he had left to work out was how to disconnect the alarms without them going off once they were inside. For this he would need Marsh again.

They turned to the getaway plan – they hadn't yet worked out the fine details of their own escape. They had to get rid of the Royal vehicles then get themselves and the jewels away from the scene as quickly as possible.

By late evening, they believed they had a plan but they wouldn't know until the day of the robbery whether it would work.

Christina was in the kitchen sorting through some of her mother's old letters and photographs when the phone rang.

'Could I speak to Edward de Jersey, please?' said a voice at the end of the line.

'He's not here. Can I take a message?'

'Where is he?'

'Who is speaking?'

'Sylvia Hewitt. Who's that?'

'Christina de Jersey. Do you want to leave a message?'

'When do you expect him back? I need to see him.'

'In a few days. Does he have your number?'

'Thank you, and yes. Sorry to have bothered you, Mrs de Jersey.' Christina hung up. She didn't know why but the call had unnerved her. She'd never met Sylvia but she knew she was Helen Lyons' sister. She had been so abrupt, almost rude. She jotted down the message on a yellow Post-it and stuck it on the phone.

Liz Driscoll had just returned from a manicure when the phone rang. She picked it up.

'Hello?'

'Could I speak to Mr Driscoll, please?'

'He's not at home. Who's calling?'

'Sylvia Hewitt. Do you know when he'll be back?'

'He's out on business.'

'When do you expect him?'

'Sometime this evening. Do you want to leave a message?'

'Just say I called. I think he has my number. Sorry to disturb you.'

Liz hung up. This was the second time she'd taken a call from the woman and if Tony was up to his old tricks again she'd really have it out with him.

Marsh was pleased with the new equipment he had purchased. He had spent thousands in computer stores across London. The skimmer was well worth the five thousand he'd paid for it. He'd given his wife *carte blanche* to go shopping at Harrods with the fake credit cards he'd had a pal create, using several numbers he'd got from the skimmer and she had departed, leaving him to take care of their child.

De Jersey had travelled by public transport to Marsh's house. It was almost five thirty when they met. They discussed the phone conversations between Scotland

Yard and the safe house. Marsh was still confident they would have no problem in gaining the IRA codeword for the 2nd of May. He played the tapes he had recorded of numerous IRA informants calling in to give the day's codeword. It was usually an odd name, sometimes a place or object. The tapes reassured de Jersey that Marsh was as good as his word, and they played them again so that de Jersey could practise an Irish accent. Marsh also confirmed that there had been no changes in the Queen's official diary and the fitting remained fixed for May the 2nd. The Royal party was to depart from Buckingham Palace at ten that morning.

De Jersey looked around the room. 'You're certainly spending the money I'm paying you. Perhaps you should slow down a bit. You don't want to make anyone suspicious about all this equipment you've got. You certainly couldn't buy it on your wages.'

'I'm watching my arse, don't you worry.' Marsh swivelled round in his chair and looked at de Jersey. 'Come on, what is it? There was no real need for you to come and see me today. What else do you want?'

De Jersey put his hand into his pocket and took out a thick envelope. 'I need your help with something. Take a look at this. It's D'Ancona's visual display, the alarms, the panic buttons.'

Marsh grinned. 'You're something else, man, you really are.' He took the CD and put it into his computer. 'Fuck me! How did you get hold of this?' he exclaimed.

'Inadvertently via you. You set the cat among the pigeons when you tried to hack in so they had to check all their files, and I have my contacts.'

'This must have cost.'

De Jersey smiled. 'Not really.' He tapped the screen.

'My problem is this. I know how to get into this area here,' he pointed to the coal chute, 'and I know that's where we can get access to the panic alarms. But I don't know how to deactivate them.'

Marsh's mouth turned down as he peered at the screen. He scrolled down, then back up again. 'Well, it's simple enough to unplug lines from boxes – it's just a matter of pulling them out.'

'I can tell there's a "but" coming,' de Jersey said.

'There is, and it's a big one. The second you pull any one of those plugs, all the others will activate and notify the call centre. You'll have every copper in London down there in a jiffy.'

'What do you suggest?'

Raymond tugged nervously at his cuffs. 'I haven't a clue. You'll need to find a way to pull out all the plugs at the same moment. A fraction of a second out and it's bye-bye Crown Jewels!'

There was a moment's silence as the two men contemplated their predicament. Marsh clicked and the interior of the safe house came up again on his screen. The silence was broken by his daughter, who started howling. He left the room and de Jersey could hear him cooing and talking to her to quieten her down. Then Marsh charged back in carrying the child.

'I've got it! I think I know how we can do it – but she's filled her nappy so I gotta change her.'

Rika had just put the twins to bed and was thumbing through the *TV Times* when the phone rang. She hoped it would be Jimmy. He'd been gone all day.

'Is Mr Wilcox there?'

'No, he not back yet.'

'My name is Sylvia Hewitt. Could you ask him to call me? He has my number. Tell him it's quite urgent, would you?'

'Who?'

'Sylvia Hewitt. Are you expecting him this evening?'

'Yes, I tell him you call. Sylvia who?'

'Hewitt. Please give him the message.'

Rika got a pen and notepad. She started to write down the message then crumpled the paper and threw it into the bin. She was sure this woman Sylvia Hewitt was after her man. She had spoken so rudely, as if Rika was the maid.

De Jersey left Marsh's house grinning from ear to ear. A taxi passed him, slowing down. The inside was lit and de Jersey saw that the blonde-haired Mrs Marsh was paying the driver. She had a vast array of boxes and bags, all with the Harrods logo. He watched until she had entered the house and then, as the cab made a U-turn, he stepped out and flagged it down.

He asked to be driven to Wimbledon station and the driver beamed. 'That's lucky. I've just come from Knightsbridge. Didn't reckon I'd get another fare back.' He switched on the clock.

'That was some shopping your last fare had,' de Jersey said.

'Don't know where they get the dosh. Took two Harrods doormen to load me up. Said her husband had made a killing on the horses. Wish he'd give me a few tips.'

De Jersey sat back against the seat as his driver gave a

monologue about his lack of luck on the tracks. 'You a racing man?' he asked eventually.

'No, I'm not,' de Jersey replied.

'Best way to be. It's a fool's game,' the driver said, then turned to glance at de Jersey. He was sitting in the shadow, his face virtually in darkness. 'Not a gambling man, then, eh?'

'No.'

'Don't take risks, eh?'

'No, I don't like risks.' He closed his eyes.

CHAPTER 21

De JERSEY was loath to do it but he cut down on some more staff and sold six more horses. This flurry of activity meant rumour was rife in the yard. All were concerned for the stable's future and their jobs so no one felt it odd that just as the racing season was starting de Jersey was spending more and more time away. Fleming had told them only that he was in financial difficulty. However, he was monitoring Royal Flush as diligently as ever: he was now relying on the great horse to achieve big results. Luckily he had consistently improved during training, even if his temperament in the stable had not and he lashed out at his handlers. If he felt like it, he could fly on the flat but he was often a slow starter, not kicking in until half-way through the run when Mickey said he could feel the animal's mood change. One moment he was sluggish, the next Mickey could hardly hold him. There was not a horse in the yard that could keep up with him. So, while de Jersey inched closer and closer to the biggest risk of his life, his precious Royal Flush was prepared for the first race of the season at Lingfield. To be eligible for the Derby he had to be placed.

De Jersey received a call from Pamela. Lord Westbrook's health had deteriorated and she suggested de Jersey visit him: it would be too late to do anything about it on the day. De Jersey thanked her and hung up. He swore under his breath. Just as he had thought everything was under control, something else had gone wrong. Christina had mentioned a phone call from Sylvia Hewitt and during a morning at the barn both Wilcox and Driscoll had said that the woman had called them.

'I had to fish the fucking message out of the bin. Rika's convinced I'm fooling around with her,' Wilcox told them.

'Leave it with me,' de Jersey said. 'I'll go and see what she wants.'

'Maybe her money,' Wilcox suggested.

It was already mid-April and Raymond Marsh had been busy. So had his wife. His purchases ranged from two dozen hand-made silk shirts, suits and shoes, to computer accessories, TV sets and furniture. Marsh was preparing to leave the country. After the robbery, he would decamp to South America. His credit-card frauds were reaching ludicrous proportions, but he needed hard cash to ensure that his departure was paid for and he had funds in hand. His house was on the market. He had not thought of how his behaviour might affect de Jersey. Only one of the stolen credit-card numbers had to be recognized and he would be arrested for theft.

De Jersey still had not made contact with Sylvia Hewitt and Christina took another call from her.

'This is Sylvia Hewitt. Mrs de Jersey, would you please ask your husband to return my call? When I said it was urgent I meant it.'

Christina found her attitude most objectionable. 'What is this about, Miss Hewitt?'

'Alex Moreno. Tell him I have some interesting information concerning a man called Philip Simmons.'

As before, Sylvia hung up abruptly, leaving Christina even more confused. She couldn't understand why the woman had been so rude.

In Monaco, Dulay was ready. His boat was crewed up, standing by for the four-day trip from Monaco to Brighton. The engine had been tested and now all he had to do was wait. The weeks before the Crown Jewels fitting dragged but his workrooms were prepared. Everything was standing by, ready for the green light.

He was sitting outside a harbour cafe in Monte Carlo, on his third coffee, when de Jersey approached.

'You're late,' Dulay said. 'I've been here over an hour.'

'Sorry. I was looking over your boat.'

'She's all set. Would you like to go for a spin in her?'

'I don't have time. Did you arrange the meet?'

'Yeah. He's only in Paris for two days.'

'At the Paris Ritz?'

'Yeah, and he didn't like me asking him to meet you. You know what these guys are like about honour. You have to do a lot of bowing around the guy. He's something else. And he's got this other guy that breathes down your neck the whole time.'

'Odd Job.'

'What?'

'Nothing. Is this guy his bodyguard?'

'Yeah. He's got a driver-cum-heavy as well. I said we'd meet him this afternoon at the Louvre. He's also into art. Do you know that if a Japanese person buys a painting and holds on to it for two years, it becomes his property even if it's stolen goods.'

'No, I didn't. I want to meet him alone, Paul.'

'What?'

'You heard me. The less we're seen together the better.'

'I arranged the meet, for Chrissakes!'

'I know you did. But I still want to meet him alone.' He went on to remind Dulay to anchor a good distance off the coast the day of the robbery. De Jersey also instructed him to test the watertight crate he had told him to acquire. They spoke for another few moments, and then de Jersey left.

He caught a taxi back to the airport and hired a twin-engine plane to fly to Paris. He picked up another taxi and arrived at the Louvre at just after two thirty. He had half an hour to wait before his meeting with Mr Kitamo.

Christina waited at the open front door as Helen Lyons arrived in a taxi. Helen had called earlier, distraught, asking if she could see Christina. After Helen paid the driver she turned to Christina. 'I'm so sorry to bother you.'

'It's no bother, Helen. Come on in. I've put some coffee on.'

Helen stumbled up the steps into the house and burst into tears.

Christina put her arms round her. 'What on earth has happened, Helen?'

Helen wiped her eyes and blew her nose. 'I've been so depressed. I went to Hove to stay with a friend but she's got flu. It's just been so awful since I found out.'

'Found out what?'

The tears started again. Christina passed her a cup of coffee.

'I just need some advice,' Helen said.

'Your sister has called here a few times. She asked to speak to Edward.'

'I hate her!' Helen said, her face tightening. 'I was staying with her, you know. That's how I found out.'

Christina sipped her coffee and waited. Eventually Helen launched into an angry tirade. 'I found out she was having an affair with David. Eight years she said.'

'I'm so sorry,' Christina said gently.

'I found all these photographs of them – they'd even been abroad together. All the lies David must have told me!'

Christina didn't know what to say.

'I was going to see her last week but the porter told me she'd gone to America and I was glad. I don't think I can face her.'

'Well, she must be back because, as I said, she has called numerous times to speak to my husband and I don't think she was calling long-distance.'

'Well, if she wants to know where I am, please don't tell her. I've decided I never want to see her again.'

Christina hoped Helen was not going to ask to stay. It would be so inconvenient, especially with all the recent turmoil.

'It's strange, isn't it?' Helen said. 'You live with

someone, love and trust them, and then suddenly it all turns sour. Knowing about Sylvia and David has almost given me a nervous breakdown. First his suicide, then the fire and now . . . I hate her so much,' Helen repeated, reaching down for a plastic carrier-bag at her side. 'The reason I wanted to see you was to give you this. It used to be on David's desk. I thought your husband might like it.' She unwrapped the photograph of Edward de Jersey at Royal Ascot talking to the Queen.

'Thank you, Helen. It's very kind of you to think of us, and I'm sorry you've been hurt so much.'

Helen stood up. 'Well, I hope she gets what she deserves. They say what goes around comes around and I hope she . . . I hope she realizes what she's done to me.' She buttoned her coat. 'She's taken whatever happiness I had left. I almost hate him as much as I do her. I didn't know, Christina. That's what's so awful, I didn't know the man I was married to all those years. And I worshipped him.'

Mr Kitamo hardly ever looked directly at de Jersey. He maintained a slow walk, pausing at various paintings, sometimes stopping to read a plaque then stepping back to gaze at the picture. He appeared to be interested only in the art on display and let out a soft sigh when they stood in front of the *Mona Lisa*. The bodyguard kept a discreet distance behind them.

Kitamo finally broke the silence. 'To possess a painting of such beauty is very desirable but there are many rumours that her enigmatic smile is whispering, "Fake". I will require one of my own people to check over the merchandise. Although I trust our mutual friend, I will only agree to the terms if I am satisfied that the said item is authentic. We have agreed on the price and I understand you wish to have a show of my intention.' Kitamo turned his expressionless black eyes towards de Jersey. 'One million US dollars.'

'Correct,' de Jersey said.

'Agreed. Our friend will receive it as soon as I am informed that the item is in his possession. I will, perhaps, be prepared also to negotiate a price for certain smaller valuable pieces.' Kitamo ended the conversation as quickly as he had started it. 'I have enjoyed meeting you, Mr Simmons.' He gave a small bow, as if to conclude the meeting, and turned back to the *Mona Lisa*.

De Jersey, however, was not prepared to be dismissed and remained where he stood. Kitamo hesitated, then clicked his fingers to his bodyguard. Kitamo moved off and his bodyguard stepped in front of de Jersey, withdrawing from his jacket pocket a white envelope and passing it discreetly to him. Then he moved off to join Kitamo. De Jersey crossed to sit on one of the leather-covered benches and slipped the envelope inside the gallery's brochure as he opened it. It contained confirmation of a banking facility for over two hundred and fifty million US dollars in Kitamo's name. It was issued by the Banque Eurofin. A contact number was provided in case confirmation was required.

De Jersey remained seated for a few moments more. When he stood up and looked towards the end of the gallery, Kitamo was watching him and gave a small bow. De Jersey inclined his head back and walked out. Mr Kitamo, as Paul Dulay had said, was a legitimate buyer, and had the finance to purchase a good many of the jewels they were planning to steal. With the robbery less than a week away, de Jersey was relieved to know this.

Back in England, the warehouse remained empty but Wilcox and Driscoll timed the journey from there to the safe house several times. The day on which they would move all the convoy vehicles and the equipment was still undecided, although de Jersey planned to do it at night, one vehicle at a time, so as not to raise suspicion. After months of planning, the heist was only five days away.

Christina was at home watching television when she received a third call from Sylvia Hewitt. She again asked to speak to de Jersey and seemed angry when she was told that he was away.

'Where can I get in touch with him?' she asked.

'He usually stays at his club, the St James's, but I know he's very busy at the moment so if you would like to leave him a message—'

'I already have. I'll call the club. Sorry to bother you, but if he should return can you pass on these numbers?' Sylvia dictated her mobile, office and home numbers.

'How is Helen?' Christina couldn't resist asking just to hear what Sylvia's response would be.

'Still grieving for David. So, will you pass these numbers to your husband?'

'Yes.'

'Thank you,' Sylvia said, and hung up.

Christina had only just settled down to continue watching television when Sylvia called back. 'He's not there and they said he was not expected this evening. Have you a mobile number I could call?'

'I'm afraid I don't know it. I'm so sorry.'

There was a pause. Christina could almost feel the woman's impatience.

Sylvia sounded really angry when she asked again if Christina could get Edward to call her urgently. 'Please make sure he knows that he really should contact me.'

'I'll tell him.'

Christina went into her husband's study to look for his mobile number. She could never remember it. She had been worried to hear that he was not expected at the club that evening. She found the number and called de Jersey's mobile, but it was switched off. Frustrated, she called his club. A moment later they were speaking.

'Christina? Is something wrong?'

'No, darling. It's just that David Lyons' sister-in-law called. She said it was very urgent. It's the third time. She's really quite persistent. I said you were staying at the club and I think she called there.'

'Oh, God, that wretched woman.'

'Well, the porter at the club said you weren't there.'

He laughed. 'That's why I stay here. Good service!'

'Well, it's good that I caught you. She wanted your mobile number but I didn't give it to her. I suspected you wouldn't want her to have it.'

'Thank you. She's a real pain. Did she say why she wanted me so urgently?'

'Not really. Something about someone called Moreno and I can't remember the other name she mentioned. She left an array of contact numbers. Do you want them?'

'No, I don't want to speak to her.'

'Are you all right, darling?'

438

'Yes. Just had a heavy day. Back-to-back meetings. I'm not raising funds as fast as I'd hoped.'

'Is there anything I can do?'

'Not really. I'm having dinner with an American banker this evening so things may look better tomorrow. I'll call you later and give you an update. And perhaps after all I'll have the woman's numbers. I'll call her and get her off my back.'

De Jersey replaced the receiver, tense with anger. He thanked the porter and arranged a room for the night. The man passed him his room keys and told him about the call from a Miss Hewitt. 'Thank you, John. If she calls again, tell her I'm in a meeting and can't be interrupted, would you?'

'Yes, sir. Goodnight, sir.'

'Goodnight, John.'

De Jersey showered and changed into a clean shirt, which he had brought in his briefcase. He lay down on the bed and closed his eyes. He was relieved that he had decided on a whim to come to his club. It had been pure coincidence that he had walked in just as Christina called. He wondered what the wretched Hewitt woman wanted. It was almost eight, though, so he decided to leave for Westbrook's and deal with Sylvia Hewitt later.

De Jersey left the club unnoticed by the porter. He had already left a do-not-disturb message on his room's phone-message recorder. He hailed a taxi in Jermyn Street to Westbrook's studio flat.

As de Jersey approached Westbrook's floor, Westbrook was leaning against the banister rail looking down at de Jersey as he came up the stairs.

'Hi there. When you left the message that you wanted to talk to me, I didn't think you'd come in person. I was waiting for you to ring back,' he said.

De Jersey put out his hand as he approached Westbrook. 'Well, we're pretty close to kick-off so I thought it best to run over the finer details in person.' They shook hands.

'Come in.' Westbrook strolled ahead of him through the open door.

De Jersey didn't show how shocked he was by Westbrook's appearance. The man's face was haggard, with a yellowish, sickly pallor, and his clothes were unkempt. 'Can I offer you a drink?' Westbrook asked.

'No, thank you,' de Jersey said, and his nostrils flared at the stench of alcohol and urine. 'Stinks like a cat's litter tray in here,' he said.

'I know, it's frightful, isn't it? There are two moggies. God knows where they are. I don't see them much. Live under the bed most of the time. But they're why I'm here. I agreed with my relative to feed them and empty their shitty bins.' Westbrook slumped on the unmade bed. 'I've not been out today,' he said.

De Jersey sat on the edge of a once elegant, velvet-covered wing chair. On the mantelpiece stood rows of pill boxes and bottles. Stuffed between them were letters, postcards, invitations and unopened bills.

'Have you not been out because you're sick or because you can't be bothered?'

'Bit of both. I'm sick as hell, so I've been staying in watching the soaps. They all have such dreadful lives it sort of takes the heat off my own.' He laughed, and de

Jersey saw that even his teeth were worse than he remembered, as if the cancer was rotting his gums.

'You'd better get yourself together. You smell as bad as the cats' tray. What about clean clothes?'

Westbrook indicated an old walnut wardrobe, its door hanging off its hinges. Inside were racks of suits, plus sweaters and shirts on shelves. 'Oh, I'm flush for clothes, thanks to you, old chap. It's just getting up the energy to get dressed. It's not been a priority.'

'Make it one,' de Jersey snapped.

Westbrook stared at him, then shrugged. 'Yes, sir.'

'What do you need to get yourself together? We have four days to go and, from the look of you, I'd say you're not going to make it.'

Westbrook swung down his legs and glared at de Jersey. 'I'll make it. I'll take some booster painkillers and some high-quality speed. I won't let you down. Believe me, this is all I'm staying alive for.'

'All right, but if you fuck me over, it won't be your life I'll go after. Do you understand what I am saying?' He nodded at a picture of Westbrook's kids.

'I understand you perfectly.'

De Jersey looked over the array of medicines. 'Morphine,' he said coldly.

'Yes,' said Westbrook. 'It's not prescription but it dulls the pain. My old aunt Sarah used it for years for arthritis. Got to be careful not to take too much, though.'

'I'll have it.' De Jersey pocketed the bottle.

'Do you fancy a glass of wine? There's a reasonable wine bar on the corner up the road. Bite to eat on me?' Westbrook gave a wolfish smile.

De Jersey stood up. If he had been uneasy about Westbrook before, he was even more so now. 'You use that money I'm paying you to eat, not to get pissed.' He looked down at Westbrook's feet. He was wearing holey socks. 'Use it to get some laundry done too, and a new pair of socks. And if you've got a toothbrush, use it. Your breath stinks as much as you do.'

'I'm rotting away inside,' Westbrook said, stepping away defensively, but de Jersey held on to his jacket lapel.

'I'm depending on you and I'm watching you. Four days is all I ask for you to hold on to being straight. Then you can stew in your own shit for all I care. Four days. Look at me. Can you do it?'

Westbrook somehow found the strength to push de Jersey's hand away from him. 'Don't threaten me. I said I'd be up for it. I haven't let you down yet and I have no intention of doing so now. Like I said, I have the drugs I need to keep me on my feet and my head clear. Take the morphine. I'll suffer for you. How's that?'

De Jersey felt compassion for him. 'I'm sorry . . . but we're worried about you. I don't want you ODing on that stuff before the heist.'

Westbrook made a big effort to straighten up. It was both sad and admirable. 'I'm ready and I hope to God you are because I don't know how much longer I've got left.'

Sylvia waited until after ten and when de Jersey had still not called she was seething. She had decided not to go into work but to take another week off. By the following morning she was furious. She put in yet another call, this time to the estate. A blustering man answered. He said he was the manager and would pass on the message.

Christina was in the kitchen when Donald Fleming tapped on the door.

'Mrs de Jersey, there was a call from a Miss Hewitt for the boss. It came through to my office. Rude woman.'

'Oh, thank you, and yes, she is. She's called here numerous times. Did you say he was still at his club?'

'No. I just said I'd pass on the message, and I gave her his mobile number as she said it was urgent. I hope that's okay. I also need to have a word with him about scheduling some races. Can you ask him to give me a ring when it's convenient?'

'Sure. I'll call him now.' Christina looked at him: he seemed very put out about something.

'Are you all right?'

He gave her a curt nod and started to leave, then paused, his back to her. 'It's a tough time. A lot of the staff have been made redundant. It doesn't make for good staff relations. Some of the young lads are worried. I know it can't be helped but, like I said, it's not easy.'

'I'm sorry, Donald, but Edward is trying to make himself financially more secure. It's why he has to spend so much time in London. In fact, he's meeting with bankers this week.'

Fleming gave her a rueful look.

'He said he may have to think about remortgaging the estate,' she told him. 'If there's anything I can do, please don't hesitate to ask.'

'Thank you, Mrs de Jersey.'

Christina left a message at the St James's then called her husband's mobile. He answered. 'Hello, darling. It's a bit difficult for me to talk right now, I'm in the middle of a meeting. It's sounding as if I may have some good news. Is it urgent?'

'Not really. Sylvia Hewitt has called again and Donald gave her your mobile number. He also wants to sort out some racing dates. Also please don't forget the girls' school play. You promised you'd be there.'

'Can we talk about this later?'

'Yes, sorry to interrupt, but I felt that Donald would really like to talk to you and from what he said, Sylvia was angry that you hadn't returned her calls.'

'I'll call them both.'

She hung up, then went into her husband's study. On the desk was a large diary. She opened it, and looked down the listed races and the horses earmarked to compete. Some had lines crossed through them. She turned a few pages. She noticed that May the 2nd was circled and that a memo about a race at Brighton had been written in. She saw her own note to remind him of the school play; she picked up a pen and printed THE TAMING OF THE SHREW. She replaced the pen in the holder, and glanced over the neat desk. Then she hooked a finger through one of the drawer handles and pulled. It was locked, which niggled her, but she left the study and forgot about it.

Later, from the kitchen window, she watched the jockeys leading the horses out for their midday training. It was cold and the sun was bright. Royal Flush was playing up again, bucking and shaking his head. He kicked out, and then the long line of valuable horses was heading for the rolling acres beyond the track. It all looked so perfect, so affluent, and she sighed. She knew how much her husband loved this life. Christina threw on her fur-lined coat and dragged her riding boots out of the hall closet. By the time she reached the stableyard most of the horses were out exercising and she walked from stable to stable, then turned into the tack room. It was a hive of activity. The aroma of saddle soap was pungent and mingled with the fresh smell of hay and manure. For the first time she felt as if she didn't belong. She walked for an hour around all the stables, into the various yards and offices, and then to the garages. She stood by her husband's Rolls-Royce, which was being polished by one of the chauffeurs, ready to be sold. She asked where the driver she usually used was, and discovered that he no longer worked for them. It was only now that she realized just how many of the staff had gone. It made her feel even more inadequate. No wonder Donald Fleming was concerned. So much had happened while she had been away. So much that she hadn't noticed on her return.

'How many horses have been sold?' she asked a girl she passed on her way back to the house.

'I think about twenty, Mrs de Jersey,' she replied sadly.

'Does that include the ones from the east wing?'

'No, Mrs de Jersey, they went a while back. The latest ones went to the Tattersalls sales and over to Ireland,' the girl continued. 'But we've big hopes for Royal Flush,' she added.

Christina gave her a wan smile and walked on. For the first time it dawned on her that perhaps her husband was not going to be able to get out of his present financial trouble. It was obvious that it was a lot worse than he had suggested. By the time she had removed her coat and boots her depression had turned to anger.

Christina went into her husband's study. Even there

she felt like an outsider. The neatness and the locked drawers infuriated her. She went into the kitchen, found a screwdriver then returned to the study. She wrenched open one drawer after another, took out the contents and placed them on the desk. She was panting, half in fear, half in anger, as she set about sorting through them. To begin with she found nothing of importance: fees for trainers and purchases of horses, notes on horses he was considering buying, at least before the current financial crisis. However, there were also unpaid bills and outstanding accounts and a £155,000 VAT bill, with a warning that unless it was paid within a week legal action would be taken. At the bottom of one of the drawers she found a paper with Edward's handwritten notes. She sat down in the desk chair and scrutinized the figures. He had been neat and meticulous. He had listed and dated everything that Lyons had invested as well as everything on which Moreno had frittered the money away: meals, houses, expensive office supplies. For the first time she saw in black and white the astronomical losses, not in thousands but millions, and she felt almost faint with shock. There seemed no way they could get out from under the mounting debts. Her husband was virtually bankrupt.

Christina went into the kitchen and opened the fridge. She was thirsty, her throat dry with nerves. She poured a tumbler of orange juice and returned to the study. She began to return the documents to the drawers, at first hoping she could replace them as she had found them but then didn't bother. He would know by the marks of the screwdriver on the drawer handles and locks that she had broken into them. She stuffed loose papers into the top right-hand drawer and slammed it shut but it was too full so she snatched out a handful of papers and slammed it shut again. The glass of juice toppled over. 'Shit.' She ran from the room and returned with a wet cloth. The juice seemed to have seeped everywhere and she returned to the kitchen to fetch a cloth.

Back in the study she faced the front of the desk to scrub at the carpet on her knees. She half rose and was leaning against the rim of the desk with the palm of her hand when it moved. She stood up. 'Now what have I done?' she muttered. She tried to push the desk back into position then saw a small hinge. She pressed it and, to her astonishment, the right-hand side of the front of the desk opened. She bent down, to discover three more drawers. The lower ones were locked and even when she tried to open them with the screwdriver they wouldn't budge. She could see they had what looked like a steel rim.

'It's a safe,' she said aloud. Then she tried the smaller top drawer, which opened. It contained envelopes full of documents about the mortgage of the estate. A brown manila envelope was tucked beneath them. Her heart missed a beat. Inside it, she discovered two passports. Both contained pictures of Edward but with different names. One was in the name Edward Cummings and, when she checked it, there was a recent New York customs stamp inside. The other passport was Irish, in the name of Michael Shaughnessy. None of this made sense to Christina. She was certain her husband had been in the UK on the date marked in the Cummings passport. In another envelope, there were passports for herself and their daughters, all with different names. She sat back, unsure of anything any more. She had believed de Jersey was in London after Christmas because he had told her so, but according to the passport he had been in New York. What else had he lied to her about?

De Jersey was in the warehouse. He was inspecting the work that Wilcox had done on removing the wall that separated it from the D'Ancona cellar. Wilcox was through and had put the bricks back into position with a sugar and flour solution tinted grey to cover the missing cement. They would fall apart if a hand pushed hard against them. The work was good and de Jersey was pleased. Then a call came through on his mobile. It was Sylvia Hewitt.

'Mr de Jersey, I had hoped you would call me.'

'I'm sorry, Miss Hewitt, I've been very busy.'

'So have I,' she said softly. 'I need to meet you urgently. I have just returned from New York. I believe you were there?'

'You must be mistaken.'

'I don't think I am and I'm not playing games with you any more. This is a very serious matter, perhaps even for the police . . . or we could come to some financial arrangement. Either way, we should discuss my findings. I think you know what I'm referring to.'

'No, I don't,' he said coldly.

'Shall we say six this evening at my flat? You know the address, don't you, Mr Simmons.'

He felt the ground shift beneath his feet. She hung up. He stared at the phone in his hand, hardly able to believe what he had just heard. His heart was beating rapidly, and he felt dizzy. This was the worst thing that had happened so far and he was going to have to sort it out fast. If she knew, how many other people had she

448

told? He would have to take drastic measures. He slowly walked away from the coal cellar and into the grimy toilets in the warehouse. He splashed his face with cold water until he felt calm, then patted it dry with a grubby white towel. He stared at his reflection in the cracked mirror, thinking. He crossed to his overcoat, felt in the pocket, and took out Westbrook's bottle of morphine. He held it in the palm of his hand, as if weighing it. He would have to find out how many other people Sylvia Hewitt had told, then make a decision about the woman herself. He sighed. He would do it alone so that only he risked paying the ultimate price.

CHAPTER 22

SYLVIA uncorked a fresh bottle of wine and set it out with two glasses, a bowl of peanuts and crisps. She'd already had a few glasses to celebrate what she felt would be a sweet victory. She had vacuumed, dusted and plumped up the cushions, as if setting the scene for a play. She felt excited and powerful, and a little light-headed from the wine, as she looked over the 'stage' she had set. She went to her desk and called Matheson. He listened as she told him she had received his final invoice and would be sending him a cheque. She also told him she had successfully tracked down Philip Simmons in London.

'He's in the UK, then?' Matheson asked.

'Yes, and I'm expecting him to come and see me now.'

'Well, congratulations. Job well done. Does he know where Moreno is?' Matheson asked.

'I presume so. All will be divulged soon enough. I'm feeling very positive about it all now because I'm sure I'll get my investment repaid, perhaps even more for all the trouble it's caused me.' Sylvia was pleased with herself. 'I might even send you a little extra, Mr Matheson.'

The doorbell rang and she stood up. 'I have to go. He's arrived. Thank you so much again.'

She was still pleased with herself as she ushered de Jersey into the drawing room, gesturing for him to sit as she took his coat. She had decided not to accuse him of Moreno's murder immediately. That was to be her trump card if everything else failed.

'Please help yourself to wine,' she said, carrying his coat into the hall.

'I would prefer coffee,' he said pleasantly.

'Oh, well, give me a moment, then.'

De Jersey picked up the bottle of wine and poured some, then took out the morphine and emptied it into the glass. He had just started to pour some wine for himself when she returned with his coffee.

'It's instant. I hope you don't mind,' she said.

'No. That's fine. The wine looked so inviting after all that I've poured some for myself anyway.'

She passed him the coffee, picked up her glass and lifted it to her lips.

'Cheers,' she said, and drank. Lowering the glass, she frowned and licked her lips.

'This is very strange,' she said.

De Jersey picked up his glass and sipped. 'Do you think so?'

She took another sip. 'Yes, is it all right?'

He sipped again. 'It's fine.'

She reached for the bottle to look at the label. 'I don't know, it's not cheap,' she said, and took another gulp.

He raised his glass. 'Perhaps it should have been left to breathe a while longer.'

Sylvia reached for the peanuts, took a few and munched them like a squirrel. 'You must be eager to hear what I have to say. I'm surprised you could contain yourself.'

He smiled. 'Of course I'm eager to know and I'm sure you're about to enlighten me. It's obvious that you've been very . . . "active", shall we say? So, please.' He sat back and gestured for her to talk.

She laughed. 'Oh, you're a cool customer, Mr de Jersey, but I don't think you've given me the credit I deserve. I knew how important my discovery was when I found out you'd been to East Hampton. You have control of Alex Moreno's properties so you must be working with him, perhaps even helped him leave the country. His apartment and that estate he owned are worth millions and I dare say you have no desire to share the proceeds with any of the other investors. But you're going to share them with me.'

'Why would I do that?' he asked softly.

'Because I know who you are, and if you want that to remain our secret, I want a considerable amount more than the money I lost.' She explained how she had discovered his identity through Moreno's lover, Brian. 'Not that he knew your names. Either of them,' she said, and giggled. 'I also showed your photograph to the site foreman at Moreno's property. He was not as forthcoming as Moreno's young friend but gay men are so much more observant, don't you think?'

'How much do you want?' he asked.

'Well, I'd say it would be worth fifty-fifty, don't you? What you have been doing is highly illegal and I would love to know exactly how you pulled it off.'

'Well, it took a lot of work. Just getting a fake passport was hair-raising. You know, I've never done anything illegal in my life before this but I was afraid of losing everything I had and when you're desperate . . .' He got up and paced the room, continuing to talk about the stress he'd been under. Suddenly she felt hot and her forehead became damp. She continued to eat the peanuts and drank the remainder of her wine.

Eventually she took a deep breath and interrupted him. 'It's been hard for all of us. The reason I think you should agree to pay me, however, is the disappearance of Mr Moreno. According to his gay friend, he was alive the evening before he had a meeting with . . .' She trailed off.

'Are you all right, Miss Hewitt?' he said.

'No, I am feeling very . . .' Her body heaved and she felt as if she was about to vomit but instead she flopped forward. She gave a strange laugh as she tried to focus her eyes. 'Too much wine,' she said.

He stood up, collected his wine glass and coffee cup, and left the room. She tried to stand but her legs gave way and she fell back into the chair. Now the room blurred and she felt dreadfully sick.

In the kitchen, de Jersey washed his coffee cup and glass, dried them with a tea-towel, removing all fingerprints, then replaced them on the shelf. He filled a glass with water, then took a small hypodermic needle from his wallet. He injected the water with ketamine, a horse tranquillizer, then replaced the hypodermic in his wallet. He opened the fridge, put some ice into the glass and carried it back to Sylvia Hewitt.

'Here, drink this.'

She seemed less drugged, and held out her hand for the water. He made sure she had a firm hold of it before he returned to sit on the sofa. She drank thirstily, gasped, and looked at him in terror.

'What have you put in this?'

He took the glass from her and checked how much she had drunk. 'Just a little sedative, Miss Hewitt. My vet uses it all the time.' He walked out of the room, taking her wine glass and the water glass with him, washed them and put them away as the lethal cocktail of drugs flooded through her.

Putting on a pair of surgical gloves, de Jersey spent a considerable time gathering up Sylvia's correspondence with Matheson and any other document relating to the investment case. Then he went back to the sink in the kitchen and set light to it all. He cleared up the charred remains and placed them in the waste-disposal unit, turned it on and ground away every fragment. Then he cleaned around the sink, wiping away any possible remaining fingerprints.

When he carried Sylvia to the sofa she was unconscious. He lifted her head on to a frilled cushion, then went into her bedroom, took a quilt from her bed and tucked it around her.

Christina was in bed when de Jersey called her from his room. He knew straight away that something was wrong.

'We have a lot to talk about,' she said, rather coldly.

'Why? What's happened?'

'I'd rather not discuss it over the phone.'

'Fine. I'll be home in a few days. I have to go to Ireland,' he said affably.

'Why?' she asked.

'I'm sorry, sweetheart, I can't put it off. You know why.'

'Where will you be staying?'

'I'll be moving around but I'll be in Dublin first then go to a few auctions. I've recently sold off a filly to a friend so I need to settle her in.' He gave no hint of the tension he felt.

'Well, don't forget we have the girls' school play on the second.'

'I haven't forgotten, darling. I'll be home in plenty of time. Are you all right? You sound . . . What's happened? It's not Royal Flush, is it?'

'No, he's fine,' she said. 'We can discuss it when you get back.'

'You know I love you,' he said.

'And I love you.' She hung up.

His hand rested a moment on the receiver. She had sounded odd. If something was troubling Christina he would find out what it was, but it would have to wait. He cleaned his teeth, showered and got ready for bed. He felt uneasy, however, so he called Donald Fleming. 'Sorry to ring so late but I'm up against it at the moment. I've just spoken to Christina. Nothing wrong up at the house, is there?'

'Not that I know of, but she was around the yard this afternoon. I think she's just worried like all of us.'

'Yes, well, let's hope I come up with some extra financing, but keep your eye on her for me, would you? I don't want her unduly worried. We'll get through this, Donald.'

'I will. I see you've earmarked a runner for Brighton on the second. You gonna make it?'

'Perhaps. Depends on a few meetings.'

'But you'll be at Lingfield for Royal Flush's race, won't you?'

'Of course. I wouldn't miss it for the world. Oh, any news on the other matter?'

'She's going for a blood test in a few days,' Fleming said. 'We'll know if she's in foal then, but I think your boy may have done the business.'

'Fine. I'll keep in touch.' He hung up and sighed. He was tired to the bone but before he settled for the night, he took out the bottle of morphine and the hypodermic needle that had contained the ketamine. Sylvia Hewitt's glass of water had contained enough horse tranquilliser to knock out a carthorse permanently so he had reckoned one heavy slug of it along with the morphine was enough to ensure she would no longer be a problem. He refused to allow himself to contemplate what he had done, and concentrated on getting rid of the evidence. He wrapped the bottle and the syringe in a hotel napkin and smashed them against the wall into tiny pieces. Then he took one of the glasses in his room, dropped it on the floor and added the broken pieces to the crushed bottle and the syringe. He slipped out of his room, walked along the corridor and up another flight of stairs until he came to an unattended porter's trolley. He emptied the glass into the bin and tossed the towel and napkin into a laundry basket before he returned to his room. It was after eleven when he fell into a deep, dreamless sleep.

Over the next two nights before the raid, they began to move the vehicles one by one to the warehouse. They had disguised the Royal mascot on the Daimler so no one would be suspicious but when it was driven to the warehouse in Aldersgate at four in the morning, there was hardly a soul around. The movement of the clothes and motorbikes was simpler but also done under cover of night. The pace was on. There was no looking back now and de Jersey called to Dulay. The *Hortensia Princess* was on its way to the south coast of England with Dulay at the helm. Suddenly all the months of preparation, the working out of timings and details had begun to gel.

On 1 May, Royal Flush won his first race of the season at Lingfield by seven lengths. Mickey Rowland was sad that de Jersey had not been there to witness his victory. Fleming was surprised – he had spoken to him about it only a few days ago. They both received calls from de Jersey and gave him a second-by-second account of the race, how Royal Flush had not even been breathing hard afterwards. He had travelled home calmly and eaten his feed, and both jockey and trainer were confident.

'You should have been there, Mr de Jersey,' said Fleming. 'He did you proud. He did us all proud. You've got a champion there. You should have seen the Sheikh's trainer sniffing around him. We'll headline in the *Racing News*, I guarantee it.'

There was an awkward pause, then Fleming went on. 'With regard to the filly, Bandit Queen, she's in foal.'

'Jesus God,' de Jersey said, closing his eyes.

'You want me to ship her out to Ireland to this Shaughnessy character?'

'Yes, I'll call with the details. Well done and thank you again.'

Christina watched as the lads celebrated Royal Flush's win. Donald Fleming was cracking open the champagne. He was drinking directly from a bottle. 'Did you see him?' he asked Christina.

'Of course. It was on Channel Four. Did you speak to my husband? He told me that he had to go to Dublin.'

'He was over the moon. If our boy wins the next one he's got one hell of a chance at the Derby. Can I offer you a glass? The boss ordered a crate for the lads.'

'No, thank you,' she said, turning as one of the lads asked Fleming about arranging the horsebox for Bandit Queen.

'Be over there later with the paperwork,' Fleming called back.

'Are you selling her?' Christina asked, perplexed. Edward had bought the horse for her.

'Yep, she's being shipped out to Ireland.'

'Oh, I see. Is that why he's going over there?'

'I guess so. She's been bought by a Michael Shaughnessy, old friend of Mr de Jersey's.'

'Well, congratulations to everyone,' she said, and went back towards the house. Then she changed her mind and walked to her car. She drove over to where the brood mares were stabled and parked. She sat watching as Bandit Queen was led out of her stall as the lads drove up in the horsebox. Christina got out and crossed to them as they were draping Bandit Queen in a blanket.

'Another gone,' she said, half to herself, then moved closer to stroke the mare's head.

A young lad stood to one side holding the halter. 'Sad to see her go,' the lad said. 'We had high hopes for her.'

'Do you know this man Michael Shaughnessy who's apparently bought her?'

'No, Mrs de Jersey, but she must have cost him a packet. Like I said, we had high hopes for her and she won her maiden race almost as well as our Royal Flush.'

'Thank you,' Christina said, and went back to her car. She drove to the house and as she went into the kitchen, the phone rang.

'Christina? It's Helen Lyons.'

Christina sighed. 'Hello, Helen,' she said. 'How are you?'

'Oh, a little better now. I'm staying with a friend in Devon and she's taking good care of me. Is this an inconvenient time to call?'

'Erm, no.'

'It's about my insurance from the house. Sylvia was taking care of it. They still haven't settled, you know, since the fire.'

'Good heavens! That is a long time.'

'Well that's what I thought, but with things the way they are between Sylvia and me, I don't feel I can call her.'

'I understand, Helen, but perhaps you're going to have to. Or perhaps you should write to her.'

'I have, but she hasn't replied. I was wondering . . .' Her voice tapered off.

Christina said nothing.

'Well, as I said, I really don't want to speak to her and I was wondering if you would be kind enough to call her for me as you knew David so well.'

Christina sighed. She could see no way out of it. 'I'll call her for you, Helen.'

'Oh, thank you. Please would you ask her to send me the details of the insurance policy. I'd be most grateful.'

Christina took down Sylvia's number and Helen's number in Devon, and said she would call her back as soon as she had contacted Sylvia. She hung up, feeling irritated. She had no interest in Helen or her sister, especially when she considered what David Lyons had done to her husband. She lit a cigarette before she rang Sylvia. There was no reply. She made another call to Dublin, to the Westcliffe Hotel where her husband usually stayed. She was told that Mr de Jersey had not booked in and they were not expecting him. This time she slammed the receiver down. Another lie! She stubbed out her cigarette and lit another immediately.

The phone rang and she snatched it up. 'Yes?'

'Christina, it's Helen. Did you call her?'

'Yes, there was no reply.'

'Did you try her office? I did give you her work number as well, didn't I?'

'No.'

Helen gave Christina Sylvia's work number, thanked her profusely and apologized again.

'Helen, I'll call you back as soon as I've spoken to Sylvia. So there's no need for you to ring me again. Goodbye now.'

Christina hung up. She felt like weeping. She sat smoking one cigarette after another, then forced herself to leave the kitchen. She'd change the beds and see to the laundry. After that she'd return to the study. This time she would methodically go through every document she could find. When her husband returned home she would be ready for him and this time she wanted answers not lies.

Once everything had been transported to the warehouse, they cleared the barn. De Jersey and Driscoll spent hours cleaning up. They didn't leave a scrap of evidence as to what had taken place there over the past months. The stove, the heaters and the big lamps were all removed. They lit a bonfire to burn the waste, the paper cups, the rubber gloves. With only twenty-four hours to go, it was the calm before the storm.

De Jersey tapped the window of the Mercedes. In a chauffeur's uniform behind the wheel, Driscoll lowered the window. 'It's time,' de Jersey said. 'Let's get the ball rolling.'

The Mercedes was owned by Wilcox but had fake number-plates and would be driven to the crusher the minute they were done with it. Wilcox gave the thumbs-up and Driscoll drove out of the warehouse. It was four fifteen in the morning on May 2nd. They left de Jersey alone to wait for the rest of the team to arrive. As they drove away, he looked at his watch. In a few hours the waiting would all be over.

'It's five o'clock,' Eric said, a fraction before the alarm sounded. His wife Maureen lay next to him, her hair in pincurls. She sat bolt upright.

461

'Breakfast?' Eric asked, standing next to the bed with a tray that held a lightly boiled egg, two slices of buttered toast and a cup of tea.

'You spoil me,' Maureen said.

By six, Eric had his wife's little suitcase packed. She always took a few changes of clothes to advertisement shoots because if they supplied them the skirts were always too long. For this one she had been asked to bring her own anyway. She had chosen a blue tweed coat with a velvet collar. She also had a hat in a box and a pleated skirt and blouse to go beneath the coat. Although they usually supplied a makeup artist, she made up her face carefully as she knew the exact shade of base and lipstick required. She must never look over made-up. That would be a dead giveaway.

Eric helped her into a raincoat. Though it was still dark, he could see it was cloudy and he handed her a small folding umbrella. 'You all set, darling?' he asked.

'I am. Is the car here?'

'I'll go and check.' Eric opened the front door, walked down the path and stood at the gate. A Mercedes was heading down the road.

Eric returned to the house and called, 'They're here, dear, just coming to the drive.' He turned as the Mercedes drew up behind his own car.

The driver stepped out, his hat pulled down low, almost hiding his face. 'Morning, I've come to collect . . .' At that moment she came out of the house, carrying the suitcase, hatbox and handbag.

'I'm ready,' said Maureen pleasantly, and turned her cheek to her husband for a goodbye kiss. Another man stepped out and opened the rear door of the Mercedes, taking her case as he helped her inside. The driver asked

Eric if he could use their bathroom. Eric gestured for him to follow him inside and they went into the house. In the car, the second man placed a rug around Maureen's knees then closed the door and got into the front passenger seat.

'What on earth are they doing?' she asked, after five minutes had passed and the driver had still not returned.

'He's had a bit of trouble with his prostate,' the man replied.

At last the driver came out, red in the face, and closed the front door. As they drove out, Maureen looked back towards the house. 'That's odd,' she said. 'My husband always waves me off to work. It's a little ritual we have. I'm a very lucky woman.' She settled back. Sometimes his undivided attention got on her nerves a little. But, as he said so many times, his queen was worth taking care of.

Maureen Stanley had made her career as Queen Elizabeth's lookalike. She was almost the same age and, like her, was cutting down on the amount of work she took on. Millennium year had been fantastic and she had often had two engagements on the same night. She enjoyed the television work more, though, than the special appearances.

'Where are we filming?' she asked Driscoll.

'Close to the BBC radio studios.'

After about ten minutes, Driscoll saw that she had fallen asleep, her head lolling forward. He looked at her and smiled at Wilcox. 'Dead ringer, isn't she?' he said softly.

'Yeah. Did all go to plan back at the house?'

'Yep. He's comfortable, can't hurt himself. Tucked

463

him up on the sofa.' He glanced again at Eric's wife, who was unaware that her beloved husband had been drugged and tied up. Eric had been bending over the hall table looking at some leaflet that had been pushed through his letterbox for window-cleaning when Driscoll had placed his left arm across the small man's chest and injected his right buttock through his trousers. Eric had tried to fend him off but the sedative acted quickly and his body sagged.

'What . . . what have you done?' he had gasped.

'Put you to sleep for a few hours, pal, nothing to worry about. You'll have a bit of a headache when you wake up, that's all.'

At six thirty, the Mercedes arrived at the Aldersgate warehouse. As the doors closed behind it, Maureen woke up. 'Are we here?' she asked, looking around the large warehouse in surprise. 'This isn't the BBC, is it?'

Driscoll turned and smiled. 'No, ma'am, it isn't. Would you like to get out of the car? There's coffee and doughnuts.'

'Thank you, I've had my breakfast.' She glanced around the vast warehouse.

'I'll take you to your dressing room, then.' Driscoll opened the door for her. By the time she was settled, Wilcox was driving the Mercedes across London to be destroyed. Driscoll then set off again to pick up a rented furniture-removal van. It would play a major role in the getaway and the team had prepared stickers to cover the name of the rental company and the number-plate.

The dressing room was a small room off the main warehouse space, previously used for storing clothes and accessories. It contained a dressing-table with a mirror, a comfortable chair and a heater. Maureen was ushered inside and told to wait for someone to come and see to her hair and makeup. She nodded and put down her suitcase. She opened it to take out her clothes. A few items were already hanging on a rail. They were all expensive, with Aquascutum and Harrods labels, but she could see at a glance that they were too long. Why don't they get their facts right? she thought. The Queen is tiny.

Outside the dressing room, there was a lot of movement. The Daimlers were ready and being given a final polish. Pamela was next to arrive and de Jersey gestured for her to join him at the back of the warehouse. He told her their queen was in the dressing room still unaware of her role and he wanted her kept in the dark for as long as possible.

Pamela seemed relaxed but was chain-smoking. She poured herself a coffee. 'I'll go and get changed, keep her company.' She surveyed the warehouse. 'Westbrook here yet?'

De Jersey checked his watch. 'He's due at eight. You all set?'

'Yes, of course. It's rather like opening night at the theatre.' She chortled.

De Jersey smiled. Pamela had been a great choice. 'You're a special lady,' he said softly.

'I know, darling. Pity I can't find a decent fella who thinks so too.' She raised an eyebrow and sipped her coffee. 'Maybe with all the loot I'll get from this I'll find me a nice toy-boy.' Then she went to the dressing room, knocked and entered.

Even though she had been prepared to see her co-artist, Pamela was still taken aback by Maureen's eerie likeness to the Queen.

'Morning, darling,' she said. 'I'm your lady-in-waiting. We've got to shack up in here for a while before they take us to the location.' She plonked down her coffee and drew up the only hard-backed chair.

'Do you have the script?' Maureen asked, still fussing with her clothes.

'No, sweetheart, I don't. The director will let us know what we have to do.'

Maureen nodded. She always liked to have the script well before they filmed so she knew what she would be required to do.

'Did you want a coffee?' Pamela asked, taking out another cigarette.

'No, thank you.'

As Pamela held the lighter to the end of the cigarette she saw that her hands were shaking. For all her bravado, she was nervous. She knew she had to ignore the butterflies starting in the pit of her stomach. She had come too far to back out now.

'Do you play cards?' Maureen asked hopefully.

'I do, darling! Have you got a pack with you?'

Maureen produced one from her handbag. 'Never without! These shoots are so boring. They always get you here far too early, don't you think?'

Wilcox and Driscoll returned in plenty of time. Wilcox couldn't help but admire the Daimlers, which were polished like mirrors. The bikes stood beside them. He turned sharply as the gate opened and the two bikers entered. Hall and Short gave him a cool nod, but Wilcox kept his distance from them. To all intents and purposes, they were hired villains and to Wilcox the most dangerous to security, but de Jersey and Driscoll had assured him they were reliable. They went to change into their police uniforms, leaving Wilcox to continue checking the Daimlers. He looked up as Driscoll appeared with coffee.

'You can't get them any cleaner,' Driscoll said. He noticed the two bikers. 'Nice to see they're on time.' He moved closer to Wilcox. 'The one on the right did twelve years for that Asprey and Garrard jewel heist. The one on the left was inside for fifteen. Same kind of gig but got out over the wall about a year ago.'

Wilcox changed the subject. 'The Colonel told me he was straight with that Hewitt woman.' He tossed the duster aside.

'What do you think he meant by that?'

Wilcox gave a shrug. 'Well, he paid her off, I guess.'

'This has sure cost him a bundle.'

Wilcox nodded. Then he smiled. 'But what a pay-out we're in line for!'

They grinned and slapped hands, each man as tense as the other but refusing to admit it.

Westbrook arrived in a navy blue pinstripe suit, a blue shirt with a starched white collar and cuffs, his old Eton tie with a pearl pin, and a rose in his lapel. He had washed his hair and combed it back from his high forehead. Even his teeth appeared whiter. His pallor, however, was sickly and his luminous eyes were far too bright. He had taken his first hit of speed.

'Morning, Colonel,' he chirped, in the familiar upper-crust drawl. He executed a small pivot turn on the heel of his new Gucci loafers. 'How do I look?'

'Good.' De Jersey glanced down at his socks: no holes. 'How are you feeling?'

'Fine, thank you. Is HM installed yet?' He fiddled with his kid gloves.

'She's in the dressing room with Pamela. She's not been told her script yet so take care what you say to her and remind Pamela not to remove her gloves. That goes for you too. The place has been cleaned.'

'Fine. Any coffee on?'

'Help yourself.' De Jersey looked at his watch. It was coming up to eight o'clock. They would leave the warehouse at ten twenty-five exactly. He watched Westbrook stroll across to the coffee pot and his heart went out to him. He was so well dressed it was hard to believe that he was the same messed-up creature de Jersey had been worried about. He just hoped to God that his lordship could keep up the pretence.

Westbrook tapped and entered the dressing room, and de Jersey heard Pamela shriek at how gorgeous he looked. So far, so good. Everything and everyone was on time. De Jersey changed into a cheap grey suit, black shoes and socks, a white shirt and black tie. He used a nasty silver tiepin and tucked a handkerchief into his breast pocket. He stared at himself. He looked every inch the private security guard, down to his large frame. He sat down, opened his briefcase and removed an expensive wig of fine reddish hair. It was the one he had worn in the Hamptons, along with matching moustache and eyebrows. He spent some time carefully gluing the moustache into place and even longer adjusting the eyebrows and wig. Satisfied, he peeled off the surgical gloves, replacing them with soft black leather ones.

He spent another half-hour spraying every surface that might reveal fingerprints or DNA. He had already sprayed and cleaned the coffee mugs and food area. The trash had been collected in a black bin-liner, which he would incinerate. He wanted to be sure that there wasn't a single print or clue left to identify him or anyone else in the team. He put down his briefcase and clicked it open. It contained his mobile phone – the vital link to Raymond Marsh. Now all Marsh had to do was get the right codeword. De Jersey hoped that he had identified the right phone line to be used today by the IRA. If he didn't come up with the goods, they were screwed.

At ten to nine, he went into the dressing room. He gave Pamela and Westbrook a nod to leave him alone with Maureen. He apologized for breaking up the party and explained it was time to leave for the location.

'Well, I can't say it's not before time.' Maureen started to gather her things. 'What do you want me to wear? You're the director, aren't you? I've been here since just after six and I haven't even been shown a script yet!'

De Jersey stared at her. 'I think the coat you're wearing would be perfect, if that's OK with you. Do you think you should wear a hat or a headscarf?'

'Well, that depends on the script. I mean, is it interior or exterior? She doesn't wear a hat all the time but I've brought a selection.'

'It's exterior moving to interior.'

Maureen displayed her hats but he chose a pale blue

headscarf that matched her coat and gave the right casual feel for the occasion. He asked her not to wear it until they reached the set. Then he chose a large brooch for her to wear on the coat lapel before hurrying her to get into the car.

'It's just typical this, you know,' Maureen complained. 'I've been here since after six and now it's all hurry-hurry. I've not even had my makeup checked. I need at least to freshen my lipstick. Will we rehearse?'

'Yes. I'd like you to come to the car.'

She chattered on as he guided her to it. His lordship was seated in the front and Pamela was waiting in the rear passenger seat with the door open. Maureen got in beside her, remarking on how unusual it was to be driven with the director.

'Oh, we're not moving yet. We just want to rehearse getting in and out of the Daimler.'

'Well, I've certainly done that many times,' Maureen said. She and Pamela got in and out as Westbrook oversaw the rehearsal.

De Jersey checked his watch and looked at Pamela. 'I need to have a chat with the artist.' Then to Maureen he said, 'Would you please get back into the Daimler?' Maureen hesitated and looked at Pamela, then climbed in. De Jersey got in beside her, leaned back and took a deep breath. He could smell the glue he had used to stick his wig and moustache in place. 'Do you love your husband?' he asked quietly.

'Pardon?' Maureen said.

'I asked if you loved your husband,' he repeated.

'Of course! We've been married forty-two years.'

'Good. Now, I want you to remain as calm as possible

470

and pay attention to what I'm going to tell you. Your husband is being held at gunpoint. He's perfectly safe and will not be harmed if you do exactly as I tell you. If you do not, he will be shot.'

She stared, her mouth open. She blinked rapidly.

'Do you understand? It is up to you whether or not you ever see your husband alive again. If you cry out or give any indication that we are holding him captive, you will never see him alive again. If you do not obey to the letter exactly what I am going to tell you to do, your husband's life will be in danger. If you do exactly as I say, no harm will come to him or you. Do you understand?' de Jersey asked. 'This is not a game. This is not a film. This is happening, right now. Give me your hand.'

Maureen lifted it as if she were a robot, and he clasped it tightly. 'We are all about to commit a dangerous robbery and we need you to portray Her Majesty the Queen.'

Driscoll glanced at the Daimler. They had been in it for ten minutes. He had heard no sound, no scream or shout, nothing but the low murmur of de Jersey's voice. It was now almost nine o'clock. He reckoned they were taking one hell of a risk with the woman. What if she fell apart and couldn't keep up the act? He began to feel sick.

The car door opened and de Jersey got out. He closed the door again, leaving the woman inside and crossed to Pamela. 'Go in and sit with her. Go through the routine.' He nodded to Westbrook, who stood up. Wilcox looked at him nervously.

'She's going to be fine. Maybe a little drop of brandy will set her up but she'll be just fine.'

In the car, Pamela sat beside Maureen.

'Are you part of this?' Maureen said, hardly audible.

'No, but I don't think they'll hurt us. We just have to do exactly as we're told and nothing will go wrong.'

'They've got my husband.'

'Yes, I know.'

'Have they got yours too?' she asked.

Pamela turned and took her hand. 'Yes, darling, so we're in this together. We just have to think it's a film. It's the only way we can get through it.'

The door opened and Westbrook passed in a small silver flask. 'Have a nip of this, ladies, we've got about half an hour to go.'

Pamela winked at him and unscrewed the flask. Maureen clutched at it with both hands and gulped down the brandy. It made her cough and splutter. Her hands were shaking and her knees were jerking in spasm. 'I'm so frightened. This is terrible, terrible.'

Pamela gripped her hand again. 'Now, stop this, stop it now. We have to do what they say. It's my husband as well, you know.'

Maureen nodded and closed her eyes, terrified. 'I need – need to redo my lip-lipstick,' she stammered.

De Jersey's mobile rang and he snatched it up.

'All on course, are we?' came Raymond's chirpy voice.

'Just waiting for you,' de Jersey responded. He glanced at his watch. It was ten past nine.

472

'Well, I'd hit your coal bunker. I've just sensed activity on the alarm phone lines, which means they've done their tests. You'll need to do your IRA threat in about three quarters of an hour.'

'Fine, but what's the codeword?'

'They've not phoned it through yet. Don't panic. I'm on to it.'

'You'd better be.'

'Over and out.' Marsh clicked off.

De Jersey stood up. He knew that the wait would get to them all now and he also knew that, above all else, he had to remain in control and show no sign of his own tension. He turned to Wilcox and nodded for him to get ready to climb through into the D'Ancona coal room. Wilcox was wearing an overall, thick gloves and a helmet with a light attached. 'How long have I got?' he asked.

'It's nine fifteen now. I'll make the threat call at ten and Marsh will intercept to the safe house shortly after that. Then we've got twenty minutes before we move out.'

Wilcox walked down into the cellar and made his way to the opening between the two buildings. He switched on his lamp and started to remove the loosened bricks.

'How we doing?' came a soft whisper. Wilcox whipped round. De Jersey looked like a ghost in a white paper suit to protect his clothes from the dust.

'Just breaking through now. How am I for time?'

'We're fine.'

As de Jersey spoke, Wilcox pushed another brick loose, cringing as it dropped to the other side. He pulled other bricks towards him on to an old duvet he'd laid on the floor to dull the noise.

'They're doing the final clean-up of the warehouse,' de Jersey told him.

'Great,' said Wilcox, working hard. Both men remained silent for a moment. 'We're in,' he said softly. 'Shouldn't you be upstairs making a call, for Christ's sake?'

'I'm on my way. Just get in and see if it's going to be a problem.'

'Bit late for that now, isn't it?' said Wilcox, and crawled out of sight.

He had already seen inside the room when he had first opened up the wall, so he knew what he would find. Marsh had been correct. There was the box with all the lines plugged into it, each neatly labelled with the location of the related panic alarm, such as 'under floor reception' or 'vault walls'. On the far side a steel door led into the safe house. D'Ancona had never suspected anyone would be able to gain access from the opposite side. That had been their mistake.

Wilcox was dripping with sweat. If one of the plugs was pulled a fraction earlier than the others, the police would be round in minutes, the heist would be off and they'd be on the run without the reward. The technique Marsh had come up with for removing the plugs was brilliantly simple. At the end of each plug was a small loop where it met the cable. Wilcox took a piece of stiff wire from his belt and began to thread it through each loop. He took his time. He didn't want to jolt any of the plugs, pulling them from their socket prematurely. After five minutes, the wire was in place, carefully threaded through all of the loops. This was the moment of truth.

If it went wrong their cover would be blown. He took hold of each end of the wire and pulled.

Driscoll was ready, pacing up and down beside the Daimler. The two bikers sat with their helmets in their hands. Wilcox seemed to be taking ages. Eventually he emerged, covered in dust, and gave a thumbs-up. The panic buttons were disconnected. The team gave a collective sigh of relief and Driscoll patted him on the back.

Westbrook checked the time. It was five to ten. He was starting to sweat and unsure if he should take his last hit of speed now or wait.

'Is there a bog in this place?' Westbrook asked. Driscoll pointed to the rear of the warehouse. Westbrook walked off and let himself into the dirty bathroom. He was just a few minutes behind Wilcox and heard him snorting up a line of cocaine through the door. 'I wouldn't mind a line if you have one to spare,' he said quietly. Wilcox opened the door and beckoned him in. They huddled together as Wilcox chopped up two very long lines.

'For Christ's sake, don't let the Colonel know I'm doing this,' Wilcox said.

'He knows I need it.' Westbrook was already rolling a rather creased five-pound note in anticipation. Wilcox produced a short silver straw and hoovered up his line. He was still wearing his overall, his face filthy from the dust.

De Jersey checked the time again and again. He was very tense. They had half an hour to go and there was still no word from Marsh. It was insanity to have depended so heavily on him and he knew it. He was starting to think about leaving the warehouse and killing the man with his bare hands when the mobile rang. The IRA codeword for that day was 'Boswell'. With trembling fingers, de Jersey made the call. When someone answered, he said, in a mild Northern Irish accent, 'Boswell, I repeat, Boswell.' The officer taking the call did not question the authenticity and put the receiver down fast. De Jersey sighed with relief.

Marsh was listening in to a call from the Commander at Scotland Yard to Buckingham Palace informing them of the IRA threat and putting a halt to the day's plans. His final task was to intercept the call from Scotland Yard to the safe house, which would inform them of a delay. If he succeeded, D'Ancona would be none the wiser.

The team waited in silence. Wilcox had changed into his chauffeur's uniform in preparation for driving the second Daimler and stood chewing his lips. All were on edge for the last call to come in. When it did, everyone stared at de Jersey as he answered. Marsh had intercepted the call and the safe house had no idea that the fitting had been cancelled. They were still awaiting the Royal visit on schedule at ten thirty.

De Jersey checked his watch: it was exactly ten twenty. They prepared to move the short distance from the warehouse to the D'Ancona safe house. De Jersey climbed into the Daimler beside Wilcox. Driscoll took his position in the second Daimler containing Pamela,

Westbrook and the silent, terrified Maureen. The bikers lowered their helmets and sat astride their police bikes. The minutes ticked by slowly.

'Open the doors,' de Jersey said, and the biker nearest pressed the automatic button to slide back the warehouse doors and they were on the move.

The convoy turned left into the road. Maureen could not speak. She sat beside Pamela, clutching her handbag, her blue headscarf tied round her head, her lipstick badly reapplied. She wanted to go to the toilet, but she was too scared to open her mouth. Her eyes were wide with fear. Pamela occasionally patted her knees, which were still shaking alarmingly.

'Well, we got the show on the road,' de Jersey said, resting his arm along the back of the front seat, just touching Wilcox. 'We got the show on the road,' he repeated, when Wilcox didn't respond. He gave him a sharp look. 'How much of the stuff did you take?' he asked.

'Enough to keep me steady. I needed it. My nerves were shot.'

De Jersey stared at him and withdrew his arm. 'Fuck up and I'll kill you.'

Wilcox licked his lips.

'Bikers are still in position,' de Jersey continued. He picked up his mobile and dialled. 'How's Her Majesty?'

'She's doing just fine,' Westbrook told him.

They passed the traffic cones, which had been placed by the two bikers earlier that morning. This was the only road leading to the safe house. They passed the no-entry sign at the end of the street, again placed by the bikers to avoid any other traffic entering it. The journey took less than three minutes.

De Jersey looked out of the window then spoke into the phone. 'Stand by, we're there.' He switched off the mobile and pulled at his glove. Ahead he could see the security guard in his uniform and cap waiting at the entrance to the safe house.

'The show is on.' De Jersey laughed softly and Wilcox gave him a small, covert glance. He seemed relaxed, as if he was enjoying himself. De Jersey caught the look and patted his shoulder. 'Three Musketeers, eh? Just like the old days.'

Wilcox dropped down a gear to move slowly to the side of the road just ahead of the entrance so that the Queen's Daimler could park with ease directly behind him.

'Good morning,' de Jersey said to the waiting security guard, as he climbed out of the car. The heavy studded doors of the safe house were open, a red carpet placed on the steps up to the entrance. Lined up inside the reception area were the D'Ancona employees, waiting for the Queen. 'The road should stay closed until we leave,' de Jersey said to the guard, in a quiet but authoritative tone. One of my officers will stay out here to help you if there's any trouble.'

'Yes, sir.'

At this moment the head representative from D'Ancona appeared in the doorway, wearing a pinstripe suit and a rose in his buttonhole. He stood to one side, waiting. There was just a fraction of a pause, just two or three seconds, which felt like minutes. Then Lord Westbrook stepped out of the front seat of the Queen's Daimler. He gave a cold, arrogant look to the guard. Then he opened the passenger door to allow Pamela to exit first. She stood to one side, holding Maureen's handbag, as Maureen stepped from the Daimler with a frozen smile.

The guard bowed and, as rehearsed, Pamela fell into position behind Maureen. Lord Westbrook stepped to her left, with de Jersey behind him, and Driscoll brought up the rear. They began to proceed into the safe house as one of the bikers, Hall, stepped forward to check the road and the buildings opposite for any signs of disturbance.

As the Royal party moved into the entrance hall then down the stairs and out of sight, the D'Ancona security guard decided to go back to his workstation. Within four feet of the safe-house main doors there was a cage, grilled on all three sides. Inside it were banks of monitors, all showing the Royal party heading slowly down the thickly carpeted stairs to the lower floor reception area. As the guard went to enter the cage, Hall, still with his helmet in place, moved in close behind him, so close that he unnerved the guard, who turned to find the muzzle of a handgun pressed into his neck. 'Back into the cage and do exactly as I tell you or this blows your head off,' Hall hissed.

The man put his hands up, and obeyed, but trod on a concealed panic button.

'Further in, pal. Move it!'

The Royal party was displayed on every monitor. They were now being led into the reception area. Other banks of monitors showed virtually every inch of corridor and office, plus the vault on the lower level, which was standing wide open. Hall's thuggish bulk came close to the guard. 'Pull the fucking camera controls, pal. The alarms are dead. And so will you be if you make me wait another second. Do it!' The guard hesitated, but got a rough push from the gun pressed now in the small of his back.

One by one he unplugged the cameras and the monitors went blank. Hall pushed him roughly into the chair, tied his hands and feet with tape and gagged him. He then crammed the man's hat down on his head and turned the seat slightly so that anyone passing the cage would see him sitting 'on guard'.

Wilcox was still seated in the Daimler in the chauffeur's uniform. Eventually Hall left the cage and signalled to Wilcox that the coast was clear. Wilcox turned on the engine of the Daimler and drove back to the warehouse. He opened the doors with the electronic buzzer and he drove in. The Daimler had served its purpose and he moved fast; he poured acid over the bonnet, removed the number plates and stuffed them with the chauffeur's uniform into a black rubbish bag that already contained the paper suit de Jersey had worn. He carried it to the rear of the warehouse and placed it in a bin. He poured more acid into the bin then replaced the lid and left it to smoulder. Minutes later he walked out to take up his position in the driving seat of the second Daimler in front of the safe house. Spittle had formed in small globules at the side of his mouth and he kept licking his lips.

As the robbery was going on, Raymond Marsh walked out of the Scotland Yard telephone exchange and prepared to perform his last task. He travelled by underground to Edgware Road then caught a bus to Kilburn. He let himself into de Jersey's flat, and dismantled the satellite link-up. Once the connections to de Jersey's home computer were broken, he poured acid over the controls, the keyboard and the printer. He took off his gloves as the acid was burning through the leather, then appraised the flat room by room. Nothing was left of a personal nature, just old newspapers and journals. He left to return to his own home.

His wife had already packed. Only his precious guitar collection and Elvis memorabilia were going with him and his family to Brazil. These items were crated up ready to be collected and shipped out. A friend had the house keys and contact number for the shippers. Simmons had his banking details. When pay-day came his cut would be transferred to his account via the Internet.

Marsh had taken great care to look after number one, even down to arranging holiday time for himself and his family, but he knew he was still traceable. The police would discover that someone had had access to the phones to hack into the safe house and Scotland Yard lines. By then, however, he would be long gone. Like Ronnie Biggs he had chosen Brazil as his first port of call. Unlike Ronnie, however, Marsh didn't run solo. He had first-class tickets for himself, his wife and daughter, all under assumed names. He gave no thought to the men and women involved in the robbery as he prepared to make his getaway. He just hoped they would pull it off.

CHAPTER 23

THE LINE of expectant, well-groomed staff in the D'Ancona safe-house reception area reminded Lord Westbrook of a school assembly. The two nervous secretaries were like his old headmaster's daughters, flushing and dressed in their best. Next to them stood a large-bosomed, round-faced woman, who held her plump arms flat to the sides of her ample body like a military officer. She resembled his old matron. She was, in fact, one of D'Ancona's chief gem experts and head of marketing. Three men reminded Westbrook of beaks at Eton. They were all waiting to acknowledge Her Majesty as she passed by.

De Jersey was worried by the line-up: there were far more people than he had anticipated. He could feel the sweat breaking out as he wondered whether Hall had done his job. The only way de Jersey would know he had been successful was by the lack of movement of the cameras. He glanced up at them. If Hall failed, they would all be caught on film. On his third glance he was relieved to see the cameras stop tracking them, their red lights disappearing.

The royal-blue carpet swirled down the stairs and covered the reception floor. Vast displays of lilies were arranged prominently. The Royal party was greeted with polite bows from the two fitters, who wore immaculate pinstripe trousers and dark jackets, with pristine white shirts and ties. They held white gloves, which they would put on when measuring and fitting.

'Good morning,' Maureen said, passing down the line-up. She smiled, but her eyes were like a frightened rabbit's. Pamela remained close by, almost able to touch her. Lord Westbrook now took the floor, his charm and breeding shining like a beacon. His soft, aristocratic tone rang out as the party moved along the line, shaking hands and smiling.

The head representative, Mr Saunders, a small and nervous man, took Westbrook aside. 'The vaults are being opened. Her Majesty can view the jewels at her discretion.' Saunders bowed to Maureen, who was frozen-faced. Her manner made the man even more nervous.

'If you would kindly follow me down to the lower level, Your Majesty, we have the vaults prepared for you.'

Much to de Jersey's relief, as soon as 'the Queen' began to move down the second set of stairs to the vaults, most of the staff dispersed. The matron figure ushered the girls towards the stairs and de Jersey watched them with bated breath: if they passed back into the entrance hall they would see the security guard bound and gagged. They didn't glance in his direction, however, instead moving up a second flight of stairs to their offices.

The inner reception area was now empty, the outer hallway guarded by Hall. Short and Wilcox were ready to act as backup.

There were ten steps down to the vault with a polished brass banister rail on either side. They passed more unseeing cameras poised at every corner and recess. None moved. Satisfied now that Hall had done his job, de Jersey hoped that no one would notice that the cameras weren't functioning.

Maureen leaned heavily on the shining banister rail, Pamela close behind as she continued down into the basement vaults. De Jersey and Westbrook kept her closely guarded and protected. Saunders kept up a rather stuttering speech, detailing the security surrounding the vault. Thankfully he and the fitters kept their eyes directed deferentially to the Royal party. They did not glance up at the cameras. When they reached the basement, a man stood waiting beside a trolley laden with iced water, fruit and coffee. Saunders suggested a pause for refreshments but Westbrook smiled and tapped his watch to indicate that time was of the essence.

The party now approached the vast vault with steel doors and two protective inner cages. The vault's first thick steel door stood wide open and the shining steel bars inside it were also open. Above the reinforced steel door was the edge of the grille that would slam down if an alarm button were pressed, protecting the contents of the vault and trapping anyone inside.

Westbrook kept the tension to a minimum by keeping up a steady flow of conversation which de Jersey hugely admired. He constantly referred to Her Majesty as he recalled anecdotes of when he had been a page at the Coronation. Whether he had or not was immaterial: the ease of his conversation made the short journey to the vault less traumatic.

The vault was enormous, with banks of steel boxes

surrounding the large central cage. Inside it was a massive steel-framed display case, lined with black velvet, where the spectacular jewels had been laid out for viewing. The breathtaking sight stunned all of them into a strange silence, which was only broken when Westbrook exhaled audibly then whispered, 'Dear Lord above!'

This quiet expression of awe somehow made it easier for de Jersey to continue in the same tone: 'Ladies and gentlemen, do not call out, but remain silent and no one will be hurt.'

Saunders half turned, as if he had not heard correctly, and at that moment de Jersey revealed his automatic. 'I need you all to lie face down on the floor.' He pointed at Saunders, 'You first. Do not make a sound.'

Saunders looked in confusion at his assistants, and his face drained of colour. Driscoll opened his jacket and pulled out his shotgun. 'Obey every word or I won't hesitate to shoot. Get down, face down!'

Maureen dropped to the floor, twitching. Her bag fell open and cosmetics rolled across the vault. Pamela drew out a replica gun from her own bag, and directed it at Maureen's head. Driscoll ran back up the stairs, signalling to the waiting Hall to join them. He moved away from the door and his position was taken up by Short, who stood guarding the open doorway.

Inside the vault, Saunders raised his hands and shouted, 'No! You can't do this. For God's sake, *no*!'

'*Down*!' de Jersey commanded, and took off his coat to reveal a large, lightweight rucksack. He tossed it to Westbrook. Driscoll and Hall held the frightened staff at gunpoint as Westbrook lifted the platinum crown containing the Koh-i-noor diamond and stashed it in the rucksack. De Jersey handed Westbrook the gun and began to drag more jewels from the display into a second rucksack held open by Driscoll. When all the jewels were in the rucksacks he gave the signal to move out.

The team backed towards the stairs as Driscoll shut the heavy steel doors, leaving Saunders, Maureen and the two terrified fitters captive. Then the gang walked boldly up the stairs, through the reception area, into the small hallway and past the bound security guard.

The bikers started their engines and moved off in different directions, although their destination was the same: the speedboats at the Tower Bridge Marina. Pamela and Westbrook left Newbury Street on foot. Neither could speak and their legs were wobbly, but they walked towards the City Thameslink station, constantly looking over their shoulders.

Driscoll walked straight into Barbican station and went down to the Hammersmith and City line. It seemed an interminable time before a train came and he shook as he paced up and down. After three minutes he stepped into a carriage and cursed under his breath until the train doors finally closed and it left the station. He was dripping with sweat and his shirt clung to him.

Wilcox and de Jersey knew they needed to distance themselves from the crime scene as quickly as possible, but they couldn't leave the Daimler behind. It was too risky and time-consuming to take it back to the warehouse and they didn't want to drive it through town. This was where the furniture van came into play. It was parked nearby on a meter.

De Jersey climbed into the Daimler with both rucksacks. Wilcox slammed his foot down and they screeched round the corner, sending the no-parking signs and cones flying.

'Slowly!' de Jersey snapped. The last thing they needed was to be picked up for speeding. The tense Wilcox managed to slow down, and they drove through the back-streets until they reached the furniture van. De Jersey leaped out and opened the van's driving side, threw in the rucksacks and got in. At the same time, Wilcox opened the rear doors, dropped the tailgate, returned to the Daimler and drove it in. There was so little space to move that he took a while to squeeze out of the car. He drew up the back and shut the doors, with himself inside, then banged on the front of the van for de Jersey to move off.

As de Jersey drove, he ripped off the wig, eyebrows and moustache, keeping the van to thirty miles an hour. It felt like a snail's pace. He headed towards the river, crossed it and turned right to drive alongside it towards Battersea.

The getaway had taken only fifteen minutes so far but he could already hear police sirens blasting in the distance. As they passed the heliport in Battersea, de Jersey saw his two decoy helicopters take off. He checked his watch: it was perfect timing. The confusion should provide cover for his own helicopter.

The officials locked in the vault had screamed and shouted to no avail. They could not get out and the lack of air inside the vault was becoming asphyxiating. Maureen was hysterical, screaming and shouting that they had got her husband. The others in the vault had realized at last that she wasn't talking about Prince Philip.

The staff from the upper floors carried on working, unaware of what was taking place downstairs in the vaults. However, when the secretaries entered the reception area at the time when the Royal party was due to leave, they were confronted by an overturned plinth of lilies and the bound and gagged security guard. With trepidation one of them opened the outer vault doors.

By eleven o'clock the City was wailing with sirens as the manhunt began. No one could believe what had happened. It was one of the most audacious robberies in history. The first thing the police did was send up their helicopters to monitor the area. They were on the look-out for two Daimlers and two motorbikes.

The entire area surrounding the safe house was cordoned off. De Jersey was still driving the furniture van and was now passing Kingston, moving on towards the A3. He still had a way to go before he would reach his helicopter to lift the jewels away from London.

At the same time, two speedboats raced from separate moorings near Tower Bridge. Hall had dumped his motorbike and placed his helmet and leathers into a holdall. He now wore a thick cable-knit sweater and a baseball cap. He had walked to the first boat, which had been brought from the old boat-house in Putney. Before leaving, he had tied weights to his holdall and dropped it into the river. He steered the boat towards Putney, intending to stash it back in the boat-house and catch the tube back to his east London home from Putney Bridge.

Ten minutes later Short followed almost identical orders. He left his bike in a car park near Blackfriars and changed in the toilets. He walked down towards Temple, pulling his cap low over his face. When he reached his mooring he had trouble with the engine. After a few panicky moments and false starts, however, he eventually got it going and sped off after Hall, just as the sirens started. Short had to drop the boat at the boat-house, then use a can of petrol to set light to the building and its contents. Hopefully the fire would provide another distraction.

Short spent considerable time inside the boat-house dousing rags in the petrol before he set them alight and exited quickly. He was a good fifty yards away when he saw the flames take hold. He was to continue on foot along the New King's Road, catch a bus to Sloane Square and from there a tube to his flat.

Driscoll walked out of the tube station at Shepherd's Bush and picked up his car from a car park. He drove home, calm now, although his shirt was soaking. He wondered if de Jersey had made it. He wanted more than anything to call Wilcox, to know that everyone was home and free, but he resisted the urge and kept on driving.

De Jersey had parked his helicopter at Brooklands air-field. It was used mostly at the weekend so it was deserted, with just a small office in operation across the car park. Wilcox jumped down from the back of the van, climbed into the driving seat and drove out of the airfield, catching de Jersey's eye as he left. Both allowed themselves a half-relieved smile, but they were not in the clear yet.

An experienced pilot, de Jersey knew that there would be no problems with air-traffic control. Contrary to popular belief, most low-level airspace in the United Kingdom is uncontrolled. He had used the Brooklands airfield a few times when he had horses racing at Epsom and Goodwood. Today he was expected at Brighton for a two-year-old's maiden race. He used the airfield's bathroom to wash off the wig glue, put on a camel overcoat and his brown trilby, stashed the rucksacks in two suitcases and loaded them into the helicopter, which contained an incongruous-looking crate. It was water-tight, lined with polystyrene squares, held together with waterproof glue.

De Jersey saw only one person by the hangars, a man cleaning a glider, who didn't pay him any attention. As he left the washroom the caretaker, who was sitting in his office eating his lunch, asked if he had a tip for the races. De Jersey laughed and said perhaps an each-way bet on his colt, Fan Dancer, but he wasn't optimistic as it was his first time out.

As de Jersey started the engine and the propellers began to move, Wilcox was six miles away, heading towards the old barn. Once there he drove the furniture truck in through the large doors, drove the Daimler out and removed the number-plates. The registration on the engine had already been removed. He used four cans of acid to destroy the seats, paintwork and all the contents of the boot. He smashed every window with a hammer and attacked the dashboard. The exertion felt good and released his tension. Then he stripped the stickers off the sides of the removal van to reveal its true identity. The 'Double Your Time' rental company did not expect it back until later that afternoon. Their headquarters were in Leatherhead, so it was just a short drive back down the A3. Wilcox left the truck in a large car park and posted the keys into a box at the gates. Philip Simmons had hired it after seeing the company's advert on the Internet and had paid for it. Then Wilcox caught a train home from Leatherhead.

De Jersey's horse was running in the three o'clock at Brighton. It was the perfect opportunity to show his face and establish an alibi, but he had to do the drop first. As he headed for the coast, he looked down on the busy motorway traffic heading in and out of the centre of London. He wondered if it was his imagination or whether there was a glint of flashing blue light in every direction. He didn't dwell on it, knowing that by now every airport would be targeted by the police as a possible getaway route, likewise the ports. It would take a long time to organize a full search, however, and by then he hoped they would be home and free.

Way below, Pamela and the now sickly Westbrook had travelled from the City Thameslink station to Brighton. There they switched to a second train for Plymouth. Pamela was concerned by Westbrook's depleted energy. He was sweating profusely and had twice staggered to the lavatory to vomit. His face was yellow and sweat plastered his hair to his head. The journey would take at least five hours and they would need a taxi to get them to the safety of her flat. De Jersey had instructed them to separate and Westbrook to return to London, but Westbrook was too unwell to be left alone.

When they reached the station they flagged down a taxi and took it to a street near her apartment. She had constantly to feed him his painkillers so that he had enough energy to walk unaided to her flat. She had made the taxi stop two streets away, not wanting to give the driver her address. Westbrook leaned heavily on her as they walked, his arm around her shoulder. He hardly spoke but when she opened her front door and helped him collapse on to the sofa, he gave a dry sob, his face twisted in pain. Her heart went out to him. 'We made it,' she said softly.

The helicopter, too, was reaching its destination. The yacht was anchored almost nine miles off Brighton Marina and as he flew overhead de Jersey used his mobile to call Dulay to stand by. He put the engine on remote control, slid open the side door and tossed out the crate. He didn't wait to see it hit the water. Instead he did a wide arc then headed for the helipad at Brighton racetrack.

Dulay watched the crate hit the water and bob to the surface. It was just a few yards off its marker. He gave the signal to start up the engines and the big yacht moved majestically towards it. Dulay and two crew hauled it aboard and then they were on their way back to the Riviera. Dulay spotted a small yacht a good distance away, but realized he could do nothing about it and hoped to God that no one aboard it had seen the drop.

Three boys were testing the little yacht for the nationals. They had taken it without their parents' permission and were smoking a large joint when the helicopter flew overhead. Through binoculars they watched as in stunned amazement the crate fell out. At first they were unsure what they had seen as it had happened so quickly, and they passed the binoculars between themselves, wondering if they had witnessed a drugs drop. They did not, however, have a radio, and as the large yacht turned to head out to sea they reckoned they were wrong. If it had been drugs, surely the boat would be heading inland, not out. Suddenly they felt a flurry of wind and galvanized themselves to set sail back to the marina.

At the racecourse de Jersey went into the weighing room to see Mickey, surprising him. Mickey was heading towards the locker rooms carrying de Jersey's racing colours, ready to dress. He thought it was odd that de Jersey was here to see Fan Dancer when he hadn't made it to Royal Flush's race at Lingfield but he didn't say anything. It wasn't his business where and when the boss showed up.

He shook de Jersey's hand and told him that Fleming was heading over to the saddling enclosure. He watched de Jersey stroll out, smiling and acknowledging a few of the jockeys he knew. He also saw him pause by the Sheikh's jockey and take him to one side. He felt a bit gutted and wondered if his boss would go back on his word about his ride in the Derby.

De Jersey walked into the owners' and trainers' bar, acknowledging a few people he knew. He bought a gin and tonic, but hardly touched it and, moments later, crossed to the saddling stalls. He stopped beside the Sheikh's trainer. They discussed a few race meetings and the conversation came round to Royal Flush. Evidently his progress was being carefully monitored by everyone in the business. De Jersey felt a rush of pride and said casually to the trainer that it was his turn for the Derby. He paused as the trainer's quiet, almost lisping voice said, 'Yours, Mr de Jersey, or Royal Flush's?' It was an odd statement and he would have replied to it but he saw Fleming waving to him.

He excused himself and joined his trainer. 'Seen him fishing around. Any money he was asking you about Royal Flush. He's got his eyes on him, you know,' Fleming said.

'So would I, if I had his money and history of success.' De Jersey was referring to the Sheikh's domination of the racetracks and his record of breeding champions. He had the finest stud in England, if not the world. The Arabs were well known for their love of the races. Their animals were kept in luxurious surroundings with the finest trainers and jockeys under million-pound contracts to race exclusively for them. One of their studs was not far from de Jersey's.

'What brings you here?' Fleming asked, as they headed across the green towards their allocated stall.

'I missed my boy's last race so I felt I should make an

appearance. Don't want the gossip-mongers spreading it around that I'm not taking an interest any more.'

Fleming saddled Fan Dancer and together they went to the ring to watch him being led out to wait for their jockey. There were ten horses racing, so nine other owners and trainers stood waiting, like de Jersey and Fleming. Mickey walked out, fixing his helmet strap beneath his chin. He stood with de Jersey and Fleming for a few moments, listening to his last-minute instructions, which were to give Fan Dancer an easy race. He was helped into the saddle and they went out of the parade ring to watch him canter up to the starting gates.

De Jersey and Fleming stood side by side in the owners' and trainers' stand. Fleming had to lend his boss his binoculars.

'I can't stay too long. Christina and I are due to watch the girls in *The Taming of the Shrew*,' he said, monitoring Fan Dancer. 'After the race I'm going to have to shift myself to make it.' Then he focused the binoculars on the Sheikh's trainer, who stood nearby, studying the racing form.

They were under starter's orders and then they were off. Fan Dancer ran a good race but seemed to get boxed in early at the rails. De Jersey watched Mickey move him out but the horse didn't like pushing his way between two others. Then Mickey moved him through a nice gap and, hardly touching Fan Dancer with the whip, rode him into fifth position. He dropped back to sixth then moved up again to remain in fifth as they crossed the finishing line.

'He's no Royal Flush,' de Jersey said, returning Fleming's binoculars to him.

'Few are,' came the reply, as they turned to walk back

to the stables. De Jersey excused himself, asking Fleming to tell Mickey he'd ridden a good race. He couldn't be late for his daughters' play.

De Jersey left the Brighton track at four o'clock and did not relax until he was alone. He gave his pocket an involuntary pat and felt the weight of the object cushioned against his leg. He knew the exact weight was 105.6 carats, but it had felt even heavier when he had prised it out of the crown. If they lost the bulk of the jewels he had dropped for Dulay, he would still retain the prize Koh-i-noor diamond.

The City of London learned that the most daring robbery in history had been pulled off through the numerous news flashes that interrupted TV programming for that day. There was a public outcry. The *Evening Standard* ran the story on the front page and the police were stunned at the audacity of the raiders. They gave away little about the robbery, but Maureen was pictured on the front page dressed as Her Majesty with a fake crown and a frozen smile. She was currently under sedation and unable to speak coherently. Her husband, she had been told, was safe if badly shaken. Though she was hysterical, she had been able to tell the police how she had been kidnapped and her husband's life threatened. She had also given a description of the man she said headed the robbery. Although she had never heard his name, she described de Jersey as a 'military kind of man'. He was in his mid-fifties, had red hair, a moustache and was very tall. The description fitted the one Saunders had given in his disturbed state.

The public marvelled at the robbery, wondering how

it had been achieved, but most were confident that the culprits would be caught. The Metropolitan Police Special Branch and the Army announced that they would join forces to recover the jewels. Operation Crown began immediately.

The police were excited when they processed a section of the security film that had been recorded just moments before Hall had forced the guard to pull the plugs. The team were caught on film entering the hallway and heading towards the reception. Their initial excitement was somewhat deflated when they got the film back from the labs. There was a clear shot of Maureen, but no single frame in which her lady-in-waiting could be seen because of the large hat the woman had worn. They could only see a part profile of Driscoll and a shoulder and body shot of de Jersey, his face obscured by the only member of the team caught fully on camera. Lord Henry Westbrook was shown smiling and talking, before the screen went blank. It was only a few hours before he was identified by a police officer who had been involved in his fraud case.

At a press conference, the reporters were informed that progress had already been made. There was a warrant out for the arrest of Lord Henry Westbrook. Meanwhile the staff at the safe house were all asked for detailed descriptions of the men and the woman involved in the heist. Their descriptions of Pamela varied so the police were relying on Maureen for details when she recovered from shock. She was still sedated and remained in hospital, her husband at her side. He gave a description of the driver of the Mercedes that had picked up his wife and helped the police artist draw a likeness of him. He could only give vague details of the man's companion.

No one could give a decent facial description of the two bikers as their attention had been focused on the 'Queen'. The sketches depicting the tall man hardly seen on the videotapes were confusing. All agreed that he had red hair and a moustache but none could give a clear description of his face. Mr Saunders from D'Ancona maintained that he was their leader. His voice was cultured and he had a military manner. He had been the first to leave the vault.

A massive search for the cars was mounted, and witnesses were asked to come forward if they had seen the convoy driving towards the safe house but no one called.

Christina was selecting what to wear for her daughters' school play when the phone rang. She was tight-lipped, sure it would be her husband making some excuse why he couldn't make it.

It was Helen Lyons. 'Have you been able to contact Sylvia yet?' she asked.

'I've called her home and her office, who told me she's taking some time off in America. I told you this last time we spoke. I got no reply from her flat so it's obvious she must still be away.'

'I'm sorry to bother you but I'm really worried about my money situation. I'm not broke but David always took care of all our finances.'

'He certainly took care of ours,' Christina snapped, unable to contain her anger any longer. 'I've called your sister for you and I don't want to get involved any further. I'm sorry, Helen, but just as you have money problems so have we, and that is due to your husband's misappropriation of our finances. Under the circumstances, the more I discover about just how much David did steal from us the more I find these calls very tedious. I suggest you ring Sylvia yourself. Now, I really have to go.'

She replaced the receiver, then felt dreadful. She knew she was taking out her own anxiety on the poor woman – but what she had said to her was true.

Just after three she drove away from the estate to do some shopping.

De Jersey got home in the helicopter at five o'clock. He stashed the wig and moustache in a briefcase and hurried towards the house. He seemed outwardly calm and collected, but his adrenaline was still pumping. When Christina returned with her shopping he had bathed and changed and was in the kitchen.

'You're back,' she said, surprised.

'I am, my darling. We have a date tonight, don't we?'

'The girls' play, yes. I thought perhaps, with all your problems, you might have forgotten it.' She walked past him to unpack the groceries.

He turned, surprised at her tone. 'You make it sound as if I'm in the doghouse,' he said.

'You are, if you must know.' She joined him at the table. 'I might as well tell you because you'll find out soon enough.'

'Find out what?'

'I was in your study and broke . . .' She paused. She

looked at him, frowning, then leaned forward and rubbed his sideburns. 'You've got glue or something stuck to your face.'

He backed away. 'It's shaving lotion. Go on, what have you broken?'

'I haven't broken anything,' she said petulantly, then faced him angrily. 'Please stop treating me like a child. I broke into your desk drawers.'

He hesitated a moment. 'Really? And why did you do that?'

Christina chewed her lip, then took a deep breath. 'I don't know – no, I do. I'm sick of your lies. I just wanted to know what was going on.'

'When was this?'

'Does it really matter? I used a screwdriver. Anyway, what I found upset me. I wanted to discuss it with you face to face. That's why I didn't mention it to you when you called. Why didn't you tell me, for God's sake? If you can't be honest with me after all these years . . . You're virtually bankrupt!' Christina said.

De Jersey relaxed a little. 'Why don't we go and sit in the drawing room and you can tell me about it?'

'You go ahead,' she said. 'I'll make some tea.' He nodded and walked out.

She took a deep breath. Her nerves were in shreds but she was determined not to let him off the hook this time.

De Jersey listened as Christina detailed her discoveries. 'I don't understand why you would need fake passports.'

'I've been using aliases off and on for years. It's been a sort of ploy to allow me to move in and out of the horse auctions without my real name attached.'

500

'That can't be the reason,' she said angrily. 'You even had passports for me and the girls, all in false names. There are recent stamps in one passport to New York. You never told me you'd been to New York. What's going on?'

'I didn't know I'd be going there myself and I got the passports for you and the girls just in case you accompanied me on one of these undercover buying trips. You know I hate being apart from you. That's the only reason.'

'So what were you doing in New York?'

De Jersey decided to come partially clean. 'I went to see the man who ruined me. I didn't want it to get out that I had.'

'Why not?'

'He used me, Christina. As you know, he let his company go belly up and consequently did the same to my whole life.'

'So you went to see him?'

'Yes, but I used a different name because I didn't want to alarm him or forewarn him about who I was. Turned out he still had some of my money invested in some properties out there. He was a cheap con-man. I caught him just about to skip the country for South America. He got scared I'd get the cops on to him so he coughed up. Not all of it, just a fraction, really, but enough to keep my head above water for a while.'

'Does Sylvia know?'

'No. If I'd told her I would have had to pay her off and then the other creditors would be hounding me for their cut too. This way, I got some of my losses back and Moreno took off, hopefully never to be seen again.' He shrugged.

'So how are things now, financially?' she asked.

'Well, not good, but they're a hell of a lot better with Moreno's cash. At least I'm not forced to sell this place, which I would have been if I hadn't got to the bastard.'

'Did you have to do it illegally?'

'Of course. I had to carry the money back into England in a suitcase, which is another reason I thanked God I'd used a false name. It was all done to protect us. Legal or not, the fact is I did it, but who is Moreno going to cry to? Not the police. He's the criminal, not me. He committed a massive fraud that bankrupted a lot of people. I know I've told you a few lies but, darling, I had to do this on the spur of the moment. I didn't have any time to waste and the fewer people who knew of my intentions the better.'

'On the spur of the moment? Do you think I'm stupid? Some of the dates on the passports go back years and who is this Michael Shaughnessy character?'

'Well, having a fake identity worked once so I did it a few times. As I said, it was to protect myself. You buy horses in Ireland and it's all over the racing news! The fewer people know what I'm doing the better.'

'But I'm your wife!'

'And if I hadn't pulled it off, you'd have been run through the mill with me. I was only trying to protect you.'

'Treat me like an idiot, more like,' she snapped.

'If that's what you call protection, then yes. I didn't want to involve you in case it went wrong. I might have been arrested at Heathrow with the cash. Fortunately I wasn't, so there was no harm done. I also couldn't put the cash into a bank because I'd be hauled up for taxes.

But we're not bankrupt yet, my darling, so as I said, no harm done.'

'There is, though.' He frowned at her. 'You've made me feel inadequate and helpless. You were in trouble when we went to Monaco but you never discussed it with me and instead bought me expensive gifts as if nothing was wrong, when all the time you were in dire trouble. How do you think that makes me feel?'

'Loved?' He laughed, but she turned away angrily.

'No, foolish. But it is still not making sense to me. For instance, you've sold Bandit Queen and Fleming thinks she's been bought by this Michael Shaughnessy, which is the name on one of your passports. But that doesn't make sense because it's really you, isn't it? The passport had your photograph in it.'

'Correct. It's simple. If I go bankrupt, Bandit Queen would have been part and parcel of the debts. This way I still own her.'

'But she was mine! You bought her for me!'

'Well, that's true, but she still is in a way.' He got up, put his arms around her and kissed her neck. 'You've had so much to deal with recently, with your mother's death. I just didn't want to worry you – and,' he looked at his watch, 'if we don't get a move on, we'll both be in the doghouse because we'll be late for the girls' production. Can we go and change?'

She nodded and kissed him. She touched his face. 'That is such a weird smell, like glue. Next you'll tell me you're really as bald as a coot and you're wearing a wig.' He grinned, scooped her up in his arms and carried her out of the room. The phone rang and she shrieked, 'Don't answer it! It'll be Helen Lyons.'

503

He carried her up the stairs and set her down mid-way. His knee was throbbing. The phone rang and rang. He wanted to answer it in case it concerned him, but Christina caught his hand.

'She's called every other day. She's trying to get me to contact her sister for her.'

'Why?' He looked over the banister rail to the hall table below, where the phone still rang.

'Because when she found out David and Sylvia were having an affair, she said she was never going to speak to her again. She asked me to call her on her behalf. Did you know about it?'

'What?'

'That Sylvia was seeing David, for years apparently.'

'Good God! No, of course I didn't. What did she want? Is it to do with David or what?'

'It's the insurance money. Apparently Sylvia was hand-ling all the claims and now Helen is running short of cash.'

The phone had stopped ringing.

'Did you speak to Sylvia?'

'No. I even called her office but they said she was away. New York, I think. But when Helen called again, just before you got home, I couldn't contain myself any longer. I told her that considering what David had done to us, she could damned well call Sylvia herself!'

Christina's mood changed. 'I have felt very lonely while you've been away, Edward.'

'I'm sorry, but I didn't have any choice.' He stroked her face and kissed her gently.

'But is everything all right? I mean, truthfully. Please, no more lies. I hated prising open the drawers like some demented, jealous woman and then when it all became

504

clear how badly off we are financially, I almost hated you for being so dishonest with me.'

'The truth is that we're out of trouble now and with the expectation I have for Royal Flush . . . If he wins the Derby it'll put this place on the map. He'll be worth millions.' He kissed her again. 'We're almost in the clear, sweetheart.'

'And you didn't have to remortgage the farm?'

'Nope. I got away without having to do that by the skin of my teeth. We're safe.'

She leaned against him as they continued up the stairs. 'Things have to change between us,' she said quietly. 'From now on, don't lie to me any more.'

'I won't. Hell, you might take a screwdriver to *me* next, never mind my desk!' He drew her close to him and they walked up to their bedroom. He gave silent thanks that he had taken Philip Simmons's passport with him to Paris. If he hadn't, Christina would have found it with the others.

They left for their daughters' school an hour later and sat through a lengthy production of *The Taming of the Shrew*. Both girls were delighted that their father was there, but Christina did not tell them he had slept through most of the last act. They had wine and cheese with the other parents, then returned home. They listened to classical music on the car stereo rather than the news, and it was almost one in the morning by the time they reached home.

De Jersey was so exhausted he went straight to bed and fell into a deep sleep. Christina lay next to him, her eyes wide open, wondering how many other lies her husband had told her. She was so naïve, she realized, and this was the first time she had ever questioned their relationship or his past. She had never felt their age difference until now and wondered what he had done in the years before he had met her. She looked at him now, sleeping like a baby, and felt intensely irritated. They hardly made love any more, and he had not even kissed her goodnight. She flopped back restlessly on her pillow, the seeds of discontent beginning to grow.

Driscoll sat in the TV room with a large gin and tonic. He had been watching the news flashes, partly in amusement and partly in denial of what he had done. They were not in the clear by any means. The biggest plus was that neither he nor Wilcox had been in trouble with the law before, so, even if Maureen could describe them, she could look at mug-shots until the cows came home: they were not in the books. The news flashes described the missing vehicles, and requests for information were repeated over and over with numbers to call if anyone had any information. They were hunting Westbrook down and a warrant had been issued for his arrest. A parade of debs and his associates were interviewed on the news, telling tales of his womanizing and dealings in high society. His face was becoming as familiar as Lord Lucan's.

'What the hell were you doing all day?' his wife asked, setting down a bowl of raw carrots.

'Touting for business,' he said, then looked at her as she started to crunch a carrot.

'Christ, do you have to do that?' he asked.

'I'm on a diet.'

'Well, I'm hungry. I didn't have time for lunch.'

She stood up. 'What do you want?'

'Omelette. Nothing too rich. My gut's giving me hell.'

'You should see another specialist. You want anything in the omelette or just plain?'

'Bit of cheese.'

'That's fattening.'

'I don't give a fuck!'

'Tony!'

'I'm sorry, but I'm trying to listen to the news.' Suddenly he felt gleeful. 'You seen it?'

'I only just got in. I've been having a mudbath at the new hydro clinic.'

'Well, there's been a big robbery.'

'Oh, I know about that. Sandra had the TV on. Do you want a side salad with your omelette?'

'Sure.' He watched her walk out of the room. He wondered how Sandra would feel if she knew her last customer's husband had been in on the robbery of the Crown Jewels.

Shortly after Westbrook and Pamela arrived home, Pamela dyed her hair back to its usual bright orange. Westbrook was on her sofa bed and continued to apologize for imposing on her, swearing that as soon as he recovered he'd make his own arrangements. He had a fake passport and cash to leave the country but until he could stand up it was out of the question. He watched the television all that day and night but even the news flashes could not hold his attention and he dozed fitfully. Where on earth had they managed to get so many photographs of him, let alone of his so-called associates? He wondered where these close friends had been for the past year during his illness.

Wilcox arrived home in time for the twins' birthday party, which he'd forgotten. It was a bit of a pain as all he wanted to do was relax and watch the news but he blew up balloons and sat out with the kids as they ate sausages, eggs and chips. He left the chaos for a while to go to the local video store to rent some movies for them to watch. He returned, arms loaded with Mars bars, Smarties, cartoons, sci-fi films and all the evening newspapers he could lay hands on. The headlines all told of the robbery and everyone was talking about it, even in the video store. The shocked public seemed to view it as sacrilege and were appalled that anyone could contemplate stealing part of the country's national and cultural heritage. Later in the evening, he sneaked away to his bedroom to watch the late-night television news. The reports were filled with interviews and the hunt for Westbrook was on, but as yet there seemed to be no clues as to the identity of the rest of the team. Nevertheless, they gave out descriptions based on what little they had to go on. Wilcox sighed with relief. He wanted to call Driscoll but knew he mustn't. He ached to hear how he was coping and became paranoid that the police had to be withholding evidence. He chopped up the last of his stash of cocaine and Rika found him snorting it in the bathroom. They had a blistering row, which somehow eased his tension.

After they had made love, Rika lay beside him, her body glistening with sweat, and he leaned on his elbow smiling at her. 'The kids had a great day. Thank you. They get on really well with you, Rika. Dunno what I'd do without you, but they're gonna go to boarding-school soon. Their mother suggested they go and stay over with her for the next holidays and—'

She turned towards him. 'Vhat you saying? You don't need me no more?'

'No, I am not saying that at all.'

'Then vhy you say it?'

'No reason. Why do you question everything I bloody say?'

'I don't.'

'Yes, you do.'

'Vhy vere you so late coming home? I told you I needed things for the party.'

'I hadda sell a car. In fact, I'm selling off most of them.'

Rika pouted. 'You still got no money.'

'Yeah, but not for long.'

'Ve get married then? You marry Rika?'

He closed his eyes. 'Yeah, maybe . . . Just let me get some kip. I'm tired out.'

Rika got off the bed and put on a robe. She tightened the belt and walked out. He sighed and picked up the remote control, wondering if there was any kind of update on the television about the robbery. He switched from one programme to another and fell asleep with the remote still in his hand.

Not long after the robbery, the police discovered that the team had pulled the plugs on the panic alarms and they backtracked through the coal chute to the culprits' warehouse base. It was two in the morning when they broke in with a search warrant. Now they had their next big lead. There, rotting in acid, was one of the Daimlers used in the heist. Fingerprint experts and twenty officers were shipped in to examine the warehouse inch by inch. They were also trying to find out who had rented the warehouse, but it was a further five hours before they got the man's name: Philip Simmons.

The day after the robbery, Her Majesty made an unprecedented broadcast asking for the public's assistance in apprehending the thieves who had taken the precious items of British heritage. The interview was followed by a documentary about the Crown Jewels, watched by ten million viewers. That led to another breakthrough. An elderly man believed the Daimlers used in the robbery might have been the ones he'd sold in Leicester. He informed the police there had been two and a chap had bought the lease on his garage more than six months previously. When questioned, he gave the best description of Wilcox his memory afforded him. The police matched the garage owner's description to the description of the driver that Maureen had given.

They had also discovered that Philip Simmons had rented the Aldersgate warehouse only months before the heist. After questioning the estate agents who had negotiated the transaction they had yet another description of the man they now believed had led the gang. It was confusing, though. Most of the negotiations for the warehouse had been done by telephone, but the agent who had shown de Jersey the property was unable to verify that he had red hair as he had worn a hat. But, as far as he could recall, he had no moustache. Although the description was sketchy, he confirmed that the man was tall, well-built and spoke with an upper-class accent.

Operation Crown's initial hype was starting to slow down. The description of Pamela had yielded no response. The police knew their biggest card would be the capture of Westbrook. The inquiry now fielded a force of over a thousand officers, all sifting through statements and calls from the public. Fifty telephone operators were working round the clock.

There had been hundreds of sightings of Westbrook on the day of the robbery and after the event. Some were at Heathrow airport, some at the ferry in Dover and others at various railway stations in the south. One caller said she was sure she had seen him on a train going to Plymouth with a blonde woman. She also said he looked drunk or sick. As it had not been disclosed to the public that Westbrook had cancer, this was a valuable piece of information that might lead to the discovery of the lady-in-waiting too.

Two days after the robbery, the police gained their next vital clue. The three boys out sailing who had watched a crate being dropped into the sea off Brighton had subsequently told their father, who reported the incident to the coastguard. He thought that although it might not have been connected with the robbery of the Crown Jewels, it was an unusual event and should be reported anyway.

The coastguard had noted the report made by the

boys' father and felt the incident warranted reporting to the police. Anything that sniffed of drugs was treated seriously. The local police interviewed the boys, then contacted Scotland Yard. Operation Crown officers travelled to Brighton.

The boys had only the first part of the yacht's name, *Hortensia*. They had not been able to see the last bit but told police that it had been flying the French flag. British customs were alerted but there had been no further sightings of the vessel in any British harbours along the coast. No customs officials had boarded her to make enquiries as to why she was anchored off the Sussex coast.

The boys' report added fuel to theories about the possible getaway of the robbers. They had numerous helicopter sightings and were still checking with all the heliports as to which of their helicopters had been used at the time of the robbery. It was a slow process to assimilate all the data and when it was cross-referenced, they ascertained that four helicopters had been hired to coincide with the robbery. They had all had instructions to collect passengers from around the City of London but the pickups had made no contact. What spurred the team up a notch was that the helicopters had been hired by Philip Simmons, who had now taken over from Westbrook as the most hunted man in Britain. His description and police identikit drawings were in every newspaper, and a computerized headshot of him frequently appeared on the vast output of daily television news coverage.

CHAPTER 24

THE POLICE hunt for the robbers was further aided by a much calmer Maureen Stanley. She was taken through the details of the day of the robbery from when she was picked up at her home to the last terrifying minutes of the heist. They questioned and requestioned her.

Meanwhile, the teams of forensic experts working in the warehouse were coming to the end of a long, fruitless exercise. They had not found a single fingerprint. The debris left by the robbers was so minuscule that it was of no use. The acid had burned the clothes and articles Wilcox had placed in the bin. The remnants, however, were taken to the lab in the hope that, under closer examination, they would yield some clues. The acid cans were checked out. Someone had ordered it in bulk and paid for it. Yet again Philip Simmons emerged as the purchaser. The company from which he had bought it gave the police his credit-card number, which threw up an address in Kilburn. When the police arrived at the Kilburn flat, the landlord told them he had never met the occupant. All details had been given over the Internet.

As one team of officers drove across London with

search warrants for Simmons's flat, a second team was trying to figure out how the robbers had acquired the details to break into Buckingham Palace security and tap the phones of both Scotland Yard and the safe house. They knew whoever had done it had had access to the telephone exchange, so all employees were being questioned. One man, with the knowledge and authority to be in such a position, had gone on holiday on the day of the robbery. His name was Raymond Marsh.

The second team headed for Marsh's house in Clapham. Those in charge of Operation Crown felt that the net was well and truly closing and they were confident that arrests would soon be made.

As the squad cars pulled up outside the house, they were greeted by a for-sale notice with a sold sticker displayed across it. It was obvious Marsh would not be in and was probably no longer in the country. Lined up in the hall were various crates to be shipped out to him in South America. All were tagged and carefully packed but with only a *poste-restante* address.

The estate agent was unable to provide an address for Marsh and said the proceeds of the property were to be deposited in his bank account. She did not know anything about the crates. Marsh had said that a friend would collect them and any bits of furniture the new owners did not want.

'Do you have this friend's name?'

'No, I'm afraid not. As I said, we were just instructed to sell the property with the furniture. I presume whoever it is must have a key.'

Robbie Richards did have the key but he didn't have anywhere to store the boxes so he had not got round to picking them up. He was supposed to have moved them on the night of the robbery and, in return for helping Marsh, take whatever furniture he wanted.

He was scared to death when he drove into Marsh's street to see the house cordoned off by squad cars and cops wandering around like bluebottles. He turned his borrowed van and scarpered. He would not have been able to assist the police in the heist inquiry but he would have been able to give a lot of details about Marsh's other illegal activities, such as the hacking and the credit-card skimming.

A team of officers broke into the Kilburn flat, but the occupant had long since departed. They began to search for incriminating evidence and the damaged computer was taken away for tests. It was deemed useless: the acid had burned through the plastic controls.

Maureen Stanley, after hours of questioning, ultimately proved unhelpful. She was unable to add to the array of sketches already drawn by the police artists. They had now transferred the drawings to a computer-graphics programme, layering in colouring and features to assist her but this confused her even more. She constantly repeated that during the time before they had left the warehouse she had been in a state of shock, frightened for herself and for her captive husband. She did say that Lord Westbrook was kind and considerate, and that the woman acting as her lady-in-waiting was called Pamela, or possibly Pauline.

Led by their Commander, the police team involved in Operation Crown assembled in their large office block. The press was now demanding results and lampooning the inquiry as a failure. Where the culprits had once been vilified for stealing the Crown Jewels, they were now lauded as anti-establishment heroes.

The police knew that the two Daimlers used in the robbery had been initially kept in the Leicester garage but again a search by forensics teams had proved futile. The robbers had known how to cover their tracks. The investigating officers were aware that the longer it took for them to sift through their findings, the more likely it was that the heist masterminds would evade them. Worse than this, however, was the possibility that the precious gems would be cut up and lost to the nation for ever.

The most promising clue now seemed futile. Philip Simmons had organized his whole life over the Internet: setting up domestic bills, making numerous purchases, renting the warehouse and his flat. None of the apparently promising leads took them to the man.

The officers were instructed to spread their nets wider. The robbers would have had to have a second, larger premises in which to prepare the vehicles and store them for the robbery. Police press officers were instructed to continue to ask the public for assistance. They were looking for anyone in or around the London area who had leased a building large enough to accommodate the vehicles used in the robbery. The contact phone number was given to news programmes. They still wished to question Philip Simmons, Lord Henry Westbrook, Raymond Marsh and a blonde woman possibly calling herself Pauline or Pamela. Sketches and computer images of

Pamela and the other members of the gang were distributed widely and were continuously on the news.

Pamela was frightened. She watched the television updates like a hawk and the computer image of her was closer than she had thought possible. Added to this, they now had her Christian name. She was also worried about Westbrook, who was now desperately ill and in need of hospital treatment, but he refused to allow her to call a doctor. He was dying. His one fear was that, after all he had done, his son would not benefit. Pamela was adamant that, whatever the outcome, they could trust the Colonel. She knew that his word was his bond. They had all known it would take considerable time for the big pay-off to come through. In the meantime the Colonel had given them all enough cash to live on well and safely. He had even arranged a flight for Westbrook. But this was of little use to his lordship now. All he wanted was for his son to have his rightful, ancestral home. Without medication, he was in agony.

Pamela bought some grass from a guy upstairs, which seemed to ease Westbrook's pain. One evening she returned from shopping to find him stoned, but dressed and trying to tie his shoelaces. He was shaking badly and he looked every inch the sick man he was. His hair was plastered to his head making him look skinnier than ever. He had hardly been able to eat, sipping only watered brandy.

'Papers are still full of it,' she informed him.

'My face seems to be on every TV channel.' He grinned boyishly, and she could see that his gums were bleeding.

517

'I'll put this through the mixer and see if you can keep it down.' She held up a ready-made meal and popped it into the oven.

'No, don't. I'm leaving.' He lit a cigarette and inhaled deeply. 'I've been here too long and I don't want to put you at further risk.'

She was relieved but ashamed to show it. 'Where the hell will you go? It's already six o'clock.'

'Home.' He tried to stand but his long thin legs shook violently.

'I'm sure you'll make it in that state.' She couldn't help the sarcasm.

'Sure I will, sweetheart. I'll roll a joint, get a bit more energy up, and then you can call a taxi.'

'I can't have you picked up from here, darling. That's too much of a risk.'

'I know. Get it to pick me up at the station. I can make it that far.'

'You can't even stand up.'

He straightened and gestured with his free hand. 'Course I can.'

'But if you take a taxi to Pimlico you'll be picked up within minutes.'

'Not that home,' he said softly, and eased himself back down. 'My real home. My ancestral pile.'

'Are you joking? It's miles away, isn't it?'

'Yes, maybe the taxi isn't such a good idea. Just get me on to a train to Waterloo, and I'll sort something out from there. Please, Pamela.'

She approached him and cupped his face in her hands. 'Let me think. If that's what you want, we'll work it out somehow.'

Pamela left the flat and returned shortly with a wheelchair borrowed from one of the elderly tenants. 'It's a long walk but we'll make it. So, roll up your joints and let's get moving.'

Westbrook allowed her to shave him and give him a shirt she'd been left by a long-gone lover. He wore a polo-neck sweater over it and she wrapped a blanket around him. She put a hat on his head and pulled it down low.

At eight, she set off to walk the two miles to the railway station. Sick and emaciated though he was, Westbrook was heavy for her to push and she had to stop for a breather every now and then. His head rested on his chest and bobbed up and down as she eased the chair across the pavements until they arrived at the station.

There was a train to Waterloo in fifteen minutes so she bought a one-way ticket and wheeled him on to the platform. She didn't want to think about how he would get on and off the train. They sat together on the platform, saying little to each other. To her astonishment when the train headed into the platform he somehow found enough strength to stand unaided.

'This is goodbye, fair Pamela. Take care of yourself. I adore you, and cannot thank you enough for your care. Now, please go and don't look back. Just walk out before I blubber like a schoolboy. I never had much control over my emotions. Reminds me of saying goodbye to my mother when I went back to boarding-school.'

Pamela kissed his wet, yellow cheek and fussed with the chair to hide her own tears. She knew she would never see him again and she cared deeply for him.

She returned to her room and began to clean up after Westbrook. When she had folded the soiled sheets and hoovered around the sofa she sat down and broke into sobs, partly due to the relief that he had gone and partly because she would miss him. Without him she was utterly alone. Then she heated the ready-made meal and poured herself a large brandy. She was too afraid to switch on the television, fearing she might hear a report of his capture at Waterloo. When she found his unused plane tickets, with two thousand pounds that he had left for her, she broke down again.

Westbrook huddled in a corner of the compartment and slept for the entire journey. No one paid him any attention. When the train arrived at Waterloo he mustered the strength to walk the length of the platform towards the taxi rank. Pain forced him to sit down for fifteen minutes. Then, sweating profusely, he forced himself up and hailed a taxi. He asked to be driven to Andover, a good two hours away. At first the driver refused to take him, then he saw Westbrook's cash and promptly got out and helped him in.

'You sick?' he asked.

'You could say that. I just had my appendix out.' He rested back against the seat, amazed he had managed to come this far. 'When we get there, squire, wake me up and I'll direct you to the lodge.' He closed his eyes. He knew that from the lodge he could get through the keeper's gate and possibly manage the quarter of a mile to the house. He was too exhausted to open his eyes, but passed the time in counting how many steps it would take him to get from the lodge to the kitchens, into the main hall and from there up the stairs into his bedroom. His mind drifted back to the room he had known as a boy. He had always been terrified of the dark, shut up in the east wing. He had never received much attention from either of his parents. He could not recall his father ever showing him any form of warmth or understanding. His mother had tried, when she was sober, but when he had needed her most she was always at some society event. The one great love of his life had been the wondrous building to which he was on his way. The halls, the ballroom, the library and the vaulted, hand-painted ceiling in his room with round pink cherubs beckoning him to the clouds on which they rested. All his ventures had been a disaster, but now, with the money from his last enterprise, he was going to make sure his son and heir, living far out of his reach, would have the money to return to his rightful home. It was a fantasy, but it kept Westbrook alive for the duration of the taxi ride home.

He gave the driver a generous tip and watched him leave, then used the stone wall as an aid to make his way towards the lodge gates in the dark. The magnificent house loomed dark and silent as he walked towards the kitchens, counting each step in the hope that his strength would not give out. He made it into the house and into his bedroom, and lay down on the French quilt, his head resting on the rolled satin cushions with their gold tassels. The pink cherubs danced on the ceiling above him, their fingers outstretched. A white marble bust of his great-great-great-grandfather stood at the window: Lord Alexander Westbrook, his periwig curling down to his shoulders, stared down at him with his sightless eyes. Westbrook gave a soft sigh of satisfaction. He was home.

Westbrook's body was discovered the next day by an elderly cleaning lady. By the time the doctor was called, two family retainers, now hired by the commercial ice-cream company as cleaners, had removed his soiled clothes and washed his body. They had called the police, who arrived with sirens screaming, as the doctor finished his examination. Death had occurred some time early in the morning.

The body was taken to the mortuary and an autopsy performed. The cancer that had been seeping through him had rendered his heart and lungs useless. There were no suspicious circumstances. When the body was released one of the old retainers provided the funeral home with his uniform and sword for his burial. They felt it only fitting that he should be laid out in his uniform, even though he had been disowned by his regiment. He was Lord Westbrook, after all. His dress uniform had been on display in the hall for visitors. His family was summoned to London for the funeral. His soiled garments were taken by the police to be examined, and the retainers were questioned but released without charge.

Westbrook made headlines again, but he had left the police without clues to assist their inquiry. He had thrown away anything that might link him to the robbery or to Pamela. He died knowing that the Colonel would be impressed by his tenacity and care during his last few hours. But, then, he had always been a true gentleman.

De Jersey lowered *The Times* and allowed himself an appreciative smile. The article stated that Westbrook had died of natural causes and his death was not being treated

522

as suspicious. He had heard no word of Sylvia Hewitt and nothing had appeared about her in any of the papers. He took this as a good sign. In fact, although the newspapers still carried front-page articles about the hunt, he sensed that they might be in the clear. He was not stupid enough to think that everything the police uncovered would be automatically handed to the journalists, but at the same time, five days after the robbery, they had not arrested anyone and did not appear close to doing so. But the daily requests for information regarding Philip Simmons, the artists' sketches and computer pictures posed a risk to him, even though they bore little resemblance to him and showed him with red hair. He just hoped that all links between him and Simmons had been destroyed.

De Jersey continued his usual daily business on the estate, exercising the horses and discussing the future racing programmes with Fleming. He was attentive to Christina, who seemed less anxious about their situation as he was now at home with her. As elsewhere in the rest of the country, there were many discussions in the yard about the robbery, but eventually interest died down as the flat season got under way.

After going through a whole gamut of emotions, Helen Lyons had decided to telephone her sister. For all her faults Sylvia was the only family she had, and Helen was lonely. Her friend in Devon had suggested that perhaps she should try to sort out her finances and visit her sister, hinting that Helen had overstayed her welcome.

Sylvia, however, appeared to be away, or at least was not answering her phone. Helen had tried her numerous times. The office confirmed what Christina de Jersey had told her, that Sylvia was still possibly in New York. When she had not heard from Sylvia after a week, she caught a train from Devon then took a taxi to St John's Wood. She still had her own key to Sylvia's apartment. She unlocked the front door. 'Sylvia, it's Helen.'

She entered the apartment and stepped over the stack of mail that had been left where it fell. As she walked into the drawing room she noticed a pungent smell hanging in the air. She screamed. Sylvia's body lay on the sofa. Helen ran to the caretaker's apartment, which was on the ground floor. The caretaker didn't know what to do. Sylvia was obviously dead and had been so for some time, but they called the doctor anyway, then waited for him to arrive.

When the doctor turned up he confirmed what they already knew, and said that they would not know how she had died until a post-mortem had been conducted. He called the police and a young, uniformed officer took a statement from him and Helen. There was no sign of a break-in and no items were missing or disturbed.

Helen had to wait for the body to be removed and taken to the mortuary. She opened all the windows to get rid of the sickening stench. There seemed no real reason for her to leave as she had still not found a new apartment, and she discovered all the documents regarding the insurance on her home. They were neatly stacked in a drawer of Sylvia's desk. She also found Sylvia's will, and found that she was the main beneficiary. The apartment was now hers but until she took it over legally, she would stay in the spare room where she had slept before.

There were some unanswered questions in the police investigation into Sylvia's death and the case remained open. The initial suspicion of suicide at first seemed to be confirmed when the post-mortem revealed a heavy presence of morphine. What perturbed the pathologist, however, was the additional presence of ketamine, a powerful horse tranquillizer. Helen was dumbfounded by this and collapsed in tears. The young sergeant sitting opposite her had to wait a considerable time before he could continue to question her. They needed to determine whether Sylvia had taken it herself or whether foul play was involved. Helen told him that it was incomprehensible that anyone could have wanted Sylvia dead but it was possible she had taken her own life.

'In the last couple of days, I've learned that she lost a considerable amount of money on a bad investment deal,' Helen told them. 'It was connected to my husband.' Then the story of the affair tumbled out. Perhaps Sylvia had taken her own life after losing David, her savings and her sister. She had also told her employers that she would not be coming into work, which was another possible sign of her intentions.

Helen was asked if she knew of anyone who had seen her sister during the past two weeks, but she did not. The police were still dissatisfied and began to check phone calls she had made or received on the evening of her death. They also questioned friends and work colleagues, but it was still not a murder inquiry. No one they spoke to felt that Sylvia would have taken her life and they told the officers of her trip to New York. This tallied with the last phone call Sylvia had made, to a private detective named Matheson in New York City. When DS Jon Fuller contacted him, Matheson was truly shocked by the news. He explained that he had been hired by Miss Hewitt to trace a man called Alex Moreno who, they believed, was involved in a fraud. He was also aware she had lost a considerable amount of money.

'Did she sound depressed?' Fuller asked.

'No, far from it,' he told them. 'She was very positive because she had traced the man she believed could help her regain some of her losses.'

'Did Miss Hewitt give this man's name?'

'Philip Simmons.'

'Did you know him?'

'I never met him but I knew he had been in New York recently. In fact, we thought he was still here. He was Moreno's business adviser. Miss Hewitt also said everything was going well and that she no longer needed my services.'

'Do you have any idea where he would be? An address?'

'No. As I said, I never met him but I think he was Canadian.'

Fuller's report was passed to his superior and placed on file. He had concluded that although it was probably suicide, Miss Hewitt's death still seemed suspicious. Why would a woman committing suicide with morphine and ketamine bother to clean her kitchen before she died, leaving no trace of how she had consumed the drugs? Why was there no suicide note? He also wanted to speak to the person that may possibly have been the last person

526

to see her alive: Philip Simmons, the name entered in and underlined three times in her desk diary for a six p.m. meeting on the day she died. As yet they had found no trace of him in her address books or office files.

Fuller was told to continue the inquiry and Sylvia Hewitt's body was released for burial. Even though the robbery squad had told the media that they were searching for a man called Philip Simmons, DS Fuller did not make the connection. The suicide of a woman in St John's Wood was not the crime of the century. If he had made the connection it would have galvanized their inquiry. As it was, the name Philip Simmons was listed among many others they wished to interview in connection with Sylvia Hewitt's death.

The robbery squad took a big step forward when British Customs, working with Interpol, traced a motorized yacht named the *Hortensia Princess*, owned by Paul Dulay and anchored in the South of France. They contacted their European counterparts, whose records showed that the *Hortensia Princess* had left Cannes four days before the sighting and had returned four days later. They emailed a photograph of Dulay's boat for the witnesses to verify that it was the vessel they had seen.

The boys were questioned again by Customs and asked if the boat they had seen bore any resemblance to the photograph they had of Dulay's vessel. They agreed without hesitation that it was the same one. The investigating team realized they might be on to a major lead when they discovered that Dulay was a jeweller. Two detectives were sent to interview him and his crew.

The two crew members confirmed that they had

picked up a box dropped by a helicopter off the English coast. When they hauled it aboard it had been full of junk so they had tossed it back into the sea. They said a fault in the engine had occurred, which was why they were anchored off Brighton. They had been able to repair the fuel gauge themselves, then hauled up the anchor to return to France. When they were asked if the owner of the boat had been aboard, they said that he had and that he had instructed them to pull the package aboard.

Paul Dulay was working in his shop in Monaco when the officers questioned him about his trip to England. Dulay kept his cool, saying that he had not been ashore. He gave the names of three companies he had called from the ship to ask for assistance with the fuel gauge before they had managed to repair it. He didn't flinch when asked about the crate.

'Oh, yes. We saw a helicopter flying overhead and watched it drop something into the water. I instructed my crew to haul it aboard.' He gave a knowing look. 'It might have been drugs – anything, you know. When we opened it, it was full of empty bottles, a couple of jackets and some other clothing. We tossed it back into the water. It's probably still floating around out there.'

The police asked about the helicopter, what make it was, twin or single engine, but Dulay shrugged. He couldn't remember, possibly a twin engine as it was quite large, and there were two or three people aboard. The officers left, only to return an hour later with a helicopter manual showing different designs. Dulay took a long, hard look, then pointed to a Sikorsky S-76. 'This one.'

'Would you mind if we searched your boat?'

'No, of course not.'

'We'd also like to look over your premises.'

'I don't see why this is necessary, but by all means.'

The two officers left Dulay in a cold sweat. He called the captain of his boat and told him to reiterate the make of the helicopter he'd told the police and to say that three people were on board.

The officers reported back to England that they had searched Dulay's boat and found nothing. They had also searched his home and workplace but had found nothing incriminating there either. They did note, however, that Dulay himself cut stones and had a very well-appointed work room at the rear of his shop. He also had a successful business with influential clients. They said he had been helpful in every way and that they were not suspicious.

They were told to stay away from him until further notice, but not to return to England. They were to keep surveillance on him and to make it obvious. He might not have given them reason to doubt him but the coincidence of his profession and his having been near England at the time of the robbery and the business with the crate made him a suspect.

The same photograph of the helicopter was subsequently shown to the boys, who knew nothing about helicopters and were unable to confirm if it was the same make.

The information from Dulay was relayed to the team, who began to enquire into who in the UK owned a Sikorsky helicopter. They also contacted the companies from which he said he had sought help. All remembered the enquiry so Dulay's story could not be disproved. Launches were sent out to find the crate that had been dropped from the helicopter.

Dulay was worried. He was sure that he was being watched and his nerves were getting the better of him. He wanted to contact de Jersey but was afraid to do so. However, a few days after he'd been interviewed he received a call from the man himself. The newspapers were full of details of the helicopter, stating it was likely to have been the getaway vehicle, so de Jersey had known Dulay would be unnerved. He called him from a pay-phone at Kempton Park racecourse. He had just watched Royal Flush sail home first with ease, ensuring his place in the Derby. He had congratulated Mickey, avoided posing for photographs and watched his horse rugged up.

He was still on a high when he rang Dulay. 'How are you?' he asked.

'They're on to me, I'm sure,' hissed Dulay.

'Not if you followed orders.'

'There's some witness who saw the drop.'

'But you kept to the story?'

'Yes. They searched the boat from top to bottom. My house, the shop—'

'But it's well hidden so you've got nothing to worry about.' De Jersey maintained his calm.

'Yeah, but you're not the one being tailed. Man, I am shitting myself.'

'Just stay calm. Carry on as if nothing's happening.

Don't go near the loot, just stick to the plans. We don't collect until the heat's off. Just go about your business and see how Mr Kitamo is. We want that one million down-payment.'

'He's going to want to authenticate the Koh-i-noor but I'm too hot right now to retrieve the jewels.'

'Well, if he wants the diamond, he's just going to have to trust us. You tell him we want the million dollars before we'll let him see it. Unless he's completely out of touch, he knows by now there's some priceless gems out there to be had.'

'I hear you. Anything happening your end?'

'No. Still in the clear.'

By the end of the call, de Jersey was edgy. He had not expected this to happen so soon. Apart from the Koh-i-noor, the jewels were still in the waterproof crate, wrapped in tarpaulins and haversacks, hidden hundreds of feet down in the ocean. A lobster pot marked the place where it had been dropped off the coast of Cannes, towards a small inlet and fishing harbour. When it was time to collect, Dulay would go in single-handed with a speedboat: no crew, no witnesses.

Out on the water the coastguards retrieved a large old wooden crate and hauled it aboard. It contained boiler-suits, boots, two jackets and a pair of shoes. It provided the robbery squad with no further clues and made Dulay's explanation seem more credible.

Dulay read on the Internet that the crate had been recovered but it did little to ease his mind. He was already wishing he hadn't joined the team, but it was too late now. He had been lucky so far, but how long would his luck hold out?

Sylvia Hewitt's death looked suspicious to Fuller. He had removed her business diary and personal papers from her office, plus letters and files from her St John's Wood flat. Sifting through them he discovered from her office diary that she had had numerous appointments for the weeks after her death and had made dates for a dental and medical check-up the next day. This was not the pattern of a woman contemplating suicide.

He called Matheson again who felt certain that when he had last spoken to her in New York she was not suicidal but determined to trace Moreno in the hope of recouping her losses. Matheson added that Moreno had disappeared.

In Sylvia's office diary were listed the names and contact numbers of certain clients of David Lyons who had also suffered extensive losses. Among the names listed were those of Anthony Driscoll, James Wilcox and Edward de Jersey. These three names were underlined as if more important than the others, so Fuller decided to concentrate on them.

The first of the threesome to be interviewed was Tony Driscoll. He almost had heart failure when his wife came into his study to tell him a police officer wanted to talk to him.

'Sorry to bother you, sir. I'm Detective Sergeant Jon Fuller and this is PC Margaret Kilshaw. I am here concerning a lady named Sylvia Hewitt. I believe you were a business associate.' Driscoll hesitated, but Fuller continued, 'You should know that Miss Hewitt is dead.'

'Oh, I'm sorry to hear that, but I didn't know her.'

'Miss Hewitt recently suffered financial losses due to her involvement with an Internet company and your name was listed in her diary.'

'Ah, yes. I know who she is but I never met her. I think she got my number from David Lyons, who advised me to invest in the same company.'

'Could you tell me why she contacted you?'

'I suffered substantial losses in the same company and Miss Hewitt asked if I would be willing to hire someone to help trace the man she believed was responsible. I was rather annoyed that she had got hold of my personal details, which I pointed out to her was illegal.'

'And you never met her?'

'No, I did not. I'm sorry I can't be more helpful.'

'Just one more thing. Do you know someone named Edward de Jersey?'

'No.'

'Do you know someone called James Wilcox?'

'No.'

'Philip Simmons?'

Driscoll's heart was thudding fit to burst through his chest. 'No. I'm sorry I can't help you but I only spoke to the woman once on the phone.' He hesitated, then decided he had said enough.

Wilcox was tipped off fast by Driscoll and warned not to be alarmed if he got a call from the police.

'I warned everyone about that bloody woman,' Wilcox said tightly.

'Yes, I know, but we've no problem. She's dead.'

There was a pause as Wilcox took in what he had said. 'How come they came to you?'

'The bitch had my details in her fucking diary so that means she must have yours and the Colonel's. I'll warn him too.' Driscoll paused. 'So far so good, huh?' he said.

'Yeah. Let's hope it stays that way,' Wilcox replied.

When DS Fuller visited Wilcox that afternoon, he denied knowing Sylvia Hewitt, Driscoll or de Jersey. 'Did you know that David Lyons committed suicide?' Wilcox asked the sergeant innocently.

'Yes, we are aware of that. Just one more thing, do you know a Philip Simmons?'

'No. I didn't mix with Lyons socially so I didn't know any of his other clients. All I do know is we all lost a considerable amount in this Internet company we invested in. Maybe he was one of the losers.'

'Via a Mr Alex Moreno?'

'I believe so. But I think he did a runner. I know we have little hope of recovering any money.'

As he had said he would, Driscoll made a short warning call to de Jersey, who was abrupt and noncommittal. When he replaced the phone he was aware of a dull sensation in the pit of his stomach. He was sure that de Jersey had played some part in the demise of Miss Hewitt, but as with Moreno he hadn't asked and he didn't want to know. He was just relieved that she was no longer a problem.

However, both Driscoll and Wilcox had financial problems and were in need of a cash injection. Driscoll decided to put his house on the market, unaware that Wilcox was contemplating the same thing.

DS Jon Fuller and his PC now made the journey to de Jersey's estate. If Fuller had been impressed by the properties owned by Driscoll and Wilcox, de Jersey's took his breath away. The patrol car drew up by the side of the west wing stables. Fuller asked a boy if he could tell them where they would find de Jersey and the boy pointed to a large area beyond the east wing stables, a vast semi-covered arena with a horseshoe-shaped swimming-pool for exercising the horses.

De Jersey was watching Royal Flush swimming around the perimeter of the pool. He had seen the patrol car enter the yard and paid it no attention. As the officers approached he continued to call out instructions. 'Keep him going. Give him another two half-circles.'

'Good morning, sir.' Fuller showed his card and introduced his companion.

'This is my pride and joy, Royal Flush,' de Jersey said, gesturing to the swimming stallion. 'Put your money on him for the Derby,' he said, and gave the officers a charming smile.

He walked with them back to the house where he told them he had met Sylvia Hewitt twice, once at her brother-in-law's house and a second time when he had visited her at her apartment in St John's Wood.

'Miss Hewitt was found dead in her apartment,' Fuller told de Jersey.

'My God! When did this happen?' De Jersey stopped in his tracks.

535

'Two weeks ago. We believe it was suicide, sir.'

'Well, that's dreadful, but I fail to see how I can be of any help. I didn't really know her.' He added that he was surprised that Sylvia would contemplate suicide. Then he paused. 'I don't know if I should go into this, but her brother-in-law, as you must know, also committed suicide quite recently. The reason I am hesitant about saying anything derogatory with regard to Sylvia is because I had a great affection for David and his poor wife.' He paused again. 'I believe that Sylvia and David had been lovers for some considerable time.' He sighed. 'I am deeply sorry this has happened. In some ways I wish I had known her better. The loss of certain investments was deeply disturbing for me, but in comparison . . .'

'Did you ever think of taking legal action?' asked the detective, with interest.

'Well, David was dead. My father always used to say, "Never invest in anything you don't understand," and I wish to God I had taken his advice. This chap Moreno ran off with whatever he salvaged out of the mess.'

'Did you ever approach Moreno?'

'Good heavens, no. Sylvia was trying to find him. She wanted me to help, but private detectives can't be trusted and I just felt it was best to forgive and forget. David was dead and that was the end of it, as far as I was concerned.'

'And you do not know an Anthony Driscoll or a James Wilcox?'

'I'm afraid not.'

'Have you ever met a man called Philip Simmons?'

At this moment Christina walked in. She paused in the doorway with a tray of coffee.

'Darling, do come in.' De Jersey rose to his feet and

made the introductions. She put down the tray and shook their hands. De Jersey handed round the coffee as he explained the reason for the officers' visit.

Christina sat down, shocked. 'Good heavens. How terrible. I must call Helen,' she said.

De Jersey put his arm round her. 'Yes, of course, we should.'

She gazed at him a moment, then smiled at the officers. 'Excuse me,' she said, and left the room.

Outside the study door Christina waited to hear her husband tell the police whether he knew Philip Simmons. 'I don't think I do. Was he one of David's clients?' she heard him say.

'We're not sure,' replied Fuller. 'It's just that there are various notes in Miss Hewitt's diary with regard to this man and, according to the detective in New York, she felt that he was connected to Alex Moreno.'

'I can't recall meeting someone of that name but, then, I do meet a lot of people at the racetracks.'

'Have you been to New York yourself recently?'

'No, I have not.'

Christina remained listening until they began to discuss racing. She went slowly up to her bedroom and sat on the bed. She could understand why he had lied. He had done something illegal in New York, he had told her that. But how on earth could it be connected to Sylvia Hewitt? She went to the window to see de Jersey ushering out the officers and watched as they walked down the path to their parked patrol car.

A few moments later, de Jersey walked into the bedroom. 'I wasn't expecting you home for a while,' he said.

Christina watched him. He frightened her. 'How much did you overhear?' he asked.

'Well, I heard them ask you about being in New York.'

'And I was not likely to admit I was there and you know why,' he said, sitting on the bed.

'But they'll find out, surely.' She avoided his eyes.

'Why should they? I'll destroy those passports if you like.'

'I would if I were you, but I don't understand why all this subterfuge is necessary.'

'I explained it to you.'

'I know you did, but why did Sylvia Hewitt have notes in her diary about this man you went to see?'

'Because, sweetheart, she was trying to trace him to get her own money back. I've told you this. In fact, it was David who suggested I use a pseudonym when travelling to buy racehorses. He even got the passports for me. As soon as a seller knows my name they put up the price. I would say that the reason she kept on calling here was that she might have found out and wanted to squeeze money out of me. She really was a very unpleasant woman.'

'She's dead, for God's sake.'

'I know, and by her own hand. She was not a nice woman at all, carrying on with David behind Helen's back. Her own sister!'

'Suddenly you're coming over all moralistic,' she said, in disbelief.

'Not really, but she was only concerned about getting her money back, and she had probably discovered that she didn't have a hope in hell of seeing any of it again and it must have been too much for her.'

'How did she do it?'

'I have no idea. We didn't get into those kind of details.'

'Did you go and see her, then?'

'What?'

'I said did you go and see her after she kept calling?'

'No, I put it off. I had enough to think about – and considering that that son-of-a-bitch David has virtually bankrupted me, I would think you could understand my reasons for not wanting anything to do with her.'

'Did you?'

'Did I what?'

'Have anything to do with her?'

'Why on earth are you asking me that? I just told you I didn't go to see her. I don't want to discuss this any further. It's finished.' He walked out, slamming the bedroom door.

He was treading on dangerous ground, and now the person he cared most deeply for might also be the most dangerous to him. He was angry with himself for leaving the passports to be found, angry that the one area he had felt was secure was now vulnerable. He had to find a way to sort it out as quickly and efficiently as possible.

Raymond Marsh, unaware that he was already under investigation, had arrived in South America without a hitch. Almost immediately he had an allergic reaction to something in the climate that gave him blinding head-aches and a rash all over his body. His wife and daughter booked into a hotel with him but he decided he wanted to move on. South America was not to his liking. He called his friend Robbie with instructions on where to send his packing cases. When he was told that cops were swarming around his old house and his face was plastered all over the newspapers and on television he slammed the phone down. It was imperative to get out of Brazil. The police might have discovered from Robbie where he was. He paced up and down the hotel room, itching and sweating, trying to think where they should go, when his wife walked in with their screaming child.

'She's got a rash too. It's the heat.'

Marsh looked at her, and grinned. 'Let's get out of here, then. Tell you what, why don't we visit your place?'

'What are you talking about?' she asked, sticking a dummy into the baby's mouth.

'New Zealand,' he said.

Rio is a city where anything can be bought and within one afternoon Raymond Marsh had new passports. At ten in the evening, he, his wife and daughter flew out of Rio on tickets booked through their illegal credit cards. During the flight he began to feel worse and by the time they landed he was sick, with a high temperature. They moved into the best hotel in Auckland and a doctor was called. Marsh's allergy subsided, but the fever and painful aches persisted. He was diagnosed with a virulent form of shingles. He remained in a darkened room under sedation for two days. He felt so ill that he didn't even watch TV.

His quick exodus from Rio meant there was no clue as to his present whereabouts. When the detectives traced the *poste-restante* address on his boxes to Rio, they set

540

off with a warrant for his arrest but returned empty-handed.

In London, the headlines now blasted on about the police's failure to capture Marsh or to trace Philip Simmons, both wanted in connection with the infamous Crown Jewels heist. The articles made their way round the world to the hotel where Marsh was staying. By the time he saw it the story was already a week old.

Marsh read the articles with relief. The hunt for him had reached a dead end and it was believed that he was still at large in Rio. He was amazed at the photographs they had used of him, which had been taken from his packing boxes. Some were in Elvis mode, others showed him in school uniform. He knew he must not use any of the credit-card numbers from the UK to pay his bills.

Marsh studied himself in the mirror. Since he had been ill he'd not had time to fix his hair and it was stuck together in unattractive clumps. He went into the bathroom, stuck his head under the shower and shampooed it three times to get the grease and old dried mousse out. It had taken many years of practice to style it into a teddy-boy quiff, but now it was receding badly and hung limply to his chin. He picked up a pair of nail scissors and chopped it short. He was near to tears. It wasn't just his hair he had lost but all his memorabilia. The crates containing his hero's guitars and his autographed pictures were now in the hands of the Metropolitan Police.

His wife barged in with a dirty nappy and had to sit on the edge of the bath, she was laughing so hard. When she stopped giggling, she wiped her eyes with a tissue. 'Christ, Raymond, you don't half look different!'

'I'll get a transplant,' he snapped.

Marsh calculated that they would have real financial problems soon, but knew that to contact Philip Simmons was tantamount to suicide. He would have to monitor the papers and lie low. He moved his family into a small apartment in Wellington and applied for a job with a local computer company. It was a far cry from the dream life he had hoped for, but at least he was free.

Sylvia Hewitt's funeral took place within days of Lord Westbrook's. The latter was a more public occasion, with press and photographers lining the streets outside his family estate. He was to be buried in the family crypt alongside his illustrious ancestors and the service took place in the family chapel. His ex-wife, his son and heir, and his two daughters had returned to England for the occasion. The company now running the house and grounds allowed them to use the chapel and crypt, and the mourners were old family friends and various distant relatives. Displays of lilies sat on either side of his photograph. The police officers seated at the rear of the tiny chapel looked on with disgust: this man had been a petty criminal and then part of a robbery that still stunned the nation.

Lord Westbrook had dreamed of his son returning to the ancestral seat. The boy stood beside his mother in a grey suit. Neither he nor his mother knew of Westbrook's dream. Those more distantly related to him told the press they were appalled by his actions.

De Jersey knew that Westbrook had been in immense pain and was happy to know he was no longer suffering.

He was relieved to see the funeral on the news. It meant one major risk was gone but he would honour his promise. When pay-day came, Westbrook's son would receive his father's cut. Whatever else de Jersey was, he was an honourable man. He had still not seen anything about Sylvia Hewitt's 'suicide' in the papers and hoped to God they had closed the inquiry.

Pamela saw the televised snippet of the funeral and sobbed. She wished she could have been there. She had sent flowers with a card that simply said, 'From your lady-in-waiting, with love and fond memories'. She paid for the bouquet in cash.

The police filmed the entire funeral, hoping that some-one linked to the robbery might have shown their face but no one did. They also examined the flowers. Pamela's message was obscure, perhaps from a mistress or lover, though 'lady-in-waiting' seemed to refer to the robbery. The florist was contacted and remembered that a bedraggled red-haired lady with a refined voice and sophisticated manner had ordered the flowers. Unfortunately she had not left an address or contact number. When shown the computer pictures of Pamela from Maureen Stanley's description the florist gasped. 'Oh, my God, this is the woman wanted for the Crown Jewels robbery. I don't believe it.' She took another look at the photo-fit and shook her head. 'No, it wasn't her. The woman I met was much older.'

The police were at yet another dead end and the robbery was dropping out of the headlines. They felt their next best move was to have it profiled on a television crime programme. *The Crime Show* had given over the entire fifty-minute programme to the case, and a private benefactor had offered a reward of twenty-five thousand pounds for any information leading to a conviction. As the programme closed, the phones were ringing and the twenty-four officers on duty were hopeful that they would get the breakthrough they were looking for. The following morning, the calls were still being followed up.

Chief Superintendent Dom Rodgers, the officer overseeing Operation Crown, was feeling ill. He had been coughing for a couple of days and feared he had caught a virus. Now he felt red hot and he took himself to his local GP's surgery in Maida Vale. The waiting room was cold and uninviting, and the two patients ahead of him both had streaming colds. He sat feeling wretched, wishing he had remembered to bring his morning paper. His mobile rang and he fished it out of his pocket. 'Rodgers,' he answered, then listened. 'What?' he said, in stunned amazement. 'Look, I'm not far from their station. I'll get right over there.'

He snapped off his phone, left the surgery without keeping his appointment, and drove straight to the St John's Wood police station. His chest hurt and he was sweating beneath his overcoat but his excitement put his ill-health to the back of his mind. He asked to speak to the officers involved in the Sylvia Hewitt inquiry.

DS Jon Fuller's hand shook as he spooned sugar into a beaker of tea. 'I'm so sorry, sir, but we had a list of

David Lyons' clients Miss Hewitt had named as losing in the crash of the Internet company and—'

'Just get to the fucking point, Sergeant. Philip Simmons. You called the robbery squad and – ' he banged down a small tape-recorder then gestured with his hand ' – go on, you've lost me enough times already, son. Philip Simmons.'

Armed with the details of the Sylvia Hewitt case, Rodgers returned to Scotland Yard where his team was waiting, having received the call from St John's Wood station earlier that morning. He tossed over his tape-recorder.

'Listen to this prick, then come into my office. We've had a development and we could have had it fucking weeks ago.'

CHAPTER 25

OTHER DEVELOPMENTS now materialized in the wake of the television programme. A taxi driver was sure he had picked up Lord Westbrook from Waterloo station just before he died. He said he had driven him to his family estate but at the time did not recognize him. He was unable to say where Westbrook had alighted from to get to the station, but they had the date and time so they could begin checking which trains had arrived around that time. A hotel barman was sure he had seen Westbrook in the company of a man similar to the one described in the programme, but he was more dark blond than red-headed. He could not recall the exact day but knew it had been some time in January. A railway porter recalled seeing someone fitting Westbrook's description on Plymouth station and said that he had arrived in a wheelchair pushed by an elderly red-haired woman. A train had left Plymouth to arrive at Waterloo just before the time he was picked up by the taxi driver. The description of the woman wheeling the chair matched that of the woman who had purchased the flowers for Westbrook's funeral.

The inquiry was buzzing again. An estate agent said that a man named Philip Simmons had rented a boat-house close to Putney Bridge. The transaction had been done over the Internet and he had never met Mr Simmons. The boat-house had burnt down in a fire on the day of the robbery.

Officers were sent with frogmen and equipment to drag the river in and around the boat-house. They hauled up the wreck of a small speedboat. After examination, an identical boat was photographed and appeared on the front page of the *Evening Standard* with a request for anyone with information about a boat of this description to contact the police directly. This produced the boatyard mechanic who had sold the boat to Wilcox. He gave a description of Wilcox, whom the police identified as one of the men who had picked up Maureen Stanley, and who had purchased the two Daimlers. The mechanic, however, had never met anyone by the name of Philip Simmons.

All of this information made it look as if the robbers had escaped via the river and appeals were made for anyone who had seen these two boats on the river to come forward. More officers questioned the owners of the vast number of boats along the Thames. This yielded the location of the mooring facility rented for the two speedboats, and the name materialized yet again: Philip Simmons.

The Operation Crown officers were certain that Philip Simmons was the cyber-identity of their number-one man. But the most vital clue to his real identity came as a result of the death of Sylvia Hewitt, which now became part of the inquiry. All the statements taken from her friends and associates were read and reread for possible links. They had the names of the three men who had suffered extensive losses in the fall of the Internet company: James Wilcox, Anthony Driscoll and Edward de Jersey. Could these men be connected in some way to Philip Simmons?

Pamela became very frightened by the headlines, 'Police About To Swoop', and holed up in her grimy apartment. She felt cut off and alone. She wore a headscarf and dark glasses when she left the flat to go to the local chemist where she bought a dark brown hair dye. Then she went to the nearest off-licence and bought a large bottle of vodka. When she returned she locked and bolted the front door, put the rinse on her hair and left it to take hold for half an hour. She began to drink the vodka and chain-smoked, watching television from her bed. Her recent adventure seemed a far-off fantasy, except that the six o'clock news had implied that it was just a matter of time before the robbers were arrested.

Driscoll and Wilcox were in the same boat as Pamela, albeit a more comfortable one. They both watched the news bulletins and read the papers from cover to cover. From their different houses they had watched *The Crime Show* with equal trepidation, their confidence dented. Their families were subjected to bad moods, but their women put this down to financial pressures. Unlike de Jersey, Wilcox and Driscoll rarely left their homes. They felt more terrified with every phone call and knock on the door. They were losing control. The waiting was becoming unbearable and eventually they decided independently that they had to flee the country.

Driscoll went to Spain, telling Liz that he needed to

secure the sale of their villa, and, after a quick phone call, Wilcox agreed to join him. They were breaking the Colonel's rules but they were unable to deal with the pressure alone. They resisted the urge to contact de Jersey.

The latest developments had given Chief Superintendent Rodgers fresh energy, but by late afternoon on the day after he had interviewed DS Fuller his temperature had risen again and he was forced to go home. The doctor insisted he spend at least two days in bed. The police press office assigned to the robbery now put out a statement saying that they had acquired vital new evidence and were confident arrests would soon be made. Rodgers warned, however, that not one of the three men's names was to be divulged until they had more evidence. Above all, they didn't want them tipped off. They knew that they were still in England, from the statements taken by the young officer, but Rodgers himself made the mistake of delaying the requestioning of Wilcox, Driscoll and de Jersey when he took to his sick bed, and Wilcox and Driscoll left England.

Although Liz Driscoll knew her husband was going to Spain, Rika had no idea that Wilcox was leaving. He put the twins in his car, saying he was taking them to stay with their mother for a few days, and never returned.

De Jersey occupied himself with his horses. The friction between him and Christina had not eased and was a constant source of worry to him. It came to a head on the night of the television documentary. Christina was watching it alone in the bedroom while he saw it in his study with brandy and a cigar. Half-way through he clenched the cigar in his teeth, switched off the television set and got to his feet.

Christina heard her husband leaving the house and watched him drive away in the Range Rover from the bedroom window. She waited by the window for a full ten minutes, staring out across the paddocks, but he did not return, and by the time she went back to the programme it was over. The constant references to Philip Simmons had terrified her because, although the man was described as having red hair and a moustache, it had also been suggested that this might be a disguise. Either the man they wished to question had worn a wig or had dyed his hair another colour. Although the computerized pictures of Britain's 'Most Wanted Man' did not look like her husband, the description of his size, demeanour and military bearing made her suspicious.

Christina went into his office and closed the door. The room still smelt of his cigar and the brandy glass was half full, as if he intended returning shortly. She went to his desk and tried the drawers. All had been fitted with new locks and handles. Christina was of two minds whether or not to force the locks again. Then she saw the keys on the desk and picked them up. She opened the first drawer. It contained a few papers, but nothing of importance. The next drawer contained veterinary and feed bills, and a stack of brochures for horse auctions in Ireland. The next had details of sales at Tattersalls, all of which she had already seen. She then turned to the right-hand side of the desk, opened the secret compartment and proceeded to check through the contents in, first, the top drawer and then, finding the larger ones beneath also unlocked this time, she removed everything, placing it all on top of the desk. The envelope with the passports was no longer there. In their place was a last will and testament of Edward de Jersey. He had left his estate to Christina and their daughters. Also listed were many donations to charities and detailed personal mementoes and monies to be paid to his staff for their services. The will, she knew, must have been drawn up a long time ago, not just from the date but because she knew there was now no money for donations. She found nothing incriminating, except that he had removed the passports. Had he found a new hiding place?

She relocked the drawers, replaced the keys where she had found them on the desk and walked out. She returned to the bedroom, calmer now but still disturbed. She kept telling herself that she was being paranoid. As if she was on automatic pilot, though, she began to search her husband's dressing room. She went first to the underwear drawers, then to his socks, and the shelves containing his cashmere sweaters. She felt underneath them with the flat of her hand. She searched his jackets, his shoes and boots, feeling deep inside to the toes in case something was hidden there. It was a fruitless waste of time. She stood up in a rage and swiped at the hangers. Jackets fell noiselessly to the floor and the ineffectiveness of the search made her scream with frustration. She was near to tears.

She returned to the bedroom, opening bedside cabinets and drawers, then threw herself on the floor to look under the bed. By now she did not care about covering her tracks and frantically searched everywhere, even the girls' bedrooms. All she wanted was something, anything to stop the terrible nagging fear that her husband was somehow involved in the robbery of the Crown Jewels.

It was after twelve when Christina, exhausted from her search, finally went downstairs to get herself a whisky. She had looked just about everywhere, but as she passed the cloakroom, she paused. De Jersey's riding caps and jackets were stacked on top of each other near the rows of wellingtons and boots. She picked up one after another, turning them upside down. Something was lodged in the toe of a muddy riding boot, hidden beneath a thick, rolled-up sock. As she took out the sock, her heart pounded. She rested against the wall as she withdrew an object wrapped in an old cloth, then sank slowly to the ground as she looked at the glittering stone in her hand: the Koh-i-noor diamond. There was no denying it. She had found what she had been looking for.

De Jersey returned to the farm at about one fifteen. He was carrying a black briefcase and entered silently. He went into his study, and put the case beneath his desk. He looked down at the drawers and picked up the keys, which were still on the desk, and weighed them in his hand for a moment, thinking. Then he hurried to the cloakroom and looked inside. He didn't have to turn on the light to realize that the coats had been searched. He turned and made his way up the stairs. All the bedroom lights were on and he prowled from room to room looking inside and turning off the lights before he walked along the landing to his own bedroom. There was only a small bedside lamp on and from the doorway he could see the disturbance in the room.

Christina was waiting in bed for him, a pillow behind

her head. He leaned against the doorframe and smiled. 'Did you find what you were looking for?' He came to stand at the end of the bed, his eyes boring into hers as he eased off one shoe then the other and kicked them aside.

'You didn't answer my question,' he said. Christina turned away from him. He took off his jacket and unbuttoned his shirt, then walked into the bathroom and closed the door. She could hear the shower being turned on, and off a little later, the clink of his toothbrush in the glass and then his electric shaver buzzing. He was in the bathroom for over fifteen minutes before he walked out wearing a white towel robe. In his bare feet, he crossed to his dressing room, glanced inside and saw the fallen clothes and coat hangers, then went to the dressing-table.

'You have been busy,' he said mockingly, as he combed his wet hair, looking at her reflection in the mirror. Then he turned.

She wanted to hide from his eyes and at first she couldn't work out why she felt that way. Then it came to her in a flash. It was because she found him so sexually attractive, more so than she had for a long time. His presence filled the darkened bedroom and she was not afraid of him any more.

'We need to talk.' Her voice was surprisingly calm.

'Not yet.' De Jersey pulled the duvet off her. Now her eyes met his and, contrary to her own misgivings, she opened her arms as he knelt on the bed and moved towards her. He touched her, gently at first, kissing every part of her body, before tearing off his robe, and pulling her tightly into his arms. This time his kiss was harder and deeper and she responded, moaning softly, as he began to make love to her, hard and fast, pinning her arms behind her head until they climaxed simultaneously, moaning with pleasure. He rolled on to his side and lay there panting, his breath coming in harsh gasps.

'Well, that's made me feel better,' he said, and reached to the bedside table to pour a glass of water. He gulped almost half then offered the glass to her.

She shook her head and drew the duvet around her naked body.

'First, let me tell you that I love you, I always have,' he said, replacing the glass.

'I don't know you!' She had tears in her eyes.

'No, I don't think you do – well, not all of me.' He said it so matter-of-factly that she curled away from him. 'But it's too late now.'

'What have you done?' she said, afraid.

'So much, my darling, but, like I said, it's too late. It would take too long to explain.' He lifted his right arm. 'Come here.'

'No.'

'Come here,' he said firmly, and drew her into the curve of his body as if she were a child. 'It's safer if you know as little as possible. You already know too much and I don't know how you will be able to deal with knowing more.'

'I found what you had hidden in the toe of your boot,' she said, and leaned up on her elbow. 'What is it?' He looked into her frightened face and smiled but he did not answer her. She turned away. 'I watched the programme tonight, about the robbery.'

'I know.'

'Please tell me it isn't what I think it is.'

He said nothing, and she felt beneath her pillow, then withdrew the stone. 'I could feel it, hard against my head, when you were fucking me,' she said, holding it tightly.

He reached over and she clenched her fist over it. 'Give it to me,' he said.

'No, I won't. Not until you tell me what it is. Not until you tell me why you have it.'

He leaned over her and almost crushed her hand as he removed it from her, then held it up to catch the light. It sparkled.

'Mountain of Light,' he said softly, and his face was like a boy's as he looked at the stone. 'It is the most priceless diamond in the world.'

'Why have you got it?' she said in awe.

'Because I needed it.'

'You have to return it.'

'Do I?'

'You can't keep it.'

'I can't?'

'No, you must be insane even to think that you can.'

'Why is that?'

She sat up angrily and looked at him. 'It's stolen.'

He gave her a cold, arrogant glance that chilled her. She moved away from him and the fear she had felt earlier returned. At first it was fear for herself but he had softened again and he reached out to her.

'No, please don't touch me. I don't want you near me. I can't deal with this.' She got up and reached for a robe and wrapped it around her. 'What did you have to do with Sylvia Hewitt's death?'

'Nothing,' he replied.

'But the police want to question this Philip Simmons and I know it's you. He was the last person to see her alive, that is what they said on the programme. Why would they say that if you were not involved?'

'How do you know it's me?' he asked, almost mockingly.

'You fit the description.'

'Along with how many thousands of other men,' he said. 'Besides, you know where I was on the day of the robbery. First at Brighton racetrack and then we went to see the girls' play. I couldn't be in two places at once, sweetheart, could I?' He placed the diamond where he could see it beside him. 'I had nothing to do with Sylvia Hewitt's death, and if you want to know where I was at the time they are claiming she died, I was at my club. I dined at the club and I even spoke to you from there. If you don't believe me, ask the porter.'

'So if you had nothing to do with her death, why do they want to speak to you?'

'I have no idea. It's possibly connected to David Lyons. He topped himself and it looks as if she did the same. He lost her savings as well as mine and, as I told you before, I didn't get in touch with her because I had a good idea she was trying to hit me for money. On and on she went about hiring a private investigator, and as for this,' he nodded to the stone and turned back to her, 'it's a crystal replica I bought when we went to the Tower of London with your parents. I intended to give it to one of the girls. I carried it around in my pocket and forgot about it until I was going out riding, so I slipped it into one of my old boots.' He chuckled. 'For God's sake, darling, don't tell me you thought I was involved in the Crown Jewels robbery. You *can't* have

556

thought that. Tell me that's not true!' He chuckled again, as she stood at the end of the bed and flushed. 'Oh, sweetheart, my poor darling. What have you been doing all evening? Trying to find the rest of them?'

'Not to begin with. I was looking for the passports you had. Where did you go tonight?'

'For a drive. Then I parked the car and walked for a while. How long is this interrogation going to go on, Miss Marple?'

He laughed, tossed the stone in the air and caught it. The light from the diamond cut shafts across the room.

'Give it to me,' she said and snatched it from him. She crossed to the dressing-table mirror and slashed at it with the stone. When it cut into the glass, she began to tremble.

'I wish you hadn't done that,' he said softly, and he was no longer smiling.

'Oh, God. Oh, my God,' she said, and he took a deep breath.

'It's going to be all right, sweetheart, but now that you do know I'm involved, I will have to take great care of you. I won't let any harm come to you and I'll have to work out just how I can keep you and the girls out of it.'

'Will you go away?' she asked.

'No. No need as yet, but now you know why I had the passports in your name and the girls'. We might have to do a moonlight flit but, whatever happens, you know I'll take care that you won't be implicated. We'll have to have a serious talk about what we should do, but right now I don't think we have too much to worry about.'

'How can you say that? If I recognized you, how long do you think it will be before someone else does?'

'You are my wife, dearest.'

She swallowed. His calm made her even more afraid.

'Did you . . . I mean, did you do it?'

'Do what?'

'For God's sake, the robbery.'

'Yes,' he said simply.

Then, as if nothing had happened, he walked casually to the door tying his robe around himself. 'I'm going to put on some tea. Would you like some?'

'No.' Her throat felt as if it was burning.

'I'm starving and I'll make a toasted-cheese sandwich too. Maybe I can tempt you,' he called, as he left the room.

She remained huddled on the bed, listening to him moving around downstairs, and her head started to throb.

De Jersey busied himself in the kitchen. He took some of Christina's sleeping tablets from the pocket of his dressing-gown, crushed them into powder and layered some under the melting cheese, then put the rest into her tea.

She was sitting up in bed when he returned with the tray, plus the brandy bottle, and he poured some into both their mugs as he sat cross-legged on the bed.

'Can I tempt you?' he asked teasingly, and she shook her head, but her mouth felt so dry she picked up a mug and drank.

She pulled a face at the tea, not liking the brandy he'd put in it, but he encouraged her to drink it. Then he started to eat a sandwich and she took one too.

'This might be our last meal together,' he joked.

She turned away from him.

'I'm teasing, you know that.'

Christina turned back to him and tears filled her eyes as she sat eating with him, afraid but still loving him, until she shook her head. 'I am so frightened,' she whispered.

He put aside the tray and took her in his arms. 'Listen to me, everything is going to be all right and now I can tell you the truth. You must have pieced it together anyway by now. I have plans. We'll have to leave England. Are you listening to me?'

She nodded as tears streamed down her cheeks.

'I love you,' he said softly, and then he made love to her again. When she fell asleep he held her until he heard her breathing deeply. He lay beside her, gently stroking her hair, until he was sure she wouldn't wake. He tucked the duvet around her and checked that she had drunk most of the tea and eaten half of the sandwich. He reckoned that would be enough. He packed quickly, taking only what he felt would be necessary, and put the diamond into his pocket. He went downstairs to collect the briefcase. He left no note and didn't look back as he let himself out of the kitchen door. He walked across the silent stableyard. It was three thirty in the morning and no one was awake. He entered Royal Flush's stable and cradled the horse's head in his arms. The bond he felt with the great stallion crushed him and he was almost in tears.

'Goodbye, my son. Wherever I am, I'll be watching you.'

The sound of the helicopter woke a few of the lads

and one sat up swearing, but the noise soon died and silence returned.

Christina slept on throughout the next morning, as horse trailers drew up at the estate and took away the horses. They had been bought by the billionaire Sheikh, and the jewel in his crown was Royal Flush.

CHAPTER 26

THE ESTATE was in turmoil when it became clear that de Jersey had sold up, lock, stock and barrel, but the staff were informed that they could continue to work for the Sheikh. The stable lads watched the great horse being led into the trailer. As always, he was kicking and biting. Even his blanket had been changed and bore the colours of his new owner, who stood around, smoking and inspecting his purchases, then walked around the estate with the shattered Donald Fleming.

Christina slept until midday, unaware that, like everything else, the mansion had been sold. When she awoke she felt as if a lead weight had been tied round her neck and her fear from the previous night returned. Looking out of the window, she saw all the movement going on in the stableyard and presumed her husband must be exercising the horses. She showered, dressed and went down into the kitchen to make herself some breakfast. There, she found out what had been happening in the most deplorable way. The new owner had left a courteous letter asking her to vacate the premises with her possessions and furnishings within a week. She also discovered the almost empty bottle of her sleeping tablets

561

where de Jersey had left it along with the loaf of bread he had used to make their toasted cheese sandwiches.

By the time she went into the yard and discovered from the staff what had happened, she was too upset to talk to anyone. She returned to the house and ran to the sink to throw up.

Christina could not admit that, along with everyone else, she had not been privy to her husband's intentions. She had had no knowledge of the sale. At first she had expected him to return and explain it to her. By mid-afternoon she was still unable to face the situation with any clarity of thought. Still shocked, she called her daughters' school, only to be told by the headmistress that the girls' fees were outstanding. She was sure that it was an oversight but asked for them to be paid forthwith. If there was a problem perhaps Mrs de Jersey would kindly arrange a meeting to discuss her daughters' future. Christina was at a loss as to what to say, but asked if she could speak to her elder daughter as there had been a family crisis. She kept control of her emotions as she told Natasha that she would like her and Leonie to come home. She told her she could not discuss the reasons over the phone. They were to catch the next train and she would collect them at the station.

There were further things for Christina to deal with, as she discovered when she called the bank to discuss paying her daughters' school fees promptly: the joint bank account was virtually empty, and payments on certain loans had not been made.

Christina discovered outstanding bills from the local grocery and wine merchants, as well as those for horse feed and veterinary visits. The phone rang constantly until she took it off the hook, unable to listen to any more queries about unpaid accounts. The papers she'd found in her husband's desk only revealed a fraction of the truth about their debts. Drawing on what little energy she had left, she went to see Donald Fleming. He was as shocked as she was. Now she discovered that wages were owed to most of the staff. She felt so ashamed that she couldn't continue talking to Fleming, who broke down and wept in front of her. 'How could he have done this? Not to even discuss it with me,' he said.

'I'm so sorry,' she replied, backing out of the door. 'I'm so very sorry.'

He looked at her, shaking his head. 'I can't believe he'd do this, not take me into his confidence. It's just . . . I worked for almost twenty years alongside him,' he said.

'I was married to him for that long and . . .' She felt her chin tremble. 'I'll come back later. We'll talk. I'm sorry, I can't think straight right now.'

She ran from the office. Entering the house she couldn't even find the strength to take off her coat. The more she began to understand the severity of her situation the more it eased the heartbreak and realization of what her husband had done. She was forced to face the probability that he had planned his departure for a considerable time and it was doubtful that he intended to return. She couldn't bring herself to think about the previous night and how he had made love to her. She sat at the kitchen table sobbing. Every time she dried her eyes the tears flowed again.

Christina forced herself to go upstairs to shower, change and get ready to face her daughters. On entering the bedroom, her loss swamped her again and she lay face down on the bed where she could still smell her husband's scent. She could still feel his presence and the sobs tore upwards from her belly.

When Christina finally stopped weeping, she changed and drove to collect her daughters. She was calm, as if none of it was happening. She didn't tell the girls what had happened until they were back at the house. Then she said that it was possible their father had not just left home but them too. She found herself in an awkward position. If he did intend to come back and take them away, as he had promised, the less the girls knew the better. She went over and over in her mind their conversation of the previous night: his promises, his protestation of love. By now, though, she also knew that he had drugged her.

Christina was unable to give a reasonable explanation to her two perplexed daughters. She couldn't tell them everything she knew, but tried to soften the blow by saying that their father had been in dire financial trouble and had been unable to deal with it. Their confused, sad faces broke Christina's tight hold on herself and she was again unable to stop the tears.

Twenty-four hours later, de Jersey had still made no contact. Christina had had no time to think about a future without her husband because she had so much she had to deal with immediately. She began to earmark anything of value to sell, but his betrayal hung over her like a dark cloud. It was while she was in this vulnerable state that two patrol cars entered the drive. It had been decided that the uniformed officers would start questioning the staff around the stables while Chief Superintendent Rodgers, with a female officer, Trudy Grainger, interviewed Edward de Jersey. At the same time, Rodgers had allocated officers to interview Driscoll and Wilcox.

As they pulled up, Rodgers saw the furniture removal vans outside the open door of the house. 'I don't like the look of this,' he murmured, getting out of the car and stretching his legs. He walked flat-footed, his feet pointing outwards, his head jutting forward like a turtle's but he had one redeeming feature: incredibly bright blue eyes. Eyes that didn't seem to miss anything, eyes that could feel like they were boring into your head, eyes that crinkled up when he smiled and made him appear to be a jovial, kindly man. In many ways he was, but underneath it he was as tough as they came.

Chief Superintendent Rodgers knocked at the open door. When he received no reply, he walked into the hallway, bypassing cardboard packing cases, some open and some waiting to be made up.

'Hello,' he called, but received no reply. He went into the drawing room. The radio was tuned to Classic FM and Christina was packing crystal glasses, wrapping them in newspaper.

Rodgers knocked loudly on the door.

'If you've come for the silver, I'm not ready,' she said.

Then he showed her his ID. 'I am Chief Superintendent Rodgers,' he said, 'and this is DC Grainger.'

'Have you come about my husband?' she stuttered.

'I'd like to speak to him,' Rodgers replied.

'So would I, but I'm afraid he's not here and I've no idea where he is.' She wiped her newsprint-stained hands on her apron.

'Could I talk to you?'

'Yes, but I have no idea where he is. He sold the farm and the house so, as you can see, I'm moving out. I have no other option. The new owner has only given me a week.'

Rodgers smiled, trying to calm her. 'Mrs de Jersey, do you mind if I turn down the radio?'

'Not at all.' She took off her apron and burst into tears. Two teenage girls appeared, carrying silver candlesticks, and Christina almost shouted at them, 'Just leave those where they are.'

Rodgers nodded and moved towards Natasha. Before he could ask either girl anything, Christina put a protective arm around each of them. 'These are my daughters, Natasha and Leonie. You won't need to speak to them, will you?'

'Not immediately,' Rodgers said, and watched as Christina ushered the girls out of the room.

'They have just got home from school,' she said, 'They don't know anything about . . .' she took a deep breath, catching herself, ' . . . the sale.'

It took a while for Christina to talk herself into a calm state and eventually Rodgers led her into the kitchen where he asked if his officers could brew some coffee.

'Go ahead,' she replied, distracted.

He sat at the kitchen table. Even in this room there were packing boxes and crates of china stacked and ready to be taken out.

'I've decided to put what I have left into storage and go and stay with my father,' she said. 'My daughters are very distressed. As I said, they have only just returned home and don't know anything.' She took out a tissue and blew her nose. Rodgers bided his time, talking gently to her about the effects of moving, anything to calm her enough to talk to him. But from the few things she had said, he knew she was privy to something he needed to hear about her husband.

At last, after some coffee and a cigarette, she seemed more in control.

'I need to ask you some questions,' he said at last.

'Is it about debts? He owes money everywhere. In fact, I had to take the phone off the hook because as soon as it became known that the estate was sold, it's not stopped ringing.'

'I am not here about debts,' Rodgers said, and waited while she dried her eyes again. She couldn't meet his steady gaze.

'Do you know Sylvia Hewitt?' he asked.

Christina nodded, and said that she also knew that she was dead. 'She was the sister-in-law of my husband's financial adviser.'

'We had been treating her death as a suicide but certain matters have arisen,' he said, and opened a notebook. He asked if Christina knew Anthony Driscoll or James Wilcox but she shook her head. Then she paused and said that, if she remembered correctly, they had also been clients of David Lyons.

'How well did your husband know Miss Hewitt?' he asked.

Christina shrugged. 'I think he did know her but not well,' she said flatly.

'Do you know if he ever visited her at her St John's Wood flat?' Rodgers asked.

'No,' she said, averting her eyes.

'So he might have been to see her, if only to discuss the loss of his investments?'

Christina didn't reply.

567

'Miss Hewitt also lost a considerable amount I under-stand,' Rodgers continued.

'I believe so, but not as much as my husband. In fact, he was always very dismissive of her. I don't think he liked her.'

'Do you know where your husband was on the night Sylvia died?'

'Yes, I do,' she said sharply. Rodgers was taken aback by the abruptness of her reply. 'He was staying at his club, the St James's. He said he was there all night.'

'You seem very sure about that.'

She kept her eyes on her hands in her lap.

'We just happened to discuss it.'

'Why was that?'

'No real reason.' She reached for her coffee cup. He saw that her hand was shaking.

Rodgers tapped his teeth with his pencil. 'Did you ask him about her death?'

'I don't understand. What do you mean?'

'Why do you remember where your husband was on that specific night?'

Christina was silent.

'Mrs de Jersey, could you answer the question, please?'

'Well, I had tried to contact him and he hadn't returned my calls so I called the club. I just remember it was that night.'

'Do you know where your husband was on the 2nd of May?'

She frowned and now she was twisting a sodden piece of tissue. 'Why that date?'

She looked up and her eyes reminded Rodgers of a frightened animal caught in a trap.

'Well, Mrs de Jersey, if you need a reminder, it was the day the Crown Jewels were stolen,' he said pleasantly, and waited.

'If you'll just hold on I'll fetch our diary.' She stood up abruptly and went into the hall. She stood with her hands pressed to her eyes, her whole body shaking. She had to take deep breaths before she returned with the book. 'Well, I know he was in Brighton racing in the afternoon but he was back here by early evening. Our daughters were performing in a school play and we both went from here at around five o'clock.'

'Do you know anyone named Philip Simmons?' Rodgers caught the quick intake of breath and watched Christina closely. 'Philip Simmons,' he repeated.

'I know the name,' she said, and looked up, her eyes not so frightened now but bright and clear. 'I watched the TV programme about the jewel robbery and I know the police want to question him.'

'And that is how you know the name?' Rodgers asked.

Christina reached for his pack of Silk Cut and took one out. He reached forward to light it for her.

'They mentioned it on the programme,' she said.

'So where do you think your husband is?' Rodgers asked.

Christina shrugged and turned away. 'I have no idea.' She inhaled deeply, then turned back to him, her face angry. He noticed yet another swift change of mood. The trapped animal was fighting back. 'My husband left me. I have to leave the house. He sold it. He's sold everything. He took off in his helicopter. He left no

569

note. I have not stopped working since then. Anything to keep my mind off the way he . . . I discovered he had sold our home from a note left to me by the new owner. He has also left me in tremendous debt, so if you do find him, be sure to let me know.' She stubbed out her cigarette in the ashtray, and she sat back in her chair, clasping her hands tightly together. 'Why are you here? If it isn't about Sylvia Hewitt, what is it about? Why do you want to see him?'

Rodgers turned over the cigarette packet. 'It is about Miss Hewitt. I'm speaking to whoever knew her.' Although he was being polite, he was watching her like a hawk.

'No other reason?' she asked.

'Possibly. I am also trying to trace Philip Simmons.'

'So you believe this man is involved in Sylvia Hewitt's death?'

'Possibly.'

'I thought she committed suicide? Helen, her sister, told me it was suicide,' Christina said.

'Possibly.' He gave nothing away but still watched her. 'I would like the details of your husband's helicopter,' he said, tapping his notebook. 'And if you have any thoughts about where he might have gone, I would be grateful to hear them.'

Christina remained silent.

'So you don't expect him to return?' Rodgers said.

Christina's eyes filled with tears. She sprang to her feet and fetched another tissue to wipe her eyes and blow her nose.

Rodgers gave her his card. 'Call me any time if you think of anything that would help me.'

'I will.' He left her looking drained and defeated. He

felt sorry for her, but he was damn sure she was holding something back. He was not finished with her yet by any means.

Christina watched the officers from the kitchen window, saw them moving across the yard, stopping the stable girls, conferring with the jockeys, then entering the manager's office. Apart from the faint hope that de Jersey would get in touch, Christina hadn't said anything because she was afraid that what she knew might endanger not only him but herself and her daughters too. She decided to leave as soon as possible for Sweden. If Edward was to contact her and his daughters, they would be safer there than they would be in England.

Rodgers sat in Fleming's office looking at the lists of forthcoming race meetings, the array of cups and awards the yard had won and the largest photograph hanging on the wall. It was of de Jersey standing by his beloved Royal Flush. He then glanced over the other photographs of de Jersey with various champions and of de Jersey close to the Queen at Royal Ascot.

'He's a big chap,' Rodgers stated quietly.

'Yes, over sixteen hands,' said Fleming.

'No, I meant Mr de Jersey,' Rodgers said, pointing to the photograph.

'Yes, about six four.' Fleming sighed and joined Rodgers, who stood looking closely at one photograph after another.

'Did Her Majesty ever come to the stables?' he asked, peering closer at one particular photograph.

'Good heavens, no! That was taken last year at Royal Ascot.'

'Did anyone from the Royal household ever come here?' he asked.

'Not that I am aware of. Like someone from the Queen's racing stables?'

'Anyone, really, who was connected to Her Majesty's household.'

'I doubt it, and I've worked here for almost twenty years. Why do you ask?'

'No reason. It's quite a place,' he said, changing the subject as Fleming returned to his desk. As he did so, Rodgers removed one of the photographs and slipped it beneath his coat. He was taken aback by the emotion in the man's voice.

'I'll never understand how he could just walk away from this stallion in particular.' Fleming pointed at a picture of Royal Flush. 'He was his pride and joy and we reckon he'll win the Derby. He's an extraordinary horse.' Fleming swallowed.

'Why do you think he's done a runner?' Rodgers asked conversationally.

'Money. He lost a fortune on some Internet company. He never picked himself up from it and running a place this size costs thousands a week. He just couldn't get out of the hole he'd dug for himself. But it still doesn't make sense to me. I thought he'd at least have told me, if not the rest of the yard.'

'Apparently he never even told his wife,' Rodgers said.

'Yeah, so I hear, and he doted on her. But the love of his life was Royal Flush. He was obsessed with him. That's what doesn't make sense. I can understand flogging the rest, but selling the horse off must have broken his heart.'

'Did you like him?'

'Who? The Boss?' Fleming asked, more in control.

'Yes. What kind of a man was he?'

'Well, I'd have given him my life savings. He's a man you thought you could trust one hundred per cent. A man of his word, until now that is. But at least most of us will still be employed. Maybe that was part of his deal.'

'Deal?' asked Rodgers.

'He's sold up lock, stock and barrel to a Sheikh, but we'll all apparently have work if we want it. He saw to that.'

'How much do you think he would have got for the place?'

'The stables?' Fleming asked warily, and sat moving papers around his desk. 'Well, I dunno how much he owed on it. I think he'd mortgaged it to the hilt. Who knows? Either way, I'd say the farm and his horses were worth about forty million. Royal Flush alone cost over a million, but he'd been selling off some of his best for months, along with his cars. He'd already let a lot of staff go.'

'Do you know a Philip Simmons?'

Fleming shook his head. 'No.'

'Do you know a James Wilcox?'

'No.'

Rodgers shifted his weight. The photograph was still hidden beneath his coat. 'Have you ever met a man named Anthony Driscoll?'

'No, I've never heard of any of them. You know,

there's a lot I should be doing. Is there something you need from me? I would like to get on with things.'

'On May 2nd of this year, do you know where Mr de Jersey was?'

'Well, not all of the time, but for part of the day he was at the races with me. We had a runner in the three o'clock at Brighton. He had to leave straight after the race as his daughters were in some play.'

'How did Mr de Jersey travel to Brighton?'

'By helicopter. He flies it himself now. He used to have a pilot but he went months ago.'

'What make of helicopter is it?'

'Erm . . . I don't really know. A small one, I think,' Fleming said, looking pointedly at his watch.

'Where do you think he is?' Rodgers asked, his hand on the door to leave.

'I have no idea, I'm sorry.'

Rodgers smiled and thanked him for his time. Just as he stepped out Fleming said, 'I'll give you a tip, though. I know where he will be.'

Rodgers turned back.

'The Derby. No way will he miss seeing Royal Flush win that race. Back the horse now and you'll get a good price.'

Rodgers returned to his car, patiently awaiting WPC Trudy Grainger. They drove out in silence with Rodgers flicking through his notebook, which was resting on the photograph of de Jersey.

'He's either done a bunk with the cash he got from the sale or he's holed up somewhere with a bottle of pills,' he said flatly.

'Or he's run off with the Crown Jewels,' said the

574

driver, but that did not go down well. Rodgers gave him an icy stare.

After another lengthy silence, Rodgers flicked through his notebook again. 'Mrs de Jersey was covering something.' He tapped the book, then suggested they check out de Jersey's alibi for the night Sylvia Hewitt had died and then rested back on the seat and shut his eyes. 'Something stinks in this and it's not horse manure. We'll put out an interest report on PNC on him, see if we can pull him in, if only for his wife's sake. She's quite a looker. It must have been difficult to walk out on her.' He opened his eyes. 'Unless he hasn't and she was covering for him.' He glared through the window and ground his teeth. 'What if the man we want is de Jersey? I reckon he could be. The descriptions we've got of Philip Simmons match de Jersey.' He balanced the photograph on his knee. 'Would a man with his face in the papers at every race meeting – a man who mixed with the Queen, for Christ's sake – risk pulling off the biggest heist in history?'

Rodgers stared at the photograph and fished in his pocket for a tin of peppermints. His mobile rang. 'Well, we'll soon know if Maureen Stanley recognizes him.'

He answered the call. 'Rodgers,' he snapped, and listened, chewing a peppermint. When he was told that both Driscoll and Wilcox had left the country the previous day he swore. A lot of fingers would point at him for fucking this up. He should have hauled them in the moment he'd had the tip-off but he hadn't. This was going to look bad.

575

De Jersey knew that time was running out. He had flown to Paris using Shaughnessy's passport and booked into a small *pension*. From a call box he contacted Dulay and spoke only briefly to say that they needed to meet. He wanted the buyer's down payment.

Paul Dulay, still under surveillance, drove to Paris. Leaving the car, he went on foot and public transport until he felt certain he had lost his tail. He was an hour late for his meeting with de Jersey in a small bar across from Hôtel de la Tremouille. He had brought half of the million dollars with him in a small leather holdall. He had retained the other half for himself.

'If you knew the runaround I've had to go through to get this cash – and I got it with those arseholes on my butt.'

'What did Kitamo have to say?'

'Well, he never says a lot but he knows what must have gone down and he's asking when he's gonna see his goods.'

De Jersey instructed Dulay not to attempt to haul up the loot. It was to remain attached to the marked lobster pot as the heat was still on. It could stay there for months, if necessary.

'How long do we expect Kitamo to wait?' Dulay asked.

'However long it takes. Don't give him the Koh-i-noor until the heat has died down. As for the other stones, tell him he'll get them in dribs and drabs. You don't go near that crate.'

'How will I give him the diamond if I can't go near the crate?'

De Jersey answered by taking it out of his pocket and covertly handing it over to Dulay.

Dulay was speechless as he took it. 'Holy Christ, is it. Where in Christ's name am I gonna put it?'

'Stay calm and lower your voice. Hold on to it until I give the word and let him know that he'll be transferring the next payment via the Internet. The day it clears we pass over the stone. Not until then.'

'I like your use of the word "we",' snapped Dulay. 'It's me who's gonna be carrying the fucking thing around.' Dulay was scared and he was drinking heavily, but de Jersey remained calm. 'Where the hell do I stash it? They've been over my shop and my home like a goddamned rash!'

De Jersey laughed and leaned in close. 'I'll tell you exactly where you're going to stash it.'

De Jersey returned to his hotel and stacked in a large wooden crate the money from Dulay alongside the cash he had received after the mortgage had been redeemed for the sale of the estate. The rest he had instructed to be placed in two banking facilities he'd arranged over the Internet in New York. On top of the false bottom of the crate were three large paintings from a small gallery close to the Hôtel de la Tremouille. They were individually wrapped in oilskins and thick rolls of bubble wrap. It was then nailed down and was to be sent by sea to the US with the gallery's name and a valuation of the contents clearly posted on the side. The paintings were to be dispatched to the Hamptons, to be held and stored by his solicitors until his arrival. It was too risky to return to his helicopter and he'd arranged storage for it at Orly airport. He knew his chances of escape depended on a solitary run. He could not afford to speak to or contact anyone. He was hoping that Christina had not divulged the names on his two fake passports, Shaughnessy and Cummings, because he intended to use them both.

After the crate had been collected by the shipping company, he switched passports to become Edward Cummings, the English art dealer. He dyed his hair dark brown and put on a small goatee beard, tinted to match his hair. Lastly he added a pair of horn-rimmed glasses. As the plane took off for New York he stared out of the window. Somewhere below, bobbing on the sparkling sea, was a small lobster pot attached to a crate containing the Crown Jewels.

Christina dressed smartly. She had spent a considerable time choosing what to wear. She was still in a fragile state and unsure how she should approach the Sheikh, who had not been forthcoming about her request to see him. But she had to know, so she had persisted until he had agreed to see her at three o'clock.

His stables were even more amazing than de Jersey's. The mansion was set in acres of rolling hills and ornate gardens, white and pillared like an old colonial home with a sweeping marble-chip drive that glittered like diamonds.

Christina was ushered into a drawing room. Elaborate paintings of horses and wildlife dotted the walls among cabinets of crystal bowls and ornate china. The gilt chairs and deep-cushioned velvet sofas were edged with gold fringe. A maid offered her tea but she refused.

Christina wanted to find out what the Sheikh had paid

for de Jersey's estate. She was certain her husband would have made financial arrangements to take care of her and his daughters and she had to ask if he had mentioned this to him. The tall, elegant man who greeted her wore an immaculate suit. His black hair was oiled and combed back from his forehead and he had an austere, cold, impatient manner. When he shook her hand she smelt a sweet lemon cologne.

He stepped back and gestured for her to sit. 'You wished to see me?'

'Yes, on a very personal matter. I apologize for this intrusion but I am desperate to get some answers. My husband, Edward de Jersey . . .' his dark eyes bored into hers '. . . you purchased the stud and racing stables from him.' She gasped for breath. 'I need to know if my husband made any provision for myself and our two daughters, if he discussed the situation with you.'

'What situation?'

'Well, I am aware that the sale was negotiated in a hurry and that perhaps my husband left some kind of information for me because he has—'

He held up his hand and she fell silent. 'To the contrary, Mrs de Jersey. We have been in negotiation for some time.'

'Some time?' she said faintly.

'Yes, perhaps six weeks. Your husband refused my first offer, so I withdrew from the deal. Then we began further negotiations, as I would agree to his asking price only on the condition that he included in the sale his stallion Royal Flush, which he at first refused but then . . .' He made an open-handed gesture, smiling '. . . I made him an offer he could not refuse.'

'When was this?' she asked.

'Four days ago.'

'How much was he paid?' she asked, pressing her hands flat to her knees. There was a silence. She looked up.

'I think, Mrs de Jersey, that is a private matter and I am not prepared to discuss it.'

'I am his wife.' Her voice sounded shrill even to her and she stood up. 'I have been left with daughters to care for, no home, no bank account and bills I can't pay. I have every right to know how much you paid him.'

'No, Mrs de Jersey, you do not. If your husband cares not to tell you then I am afraid—'

'I want to know! *I have a right to know!*' She was shouting now. She needed the iced water he passed to her. She was near to fainting. The Sheikh asked if she needed a doctor, but she said no, and tried to regain her composure. It was all too much for her.

'I really would appreciate it if you gave me some indication of the sum of money my husband received for this transaction,' she said, her voice low and filled with sadness.

After a while, to calm her down and to prove there had been no underhand dealing, he showed her the receipts and the document with her husband's signature, and she realized that he had collected considerable monies on the night he had left, and had arranged for further payments to be made into a banking facility. She now knew that, when de Jersey had returned to discover that she had been searching the house, he must have already had the money and made the decision to leave her. He had known that he was going when he made love to her.

Christina returned to the home she had loved, which was now stripped bare. She had admitted to her husband that she did not know him and she remembered word for word what he had said. It was devastating to stand in rooms they had furnished together and realize the extent of his betrayal. She walked around the almost empty house until she reached their bedroom. She could hear him, his voice, his laugh. She remembered how he had said he loved her. It was torture, but she needed to feel the pain, the force of his lies, to do what she had in mind. If he had provided for her, shown some care that the love she had given him for twenty years meant something, it would have eased the hurt. But he had given her nothing and walked away with millions of pounds in cash.

Christina headed slowly down the stairs and into his study. All the furniture was gone but his cigar smoke had left a tangy smell clinging to the walls and it made her feel as if he was there to witness what she was about to do. She bent down to the phone. It was still connected and she took out the card given to her by Chief Superintendent Rodgers. She was calm and cold with anger. She dialled his direct number and waited.

'Rodgers.'

'It's Christina de Jersey and I would like to speak to you with regard to my husband.'

CHAPTER 27

MAUREEN STANLEY was not shown the picture removed from de Jersey's office but the police lab had blown up the section of the photograph that showed his face and shoulders. It was placed among eight other black-and-white photographs of men with similar build and hair colouring. They didn't yet have photographs of either Wilcox or Driscoll.

Chief Superintendent Rodgers waited as she stared at one photograph after another. She took her time, frowning and pursing her lips, as she studied each picture. She laid all eight in front of her as if she was playing patience. Just as Rodgers was about to give up on her, Maureen identified their man. 'I've got a good memory for faces.' She had now recovered from the kidnap ordeal and, bathing in the continued media interest, she was enjoying herself.

Rodgers interrupted her impatiently. 'Mrs Stanley, do you recognize the face of the man who held you captive? The man you claim to be the leader.'

'Oh, yes, without any doubt!'

'Could you please indicate to everyone here which of these eight photographs you believe to be this man?'

Maureen nodded, her hand poised over the photo-

graphs. 'Without any doubt, that's him!' she said trium-
phantly, and held up the picture of George Ericson, one
of the officers attached to the inquiry.

Rodgers closed his eyes.

Tony Driscoll signed the papers for the sale of his villa in
Marbella. The estate agent was a glamorous blonde with
an all-over tan and plunging neckline. The villa was going
to a dapper Italian, who had agreed to pay cash. That,
minus the agent's cut, plus all the contents, left him with
a hundred and thirty thousand. Driscoll knew it was
worth more but as he had been paid in cash he accepted
the loss.

He was preparing to return to England when he
received a call from his wife. She was hysterical. The cops
had been round. 'They were asking all this stuff, Tony,
about this woman Sylvia Hewitt. Then – oh, my God,
Tony – they were asking about the Crown Jewels robbery. Where you were on the day, where you are now. I
said it was all a mistake, that you were sorting out our
villa.'

'Get off the phone, Liz.'

'What do you mean, get off the phone? What the hell
is going on, Tony? *Tony?*'

But Driscoll had slammed down the receiver. He went
to look for Wilcox and found him on the patio. He sat
down on the sun-lounger beside him. 'We've got
trouble,' he said quietly. 'The cops have been round to
my place asking questions and they've got a search
warrant.' Wilcox's eyes remained closed. 'Did you hear
what I said?'

'Yeah.' Wilcox removed his shades.

'What do you think?' Driscoll asked.

Wilcox got up, reached for his towel and slung it round his neck. 'I'll go down to the harbour and call Rika, see if they've been nosing around my place too.'

'Then what?'

'Well, we'll have to think what we do next.'

'I know what I'm doing, pal. I'm getting the fuck out of here. Stupid cow told them I was here, so how long do you think it's gonna take for them to come and pick me up? One call to the Spanish police and we're nabbed.'

'What did they want?'

'They were asking about Hewitt then slipped in the date of the fucking robbery. Not hard to put two and two together. They're fucking on to us.'

'We don't know that for sure.'

'Well, I tell you one thing, I ain't going back to find out.'

'What are you gonna do?'

'Move on, lie low and wait, I guess.'

Wilcox kept his cool. 'You mind waiting until I speak to Rika?'

'Sure, but get a move on. We should separate, fast.' Driscoll went back into the villa.

Wilcox used Driscoll's jeep to drive down to Puerto Banus harbour. Once there, he went into a bar and called Rika. He said little but listened as she told him that not only had the police been round asking questions about his whereabouts but had also returned later with a search warrant.

'Vhat are they looking for, James? Vhy you leave me? Vhere are you? Tell me vhat you do.'

584

He hung up and dialled his ex-wife, Françoise. He could hear his kids shouting in the background as he said he would not be able to return to England for a while and the boys should stay with her. Françoise hit the roof. He hung up on her and walked out of the bar. He drove back to the villa, his nerves in shreds.

As he parked the jeep in the drive, trying to think what his next move should be, Driscoll came out, his bags packed. 'I'm out of here,' he said flatly.

'Where you going?'

'I dunno, but I'm not staying around to be picked up, and if you've got any sense you'll do the same.'

'On what?' snapped Wilcox, getting out and slamming the car door.

Driscoll sighed. 'Look, I'm not ditching you in the shit. I've left five hundred quid on the kitchen table.'

'Big deal. How far am I gonna get on that?'

'It's not my problem, Jimmy, but we can't risk staying together.'

'Well, it's all right for you. You just made a packet on this villa but five hundred's not gonna last me long, is it?'

'Take the Jeep – all the documents are in a drawer in the hall – then go visit one of the chicks you've been hanging out with. Leave the keys on the table in the hall. The agent's got another set but you can't stay on here for much longer. The new tenants are moving in at the end of the month.' Driscoll walked away without a backward glance.

Driscoll walked down the green gravel drive, past the kidney-shaped swimming-pool and into the half-com-

585

pleted lane beyond. The authorities had been 'finishing' the roadway to the plot of villas since he had purchased his fifteen years previously. At the end of the pot-holed road he turned right and headed towards a small row of shops where he called a local taxi to take him to the airport. He still had no plan, but he called his wife and told her to sell the house. He told her not to ask him any questions but to wait for him to contact her. She was beside herself with worry. Driscoll said little to comfort her, just that he was unable to return to England. He didn't know how long he would be away and told her that she was to buy herself a house and leave a contact number with the estate agent he had used to sell the villa. He felt wretched to leave her sobbing, scared stiff, but he reckoned that if they were on to him they'd have tapped his phone. They knew he was in Spain now, but where else could he get to without a fake passport? Wherever he went they'd track him down.

Using a false name he hired a private plane to take him to Palma, Majorca. It was the only place he could think to go without having to show his passport. Once there, he rented a run-down apartment overlooking a pottery factory. Not until he was installed in it did he relax. At least without Wilcox he felt less vulnerable. He would sit it out until the heat died down, and with over a hundred thousand in cash he would be safe for a while. He did some grocery shopping and hurried back to the apartment. Having spent many summers with his family in Spain he had a good grasp of the language, but he still sounded like an Englishman and, worse, he knew he would stick out like a sore thumb if he didn't change his appearance. Driscoll decided to stay put, grow a beard, get a good suntan and hide out. He knew he had to use his cash sparingly, but however he looked at it, life was going to be a far cry from what he was used to. There had been no big pay-day yet and there might never be one. The cops were on to him and, after reading all the English newspapers from cover to cover, he felt sick. Most were a day old but made no mention of the robbery, which scared him more than big headlines. It was always that way before the police swooped in.

Wilcox took from the villa anything he could sell: bed linen, cutlery and Driscoll's clothing. He loaded up the Jeep, knowing it would have to be the first thing he sold as it was licensed in Driscoll's name. His main problem was where he was going to hide out and he had to resolve it fast. Taking Driscoll's advice, he wondered about shacking up with one of the girls he'd met on his first night. Sharon was a waitress in a cocktail bar down on the harbour. If not her, there was Daniella, a masseuse who worked at the Marbella Country Club. She'd come on to him in a big way and he'd arranged a date for that night.

Wilcox drove to Sharon's villa in the hills but at the last minute he decided against it as she shared with two other girls and that meant more exposure. He turned round and headed for Daniella's. By that evening he had sold the Jeep to a rental company, signing it away as Anthony Driscoll, and bought an old Suzuki for cash. He drove to Daniella's small apartment on the outskirts of Nueva Andalucia. Even though Daniella was unsure how she felt about her new house guest, he was charming and persuasive, and she finally relented. She warned him, however, that if he messed around with her he would have her brothers to deal with. As it was, they wouldn't like her cohabiting with him.

Knowing he was on unsafe ground he gave her money towards the rent immediately to show that his intentions were honourable, and that night he was introduced to Daniella's family. He did not mention that he had six children and an irate mistress in England, but gave an elaborate story about falling in love and wanting to make a new life with Daniella, outlining his intentions to look for work the following day. One of Daniella's brothers offered him a job in his holiday apartment block as a general handyman, painting, decorating and cleaning up after the clients had gone home. It was a far cry from what he was used to but at least he felt safe, for now.

Neither Wilcox nor Driscoll had attempted to contact de Jersey, still obeying the rules from the old days. They had, however, kept a watchful eye on the newspapers, which were strangely silent, which made Wilcox nervous. He decided that he should not contact his ex-wife Françoise or Rika for some considerable time. At least the boys were with their mother, and he felt sure that Rika would not stay solo for long.

Christina was nervous but so hurt and betrayed that she felt her salvation lay in what she was about to do. Once confronted by Chief Superintendent Rodgers and three senior officers, however, she became flustered and tearful. She was offered tea or coffee but declined both and asked for water. She remained silent, head bowed, as Rodgers gently began the interview, trying to encourage her to talk, knowing intuitively that this was the breakthrough they'd all been hoping and praying for. She agreed to the interview being tape-recorded.

'Why have you come to see us today?' began Rodgers.

'I feel compelled to voice my suspicions of someone's involvement in the robbery of the Crown Jewels and the death of Sylvia Hewitt,' she replied, in a flat, unemotional voice.

Rodgers glanced at his officers. 'Who are you referring to, Mrs de Jersey? We have asked for the public's assistance in many areas.'

'Philip Simmons.' She did not look up.

'Do you know who he is?'

'Yes, I think so.' They waited as she coughed and sipped the water, her head still bowed. 'I think he's my husband.' She looked up and began to talk quickly, explaining how she thought she had recognized him from the television programme but that she had not wanted to believe it.

'I'm sorry to interrupt, Mrs de Jersey, but until you saw that programme did you have any reason to believe your husband was Philip Simmons?'

'No, not really. He had been worried about money and—'

'Once you'd recognized him from the depictions on the TV programme, what did you do?'

'I'm sorry?'

'Well, was he at home? Did you confront him?'

'Yes.'

'So you confronted your husband and accused him of being this man we are trying to contact, is that correct?'

'Yes.'

'You asked him if he was Philip Simmons?'

589

'Yes.'

'And what did he say?'

'He said he wasn't.'

'He denied it, then?'

'Yes, to begin with, until . . .'

The tension in the room was almost palpable, and Christina hesitated. 'Until . . . I found the diamond.'

Rodgers sat back in his chair with disbelief. 'Mrs de Jersey, are you saying you found the stolen jewels?'

Christina's hands were clenched. 'One of them. It was in the toe of one of his boots.' She described how she had found the stone and said she was now sure that it was the Koh-i-noor. She told of how she had confronted her husband, how he had said it was a fake and how she had then used the stone to cut the dressing-table mirror, proving that it was real.

'What did he do then?'

'I asked him point-blank if he was involved in the robbery.'

Rodgers and the other officers leaned forward. 'And what did he say?'

Christina paused. 'He said he was.'

The silence in the room was deafening. This was the confirmation they had all been waiting for. She continued, 'When he told me . . . I didn't know what to say. It was like I was in shock. He made me some tea and . . .' Tearfully she explained how he had laced it with sleeping tablets and how she'd awoken to discover he had left during the night in the helicopter. Then she broke down and Rodgers called for a break in the interview.

Once they resumed, she was questioned again about Sylvia Hewitt and was able to recall the night of the woman's death.

'Are you aware that Sylvia Hewitt died from a mix of morphine and ketamine?' Rodgers asked quietly.

'I didn't know how she died. I believed it was suicide. I told you this when you came to the house.'

'Ketamine is a strong horse tranquillizer, and vets also use it for putting smaller animals to sleep.'

'I didn't know that,' she said, with a dull-eyed stare.

'Would your husband have had access to this drug?'

'I suppose so . . . He did run a racing stable. You should ask Mr Fleming, perhaps. I don't know.'

'You say he fed you sleeping tablets the night before he left?'

She looked up, shocked at what he was suggesting.

'Did you suspect that he may have been trying to silence you? You have told us he left the same night.'

'Yes, that is correct, but there were pills left in the bottle and if he had wanted to kill me he would have used them all.' Her voice rose.

'So, you do not think your husband meant to harm you?'

'No!'

Rodgers remained silent, then leaned close to her. 'When we came to the house you said nothing of this to me, Mrs de Jersey. Not a word about finding the diamond, not a word about confronting your husband, not a word about his admission of guilt. And that makes me suspicious.'

For the next hour, Christina was put under considerable pressure and forced to repeat many times the moment she confronted her husband. When she was accused of aiding his escape she became angry and stood up. 'I didn't know! I didn't know! *I didn't know!*' she yelled, and broke down sobbing. 'I didn't think he would leave me,' she cried, and it was Trudy Grainger who took Rodgers aside and said that Christina should be allowed to rest.

Chief Superintendent Rodgers was fully aware that the distraught woman was in shock, but he felt only excitement at the advances they'd made. The old adage that 'hell hath no fury like a woman scorned' was bearing fruit, and their biggest break to date. As Rodgers continued to scrutinize Christina's information, he made memos and notes for further questions.

They broke for lunch and the team assessed the information. They were worried that they might have lost the big fish as they had received no word from Interpol. As for the other stolen gems, Christina had no clue where they could be. Unknown to her, a search warrant had been issued and a full-scale search of the estate was under way. To the consternation of the new owner, an army of police officers had arrived to search the house and stables. The same scrutiny was now directed also at Tony Driscoll's property and James Wilcox's house.

That evening, the police gave a statement to the press and said they were now able to name Britain's most wanted man as Edward de Jersey, also known as Philip Simmons. Warrants had also been issued for the arrest of James Wilcox and Anthony Driscoll. The police said that both men were possibly residing in Spain.

On the following day, accompanied now by her solicitor, Christina began another lengthy session with the police. They asked detailed questions about her husband's trips abroad. When they learned of the trip to Monaco they looked again at the inquiry into the *Hortensia Princess* owned by Paul Dulay, who had been under surveillance for weeks. Until now they had had only his confirmation that he owned the *Hortensia Princess* and his explanation of the 'drop' witnessed by the boys.

Paul Dulay was arrested by the French police. At first he was adamant that he had had an innocent reason for being anchored off Brighton. However, they were now armed with the fact that de Jersey had been at the Brighton racecourse on the afternoon of the heist and that he had arrived there shortly after the time when the eyewitnesses said they had seen the drop. Under pressure, Dulay refused to answer any further questions without a solicitor being present.

Paul Dulay's shop and home were searched again and eventually, under further questioning, he began to break. His lawyers agreed to a deal if he gave information and he admitted his part in the robbery. He took the police to the small cove and pointed out the bobbing lobster pot. It was a matter of minutes before they would gain access to the crate attached to the buoys. The cove was jammed with sightseers and reporters as the launches set out to make the collection.

The crate was returned to the shore and taken to the local police station where it was opened. In it they discovered the stolen jewels, except for the fabulous Koh-i-noor diamond.

Dulay was questioned round the clock and at last gave details about the sale of the diamond, and the Japanese buyer was traced. At first he refused to be interviewed but then, on condition that there would be no repercussions, he admitted to having given a large down-payment to Dulay for the diamond, but had not as yet received the stone. Dulay was questioned again, with the British police present, and admitted to paying Edward de Jersey half a million dollars in Paris; the rest he had kept for himself.

Now the police feared that the stone had already been broken up. They persisted in their interrogation, until Dulay cracked. The police could hardly believe it. The stone was hidden among pebbles by a waterfall in his garden.

When British officers reached the waterfall they found a mermaid spouting a trickle of water from her outstretched hand. Beneath her tail fin, covered with water, lay the rockery stones. There, gleaming among them was the Koh-i-noor. As the water bounced off it, refracted rainbows danced in the sunlight.

In England, the excitement of the jewels' return was dying down, but reporters had given heroic stature to the men they believed were behind the theft. Edward de Jersey's name was on most people's lips. The police were sent on one wild-goose chase after another. Two weeks later there were still no arrests, except for that of Paul Dulay. He had spilled his guts, but it became clear that he had known only so much. He had never met Driscoll or Wilcox or any of the others involved in the heist, he maintained, but when he was shown the photograph of Edward de Jersey, he identified him as Philip Simmons. He remained incarcerated in a French prison until he could be brought to England to stand trial.

After naming de Jersey as the main operator, Dulay was returned to his cell. He had not disclosed that he had met Anthony Driscoll many years before. The police still had no notion that Dulay, along with de Jersey and his team, had been behind the bullion robbery. He asked for notepaper and a pen to write to his wife. Then he tore up his shirt and hanged himself in his cell. The note he left for Ulrika and the children asked them to forgive him. It was a severe blow to the police as they had been dependent on him as a prosecution witness.

Chief Superintendent Rodgers insisted that he would not give up searching for the robbery suspects. He stated that he would arrest the culprits within the next few months. However, it was clear that de Jersey's trail had gone cold. This was a big problem. He was carrying a large amount of cash, not only from Dulay but from the sale of his estate. A man on the run with nothing was easy to pick up. A man with a fortune was more difficult. He had more than enough money to buy a new identity, a new face if he so desired. Even with the efforts of the FBI and Interpol, they had no leads. He, like Wilcox and Driscoll, had disappeared.

The now depleted team of detectives decided to focus their search in Spain and hopefully pick up Wilcox and Driscoll. Armed now with photographs of their suspects, plus a substantial reward for information, they headed off.

After days of interrogation Christina collapsed from the strain. She spent two days in a private clinic and her father came to England to care for his granddaughters. At last she was given permission to return to Sweden with the girls. The Swedish authorities agreed to put surveillance on them all in case de Jersey made contact.

Christina had been in Sweden almost a week before she went to the bank. She had her own account there, with money left to her by her mother and some small items of jewellery in a deposit box. She wished to sell the jewellery as she had decided to remain in Sweden. Christina spoke briefly to the manager, who took her to the vault. She unlocked the box in private. In it she found a letter addressed to her. She knew instantly from the writing on the envelope that it was from her husband. With shaking fingers she ripped it open and read the single sheet.

My Beloved,

By the time you read this I will either be a man you despise intensely or you may have found it in your heart to forgive me. I had no option but to sell fast and make no indication to you of my intentions. I did not ever want to implicate or harm you and our children in any way. I love you as much now as I did when we were first married and I love my daughters wholeheartedly too. I also respect you, and know you will bring them up to be as beautiful and admirable as yourself.

I know you would never betray me but to safeguard your life and ensure your future happiness, the best possible scenario is for me to disappear. I have made provision for you all. The keys enclosed belong to a lovely house I chose with you all in mind, as I knew you would return to Sweden. I will love you until the day I die and I thank you for the most beautiful and perfect twenty years. God bless you.

She held the letter loosely in her hand, reading and rereading it as the tears welled in her eyes and dropped on to the page, blurring his writing. The keys were attached to a small card with an address on it, and beneath that was a thick envelope with bank cards and accounts in the name of Christina Olefson, her maiden name. They contained one and a half million pounds. The house was valued at three-quarters of a million.

Later that day, Christina sat on the stripped-pine floors of her new home, staring out at the gardens. He had thought of everything, as he always had throughout their marriage. He had loved her and she had not trusted him. He must have known she would not, and guilt now replaced the pain she had carried with her for weeks. But there were no more tears: she had wept too many. She got up and pressed her face against the cold windowpane. She drew a heart in the condensation on the glass, wrote her name and his, then slashed an arrow through it. She walked out of the room as the heart dripped tears. She knew now that their life together was truly over. She had loved him so much, perhaps too much, and it had made her blind. Christina would not have cared if they had been penniless but he would have, and that was why he had jeopardized the happiness of his family.

Christina intended to keep secret the money she had received. She did not ask the bank manager when or how her husband had accessed the deposit box. She preferred not to know. She asked her father to move in with her and the girls: then it might be thought that her father had bought the house or at least part of it. The police, she knew, were still monitoring her, perhaps hoping de Jersey would make contact. Having found the house keys and the money in the deposit box, she knew he would not.

She enrolled her daughters in the American school in Stockholm and began furnishing and decorating her new house.

May had been one of the coldest on record, but Royal Flush was in peak condition, ready for the Derby on 8th June. The massive stallion had calmed down, and lost his frantic, often dangerous edge. He had been groomed until his coat looked like black patent leather. He left the other top-class horses a good furlong behind in training and as the build-up to the flat-racing season started, Mickey Rowland became confident that, although the owner had changed, he would still have the ride of his life. It had been written into the deal de Jersey had struck, and for that Rowland could forgive his boss's sudden departure and the salary he was still owed.

Royal Flush's new owner kept his prowess under wraps. No spectators were allowed to watch his training sessions. Having won his two trial races with ease, he was the hot favourite for the Derby, even more so because he had been Edward de Jersey's horse. The most wanted man in Britain was about to see taken from him the prize he had coveted.

To Chief Superintendent Rodgers, the lack of sightings and of public information regarding Driscoll and Wilcox, even with a large reward, was unfathomable. Clues to the whereabouts of Pamela, like so much else, had also borne no fruit until they received a call from Plymouth police. A woman had been badly burned in a fire at her flat in a run-down area known as the Fort. She had apparently fallen asleep while smoking and drinking. The neighbours had seen smoke coming from beneath her door and had tried to break in. Unable to do so, they had called the fire brigade. Pamela Kenworthy-Wright was found in a sorry state on her bed, badly burned and suffering from smoke inhalation. When the paramedics had tried to take her to hospital she became hysterical, but by then she was sinking into a coma. Beneath her bed, the police discovered a large tin box containing three thousand pounds in cash and a variety of articles that warranted suspicion. There was a shirt with Lord Westbrook's monogram and a gold signet ring with his family crest on it.

Chief Superintendent Rodgers and two officers caught the train to Plymouth and a squad car picked them up at the station. Within fifteen minutes of their arrival at the hospital Pamela died. It was a bitter blow that they had been unable to interview her, as they strongly believed she had played a part in the robbery. This was later confirmed by Maureen who identified her as the lady-in-waiting.

They spent a considerable amount of time sifting through all of Pamela's belongings but came up with no further clues. She had been as diligent as de Jersey had instructed her to be, except for Westbrook's ring, which he had left her along with the cash.

Alone, and with little contact from anyone, Pamela had taken to drinking heavily as she read the exploits of the police in their hunt for the raiders. But even that began to mean little to her as she drank more and ate less. Poor Pamela. She had died a horrible death but she made front-page headlines and they showed a photograph of her taken years ago in a touring production of *The School for Scandal*. In the photographs taken from her old scrapbook she looked beautiful, so at least she was saved the disgrace of anyone seeing her raddled, drink-blotched face and carrot red hair. She died as Lady Teazle and even long-lost friends who had known her as an actress came forward to give eulogies about her talent and her wonderful nature and humour. She would at least have liked that part.

In Spain, Wilcox was tanned and had grown his hair and beard. He was still working for Daniella's brothers, painting and decorating their apartments. One positive outcome of his new modest lifestyle, he was getting his cocaine addiction under control. One lunch-break, Daniella's brother held up a Spanish newspaper. 'There's a horse here that was owned by the guy they say did the Crown Jewels robbery,' he said, stabbing at the paper. 'It's called Royal Flush.' He showed the photograph to Wilcox.

Later, when the young man had gone, Wilcox picked up the paper and read the story about Royal Flush. He turned the page to see another picture of Edward de Jersey, still at large, and yet another lengthy article about the jewel heist. He stared at de Jersey's impassive face. It would be just like him, Wilcox thought, to turn up at

600

the Derby, bold as brass, and watch his horse run. He wondered whether the police had thought the same thing. He could not resist touching de Jersey's face and sending up a silent prayer that he did not.

Driscoll was flicking through the UK satellite channels. Eventually he settled on one where they were discussing the forthcoming Derby. At first he paid little attention as he had never been a gambling man. When he had worked in Ronnie Jersey's betting shops, the old boy had warned him to keep his money in his pocket and let the punters lose theirs. Driscoll had religiously followed his advice. Then the programme focused on a horse called Royal Flush, once owned by Edward de Jersey, and he gave the TV his full attention. Driscoll had not allowed himself to think about de Jersey, but hearing his name brought it all back. Holed up in Spain, he rarely left his apartment for fear of being recognized and had grown a full beard to hide as much of his face as possible. He had lost a considerable amount of weight, partly due to living on his nerves and partly due to the fresh salads and vegetables he bought at the market. The stomach pains and indigestion he'd lived with for years had abated and he was much fitter due to the nightly jogs he took to pick up the newspapers left on the beaches by the tourists. Over the past couple of days he had been in a panic: his own face was plastered over the papers along with Wilcox's. He sent up a silent prayer that for his sake, for Jimmy's, for the old Three Musketeers, de Jersey would stay hidden.

By late May, Christina knew that the hype for the Derby would soon pick up momentum, and this Derby would have special implications for her. She would not place a bet – she never had – but for de Jersey's sake, she hoped Royal Flush would win. Like Wilcox, she wondered if he would risk watching his horse race. She prayed he would not, but knew how hard it would be for him to resist. This was the race her husband had adored, the race he had wanted so badly to win, with its connection to his long-dead father, though exactly what the connection was she did not know. All she hoped was that he would not surface.

CHAPTER 28

THE POLICE were still maintaining a large team on the hunt for de Jersey, and were armed with recent photographs now of Wilcox and Driscoll. Liz Driscoll had no idea where her husband had been on the day of the robbery, and Rika said she was certain Wilcox had been at home because it had been his sons' birthday party. Up to this point no physical evidence had connected either of the pair to the heist and they had set themselves up for suspicion with their absence. The hunt for them was stepped up.

After nearly a month of wild-goose chases around Spain the police came up with nothing. Chief Superintendent Rodgers was now looking into leadingleisurewear and the disappearance of Alex Moreno, in case this yielded clues as to the whereabouts of de Jersey. But Alex Moreno had disappeared off the face of the earth. He was feeling depressed when he called a meeting to update his top officers. He knew he had to remind the public that de Jersey was still at large – he needed their help – but even the press were no longer eager for bulletins.

He sat in his small cordoned-off booth, knowing he

had to go and confront his equally demoralized team. They were all aware of the pressure he was under and for the life of him he could not think what his next move should be. At his last weekly session with the big chiefs they had hinted that perhaps it was time to bring in a fresh team to review the situation.

He stood up, pushed back his chair and went to the meeting room where the twenty male and two female officers on the inquiry sat waiting for him. He entered, with a scowl on his face, and stood in front of the rows of photographs assembled on one wall. 'Well, I'm going to have the rug pulled out from under my feet if we don't make some bloody arrests,' he snapped. 'They're still at large, and anyone with any bright ideas, now's the time to spill them out.'

A female detective, Sara Redmond, a small pretty blonde woman, raised her hand. 'It strikes me, Gov, that the one lead we do have is this name, Philip Simmons. Why did he use that name? Maybe there's some historical reason, some link to his past. Or perhaps he's used it before in other crimes. It's worth a—'

The phone rang. Rodgers picked it up and listened, his face changing from drawn grey to deep red. As he hung up he hit the table with the flat of his hand. 'We've got a guy held in Newcastle, brought in after a burglary went belly up. He's asking for a deal.' They looked on in anticipation. 'He's admitted to being in the heist.'

The room erupted with a cheer and they scrambled to their feet. Sara's comment was forgotten.

In exchange for a reduced sentence, Kenneth Short had given a statement in which he admitted to being one of the bikers on the raid. At first he had denied knowing his partner, but eventually he gave the second name and

604

the police picked up Brian Hall from the farm in Dorset where he had been hiding out. Short had been paid in cash by a man he knew only as Philip Simmons, twenty thousand up front with a second twenty thousand coming after the stones had been sold. After reading in the press that the jewels had been recovered, he knew he would never see the second payment, but he had got himself into debt on the strength of it. He had arranged to burgle a factory office, but he had been caught by a security guard with a dog.

Hall and Short described how they had used the boats as getaway vehicles then set fire to the boat-house. Both motorbikes were recovered from exactly where the men had left them. They also took the police to the barn, which still housed the second Daimler. In addition to providing the team with fresh evidence, the two men's arrest stimulated positive press coverage. The robbery was back on the front pages and the police hoped for further developments.

Neither of the men arrested could give details of the set-up for the robbery, but told the police that they had been brought in by Tony Driscoll. Hall had worked for Driscoll years back but had met him again when he was hired to work at his daughter's wedding. Both men identified Wilcox as the driver in the raid. Now the hunt for Driscoll and Wilcox intensified and their faces were plastered across the papers and television news in the hope that someone would come forward with information on their whereabouts.

The new spate of publicity threatened both Wilcox and Driscoll's safety. Both men were forced to sweat it out, hoping that they could remain at large. The day-to-day fear of being exposed was hard to live with and Spain was crowded with British holidaymakers. Photographs of James Wilcox and Anthony Driscoll were placed in every Spanish police station, in bus shelters and airports, with 'REWARD' in red letters printed above their faces. Anyone might recognize them at any time.

The next lucky break came from a prisoner who also wanted to make a deal. He said he had information connected to the Crown Jewels robbery. He had heard a rumour that a guy in Franklyn had had something to do with it, a Gregory Jones.

Jones was unforthcoming. He was in for life and he knew he would not get a more lenient sentence, even if he co-operated. He only agreed to talk when they promised to put in a good word for his transfer to an open prison. From Jones the team learned how he had told Edward de Jersey, posing as a solicitor named Philip Simmons, about the Royal household's security procedures. Jones did not indicate that he had been paid.

Reviewing the outcome of the past two days' work, Rodgers was back on form, his energy renewed. The recent arrests and charges meant there was no possibility of a new team taking over the case. His officers were more confident now. They felt they knew both Wilcox and Driscoll, having spent hours interviewing Liz Driscoll, and Wilcox's live-in girlfriend and his ex-wife. DC Trudy Grainger and DC Sara Redmond, the two women attached to the team, had both been very visible when they and Christina de Jersey had been interviewed.

'Well, we may be getting to know Driscoll and Wilcox, but Edward de Jersey remains an enigma,' Trudy said, as she checked over the recent statements.

'What do you mean?' Sara asked.

'Well, he doesn't fit into the same pattern as either Wilcox or Driscoll. He's a different kind of man and you can almost understand why the press make such a meal of him, of all three of them. I mean, they didn't use any violence during the robbery. Nobody got hurt.'

'You want to bet?' Sara said.

Trudy continued, 'They didn't use violence. It's a fact. All right, they put the fear of God into the security guard at D'Ancona, ditto the staff, but in the long run it's benefited that Queen lookalike. She's getting a lot of mileage out of the kidnapping. She's in the *News of the World* every week. Last Sunday they gave her a full-page spread in the magazine section on how to wear twin-sets or some such crap. Like I said, nobody got hurt and they got the jewels back so that's why the public doesn't give a toss.'

'I don't agree about nobody getting hurt. Ask the wives how they feel – in particular Christina de Jersey! They were lying bastards all of them, especially Edward de Jersey. He didn't give a damn for his wife or his two kids. How do you think they're coping?'

'Probably loving it,' snapped Trudy, irritated because she knew Sara was right.

'Loving it?' Sara asked. 'No way. He walked out on them, ditched them, and got away with millions. He's not a hero to me. He's a lying, two-faced son-of-a-bitch and I hope we catch the bastard.'

607

'Okay, you made your point. But for all his faults we can't seem to get a single person to say anything bad about him.'

Sara leaned against Trudy's desk. 'No, that's not quite right. It's not that no one will say anything bad about him, it's that they don't want to say anything at all. Maybe because they're afraid. But someone's got to know him, got to be able to lead us to him.'

Trudy smiled. 'Well, maybe you'll find them now. I've got to take these into the gov, so excuse me.'

Sara returned to her desk and sat doodling on a notepad. All the men arrested had spoken freely about Driscoll and Wilcox, but seemed reluctant or unable to divulge much about Edward de Jersey. They said he spoke little, was always polite, yet acted like an army general. They had never seen him angry: he had always been pleasant, well dressed and courteous. Brian Hall had described Wilcox as moody and volatile, Driscoll had stomach problems, and the pair hung out together, rarely talking to anyone but de Jersey; both men always referred to him as the Colonel. Sara drew a pin man with a big head and a curling moustache, and printed under it THE COLONEL. Then she tore it into fragments and concentrated on looking over all the statements from Brian Hall.

Sara was not the only person who had picked up on Brian Hall's reference to Edward de Jersey's nickname. When he was receiving all of the other information, Rodgers had not paid it much attention. Now it intrigued him and he stepped out of his cubicle. 'Sara, can you print up Brian Hall's statements for me?'

'Sure, just going over them myself, gov.'

Rodgers sat down again in his swivel chair, his desk empty but for a telephone and a notepad. He detested clutter as much as he loathed computers. He was hemmed in by boxes and filing cabinets. It was as if the hunt for the jewel thieves had been going on for years instead of weeks.

Sara placed the statements on his desk and watched as he thumbed through them, scanning the pages. 'You looking for something specific?' she asked.

'Yep. It was something Hall said. It's lodged in my brain. Did he say that Driscoll and Wilcox called de Jersey by a nickname, something like the Colonel?'

'Yes, gov. It's on page four about five lines in.'

Rodgers looked up, surprised. 'Thanks. That's all for now.'

She walked out and he frowned, rereading the sentence in Hall's interview as a bell rang in his mind. He closed his eyes and thought back to his days as a rookie officer, days when stories abounded about a mythical, untouchable robber known only as the Colonel. Could de Jersey have been that mastermind? He was the right age. Suddenly Sara Redmond's suggestion that perhaps de Jersey used the name Philip Simmons for a historical reason came flooding back to him. Could it be that if he looked again at the robberies attributed to the Colonel – the Gold Bullion Raid and the Great Train Robbery – the name Philip Simmons would crop up there too?

Rodgers walked into the main incident room.

'I need a car. I want to go to Edward de Jersey's place. Is Trudy around?'

609

'No, sir. She's just left to check out Gregory Jones's bank statements. She's going to interview his mother and—'

'Never mind. You come with me. Right now.'

Rodgers headed out to the estate again. This time he wanted to talk at greater length with those who worked there, those who had been previously in day-to-day contact with de Jersey. Up until now Rodgers had concentrated his efforts on the physical evidence and myriad leads, but now he knew that if he was going to catch de Jersey, he would have to understand the man. Until now, the overall impression he had gained from de Jersey's former employees was that he had been conscientious, expected hard work, loyalty and results but had rewarded them accordingly. But one thing everyone mentioned fascinated Rodgers: de Jersey was obsessed with Royal Flush. He had treated him like a son, they said, had given him more attention than his own daughters.

At the de Jersey estate, he was surprised to see so few people around. There were also heavy cement trucks and building equipment: the new owner had begun renovations. Rodgers went from one empty stall to another and Sara trailed after him. It was obvious that the staff, or most of them, had left. Rodgers felt frustrated, then came across Fleming talking to the vet as the empty stalls were being hosed down. The vet was there to discuss what recourse Fleming thought he might have about his unpaid bills. They watched as Rodgers walked towards them across the yard.

'Afternoon,' Rodgers said. 'Could I just ask you a few questions?'

They returned to sit in Fleming's old office, stripped now although the photograph of de Jersey with the Queen still remained on the desk. The vet told Rodgers that de Jersey had been beside himself when Royal Flush was injured and ill. He said that de Jersey himself had tended the horse's injured leg. Fleming told Rodgers that de Jersey seemed able to communicate with the horse better than anyone else. He recalled de Jersey's outright refusal when it had been suggested they geld him due to the vicious temperament that might destroy the horse's concentration on the racetrack. Instead de Jersey had moved the horse into a stable section with no others. He had then personally overseen his training for six months and gradually, to everyone's surprise, the big stallion had calmed, winning his first races as a three-year-old, proving that de Jersey had been correct. Fleming decided not to mention the 'arrangement' he had had with de Jersey or his payment of ten thousand pounds. He was too ashamed of it and knew it would not help the inquiry. As much as de Jersey loved the horse, he had risked his performance in the Derby. What he had not been able to understand until now was why: his boss must have arranged already to sell the estate and Royal Flush with it. Fleming now understood why de Jersey had used the stallion illegally to cover his champion dam. He had known that he might lose him and wanted the chance one day to own another racehorse as great as Royal Flush. So Fleming made no mention of the sale of Bandit Queen to Michael Shaughnessy in Ireland.

The vet left, and Rodgers with Sara, who had not said a word, remained in the office. Fleming was uneasy.

'Nobody wants this, then,' Rodgers said, picking up

the silver framed photograph of de Jersey with the Queen.

'I do,' Fleming said softly. He gave a glum smile. 'The Derby was the race he always wanted to win,' he told Rodgers. 'He had entered many of his horses over the years. It was something to do with his father.'

'What about his father?' Rodgers asked. 'Did Edward de Jersey inherit this from him?'

Fleming looked surprised. 'No. His father was an East End bookie.'

Rodgers was stunned. 'A *bookie*?'

'Yes. I think his first name was Ronald, not that he ever said much to me about him. The Boss wasn't the kind of man you had lengthy personal conversations with. He went to Sandhurst, but I only knew him as a racehorse owner. He hired me over twenty years ago.'

'Did you like him?' Rodgers asked. He waited as Fleming hesitated, then repeated the question.

'Did I like him?'

'As a man,' Rodgers persisted.

'I don't know how to answer that. It's hard to, after what's happened. They were a special couple, though. Ask my wife.'

'I'm asking you.' Rodgers stared hard at Fleming.

'Well, I just answered your question, didn't I? You don't work for a man for twenty years and feel nothing for him. I respected him and . . .'

'And?' persisted Rodgers.

'If he did what he's accused of, then I must never have really known him because he was always on the level with me, until right at the end. But I put that down to him having money troubles. Listen, I've got nothing more to add and I'd like to get on with things, if you don't mind. Still got some loose ends to tie up for the new owner.'

'Well, thank you. I appreciate you talking to me. I need to get to know the man I'm trying to track down.'

'I gathered that, but I don't wish you all that much luck. I hope he stays free.'

Rodgers stood up, looking angry, and nodded to Sara, who had still not said a word. 'Well *I* hope he doesn't. When it boils down to it he's a thief. A cheap con-man. And he's not going to get away with it.' He walked out. Sara gave a nod to Fleming and followed Rodgers.

Alone now, Fleming picked up the silver-framed photograph, the one his old boss had been so proud of. He did have more to say about de Jersey, but he couldn't because it would implicate himself. Right now he and his wife were looking for a new place to live. He had discussed working for the Sheikh and had been offered a job in their offices. It was a come-down, but it would pay the rent and also provided accommodation. His retirement would be a considerable time off, and now he had no bonus or pension. When de Jersey had hit his financial troubles he had stopped paying the pension scheme for his staff. Suddenly Fleming felt anger well up inside him and all the feelings of betrayal surfaced as he stared at the photograph. He wondered where de Jersey was hiding out and suddenly felt a rush of intense fury that he had put so much trust in his old boss. He smashed the photograph against the desk.

After his last meeting with Dulay, de Jersey headed back to Ireland as Michael Shaughnessy. He owned a small-holding in that name, which was managed by a local

Irish horse breeder. De Jersey had visited whenever he was in Ireland, but always in disguise. It had been his little project, a secret. Bandit Queen, now in foal, was there.

The mare had cost £125,000 and had originally been purchased from Tattersalls in 1999. She had raced only three times in the de Jersey colours. While the hysterical manhunt for Edward de Jersey continued, he was calmly arranging to send Bandit Queen to America. First he chartered a flight and paid shipping-agency and export-testing fees. He arranged the Wetherby papers, listing Royal Flush's brother, a stallion called Royal Livery, as the sire. He did everything he could to conceal that Royal Flush had been put to stud illegally. Bandit Queen was transported in a horsebox to the airport. She would be held in quarantine in America, for which he had also paid, and then taken to East Hampton. De Jersey hired a boy to travel with the horse for the duration of the trip and paid him well to make sure he took the greatest care of his precious cargo. De Jersey, as Michael Shaughnessy, then flew from Ireland to Virginia. From there he took an internal flight to New York.

After arriving at JFK, de Jersey travelled on, still as Shaughnessy, to East Hampton on the Jitney bus. He had only one suitcase and stayed at the Huntting Inn. He checked that Bandit Queen had travelled well and was undergoing tests at Cornell. He was certain they would find no discrepancies with her papers or blood tests. As with everything, he had covered his tracks well. He rented a cottage near Gardiner's Bay in Springs, East Hampton. He rarely left the property but ordered anything he needed over the Internet as he planned how to regain ownership of Moreno's property. He was careful, knowing that by now the UK police might have traced his connection to it, but he was not prepared to walk away from millions of dollars.

The hands at the quarantine stables led Bandit Queen down from the trailer, impressed by her size and obvious quality. She had a smallish head, almost Arab, with a powerful neck and a sturdy, strong, muscular body. The foal she was carrying was not showing to a great extent. She was checked by a vet, who found that the long journey had not upset her, and she ate her first feed hungrily. Her coat gleamed brilliantly in the late-afternoon sun. As she settled in, the staff were in constant contact with her owner: Michael Shaughnessy called every day. He said he was hoping to leave Ireland shortly and gave no indication that he was already living in East Hampton.

By the end of May, de Jersey, now comfortable with his new name, contacted the firm of solicitors to whom he had sent the crate of paintings, saying he would collect it personally. He drove there in a rented Jeep, walked into their offices, handed over his documents and paid for the delivery. Then he drove to a warehouse they used for storage of their clients' possessions. This was not an unusual transaction as the nomadic nature of many homeowners in the Hamptons meant that solicitors acted as 'house carers', paying bills and monitoring properties during the winter months when they were vacant. De Jersey put the crate into the Jeep, and returned to his house. He took out twenty thousand dollars then hid the rest in waterproof plastic bags beneath the floorboards.

The pressure of the last month had taken its toll on

him. He had aged considerably and lost a substantial amount of weight. Like Driscoll and Wilcox, he now had a full beard. He hardly went out unless to buy groceries. He bought from the local farmers' markets and ate good fresh food to build up his depleted strength, and every day he called to check on his unborn foal. At the quarantine stables they became used to the soft-toned voice of the man they had never met.

'Hello, this is Michael Shaughnessy. How's my lady?' he'd ask.

De Jersey waited for the birth like an expectant father and looked around for a property where he could eventually keep the mare and foal. Beneath the floorboards he had more than enough to keep him for many years, and when he eventually discovered a way to get his hands on the Moreno property, he would retire in luxury. His long-term plan was to live in Virginia and open a racing stables there. Until then, he was content to bide his time. The locals were aware that there was a new resident along the bay but they made no approach. That was part of the joy of the Hamptons, the privacy: you could be social if you liked, or remain incognito. It was an artists' colony, too, and the gaunt man with the long coat and beard fitted in. The beaches were always empty and he took early-morning walks to watch the sun rise. He clambered over the rocks and sat contemplating his life, his future, and thinking of Christina, of his daughters, and wishing that it had turned out differently. This, however, was the only way he could stay free, if lonely too.

De Jersey had plenty of time to think about Driscoll and Wilcox, but there was no remorse. In fact, he had none for anything he had done, except perhaps Sylvia

Hewitt, but that had been necessary. Believing that helped him come to terms with her death. He had no intention of returning to England, or watching the Derby, whatever anyone hunting for him might think. He had no need to go home. Bandit Queen was expecting his champion's foal. He was certain he had got away with it and that one day he would win the Derby with Royal Flush's foal.

His conversation with Fleming and the vet was further confirmation to Chief Superintendent Rodgers that he was dealing with a complex man in Edward de Jersey. His father had been a bookie, yet de Jersey was able to mix with royalty at one moment then steal the Crown Jewels at the next. As the squad car drove away from the estate he looked at Sara. 'What do you think?'

She gave a rueful smile. 'I don't think anyone really knew him.'

'Well, I'm damn well going to because I'm gonna catch the bugger if it's the last thing I do. Then I'm gonna retire.'

Rodgers decided he had to go back into the past to find out what made de Jersey tick so he spent time sifting through the records with Sara's help. De Jersey had no previous criminal record, but Rodgers found old news coverage and articles on his father's betting shops and the resulting feuds between rival East End gangs. There was little information about either father or son, but there had been a memorial service for the well-liked bookie. He had asked for his ashes to be spread over the

Epsom racecourse on Derby Day but permission had been denied.

Rodgers, again with Sara's assistance, now checked out births, marriages and deaths, and discovered de Jersey's birth certificate. He was older than Rodgers had believed, which fuelled him to unearth even more about the man. He checked medical and school records. He checked Fleming's comment that de Jersey had been at Sandhurst, and found out that he had been discharged due to a complex knee injury that had required delicate surgery. It was Sara who discovered that James Wilcox had been at Sandhurst at the same time as de Jersey and, like him, had been forced to leave, although for different reasons.

At night in the privacy of his home, Rodgers pieced together the paper trail that led to de Jersey's background and it fascinated him. Sara helped to uncover further details of his past on the computer and Rodgers studied his career in the estate business. Sara acquired tax records, which showed his growing affluence, but nothing told them how he had acquired wealth enough to buy the luxurious estate. Now Rodgers concentrated on finding a past link between de Jersey and Driscoll. After hours of diligent checking and cross-referencing, Rodgers was certain he was on to something. Although he hadn't determined when Driscoll and de Jersey had met, both Driscoll and Wilcox's affluence coincided with de Jersey's, all shortly after the gold-bullion robbery. Before he discussed his findings with his team, Rodgers instructed Sara to try to find more details about de Jersey, when he had acquired the 'de' in his name. She produced details of his first wife Gail, whom he had married when he was still called Eddie Jersey. She had remarried twice.

She was now divorced and living in a mews house in Chelsea. Sara gave Rodgers her phone number.

The ex-Mrs Jersey did not at first agree to be interviewed but eventually acquiesced, albeit in a disgruntled way. Rodgers hung up and looked at Sara. He would take her with him. After all, it was she who had put the idea of tracing de Jersey's history of crime into his head. 'You busy, Sara?' he asked.

'I was just about to type up the interview statement from the farmer who leased de Jersey the barn,' Sara said. 'The forensic team is still at work, though it's looking like their efforts aren't producing much.'

'Trudy, can you take that over? Sara, I want you with me.'

Trudy pulled a face. 'I can,' she told Rodgers, 'but I've got information that Philip Simmons, a.k.a. Edward de Jersey, paid money into Gregory Jones's mother's account. Fifty grand!'

'Good work, and if that lying bastard thinks he's going to a cushy open prison he's got another think coming.' He turned to Sara. 'I need you for maybe a couple of hours, okay?' he said, and she closed down her computer. 'Order a car for us, will you?'

Sara hurried out after Rodgers, who was pressing the lift button. 'I need you to come and interview de Jersey's first wife with me. She's agreed to see us.'

'Why? You think she knows where he is?'

'I just want a clearer picture of the man.'

The small but expensive house was in Glebe Place and Gail Raynor herself opened the front door. She was rather brittle and unforthcoming as she led them into a pleasant sitting room. She did not wait to be asked but went into a terse speech, saying that she realized they had come about her ex-husband, but that she had not seen or had any contact with him for over twenty-five years. She had read the news coverage regarding his connection to the robbery, so she had thought they might want to speak to her, but she was not harbouring him, she assured them. 'And if he did make contact, I would waste no time in calling the police. It was a despicable crime and I'm glad it failed. The stolen gems are now back, I hope, in safer hands than they were before.'

At one time she had obviously been beautiful, but she had not aged well. She had tinted blonde hair, arched eyebrows and vivid blue eyes. She seemed to prefer to talk about herself rather than her connection with de Jersey. She had married young and had soon realized that he wanted her more for her contacts than for love. Her father had owned estate agencies around Chelsea and Fulham and de Jersey had taken over the running of them. Following the death of her father, he had control of the business. She was still disgruntled after all these years, despite the generous divorce settlement she had received.

'Did he buy the estate then?' Rodgers asked.

Gail shrugged.

'It was worth forty million,' he said softly, and her jaw dropped.

'The lying son-of-a-bitch. Forty million! Jesus Christ.' She ran her fingers through her hair.

'Can you tell me anything about his background, his family?' asked Rodgers.

'His father was a bookie. He apparently made a killing

on Derby Day, which enabled him to open his first betting shop, but apart from that I know nothing. In fact, oddly enough, Eddy didn't have many friends. Forty million! I know the estate must have increased in value since he bought it, but it's just unbelievable. He told me he only earned fifty thousand a year from Daddy's business.'

Rodgers's theory that de Jersey had acquired the estate using illegally procured funds seemed to hold water and a knot of excitement formed in his belly. 'So where do you think he got the finance to purchase it?' he asked, tentatively.

'I have no idea. He sold all Daddy's agencies, so probably from them. I really don't know. He always had money, though, very good at investments. He remarried some model young enough to be his daughter.'

'Did you ever hear anyone refer to him as the Colonel?' he asked.

'The Colonel?' Gail repeated. 'He went to Sandhurst for a while but got kicked out. Injured his knee or something. He was always complaining about it, but that was his only Army experience. He was never a colonel. Though, knowing him, I wouldn't put it past him to say he was. He may have played one once, I don't really know.'

'Played one?' Rodgers asked.

'His mother was in some amateur dramatic society and he used to be in their productions when he was a kid. I don't know much about it, but he had some photographs of himself in costumes and wigs. He didn't do it when he was married to me. Too keen to get on Daddy's good side.' She stood up and looked towards a small antique desk. 'I've got a photograph, I think. I'm sure I have.'

She opened a drawer and began removing letters, books and old diaries, searching for a photograph album. 'I'm sure I had it somewhere.' She looked around the room, then crossed to a bookcase.

'Did you ever meet James Wilcox?'

'James?' Gail asked. 'Yes, I knew him from the days we used to hang out in the clubs. He introduced me to Eddy.'

'Tony Driscoll?'

'I read about him in the papers but I never met him.' She continued searching along the shelves, then pointed to a row of books. 'There it is.'

Sara, who was taller than Gail, reached up and took down a leatherbound album. She handed it to Gail who began to turn the pages.

'Maybe I'm wrong. After he left I made a point of throwing out anything connected to him. Ah! I've no idea why I kept this but here it is.' She lifted the plastic covering off three black-and-white photographs. 'It's a production he was in when he was a kid. See for yourself. He's standing at the end of the row.'

Rodgers looked at the picture.

'They did *A Christmas Carol*. He's the one next to the little boy on crutches.'

Rodgers could see no resemblance to the man he was hunting in the tall, thin boy standing shyly to one side. He turned the picture over, and scrawled on the back were the names of the actors in the show. He passed it to Sara. One of those listed as playing Tiny Tim was H. Smedley, and de Jersey had written 'Me' for himself. She gave the photograph back to Gail. 'Thank you.'

Rodgers knew instinctively that Gail didn't have any more useful information so he stood to leave, and thanked her for her time. But she hadn't finished her tirade. 'He walked out on me, you know. He never had the guts to say to my face that he was leaving. I woke up and found he'd packed and gone. The worst part was that he'd been preparing to leave me for ages. My lawyers said he must have spent at least six months arranging it all and that made it worse because I had no idea. That's what kind of person he is, a devious liar.'

Rodgers murmured his thanks again, then said, 'Well, I hope we catch him this time.'

To which Gail replied, 'No point, really, is there? I mean, he's almost a national hero, according to the press, and they got the jewels back. It's not as if he killed anyone.' She gave them a watery blue-eyed stare as she closed the door.

'Do you believe that?' Rodgers asked Sara as they returned to their car.

She hesitated. 'No, I don't. I think he killed Sylvia Hewitt. I also think he might have killed Alex Moreno.'

'Why do you say that?'

'Well, I know everyone thinks Edward de Jersey is some kind of hero but to me he's just a thief. Maybe he's been one for many years, and the more I hear about him, the more I uncover, the more I get this nasty feeling about him. I wouldn't trust him an inch, but if I met him I think I might just as easily fall in love with him. That's why he's so dangerous. I'm certain that if Alex Moreno did steal from him he wouldn't let him get away with it.'

He gave her a sideways glance. 'Lemme tell you something, Sara. Maybe I think the same, but if we start an investigation in the United States, they'll get in on the act. We've come a long way to catch this bastard and

I want to be the one who does. I'm retiring after this and no one else is gonna get the credit for weeks of round-the-clock work. I'll get this son-of-a-bitch. I'm close to it. I know it.'

'Unless he's in the US.'

He gave her a dull-eyed stare. 'If he tries to get his hands on the Moreno property, we'll know about it. I've got the contractor over there keeping an eye open for us. You've got to understand, though, that if he did kill Moreno, it's gonna be their case, not ours. Right now, all I'm interested in is catching the bastard myself. I honestly think I know Edward de Jersey now, really know him. He's a cold fish. He dumped his first wife and did the same with his second.'

'He does sound ruthless. To do that to his two daughters is just unbelievable,' Sara remarked, with distaste.

Rodgers unlocked the car doors. 'Yes, he's ruthless but he has one vulnerable area. I realize that now.'

'His daughters?' she asked, getting into the car and slamming the door.

He got in beside her. 'No. Somewhere, somehow he was able to cut out normal everyday emotions like that. Sure he must care about them, but the man is calculating. He spends months working out every little detail. The planning of that robbery was a work of art.'

'So what's vulnerable about him?'

'His racehorse, Royal Flush, and if my gut feelings are correct, the bastard won't be able to stay away from the race of his life.'

She gave him a sidelong glance. 'I've got a little straw number,' she said.

He frowned, not understanding.

'I'll need a hat for the races.'

He gave an odd snorting laugh. 'Get a good one on expenses. If he's there he might be in the boxes. I'm thinking of getting kitted out with a top hat and tails.'

She laughed, and he turned to her with a scowl. 'I'm not joking. If he's there, the bastard won't be crawling like a rat in and out of the punters' legs, he'll be moving with the high-flyers – and, knowing the fickle aristos of this world, they'll probably welcome him, just like they covered for Lord Lucan. They'll think it's all a good laugh.'

She nodded. 'I hope to God the laugh's not going to be on . . .' She was about to say 'you' but instead she said 'us'.

'It won't be, I'm sure of it. He's going to be there and it's not gonna be funny. He's going to get thirty years just like the Great Train Robbers and I'll be right there watching him as he's taken down. That'd wipe the smile off anyone's face.'

'I wouldn't know.' She smiled sweetly. 'I wasn't born when that happened, gov.'

'I was,' he said softly. 'I remember it all. I was also around for the Gold Bullion Robbery.' He took a sharp breath. He had been about to say they had never caught the man nicknamed the Colonel, but he stopped himself, knowing he still could not prove his suspicions. But what a retirement bonus he would get if he could!

His superiors took some persuading to allow Rodgers to carry out a large operation at the Derby, but Rodgers was so convinced that he knew what made de Jersey tick that he eventually won them over. Now he felt that the

625

end was in sight and he would be glad when it was over. It was true that de Jersey appeared to be the perfect gentleman, but Rodgers was certain that beneath the cloak of geniality lay a much colder, harder, more dangerous man. But he had one weakness. Rodgers believed that he wouldn't be able to resist witnessing Royal Flush's biggest challenge. If he had known about the foal, however, he would not have been as confident.

Two weeks before the race Rodgers asked Christina to be at the Derby. She tried to refuse, but he was insistent. They needed her to help identify him and who would be better able to do that than her? She did not want them to look too closely at her financial situation so she agreed, but did not tell her daughters. She looked over the invitations that had been sent to her, and was touched by how many people had asked her to join them in their boxes. Until she had been contacted by the police, she had planned to refuse them all. Now she accepted one, saying how much she appreciated the hosts' kindness in asking her and that she looked forward to seeing them.

The police operation was planned and outlined. They would have the racecourse covered with officers in plain clothes, mixing on the lower levels, wandering around the tic-tac men, hanging out in the oyster and champagne bars. They would be by the main Tote betting shop. They would be planted in every area, even up in the Royal balconies. They would be in the restaurants and private rooms. They would be, as Rodgers said, everywhere de Jersey might appear. They had installed several separate cameras at the finishing line, covering the winner's enclosure, the owners' and trainers' sections in the stands, the bars, and the small helicopter landing pad. It was a massive operation just to catch one man.

CHAPTER 29

I T WAS after one of de Jersey's morning walks that the unexpected happened. The beautiful weather at the beginning of June had changed to a thick, muggy heat and the constant rain made the house cold and damp. The sound of the sea crashing against the rocks below, which usually filled him with a sense of freedom, now got on his nerves. Checking the calendar, he saw that there were only days to go before the Derby. For the first time since he had been on the run, he felt the terrible loss of his family, the life he used to lead, and was enveloped in a deep depression. For months he had been moving and under pressure but now, with time on his hands, he felt listless and empty.

The weight of the darkness made his shoulders droop. He found it difficult to raise his head. The tears that had never come before now trickled down his cheeks, but he made no move to wipe them away. He could hear Christina's voice when she told him she had found the Koh-i-noor diamond in his boot. He had known then that he would have to leave her. He had already planned his departure by then, as he knew they were closing in, but he had not anticipated what losing her or his daughters would feel like. Slowly he got to his feet and walked to the window to look out across the ocean. The mist hung there like a dark grey blanket.

He had no notion of what had shaped him into the man he was and he did not know why he had done what he had done. The only thing in his life that had held him in a vice-like grip was winning. The emotion he had felt when he had seen his horses pass the post first was exhilarating in a way that nothing else was. He began to pace up and down the room. He was still a winner, he'd got away with it, he was free, he had won, he would win again. But this was not about money, not about what he had stashed beneath the floorboards, not about what he would get from selling Moreno's house.

As he paced, the darkness lifted and he began to laugh. His passion for his family and Royal Flush surpassed anything he had known and he'd give anything just to glimpse them again. The adrenaline pumped into his body like a bolt of electricity. Gone was the restriction that felt like a tight band around his brain, gone the depression, and his body tingled. He snorted out a strange, guttural laugh, because it truly felt as if he had the last laugh on them all. De Jersey knew they would all be waiting for him at the Derby. He also knew that if he showed up he would be arrested within moments, but it amused him to think of the furore it would create. And Bandit Queen would not be his future but his last laugh – even more so if Royal Flush won the Derby. Her colt or filly would be unstoppable.

He longed to attend the Derby, to hear the massive crowd. As at no other race meeting, they were as integral a part of the day as the race itself: the gypsies and punters, the tic-tac men, the boxes, the women in their extravagant hats, the men in their toppers and tails, the smell of chips, cockles and mussels, the pop of champagne corks.

He had been taken there as a kid by his dad, thronging on Gypsy Hill with their East End friends and their beer and their picnic hampers. He had never thought then that one day he would be on the other side, greeted by the Queen, tipping his hat to her as she murmured, 'Mr de Jersey.' He could hear his father weeping with joy, cap in hand, as the horse he'd bet on romped home the day he'd put his life savings on it. His father had cried tears of disbelief, then joy. He had sworn he would never lay another bet, that this was the last one and that with his winnings on the rank outsider he would open his first betting shop. He had been true to his word. But the one race Ronnie Jersey would not miss for the world was the Derby. Now, to own the odds-on favourite, to have trained him and to know in his heart that nothing was going to stop that horse passing the post first, hit de Jersey harder than he would have believed possible.

'How's my lady?' came the familiar voice to the stable girl.

'Is this Mr Shaughnessy?'

'It is, just calling to check on my girl,' he said, and she could almost feel his smile through the phone.

'Well, sir, I have to tell you she's incredible. She eats like a Trojan and she's getting to be a fair size. We had the vet check her out and she should be out of quarantine soon. He thinks the foal's gonna be a whopper but he's not worried. She's a big mare and he thinks there'll be no complications, even though she's got another four months to go.'

'But she's not too big?' he asked, with concern.

'He says there's no worries and we had her scanned as you wanted.'

'I'll come by this afternoon,' he said abruptly.

The staff at the quarantine stables had not met Michael Shaughnessy before and were somewhat surprised by the tall gaunt man in his old overcoat. He drove up in an equally decrepit Jeep, covered in mud. He wore thick boots and looked as if he'd not had a good meal for a while, but his manner didn't match his appearance. He was authoritative when he asked to be left alone to view his mare.

The word went round that Shaughnessy was at the stables and they watched as he went into the manager's office. There was a lengthy conversation, after which Shaughnessy came out, went back to his Jeep and drove off. The manager walked out, shaking his head. 'He wants the mare and the foal shipped back to England when it's born.'

'Where's he living? Is he local?'

'Says he's leased a house on Gardiner's Bay up in the Springs, but he's going back to London.' He checked his watch. 'He's cutting it fine. He'll only just make it. Says he's going back for the Derby.'

The Derby always drew a massive crowd. The Royal Family's own security was tight. Their Daimlers and Rolls-Royces drew up and the occupants were ushered out and into the Royal enclosure. Their boxes were hemmed in by security guards and police. The same amount of security would be present in all the car parks surrounding Epsom and extra officials had been hired to check and double-check all the passes. All major parties hiring buses and other means of transport were to be checked out, as were the gates, though monitoring the thousands entering the track would be difficult.

The Queen had a horse running in the Derby. It was the second favourite. The favourite, with days to go, was still Royal Flush. It was hardly ever mentioned that the horse had changed hands and was now owned by the Sheikh. It was always referred to now as the 'Royal Thief's Horse'.

The bookies would have a field day if Royal Flush didn't win. The punters were betting on him frantically and the bookies had been asked by the police if they would tip off any single bet that might have been laid by de Jersey. They retorted that it was against the privacy laws to disclose a private gambler's bets and any card-carrying member of Ladbrokes or any member of any of the established betting brokers would adhere to the code. They did, however, gain possible confirmation from the United States that any substantial-sized bet placed on Royal Flush from that side of the ocean would be reported.

Christina travelled from Sweden to stay at the Dorchester, giving herself time to purchase a new outfit. She had travelled alone and was met by officers at the airport in case she was pestered by the journalists, but none were there. She moved into her suite. Alone and back in London she felt a terrible sense of loss. If she saw him, she had no notion of how she would react and what feelings would surface. And if he did show, she was expected to give him up. Now she did not know if she could do it.

The officers were ready. It had taken weeks of preparation and it was still only an outside bet that de Jersey would turn up, but it was one on which Rodgers was now risking his career. The astronomical cost of the investigation and the massive surveillance operation to take place at the racecourse were under review, as were his actions. He had prepared his morning suit with his grey silk top hat. At least he would go down looking like a gent, or up looking like one, depending on the outcome of the day.

At last it was Saturday June 8th – Derby Day. The Derby was the fourth race. The first race had been over for twenty minutes and the horses for the second were cantering to the start. There had been no sighting of de Jersey, but there was a bigger crowd this year than ever before, swelled by the press's anticipation of a win by Royal Flush, and the fact that everyone felt sure the most wanted man in Britain would be there. Some hoped to see a dramatic arrest. Others hoped he would be seen but get away.

De Jersey walked up to a rather drunken reveller and offered him two hundred pounds to exchange suits with him. When he hesitated, he upped it to three hundred. They went into the men's cloakroom and while they switched clothes the flushed boy asked why he hadn't got a suit already.

'Because I'm Edward de Jersey,' he said, and walked out. He disappeared into the crowds.

The boy became hysterical. He forgot to do up his flies because he was so eager to find someone to tell and grabbed a uniformed officer, who tried to fight him off. 'He's here, that man they want, the guy from the jewel robbery!'

'What?'

'What about the reward? Will I get the reward? I've just seen him!'

'Oh, yeah, right, you and two hundred others, mate,' said the copper.

'I'm telling you the truth. He's wearing my bloody suit.'

The rumours started and the police were galvanized into searching the men's cloakroom and surrounding areas, but by this time de Jersey had made his way over to the saddling area. He approached his former trainer. 'Hello, Donald, it's me.'

Fleming turned and almost dropped the saddle. 'You're crazy. The place is crawling with cops.'

'I know, but I wanted to give you this. It's ownership of a certain horse. She's in the States, Donald, in quarantine and the foal's doing well. The foal is yours and Mickey's. It's gonna make you both rich.' Fleming didn't know how to react or what to say. Suddenly he was close to tears. 'I'll tell Mickey. His wife's pregnant and—'

De Jersey moved off without another word, and Fleming watched him go. He'd not even had time to shake his hand.

They had de Jersey on camera, heading out of the saddling area, but when they got there he had disappeared. It was not difficult as the place was thronging with people. The next sighting was at a booth selling cockles and mussels. He bought some and paid with a fifty-pound note, telling the vendor to keep the change. Rodgers, accompanied by Sara Redmond, was apoplectic as one sighting came on the heels of another.

The Derby runners were now being paraded in the ring as the jockeys came out to meet the owners and trainers. There was uproar as Royal Flush's jockey walked out. It was Mickey Rowland. No matter what he thought about his former boss being a jewel thief, de Jersey had secured him the ride as part of the contract and Mickey wanted to show his respect. He got on to Royal Flush and rode out carrying de Jersey's colours, holding the silk shirt high above his head. He waved it around madly before it was wrenched away from him by the Sheikh's bodyguard, but it had been caught on camera, seen by the crowd and by TV viewers around the country.

The police continued searching for de Jersey but it was like hunting for the Scarlet Pimpernel. He was sighted virtually all over the track as the riders assembled at the start.

Christina, in a box belonging to a major racing family, watched the television broadcast. It was obvious that de Jersey was there, but where was he? She was very distressed and sat down by the TV screen as an officer entered the box and asked if she had seen her husband.

'No, I haven't. Please, leave me alone.'

He left, but two officers were positioned outside. If Christina walked out they would be right on her tail, but she remained seated, holding an untouched glass of champagne, her eyes on the screen. When she had seen Mickey Rowland wave her husband's colours she had almost dropped the glass. The owners of the box had given up attempting to make her feel part of their celebrations. To some extent her presence made everyone anxious and the thought that her husband might appear heightened their excitement to fever pitch. In the end Christina excused herself and said she was going to the cloakroom.

She knew she was being followed, and when she got to the ladies' she turned to the officers and gave them a charming smile. 'I won't be a moment but I don't think it would be in order for you to join me in here.'

She went into one of the cubicles, closed the door and leaned against it. The tension was unbearable and she was trembling. She talked herself calm and walked out to look at her reflection in the mirror. The face that gazed back at her was so pale that her eyes seemed over-large. Her hands shook as she reapplied her makeup and adjusted her wide-brimmed hat. She took a deep breath and walked out. The two officers stood aside as she joined them. 'I think I'd like to go and watch the race in the owners' and trainers' stand.'

'OK, Mrs de Jersey, but we will have to accompany you.'

'I understand.'

They moved off and the crowds knew something was up. Even if they didn't recognize the beautiful woman with two uniformed officers at either side of her, they moved aside to allow the three to pass. A steward tried to bar their entry but the officers showed their ID. One used a walkie-talkie to report that Mrs de Jersey had requested to move to the owners' and trainers' stand and to watch the race close to the fence. The officers were given permission to take her there but on no account to leave her side.

The horses were under starter's orders and although the police now had twenty-five sightings of de Jersey, he remained at large. What they didn't know was that he wasn't in the boxes or on the balconies. Instead, he had made his way towards Gypsy Hill where the buses, the funfair and all the East End families were gathered. He stuck out like a sore thumb. No one there was in top hat and tails and they started to call his name as they ushered him closer and closer to the rails to watch the race. Among the East Enders, his own people, he felt at home and they gathered around him in an almost protective circle.

One man pushed, shoved and elbowed his way towards the tall figure. He had broken out in a sweat in his eagerness to get to de Jersey, to touch him, to let him know he was there.

'Eddy, Eddy,' he shouted, standing on tiptoe. He bent down and tried to squeeze between the pressing bodies. 'Eddy. *Eddy*!' He was hoarse from shouting. He could just see his quarry through the crowd.

'Eddy, it's me! *I know him, let me through*!'

De Jersey, hemmed in by men and women, some asking for his autograph, did a half-turn and saw the round sweating face of Harry Smedley. 'Let my friend through,' he said, and raised an arm as Harry Smedley reached his side.

'It's me, Harry Smedley,' he gasped. 'We was at school together. Remember me?'

De Jersey looked down and smiled. He still had no recollection of the little man. 'Of course. Come on, Harry, the race is about to start.'

This was to be the greatest day of Harry Smedley's life, standing right next to the most wanted man in Britain. His wife was not going to believe it, or his sons and grandsons. This was a moment he would never forget. 'I got two hundred quid on the nose,' he yelled, as he was jostled and pushed.

The crowds grew even more boisterous as de Jersey opened his wallet and threw fifty-pound notes to those around him. 'Royal Flush is going to win,' he shouted, and they scrabbled for the money as they cheered and shouted.

On the other side of the track, the police telescopic cameras finally picked him out, but, with the race about to start, it was impossible to get cars and officers across the track to pick him up. All the officers positioned in and around Gypsy Hill were instructed to move in and arrest him. The newscasters and racing correspondents were having the day of their lives.

'Added to the excitement felt around this wonderful race is the news that the most wanted man in Britain is here, mixing with the crowds. His horse, Royal Flush, is now at the start and until the race is over it seems that there is nothing anyone can do. And they are under starter's orders and they are *off*.'

Royal Flush came out of his stall badly, pushed to one side by the horse to his right. He took a while to adjust before he gathered his stride. Rounding the bend, he was in sixth position but holding the ground well. De Jersey stood, surrounded by men and women like those his father had known, his infamy forgotten as they concentrated on the race. Harry Smedley cheered and shouted until what little voice he had left became a croak. Most of them had bet on Royal Flush and the cheers and yells for him to come forward were deafening. The horses rounded the bend, then faced the hill climb but it was starting to look as if Royal Flush would be left far behind if he didn't make his move.

Harry Smedley was now almost in tears. He looked up at de Jersey, who stood as if frozen. He was willing his boy to move up, willing him with his hands clenched at his sides. 'Come on. Move him up, Mickey. Come on, my boy, come on, my son,' he whispered.

Then, out of nowhere, the big stallion eased forward, whipped on by the jockey, and was now lying third. As he took second position the crowd roared their approval.

De Jersey stood immobile. Not until his beloved Royal Flush moved up into first position did he begin to yell with everyone else. Royal Flush was neck and neck and then, there he was, out alone, winning easily and with such force that the roar of the crowd was deafening. It had been worth it. Seeing him cross the finish line was a moment of such glory that it would surpass anything that was to come.

Harry Smedley was weeping, leaning over the rails. 'He did it. He did it,' he said, but when he turned to de Jersey, it was as if he had disappeared into thin air.

De Jersey couldn't have pushed his way back through the crowds behind them. They were twenty deep and, being so tall, he would easily have been seen. Harry turned back in confusion and then his heart stopped. 'Oh, my God, he's gone over the fence!'

'And the winner of the 2002 Derby is . . . Royal Flush.'

As the Sheikh entered the winner's enclosure to be honoured with the most coveted award horse-racing could offer, a solitary figure was seen climbing over the barrier at Gypsy Hill, walking with his hat raised high. He swaggered along the track and was cheered almost as loudly as the winner.

'We got him,' said Rodgers, red-faced and sweating, as he spoke orders into the radio microphone to pick him up.

'No, we didn't,' Sara said, holding on to her flowered hat. 'He gave himself up.' She sounded strangely close to tears. She turned to look at Christina de Jersey, still between the two officers. She was standing close to the rails by the winning post.

Rodgers had made sure she was visible to him, certain de Jersey would try to see her. He now watched her as the figure of de Jersey walked closer and closer. He crossed to ask her the unnecessary question. 'Is that man Edward de Jersey?' he asked.

She turned to face him but he couldn't meet her eyes. They were full of pain. 'Yes, that is my husband,' she said.

They all turned back to the track to see the officers now streaming from all sides towards de Jersey who was still audaciously acknowledging the cheers.

De Jersey was arrested on the track, surrounded by plain-clothed and uniformed officers. Once he had been cautioned, he was handcuffed and removed from the ground in a police van to be taken to Scotland Yard for questioning.

'Do you want to see him?' Rodgers asked Christina, but she shook her head.

'No. I want to go home.' She was led away and he ordered the officers to shield her from the photographers. He felt such compassion for her, and admiration at the way she had behaved.

Her Majesty had also witnessed the arrest. She gave no indication of what she felt, but seemed annoyed that her own horse had been placed fifth.

Edward de Jersey spent many months in prison waiting for trial as bail was refused. He was tried eventually for his part in the infamous robbery. He never named any of his associates and never spoke on his own behalf, refusing to give evidence. He was not charged with Sylvia Hewitt's murder as there was insufficient evidence to take the case to court. He was sentenced to twenty-five years.

EPILOGUE

ANTHONY DRISCOLL is still at large. He lives with a Spanish woman named Rosa. She works in a local restaurant and he is employed as a night-watchman for a local pottery factory.

JAMES WILCOX is also still at large. He is now married to Daniella and has a baby daughter. He continues to work for Daniella's brothers, refurbishing holiday apartments.

CHRISTINA DE JERSEY divorced her husband after he was sentenced. He refused to see her or his daughters, encouraging them to start a new life. Christina subsequently discovered that he had placed three million dollars in an account in the North Fork Bank in East Hampton, to be given to his daughters when they reached the age of twenty-one.

RAYMOND MARSH is still at large, now working for an IT consultancy company in New Zealand.

HARRY SMEDLEY was paid ten thousand pounds for his exclusive story in the *News of the World* based on his childhood memories of Eddie Jersey. His book was entitled *My Friend Edward de Jersey*.

ROYAL FLUSH went on to a stunning career, winning at Royal Ascot and Goodwood. He was then shipped out to Dubai, where he won the great Dubai championship. Returning to England, he suffered abdominal pain, sweating and fine muscle tremors, and acute grass disease was diagnosed. He died never having been put to stud. Bandit Queen's colt was Royal Flush's only progeny.

BANDIT QUEEN'S colt was born safely in the US. He was a healthy, magnificent foal and was later shipped to England to be trained by his new owners, Donald Fleming and Mickey Rowland. He was turned out to graze as a yearling, until he was ready to be trained. His photographs dominated the cell walls of the man who had bred him illegally, the man who, unlike most men, had seen his dream come true. That, in the end, had been the fulfilment he had always coveted.

CHIEF SUPERINTENDENT RODGERS retired from the Metropolitan Police after watching Edward de Jersey sentenced. He had spent many hours interrogating de Jersey and was pleased to see him go down, yet he remained dissatisfied that two of the robbery team members remained at large. As they were about to lead away the handcuffed de Jersey, Rodgers asked if he could have two minutes alone with him. He knew that even if de Jersey admitted it, there was little he could do with the information but he asked him anyway. Was he the Mr Big behind the Great Train Robbery and the Gold

Bullion Raid? De Jersey looked Rodgers straight in the eye. After a long pause he smiled and held up his handcuffed hands. 'You'll have to wait for my autobiography.'

SLEEPING CRUELTY

To my mother, sweet Flossie

Acknowledgements

MY SINCERE THANKS to Suzanne Baboneau at Macmillan for her constant support and enthusiasm for my work, a friendship I value greatly. Many thanks also go to Hazel Orme, Philippa McEwan, Esther Newberg and Peter Benedek. Thanks also to my agent Gill Coleridge, who steers my career and reins in some of my more erotic writing.

I'd also like to thank the team at La Plante Productions. The rough draft of *Sleeping Cruelty* bounced around the office until it fell into the capable hands of Alice Asquith, head of research, Kate Fletcher, Nikki Smith, Kerry Appleyard and George Weatherill. After testing some of the sequences out on random passersby, the team found some of my more steamy scenes too hot to handle, so these scenes will be forever left to the imagination! A big thanks to Liz Thorburn, MD of La Plante Productions, 'mother' to us all.

Further thanks to my financial advisor Stephen Ross, who was disappointed not to have been allowed access to the censored sections!

Special thanks to the following for their generous contribution: Juliet Battersby, Bulgari, Hugo Waring for his wine expertise, Professor John Henry at the

Poisons Unit at St Mary's Paddington, the Ritz, the West Indies Tourist Office, British Virgin Islands Tourist Office, French Antilles Tourist Office, the Necker Island Office.

All characters and events in this book are fictional. Any resemblance between them and any real character or event is coincidental; it is not intended and should not be inferred.

PROLOGUE

Summer 1977

THE VILLA was nestled in a hollow cut into the side of a cliff, overlooking the sea. A strange, low, sprawling building, it was shaded by the massive fir trees that surrounded it, almost encroaching on to the small paved patio at the front. The grounds of the house curved upwards steeply so that you could look in through the windows on the top floor. The nanny could tell that the villa must have had another storey at one time, a third floor, high enough to overlook the forest and give panoramic views of the sea and maybe even a glimpse of the beach below.

Though highly experienced, and with tip-top references, she was surprised when she received a call in answer to the advert she had placed in the *Lady* magazine, asking if she could start work immediately before she had met either parents or children. The wages were almost double what she had anticipated, and a first-class ticket and travel expenses were sent from a reputable firm of solicitors in Paris. She was told that her duties would be outlined to her on her arrival. It seemed a wonderful opportunity, and she felt fortunate.

The children's father, a handsome man in his late

1

forties, had shown her in. He was aloof and rather condescending, especially when she had questioned the weight of the household duties he was expecting her to take on. He spoke slowly, not looking into her face but staring over her head. 'I checked your references. Previously you have been paid a standard rate. I am offering substantially more. Surely it is not asking too much of you to run the household. There will be no interference. I will not be here. I have business commitments in Paris.' He went on to say that he would spend only the odd weekend at the villa but would always give her warning if there were to be any guests and then, if necessary, he would bring staff from his Paris home to cook and assist with the cleaning.

The interview was brief. She felt guilty about even mentioning the household tasks, especially when she saw her luxurious quarters: a huge bedroom with vast wardrobe space and *en-suite* bathroom. What a change from her London bedsit! She looked forward to spending days on the beach with the children and perhaps going for rambles and picnics.

No sooner had she unpacked, showered and changed ready to meet her charges than she heard a car departing. He had not even introduced her to his children. There was a sound at her door, a child's knock. It opened and there they were. The children stood together, sweet and shy. They shook her hand, welcomed her with downcast eyes and, as if rehearsed, said they hoped she would enjoy working at the villa. They looked so vulnerable that she was fired with enthusiasm to make the most of this job.

As she got to know them over the next few days, however, they began to make her feel uneasy, sometimes downright scared. Both children were astonishingly beautiful, but their faces were chillingly devoid of emotion and their wide, clear blue eyes oddly expressionless. Both had ash blond hair, bleached white by the sun. Their slender bodies had a golden tan, and for two such young children they were remarkably clean and poised. She soon realized they were both neurotically fastidious about their clothes. Though she was only eight, the girl changed numerous times during the day. The nanny also noticed that she washed her hands and face repeatedly. The boy, at ten, was just as meticulous about his appearance. But there was nothing feminine about him: he had an unusually mature masculinity, giving the nanny sidelong glances when he thought she wasn't looking. If she caught his eye, he would give a slow adult smile.

The nursery was always tidy, the toys lined up with military precision. They made their beds without having to be told, and asked for fresh sheets and pillow-slips every two days. The amount of washing and ironing ensured that the nanny's working day stretched well into the evening. When she questioned them, it soon became clear that they had not been forced into this disciplined lifestyle. It was how they liked it, they said in unison. They were always whispering and giggling together but fell silent when she approached. They ate sparingly, simple food with lots of salads and vegetables. She presumed the menus had been established by their previous nanny. But when she asked, they changed the subject. Once they spoke briefly of their mother, who had died two years before, they said, in the villa, in a fire. They didn't seem distressed, just stated the fact, then asked if she would like to come swimming. She

3

agreed to meet them in the garden as soon as she had put on her swimsuit.

They were waiting for her, but not in their swimsuits. They were still dressed. The boy strolled ahead, the girl took her hand and led her towards the pool. 'Dive in,' she piped.

The nanny was puzzled that the pool should be in such a shaded area, and from where she stood the water appeared murky. But the children told her again to dive in.

'Go on, close your eyes,' said the little girl. 'I'll guide you right to the edge.'

The nanny's toes were gripping the edge of the pool when she looked, *really* looked, at the water. It was infested with wasps and bugs, a seething, green, moving carpet. She was so shocked that she almost lost her balance as the children ran away, laughing.

Later she served them supper and watched them get into their beds before returning to her own room to read. The heat was oppressive and when she opened a shutter to let in some air, she was taken aback to see the children in a dark corner of the garden. The little girl, wearing a white nightdress, dragged a large doll with curly blonde hair, behind her. The boy pointed at the ground with a spade. In silence, she watched the children until they came back inside. Then she went out to see what they had been doing. Handmade crosses marked what appeared to be a row of graves. One cross, made from rough twigs and bound with string, had a piece of pink writing-paper pinned to it, with the word 'Papa'.

The following morning as she served them breakfast, she mentioned that she had seen them playing. The boy

4

pushed his plate to one side. 'You must have been dreaming. We were in bed.'

'Yes,' said the girl. 'We always do as we're told. We weren't outside.'

The nanny didn't want to make an issue of it, but after breakfast was cleared away, she went in search of the garden graves and discovered they had gone.

She was frightened. She knew she hadn't imagined it.

She tried to be cheery and inject some fun into their strict lives, but they weren't interested. They didn't want to go to the beach, or for walks. They preferred to sit together, reading or whispering. Their routine remained the same day after day, and she felt like an intruder in their world. She hoped their father would return one weekend.

No one ever came to the villa. There were no calls, there was no mail. The groceries were delivered on Friday, so she had no need to go to the nearest village. She was pleased when she saw the deliveryman roar up the drive. But he seemed in a great hurry to get the receipt signed and leave. He didn't even turn off the van's engine. 'Did you know the children's mother?' she asked, as he laid the carbon paper between the receipt and copy.

He shook his head. 'She burned alive, up there.' He used his chewed ballpoint pen to point to the flat roof of the villa. 'It used to have another storey – that's why the roof is flat.' His face glistened with sweat as he then leaned close. 'No one stays there now, not for more than a few days anyway. He stays away for months at a time, the father. He hates it here.'

'But what about the children?'

5

The deliveryman gave her a strange look. 'They're the reason no one stays. It was them that started the fire they reckon. They're . . . not normal.'

Later when she entered the nursery she found them lying side by side, their arms entwined around each other, whispering. They parted quickly and fell silent, as if annoyed by her intrusion.

'This afternoon we're going on a picnic,' she said. 'Which would you prefer, the beach or the heath? You choose.'

As if on cue there was a clap of thunder and heavy raindrops began to fall. The children giggled.

'Ah, well,' said the nanny, 'maybe tomorrow. These storms never last long. Let's see what's on the television.'

She turned on the set, but it was crackly and unwatchable, so she offered to play a game with them, but none of her suggestions drew so much as a flicker of interest. The two children sat, hand in hand, dead-eyed, until she became angry with her own inability to cajole them into animation.

'Why don't you want to play?' She couldn't stop her voice rising. 'Have you ever played like normal children? What on earth is the matter with you both? Stop looking at each other and look at me. *Look at me!* Now, tell me what's the matter. You behave as if you hate me.'

The boy kicked at a chair leg. 'We don't hate you,' he said. But he had a strange smile on his face.

'No, we don't hate you,' piped up his sister.

The nanny took a deep breath. 'Are you like this because of your mother? Because of what happened to her?'

6

The children held each other's gaze for a long time, as if having a silent conversation. Then the boy eased away from his chair and crossed to her. Reaching for her hand, he began to stroke it. His skin felt almost silky. He pressed his body closer and closer to her as if wanting to slip his arms around her waist. She found it moving, as if he was trying to comfort her.

Apparently encouraged by her brother, the girl crossed and hugged the nanny's knees, so tightly that she could feel the child's hot breath against her thighs. Suddenly her joy turned to panic as she realized that this was no show of juvenile affection.

The boy was easing up her skirt, his small hands rhythmically stroking her thigh, as his sister's hot breath centred at her crotch. Just as the boy's hand reached for her breast she pulled away. 'Stop this,' cried the nanny, standing and smoothing her skirt. '*Stop this right now.*'

They looked up at her, puzzled.

'But you said you wanted to play with us,' said the boy petulantly. Then he punched her in the stomach while his sister sank her teeth into her hand. The nanny let out a yelp of pain. The children responded with high-pitched shrieks of delight.

'Get away from me,' screamed the nanny. '*Stop this.*'

She ran to her room. She put a call through to Paris, to their father. He was curt, dismissive, and did not question her reason for wanting to leave. He asked if she would please remain at the villa for that evening until he had made alternative arrangements. The nanny stayed in her room, packing her suitcases, not wanting to face either child again. She was ashamed that she couldn't deal with them but she knew that someone far more experienced than her would have to unravel their psyches.

As dusk drew in she went into the kitchen and made up a tray of cold chicken and salad for herself, leaving the children's food laid out on the table. She could hear no sounds from the nursery, and was unsure if they were inside the villa or not. Then she returned to her room and locked the door. The rain lashed down: the storm had returned.

Later that night she awoke to a loud bang. The thunderclaps seemed to be centred on the villa itself. She moved around the house, checking doors and windows. A light was showing beneath the nursery door. She paused to listen, then bent down to peer through a crack in the door. An eye peered back at her and she straightened up fast as a high-pitched laugh echoed across the corridor.

She made her way to the master bedroom suite. The room was in darkness. The furniture was oak, as oppressive as the night itself, and a wardrobe door hung open. She looked inside. Rows of shirts, suits, trousers, racks of ties and handmade shoes, bottles of cologne with silver-backed hairbrushes were neatly lined up in open drawers.

She jumped in fright as a loud bang came from the bathroom. The shutters had come loose. Standing in a puddle on the blue and white tiled floor, she reached out to close them. At that moment the lights went out. She groped around for the switch. It must be a power cut. She found a hand towel and knelt to mop up the water – she didn't care that she was using a pristine white towel to dry the floor. Whoever had the misfortune to work here after her could deal with it. She was glad to be leaving. She wrung out the towel into the bath. Then she froze.

A sound came from above her, from the flat roof. It was as if something was being dragged across it, like a heavy, unwieldy sack. Frightened, she listened and, still carrying the sodden towel, she left the bedroom. On the landing outside she listened again, looking upwards. She wondered if perhaps an animal had jumped on to the roof. But as she could hear nothing, she hurried along the corridor to her own room, went in and closed the door behind her.

Then she heard the sound again, coming from directly above her room. She stepped out into the corridor again. Looking up, she inched towards the old staircase that once led up to the third floor, but now terminated at a bolted wooden trap-door.

A sudden flash of lightning momentarily flooded the corridor with a bluish light, but the staircase to nowhere remained dark and shadowy.

'What's happening?'

The voice came from behind her and she spun round. Both children stood there hand in hand.

'There's something on the roof,' she screamed. 'There's something *up there on the roof*.'

At that moment the lights flickered on. She felt foolish, standing barefoot in just her bra and slip. 'Didn't you hear it?' she asked lamely. 'It sounded as if someone, or something, was trapped up there.' She looked into their impassive faces. 'I'm sorry if I frightened you, but I was scared.'

The two children stared in silence.

'I'm sorry. You'd better go back to your room and try and get some sleep. Your father will be here tomorrow.'

They looked at each other. 'Why?'

The nanny wiped her face with the back of her hand. 'Because I asked him to come. I'm leaving.' She headed towards her room.

The children remained watching, their eyes wide.

'I'll be leaving in the morning, as soon as he gets here, so please just go back to bed.'

As she closed her door behind her, she was sure she heard the boy call her a stupid bitch. She looked at her watch. It was almost four in the morning. She shivered as she remembered their hands on her body. Was it possible she had been mistaken? But when she relived it, she knew she had not. Then the noise on the roof started again. She felt the draught as soon as she stepped into the corridor. The trapdoor was open. She climbed the stairs to peer out and scan the roof. What she saw froze her to the spot.

Their small frames doubled under the weight, the two children were dragging a body, using all their strength, and trying to roll it over the edge of the roof. The rain had left pools, which were now blood red, as were the awful marks where they had hauled their burden across the roof. The children seemed wounded; their blond hair was matted with blood, their night-clothes were drenched.

'Dear God, what's happened?' she whispered.

The boy spun round. 'It's all right,' he said, continuing to heave the body closer to the edge of the villa roof.

'No one will do anything,' added the girl, helping her brother. 'We're only children.'

The nanny knew without even seeing his face that the body was their father's. 'Just like they did nothing about Mama.' The little girl strained as she pushed at the dead weight. As the body rolled over the side on to the ground with a dull thud, both children smiled, as if congratulating each other, then turned to face their nanny.

'Nanny, will you help us bury him?' they asked in unison.

CHAPTER 1

WILLIAM BENEDICT was fifty-three, and regarded himself 'well preserved'. He had never been a vain man, but recently his creeping paunch and loss of hair had started to play on his mind. It was the latter that he really hated. His blond hair had always made him look younger than he was and although you could never have described him as handsome, his boyishness had given him a certain attraction. Even the press nicknamed him 'Boy Wonder'. But his youthful looks had gone.

Standing just under six feet tall, William stared down at the scales: despite hiring a personal fitness trainer he had not lost a single ounce. Why waste time and money on press-ups and weights for nothing? And the pills, at least thirty different vitamin and mineral supplements, irritated him too – they seemed to stick in his chest for half the morning.

William muttered with annoyance as he inspected his face in the mirror. He struck a pose, sucking in his cheeks and raising an eyebrow. He was all right, really. His pale blue eyes were as bright as they ever were – his mother always said they were his best feature. They had a permanently alert quality that could be unnerving, particularly when they darkened in anger. He glared at himself: he was beginning to feel as if someone else had sneaked into his body and blown it up. He drew his lips back to inspect his teeth, which had come courtesy of one of the best dentists in Los Angeles. He had smoked cigars all his life but his second wife had been particular about teeth and had made sure that his never bore the tell-tale stains.

Clothes were a different matter: he dressed for comfort rather than style. He had always been told what was fashionable, and both his ex-wives had sent him to the tailor in an attempt to improve his sartorial sense. He had wardrobes full of tailored shirts, suits and handmade shoes – even his tracksuits were made by Armani. Everything looked fine on the hangers in the wardrobe, but once it was on William it gave the impression of sloppiness. The truth was, he had never really been interested in clothes. He felt he didn't need to be. William was a man to be envied. Few could match his fortune. He had recently floated his computer company and made a five-hundred-million-pound profit, and he had numerous other interests in property and industry.

His new project was politics. He had never been a political animal, but had voted Labour throughout both his marriages simply because it infuriated his in-laws. Now he had switched his allegiance, more or less on a whim, to the Conservative Party due to Andrew Maynard. He had heard the tall, pallid Maynard speak at some tedious charity function and the hairs on the back of his neck had stood up. It was almost as if something about the man reminded William of himself – not physically, more because, to all intents and purposes, he was an outsider. He made a note to watch the young man's progress. When he found himself in Brighton during the 1997 Tory Party conference and noticed that Maynard was to speak, he surprised himself by going to hear him.

As just another hopeful politician attempting to gain notice, Maynard might easily have been overlooked that week. But to everyone's surprise, though not to William's, he swept the entire conference hall to its feet for a standing ovation. The young man mesmerized his listeners.

The third time William saw Maynard was at a fund-raising dinner at the Grosvenor Hotel. Having decided to back the Conservative Party, William had made generous donations to Party funds, which had warranted an invitation. Once again the young man enthralled him, this time as a guest at the same table. Maynard, William noticed, drank little and hardly touched his food. It was not until coffee was served that William had the opportunity to talk to him. Maynard seemed shy, explaining that he held out little hope of gaining a seat at the election, but added that he fully intended to give the opposition a good run for its money.

Over the following weeks William continued, albeit half-heartedly, to monitor the young politician's career as the pre-election fever grew. However, Maynard lost, by a narrow margin, as the Labour Party swept to victory. His loyal supporters commiserated with him at a breakfast they had organized. They didn't stay long, and Maynard shook their hands as they departed, maintaining that he would fight on, and that next time he would win.

At the end only William remained with him in the

restaurant. He lit a cigar, feeling depression hanging in the air. Maynard loosened his tie and unbuttoned his collar. He picked up a lipstick-rimmed champagne glass and downed the remains. Until now they had hardly spoken more than a few words to each other, although Maynard had written William an appreciative letter thanking him for his financial backing.

Maynard turned to him now with a doleful expression. 'It was close. I'm sorry . . . you've donated so much. I'll never be able to thank you enough for your support.'

'Why don't you let me take you home?' William offered and ushered him to his car.

Maynard sat, head bowed, beside William in his Rolls Royce. They turned into Ladbroke Grove off Notting Hill Gate, and headed towards Maynard's small terraced house.

William cleared his throat. 'I donated to your campaign even though I didn't think you were ready. You were always an outside bet, but I don't regret it or worry about losing my money. It may still bring opportunities, so let's just put it down to experience.'

Maynard was clenching and unclenching his fists. He muttered that the new Prime Minister was young too, then turned to William. The weeks of day-and-night canvassing had taken their toll, and Maynard was thinner than ever. With his tie askew, and his unflattering black-rimmed spectacles he seemed like a fragile petulant boy. But when he spoke, his voice was cold with controlled anger. 'I appreciate your generosity, but I am sad that my political aspirations are not the reason you have supported me. It makes me wonder what strings you might have tried to pull for your own gain if this rank outsider you bet on *had* won!'

The chauffeur stopped outside Maynard's house, but before he could get out to open the door, it had been slammed shut.

Maynard opened his front door and just managed to close it behind him before the adrenaline that had been keeping him going for days evaporated. He leaned against the wall then slipped down it to the floor. He had not just failed to win his parliamentary seat but, without the continued donations from billionaire William Benedict, he had also lost future assurance of financial backing. With his rude remark, he knew he had made a foolish tactical error.

The following morning, Maynard's cleaner arrived as he was leaving. By eight fifteen he was at Claridge's – William's regular haunt for breakfast meetings. This morning when Maynard joined him he had every newspaper piled on the table and some stacked by his chair.

'I want to apologize for the way I spoke to you,' Maynard said, and flushed as he sat down.

They discussed the news coverage. The rival Labour candidate had expressed concern at beating Maynard by such a narrow margin. 'But he still won,' Maynard said, buttering his toast.

'Listen,' said William, 'I'm going to give you some advice. Take no favours, you'll have no debts. Show respect. A friend is useful, an enemy takes up your time. With that in mind, I have forgotten what you said to me last night.' Before Maynard could respond, he took out a pocket calculator, and a computer no larger than a wallet. Intent on the screen, he tapped away. Then he turned it to face Maynard. 'Is that up to date?'

On the tiny screen were Maynard's private bank statements, details of his mortgage, life assurance policies, the accounts for his office and staff during the campaign, lists of queries on personal expenses, claims, then details of tax and VAT payments, and sums owing to him.

'I pay my cleaner twenty quid a week,' Maynard said. It was the one item not listed. But he was angry, confused and dismayed by all the information William had amassed. He continued to scroll through the personal details: his school, his scholarships, university degrees, even the odd payments for speeches he had written for various MPs. He had been so engrossed he had not really listened to what William had been saying. But now it dawned on him. Had he heard correctly? He was not withdrawing any further donations? 'You will be in financial difficulties within months,' William said. 'You've taken out a second mortgage, you've no collateral left, and no fairy godmother in the wings to leave you a big inheritance. You need me, Andrew, more now than ever, and I'm offering you the deal of a lifetime. I'm going to back you to the hilt, all the way. Just you.'

William scraped back his chair and Maynard looked up. William needed a smoke, and it was not allowed in the dining-room.

Maynard joined William in the foyer where he sat with his cigar. He was unsure what William had meant by 'just you'. He felt as if he might be walking into a trap. What was the deal? What strings were attached?

William puffed until a halo of smoke formed round

his head. He suggested that Maynard should go for a good long holiday to recharge his batteries and think clearly about what he should do. William was certain that his election campaign had got him noticed; it would be up to him now to approach the Tory leader to discuss his future.

Maynard leaned forward. 'Why are you doing this?'

William stubbed out his cigar, only partially smoked, in the big silver ashtray on a stand by his chair. 'I have my reasons.'

'I need to know, sir. Please, you're offering me so much – why?'

William frowned. Then after a long pause he cocked his head to one side. 'Okay. It was just before lunch, a few years back, at the Party conference. Margaret Thatcher was sitting next to me. I watched her watching you. I saw her backbone stiffen. She never took her eyes off you until the end of your speech. You impressed me, and I saw that you had impressed her. That's it, really. Now, I have to go, old chap. You think about it. Call me tonight, or whenever.' He grinned at the confused young man, stood up and walked into the foyer.

William had to go only five paces across the pavement to reach his car. The passenger door was already open, his chauffeur standing by. He touched his cap when he saw Maynard.

Maynard stood rooted to the pavement, his heart thudding. William was getting into the car. 'Can I come with you? Could you drop me wherever you're going? Please?'

William shrugged, a little irritated: he wanted to get on with the day, but Maynard was fast off the mark, leaped in beside him and slammed the door.

19

'This is a Rolls Royce,' remarked William as the car glided away. 'The doors are perfectly balanced and hinged. They do not require a heavy-handed slam. You should learn that. One day, perhaps, you'll have one of your own, if we play our cards right.'

Maynard swallowed. His throat was bone dry.

William continued, leaning back against the soft leather seat. 'You need a makeover. It's all about image – get a professional. Lose those bloody glasses for a start. And you need a red hot PR person.'

Maynard felt as if he was hyperventilating. William leaned forward and opened a small compartment built into the back of the seat in front of him. Maynard saw that the compartment was stocked with all kinds of drinks, a cut-glass ice bucket, cigar boxes and cutters and cut-glass decanters with silver tops designed by Dunhill. William took out one of the decanters, poured a glass of water, and passed it to Maynard, who sipped it gratefully.

At last Maynard had pulled himself together. 'I have never done anything illegal in my life,' he said. 'As a politician I have to be scrupulously honest – and everything you're offering might be a potential trap – might ruin my career prospects. I'll get there the hard way, if I have to, no matter how long it takes. I have no interest in personal wealth – or a "makeover".' He took a deep breath. 'All those things are insignificant in comparison to the kind of changes I want to make to this country. Our current system is corrupt, we need to—'

'Stop the car, please.' William cut Maynard off before he could finish his sentence. He'd heard Maynard's speeches repeatedly during the campaign, and applauded the radical ideas he had urged on his supporters. But now he was trying William's patience. He leaned over and opened the young man's door. 'Get out, I've heard enough. Some people like to spend two million on a racehorse, but they never place a bet. It's not the money they want, it's not the winnings that excite them, it's the enjoyment of watching the horse race, and the thrill of when – *if* – it wins. That's all there is to it. That's all you are to me. Now go home.'

'Your *racehorse*? I jump when you say so?'

William shook his head in exasperation. All he wanted, he said, was to see Maynard win his seat in the next election and to be there to watch him do it. Then he took pity on him. 'No strings, no traps. *I believe in you*, you dumb bastard!'

William held out his hand for Maynard to shake. 'I mean it, I believe in you, son. You shine brightly, and you're right to be cautious. This is a career you've wanted since you were a kid. Well, I'll give it to you, with no ulterior motive. Now push off, I have work to do.'

Maynard walked away, his hands stuffed into his coat pockets. He must have looked such a wimp, but in fact he was highly ambitious and, at times, aggressive. Nevertheless, he would not allow himself to be treated like a commodity: he was not for sale. His career could not be compared with a racehorse. He had suffered too much already to get to where he was. Then he stopped and gave a humourless laugh. What career? In the cold light of morning, after all the hype, he knew he was still low on the political ladder. But maybe he had just stepped up a rung.

It took him three further days to contact William

Benedict. His excuse for not calling earlier was that he had been busy with post-campaign work. In reality he had taken legal advice. He told William that he had decided to accept his offer and made it clear there must be no possibility of any backlash against him. Then he relaxed. He had a benefactor whom most ambitious men would give their right arm for.

He was a little taken aback by William's non-committal response. He was quite cool; it appeared that his mind was elsewhere. All he said was: 'Good, but you realize it'll have little to do with me personally? Apart from the money, it'll all be down to you. I'll see you at my lawyer's tomorrow.'

Maynard's cosmetic makeover took more time to finalize than the legal accountancy and drawing up of acceptable bank accounts. It was imperative that the monetary transactions could not possibly be construed as a bribe from William, especially considering the fuss that had been made over the recent Aitken case. As Maynard had insisted it was all above suspicion: no ulterior motive could be detected behind his benefactor's generosity. The contract went back and forth and Maynard pored over it for anything that might be misconstrued if it ever became public knowledge.

Six months after their breakfast at Claridge's the change in Maynard's appearance was beginning to pay off. The fact that the tailoring and the dental work had taken so long was a blessing, because no one was able to pinpoint any dramatic change in Maynard and therefore didn't whisper about his growing show of confidence and polish, and William enjoyed watching his protégé emerge.

Neither did success come overnight – it took a great deal longer. Three years after that breakfast meeting, Maynard's star at last rose. He took his seat in a by-election, and became the young hope of the Conservative Party. Aged thirty-eight he was now courted by the Party elders, who showed interest in grooming him for a big political future.

For William, it was not a question of basking in the young man's glory, but of watching his protégé quietly from the sidelines with almost fatherly pride. Maynard became well known for his fearless stance, and was an almost constant media focus. Acting classes and elocution lessons improved his pose and diction, which meant that his television appearances gained him respect and attention. He ate up his fame with relish. Without doubt Andrew Maynard was earmarked to rise to the top.

Even though William had never hinted that he wished to be repaid for his generosity, it was at this time that he was knighted for his constant support to the Party. His charitable donations brought him to the attention of the peripheral socio-political scene and he was more socially active than ever before.

Sir William was inundated with invitations to fundraising events and charitable functions. He couldn't calculate on how many boards he now sat as an 'honorary member', and he enjoyed his new standing. He was a wealthy man but, until this stage in his life, had kept a low profile. It was not until Maynard had crossed his path that he had appreciated his fortune or used it for anything other than to expand his own companies. He continued to work on pet projects but only when he felt so inclined.

William knew that his seemingly bottomless wallet was his biggest social asset but he nevertheless found most of the company he attracted delightful. A number of ladies used him as their escort, and he took on this role with enthusiasm. Not that he found any of them sexually attractive – far from it. It was being at the hub of the social world that he liked, and he took to collecting all the newspaper photographs and articles in which he featured. And all of the changes in his life had come about through Andrew Maynard, who now occupied the place of the family he had lost. He had little contact with his own children due to his ex-wife's bitterness, and at times he looked on Maynard as a son. It was as if Maynard had opened a door inside William that allowed him, at this stage of his life, to enjoy living.

Even with all his millions, William had always felt second rate. His self-consciousness when moving in his ex-wives' aristocratic circles made him uncomfortable and aware of his social shortcomings. Now he blossomed, and for the first time discovered he was comfortable with himself. His background, which had been an embarrassment to his wives, was acceptable. As a self-made businessman he was applauded in the post-Thatcher line-up. And it was all due to Andrew.

Niggling doubts arose only on the odd occasion when he had dinner with Maynard. Sometimes William felt as if the young man only accepted his invitations out of politeness, but they were still pleasant evenings. The pair would discuss the present day's news, Party developments and so forth, but nothing personal. In fact William could not recall ever having any conversation with Maynard that embraced his private life, apart from on one evening. Maynard told him of how he had lost both parents and then, shortly after his mother's death, his elder sister had been killed in a car accident. William had commiserated, hoping for more details, but Maynard had been his usual reticent self: he said that his sister was much older and they had little knowledge of each other's lives – she worked abroad as a nanny and had never shown any interest in his political hopes. He invariably turned conversation back to William, fascinated by how he had accrued his wealth.

William had never known anyone to take such an interest in his career and enjoyed talking about his success. The first company he founded designed and developed computer chips, sold software programs, and designed and built computers. He had recently, partly out of boredom, begun manufacturing CD-ROMs, and had opened up a four-storey factory to develop computer games with experts brought in from Japan and the USA. He was selling on the Internet, and opening more factories to take over the European market. William had made his first million before he was twenty-eight.

Maynard, however, even in the relaxed atmosphere, would never talk about his own life and William did not like to press him. In some ways, though, their relationship was moving closer, albeit at a mutual-admiration level. It was, however, a deeper friendship than he had ever shared with another man. Yet after five years, all William knew about Maynard was what every newspaper reporter knew: his age, where he was brought up, and that he had been to grammar school outside Leatherhead before winning a scholarship to Cambridge.

At one dinner party hosted by a famous novelist and paid for by a glossy magazine, William defended Maynard when a gossip columnist, Meryl Delaware, spoke in a derogatory fashion about his lack of private life and his colourless background. 'My dears, that young man is like one of those awful Russian dolls. You keep on opening it up and out pops another and another, and they are all as *boring* as each other!'

At this point William leaned across the table and asked if perhaps she was confusing Maynard with herself: she appeared to have more in common with a rotund Russian doll than the intelligent young politician.

She sat back and glared hard at him, her mascara-caked eyelashes like tiny spikes. He should perhaps have taken this as a warning: the tentacles of Meryl Delaware's journalism crawled a considerable distance, and what might not do for her society magazine would perhaps find a place in a number of downmarket newspapers. Now Meryl Delaware leaned closer to William. 'Sweetie, you should be careful. Your protégé is *very* cagey about himself. Perhaps one of his layers will be peeled off to reveal a deep and nasty secret . . .' William laughed dismissively, but later that evening Meryl Delaware sidled up to him: 'I meant no offence, dahling. Perhaps the reason he's so hush-hush about his private life is because he's as flawed a human being as the rest of us.'

William gave a stiff smile. 'Speak for yourself, Miss Delaware.'

'Oh, sweetie, don't tell me you won't admit to having flaws?'

William shook his head. 'I doubt my faults would be of any interest to anyone, especially your readers.'

'You'd be surprised, Sir William . . .' And with that she swanned off into a small throng of people.

On his way out, William overheard someone say, 'God help this country if people like that vulgar fool and his protégé can buy their way into the cabinet!'

With clenched fists he walked out of Claridge's into Brook Street and signalled for his chauffeur.

CHAPTER 2

WILLIAM WAS always up and dressed by six, his chauffeur standing by to take him to his first appointment of the morning. Recently he had been planning a takeover of a German electronics company. It was part of a large corporation owned by Baron von Garten, whose steel empire had been in his family for generations. However, it had been hinted that they were selling off their smaller electronics bases. Three previous meetings had been cancelled so William had sent his private plane and an invitation to breakfast at the Connaught. He was determined to get his hands on the prime site, sniffing out, with his fine business acumen, that von Garten was in financial difficulties. He knew that once he had his foot in the door he could make further inroads into the von Garten companies.

Sir William arrived at exactly nine for his breakfast meeting. He had been so busy making calls he had not noticed that one shoelace was undone and in danger of tripping him up as he marched through the Connaught Hotel reception into the dining room. William sat down at a table with a pristine pink cloth and a single rose in a tubular silver vase. He tossed aside the menu and ordered grapefruit, coffee, wholemeal toast and kippers.

He always had the kippers at the Connaught: they were perfect, not too smoked, and grilled with just a dab of butter. Just thinking about his breakfast, his mouth watered and he'd eaten two rounds of toast before his guest sauntered into the dining room.

Baron von Garten was accompanied by a shrewish little man wearing rimless glasses and carrying a soft leather briefcase. William waited, tetchily drumming his fingers on the table, but the Baron made no apology either for being half an hour late or for the previous cancelled meetings. His companion introduced himself as Herr Eric Kramer, the Baron's lawyer.

The elegant Baron said only a few words and left his lawyer to do most of the talking. Kramer explained that the Baron's family had to be a hundred per cent certain that, if they did agree to the sale, their name would not be connected to any of the factory's future products. He gave a blow-by-blow account of the Baron's ancestral history, emphasized how well connected the family still was, and declared that a transaction would be withdrawn at any whisper of scandal. He wanted a confidentiality agreement signed to ensure that any dealings would never be made public.

William was pretty sure that the Baron's Board of Directors had not been asked to approve the deal, so that when the business was sold to William it would be too late for anyone to do anything about it. He guessed that the Baron, for all his family connections, was hurting for cash.

'How much?' he asked softly, and both men leaned forward as if afraid to be overheard.

William shook his head. 'Gentlemen, that is a preposterous asking price,' he said, and withdrew from his own briefcase a detailed document about the property: its location, its present dilapidated condition. It emphasized that William was buying the shell of the old factory to tear down and rebuild; his major interest in the purchase was its location. He wished to turn it into a computer works, offering four hundred jobs, and bringing a team of experts to train the employees to his standards. He showed them a brochure about a similar factory up and running in Paris. As they glanced over it he signalled for the bill.

The deal was concluded quickly. William would arrange a banker's draft to pay a percentage of the fourteen million dollars he had agreed – exactly half the amount they had asked for. They would receive this as soon as all the documents were signed and the surveyors had completed their inspections.

Throughout the entire transaction the Baron had remained aloof, treating William with contempt. It was as if this business deal was beneath him. Perhaps it was no wonder that – if the rumours were well founded – he had got himself into dire financial difficulty.

William had to wait only a moment outside for his Rolls – Arthur was heading towards him immediately. The Baron walked out of the hotel accompanied by a rather well-preserved blonde woman. He introduced his wife frostily, and the Baroness smiled vacantly in William's direction as the doorman hailed a passing taxi. The taxi drew up at the same time as William's gleaming car, but he was already speaking into his mobile so they had no further interaction. Not that William desired any: his mind was already on his next appointment with his bankers.

After lunch Andrew Maynard joined him for coffee.

He seemed relaxed and confident, his face slightly flushed, although this was noticeable only to William, who knew him well enough to realize that Maynard was drinking more than usual. But the warning bells still did not ring and William was merely pleased to see his protégé looking almost handsome: he'd been away in France and the suntan suited him, and he had started taking more interest in his clothes. Maynard was wearing a slim gold watch and the lining of his expensive new suit was of a dark emerald green satin.

The conversation turned to the predilection of the British press for public hounding, and to the most powerful man in British journalism, the newspaper magnate Humphrey Matlock. Matlock's powerful control of virtually every newspaper in the UK made him a formidable opponent. Although William didn't know him, he admired Matlock's tenacious strength of mind. Maynard, however, believed that no single individual should be allowed such control of the national media. William pointed out that as long as Matlock was on their side they had no reason to try to stop him.

'We'll never know exactly which side he's on. And now that everyone is afraid to get on the wrong side of him, whichever party they belong to, he's unstoppable,' Maynard insisted.

'I don't understand why you suddenly feel the need to attack him. As I recall, he's never done anything but enhance your image,' William replied, then stood up to leave – he had a three-thirty appointment.

The next morning at five fifty-five William had had his morning shower and was throwing on his clothes. He

31

caught sight of the documents he'd been reading in bed the night before, and his heart leaped with pleasure. He owned numerous sumptuous homes around the world, all run by a permanent staff and ready for occupancy at any time of the year. But his latest purchase was the jewel in his crown. He was looking forward to showing it off to Maynard. He wouldn't approve, of course: he maintained that one home was enough for anyone. William had bought a small island in the British Virgin Islands. In the sixties it had enjoyed brief fame as a jet-set getaway, and appeared in all the top magazines as one of the most exclusive playgrounds in the world. But in the intervening years the owner had grown infirm and his money had gone on health care rather than upkeep. Now the island was in a state of total disrepair.

William had spectacular plans to make his paradise rise from the ashes like a phoenix. He had bought it at a good price because the refurbishment costs would be astronomical. He invited a select group of designers to tender for the renovations, and took great delight in poring over their Toytown models. It was a huge job and, judging from the way the companies fell over themselves to produce their designs, a desirable one. Maynard would be appalled at the fact that no expense would be spared to make William's dream come true.

It was six thirty and William went downstairs for breakfast. As he sat at the table and shook open that day's *Times*, he smiled to himself. He was where he had always dreamed he would be, right at the top of the world, and he had, as he constantly reminded himself, got there solely by his own hard work. He read the social column: 'Not So Idle Rich' was the headline. William Benedict already had a knighthood they said, how long would it be, at this rate, before he moved into the Upper House? William raised an eyebrow. He'd like that. He'd like to sit in the House of Lords, perhaps become one of the government's advisers ... and maybe, with the help and guidance of Andrew Maynard, it was within his grasp.

Andrew Maynard's cleaner, Mrs Skipper, always arrived promptly at six a.m. She would tidy the house, prepare breakfast and cook an evening meal he could heat when he wanted it. Andrew Maynard was meticulous about his domestic routines. He did not like her to be there all day, or to stay overnight. He hated to work in his study with the sound of vacuuming, or the smell of cooking lingering in the air. By nine he had jogged, showered and breakfasted and had given Mrs Skipper a list of shopping, laundry or dry-cleaning collections. By ten his secretary was installed, the coffee percolating and the newspapers neatly laid out, and Maynard was ready for work, as immaculate and fresh as his small terraced house. Maynard had chosen the house because of its location and politically correct lack of ostentation. William had offered to buy him a larger property, but he had refused point-blank.

Mrs Skipper had been working for Maynard for the past five years. She knew as little about his private life now as she had when she started, and what she did know she had gleaned from the newspapers: when he took her on, she had signed a confidentiality agreement. He had explained that in his profession it was imperative he could trust those closest to him. As far as she knew, Maynard was a man of unimpeachable character, a young man on the threshold of a glittering political career, which even she could see was about to soar.

That morning Mrs Skipper picked up the single bottle of skimmed milk left by the milkman and, frowning, noticed that the bedroom curtains were still drawn. She let herself into number twelve. Mr Maynard was always up by this time so that she could make his bed and collect the dirty laundry. She went into the kitchen, which was as she had left it the evening before. This, too, was unusual: he always put his dirty supper dishes into the sink ready for her to rinse and load into the dishwasher. As she put the milk into the fridge, she noticed that the evening meal she had prepared yesterday was still in its tin-foil-covered dish. Mrs Skipper began to unbutton her coat, looking around for the note that was left each day on the kitchen table.

There was no note. She hung up her coat and fetched her apron, then walked back down the narrow hallway towards the stairs. She looked up, listening, wondering if her employer was upstairs in the bathroom – perhaps something had made him late for his morning jog and he was still out. Maybe he was ill. 'Mr Maynard?' she called tentatively.

The house was eerily silent – she was used to hearing the radio or television news when she came in. She began to mount the stairs, pausing midway to call his name again, but there was no reply.

His bedroom was dark and the bed had not been slept in. The bathroom door was open, and a suit, shirt and underwear were laid neatly across the bed. She went back out into the hall and tapped on his study door. It swung open, revealing the tidy desk, a stack of memos and mail lined up by the bank of telephones. She pulled the cord to open the curtains and, in the light, looked at the desk for some kind of sign. A yellow Post-it had been stuck to his blotter with a phone number. His address book was open and another sticker on the open page bore the same number and, underlined, an odd message: 'Call this number. Do not go into the bathroom'.

More worried by the minute, Mrs Skipper returned to the kitchen. Now she noticed that the back door was ajar. She opened it wide and looked out into the garden, which was empty. Mrs Skipper closed the door and locked it. It was then that she felt the drip of water from the ceiling above. She looked up and listened. Maynard's bathroom was directly above the kitchen.

Mrs Skipper went upstairs again and listened at the closed bathroom door. Now she could hear water running softly and, looking down saw the creeping stain growing darker as it seeped into the carpet and edged into the bedroom. She turned the bathroom door handle. It was not locked, and she pushed it open and froze in shock at the sight of Maynard's body, partly submerged, and his hands, floating, with deep gashes at the wrists from which blood still trailed.

'Call this number. Do not go into the bathroom,' the yellow note had said, each word heavily underlined. Mrs Skipper moved back into the office, reached for the phone and dialled.

The telephone's shrill ring woke William from his reverie. He waited a beat, hoping his housekeeper would pick it up, but eventually got up and answered it himself. 'Yes,' he snapped.

It was an hysterical woman, babbling incomprehensibly.

'Who is this?' he said coldly. It was William's personal phone. Only a handful of people had the number; this woman must have misdialled. Then William heard Maynard's name. He tried to slow the woman down. 'I can't understand what you're saying,' he said, and told her to take a deep breath.

'He's dead, sir. Please come.'

'Has there been an accident?' William asked. The phone felt clammy in his hand. When he realized what she was telling him, his heart lurched. 'Listen to me! Do nothing until I get there, do you understand. Wait until I see you. Do not call anyone until I get there.'

His heart was still thudding as he drove from his four-storey house in The Boltons towards Ladbroke Grove.

When he saw Maynard, he became icy calm. Mrs Skipper was sitting at the kitchen table below. He could hear her sobbing. She had refused to accompany him up the stairs, so William was forced to confront the grotesque sight of Andrew Maynard's body alone. His first reaction was of stunned horror, as if the scene before him was some sick theatrical set-up. Nothing he knew about Maynard had prepared him for this. He didn't touch the body, but looked down into the open eyes, the dark hair floating around the head, and reached forward to turn off the taps. Maynard's blood had stained the water a soft shell pink. The cuts in his wrists were deep and blood had sprayed down the bathroom tiles. Beside the bath was an empty gin bottle, and an overturned crystal glass with a slice of lemon still resting at the bottom.

William went to Maynard's study, pocketed the note with his phone number on it, and looked around for Maynard's diary, address book and any personal papers. He placed them in his own briefcase, and searched for a suicide note before returning to the bedroom. He found it partly hidden beneath the bathtub. It was sodden from the overflowing water and the ink was blurred, which made the few hastily scribbled lines hard to decipher, but William could see it was addressed to him.

Dear William,
  I have no ambition left, just heartbreak and terrible longing.
  I am sorry,
  Andrew

William read and re-read it. It made little sense to him. What heartbreak, what longing had made Andrew take his own life? He felt numb and confused, as if he still could not believe what had happened. Eventually he called the police and sat waiting for their arrival, studying the note as it dried in his hands. Maynard's death would create a media frenzy, and one part of his brain was already wondering who would be the best man to hire for damage control.

Five hours later William returned home. He had his own press office prepare a statement, but no matter what he said, Maynard's death would cause one hell of a scandal. William poured himself a brandy, retired to his drawing room and started checking through the papers he had removed from Maynard's study. He had made no mention of them to the police, but they had taken the suicide note. They had asked if it was

Maynard's handwriting, and William had nodded, but in reality it was so smudged it was hard to tell. The large bundle of personal letters he placed to one side as he flicked through the first leatherbound desk diary filled with appointments, then Maynard's private diary.

He couldn't believe he had been so blind, that he had failed to detect this other side of Maynard. It confused and angered him, yet he found the details of the man's bizarre, hidden life strangely compelling: the neat, meticulous handwriting, the lists of names, lovers, descriptions of sexual practices and a detailed account of monies paid out for years on sexual gratification. One name, Justin Chalmers, featured more often than most. This man had accompanied Maynard on trips to Paris, Vienna, Jamaica and Morocco. Maynard's bank statements recorded payments to Chalmers; large sums over several years. William wondered if he had been blackmailing Maynard. What else could account for the thousands of pounds Maynard had spent on him? What else could account for the lists of fictional companies, whose names he had used to redirect campaign funds to a bank account in France? The recipient was always J. Chalmers. Was Justin Chalmers the person Maynard 'longed for'? Had Chalmers broken his heart?

It was lunchtime before William moved through to his office and checked the answerphone. There were twenty-four messages, but he felt disinclined to play them. It was imperative that he found Justin Chalmers. Of all the names in Maynard's diary, this one had leaped out as the most dangerous. Slowly William punched in the number and waited. The phone rang three times, then an answerphone clicked on and a soft, drawling voice announced, 'Hi, I'm afraid I am unable to come

38

to the phone right now. Please leave a message and the time and date you called and . . .' there was a pause, followed by a laugh '. . . if you're lucky I'll get back to you.'

At two fifteen, William let in his damage-control expert, Myers Summers. 'Well, this is a fucking mess all round, isn't it? You know the world and its mother are trying to contact you, old boy?' Summers shrugged off his coat.

'I guessed as much, but I'm not speaking to anyone until we've sorted something out. Come and have a drink.'

'Not for me, thanks, if we're to concentrate on making sure you escape the flak.' Summers sat down. 'Right, let's have it from the top, shall we?'

It was just after midnight when Summers left, by which time William was flushed with brandy – not drunk, but he had consumed more than usual.

Summers's parting shot was that it was imperative to get the boyfriend, or whoever he was, tucked away and out of public grasp no matter the cost. Especially as, according to the diary, he would have been the last person to have been seen with Maynard. He might even have had an argument with him that had resulted in Maynard slashing his wrists.

'I suppose he did slash them himself?' Summers asked, as if it was just an afterthought.

'How the hell would I know?' snapped William.

'Well, let's hope he did. It's murky enough as it is. If murder was mentioned, it would really whip up a frenzy. Is this Justin fella around at all?'

William shrugged. He obviously had been, and with Maynard on the night he died. But where was he now?

As the police did not have access to Maynard's private diaries, William was confident that he could deal with Justin Chalmers. Money, he had learned over years of having it, always had the desired effect on a certain type of person. He had no doubt that Chalmers could be bribed. He was about to turn off the lights in his study when he checked the time. It was two thirty. He hesitated, then picked up the phone and dialled, leaning back against the desk, staring at his brown brogues. There was no immediate reply, and he was about to hang up when a sleepy voice answered, 'Yes?'

'I called and left a message earlier today,' William said, then had to clear his throat as he was so nervous. 'Is that Justin Chalmers?'

'I believe so . . .' came the reply, followed by a yawn.

'I need to see you.'

'Really? You want to come over now?'

'No, in the morning, early. This is a most urgent matter, which concerns a mutual acquaintance. I cannot discuss it over the telephone.'

'Mmm, well, come whenever you want, and . . .' there was a pause, then what sounded like a giggle '. . . I can't wait.' The phone went dead. At no time had Chalmers even asked who was calling.

Exhausted, William went to bed and was asleep as soon as his head hit the pillow. He slept, untroubled by dreams, but his serenity was not to last long.

CHAPTER 3

I T WAS six a.m. when William drove into the mews. As yet the news of Maynard's death had not broken: it had not made the previous night's programmes, but there was no doubt that it would be this morning's main item. William arrived at Chalmers's address in Kensington. Flower-tubs and urns decorated the doorsteps of the row of pretty two-storey mews cottages. If he lived in that sort of house, in this part of town, William thought, Chalmers must be pretty well off. But as he reached the end of the street, the houses began to look seedier, obviously leased. Number thirty-two had the obligatory doorstep tub, but the plants were dead and the front-door paint was peeling. The bell was out of order, so William knocked. He did not have to wait more than a few moments before the door opened. A tall, tanned young man beckoned him in. He was wearing a pristine white T-shirt with pale washed-out denim jeans. His bare feet were encased in velvet monogrammed slippers and he wore a heavy gold bracelet on his right wrist. The interior was dark, all the curtains still drawn, but the furniture was antique and the carpets, though threadbare, were good-quality Turkish. Velvet cushions were scattered over the floor, and there was a sofa with stuffing protruding from its arms. 'Justin Chalmers? Sir William Benedict,' William said, and thrust out his hand.

The young man glanced down at it and, without a word, went through a bead curtain into what William supposed was the kitchen, from where the smell of coffee emerged. William stood uneasily in the middle of the room.

Minutes later the young man reappeared with a tray and put it down on an Indian brass coffee-table. 'Do sit down. I rarely entertain at this house, so excuse the mess. You obviously have something of . . .' He swallowed the word 'urgency', then smiled, and gestured to the coffee pot. 'Black or white?'

'Black, please.'

William sat gingerly on the edge of the sofa. 'Thank you for agreeing to see me.'

'I'm intrigued by how you got hold of my number and address.' Chalmers handed William a cup.

He was tall, at least six foot two, with a lean torso. He had exceptionally blond hair, not the same colour or texture as William's but naturally thick and streaked by the sun, well cut and worn quite long, touching his shoulders. He had penetrating wide-set eyes of so vivid a blue that the whites seemed brilliant. The deep lines at the side of his eyes and mouth did not detract from his overall youthfulness, but he was, William guessed, in his early thirties.

As he passed a chipped porcelain cup and saucer, William noticed that his fingers were long, slender and as tanned as his chiselled face. His nails were clean and manicured and he had a large embossed gold ring on the little finger of his left hand.

'You needed to see me urgently,' he said, 'so let's not waste time. What's the problem?' He curled up on a cushion opposite William, and looked at him over the rim of his cup. He took a sip, then tossed his hair back from his face.

William watched him carefully as he began. 'You know Andrew Maynard?'

'Yes, I do.'

'He was found dead yesterday morning.' Chalmers showed no flicker of emotion. 'With his wrists slit in his bathtub.'

'Really? Sorry, I forgot to ask, do you take sugar?'

'No, thank you.' William took a sip of coffee. 'I'm aware that you had an ongoing relationship with him.'

'So?' Chalmers sank back into his chair and blew on his coffee. 'There are biscuits too, if you'd like one.' William was alarmed by the young man's response. This was not how it was meant to go. Chalmers pulled a face. 'So you found him, did you? Must have been unpleasant. A lot of blood, I suppose? Cutting your wrists sends a massive spray.'

'You saw him last Thursday. What time did you leave?'

There was a pause as Chalmers gazed intently at William. 'You seem very well informed.' He leaned back and closed his eyes. 'I went round at about seven thirty in the evening. I was having dinner elsewhere, but Andrew wanted to see me, so I obliged. I left about an hour later. Around eight thirty, perhaps a quarter to nine.'

'Did you have an argument?'

'I don't think that's any of your business.'

William placed his cup down and leaned forward. 'You mind if I call you Justin?'

43

'I don't mind if you call me Jack the Ripper.'

William talked across Chalmer's laughter. 'You see, Justin, the press will hound you if they discover what was going on between you and Andrew Maynard. I am aware that he paid you large sums of money.'

Chalmers stared. William was unnerved by his assurance and turned away. He chose his words carefully. 'It would be preferable, Justin, if your relationship was not made public.'

'I have no desire to discuss my relationship with Andrew. We were good friends and I was very fond of him, although not as exclusively as he wanted.'

'Did he kill himself because of you?' William blurted out.

Chalmers shrugged. 'I have no idea. He seemed quite together when I saw him but, then, one can never tell another person's real feelings, especially when that person is a politician.' He laughed, softly, leaned back and stretched like a cat, his sexuality and sensuality filling the room.

William felt distinctly uneasy in his presence. Suddenly doubts started to filter through his mind. *Could* it have been murder?

As if reading William's mind, the other man leaned forward. 'I didn't kill him. I can tell you're thinking it's a possibility, but I didn't. He was too useful and, as you so rightly pointed out, I received a considerable amount of money from him and hoped to continue doing so.'

William stayed another fifteen minutes, in which time he agreed that a sum of money would be paid into Chalmers's bank account on the condition that he left London immediately and did not speak to the press or anyone else about his relationship with Andrew

Maynard. The young man did not quibble over the amount, but accepted a hundred thousand pounds immediately and said he would be on the next flight. William was relieved that the negotiations had gone so smoothly, but as he shook Chalmers's hand, he felt the man's fingers grip his own.

'You have his diaries?'

'Yes.'

'Do the police know you removed property from the scene?'

'No. They will be destroyed. No one will know of their contents.'

'Ah, yes.' Chalmers sighed and smiled simultaneously. 'But *I* know . . . and I also know I could make a lot more than a paltry hundred grand in one exclusive to any number of tabloids.' He let the veiled threat hang in the air briefly then continued, 'Because I *did* care for poor old Andrew, I'll accept your offer – but I'd appreciate it if you remember you're getting off very lightly.'

'I have nothing to worry about,' William said, removing his hand from Chalmers's grasp.

'Really? Then I've misjudged you, Sir William.' He crossed his arms and propped himself against the door-frame. 'Look at the facts. You have come here personally and you have taken possession of his diaries. It can only mean one thing: you are worried that Andrew Maynard's private life might contaminate your own.' Chalmers chuckled to himself. 'After all, you did finance his career and, knowing the gutter-press, they will dig deeply into your . . .' he snorted before continuing, making speech marks in the air '. . . "predilections". Perhaps they will assume that you too are a "friend of

45

Dorothy" as they say. They may force you to come out.'

He smiled at William's discomfort, but his eyes showed no signs of amusement. William grasped the subtext and reluctantly upped the kiss-off price to a quarter of a million. It was accepted.

William drove back to The Boltons in a fury. He didn't mind spending the money – that had not irked him – it was the arrogance of the man, the confidence with which he had played his hand so perfectly. Justin Chalmers had class and William knew it. No matter how rich he was, he would never be able to match that sort of man's aristocratic air, and he felt sure that that had not been the last time he would see him.

The crisp morning made William feel a bit better. The traffic in Park Lane was still moving freely, enabling the gleaming Rolls to move swiftly down and round Hyde Park Corner. On occasions, William enjoyed driving himself instead of being chauffeured and already he felt more confident, as if the power he was wielding over the car was somehow mirroring the control he had taken over his life. Two hundred and fifty thousand pounds was chicken feed to a man as wealthy as William, and he had been prepared to pay a lot more. He would clear up this unfortunate Maynard business quickly, and that would be that. A minor setback. He slotted a CD into the stereo and drummed his fingers on the steering-wheel as Beethoven exploded from the speakers.

As he drove towards The Boltons, his mood lifted even higher. He had a full day ahead: a luncheon with Lady Thorn to discuss a charity benefit, then back-to-back business meetings for the rest of the afternoon before dinner with a senior member of the Royal Family to discuss sponsorship for the Royal Horse Show. As he mulled over the day ahead he succeeded in putting Maynard's suicide to the back of his mind.

However, as he turned into The Boltons, it all came flooding back. The roadway outside his house was swarming with reporters and photographers, and a TV news team was setting up its cameras. William was forced to slow to a crawling pace as the hordes converged on his car. The flash of cameras made his eyes water, and there was a sudden burst of voices as they recognized him and attempted to stop the car to interview him there and then. 'Sir William, SIR WILLIAM . . . *Daily Mail* . . . *Daily Telegraph* . . . the *Sun*.' They surrounded the car, shoving microphones towards him, and he almost ran over a few as he attempted to get into his driveway. The electronic gates half opened, but the journalists took that as an invitation to move further on to his property.

He lowered the window, and barked, 'You are trespassing. Please move out of the way of the car. *Move away from the car*. No comment. *No comment*. Get out of my way, please.'

Not until the gardener, the valet and Michael, his secretary, came out did William try to step out of the car. As the gates closed behind him, he saw his employees trying to remove two men who were attempting to squeeze past them.

Michael opened the driver's door and gestured for him to hurry inside. 'We've been inundated, sir. The phones are ringing, the fax machines haven't stopped, and there are people trying to get over the back wall.'

47

Inside the elegant hallway, William headed straight for his study. 'Call the bloody police, Michael. They're trespassing, for God's sake. Legally they can't put a foot in the driveway.'

'I know, sir, but they've been out there since you left this morning. We have contacted the police and they—'

'Call the Chief Superintendent. No, get me Commander Jameson. I'll talk to him.' Michael bustled around the study, stacking documents on the desk. Every single phone was ringing. 'Turn the bloody phones off! This is ridiculous. Get Mrs Fuller to bring me some coffee and—' William snatched at one of the telephones and barked into the receiver. 'Yes?'

It was an irate Myers Summers. 'Where, in Christ's name, have you been? I've been calling since seven o'clock. Have you seen the papers?'

'Not yet. I've been trying to get rid of the press. They're like hornets outside.'

'Well, read them and call me straight back.'

William took half an hour to get through every newspaper. By the time he had finished, Myers Summers was sitting in his study.

'You're telling me you went to see this Chalmers in the flesh?'

'Yes.'

Summers rested his head in hands. 'Did anyone see you?'

'No. Why are you getting into such a state?'

Summers took a deep breath. 'This is serious, William. You walk off with diaries and documents. You

48

spend – how long at Maynard's place before you call the police? You then pay some fucking fruit half a million—'

'Quarter of a million.'

'Why? What the fuck for? I mean, who is he?'

'The last person to see Maynard, that's who. And he's a screamer so I got rid of him.'

'Do you think he killed Maynard?'

'No, Maynard cut his own wrists, Myers, with—'

'Yeah, yeah, I know, with an open cut-throat razor, silver and bone handle, inscription from you! Now, it seems to be a bone of contention that the cuts were deep, and to both wrists. Apparently that's odd. If you slash one open it's pretty tough to slash the other. So we won't be certain it was suicide until after the post-mortem. He could have a six-inch blade shoved up his arse for all you know, and this poofter might have done it! And you go round personally and pay him off!' He sighed and flopped back in his chair. 'Why?'

'To minimize the risk of scandal I bought his silence.'

'Are you *joking*?' Summers sat forward again. 'Don't you *see* the implications of that?'

'Quite frankly, no, I do not. Right now the "poof-ter", as you call him, is probably on his way to Paris. Gone. Finished with.'

Myers Summers closed his eyes. 'Well, I'll have to find out more about him. You're sure no one else saw you visit him?'

'Certain. I told you, it was six o'clock in the morning, there wasn't a soul around. Just milkmen, newspaper boys . . .'

'All right. Now, yesterday, did Maynard's cleaner see you remove anything?'

49

'No, she wasn't in the room.'

'Well, that's something. And she called you as soon as she discovered the body?'

'Yes, there was a memo stuck on his desk telling her to call my number.'

'What? He left a memo? With some kind of instruction?'

Suddenly William found himself blushing: it hadn't occurred to him how strange it was that Maynard should leave a sticker on his desk for his housekeeper to find, with William's private number and instructions not to enter the bathroom. Of course it was suicide. Maynard must have known exactly what he was doing.

'Come on, man, was there anything else this woman might have seen you remove?'

William was irked by the way Summers was speaking to him. 'Listen to me, Myers, I took the personal items because there were details of how much he had been forking out to this guy and it was a lot of money. Whether it was blackmail or not is immaterial now. Chalmers is out of the loop. I was just trying to protect Maynard's reputation, and mine and the Party's. He'd have been misappropriating funds, for Chrissakes.'

Myers Summers got to his feet and walked round the room as he spoke. 'All right, then, let me put it to you another way. His bank will have particulars, won't they? His bookkeeper, accountant. Maybe friends of this Justin Chalmers character knew about the money. Maybe there are other Maynard pick-ups in other diaries – last year's for instance. The police will be looking into everything.' He laid a hand on the mantelpiece and turned to face the desk. 'Can't you see, Sir William? This is a huge story. I mean, the man was supposed to be some great political hope, and he's climbing the ladder like a trapeze artist when he tops himself because he's heartbroken about some bloody poof. How much sleaze do you need to make a juicy front page?'

Myers pulled at his pinstriped waistcoat, then his tie, then his jacket, as if to calm himself. 'Okay, Sir William, I'll tell you what'll happen. You give a statement – I'll get my people to write it for you – and in it you say nothing about the diaries or documents you took. Nothing. You happened to be there as you had a meeting scheduled. After finding the body you were deeply distressed and needed a few moments to collect yourself before calling the police. I'll talk to the house-keeper. I'll also run a trace on Chalmers. List the other names you found in the diaries and I'll give them the once-over as well.'

'Is all this necessary?' William asked.

Myers Summers picked up his bulging briefcase: he was already running late for his next appointment. 'If Andrew Maynard was murdered, then it's abso-fucking-lutely necessary and even if he committed suicide, drunk or drugged up, whatever, it's still gonna be headlines for weeks because the press will want to find out who his boyfriends were, what his relationship was with every male he knew, in fact. And you can bet they'll come after you. You found him dead, you financed him to the hilt, and it's public knowledge that he's your mentor when it comes to public-speaking. Everyone knows you scratch each other's backs. What they'll wonder is just what else you've mutually scratched.'

'It's OK, Myers. I get the picture. But no one's going to think *that* of me.'

Myers Summers raised an eyebrow. 'They'll believe

anything, if they're told it often enough. Isn't that why you have a publicity agent?' He rested his hand on the door-handle. 'I'm just warning you, as one of the mega-rich, you are just the type the tabloids will go for. The bigger they are, the harder they fall. And all those little people you may have forgotten treading on when you were climbing up will come crawling out of the woodwork.' He paused and faced William. 'Just for the record, were you having a scene with Maynard?'

William gasped. '*What?*'

'Are you queer?'

William sucked in his breath, shocked. '*No, I am not.* And how dare you speak to me like that!'

'Well, that's the best news so far. I'll deal with it,' Myers said, and with that he opened the door to the hall. 'I'll be in touch shortly – if I make it through that mob and live to tell the tale.'

William remained in his study. Up to now, he would have described himself as unshockable; a tough man who had made it to the top by his own hard graft but who now enjoyed rubbing shoulders with the British aristocracy. For the first time, he realized the depth in him of a naïvety he had never previously suspected. He checked his watch and buzzed for his secretary.

Michael scooted in. 'Yes, Sir William?'

'I'm due at lunch. Can you call the Ritz and—'

'Oh, I'm sorry, Sir William, Lady Thorn called, but I didn't want to interrupt your meeting with Mr Summers. She sends her apologies, but has come down with flu.'

William sat down behind his desk. 'Perhaps, under the circumstances, it's a good thing.'

'Yes, sir, I've got sheets of messages. There are also

numerous faxes, e-mails and an urgent call from Super-intendent Hudson, Metropolitan Police. He's left his home number and direct line.'

Michael left the study and William unlocked the drawer that contained Maynard's business-appointment diary, and wondered why Myers hadn't asked to see it. It soon dawned on him that such a devious man wouldn't want to touch it. If the story did get out, Myers could say he knew nothing about any diaries being removed. William's eyes travelled to his wall-safe, which held Maynard's personal diary. It was as if he could see the red leatherbound cover through the steel door. It was dangerous to keep it, but he could not bring himself to destroy it.

Later, Myers Summers phoned William to give him details of the post-mortem: Andrew Maynard had died from loss of blood due to both arteries being severed on right and left wrist. Tests showed that his blood contained a vast quantity of alcohol and cocaine. There were no signs of physical violence. It was determined that he was a practising homosexual but no traces of semen were found apart from his own. His naked body was devoid of pubic hair and smothered with Johnson's baby oil. Myers hesitated to draw breath. 'They also found numerous bottles of pills. You name any kind of speed and your friend had it, plus five grams of cocaine. Oh, and another tasty morsel that will, no doubt, be fucking leaked is that Maynard was suffering from geni-tal herpes.'

William couldn't listen to any more. He was sweat-ing. Only the announcement of a Third World War would knock this lot off the front page.

'The housekeeper's blabbed,' Myers went on. 'She's

told the cops about a diary and drawers full of letters and that you were the only person with access to them before they arrived.'

'I suppose the police will want to question me,' William observed.

''Course they will, but wait, just fasten your seatbelt. So far strong-arm tactics have kept it all under wraps in case it was murder, but it'll all hit the fan tonight. So far the press have only had the most meagre details. They only know he died at home. But tonight they'll have the titillating details. You know anything about his family?'

'No, I don't. His parents are dead. I believe he had a sister, but she died in some car accident. There's just an aunt in Bournemouth, as far as I know.'

'Ah, well. No doubt we'll know a lot more by tonight.'

William shrugged. 'You sound very sure. Why?'

'All right then,' Summers grunted. 'How about this? Someone has managed to get photographs of the body from the mortuary and some other bloody hack paper has been sent photographs of Maynard dancing in some gay night-club in Morocco, so Christ only knows what else they'll get from some bloody perverted bastard trying to make a few quid.'

'Well, what's all that got to do with me? I financed him. I didn't go down the Palais with him, dancing on a Saturday night.'

Summers hesitated. 'We only have your word for that.'

William was starting to get angry. 'I've told you, Myers, I knew nothing about his pervy life till yesterday, and I will make a statement to that effect and hand it

54

over to the police. I've already spoken to them anyway – at his house before I left.'

'That won't satisfy the papers,' Summers was impatient. 'You were closely associated in life so you will be in death.'

'So what do you suggest I do?'

'Give a statement and, thinking about it, perhaps it'd be better in your own words.'

'You fucking said you'd write it!' William said angrily.

'Maybe I did, but standing back a bit, I think it should come from you. You knew him better than anyone else.'

'What's that supposed to mean?'

'One minute you were calling him the political saviour of the millennium, next he's pictured dancing with twelve-year-old boys in Morocco! You work it out. I can't be involved.'

'Can't or won't? Which is it, Myers?'

There was a pause. 'My wrists are tied.' Summers gave a humourless laugh. 'Sorry, under the circumstances, that was a rather crass thing to say.' He continued, 'I've been warned off you, William. I'm sorry, but a word of advice. For God's sake keep schtum about the diaries and stuff. Burn them, get rid of them, deny ever seeing them. And don't mention the note. Why did Maynard want *you* to find him, before the police? And don't mention this Chalmers bloke either.' There was a pause, this time at William's end. 'You still there? Hello? Hello?'

William had hung up. He'd never liked the squint-eyed son-of-a-bitch anyway. It was just that he was so well connected. Well, fuck him! William hadn't become one of the wealthiest men in England without being able to take care of some jumped-up journalist – or a pack of them come to that. And if they wanted to dig around in his past, let them. He didn't have anything to hide.

'Michael,' he bellowed. 'Call a press conference.'

'For when, sir?'

'First thing in the morning. Meanwhile I want you to cut out every newspaper article on Maynard and record every piece of television news coverage to date, even if it takes all night.'

'It's all over the Internet,' Michael said nervously.

'Then print out whatever anybody's saying. I want to read it all, no matter what it says. Is it bad?'

Michael nodded and his lips trembled slightly. 'Some of it's downright sick. Er . . . will you be arranging his funeral?'

'What?'

'Andrew Maynard's funeral, sir.'

William slumped into his chair. 'Yes, yes – well, you sort it out, I can't think about that right now. Go on, do what you have to, no expense spared, but keep it simple.'

Michael left the room, as William lowered his head into his hands. He had been too preoccupied, too shocked for it all to have sunk in. He had been blocking out the emotional impact of losing a man he had grown to admire and love like a son, and now the floodgates opened. The tears trickled down his cheeks, as he murmured his protégé's name in despair and bewilderment.

He tried to hide his tears when Michael tapped and re-entered. The police were waiting to see him.

William blew his nose, wiped his face and nodded for Michael to let them in. He stood up, hand outstretched to meet Superintendent Hudson and Detective Inspector Joan Fromton. He offered them tea or coffee but they refused, seating themselves in front of his desk on two hard-backed chairs that were usually placed against the wall.

The interview lasted two and a half hours. They questioned William in detail as to how he found the body, what the housekeeper had said, why she had called him before contacting a doctor or the police. William had no need to lie. He just did not mention that a note had suggested she call him: it was feasible that she would have anyway as he was so closely associated to Maynard.

Then came the obvious question; 'Just how closely?' With dignity William dismissed from their minds any notion that he was homosexual. All he was, and all he had been for the past few years, was a friend and business associate. There had been nothing more between them than friendship and admiration. He had had no inkling of Maynard's private life.

He was asked whether he had removed any items from Maynard's property and he said that he had not.

When questioned about Maynard's associates, he again extricated himself well by saying that, as he had already stated, he did not know of Maynard's private life so did not know any of his close male or female friends. The officers were polite, at times appearing genuine in their sympathy with his grief. Twice William came close to tears as he repeated that he had not really taken in the loss of someone he had greatly admired, and felt sad that, despite their friendship, Maynard had not spoken to him about his depression. This led the officers to ask William if he had been aware that Maynard used certain substances, and that a substantial amount of cocaine had been found in his house. William said he had not. The interview eventually ended with William admitting, 'It is hard, I suppose, for you to understand how someone like me could be foolish enough not to see what Andrew was, but I didn't. You see, I cared for him deeply, as a father would. He was special to me, but now I have to face the awful truth that I never really knew him at all.'

The Superintendent thanked William, and said that he would have Maynard's note sent to him as soon as it could be released. Hudson had a habit of appearing to dismiss a subject, then hopping back to it. 'You recognized the writing on the note as Maynard's, is that correct?'

William nodded.

'It was very blurred from the water, but you still believe it to be Maynard's own handwriting?'

William's nerves were ragged. 'Yes, I do. Is there any reason for me not to? He had very distinct, looped writing.'

'Yes, we are aware of that. But the letter was submerged in water so it's quite difficult to ascertain for sure . . . That said, the forensic experts believe it to be Maynard's.'

The policeman assured him that foul play was not suspected and offered William his condolences. When he was ushering them from the room, Joan Fromton asked if William would please contact them should any of Andrew Maynard's associates approach him; they would still like to make enquiries about the drugs discovered at Maynard's home. Then she threw William. 'Does the name Justin Chalmers mean anything to you, Sir William?'

William knew that he had flushed but he shook his head. 'I can't say that it does, may I ask why?'

'He is the main beneficiary in Andrew Maynard's will. He had no family, but no doubt Mr Maynard's lawyers will be able to assist us. Thank you very much for your time.'

William gave a long, weary sigh. Chalmers worried him greatly but, as the police had said, there were no criminal charges under review. But yet again, just as he went to shake the Superintendent's hand, he felt the carpet tugged from beneath him.

'Sir, if this case had proved to be other than suicide, and you had removed items from the deceased's premises, it would be a criminal offence. I am sure you are aware of that. I take your word for it that you did not remove any such items such as diaries, private letters . . .'

There was cold appraisal in the balding Hudson's hazel eyes. He knew William must have taken a diary, perhaps even letters, and he also understood why. These society types were all the same; their sole priority was saving their own backsides, and it infuriated him that he had been ordered to clear up the investigation as quickly and with as little scandal as possible. He knew that William was somehow caught up in this and given half a chance, Hudson would come down on him like the proverbial ton of bricks.

'Thank you for your time, sir,' the Superintendent said as he left, ushering his inspector ahead of him. He kept his head down as he walked out into the street beyond the high barred gates. The vultures hovering there with their cameras and microphones, screamed for him to stop and say a few words.

'No comment. No comment.'

A uniformed officer stood by the plain patrol car, the door open. Joan settled in the back seat, Hudson in the front with the uniformed driver.

'What did you think of him?' she asked, checking over her notes.

'Not a lot. Lying through his teeth about the "no items removed from victim's premises". He certainly had time enough to clean the place up. He's probably scared his own sexual peccadilloes will get out – every politician's hiding something or other.'

'He's not a politician, though. He was Maynard's benefactor. He's rich as Croesus.' She paused. 'Didn't you think he reacted strangely to Justin Chalmers's name? I wonder why.'

'Justin Chalmers . . .' the Superintendent mused. 'You ran a check on him, right?'

'Yes, sir, clean as a whistle. Neighbours say he keeps himself to himself – not at home much, apparently. He has a sister who visits regularly. She has some sort of psychiatric complaint. I think he looks after her pretty well. Oh, and he's openly gay, which explains Maynard's generous will. Probably partners.'

'Oh, well, there you have it. That probably explains Sir William's reaction then. Maybe he had a scene with him too and doesn't want it to come out. Half of the society set are in the closet, not that it concerns me.'

Joan smiled. She'd liked Sir William, and felt sorry

for him, but she said nothing more as they drove past the flashing photographers. She often wondered what they did with all the photographs they took, and laughed to herself.

'What's so funny?'

'Oh, I just wondered if they'd caught my best side.'

He grinned. 'Don't let it concern you. They're not interested in us – we're not rich or famous enough. Now, if it had been a murder, we might have made the front page departing from Sir William Benedict's mansion!'

CHAPTER 4

O N THAT evening's news programmes William did not come across well. Blustering, he denied any knowledge of Maynard's sexual predilections, and refused to be drawn into any discussions on weird sexual practices. He said he was saddened by the death of a friend, and hoped people would remember Andrew Maynard as a young, highly intelligent, well-meaning man. When asked whether he had removed any items from Maynard's home, he remained silent.

The press had a field day. They printed exclusive interviews with Maynard's cleaner, Mrs Skipper, and his secretary, Sara Vickers. Both women spoke of Maynard's private life in a way that was easy to embroider. William's next few days were beyond his worst nightmare. The affair mushroomed and dragged in people from under every stone of his own past. A photograph of William with his arm around Maynard appeared on the front page, an innocent photograph, with four other people cut from it to make it appear over-affectionate, if not loving. Headlines screamed, 'GAY MP'S SUICIDE', and further details of Maynard's life appeared, more photographs of him taken in seedy nightclubs, and on beaches. Where they came from was a mystery, but they kept appearing, and William constantly featured in one doctored picture or another. The trouble the press took to make it appear that William was the lover over whom Maynard had slashed his wrists was beyond belief. His first wife, Lady Margaret Pettigrew, gave an exclusive interview for one of the Sunday colour supplements headlined 'My Husband – The Adulterer'. She had waited twenty years for her revenge and she took it with relish.

William's humiliation did not end with her revelations. His second wife, Katherine, the mother of his two children, jumped on the bandwagon with equal enthusiasm. It was as if the two women had got together to destroy him. In a double-page spread in one of the tabloids, Katherine painted him as a mean, vicious, brutal man who spent his days trawling the streets for nubile flesh, neglecting his two children in favour of prostitutes.

Every day brought another outrageous defamatory onslaught, another person creeping out of the woodwork to tell their story. Maynard's suicide was beginning to take second place to the hounding of William, as if his death had simply acted as a catalyst. William could do nothing but look on with stunned helplessness. None of the sexual slanders was true, but the fact that he had indeed used a few girls made it impossible to sue.

In any case his lawyer, Brian Sutherland, appeared frightened for his own reputation. William felt as if he was hitting his head against a brick wall. 'For God's sake, yes! *Yes*, I've hired a few call-girls over the years, but who hasn't? It doesn't make me some insatiable sex addict! If I'm not a homosexual, I'm a lusting pervert.

Something has to be done to stop them printing these lies about me.'

Sutherland was one of the most respected lawyers in England. He warned that if, as William had admitted, he had occasionally used call-girls, then to bring a massive and costly lawsuit against someone as powerful as Humphrey Matlock, the proprietor of the newspapers, would end in catastrophe: '. . . the reason being, William, that any one of the girls you've known in an intimate way could be tracked down and offered money to refute these denials of yours. And as you have admitted, albeit in the privacy of my office, that you have occasionally used the services of certain illegal agencies for, ah, intimate massages and so on, you could not swear otherwise on oath.'

William interrupted, 'But no more than any other man has, for fuck's sake. Name me anyone you know who hasn't,' he snapped.

'That, old fellow, is not the issue, because you are not "any other man" but Sir William Benedict. So I suggest, and this is my best advice, that you lie low and ignore the slanders. Look at Jeffrey Archer! For God's sake, don't antagonize them, just let it blow over.'

'But it's a bloody outrage,' William stormed.

'I admit that it is,' said the suave Sutherland, in mellifluous tones as he wandered around his elegant Mayfair office, 'but you must look at it in a logical way, old man. The fact is that you don't want any of these women with whom you have had sexual relationships, albeit infrequently, to testify against you. And as they will want their fifteen minutes of fame while Humphrey Matlock is known for cheque-book journalism, I really do think you should just let it blow over.'

The meeting was at an end, and William knew he should heed Sutherland's warning. He agreed angrily to do nothing, but he couldn't help wishing for a minute alone with Humphrey Matlock so that he could swing a punch at him.

The final straw came the following weekend, when yet another Matlock-owned newspaper gave centre-page coverage to interviews with William's children, who said they hated him for betraying their mother. He noted bitterly that neither made any reference to the substantial allowances he made to them, way over what he was obliged to pay, and that he maintained the entire family in a luxurious lifestyle.

Desperate to stem the flow, William tried to contact his ex-wives. Margaret refused to speak to him, and when he threatened Katherine with reducing his maintenance payments to the amount stipulated by the courts, he was met with screams of 'Do that, you bastard, and I'll make up the difference by selling the rest of our story to the highest bidder.'

For six weeks after Maynard's death – six horrific weeks of humiliation and degradation – the country was privy to the personal details of his two marriages, his household costs, his earnings and even his children's school fees. Now everyone thought he was an obsessive, sex-crazed man, hell bent on personal gain and even using his own children to achieve it. However, in every single article, there was still a kernel of truth, no matter how distorted, which made his lawyers balk at legal action. Had Matlock got to them, William wondered. Was there no one he could trust? Was he really so despicable?

The answer came from his sixteen-year-old son,

Charlie. William drove to the school to take his son to lunch. It was an awkward, strained occasion and Charlie was unable to look his father in the face. It was not until pudding was served that William asked, 'Why, Charlie? Why have you said these terrible things about me?' The boy shrugged, still refusing to meet his father's eyes. 'I've never stopped loving you, providing for you. You've wanted for nothing.'

Charlie looked up at last, and William noticed for the first time his son's resemblance to himself. 'You left us. You've never been a father. All you were ever interested in was making money. And now I think we should go back, Dad,' he said. 'My band's got the music room booked this afternoon.'

William drove his son back to school in silence. When he leaned forward to embrace him, Charlie recoiled. 'Bye,' he said stiffly and got out, slamming the car door. He walked straight through the gates, hands clenched at his sides. He was hoping and praying that none of his friends had seen him. Even the car was embarrassing: no one who was anyone had a two-tone Rolls Royce with a gold Spirit of Ecstasy.

The following day William had an equally excruciating luncheon with his daughter, Sabrina. She was more aggressive than her brother, refusing to eat, and sitting with pursed lips – so like her mother's. William had married Katherine because he wanted to be accepted in high society. She had bubbled with delight at the balls and at the races. She enjoyed posing for photos with William in the winner's enclosure, and showing them to her friends when they appeared in the society columns. But the effervescent, giggling young socialite of courtship had vanished immediately after the wedding. She began to reprimand him as if he were a child for the way he held his knife and fork, the way he dressed. She made little jibes that exploded into huge rows. Eventually she had hired Miss Drumgoole to teach him etiquette. The truth was, William had needed to learn from Katherine so that he could feel at ease in the social circles to which she introduced him, but her scornful carping made him uncomfortable and afraid to open his mouth.

And here was Sabrina, his offspring, as like the whingeing Katherine as if she had been spat out of her mouth. She was pale, with straight blonde hair, heavy-lidded eyes with fair lashes and braces on her teeth. She might have been attractive but her long, thin nose and full lips made her face lack animation and she seemed loath even to attempt a smile. William had no one to blame but himself: it had been his choice to divorce one vacuous titled blonde and marry another. Out of the frying pan and into the fire.

'I can't stay long,' lisped Sabrina. 'Besides, Mummy said I really shouldn't have agreed to see you at all. We've had these press people everywhere.'

'I am sorry,' he said flatly. 'Perhaps if your mother hadn't been so eager to spill her vitriolic lies about me, this would all have blown over.'

'I have been teased unmercifully because of you. The other girls do nothing but giggle about you, and mince around like willy woofters, pointing at me. It's embarrassing having someone like you for a father. They call me "Rough Trade", because of you and your boyfriend.'

'I'll take you back to school.' William folded his napkin. He was too tired and too hurt to argue.

Had he brought all this vituperation upon himself? Surely there had to be someone he could call a friend. He went through lists of names, people who had stayed on one or other of his estates, all those he entertained regularly. But then it dawned on him that no one except his employees had made contact in the past few weeks. He kicked at the sofa in a drunken fury, as his father had when the bailiffs arrived to remove the family's few possessions. Unlike his father, he had no woman on whom to take out his frustrations. At least his mother had always been there, even if it was only as a punch-bag.

His mother had scrimped and saved for him to stay at school for extra tuition, and it was she who had told him there was a way out. She always said, 'Get your maths, Billy. You got to have maths.' Why she had this fixation with maths he never discovered, but his high grade in that subject netted him a scholarship to Liverpool University. Sadly, she had not lived to see this and his father's advice was that he should go out and work, rather than 'loll around at university with a load of ponces'. Billy had rolled up his sleeves and punched his father – so hard that he sent him sprawling into the fireplace – and walked out. He never saw his father alive again.

Fortified now by anti-depressants and sleeping-tablets, William remained closeted in his bedroom where his past became his focus. There had been around forty mourners at his father's funeral from the bars and clubs at which he had virtually lived. They all told funny anecdotes about him, what a character he had been, what bad luck he'd always had in his business ventures, how near he had been to doing well, and how many times he had tried to earn a decent living. Hidden among various drawers at home, William had found the remnants of his father's so-called 'business ventures'. Most were unpaid bills, but astonishingly he found a life assurance policy worth four thousand pounds. William sold the family house and made a further three thousand. Throughout his university life he hardly touched the money; his grant was sufficient to live on, and he was too scared to mention his nest-egg in case it was taken away. Not until he graduated, with a double first in mathematics and electronic studies, and moved to London, did he begin to utilize it.

In 1968, seven thousand pounds was a lot of money. Today it would have been worth almost ten times as much. William began to study the *Financial Times* share index as meticulously as his father had studied the dogs and, still only twenty-three, he began to accumulate a small fortune. He invested it in a small factory to make a computer circuit board he'd worked on at university. In those days the most elementary computer filled a room, but William's circuit board was set to change that. By the time he was twenty-eight he was a million-aire – not in the same league as Bill Gates, but rich none the less. By thirty he was one of the most eligible bachelors in Britain.

But William wasn't very interested in women. He preferred a brief fling, usually with one of his employees. It was easier, because all he really thought about was work. It had been Angela Nicholls, one of his secretaries, who had first encouraged him to attend social events, go to the theatre or the opera. On her advice William bought an apartment in Knightsbridge and joined a golf club, a tennis club and a luncheon club, and soon had a wide circle of friends. Angela gave him a confidence in himself that he had previously lacked. She was an attractive girl from a good family, the sex was easy and comfortable, and William was fond of her. When Angela fell ill with glandular fever and was forced to take time off work, he was caring and considerate, sent flowers and paid for the best medical attention. He had imagined when she recovered that they would pick up where they had left off. But hadn't reckoned on Harriet Forbes, the willowy blonde sent by the agency to fill in.

William remembered Harriet clearly. Only twenty years old, she had an insatiable sex drive and represented all the girls he had lusted after when he was a teenager but was too shy to date. Harriet was the youth he had lost in making himself rich. He was quickly and foolishly besotted with her; Angela was forgotten. He was surprised to discover how well connected and wealthy Harriet's family was. One evening, as they strolled home arm in arm, they stumbled upon Angela. Harriet made some stinging remark about how plain she was, and Angela ran up the street in tears. William did not follow her. He was too intoxicated by Harriet. Too intoxicated to see his relationship with Harriet for what it really was.

One day Harriet arrived at William's apartment with an astonishing collection of ballgowns from some of the most exclusive boutiques in London. 'For the Berkeley Square Ball tonight,' she gasped, tugging at a zip.

'But you know I've got dinner with the Japanese.'

She looked up at him with amazement. 'Don't be ridiculous! I couldn't take you with me – it's a Society do.'

So he was good enough to fuck and pay for endless champagne, meals and clothes, but even with all his millions he was not good enough for her precious aristocrats! 'I don't want to go to some tin-pot ball with a load of overdressed slags cavorting round with a bunch of chinless twats anyway,' he snapped petulantly.

Harriet laughed, picked up her purchases and made for the door. 'You obviously do or you wouldn't be getting so uptight,' she said, over her shoulder. Then she flounced out, banging the door behind her.

He remembered how he had smarted with anger, and then how he had told himself that it was time he straightened out and got back to work. For the first time in months, he called Angela, but was told she had gone to Yorkshire to stay with her family. A month later he saw her at the opera, a few seats in front of him. He was alone, and during the interval asked if she would have a glass of champagne with him. She introduced him to her party of friends, one of whom was Margaret Pettigrew. That evening they all dined together: he was attentive to Angela, but intrigued by Margaret. As he helped Margaret into a taxi she slipped him her phone number.

Two months later William and Margaret were married. William paid for the wedding, an elaborate affair that made all the society columns, even 'Jennifer's Diary'. Margaret's family, it turned out, owned a stately home and acres of Hertfordshire, but didn't have two pennies to rub together, so it was an advantageous union on both sides. The Pettigrews needed the money; William desired the social status. Again Angela was dismissed from his thoughts. In a moment of madness, William invited Harriet to the wedding, thinking she would never come, but she did, in an overlarge hat and tiny dress in skin-pink. She strode up to him, kissed him on the lips, and whispered, 'She looks like a fucking horse!'

He smiled down at her. 'Do you think so? She reminded me of you.'

Harriet shrieked with laughter. She was later seen leaving hand in hand with one of the waiters.

Apart from William's business associates and staff, the rest of the guests had been from Margaret's side: dukes, earls, judges and Members of Parliament. Everyone knew William as a business tycoon, a multi-millionaire IT magnate, and he relished the attention. During the wedding luncheon he bought his first racehorse, and was invited to the Dunhill polo match. Later as they boarded his private jet, bound for St Lucia, William was convinced that marrying Margaret had been the best business and social move he had ever made. On the plane she made a toast: 'To Angela, for introducing us.' William raised his glass but felt a dreadful pang of guilt. Angela had been at the wedding, but he had not even spoken to her. He knew he had hurt her badly, but she gave no indication of this, just a shy smile when their eyes met over lunch. 'To Angela,' he had said, and quaffed the glass in one.

During the honeymoon, after their brief consumma-tion, Margaret suffered a bout of cystitis. William slept in another bed for the entire two weeks. During the days, while Margaret stayed inside 'in the cool', William remained at the bar, wondering now if he had just made one of the biggest mistakes of his life.

Back in London, Margaret devoted herself to the marital home, lavishly decorating it to the tune of nearly a million pounds. She also found a country house in Berkshire with stables and twenty-two acres of land. The cystitis recurred virtually every time they had fumbling, dutiful sex. After a year they were sleeping in separate rooms.

Gradually William spent more time away from home, and this was when he began to pay high-class prostitutes for what he neither got nor wanted at home. At Royal Ascot he saw Harriet again. As usual he was alone: Margaret had a headache. Harriet was wearing a novelty hat and the usual short, tight skirt, her pregnancy visible to all. She was not in the Royal Enclosure, and was accompanied by a rather seedy-looking young man. William spent a considerable time with his binoculars trained on her. The sight of her made him wonder if theirs might have been a long-term relationship, but that was foolish.

'William, come and join us!' It was Cedric, Lord Hangerford, making drinking gestures with his hand. As he entered the private box William was struck by a beautiful woman sitting alone in a corner, studying form. 'What do I get for twenty to one?' she called, pen poised over her card.

'Put one pound on, you get twenty back,' William replied.

'God, I'm stupid sometimes,' said the beautiful blonde, without looking up.

William bought two more horses from Cedric Hangerford, and went home to find Margaret out, playing bridge with friends. 'She may stay with Mrs Castleton tonight,' said the maid, grimly.

William nodded as she shut the door behind her, then flicked at the blotting pad on his desk. Bored, he looked around the room at the décor, so carefully chosen by Margaret and that terrible old queen who claimed to be an interior designer. It was an elegant study, lined with hundreds of leatherbound books. White linen was draped as curtains and a large antique mahogany desk was placed beneath the window. Margaret loathed reproduction furniture: she said it was made for the middle classes. William had a sudden urge to swipe everything off the desk and hurl the Georgian ink-well at the curtains. He put his head in his hands: he was rich, successful, and bloody lonely. He dialled Madame Norton, who ran an up-market call-girl agency. He told her what he wanted, then informed the staff that they could retire for the night. Half an hour later the doorbell rang and William answered it personally.

Nina strutted in and followed William up the marble staircase towards the bedroom. She let her coat fall to the floor, stepped over it and threw a cheap black bag on to the damask-covered king-size bed. William poured two glasses of champagne and glanced at the girl, who was looking around the room. 'It's on the bedside table,' he said casually, and watched her pick up the roll of money then stuff it into her bag. She smiled sweetly as he passed her the champagne. His notion had been to try to re-enact the moments he had enjoyed with Harriet, but this girl was too cheap. He realized he had made a foolish mistake in asking her to come to his home.

'Cheers!' She took a sip and kicked off her shoes.

William was about to tell her that she could keep the money and leave when the bedroom door opened. He caught Margaret's reflection in the mirror and turned, holding out his glass of champagne. 'Why, Margaret,' he grinned, and went on with characteristic bravura, 'would you like to join us?'

Margaret was frozen to the spot, mouth hanging open in stunned amazement. Then she started to scream.

The divorce cost William the house and a substantial pay-off, negotiated by her weasel of a lawyer, who could hardly stop rubbing his hands in anticipation of his cut. However, William's own lawyers were clever enough to insinuate that if she did not accept his offer, they would issue a counter-action accusing her of frigidity and denying her husband his conjugal rights. He celebrated the decree nisi with Cedric Hangerford over dinner at Rules. Cedric brought along his cousin, Katherine, the leggy blonde William had met in his Ascot box. 'Twenty to one, you'll say yes to the coffee at my place,' she quipped, as they left the restaurant.

William married her within the year. It was a small register-office affair, with a private dinner afterwards. But that evening the couple threw a ball at the Ritz, ensuring the marriage made not only the social columns but the glossy magazines too. Two days later they were honeymooning on safari.

It was far from the disaster of his first marriage. During their ten days in Zimbabwe they enjoyed each other's company. Katherine's genuine interest in wildlife and her inability to handle a camera were endearing. However, the sex was unsatisfactory. Katherine was not exactly frigid, just unloving. She evidently felt that the sooner it was over the better. William's inexperience of dealing with someone like Katherine made it impossible for him to discuss his frustration with her.

When they returned home and moved into their new house, William discovered that Katherine was no house-wife either. She was useless at organizing, hopeless with money, loathed shopping, never read anything other than *Tatler* and was generally bone idle. After a few months she was pregnant, and demanded that they sleep in separate bedrooms and expected to be waited on hand and foot. William soon realized that he had traded in one nightmare for another. When Katherine gave birth to a boy, they moved to a larger house. Although they employed two nannies she complained incessantly that she was tired and depressed, and spent all day in her bedroom watching television. He noticed that she was always lively enough to attend the dinners, balls and society parties she was invited to, but when he asked her to accompany him to a business function she always had a migraine. According to her, his business associates were 'middle-class and boring', which made William acutely ashamed and aware once more of his background.

Two years into their marriage, to Katherine's horror and William's surprise, she was pregnant again. After the birth of their daughter, Sabrina, Katherine locked herself in her bedroom, complaining of post-natal depression, but was overjoyed to have a daughter. However, he had had enough of the marriage. Despite that he did not file for divorce for another two years, and then only because he had found out his wife was handing over thousands of pounds to her cousin Cedric, whose stud farm was in financial difficulties. It wasn't that William didn't have the money to 'donate', it was just that every relative of Katherine's seemed to treat him like a soft touch.

The divorce was drawn-out and costly. For all Katherine's perpetual inertia, when William decided to leave she found the energy of a maelstrom. She wept, screamed and threatened to take the children abroad so that he would never see them again. He fought for custody, but Katherine threatened to tell the court of his trips to Madame Norton's, determined to prove that he was not a fit father.

Since his last divorce William had been almost content. He had concluded that marriage was not for him and had vowed that he would never contemplate it again. He didn't acknowledge that he was lonely, but buried himself in his work. Then he had met Andrew Maynard and his life changed. He found he had not only a face and a purse, he had a voice too. In return for his sponsorship, Maynard had helped him realize that he should be proud of his achievements.

After Maynard's death William felt as though the light had gone out of his life. Now he sat alone in his study and thought. He poured himself a large Armagnac, lit a cigar, and decided to set fire to Maynard's diaries. Then, on impulse, he decided to read them. He needed answers. Deep down he could not believe he had so misjudged the man for whom he had cared so deeply. As he unlocked the safe and took out the first diary he felt strangely calm.

In the months before Maynard's death the diary

contained frequent references to 'JC'. William assumed this was Chalmers.

> *Lunched here in Grimaud. They used to live here with their parents. They are the most astonishingly beautiful couple. She is as blonde as he and just as charming. I never believed in love at first sight until this moment. It was as if every movement was held under a bright magnifying-glass. I could not take my eyes off them, it was all I could do to stop myself kneeling at their feet. It is so rare to find such perfection. I am an adoring slave, nothing in my life meant anything, all I wanted was to*

The rest has been blacked out, making it impossible to read.

William began to feel cheated as he turned the pages: there were more blacked-out passages. Then he read,

> *... took me to a place that I could not believe. I am ecstatic, I am flying, I am a slave. I have never known such total peace and tranquillity. I want nothing but to be embraced and tortured in such sweet pain. I am a dog to be chained and beaten into total submission.*

There then followed a long sequence of dreadful adolescent-style poetry, in which the word 'torture' featured over and over again. Maynard never referred to a 'he', or specifically named Chalmers, but wrote often that he was desperate to hear from JC. William found a note at the top of a page, decorated with a heart, that read, 'JC called. I am in heaven, must get more money'.

There followed a long list of items of clothing he had purchased, gifts for JC, and then

I am beginning to realize that beneath the drugs and the debauchery, beneath his perfectly handsome, stunningly beautiful profile, his face sometimes takes on a coldness, just as hers does. Sharp like a knife-edge. I feel frightened . . . Justin was so sour to me today, he made me weep.

Then more blacked-out lines, and then over the page, the ink was blotched, from tears perhaps.

I think Justin hides in a bottomless well of cynicism, which at times is so deep there is no sun, there are no stars, only darkness, and I have such a need to reach out to him, as he has become the centre of my universe.

William sighed at such twaddle, hardly able to believe this had been written by the man he knew. He flicked through the pages, then stopped at the sight of his own name.

Mr Need-to-be-accepted, Sir William B, came round today. A tedious, wretched man with too much money. He believes I will be his political hero. If only he knew what I really felt about his persistent intrusion into my life, this inarticulate buffoon who got lucky with some computer chip and believes himself to be my equal.

William felt sick. A buffoon! He had ploughed hundreds of thousands of pounds into this egotistical pervert. How could he have been so stupid? He hurled the diary across the room.

Alone in his vast bed, William tossed and turned, asking himself over and over why he had allowed himself to be subjected to such abuse. Did he have such an inferiority complex that no matter what success he achieved he felt unworthy of it? Why had he allowed himself to be humiliated by virtually everyone who had entered his life? He had been living in some fantasy world since meeting Maynard. He had deluded himself that at last he had found contentment. Eventually he fell into a restless sleep.

He woke feeling tired, wretched, unwilling to face the day, and stayed in bed with the curtains drawn. He told the servants not to disturb him, and refused to eat. For two days and nights he cried as he never had before, until at long last he felt he had no more tears to shed. Then a calm sense of relief washed over him.

When he got up for a pee, he saw his reflection in the full-length mirror. He was in appalling shape: his eyes were puffy and dark-ringed, his face was pasty. William had never been handsome, but he had believed he was attractive, particularly since his success. He laughed bitterly to himself. Who would want him now? The depression returned. He had never been in love, had never felt passion the way Maynard had. He had wanted sex and been willing to pay for it, but he had never experienced ecstasy. Now, he thirsted for love.

He walked back into his darkened bedroom and threw on some clothes. First he called his office to say that he would be away for some time. Then he instructed his valet to pack a suitcase with evening suits and casual wear. He asked Michael to arrange for his jet to be fuelled and made ready to depart from Heathrow's private airfield.

'What destination shall I tell the pilot, sir?' Michael asked.

'Nice.'

'Will you need your apartment prepared?'

'No, I'll be at the Hôtel Negresco. Book me a suite.'

'Would you like me to arrange meetings?'

'No, this is not business. I need . . .' he gave the ghost of a smile '. . . need some space, as they say. I'm taking a break.' He gave another wan smile. 'Taking a break from my life, Michael. No more questions.'

The flight to Nice was comfortable, and the drive to the hotel uneventful. On arrival he didn't unpack but telephoned the villa in Grimaud. Justin Chalmers' villa. Part of him denied what he was doing, but the other part knew perfectly well: he was going to find water in the desert. He believed that here he would find solace for his lost soul.

A woman answered. 'Countess Lubrinsky speaking.'

'Sir William Benedict,' he said. 'A friend of Justin Chalmers. I'm going to be in Grimaud at the week-end . . .'

'Really?' crooned the Countess. 'Then you must join us. We are having a small dinner party.'

'I'd be delighted, thank you. If your plans change, I'll be at the Negresco.'

'I look forward to meeting you.'

The phone went dead and he replaced the receiver on the cradle. He had no idea what he was doing. It was the beginning of an adventure. He liked the sound

81

of Countess Lubrinsky's voice, but he really wanted to meet whoever had accompanied Chalmers to meetings with Maynard. Was this countess the beautiful woman to whom he had referred in the diary?'

He thought again of how Maynard had described him, and his lips tightened. A buffoon! His whole body flushed with indignation. Was that what they all felt, how they all saw him? God Almighty, he wanted to get back at Maynard – at them all – and he would start with Justin Chalmers. That was why he had come to France. It was because he needed space to think, to make plans for how he would take his revenge. He would pay back *every one* of the bastards. No one was ever going to call him a buffoon again.

CHAPTER 5

THE COUNTESS Lubrinsky tied her silk sarong tighter round her slim waist, and stared at her reflection in the mirror above the telephone table. She ran her fingers through her thick auburn hair, the curls in ringlets around her neck. She had long tapering fingers with short, unvarnished nails, and wore no jewellery apart from a gold ankle bracelet. At forty years old, Sylvina was proud of her figure, and her sculpted face was without a wrinkle. Her slanting green cat-like eyes, fine straight nose and high wide cheekbones gave her the look of a mystic. She lit a cigarette and, turning to the right, caught Sharee's reflection behind her. 'Hello, darling, have you had your swim?'

'No, just about to. Who was that?'

'Some friend of Justin's. I invited him to dinner.'

'Oh, God, why do you always invite every stray he gives our phone number to?'

'Because I presumed he'd arranged it.'

'Well, don't presume. Ring the bastard up and ask.'

'Don't start. It's just for dinner, and I've left a message on his mobile.'

Sharee, blonde and fair-skinned, was twenty-four.

She had a fuller figure than Sylvina, slightly plump around her bottom and thighs, with full, perfectly shaped breasts. Sylvina stared at her, took a long drag on her cigarette and blew out a perfect smoke ring. It coiled around Sharee's right nipple.

'You smoke too much, Sylvina.'

'I know. Keep still. Let me see if I can circle the left one too.' She sucked at her Gitane, held her breath and pursed her lips. The smoke ring floated in the air and Sharee wafted it away, strolling out on to the patio.

She leaned against the balustrade and, one hand shading her eyes, watched the butterflies in the garden. Sylvina, not knowing their correct names, had called the various species after parisian couturiers: the blue was Dior, a deep black, brown and orange one Schiaparelli, a remarkable multicoloured one Versace, and a rather dull moth type she found amusing to nickname Chanel.

'Penny for them, sweetie,' Sylvina said now, pouring herself a Dubonnet.

'I was looking for a Gaultier,' Sharee said, and turned back to the garden.

'Did Justin use all those trees he cut down to build the bridges?'

'No idea, darling,' Sylvina said, flopping on to a teak sun-lounger. Its cushions were hot from the sun, and she yelped.

'You should open the parasols,' Sharee said, and started towards the curved narrow staircase that ran round the outside of the house like a spiral of small white marble pillars. 'I'm going for a swim,' she said, and Sylvina watched her climb upwards to the rooftop pool.

'I love you,' she called out.

'I should hope you do,' came back the reply.

Dinner was to take place in a vast room with floor-to-ceiling windows draped in white muslin, lit by hundreds of candles. The huge table had a gold swan as a base, its wings balancing a slab of green-tinted glass. A vase of wild flowers, ferns and lilies sat on a large side table giving off a sweet and heady perfume. Sylvina, wearing a white robe, moved around the table placing name-cards in gold butterflies. Satisfied that the table was perfect, she moved to the ornate stone hearth and lit the fire. She would have to turn up the air-conditioning because it was a very warm night, but the fire was such a focal point that it was a shame not to light it.

It was a stunningly beautiful room, every item chosen with great care. The heavy oak floor had been shipped in from England. It had once been in a castle but now looked as if it had always belonged here. The carved oak doors had been brought from a temple in Indonesia. Content, Sylvina walked upstairs to find Sharee.

She found her soaking in the bath, bubbles up to her chin, a towel wrapped around her hair and wearing an eye-mask. 'You should get out, sweetheart – you'll be wrinkled like a prune if you stay in any longer.' Sylvina sat on the edge of the bath. 'I called Justin again,' she said.

'And?'

'He wasn't there, and nobody seems to know where he is. But I have a feeling he might turn up, the way he does!'

85

'Will she be with him?' Sharee tossed the towel from her hair, and sat up in the bath.

'How should I know?' Sylvina snapped.

'Don't get ratty, I was only asking. She's so difficult. I mean, I can take him on his own but when they're together it's just awful. They're like . . .' She frowned, pursing her lips in an attempt to find the right description, but none came. And, anyway, Sylvina had walked out.

Alone in her room, Sylvina chose a cerise Valentino tunic, tight-fitting with a split to her thigh and a mandarin collar. Her high-heeled sandals, which made her almost six feet tall, had been dyed to match. She coiled her hair into a pleat and placed a fresh freesia on either side of her head. Lastly she clipped on a pair of sparkling diamond drop earrings that had belonged to her grandmother.

Sharee came in wearing an ice blue, figure-hugging dress with T-bone straps.

'You look cute,' said Sylvina. 'Are you going to put on some make-up?'

'No. If I look and feel terrible, maybe I won't eat.'

Sylvina laughed and wrapped her arms around Sharee. 'I love you the way you are. I wouldn't want you to lose an ounce.'

'I look like shit.'

'You don't, honestly.'

'Yes, I do. I wish you'd help me buy some decent things,' Sharee muttered, checking her appearance in a long carved wooden mirror.

'When I have the funds, darling, you'll have whatever you want.'

'Yes, I know. But in the meantime you look a million dollars and I look like some cheap hooker.'

Sylvina closed the wardrobe then bent to pick up the various shoes and sandals lying about on the floor. 'God, you're so untidy. Don't you ever put things away?'

In fury, Sharee bent down and started gathering up shoes. When she had an armful she went on to the balcony and threw them over the rail. 'Happy now?' She turned, but Sylvina had left the room and Sharee felt foolish. She followed Sylvina out to the patio.

Sylvina passed her a glass of champagne. Sharee's mood was beginning to irritate her. There wasn't anyone special arriving, thank goodness, because actually Sharee did look cheap. Sylvina checked her watch: the guests were due in under an hour. She always liked to be ready in good time, and went in search of the housekeeper, Marta, to check that all was as it should be. Marta, who lived at the villa full-time, had hired two local boys as waiters. The chef was tutting round the various tureens and dishes laid out on the large wooden kitchen table. When she was satisfied that everything was on schedule Sylvina had a quiet word with Marta about Sharee's shoes, then returned to the patio.

The grounds were floodlit, spotlights carefully placed round the fountain to make the spray look like shooting stars.

'Isn't it beautiful?' Sharee was happier now, reclining on the chaise, sipping champagne. She asked again who they were expecting, even though Sylvina had told her numerous times.

'Baron and Baroness von Garten, Meryl Delaware,

Count Frederick Capri and his guest Princess Constantina with her guest the actor Terence Hampton, and the unknown Sir William Benedict.' Sylvina was a regular in the cheap French and English gossip magazines. She no longer even bothered to read them. However, now that she was broke, she tried to maintain some exposure so that the invitations kept pouring in. It was only at social functions that she was offered these house-sitting jobs. Sylvina's relationship with Sharee was not public knowledge and she was keen to keep her sexual proclivities quiet. Luckily, so was Sharee, who entertained hopes of becoming an actress and knew how things like that could damage your chances – unless of course you were famous enough for it not to matter.

William sat back in the hired Mercedes. Mercifully the driver had not spoken a word since he had opened the door for him to get in. He looked down at his linen suit and wondered whether it was the right thing to have worn – linen creased so badly. He switched on the lights to examine his trousers, then worried that his shirt was too formal for the suit. By the time the car pulled up outside the gates he was sweating with nerves. He felt hot, badly dressed and wished he had not pushed himself on Countess Lubrinsky. And what if they didn't speak English? But of course she did – he had spoken to her on the telephone. Should he have brought champagne or flowers? It was too late to do anything about that now. He'd have Michael send an arrangement the following day.

'*Magnifique*,' said the driver.

William leaned forward and looked out at the gar-

dens. What a beautiful place! From the road there had
been no indication of what lay hidden behind the trees.
A crescent of vehicles was parked in the wide horseshoe
drive to the right of the villa's front door, two Rolls
Royces, a Porsche and a Citroën. The driver parked the
Mercedes beside the Citroën, stepped out and opened
William's door. He stood to one side deferentially as
William gave a nod of thanks, and made his way to the
porch. Flowers in large white tubs were placed either
side of the white steps, and the pillars were draped with
pink blossom. William was about to ring the bell when
the door opened and Marta, in a black dress and white
apron, stood before him, smiling. 'Good evening,' she
said. 'Please do come in.'

William walked past her into the hall as she closed
the door quietly behind him.

'Who may I say it is, please?' Marta asked sweetly.

'Sir William Benedict,' he said gruffly.

She handed him a glass of champagne from a tray
held by a young waiter, then ushered him into the
drawing room where the smell of perfume mingled with
lilies, Havana cigars and incense which made his head
spin. Immediately he wished the ground would open
and swallow him. The male guests were all wearing
black or white tuxedos and the women, as far as he
could see, long evening dresses.

'Sir William Benedict,' Marta announced.

The stunning woman in a cerise dress who
approached him with a wide welcoming smile was the
Countess. She introduced herself as Sylvina and said,
'How very kind of you to join us.' William saw immediately that she had recognized him from the magazines
and glanced round the room. He spotted the horrified

expressions on the faces of the Baron and Baroness von Garten.

'It's the ghastly parvenu who was going to buy one of the factories.' The Baroness's stage whisper to her husband echoed round the room. The Baron's lawyers had ceased all negotiations as soon as the scandal had become public. He had not wanted his family name tarnished by association with misdemeanour, particularly one with homosexual undertones.

William's smile froze on his lips. The Baron had cost him a lot of money by withdrawing from their deal. Worse still, he had sold instead to William's strongest competitor. It was not just a financial slap in the face, he had also lost out on a vast potential European market. He had not yet found another suitable site and, more infuriatingly still, the rival company that had bought the factory had made offers to the staff William had earmarked for positions and interviewed in Germany. The Baron and Baroness now turned their backs on him. If he compiled a list of people to take a swipe at, these two stuck-up sons-of-bitches would be close to the top.

Silvina had noticed William's embarrassment and now linked her arm through his and guided him towards the other guests. 'I am sure you know Meryl Delaware?' she purred.

William felt his belly turn over. It was bad enough to have the von Gartens cut him dead, but now he was faced with this fat, painted bitch with her gossip-tuned ears. Meryl, dressed in black lace with too many fake diamonds around her neck, turned to face him. Her red mouth dropped open in shock. Then she forced a brittle smile. Meryl Delaware had written one of the most unsavoury articles about him and Maynard for one of the glossy magazines. In it she had hinted that Sir William had appeared very close to his protégé, and had illustrated it with a photograph of William leaning forward to talk to Maynard. As with many other photographs, it had been doctored to exclude the other members of the party to make it look as if the two had been having an intimate, candlelit dinner. 'How do you do?' she said, before turning back to face the wall.

The atmosphere changed swiftly from sophisticated elegance to the deep silence of unease. Everyone but Sharee was fully aware of who William was and unsure how to react.

Sylvina gestured to Marta to refill her champagne glass, and told her to adjust the place settings. Sir William should sit next to her with Terence Hampton on his other side. Terence was a social 'actor': you could put him next to anyone and the conversation would never dry up, as long as it revolved principally around himself.

As the guests were ushered towards the dining-room, Sylvina fell into step beside William. Suddenly the von Gartens were standing in front of her. As though William was not there, the Baroness announced, 'I'm afraid it is inappropriate for us to dine here, after all.'

Nothing like this had ever happened to Sylvina. 'I'm sorry, Baroness. Are you feeling unwell?' she said. 'Please do stay, dinner is served.'

'Maybe if someone was asked to leave . . .' said the Baron, eyeing William.

'I'm sorry,' said Sylvina. 'Sir William is my own personal guest.'

William was appalled. He shifted from foot to foot and stammered, 'It's all right, I'll go.'

Sylvina gripped his arm. 'No way, baby.'

She was still smiling as the Baron and Baroness huffed and puffed their way out of the door. 'I hope you don't mind but I have seated you beside me, so we can get to know each other.'

William murmured that he could think of nothing he would like more. He felt even better when she patted the sleeve of his jacket. 'This is from the new Armani collection, isn't it?'

'Yes, it is,' he said, flushing deeply.

'I thought so, and so much more comfortable in this heat than a dinner-jacket.' She whispered, 'No smell of mothballs.'

He caught her warmth and her wonderful, genuine smile, and began to feel more confident.

'I'm sorry about that little unpleasantness earlier.' She leaned right into him and added, 'The Baron is no paragon of virtue and neither is his wife. How odd that they should show such bad manners.'

But as the chilled avocado and mint soup was served, the conversation became stilted. The other guests were talking under their breath about the von Gartens' exit or William's tabloid exploits. Aware of the awful silences around the table, Sylvina told Marta to bring in a very special wine she had been saving for such an occasion. Her energy and charm immediately lifted the atmosphere, and Marta bustled off down to the wine cellar. She wasn't sure what bottle of wine Sylvina was talking about but she scoured the shelves and selected a Château Margaux '78. Leaving the cobwebs and thick layer of dust behind, she hurried back to the dining room and passed Sylvina the dusty bottle. 'Marta! The cob-webs! You know I hate spiders.' She rose to her feet and raised her arms above her head. 'Never mind, at least we know it's authentic. Now, dear, please decant it and let it stand. We are all eager to taste it.'

Marta left the dining room and immediately replaced the bottle with a vastly inferior one. She decanted it, as instructed, into a Victorian cut-glass decanter, which was taken to the table by one of the waiters. Sylvina had often laid wagers with her as to who would detect a first growth from a simple Médoc. She looked around at her dinner guests as they peered and sipped at the wine and discussed its attributes. William picked up his glass and turned to face her. 'This really is so very kind of you,' he said, and obviously meant every word.

'It is my pleasure,' she said huskily. She had to wriggle in her chair because the thought of his money made her feel orgasmic.

'To our mutual friend, Justin Chalmers.'

They sipped their wine and smiled. When she asked him what he thought of it he held the stem of the glass loosely in his fingers. 'Not too heavy or fruity, quite light for a Pomero.'

William reached for his water. The wine was ghastly. If he had ordered it in a restaurant, he would have sent it back. He felt unable to bring up the subject of Justin himself, and hoped someone else would do so, but the conversation remained on the quality of the wine. It amused him to see them sipping and nodding.

Sylvina leaned closer to him. 'I've even started making my own cobwebs – you know, from that stuff they squirt over you at kiddies' parties. It's cheap plonk, but you knew that. I could tell from your face.'

He smiled, pleased, then leaned closer to her. 'No one else seems to.'

'Even if they did, dahling, they wouldn't say so just in case they were wrong.'

'Are you expecting Justin for the summer?' Terence Hampton enquired, after enthusing loudly about the wine.

Sylvina shrugged. 'Well, it is his villa, but you know Justin. I hear he's in Europe, so perhaps he will appear at some point, unless . . .' She turned pointedly to William. 'What do you know of our Scarlet Pimpernel, William?'

'They seek me here, they seek me there.' Between the arched oak dining-room doors stood Justin Chalmers, his shadow from the flickering candlelight falling across the table. He was as blond as William remembered, but his hair was short now, almost in a crew-cut. He was deeply tanned and wore a black T-shirt with one sleeve almost ripped from the seam, a pair of tight black leather trousers and black motorcycle boots. He had a row of fine gold bracelets around his wrist and a slender gold watch. He shook the bracelets in a theatrical gesture then yawned. 'Eat up, and excuse the interruption. I need to bath and shave before I join you.'

William felt apprehensive. He had only ever met the man once, and then it was to tell him to get out of England. Now, driven by loneliness and relentless curiosity, he had blustered his way into his villa, having lied to the Countess. To his astonishment, Justin gave him a dazzling smile. 'How nice to see you, Sir William. Quite a surprise.' Then he turned and walked back into the hall calling over his shoulder, 'Don't let me interrupt your dinner further.' He caught Marta as she was about to wheel in the trolley with the main course, cupped her chin and kissed her lips. 'Who's a good girl?' he said.

'I thought you'd want to know. I think he invited himself,' Marta said, then asked hesitantly, 'How is she?'

He twisted his gold bracelets and his eyes brimmed with tears. 'She's going to be fine, but it'll take a while longer.'

'She'll be coming home then?'

He nodded, and said caressingly, 'Yes, our beautiful lily will be home, but you know how these clinics like to take their time and my money. They said she simply needed rest. She's doing some new therapy with crystals, and she sounds much better. It wasn't such a bad one apparently, but I like to be careful.'

Marta touched his hand gently. 'You know I am always here for her.'

He started for the stairs. 'I'd better get showered. Oh, is the fat man staying or is he just here for dinner?'

'Just dinner,' Marta said, as she wheeled the trolley towards the dining room. Two waiters came out to take it from her, and both looked to the stairs. Justin always had an effect on young men: the aura of danger that hung about him acted like a magnet.

Justin stood beneath the shower jets, eyes tightly closed, and pondered. Why was Sir William Benedict sitting at dinner? What did he want? What did he know? Or maybe it was all going according to plan. Maybe he was ripe for the picking already. Justin sighed. He knew he would find out sooner or later. And Sir William could not have appeared at a better time: Justin was broke again but downstairs, sitting at his dining-room table, was the man who had financed the reconstruction of this villa and paid off his debts. Justin spent money like water, and the cash William had given him was gone. He reached for a soft white towel and wrapped himself in it from head to toe. He was not sure yet how he could use his golden goose. The plan only formed later when everyone except William had departed.

William had drunk too much, and the combination of alcohol and anti-depressant pills had made him red-faced, sweaty, and unable to stand unaided. Every time he rose, the room spun and he felt ill. Justin helped him to his feet, and they went out on to the balcony into the cool night air, which made his head spin even more. He almost fell, but Justin caught him, guided him to a chair and went to brew some coffee. Marta had gone to bed, as had everyone else at the villa, and they were alone.

William tried desperately to sober up. With his head in his hands, he took deep breaths and tried to concentrate on his own shoes. He felt wretched. When Justin returned, he placed the steaming mugs on a low table then went to stand behind William's chair and began to massage his shoulders.

'I'm sorry about this,' William said hoarsely. The strong hands were soothing.

'Don't worry about it. Just relax. You're very tense – your shoulders are rigid.'

Justin leaned over to the table, and passed William his coffee. 'This'll make you feel better, and maybe you should take a couple of these. They're just aspirin, but they'll stave off the hangover.'

'Thank you,' William said. 'I'm sorry to have just turned up on your doorstep like this. To be honest, I don't really know why I came.'

'I'm glad you did. And you're most welcome to stay over if you would like.'

'No, no, I must get back.' There was an awkward silence. William lifted his eyes to Justin's and flushed as the handsome man smiled. It was extraordinary, he thought. Even though Justin was in his early thirties he had the look of a well-scrubbed youth. 'I think I'm very tired,' he said lamely.

'You must have been through a lot,' Justin said, sitting opposite.

'That's putting it mildly!' William leaned back and gazed over the garden so that he would not have to look at Justin, whose handsomeness unnerved him. 'I just needed to get away to try to recharge my batteries. I've made a fool of myself.'

'It's understandable. Anyone would feel the same.' Justin lit a cigarette, watching him with lizard-like attention.

'Can't show my face anywhere in London without being ridiculed. Not that I'm asked anywhere any more. I'm like some kind of plague. The people I thought were my friends have turned their backs on me, scared to be tarred with the same brush, I suppose. Dear God, I'm normally so in control of my life.'

'Why don't you do something about it?'

William sighed and drained his coffee mug. 'That's why I feel so wretched. The Baron and his wife walked

97

out before dinner rather than sit at a table with me. So, in answer to your question, what the hell can I do about it?'

'Well, instead of accepting it and weeping into your cup, so to speak, turn it round.'

William rose to his feet. He felt steadier now. 'Oh, I dare say it'll all blow over. At least my wealth is still intact. It'd be much worse if I'd lost that as well as my respectability.' He chuckled a little.

'It would be nice though, wouldn't it, to make all those two-faced society cunts eat their own shit.'

William stared at him, a little shocked by his language and his icy tone. 'Yeah, but well, my lawyers warned me the best thing to do was ignore it, and it'll blow over.'

'But it would be nice to lead them by the nose and rub it in the trash they've written about you. You see, Sir William, you made the biggest mistake of all. You got caught.'

'Caught? The only thing I did wrong was trust Andrew Maynard,' William snapped. 'He was probably scared that his private life was about to come out. But what a terrible waste to kill himself!'

'Yes, maybe, but you shouldn't have tried to cover up for him.'

'I think that's enough.' William had regained some of his decorum. 'I should be on my way.'

Justin stood up and moved closer to him. 'You could get back at them, you know. You just need the right connections.'

'And you have them, do you?' William said, with some sarcasm.

Justin moved closer still, and patted his shoulder. 'I have them, Sir William, and I'll tell you something else.

98

If you just swallow the situation, wealth intact or no, you'll hate yourself for the rest of your life.' Justin's voice was soft and persuasive, and he had the most hypnotic eyes William had ever seen. It was impossible to look away from him, even if what he went on to say was rather insulting. 'Regaining your social acceptance can be arranged. It's easily bought. But that should not be enough for a man of your standing. You want to regain the respect of others because, right now, you don't have any. I don't think you even have any for yourself. They've beaten you into running away, which is why you came here. Correct?'

'You're very intuitive.' William was more and more intrigued by the young man, but not yet prepared to discuss his situation in any greater depth, especially not with Andrew Maynard's ex-lover. But he sat down again.

It was then that Justin knew he had been right. He had an immensely rich fish on the end of his line, and the next few moments would be crucial in making him take the bait, and swallow it so that the hook lodged firmly in place. He must not wriggle free. Justin wondered how many more photographs of Andrew Maynard he could leak to keep it an ongoing front-pager.

'So, Mr Chalmers, if you were in my position – and pray God that you never will be – what would you do?'

Justin smiled. He'd got him. 'Pay every one of the bastards back twofold. Only then would I feel capable of getting on with my life. I wouldn't let anyone get away with treating me like a buffoon!'

By William's reaction, Justin knew that Maynard's nickname had hit him like a dart. William leaned forward. 'So what would you do?'

Justin looked deep into William's eyes. 'You own an island, don't you?'

'I do.'

'Then that is where you will lay the trap.' He laughed, throwing his head back and clapping his hands. Once more he became serious. A slender finger tapped William's knee. 'I have an idea. It'll take a long time, but you will need that time to get ready, and I can guarantee that it will work. But you must be prepared to arrange it, down to the smallest detail. Then you can step in for the kill.'

'I don't want to kill anyone, for Christ's sake,' William squeaked.

'Hypothetically you do, but if you won't admit it, then forget it.'

'Okay, carry on, I'm all ears.'

Justin lay back in his chair and closed his eyes. The flickering candles played across his beautiful face. Then his eyes opened and William recalled what he had read in Maynard's diary about a darkness, both frightening and exhilarating. Now he felt it. His stomach churned and the bile of his humiliation subsided as he felt excitement rise. 'Go on,' he said softly.

CHAPTER 6

SYLVINA CARRIED her coffee and rolls out to the pool where Justin was swimming. He didn't acknowledge her until he had completed twenty lengths, then he stopped, resting his elbows on the edge of the pool. 'I have a brilliant idea,' he announced.

She slid on her sunglasses, and poured coffee as he heaved himself out, splashing water everywhere, then padded towards the sun-lounger next to hers.

'Go on, ask me what it is.' He picked up her roll, bit into it, then reached for her coffee.

You always do this.' She was irritated. 'Why don't you ever ask if you can eat my breakfast? Better still, get your own.'

'You, my darling, will have a retinue of servants to bring yours in the future.'

'Really? Won the lottery, have you?' She picked up the pool telephone and asked Marta for more coffee and rolls. Justin was towelling himself dry. He was obviously pleased with himself about something.

He flopped down on a sun-lounger. 'This is how it's going to work.' She sat next to him as he smothered himself in her suntan lotion. 'You're going to get engaged to William.' He gave her a wide grin.

'Really? And is he aware of this development?'

'No, but he'll be thinking about it. I'll get him to come by this evening so we can arrange it.'

'Really? Well, that is fascinating. What if I'm not interested in attaching myself to him and, more to the point, what if he's not inclined to attach himself to me? I'm not going to open my legs for him. I've refused a lot better and—'

'Not that much richer,' he interrupted, then lay back to sun himself. 'This is the way it will work. You will get engaged and start to iron out his social ineptitude. You will become the society hostess of the season: parties, balls, the works. You will begin to entertain on such a lavish scale that anyone refusing to be associated with William will be won around. With your contacts and mine we'll make them cream themselves to get close to him!'

She laughed, leaned over and rubbed his flat muscular stomach. 'You're such a dreamer, darling.'

He swiped her hand away. 'This is *not* a dream! We can make it a reality.'

She shrugged. 'Fine. I'm riveted. Is there a purpose to all these immensely costly social functions you intend to sweep the world with, or do you just fancy dressing up?'

'I swear to you, he'll pay you for the privilege of your company.'

'Sounds very Mills and Boon to me, sweetheart, but do go on.'

Justin began to pace, skipping between the cracks in the marble tiles. 'Payback time. You will be his reintroduction into the world he has always wanted to be part of. He could never get there on his own and needs you to get inside the inner sanctum. Once he's there . . .' he gave a shrill, almost hysterical laugh.

Sylvina couldn't follow what he was talking about and Justin was interrupted by Marta's arrival.

'I'll go and shower,' Justin said suddenly, sunbathing forgotten. 'We'll ask for a million in cash, all expenses on top of that, a new wardrobe, a car, anything you can think of to enhance your performance as the most beautiful, eligible and sophisticated society hostess.' He was still chattering to himself and, as he disappeared, she could hear him laughing at his own fantasy.

'He's crazy,' Sylvina said. Then, 'Do you know when she's arriving?'

'I think perhaps tomorrow,' Marta replied. 'He has asked for the white linen sheets to be aired, plus her lilies, and that bottled water she prefers.'

Sylvina sighed. 'I don't know why he wanted me to house-sit. It looks like he's going to be here for the summer. He really is annoying.'

Marta said nothing, but cleared away the dirty crockery and headed back into the house.

Sylvina picked at a roll. She was suddenly depressed. She hated being so broke she couldn't leave here. She'd let her Paris apartment for the summer and her family château was uninhabitable. Even the vineyard that had once flourished was now suffering from blight. She rummaged in her pocket for her cigarettes and lit one. It would be nice to have some of the fat man's millions. She knew she had borrowed too often and, in so doing had limited her circle of wealthy friends by exploiting their generosity. But she still had many high-powered contacts. She was still on the invitation list of society's upper echelon, but of late she had been unable to afford the price of the charity tickets. She stubbed out the cigarette.

'Is that coffee hot?' Sharee said, making Sylvina jump.

'Yes.' Sylvina closed her eyes.

Sharee, using Sylvina's cup, poured herself a splash, sipped, then filled the cup. 'You were miles away,' she said, sitting down on Justin's vacated sun-lounger and squinting up at the sun. 'It'll be a boiler of a day. We going to the beach? Are you listening?'

Sylvina looked over her dark glasses at Sharee. 'Justin's got this crazy idea.'

'Hasn't he always?' Sharee said, concentrating on a few leg hairs that had been missed during waxing.

'It's about William Benedict.'

Sharee took out a pair of tweezers and began to pluck out the stray hairs with relish. 'What would you think if I got engaged to him, for money? I mean, we wouldn't fuck, it'd be a business arrangement for me to introduce him into society.'

Sharee's head was bent low over her left leg. 'Well, he's not exactly a teenager, is he? I thought only debs and young guys got into that society thing. He's gotta be fifty if not more.'

'If it's what he wants.'

'Is it?'

'I don't know.'

Sharee laughed. 'You know, sometimes I think you're as bad as Justin. He's nuts!' She looked up. 'Maybe *I* should offer. I mean, I'm younger than you and if he's got that amount of money to throw around, I'd get engaged to him. I'd even fuck him if it made him happy.'

104

'You've missed the point,' Sylvina snapped.

'Oh, yeah, so what is it?'

'I am a countess. I know everyone one needs to know. I am socially accepted, sweetheart.'

'Who you kidding? You've not got two cents to scratch yourself with, and I wouldn't say the Euro-trash I've met with you are exactly the top social order. You're not exactly mixing with King Thingy of Spain!'

'I was invited to his son's wedding,' Sylvina said.

'Oh, were you?' Sharee laughed.

Sylvina became inceasingly angry. 'Yes, I was, and the *Euro-trash* you have met are about the only people I could introduce you to as, quite honestly, you and your appearance leave a lot to be desired. Looking like a shop assistant is not exactly—'

Sharee hit her so hard she fell off the sunbed. 'This shop assistant, you bull-dyke, hates your fucking guts, and unless you apologize I'm walking right out of this fucking Mickey Mouse villa.'

Sylvina lay stunned on the marble tiles as Sharee got up and stood over her. 'Apologize or I'll kick you.' She glared down at Sylvina.

'Go on. Kick me.'

'You're sick, you know that? Sick, perverted and *old*.' Sharee bent down and began to drag Sylvina by her leg towards the pool. Sylvina struggled and wriggled as the skin on her thigh was scraped raw.

'Is this a private party or can anyone join in?' Standing in the doorway, Justin laughed.

'Fuck off,' screamed Sharee.

Justin watched as both women fell into the pool and continued the fight in the water. Eventually they bobbed up, gasping, spluttering and exhausted.

'Are you going to . . .' Sharee puffed '. . . apologize for calling me a shop assistant?'

'No,' Sylvina spat. Sharee hauled herself out of the water, her bikini hanging off.

'You are not a shop assistant, you are the woman I love more than anyone else in the world.' Sylvina held out her hand and Sharee took it, helping her out of the pool. They embraced passionately as Justin watched. Sylvina's soaked robe was torn and he could see her body shape through the thin cotton. Suddenly Sharee ripped it away, dropped to her knees and eased Sylvina's thighs open and began to part her glistening pubic hair with her tongue. Sylvina gasped. The next moment, Justin had cupped her breasts in his hands and she moaned as he thrust into her from behind, guided by Sharee. They were both intent on Sylvina, thrusting into her and caressing her until she climaxed with such a howl of pleasure it disturbed a flock of white doves, which fluttered up over their heads.

Justin pulled back and zipped up his trousers. 'Well, that was most pleasant and so unexpected,' he said, as he wiped the sweat from his forehead. 'I'll not be in for lunch. Back around four.' He moved towards the door.

'Justin!' Sylvina called, wrapping a towel around herself.

'Talk later,' he said, without turning. 'William will be here for dinner.' He paused. 'I'd say he'll be hard to move out if you put on a display like that, girls, but please have a little more decorum. Make him wait . . . at least a couple of days.'

'You mean he's staying?' Sylvina asked.

'Yes – and he jumped at the invitation. We're to discuss our proposition with him,' he said, and disappeared from view. Moments later he called Sylvina's name. She stood up and followed him into the house, leaving Sharee now collapsed on a sun-lounger. 'One little thing my love. Get rid of the shop assistant. She really does let you down. Make some excuse. I would prefer it if she wasn't here when I got back.'

'But, Justin, she thinks she's here for the summer.'

He sighed with irritation. 'Tough.'

'What about your other guest? How do you think she's going to cope?'

He checked his appearance in the mirror, then his eyes strayed to hers, cold, expressionless. 'She will be part of it. As I said, sweetie, I have been planning this for months.'

'But you didn't even know he was coming here,' she said.

Justin gave one of his sly crooked smiles. 'Didn't I? Well, let's just say it's all worked out perfectly, or I'm just lucky.' Sylvina flinched as he twisted the skin on her forearm until it hurt. 'So get rid of the slag.'

Sylvina stepped back. 'I'll think of something,' was all she said, and he brushed past her before she could add anything else.

Sylvina showered and changed. She went into Justin's bedroom. It was tidy, apart from a stack of magazines strewn over the bed. She picked up an old issue of *Vogue*, and turned to where a yellow sticker protruded. It was in the property section, where she found, ringed in red felt-tip pen, an advertisement for an island in the Caribbean, for sale, price on request. She looked over numerous other articles, all referring to William Benedict's purchase for eight million of a paradise island. Sir William was quoted as saying he intended to refurbish the island, and there were lists of the designers he had approached. She laughed softly. Perhaps Justin was not as crazy as she had thought. It was obvious now what his intentions were. He wanted the job. And maybe, just maybe, he was going to use her to persuade William to give it to him, for a fee. Well, she'd do whatever she needed to – like Justin, she could smell money dripping from the glossy pages he'd underlined and flagged.

By the time she returned to the pool, Sharee was lying topless, smothered in oil, her big breasts flopping wide across her chest. Her tiny bikini briefs were still untied and she looked, as Justin had said, like a slag.

'You want to go down to the beach for some lunch?'

Sharee wafted her hand. 'Nah, I'm knackered. Let's stay here and flop around.'

'I'm going. Come on, take a shower. Make yourself look good.'

'I don't feel like it.'

'Terence Hampton just called, he's getting a party going. The producer of *Babylon Baby* will be there, with a whole bunch of actors. They're looking for locations.'

Sharee sat up and stretched. 'In that case . . .' She laughed '. . . will you gimme one of those tiger-motif sarongs to wear and those big mules with the white tie strap?'

'Sure. Have anything you want, but don't be too long. I've ordered a taxi.'

'Okay.' Sharee breezed past, catching her hand. 'You look real classy, Countess.'

Sharee had not the slightest idea that she was about

to be persuaded to leave. Her lover might care for her, but she loved money more.

The private beach area had a small but elegantly styled Moorish marquee, in which tables had been set. The champagne was on ice and plates of fresh shellfish laid out. A guitarist was playing bossanovas. In the evening, there would be a disco and the party would continue until dawn. Sylvina arrived neither too early nor too late: she timed it so that she was seen by the optimum number of guests, and could do the rounds of cheek-kissing and introductions. Today's guests were mixed, mainly actors and actresses, a few producers and studio executives. It was rent-a-crowd time. The guest list had been compiled by Meryl Delaware, who held court in a flowing white cotton kaftan with platform shoes, Armani dark glasses, a silk scarf tied round her hair and jangling gold bracelets. The outfit successfully disguised her squat body.

'Darling, that was a lovely dinner party,' she cooed to Sylvina. 'My dear, you do know about that awful Sir William, don't you? His appearance at any function will clear the room. Ghastly creature. I used to be at school with his ex-wife, Katherine Hangerford. Sweet, sweet woman and such adorable children. It's just too awful the way he's dragged them through the gutter press.'

Meryl's lipstick was already running into the rivulets that had formed around her collagen-boosted lips. Sylvina let her prattle on while she scanned the crowd for Sharee. She managed to catch her eye, and gestured for her to join them. 'You know Sharee, don't you,

Meryl? I've promised to get her an introduction to Bernard Goldberg.'

Meryl smiled bleakly. 'Such an adorable man.' She ushered Sharee ahead of her and glanced back to Sylvina, just a flicker to register that she was owed a favour in return for this intro.

Sylvina looked on, as her lover shook hands with the large balding man in a T-shirt, huge baggy shorts and a backwards red baseball cap. At least he had the manners to remove the cigar from his lips as he leaned forward to catch Sharee's name. He was in a huddle with Terence Hampton, a Brad Pitt lookalike – one of the many dotted around – and one of the Baldwin brothers, no one seemed to know which one.

Sylvina waited half an hour, moving around unobtrusively. She was asked to a couple of dinner parties that evening, but to everyone's surprise she politely said she was otherwise engaged. The joke about Sylvina was that even if she was stranded in the Sahara desert she'd know someone there who would give her a free meal. Eventually she made her way back to Sharee.

'This is Countess Lubrinsky,' Sharee said to Goldberg, who beamed and offered Sylvina a glass of champagne.

She declined politely, raising the half-filled glass from which she had taken no more than a few sips. 'I have a terrible headache. Do you mind if we leave?' she whispered to Sharee.

'What? Now?'

'Sorry.'

Sharee put on a sympathetic face. 'You go and lie down. I'll come later.' She leaned in close. 'They're all

110

dining on his yacht later and he's asked me. What do you think?'

'Go for it.' Sylvina smiled and left her.

Just after six Sharee returned to the villa to change. She was quite drunk, and was with three of Goldberg's guests in their Rolls Royce Corniche. The volume of the CD player was so loud that Sylvina was forewarned of their arrival well before they appeared on the drive. Sharee was flushed with excitement at the prospect of the party on the yacht. The plan, she told Sylvina, was to potter around the bay then maybe sail along the coast to Monaco. She was hot, feverish and angry in case Sylvina threw one of her moods and insisted that she stay.

'It's entirely up to you,' sighed Sylvina. 'Go, if you want. They seem a great group of people.'

'They are. And Terence is coming along. Why don't you come too?'

'Oh, sweetheart, I don't want to move. Head, you know.' She sank dramatically into a chair. 'Pack your things, don't worry.'

Sharee blinked, swaying. 'Well, there's no need for me to pack everything. I mean, it's just a night or two.'

Sylvina smiled weakly. 'Make the most of it. This could be your movie break, darling, what you've dreamed about. He's very famous, isn't he? Go and have a lovely time. And you know I hate having Justin looming over my shoulders so I'll probably go back to Paris if you stay on board any longer. If you've got all your things there'll be no problem.'

111

'Sure you don't mind?'

Sylvina picked up her case and walked her out to the car, whose stereo was still playing Guns N' Roses's 'November Rain' at an ear-splitting volume. The Corniche vanished up the drive, leaving Sylvina waving wanly on the porch. It had been so easy.

By seven o'clock there was still no sign of Justin, and it didn't look as if the planned dinner with William would be going ahead. The headache Sylvina had faked earlier was now coming on for real so she decided to go up to the roof for a cool swim. She paused as she passed her suite: her clothes had been taken to Sharee's room earlier in the day. Vast clear glass bowls now held bunches of white liles, which complemented the white bedspread, white lace cushions and the white muslin curtains that billowed out over the polished wood floor. The room was looking bare to the point of bleakness, but Justin's impending house guest hated clutter. He always had to rearrange the furniture when she was around. He said she suffered from claustrophobia – or was it agoraphobia? Over the years she had had every phobia known to man. She was the most neurotic woman Sylvina had ever met.

Continuing up the stairs to the roof, Sylvina walked out into the clear night air, stripped off her clothes and eased her body into the pool. She loved to swim naked at this time of the evening. It was so perfect; the water cool and refreshing. She swam a few lengths then lay floating on her back, eyes closed.

'She's very beautiful, isn't she?' It was Justin, whispering to William.

Sylvina had not heard them walk out onto the roof, but hearing the whisper, she opened her eyes and smiled. 'I didn't hear you arrive,' she said softly.

'We got held up in some traffic,' Justin said nonchalantly. 'Then we did a tour of the villa, and here we are.'

'It's nice to see you again, William.'

William smiled shyly. 'I'm sorry if I'm intruding.'

Sylvina swam to the side. 'Don't be. I'll go and shower. Are we going to dine at home, Justin, or would you like to book a table?'

'Eat in,' he replied abruptly.

As Sylvina strolled past them she heard Justin speaking to Marta on the poolside phone and asking for chilled champagne. William looked even more uncomfortable this evening than he had on the previous night. He was wearing another crumpled suit, with a creamy shirt left open at the neck to reveal a patch of pale skin.

By the time they sat down to dinner, Sylvina observed that he looked marginally better having removed his frightful open-toed sandals in favour of canvas rope-soled shoes. She also noticed that he hardly touched his champagne but instead consumed copious amounts of water. She was quiet and thoughtful, allowing Justin to regale them both with one amusing story after another about his travels, then listened to him describing the numerous villas he has redesigned including his own. He told William that at one time fire had destroyed the entire top floor, and he had redesigned it. He 'happened' to have some of his designs on hand to show William, who seemed impressed, but not overly interested. Justin had already

113

driven him around to show him various villas and gardens he had refurbished.

Eventually William leaned across to Justin and tapped his hand. 'No need for overkill, you've already got the job.'

Justin laughed with delight. 'I can't stop thinking about what I'll do.'

'Just give me some plans to look over, and an estimate of what it'll cost to do everything you've suggested.'

Justin turned to Sylvina. 'William has a wonderful paradise island . . . Well, it's not a paradise yet but I intend to make it into one.'

'For a price,' she said softly, and caught the ice in Justin's eyes. But then she made him smile. 'Justin's the best interior designer I've ever known. Exciting, inventive and, considering what he's made of this villa, a genius.'

'Thank you.' He grinned like a delighted schoolboy and then gave her a small wink. 'We've had long talks about you.'

'Really?' she said nonchalantly.

On numerous occasions throughout the meal, she felt William's eyes on her, but if she returned his gaze, he immediately looked away. Whenever possible, Sylvina took the opportunity to reappraise his looks. He had nice hands and wore an expensive slim gold Bulgari watch. On his left hand he wore a heavy signet ring on his little finger. His cufflinks, however, were multi-coloured enamel; not so good.

'Shall we go into the drawing room or on to the roof?' Justin asked.

'Drawing room. I seem to have been on the roof all day,' said Sylvina, smiling. William, very much the gentleman, eased back her chair to allow her to move from the table. He stepped aside and she walked ahead of him from the room. It was sweet that he was on his best behaviour, Sylvina mused.

As they headed for the drawing room, William disappeared to the bathroom, and Justin gripped her elbow. 'He's on the line, sweetheart.'

'I can see that,' she said coolly.

He whispered, 'Not just for me. I've worked him over for you too. You're gonna do the Pygmalion on him, and for one million.'

'What? Are you joking?'

'No. Ssh, he's coming back.'

Marta had set out coffee, brandy and port, plus chilled lemonade and more iced water beside the two large white canvas sofas. Justin and Sylvina sat on one, with William opposite. William lit a cigar, took a few deep puffs and then leaned back, crossing his legs as the smoke curled above his head. Sylvina was taken aback when he announced softly, 'One million.' His face was impassive as he went on, 'Would you like to tell me what you are prepared to do for that?'

Justin answered for her. 'I think it is right that you should know she's a lesbian.'

'My loss,' said William, and gave a wonderfully engaging chuckle. 'But I think I've had my days paying for sex. This will be purely a business deal.'

Justin gave her a sidelong glance.

Sylvina said, 'But you'll have to agree not to have any sex with another woman whilst I am with you, so there will be no hint of a scandal attached to your liaison.'

William nodded. 'How well known is your sexual orientation?'

'What?' she was puzzled.

'I'm prepared to buy your services to re-establish myself as a respectable member of high society, but you can guarantee that after we announce our engagement, the British press will start digging up your past. If it is public knowledge that you are a lesbian, I'm back to square one.'

'It isn't,' she snapped and, to her annoyance, felt herself blushing.

'Any recent affairs?' he asked, with a half-smile.

'One, but she's history,' she said, glaring at Justin. 'And it wouldn't be in her interest to let it out. She wants to get into the movies, you see.'

William was not entirely convinced. He had taken out a small black notebook and was flicking through the pages. Sylvina glanced at Justin, who raised an eyebrow.

'Justin said you will need a dress allowance, a car, servants. These will be listed as expenses, correct?'

'Yes,' Justin said.

'What figure are we talking here?'

Sylvina shrugged and looked again to Justin.

'Don't look at me, Sylvina darling, you know what designer clothes cost. Anyway, William, it'll be a good teaser sequence. You know, being see together at the Paris fashion shows.'

'My apartment's leased for a year,' Sylvina said, toying with her necklace, 'but my château is always good for name-dropping, even if it is only occupied by cats and fieldmice. The exterior is still magnificent. We could have some wonderful publicity shots taken together there and . . .' She was hardly able to take it in: he was paying her a million!

116

William jotted a note and turned to the next page, which was filled with neat lists. He had spent the afternoon working out whether Justin's proposition was viable. 'How much would it cost to refurbish?' he asked.

'I have no idea.' Sylvina sighed. 'It's in an appalling state. No one's lived there for ten, twelve years. Roof, plumbing, electrical wiring from the thirties. It was occupied by the Germans during the war . . .'

'I think I get the picture.' William made some more notes and pursed his lips. 'You know, I think it might be a possibility. My humiliation at being made such a public laughing-stock fired up an immediate need to get my own back, which I felt was rather childish. But I have now become genuinely excited by the prospect. I've decided to take a lengthy period away from my work. If I am going to be reintroduced to society life, I might as well enjoy it. How long do you think we'll need?'

Justin jumped in. 'Oh, quite some time. Don't forget, I'll have my hands full redesigning the villa. That could be at least six months.'

'Six months?' she gasped.

'Six months?' William said, astonished.

'Of course. I'll have to ship in most of the fabrics and furnishings, and I'll need time to prepare my plans.'

Sylvina was now in tune with Justin. The longer it took, the more money they could squeeze out of him. 'To ingratiate yourself into the top level of society takes time and patience. You'll need to get to know an awful lot of people. I can arrange dinners and parties to introduce you, but you also need a bit of refurbishment yourself, William. To get a perfect suit made up nowadays takes six to eight weeks.'

'So we're looking at even longer than six months,' William said, shutting his book and slipping it into his breast pocket. 'But in the cold light of day, let's face it, the proposition is a farce and mightly easily backfire. To play out such an expensive game would make me even more of a loser if it goes wrong.'

'It won't,' Justin interjected.

'I'll make sure of it,' Sylvina said firmly.

William was beginning to feel in control again. Clearly Justin and Sylvina needed him – or his money. The game might work, but William's business brain was still functioning at full speed. He would pay, but he would make sure he got his money's worth.

'Obviously the ball is firmly in your court, William, but last night when we talked you seemed so frustrated by all the crap you'd been subjected to,' Justin said casually. 'If you can live with it, that's your business. I couldn't – but, then, I'm not you.'

'No, you're not,' William said. He rose, and glanced at Sylvina for permission to help himself to a brandy. 'This would be a totally new venture for me. Even if I win the game, it will provide me with satisfaction but no financial remuneration.' He swirled the brandy in his glass. 'On the other hand it might be fun.' He smiled and leaned against the back of the sofa. 'Fun is not something I've had much of. What I had previously regarded as fun now seems rather wretchedly mundane. However, it sounds as if you wish to be the "ringmaster" – because you instigated the game you would automatically control the events. I can't let that happen. It is imperative that I am in control. I must be the manipulator, as I am in my business dealings.'

'So what are you saying?' Justin asked tentatively.

'That I'll play . . . but with ground rules that I set down. And if you do not come up to expectations, I walk away. Your pay-off will be dependent on success. In other words, I am perfectly willing to pay for the privilege of becoming . . .' he chuckled '. . . your Eliza Doolittle, with a very attractive Professor Higgins.' He beamed at Sylvina. His face was alert, his eyes bright. 'So, here's the proposition. If within eight and twelve months you can help me regain my standing in the upper echelons of UK society, you get your money.'

He had one final query. 'One thing I do need to know, though, and whether or not I agree to all we have just discussed will depend on your answer.' They waited with baited breath. 'Tell me about Andrew Maynard. You first, Sylvina.'

She glanced at Justin, then fingered her necklace. 'I know what happened to him, obviously. Very tragic, even more so because I had met him here, just the once, and he seemed to be a genuine and interesting young man. That's all, really, I didn't know him at all.'

William turned a cool gaze to Justin, and gasped. Tears were streaming down his cheeks.

'What happened, Justin? I need to know.'

Justin paused for some minutes before he spoke, his voice low. 'I met him about two years ago. It was his first time in France and he was trying to buy some batteries for his camera, down on the quayside. His French was appalling, so I introduced myself and—'

'And?' William interjected.

'We became friends. He moved in here to stay for the rest of his holiday. Then we became lovers.' Justin closed his eyes and sighed. 'He was obsessed with this place, with me, with France. It was like he had never enjoyed a moment of his life until then. But he was just a summer thing for me. I had no idea what I had . . . encouraged. I mean, I'm a free spirit, but he wanted to own me, and because he couldn't, he got into some weird sex-trips with rent-boys. Andrew had been sexually naïve, but he made up for it and, from then on, whenever he could he came here. Sometimes I never even saw him.'

'But you were the last person to see him in England the night he died.'

'He was in a depressed state, and I will always feel guilty because I probably made him even more so. I suggested that perhaps I shouldn't see him any more. I told him I couldn't reciprocate, I didn't want him. That evening I told him not to be foolish, he was taking too many risks, especially in his career. So I left him. The rest you know.' William sighed and Justin added, in a soft, emotional voice, 'I will never forgive myself. The way he has been written about is unfair, so cruel. He did not deserve it. You want to get even, William, well, maybe I do too, not for me but for Andrew.'

Sylvina had not been paying much attention to Justin. He was putting on a show for William's benefit, obviously. All she knew was that Justin had got thousands out of poor foolish Maynard, the way he had with so many lovers; he used them and discarded them, enjoying their desperation almost as if that was what turned him on.

'Does this mean you won't hire me to refurbish your villa?' Justin said now, in a boyish voice.

'No, of course it doesn't. But, as I said before, I will need professional estimates. Truth is, with the problems

I've been through I've not had time lately even to consider the island, but if you have ideas and experience, and you evidently have, then yes, you can do it. Why not? As for you, Sylvina, here's a list of people who are high on the social agenda that I want to see eating out of my hands!'

The first two names on the list she knew. 'Well, this will be no problem at all, Baron and Baroness von Garten are friends of mine.' She recalled the way they had left dinner in front of William, and added hastily, 'Not close friends, of course. But . . . yes, I know most of these names. It'll be no problem at all.'

Justin rested his hand on Sylvina's knee and gave it a small triumphant pat. He knew now his fish wasn't even wriggling. The game was about to commence, and William, for all his business acumen, had no notion of where the ground rules began and ended.

It was quite some time before Sylvina was able to corner Justin alone, and ask him just what this deal to refurbish some villa was about.

Justin shrugged. 'Well, sweet face, you are getting paid for Sir William's entry into society, and I am doing the same for some island he's got in the Caribbean. Nothing wrong in feathering my own nest – I've certainly feathered your bankrupt one.'

'There's no need to rub my nose in it.' She moved closer. 'But what was all that about a game, taking revenge? He's not a crook, is he?'

'No, straight as an arrow, pussy.'

'So what were you talking about?'

'Mind your own business.'

'But if I'm going to be living in his pocket, so to speak, don't you think I should know?'

He turned to her, and his eyes were so cruel that she stepped away. 'You don't want to know because it doesn't concern you.'

'But it is something that concerns you, right?'

He glared, refusing to answer, but under his breath he whispered, 'It does, but he doesn't know it . . . yet.'

CHAPTER 7

JUSTIN WAITED until he thought William was asleep, then crept into Sylvina's room. He eased the door closed and flew on to her bed. Lying on top of her, he gripped her face with his hands. 'We are rich, rich, rich, sweetheart! Didn't I tell you it would work?'

'Yes, you did, but it's going to take a long time. He's no pushover, and he'll be counting every penny in that bloody little notebook.'

He rolled away to lie beside her, a big smile on his face. 'Listen, he's up for it, and you'll not see that book out again. Just take your time and enjoy it. You'll never have had so much money to throw around in your life!'

She leaned up on her elbow and looked down into his face. 'Where will you be when I'm with him?'

Justin stretched and yawned. 'I am heading for the British Virgin Islands. Preparing the island for his future house-guests.' He giggled. 'Obviously my fees for refurbishing it in my own inimitable style will be exorbitant, but style never did come cheap.' He swung his legs from the bed and sat with his back to her.

Sylvina stroked his shoulder. 'I don't want any repercussions. I was serious about not wanting to get involved in anything illegal. I mean, he's not going to be hurling people off the cliffs, is he?'

'No, of course not. You heard him, he just wants to . . .'

'Mmm, go on. William wants to what?'

Justin walked across to the window and opened the white muslin curtains. He twisted one round him so that it hid his face. 'Everyone has a sexual fantasy. Everyone has wondered what it would be like to be taken to the ultimate erotic high. Unbridled lust and lechery is what is going to happen on the island.'

Sylvina laughed. 'My darling, I know you're an experienced screw, but you're not everyone's idea of the ultimate sexual partner.' She sat up. 'And don't think for one second that I'm interested in any of your erotica. I've agreed to spend as much time as it takes with William, but no sex. Then I'll be off, as soon as I've collected my fee. Do I really need a whole year with him?'

'Yes, it'll take that time to work over the island. I have to have enough time to prepare it.'

'This list of names he gave me – I mean, they're a bit ridiculous. I know the von Gartens, he met them here. What's so special to him about them?'

'No idea,' he said, shrugging.

'Cedric somebody, who's he?'

'Breeds racehorses, English aristo.'

She continued reading from the list: 'I mean, Meryl Delaware? Dear God, everyone knows that wretched scribbler.' One name had been underlined three times. 'This Humphrey Matlock, who's he?'

'Newspaper magnate. I'm surprised *you* haven't heard of him – you read his grubby papers.'

124

'Oh, well, he shouldn't be a problem, then. But no one on this list is remotely "high society". She put the list aside. 'Is she going with you? She's very fragile, you know.'

He let go of the curtain and sauntered to the door. 'She's never done anything she didn't want to,' he said quietly.

'Don't you mean she's never does anything without you pulling the strings? What is she going to be doing?'

'Mind your own damned business.'

'Fine, I will. But be careful because I know she had another fit and one day she might just snap. Be prepared for when she turns on the hand that operates her. I hope your devious little mind isn't setting me up to prepare William for her, marry her off for his money.'

He giggled. 'Don't worry. I'll keep her away from him until the time is right. She's my *pièce de résistance*, the perfect foil, my beloved sister.' He opened the door and blew Sylvina a kiss. 'Goodnight,' he said, and closed the door softly behind him. Then he swung it open again. 'Don't you even contemplate marrying him either. You can announce an engagement but then you have to ditch him publicly. Understand?'

'Oh, go to bed. One year with him will be sufficient, thank you.'

He closed the door again, and she lay back on her pillows. She'd done some crazy things in her life, but this one took first prize. Still, one million . . . *one million*!

Five days later, Sharee returned to Nice. She called the villa to be told by Marta that Sylvina had gone to Paris and had left no forwarding address. When she asked after Justin, she was told that Monsieur Chalmers was collecting his sister and would be departing for the British Virgin Islands, again with no forwarding address. She felt a little guilty about taking off for so long, but as no one was here, she couldn't apologize. Her sojourn had turned into a sordid group-sex session, which in itself had not worried her, except that she had been unable to get off the yacht. Still, she'd made friends with Terence Hampton, or thought she had – although when she'd called to ask if he could run her to the airport, he had been unable to come to the phone.

Sharee eventually flew back to London and her small studio apartment. She continued to phone Sylvina on her various numbers, but her calls were not returned. It baffled her at first, but then made her feel that somehow she had been moved aside, as if Sylvina had instigated the boat trip. Although she knew it had been her own decision to go, doubts began to surface, and Sylvina's rejection angered her. Not only had she been used like a whore on the movie producer's boat, Sylvina had treated her in the same way.

William's apartment in avenue Hoche was already lavishly decorated with the finest antiques and paintings. All it required were floral displays. Sylvina moved in and, for the moment, William stayed in a suite at the Ritz.

Sylvina checked every society-function guest-list, making copious notes of the hottest faces on the circuit and the most fashionable venues. She had not expected to enjoy herself quite so much, but having a man so dependent upon her was a new experience she relished. And with no sexual chemistry to complicate the relationship, she and William were surprised to discover a genuine mutual friendship growing.

That William knew from the outset that sex with Sylvina was out of the question made him much more relaxed when she questioned him about his affairs. He found himself admitting that perhaps the disasters of his loveless marriages had been his fault. He had been too eager to move up the social ladder.

'What on earth for?' Sylvina asked, never having had to climb so much as a single rung herself. Her own family had been titled and she had married Count Lubrinsky at an early age. She had not seen their union as social climbing, because it was his wealth more than his title that she'd married.

Sylvina's château had never really been a home, just a rambling, cold megalith, and one morning they drove down to the small hamlet where it was situated outside Tours. Even with its high turrets and splendid balcony, it seemed tired and grey.

'This is where I was brought up, apart from the years I spent at school in England, of course, which I hated but it was still preferable to spending time here.' It had been years since she had visited the place and she felt an unwelcome surge of emotion as she stopped the car. 'Do you want to see inside?' she asked, almost hoping he would say no.

But William got out and looked around, smiling. 'Yes! This is wonderful!' They wandered through room after room with empty walls and rotten floorboards.

Trees and shrubs sprouted in corners, as if nature had taken over like a secret army. It was a sad wreck of a once beautiful palace.

'My father gambled away his inheritance. I was never sure whether he married me off to a count so that he could still live here or so that he could still gamble. The Count was an elderly cousin. The marriage was not consummated, and he died a few months after my twenty-first birthday.' She fell silent. Then she said flatly, 'They should bring in the demolition people. It's dangerous.' Seeing it again, after so many years, had brought home to her her lonely childhood. The barriers placed across the stairs, cutting off rooms too dangerous to enter, were like the emotional barriers that divided her family.

'This is all I have left,' she went on. 'My father spent the money I was left by my husband. Papa was a wastrel,' she said, looking up to the massive barrel-vaulted ceiling where once chandeliers of the finest crystal had tinkled. The fact that William wanted immediately to restore the château while Sylvina wanted it torn down epitomized their differing attitudes to the past: he was awed; she was indifferent. 'Why live in the past? It's better to look to the future,' she said.

'But generations of your family lived here.'

'So they did, and they're all dead.' She was starting to feel depressed by it, and over everything loomed her hatred of her father.

On the drive back to Paris William said he could not believe that when she received her money she would not rebuild the place. Sylvina couldn't contemplate the idea. 'No one can live in such a monster of a house,' she said. She had no children to inherit it. Why would she want to resurrect something that was dead? It was a pointless exercise, as pointless, to her, as being overawed by wealth and a title.

'That's because you have it, and I haven't,' he said, as they returned to avenue Hoche.

'No, it's because you think it will give you something. I am telling you it won't. All you saw was a large white elephant.'

'No, I saw your past, your family's past. It's in every stone of that château.' She cupped his face in her hands and kissed his cheeks. 'They are dead and I am alive. The world has changed. I want to live in the present. If I were to spend all my money renovating the château, I would be living in the past. You should be angry that you wasted a second of your time worrying about what has happened to you. You are a rich man. You could have anything, be anything. Go and find yourself a young, beautiful wife. Have more children, and don't dwell on the past. It will swallow you up.' Suddenly she stopped. All this had made her forget why she was with him, which, as she had said, was all to do with the past.

'What are you thinking about?' he asked.

'Oh, nothing. Memories.'

Sylvina was still anxious when William left for the hotel, convinced she had made him think about what they were doing and worried he might pull out. Why had she been so bloody truthful? The million pounds looked as if it might disappear. But at the same time the images of her childhood would not lie quiet. Tomorrow she would have to work extra hard, just in case she had placed doubts in his mind.

*

Sylvina need not have worried. William too was caught up in the past he had always tried to submerge. The voices would not lie quiet. He wasn't thinking about what Sylvina had said, just hearing the cries, seeing his mother press the ice-pack against her swollen cheek. He vividly remembered a particular night when, in tears, he had asked his mother if he should go to the police. She had slapped him and said, 'You'll do no such thing. This is private business. It's nothing, do you hear me? Nothing happened here.' He knew it had, but his drunken father was sleeping off the booze. 'Don't pay any attention to what you see, Billy love, just you get out. If you get to be somebody, this will all have been worthwhile. You can say it made you. Because if there isn't a reason for it, he might as well kill me now.'

What had his mother meant? He had never stopped asking himself that question. Now he thought of the abuse he had suffered at the hands of the bloodthirsty media. He didn't need to take their insults, as his mother, who'd had nowhere to run, had accepted his father's brutality. It frightened him now to think that perhaps he had inherited her wretched acceptance of fate. She had never fought back, and neither had he. Paying out a million pounds to save his face was a cowardly revenge, perhaps as bad as his mother telling him that his success was worth her pain. He was ashamed that he had not fought back, ignored the lawyers by suing, even if it had meant losing money. At least he would have had some respect for himself. And what had he done instead? Run to Justin at his villa.

He picked up the phone and called Sylvina. 'It's me,' he said hesitantly. 'I don't want to be on my own,

Sylvina, just tonight. It's not . . . Can I come round to see you?'

'Yes.'

There was a long pause before she surprised herself by saying, 'I was just about to call you.'

'Well, I beat you to it.'

When Sylvina opened the apartment door, they looked at each other then embraced. It was not a sexual gesture, just mutually comforting.

'After I left you,' he said, accepting the brandy she held out, 'I started remembering things that I didn't want to think about. And then I couldn't stop.'

'Me too.'

They clinked glasses.

As they lay next to each other in the big Louis Quinze bed, William felt an unfamiliar warmth. 'My mother . . .' he said shyly.

She snuggled against him. 'I was thinking of mine too.'

They slept that night in each other's arms. They had not found the answers, they were not even sure what they were looking for, but they had found a deeper friendship.

The following morning they had breakfast together. As Sylvina poured his coffee she gave him an affectionate smile. 'Had any more thoughts on what we talked about last night?'

He looked at her, surprised, a glob of marmalade at the side of his mouth. 'What? What do you mean?'

She sipped her chilled *citron pressé*. 'You're not having second thoughts . . . about going on?'

'Good heavens, no!' he said, slurping his coffee.

It almost made her wince. In a formal setting his eating habits were acceptable, as she had observed at the dinner party, but when he was relaxed, he reverted to childhood table manners; eating with his fingers and dropping crumbs everywhere.

'For one thing, the island isn't anywhere near ready, and for another, as good as you are at bolstering my confidence, I've still a long way to go. Besides, I'm enjoying myself. This is the longest period I've ever spent away from my work.'

She smiled. 'Well, you're not entirely away from it. You spend hours every day on the phone barking instructions, and I've seen the faxes at the hotel for you every night.'

'Ah, yes. Well, I've got to keep my beady eye on everyone. I've got damned good staff, but you can never trust anyone else to make your decisions.'

'You mean you can't delegate.' His sharp tone unnerved her.

'Oh, but I can, my dear. If I couldn't, I wouldn't be worth the fortune I have accumulated over thirty years. I have thirty-five board members, even more top-level executives. Some have been working for me for years. I believe in giving tremendous responsibility to my team – it's one of my talents. An even better talent is spotting new blood . . .'

Sylvina listened for a full ten minutes as William outlined his numerous business deals, down to the location of each of his endless factories. Then he described the new Internet site he had set up to sell his games on-line, even drawing with his sticky knife on the pristine tablecloth to demonstrate some new hi-tech computer link that kids could use to play for serious prizes across the world.

She gritted her teeth. The question on her lips was why William was playing around with her, albeit at a price, and why he was allowing Justin free access to his island at what she knew would be an astronomical cost. Darling Justin Chalmers could spend other people's money even better than she could steal it. He had no morals, unless . . . Was it some kind of blackmail?'

'Is Justin hitting you for cash?' she asked sweetly.

'Bloody fortune.' William stood up and tossed his napkin on to the table. Then he beamed. 'But he's building me a paradise.'

'Really? Well, far be it for me to give you any advice, if that's what you want . . .'

'Ah, that's only part of it.' He glanced at his wristwatch.

Sylvina couldn't resist asking, 'Part of what?'

He walked to the door as if he were not going to reply, but as he reached it he looked back at her. 'It's a private matter.'

'To do with Andrew Maynard?'

His face darkened. There were many layers to William, she thought, and from his expression, she knew that whatever Justin was up to had something to do with the death of Maynard.

'Indirectly,' William said quietly, and swung the door with the toe of his shoe. 'Most of all it's to do with me, and if Justin hasn't enlightened you then I feel I shouldn't. Now, it's getting late and we don't want to miss the entire morning. We're going to the galleries today, aren't we?'

133

'Yes, it's a private view,' she said, stubbing out her cigarette. Not that anyone would be examining the paintings, just who was there. The publicity wheels were already in motion and she and William would be photographed. 'I suggest you take your time over dressing. Wear the new Valentino dark grey suit, white shirt and silk tie. I'll meet you in two hours. I must have my hair done, my nails . . .'

'Okay, whatever you say, Ma'am.' He walked out, leaving her deeply frustrated and still no nearer the real reason behind her 'contract' with him and whatever the devious Justin was doing.

William had arranged a bank account for Justin to use during his work on the island. He did not place any limit on expenditure, but gave strict instructions that any new acquisitions must be agreed in advance. These were to be dealt with through his office at home, where Michael would monitor Justin's costs. Justin sent faxes several sheets long on the refurbishments, detailing everything from art purchases down to the price and size of each towel to be placed in the suites. Time and again Michael gasped with amazement as the costs soared, but whenever he mentioned it to William he was simply told to pay. So he did. The figure mounted daily.

That evening William and Sylvina were to dine with the British ambassador, after a first-night performance of *Dido and Aeneas* at the Bastille Opera. A photographer leaped forward when they alighted from their limousine, drawing the press-pack towards them, the battery of flashbulbs making them feel like royalty. Sylvina was pleased they could not be photographed inside the theatre, as William slept through the entire programme. Returning to the hotel he yawned until she wanted to slap him.

'I think I've had enough of Paris,' he said eventually.

She would have liked to tell him that she'd had just about enough of him, but instead she said she would need a couple of days to pack and make the arrangements to move on. He didn't argue. For two days he left her in peace as he took himself off to toy shops. Toy shops! At times he behaved so childishly.

William returned with his arms full of mechanical toys. Sylvina found him sitting on the floor winding them up and crawling around after them on all fours. A few hours later he had taken them all apart. He made fast sketches of each and beamed with delight. 'I can rip off every one of these. My factory can knock them out at a quarter the price. Obviously we'll have to make them slightly different, or I'll be sued, but—'

She interrupted, 'I have some shopping to do. Would you arrange with your pilot to take off later? I've had some alterations done and they won't be ready for collection till four.'

'No problem, dear heart.' He was squatting on the floor with an electronic device that made four toy mice scuttle across the carpet, followed by a larger creature representing a cat. Sylvina walked out as he yelped, 'Gotcha!' The furry cat scooped the little mice into its open mouth, and emitted a high-pitched screech.

'Bloody clever,' he muttered. Although William had never had toys in his childhood, he was not making

135

up for it now, as Sylvina thought. This was money: this was what excited and cheered him. At long last he was looking forward to returning to work: his energy was back.

Sylvina was loath to leave Paris but now she saw that she had little choice: William was impatient to go home. She decided that Justin was getting a better deal than she was and feverishly upped her spending sprees. She ordered a new wardrobe from Valentino, Givenchy and Christian Dior, with matching shoes, hats and handbags. She had never liked London, but at least she was returning to it in style.

William got back to The Boltons with so much luggage that his chauffeur had to order another car to follow the Rolls. His servants looked on, speechless, as Sylvina was introduced, her suitcases filling the hallway. 'Michael, this is Countess Lubrinsky.' William's secretary gave a small bow, flushing as she acknowledged him with a glacial smile. She told the chauffeur to make sure that all the cases had been removed from the second car, and asked the housekeeper to see that they were taken up to her suite. Her perfume hung in the air, sweet and heavy. From her body language alone, everyone could see that she loathed the house.

A few days later William burst into Michael's office, demanding an update on his business. Michael wanted to discuss the exorbitant outgoings of Justin Chalmers. William dismissed his worries with a waft of his hand: he had little or no immediate interest in the island.

'Don't fret, for God's sake, Michael. I certainly won't be having financial worries for a fair few years yet. Just get me up to date on the business.'

'But, sir, this Justin Chalmers—'

'What about him?'

'Well, his bills are vast! Purchases being shipped in from India and heaven knows where else.'

'He's an interior designer, Michael.'

'So all the accounts I've sent you are acceptable? Fine. I'll confirm that with the accountants.' He hesitated before continuing. 'Er, what about the account you opened in the name of Countess Lubrinsky? It's already in the red.'

'Top it up,' said William, bored.

'But it's another twenty-five thousand.'

'Michael, she is to be my wife.'

'I'm sorry?' Michael's voice sounded strangled.

'You heard, Michael. Countess Lubrinsky and I are engaged to be married.'

'*Engaged*?' Michael stuttered.

'Yes, that is correct. Beautiful woman, isn't she?' Then William began to pass the sheets of drawings he had made of the toys in Paris. 'Get these over to the art department, then on to the factory. I like the cat and mouse one. But we'll have to come up with a different concept. Tell the artists to make it up as a fox and chickens.'

William tapped on Sylvina's door. He was told to enter and found her trying on a gown.

'Whoever did your décor should be shot,' she said. 'This is so ghastly, I feel ill.'

'I told my secretary,' he said, looking around irritably. He'd never noticed the blue and white flock wallpaper, depicting Chinese fishermen with little rods.

'Told him what?' she asked, as she looked at herself in the wardrobe mirror. Even that was hideous – and, worse, the mirror was so cheap it made her look fat.

'That we're engaged.'

She turned sideways for a different angle of herself in the spectacular black velvet sheath dress. 'Bit premature, isn't it? Weren't we supposed to discuss it first? I thought we'd only make an announcement if it was essential. They don't even know I'm in England yet. We need to be seen around a lot first.' She smoothed the velvet over her hips. 'Let's hope he doesn't run to the press, because we're not ready to make any announcement yet.'

'Christ, it's an engagement, not a wedding date. It's covered in your fee and you agreed.'

'I'm not saying I didn't but, I think you might have had the manners to *discuss* it with me first. It was a silly thing to do, especially after we've spent so long working on your profile.'

He flopped into an armchair and opened a magazine. 'Oh, Michael's not going to tell anyone. He's worked for me for years. Have you seen this month's *Paris-Match*? There's a photo of us at the races. Very good of you, but not so flattering of me.'

Sylvina peered at the series of photographs. 'Darling, it's me who has to be the catch of all time. And, besides, I think you look very sophisticated.'

'I think I look a bit of a prat.'

Sylvina told William she had hired a well-known PR agent who would ensure that wherever they went a paparazzo would be at hand, the flash of whose camera would draw attention to them. But William seemed to have forgotten that this had been paid for. Like a young movie-star, he had started to believe his own publicity. And he loved it.

'You never cease to amaze me,' she said, turning her back for him to unzip the dress.

'Why? Is it seeing the man emerge before you? Well, I've done everything you told me to do.' He chortled.

It was hard to believe that in such a short time he had changed so much. There was a confident air about him, and his voice was louder than it had been in Paris.

'You're very cheerful,' she said.

'I'm glad to be home.'

Sylvina let the gown slip to her ankles and stepped out of it, naked. William reached out, as if to touch her, and she stepped back. 'Don't get too confident, William.'

He snatched away his hand as if she had slapped it. 'It was just a bit of lint on your shoulder,' he snapped. 'I should be allowed to touch you, considering the money I'm paying you. But don't worry, I don't want to.' He walked out and slammed the bedroom door shut behind him.

Sylvina sighed. He'd done it to her again. It unnerved her, the way that at one moment he was under her control and at the next she would realize that he could get rid of her whenever he liked. She had to be more careful now they were on his turf.

The couple had dined with film stars and cabinet ministers in Paris, attended premières, had been seen at

Longchamps and Auteuil. Now that they were in England the wheels of publicity were turning here. Michael monitored the growing frenzy around the pair with trepidation. He couldn't grasp what was going on, but knew it was building towards something. Perhaps it was just the announcement of their nuptials, but he had detected that the Countess, far from caring for William, was at times almost disdainful of him. He was sure she was simply bleeding him of a lot of money. And Michael was aware of how much, because he oversaw her accounts. *Nothing* quite made sense – not just the Countess, but the vast fortune being paid out to Justin Chalmers. And when he took a call from William's financial adviser, who was fishing for information, Mr Flynn appeared as nonplussed as himself at the astronomical sums being moved to the British Virgin Islands. He asked if Michael had any notion of what was going on.

'I believe he's having the island refurbished.'

'The amount he's shelling out could refurbish bloody New Zealand. This is just a small place, isn't it?'

'I'm not aware of the detailed instructions, just that the island is being prepared for Sir William to stay there with some guests.'

'Well, please ask him to contact me. He's not returned any of my calls . . .' There was a long pause, then Michael heard a light cough. 'Just between you and me, Michael, I know he took quite a public thrashing over this Maynard business. He's not having some kind of breakdown, is he?'

'No, he seems in very good spirits.'

'Ah. Well, get him to call me because I don't want to continue throwing money at this chap Chalmers until I've spoken to him. I need more details.'

Michael hung up, and addressed himself to another of Sir William's scrawled messages. The Countess did not wish to remain in The Boltons so he had arranged to rent a house for her in Mayfair. Having now formally announced their engagement in *The Times*, they were at last holding centre-stage, and Sylvina felt it would look better if they did not appear to be cohabiting.

'We're not,' William had said petulantly.

'We're under the same roof, dearest, and that to Meryl Delaware means we're swinging naked from the light fittings. We must appear to be above reproach, exceedingly respectable.'

'Fine. Go ahead and do what you want.' William was growing bored with her constant requests for hand-outs.

Sylvina insisted on installing a maid, cook and butler in her new home and ordered that the floral displays be changed every three days. She adored her luxurious surroundings, but William was irritating her. She tried to contact Justin, but after leaving several messages she gave up. She knew that William and he kept in regular touch, but when she asked how the 'project' was coming along William said simply that it was costing enough to be more than just 'coming along' and he hoped it was almost completed. So did his financial adviser, who had demanded a meeting to discuss the island situation.

'I have the money, haven't I?'

'Well, yes, of course, Sir William, but I also have to do my job, and I am advising you—'

'Don't. I know what the costs are and I have agreed to them. That is all you need to know.'

'And the house in Mayfair?'

'That is also acceptable. My fiancée requires her own establishment so, if there is no other business, please excuse me.'

Yet again, the idea occurred to them that perhaps Sir William was having a breakdown.

As they left his office, Michael was waiting to usher them out. 'What do *you* know of this Justin Chalmers?' Mr Flynn asked. He and his company had worked with William for many years, but Mr Flynn had never been spoken to so brusquely or kept so much in the dark by William as he had today.

'I've never met him, Mr Flynn,' Michael said quietly, afraid to be overheard. I did check up with some interior designers I know of, and they have no idea who he is, but . . .' Michael hesitated '. . . I think he was an associate of Andrew Maynard.'

Mr Flynn nodded. 'I see,' he said, but he didn't really, and he was rather annoyed at the way he had been treated. But, as Sir William had said, he had the finance to do what he wanted, so if this island was what he wanted then so be it. Mr Flynn would keep the money flowing out.

The past months in London had been enjoyable to begin with, especially as William watched people's attitudes change towards him. But the 'intended marriage' was now constantly raised by the press. Reporters asked ceaselessly for an announcement of the wedding date. But there was to be no date, no marriage. William knew he must do something radical. Sylvina just repeated that he had jumped the gun in announcing it. She felt that to all intents and purposes she had done her job: it appeared he was already accepted socially again.

'You were invited to Baron and Baroness von Garten's summer festival, two people you had on your list. You wanted to be acknowledged by them. I just don't understand why, after the lengths we went to, you turned down their invitation.'

'That, my dear, was the whole point. I wanted to turn it down. I can't stand the bloody sight of him, or his stuck-up bitch of a wife.'

She sighed. 'Fine. Well, what about Lord Hangerford? He's underlined on the list, and I've made contact. You've been asked to dinner and the races. You've turned him down too. I thought you wanted to get to know these people.'

'I did know them,' he said angrily.

'So why have you had me pulling these strings?'

'*You're missing the point!*' he shouted.

She sighed. 'William, what *is* the point? You pay me to have you reintroduced and accepted socially, and now you tell me you don't want to be.'

'I don't want to socialize with them . . . not yet.'

'Oh. Well, why don't you tell me when you do? In the meantime I'll just stay at my house and wait for your call.' In a flash she regretted having said this. 'Are you backing out of the deal we had?' She was panicking.

'No. All I feel is that it's got out of hand. I'm grateful, you've done a good job, but I think maybe it's boring me now, as much as it is you.'

'Is that my fault?'

'No, I didn't mean that. It's just . . . I'm tired of it all.'

'*You're* tired! Well, let me tell you, I'm exhausted.

All right, you're paying me, but I'm not only exhausted. Most of the time I'm bored out of my mind by these people.'

'Don't get tetchy,' he said.

'I'm not tetchy, I just want this all over and done with, and it appears you do as well. So, pay me off, and let me get back to my own life.'

'That's all this has really been to you, isn't it? Money,' he said glumly.

She wanted to scream, but she took a deep breath, crossed over to him and slipped her arms around his neck. 'Sweetie, I am what I have always been, and I have never led you to believe otherwise. You've always known this was a game. You instigated it and I have played my part. I have not had an affair, I have remained, ready, willing and able, at your beck and call. But it's almost a year . . . so let's part as friends.'

He removed her arms from around his neck. Yet again she was taken aback. His voice was soft, hardly audible. 'If I'd offered more money, would you have fucked me?'

She laughed. 'Christ no. Well, maybe. If the price was right, who knows?'

'Someone of your age should be–' He never got out the word 'grateful' as she slapped him across the face.

'Don't throw crass remarks, Willy. If I'd have opened my legs, you'd have dived in. I've earned every penny, so please don't try and back out.'

'Not just yet. There's one person you've not brought to the table. Humphrey Matlock. You've not even got close to him.'

Sylvina clenched her teeth. She had really tried, but

Matlock was a hard man to get to. He appeared to loathe social functions and, in any case, was often abroad. When he was in London, he went fishing at weekends or whenever he could get away.

'William, Humphrey Matlock's a very unsociable creature and, to be honest, I wouldn't include a newspaper magnate as high priority for social standing.'

'Bullshit! Newspaper magnates are high in the social pecking-order. I want to meet him,' he said pettishly, 'but on my terms. I want that son-of-a-bitch to want to meet with me.'

'Right. Come hell or high water, I will arrange for you to do that. But please pay me, William, and let me get out of here. Otherwise we'll end up hating each other and I honestly don't want that.'

He took out his cheque book, and dangled it in front of her. 'You get me to Humphrey Matlock. Forget everyone else.'

She pursed her lips. 'Have you tried picking up the phone and calling him? You're on the front page of every bloody glossy magazine, some of which he owns. Meryl Delaware's been working overtime for you.'

'What?'

'Pay her and she'd work for Jack the Ripper – she even works for Matlock but she can't get close to him either. She's never met him.'

'I want him to *want* to know me,' he said again, thrusting out his lower jaw.

Sylvina looked at the cheque book, and bit her lip. 'Okay, I'll arrange it. I'll see if Meryl Delaware can help, but it'll cost.'

Two days later an innocuous piece in one of the gossip columns said that all seemed to be going well for the new 'golden couple', Sir William Benedict and Countess Sylvina Lubrinsky. Shortly afterwards, William received a gold-embossed invitation to a midsummer fête at the Matlock's country home. He propped the invitation on the mantelpiece and stood looking at it, his hands stuffed into his pockets. When Michael walked in, William pointed to it. 'What a two-faced piece of shit, eh?' Michael took the invitation down to read it. 'That's the son-of-a-bitch who ran filth about me for months. Every one of his papers ran lies about me, and now, a year later, he invites me to his home.'

Michael shook his head in disgust, and replaced the invitation. 'So you won't be going, sir?'

'You accept, Michael, and send a bouquet of flowers to his wife. Then, nearer the date, you can telephone and say I have been unavoidably detained.'

Michael gave a quizzical look, but noted down his latest instructions. They were getting more bizarre every week – and he had detected a frosty atmosphere between Sir William and his countess.

Sylvina was looking ravishing, and William thanked her for the scrapbook of press-cuttings she had sent him.

'It was really just to make a point,' she said. 'All that coverage was hard work, and sometimes I thought you didn't know how much time it took.'

William smiled and passed her a white envelope. 'You'll find a cheque inside, certified, of course, plus a list of the extra expenses that I did not agree to pay. I have deducted them from the fee we agreed.'

Sylvia gasped. Three hundred thousand pounds had been deducted from the million-pound payment. Even the solitaire diamond engagement ring had been charged to her. He had a funny crooked smile on his face.

'You fat bastard!' she snarled.

'Maybe I'm fat but I'm not stupid. Not stupid enough for you to rip me off anyway.'

After Sylvina left, still cursing, she phoned Justin and at last managed to speak to him.

'Hi, gorgeous, how's things?' he drawled.

'My cheque was short. The mean bastard deducted three hundred thousand grand.'

'He's got *some* sense, then?' He laughed.

'Soon you might be laughing on the other side of your face too,' she said angrily.

'What's that supposed to mean?'

'Exactly what I said. He's back doing business again like a demented kid. Every time I got him invitations from those wretched names on his pitiful list, he did nothing about it.'

'Did you get to Matlock?' Justin asked sharply.

'Yes. He's going to some function at the man's home. That's why I'm out of here.'

'You're leaving London?'

'I'm on my way to the airport right now.'

'He's going to Matlock's?'

'I just told you so. He's got the invitation, squeezed out of Matlock's prune-faced wife. What a dull woman she is.'

'Shit,' Justin hissed. Sylvina laughed. 'Goodbye,' she said, as she switched off her phone. She leaned back smiling. She had just made herself a tidy sum and could look forward to enjoying herself. She certainly had the wardrobe for it, and all the press she had engineered for William had benefited her too. Life was good.

Meanwhile, far from feeling relief at Sylvina's departure, William felt seedy and foolish, and more so when he considered that *he* had instigated the madness of the past year. But for what? He thought of other men who had been publicly vilified by the press: Profumo, Lambton, Archer and, of course, Aitken, now released from his prison sentence. Admittedly, the scandals in which they had been involved were more sensitive than his. In fact, he hadn't even been involved in a scandal. He was innocent, but he wondered if those others felt as he did. Had they at some time wanted revenge for the way they had been treated, or had they simply accepted it and got on with their lives? The public hounding as journalists dug into their families' lives must have hurt each of them, just as it had hurt him.

William looked at the array of invitations to high-society functions that had come in daily while Sylvina was at his side. How ridiculous to have coveted such meaningless things. He knew that if he continued to lavish money on certain charities he would remain on their lengthy, highbrow guest-lists, but he no longer cared. Maybe that was what he had learned from Sylvina: all it took to penetrate the higher echelons was money and 'face'. He had been a self-made mega-rich tycoon with one fatal flaw: his need for social acceptability. Now at last he realized how hollow that had been. How could he find a real purpose in life?

William, too, placed a call to Justin. He asked,

uninterestedly, how the work was coming along. Justin assured him that everything was going according to plan, that the game would soon be ready to begin. William told him quietly that the game was off. It was pointless. Sylvina had gone, and as soon as Justin was finished with the refurbishments he was to go, too. Justin flew into a rage, but knew better than to show it. When William hung up Justin let out a furious scream.

'I'm off home now, sir,' Michael said, popping his head round William's study door.

'Goodbye.' His employer's voice sounded empty.

Michael stepped into the room. 'Everything all right, sir?' he asked, with some concern.

'Yes, everything's fine. Goodnight.'

'Will the Countess be coming back?'

'No, she won't. She's gone.'

William gave a small, sad smile. 'Not much luck with the ladies. See you in the morning.'

Michael closed the door quietly. He could think of nothing to say.

If he had seen William opening his locked desk drawer and taking out a Luger pistol, he would have been more than concerned. William placed it on his leatherbound blotter and stared at it. The awful loneliness had something to do with Sylvina's departure but more to do with him. He contemplated ending it all. All he had to do was pull the trigger. But that was easier said than done. The pistol had belonged to his father. It had not been used for thirty years, and the firing pin was bent out of shape. He held it to his head as he stared at his reflection in the mirror, and remembered the discovery of Andrew Maynard's body. Had he really died of heartbreak . . . or through fear of his private life being exposed? Suddenly William focused on Humphrey Matlock's invitation. He lowered his useless pistol and tossed it back into the drawer. A spark of anger ignited amid his spiralling depression. 'I want to get that bastard,' he muttered.

William decided then that, after all, he was going to fight back because he was an innocent man. He had not stolen, lied or destroyed anyone in his climb to success yet he had been vilified. He was still wary of Justin's plan, but the dream of revenge on Matlock had pulled him away from the edge.

In the middle of the night, an enraged Justin placed a call to Meryl Delaware. She was about to launch an angry tirade at him for waking her at such an hour but he didn't let her get a word in. Speaking in a low, urgent voice, he gave her a front-page scoop. It concerned a young actress called Sharee, and her relationship with Countess Sylvina Lubrinsky, Sir William Benedict's future wife.

Two days later, as William was sitting down to breakfast, he was surprised to hear Michael arrive and tap on the door. 'I'm sorry, sir but I couldn't have blanked it. It came right out of left field.'

William looked up expectantly. 'Blanked what?'

In an exclusive that seemed exclusive to every tabloid paper in Europe, Sharee had disclosed her sexual relationship with William's fiancée. The headlines were beyond belief – 'Britain's Bad Boy Falls Prey to Sex Goddess' – but the articles were explicit, and accompanied by photographs of Sharee either in a sexy pose, pouting, tits to the fore, or as an angelic baby 'used and abused by lesbian temptress'.

The nightmare began again. William's home was surrounded by pressmen. He couldn't move outside without cameras flashing and microphones being thrust under his nose. The press regurgitated all his past indiscretions with hookers, and his ex-wives' quotes were rehashed. The onslaught was relentless. This time Michael was impressed by the way William handled it all. He remained composed and quiet. His demeanour when he left the house was sad, resigned, and that belied his abject humiliation. Eventually he decided to give a press conference. The battery of cameras and television crews with reporters fighting for front-row positions was sickening, all for some ridiculous article that might titillate a few readers.

Fortified by a few glasses of wine, William walked out to face the baying mob. He read a short statement he had written himself, and felt his anguish rising. Eventually he broke down. The flashbulbs popped. On returning to his house, he felt that the press conference had been the straw to break his back. He was appalled that he had lacked such self-control, and refused to watch any newsreels or read another paper. Now he was seriously contemplating ending it all.

Then everything changed. The fickle world turns on a fivepenny piece. The press began to depict him as a wronged lover and the public loved it.

Michael hired a PR agent, who played heavily on William's shock and trauma at the revelations. William

151

was amazed by an avalanche of sympathy letters and articles. He was now seen as a man seduced by a gold-digger who had betrayed him. The débâcle went on long enough for William to be sickened at first then amused that without making any effort himself he had come out smelling of roses.

Sylvina and Sharee had unwittingly given William a new public image, and to Justin, this turn of events was a gift from heaven. He had dropped the scoop to Meryl to spite William for dropping the plan. But the miraculous turnaround also meant that William's putative guests would be sure to accept an invitation from such a popular media star. He called William to talk him into leaving London to visit the almost completed paradise island.

'I can't right now, Justin,' said William, tired from all the interviews and phone calls.

'Right now is the perfect time. William, are you there?' There was a pause. 'I want you to think about our plan,' Justin began.

'At the moment I can't think about anything.'

'But you have to.'

'Justin, I can't talk now. Call me later.' He hung up.

At the other end of the line Justin's face twisted into a paroxysm of fury. Then, in a fit of rage, he smashed the receiver to pieces against the wall. He berated himself for acting too rashly.

He had been sure that the exposé would make William even more eager for revenge, but it seemed to have had the reverse effect. 'Will this idiot never come to his senses?' Justin muttered to himself. Gradually he calmed himself. It was just a setback. He'd leave it a day or so then call again. The fish was still on the line, he assured himself, just wriggling dangerously. Justin would land his quarry, even if it meant drawing him out to the island and slitting his throat himself.

CHAPTER 8

A FEW DAYS later Justin called William again.
William was surprised to feel genuinely
pleased to hear from him, but with the Sharee
story, he was desperate to get out of London. He
couldn't face going to work. 'I'll get the next flight
out,' he said.

'What?' Justin asked loudly.

'I said I'll be flying out as soon as I can.'

'Oh, fantastic. By the way, I've ordered four jet-skis,
and I told you about the speedboat, didn't I? Expensive,
but out here it'll be an eye-popper. Hopefully it's
arriving today. Let me know what time your flight gets
in, and I'll have a boat fixed up to collect you, if yours
hasn't been delivered. Hello? Are you still there?'

'I'll have Michael call you, Justin.' William hung up
and pressed the intercom. 'Michael, arrange a flight for
me, would you? I want to leave as soon as possible.'

'Where to, sir?' came Michael's clipped tones.

'The island. So get Mrs Thingy to pack enough
suitable clothes for a fortnight.'

'You have board meetings the day after tomorrow.'

'Cancel them.'

Michael accompanied William to the airport, osten-

154

sibly to take notes and instructions, but his boss seemed distracted.

'The new mechanical toys are ready for you to test, sir. Do you want me to send them out to you on the island?'

'What toys?' William asked.

'The fox and hens, remember?'

'Oh yes, yes, just go ahead.'

'What about the patent?' Michael asked, aware that they had been copied from some William had bought in Paris.

'Well, I reckon we can get away with it. I'm sure I remember seeing some designs for a similar toy done by one of my boffins years ago. If they do decide to take on the Benedict Corporation, which I'm sure they won't, we'll be able to pass it off as ours anyway. In fact, Michael, get my lawyers to look into the company that made that cat and mouse thing and root out our old files. Maybe we can sue *them*!' With that, they arrived at the airport.

The speedboat's engine was cut and it cruised into the small, immaculate dock. It was late afternoon and still blisteringly hot, but a sea breeze kept the air fresh. Justin, deeply tanned, was wearing cut-off blue jeans, a white T-shirt with torn seams and a faded pair of flip-flops. His gold Rolex wristwatch glistened in the sun, and a pair of black Armani shades hung from the neck of his T-shirt. A boy in white shorts and dirty sneakers was at the controls. He jumped deftly out of the boat on to the quay, and Justin hurled him a coiled rope, which he tied around a wooden post.

William was sitting in the small harbour café with a whisky and soda. He had landed in Miami, then booked the Cherokee two-seater to taxi him to Tortola, the adjacent island; his own had no airstrip. Another sea-plane landed at the same time, and William was irritated to see Count Frederick Capri, whom he recognized from Justin's villa in France, greet the disembarking passengers.

His mood darkened as he watched the lithe, handsome Justin strolling towards him. He seemed to know everyone who passed, waving and laughing, speaking fluent French one moment, Spanish the next. William sipped his drink and squinted into the sun as Justin made his way towards the café veranda and leaned against the railing. 'You made it,' he said, smiling, his white teeth dazzling against his dark skin.

His hair had grown quite long since William last saw him and he wore it combed back from his high forehead. It was bleached almost white.

'The boy'll get your cases,' Justin added, slipping on his shades and checking his watch. 'We shouldn't leave it too long, there's a bit of wind and it might get choppy. Besides, I want you to see the island in the best possible light – when the sun is just slipping down.'

They walked to the quay, got into the boat and surged off. William pressed his back into the leather seat. Justin sat next to him, tilting his face to catch the last rays of sun. 'So the Countess buggered off,' he said.

William shrugged. He could smell Justin's sun-oil, and glanced at the small diamond ring he wore on his little finger.

Justin hooked his arm around William's shoulder.

156

'This is nerve-racking for me. It's been almost eighteen months, did you know that?'

'Time passes quickly,' William said, uneasy with the man's closeness.

'I have created a paradise,' Justin said, tightening his arm. 'Sometimes it was hard for me to remember that I was creating a place for you, not me. I've grown to love this island with a passion.'

William would never forget the next few moments. The boat cut through the water, passing between two jagged rocks. A mist began to sweep towards them, blurring the ocean and the sky, creating an illusion of nothingness. Then the island appeared, like a mirage. White turrets, boundary walls, white cliffs and sparkling latticed windows. As they drew closer, the mist parted, and William made out undergrowth, trees and shrubs in a blaze of different colours.

The quayside, jetty and pathways leading to the mansion were as white as the turrets. Large Chinese lanterns hung from ropes, swinging gently in the wind, and the tinkle of wind-chimes and bells echoed across the water. William half rose, his lips parted, as they cruised past man-made beaches and cascading waterfalls. The perfume from the lilies was so strong that the heady smell wafted over the water like incense. The boat passed hidden coves equipped with small jetties and lines of jet-skis, sailing dinghies and windsurfers. Sun-bathing terraces, covered with brilliant white canopies, rows of polished sun-beds and picnic tables, jutted out from the rocks; diving boards reached out into the sea. As the boat curved inwards to the main landing, jetty-boys in white blazers and shorts stood like sentries waiting for their arrival. The boat-boy eased into the jetty alongside a sleek cruiser covered in white tarpaulins and a small, elegant launch. Five white golf carts were parked nearby.

Justin climbed up on to the jetty, speaking in French to the boys, who then assisted William from the boat, collected his luggage and stacked it on a golf cart. William stood still, taking it all in. 'Stunning,' he said, in awe.

Justin was delighted at the impact of his creation. But this was just the beginning and he was determined to milk every second. 'I'll show you the grounds first.' He veered off the pathway into a shaded, narrow, rough lane where the ferns and the palms made it darker and more mysterious. They turned a corner on to a clearing with an Olympic-sized marble swimming pool. The water, lit from beneath, was a vivid turquoise. Sun-loungers were covered in the same brilliant colour; parasols and tables were placed on different levels. A straw-covered gazebo accommodated a bar, where a man stood waiting to serve drinks. Crystal glasses glittered, and mountains of fruit in ceramic pots were dotted on the tables around the pool. Justin escorted William to a jacuzzi built on a higher level, and a large swirl pool with an elaborate mosaic floor.

The tour continued round the entire island, taking in secret pathways, or 'lovers' walks', as Justin described them, until at last they headed around the rear of the mansion, past the servants' quarters to a shady cobble-walled yard. 'The servants live in the area away from the master rooms, but they're connected by phone and intercom,' Justin said, pointing out the hidden wires. Following his gaze, William looked upwards. 'The cameras are for the security monitor in your master office. You can see what's going on over the whole island with one flick of a switch.'

They returned to the cart and headed back towards the main mansion entrance. Justin had restructured the building, turning a warren of small rooms and corridors into vast open spaces. The doors leading into the main hall were thirty feet high and had come from an Indonesian monastery. They were carved with spectacular fretwork, and in the centre of each was a wooden lion's head, its jaws wide open, holding a gleaming brass knocker. Justin had a flair for mixing the old with the new and the combination was perfect. The hallway was tiled in black and white marble. Above, a huge domed ceiling was vaulted with thick wooden beams, a minstrel's gallery snaking its way around the hall. Overhead, fans whirred quietly, and carefully positioned lights cast beams on paintings the size of living-room walls. Tapestries, oil paintings and a full suit of armour gave the feeling of a medieval castle, yet the room was light and airy. The wide double staircase was made of polished Japanese pine and had a frail appearance that belied its strength and weight. The windows opened on to balconies and verandas. All the rooms seemed to be interconnected: one wall slid back to reveal a modern, open-plan drawing room with white cushioned sofas, low tables, paintings, china displays on plinths of polished wood, Japanese bowls, rough local pottery, and, dominating each room, a wide open fireplace. 'I've installed the finest air-conditioning system. The engineers were here for months.' Justin pointed around the room, to the floor and ceiling, but William could see no grids or outlets – they were all hidden from sight.

Besides a row of six small bungalow-type residences for staff and guests, there were eight suites, each with their own bathroom. There was also a drawing room and a dining room with a long monastery table and big carved chairs, plus a smaller table for more intimate dining. The breakfast room had no walls, and was designed so that guests could drink their morning coffee with spectacular views on every side. However, when it was windy or wet, the touch of a button would electronically activate glass panels to shield them.

Nothing in his wildest dreams had prepared William for this extravagance. Justin insisted on tours to the servants' living-quarters, going into long descriptions about the kitchens and wine cellar, which he wanted William to see. Then he led William into a gargantuan study. It was a modern room, with a futuristic-looking desk, a hi-tech computer and printer, a huge television and a bank of security monitors. Although William was now aching with tiredness, Justin gestured for him to sit. He crossed to the desk, spread out the architect's drawings of the mansion, and with a red pen indicated the areas they missed on the tour and the positions of the hidden cameras. He began to fiddle with an array of switches in the large panel at the side of the desk. The monitors fizzled into life, revealing every possible area of the island.

'You can keep an eye on everything, William,' Justin said, unable to hide his pride in his work.

'Very impressive,' William said, so exhausted he could hardly keep his eyes open.

'We need to discuss the finances,' Justin said, rolling up the drawings.

'Not now. I need some sleep. Perhaps in the morning.'

Justin checked his watch. 'Will you want to dine? Only you should really meet all your staff.'

William removed his jacket. His shirt was stained with sweat. 'A light supper in my suite. Offer them my apologies. I'll meet them tomorrow.' He looked around, unsure where to go.

'I'll send the chef to your room,' Justin said, opening a door in the corner of the study. 'Tomorrow we'll discuss the grand plan.'

William took a deep breath. 'No, we won't, I'm here for a holiday, nothing more. All that revenge stuff was nonsense, as stupid as my arrangement with Sylvina.'

Justin's heart sank, but he kept a smile on his face. 'You get a good night's sleep. Maybe you'll think differently in the morning.'

William glared. 'No, I won't. As I said, I'm here for a break, and God knows I certainly need one. All that silly stuff is best forgotten. I don't even want to discuss it again. Goodnight.'

As William made to leave, Justin gave a small bow. 'Welcome home,' he said softly.

'Thank you. You've done one hell of a job.'

Justin directed him to his suite, then closed the door and leaned against it. 'You've done one hell of a job,' he repeated sarcastically. 'Fucking prick,' he muttered, under his breath. The dumb bastard didn't want to play! Well, so be it, *he* would play. He hadn't spent eighteen months setting it up and half of his life waiting for this opportunity just to let it slip away. It might take a little longer, but he was sure he could persuade the buffoon to do exactly as he wanted. No one was going to stop him now.

William showered and changed into a pair of cotton pyjamas that had been laid out on his bed. His suite seemed bigger than the first floor of his London house. He padded to the balcony, opened the doors and walked out. Like a golden globe sinking into the sea, the sun's last rays reached out like tentacles into the darkening sky before it disappeared. William gasped. It was the most extraordinary sight he'd ever seen. Soft lights came on automatically, and he rested his hands on the veranda rail. He breathed deeply. The air was cool and sweetly perfumed, the night caressing, almost like a naked woman reaching out to hold him. As emotion welled up inside him he felt close to tears and gasped to regain his composure. He felt as though he were caught in a dream. But it was reality. This was his paradise. It belonged to him and no one else.

There was a light tap on the door and William let in a small Frenchman who introduced himself as Monsieur Dupré, the chef. He handed William the menu, a thick sheet of manila paper with looped writing. William barely glanced at it. 'I'd like some melon, a little scrambled egg and maybe some salmon.'

'Of course, Monsieur, and . . .' He passed William the wine list. One glance told him it was on a par with that of the Ritz. He asked for a bottle of chilled Pouilly Fumé and some iced lemon tea. Dupré bowed and backed out, closing the door silently behind him.

The tray arrived on a steel trolley with silver domes placed over delicate pale blue porcelain. The cutlery, of silver and eighteen-carat gold inlaid with ivory, was laid out on the damask cloth. The fluted goblet was chilled and frosted, and the wine stood in an ornate silver bucket.

'I'll serve myself,' William said briskly, anxious to be left alone to savour yet another of Justin's touches of elegance. The eggs were cooked to perfection, the salmon melted in his mouth like butter. The warm crusty rolls were fresh, just as he liked. The melon, cut into fine slivers, was garnished with segments of lemon, strawberries, pineapple and apricots. William ate sparingly, and after a glass of wine, his eyes drooped. He didn't finish his meal but went into the bedroom, fell onto the damask-covered bed and into a deep, dreamless sleep.

At some point during the night, the tray was removed and the hand-made mosquito nets released above the bed. William turned and his eyes opened and, for a moment, he was unsure where he was. The netting above him felt like hands touching his face and he cringed. He must make it clear to all the servants that his rooms were not to be entered unless at his express permission. Returning to a half-sleep, he saw winding dark corridors, secret rooms – eerie, frightening places. He felt so cold he woke up. Pushing the netting aside William reached for the bedside lamp, patting its base to find the switch. The lamp filled the room with a soft yellow glow. Looking around, he suddenly noticed a painting.

For a moment it looked like a mirage, suspended in the air, but then he realized that it had been framed to stand away from the wall and was intended to appear to float. It was of a woman, her blonde hair cascading from a central parting almost to her waist. A pale blue chiffon scarf covered her shoulders, revealing her perfect breasts. One hand, with long fine fingers and short oval nails, held a white lily. The other rested against the side of her pale neck, as if she was touching her pulse. The painting was in washed, muted colours. Only the face had clarity, as if the artist wanted it to be the focus. It was a childlike, innocent face. Pale blue eyes stared out above a small, delicate nose and the full lips were slightly parted. William turned off the light, but kept staring towards the painting, unsure whether he wished it to remain in the room. Eventually he fell asleep, her face the last thing he saw that night and the first when he woke next morning.

Standing on the veranda, William saw Justin in a white robe heading back towards the house.

'Morning,' Justin called up.

'Morning,' he replied.

'I've been for a swim,' Justin said, shading his eyes. 'Have you had breakfast?'

'Not yet, will you join me for coffee?'

'Absolutely,' said Justin, disappearing.

'Justin!' William called after him. 'The woman,' he said, as Justin reappeared. 'The painting of the woman in my bedroom.'

'Ah, yes,' Justin called up. 'Beautiful, isn't she?'

'Who is she?'

'My sister,' Justin said. Almost as an afterthought he added, 'Her name is Laura.'

At breakfast, William was wearing a pair of Bermuda shorts and a loose floral shirt. On his feet were Gucci sandals, leather uppers with rope soles, but his legs above his socks were unhealthy pinkish blobs. His pale freckled skin never tanned, but turned red and blistered if he sat in the sun too long. His fine blond hair, thinning at the back in a neat round crown, was perhaps the only thing the tropical sun enhanced, turning it from mousy blond to white-silver. Justin, in comparison, was so deeply tanned from months of working outdoors that it was hard to tell what race he was. He was wearing a cheesecloth kaftan and the flip-flops he had worn the previous day. He hitched up the kaftan around his thighs as he stretched out his long legs beside the table.

A large trolley loaded with fresh fruit cascading from iced bowls had been wheeled to within easy reach of the table, with fresh rolls, pastries and home-made breads under a covered silver warming-dish. Various jams and sweet and sour marmalades in silver basket-weave jars, matching silver coffee- and tea-pots with hot-water jugs in the same but larger-woven pattern sparkled in the morning sun. The table wore a starched pale blue linen cloth, with matching napkins and heavy cutlery. Added to the array of knives and forks were diamond-shaped grapefruit spoons. Iced flutes held freshly squeezed orange juice. Jugs offered lemon water, or grapefruit juice with sprigs of mint. A small, heated tray held covered tureens with bacon, sausage, scrambled eggs, liver, kidneys and onions.

'No cornflakes?' William said, looking over the trolley.

'I'll send down for some,' Justin said.

'No, don't bother. It was a joke.' William poured more coffee and proffered the pot to Justin, who shook his head, holding up a glass of iced water.

'Not until midday. Gets me too speedy.' He sat munching at an alarming rate.

'Is she dead?' William asked, out of the blue.

'Who?' Justin enquired.

'The woman in the painting.' William dabbed the corners of his mouth with his napkin.

'Laura? No, she's very much alive.'

'You've never mentioned her.'

'I'm sure I have.' Justin took out his cigarettes, noting the way the debris from William's breakfast now dominated the table. He had read somewhere that the space a person took up on a table was representative of their perceived status in relation to their fellow diners. William clearly felt he was the dominant personality here.

'Laura?' William said, his head cocked to one side. 'The name suits her. She's very beautiful.'

Justin nodded, picked up a book of matches and lit his Gitane. He drew the ashtray close and laid the match in the bowl then slid it, with a half-amused smile, directly in front of William. He had now reclaimed his space. 'We should go over the accounts,' he said quietly.

'Fine. Whenever.'

Justin stood up and stretched his long arms above his head. 'Half an hour? Your study would probably be best. Then I can lay out all the plans.'

'What does she do?' William asked, looking up at Justin.

'My sister?' Justin drew deeply on the cigarette, then let the smoke drift from his nose. 'She fucks.' With that he strolled away, the smell of his cigarette hanging in the air.

*

166

Justin was waiting in William's study. He had changed into a pair of white shorts, frayed at the edges and a washed-out blue vest. William pointed to a stack of receipts and invoices. 'Has Michael been privy to all of this?'

'Most,' Justin said, concentrating on the account books.

'He'll need copies of everything,' William said, wandering around the room, noting the contents of the bookshelves and cabinets.

'Absolutely.'

William stared out of the window. 'Christ, it's a wonderful view from here,' he said.

'From every room,' Justin corrected, concentrating on his papers. 'Shall we get started?' He stepped away from the desk, gesturing to the carved chair behind it. William sat as he placed an open, leatherbound account book in front of him. He pointed to the control panel on the desk. 'You have a high-tech calculator there if you need it. It'll give you the costs in any currency, plus exchange rates. This is the master copy.'

William nodded and flicked briskly through the pages of neatly handwritten accounts until he got to the last page and glanced down. Justin was becoming irritated. He knew that William was looking for the final total. 'If you have to look for it, you can't afford it,' he said. 'The truth is, it's peanuts compared to what some interior designers would have charged.'

'Jesus Christ!' William uttered under his breath. The total was one hundred and twenty-six million dollars. 'Peanuts?' He looked up as Justin averted his eyes.

'I'll start at the beginning. Go to page one, structural repairs,' he snapped.

'Yes,' William said flatly, adding a curt, 'I think you had better do just that!'

At last there was some energized response from William, even if it was not necessarily a good one. His depression hung around him, pervaded the island and infuriated Justin. He simply could not understand his lack of energy and enthusiasm. He was like a dead man set in cement. Only the money angle seemed to have given him a spark of life.

Later, a business lunch of crisp salad and chicken breast wrapped in spinach leaves on a bed of saffron rice was brought in to them. William did not want a break, and Justin, under a barrage of questions, didn't eat a morsel. William demanded to know the cost of every item. By mid-afternoon Justin had to get out. He needed to clear his head. He'd not even left the room for a piss. Neither had William.

No wonder the man was rich, he thought. Nothing went unnoticed – he even inquired about bars of soap.

'Look, Sir William, we must discuss more than nit-picking costs. There is more at stake here.' William peered at him quizzically. 'I suggest we both take a break. I'll arrange for a drink to be brought up to you at the jacuzzi.'

Reluctantly William acquiesced. He didn't like jacuzzis and he could have easily continued all day and into the night.

'I'll take some of these folders,' he muttered.

'Fine. Just don't get them wet.' Justin was trying hard to control his temper.

Justin walked to the edge of the pool, kicked off his shorts and dived naked into the cool blue water. William was sitting in the jacuzzi on the higher level, wearing

Justin's baseball cap with a cigar clamped in his teeth. He was checking through the lists of paintings and tapestries that had been shipped in from Sotheby's and Christie's showrooms in New York and London. The hot water was pumping and shaking over his rather flaccid thighs and buttocks. He had put on at least two and a half stone since Maynard's death, partly due to Sylvina's constant round of dinners. His pot belly hung over his maroon bathing shorts. He watched Justin swim length after length.

After about half an hour William showered and changed, gathered up the folders and returned to the study. He was surprised to see Justin already at work, bent over the computer, with a glass of chilled wine.

'You mind?' Justin asked, holding up the bottle, which was already three-quarters empty.

'Not at all.' William gestured to the chair beside him. 'I need you to run these by me. Mexican artefacts? Were they necessary?'

'No, not at all, but rather nice, don't you think?' Justin slumped down into the chair.

'At this price they should be.'

And so it continued.

At last, by nine that evening, William was satisfied that he had covered the entire expenditure on his island paradise. He closed the last book and reached for a cigar from the specially designed humidor, embossed with his initials in gold. 'You took some liberties,' he said quietly.

Justin leaned forward. 'I'm sorry?'

William pushed back his chair. He puffed at his cigar then spat out a fragment of tobacco. 'I said, you took liberties. Some of the costs are ridiculously high.'

'You'll find it worth it.' Justin handed William a pen and blank piece of paper. 'Now, can we discuss the original reason for my rebuilding this place?'

William wrinkled his brow. 'We did. I thought I'd cleared that up on my arrival.'

Justin smiled. 'Fine. You're the one who's been made to look the arsehole, so it's your decision. I mean, I've seen you publicly humiliated. If I were you I'd want revenge. But I'm not you, obviously, and it's always been your decision about everything.'

'Revenge?' William shifted uneasily, recalling that late-night conversation all those months ago in the South of France. 'It's been too long now.'

'William, everyone has called you a wanker. The press, your family, everyone. Doesn't that bother you? Even with all your money, you'll never be free of that. The only thing you can do is pay the bastards back, but you're too much of a pussy to do it. I've set it all up for you, worked my butt off.'

'You'll be paid.'

Justin lifted his hands in exasperation. 'Fine, pay me off like Sylvina and I'll walk out of your life. I don't care any more, I just don't want to waste any more of my time on you.'

William sat down, head in his hands, and fell into the trap. 'This grand plan you've conceived . . .'

'I didn't, you did. It was your idea.'

'Refresh my memory.'

Justin's eyes narrowed as he wondered how much to elaborate. He must choose his words carefully.

'Okay, the original plan was for you to become socially accepted again, which partly worked via Sylvina.

170

You listed the specific names of people who had, to your mind, done the dirty on you. People like—'

'Baron von Garten,' William muttered.

'Exactly. Then everyone on the hit-list would subsequently be invited to join you here on your island, where they would be at your mercy.'

Justin looked for a reaction, but there was none.

'Once here, they would be lulled into a false sense of security, entertained on such a lavish scale that they would relax . . . unaware that you had another motive. Pay-back. You would systematically get every single one of them.'

'Caught in a sexual scandal,' William added quietly.

'Exactly,' Justin said softly, then got up and touched William's shoulder. 'That was what we hatched up. Don't tell me you've forgotten.'

'Of course I hadn't,' William said hoarsely. 'I hadn't forgotten, Justin, but so much has happened, and the Sylvina débâcle turned round to my benefit. Sometimes the press that I despise so much—'

'Makes you look even more of a buffoon,' snapped Justin.

There was that word again. William clenched his hands in anger.

'Go to bed. You think about it tonight. Then if you decide to go with it, we can start things rolling. If not, then I'll be finished here and I'll leave, with no hard feelings.'

Justin strolled out. He might have been discussing something as mundane as cushion fabric, not a complex revenge plot.

William felt as if he had been holding his breath too

long, and let it out. 'Oh, my God,' he whispered. He wondered whether Justin was unbalanced. But it was himself who had sown the seeds of the plan. That night in France he had wanted to make someone pay for what had been done to him. His injuries had still smarted then. But did he still want that? William patted his pockets and removed his wallet. Neatly folded into a small square was the original list he had made out of people whom he believed should pay for what he had been put through. But now that he had just such an opportunity, he found it didn't make him feel good. Instead it disturbed him. He needed to think hard before he made any decisions.

The sound of speedboat engines drew William to the balcony of his room. The night-lights and lanterns illuminated the path all the way to the water's edge creating a carnival feeling. He could see a group of people on the jetty watching the Sunseeker Hawk 34 being tested. Justin was shouting instructions to Sammy at the wheel, and the engine came to life with a sound almost as loud as Concorde. The boat lifted out of the water leaving a foaming wash behind as it disappeared out of sight.

After a moment, the Sunseeker returned with Justin at the wheel. He circled the boat, putting it through various fast turns and surges, laughing and waving to the boys on the jetty. Then he cut the engines, drifted back to the shore and tied it up. He jumped out, then walked away from the jetty, each arm hooked around a boy's shoulder. As they disappeared into the darkness, their disembodied voices and laughter hung in the air.

William wondered where Justin slept. Perhaps he was living in the servants' quarters or in one of the thatched bungalows. He decided to take an evening stroll. Walking through the hallway, he paused and looked up to the ribbed ceiling, then at the paintings and tapestries. The elegant flowers, plants and ferns that hung and draped the stairs and balconies were so thick and voluptuous they might have been growing there for years. He had to admire Justin's artistry, the way he had made the hallway a powerful, but not daunting, centrepiece of the mansion.

'I like this,' he said. He thought again of the Grand Plan as he surveyed the hall. It might just work. He had laid the groundwork during his year with Sylvina and the press had unwittingly made him a social star. He was sure the people on his list would accept his invitation to stay. It was just a matter of deciding when.

William stepped through the massive oak and iron doors, which appeared to be left open at all times, and walked down the white stone steps. He turned back and looked upwards: the night-lights threw gentle beams across the roof of the mansion, illuminating its magical structures. Plants cascaded in tumbling waterfalls of colour, and thousands of lilies, in hanging baskets and ornate pots, gave off a powerful aromatic scent. William had never given a moment's thought to plants or flowers before, but now he touched, smelt and admired them. His pleasure grew as he walked along the main pathway to a smaller, darker lane that Justin had called Secrets Avenue.

William walked for about a quarter of a mile, and calculated that he was heading to the east side of the island towards one of the small coves. As the pathway sloped downwards, he could hear the thunder of the sea.

It will work. They'll be bewitched by the place. He took such a deep breath of fresh air that he felt light-headed. It's even got to me.

The path curved to the right and a white wooden railing with a thick rope marked out the steep slope to the side. The pebbled path was also slotted with thick wooden slabs, each one lower than the next, to create a set of steps down to the beach. The cove was carved out of the white cliffs, discreet lamps and platforms built into the rocks. The sun-loungers and cushions were lined up like soldiers, and tables with white parasols had been positioned to accommodate diners who wished to eat in the shade. Then, to his surprise, William thought he heard Justin's laughter, carried on the wind, then the clink of glasses and a guitar playing softly in the dusk. He stayed in the shadows, scanning the darkness for him.

He spotted Justin lying stark naked on a small wooden jetty that extended into the sea. Sammy was with him, wearing an orange sarong tied loosely around his waist and a crown of flowers around his head. He was smoking a long joint, leaning back with his eyes closed. A beautiful girl with long braided hair entwined with flowers was massaging Justin, while another with red and white beads in her hair was dancing nearby, dressed only in a white chiffon scarf. A small girl was sitting between Justin's legs placing strawberries along his thighs and eating them off him, one after the next. A fourth exotic creature, wearing Justin's white kaftan, was playing the guitar. William watched in awed silence. The scene was like a painting by Gauguin.

He was just about to make his presence known, when the girl eating the strawberries began to eat Justin. For a moment William felt deeply embarrassed, then so shocked he couldn't move. All of Justin's beauties had begun to massage, suck and lick him. But when the girls stripped off their gauzy garments, William was aghast. The figures unintentionally revealed to him were male. William turned and ran away like a schoolboy.

The next morning William had already had breakfast and was sitting by the pool when Justin sauntered towards him. 'Morning,' he said, and flopped down on the sun-lounger next to William. 'I've ordered corn-flakes and every make of cereal you insist on crunching at breakfast. There's also a selection of muesli. Did they leave them out for you this morning?'

'Yes,' William said. He hated muesli: all those nuts and bits got stuck in his bridge.

'So, did you sleep well?' Justin enquired, yawning.

'Yes,' came the crisp reply.

'That's good.' Justin scrutinized William's pink flesh. 'You need some protection cream – there's plenty in your room, plus some self-tanning lotion.' He touched William's thigh. 'Look. You're already burning.' William pulled his legs away. Justin stood up. 'Finish your breakfast while I have a swim,' he said, heading back inside. 'Then we can talk business.'

William tried to stop himself watching Justin stroll away through the double doors.

*

Twenty minutes later, William appeared at the pool, dressed in a dreadful pair of khaki shorts, a white shirt, loafers and a Panama hat. Justin clung to the rail at the side of the pool. 'Going on safari, are we?' he remarked.

William flushed and hitched up his pants in a defensive gesture. 'I need to do some exercise,' he said lamely.

Justin hauled himself out of the pool and placed a dripping arm around William's shoulders. 'There's a well-equipped gym, and one of the boys is a fitness trainer. He'll have you in shape in no time at all.'

'I used to work out regularly,' William muttered, ashamed of his body next to Justin's.

'I can see there's still some muscle tone, so it won't be too much of a strain,' Justin lied. He felt sorry for William, surrounded by beauty but so deeply uncomfortable with himself. He led him through to where a large woman sat flicking through a magazine. 'This is Ruby, Sir William. She's the skin expert.' He turned to her. 'Check his sun lotions. And use some of that self-tan on him.'

'Yes, sir, will do, sir.' Ruby bobbed up. 'Any time you wish, sir.'

Justin smiled at William. 'Before you go outside again, Ruby will see to you. That's an order.' He threw his head back and laughed. 'Now, let's have that talk.'

Settled in the study, William tried to resume his authority. 'I've given this thing a lot of thought, and no matter which way I look at it, it's farcical. I mean, do I really want to invite these people here?'

Justin sighed. 'You'll never get it, will you?' He leaned forward and looked William in the eye. 'It's a scam, William. We're going to pull a scam that exploits the greed and selfishness of all these ghastly people.' He gestured expansively towards the open window. 'Look at the place. It's the nearest you'll find to paradise on the planet. We publish pictures, get a few articles in the press. It'll be easy. "The Most Exclusive Villa in the World. The Most Expensive Villa in the World". They'll all fall for it. They'll be over here and ready for the plucking.'

William slapped his hand down hard on the desk. 'Read my lips. I *do not* want them here. And even if I did agree, and we got everyone here who has made my life hell—'

Justin put his face in his hands, screeching, 'No! No! You've got it wrong. You still don't understand. Let me give you an example.' He sat back again, talking deliberately as though addressing a simpleton. 'Your ex-wife is at the hairdresser's. She picks up a copy of *Hello!* magazine. The page falls open at the headline that has grabbed everyone's attention: "Tycoon's Island Paradise Affordable Only By Mega-Rich". She sees the pictures of the beaches, the rooms, the pool. Then she sees the words: "Exclusive – only multi-millionaires, pop mega-stars, the top fifty wealthiest people on the planet will ever be given the opportunity to see this playground for the world's élite."' William couldn't help but smile as Justin pressed on. 'The pictures and the words will stay in her mind, haunting her, tempting her. What wouldn't she give to be a fly on the wall, just to see the place, *see you*? Until one day, opening her post . . .' Justin mimed a bored woman opening an envelope, then feigned surprise and delight '. . . what should she find but an invitation. A *free* invitation to taste for herself the delights of this paradise on earth.'

'Sorry. Don't buy it.' William shrugged. 'If she knows it's my place, she'd never accept, even if it was free. Besides, I have no desire to have either of my ex-wives set foot on the island.'

'Fine, cross them off your list.'

'I already have. I've crossed them all off. We're not doing it.' With that, William stormed out of the room.

William ate alone at lunch, Justin having taken the boat to pick up some stuff from Tortola. He tucked into a lobster salad followed by a sorbet, and sipped a light sparkling rosé from a small vineyard in California. Afterwards he could hardly keep his eyes open, and decided to take a rest.

Ruby was waiting in his suite. A massage-table covered with white towels was positioned in the centre of the room, an array of oils and lotions laid out on the table. William just wanted to crash out, but Ruby assured him he would sleep even better after a massage. After a quick shower he lay face down on the table. The oils were cool against his hot skin, and Ruby's touch gentle and soothing. First she massaged him, then applied an astringent lotion to remove the residue of oil from his back. She removed the small towel from his waist, and continued to massage him, gently easing the tension from his muscles. Then she rolled him over, and started to masturbate him. When he came she wiped away his semen and continued the massage. William drifted into a deep sleep, unaware of the slices of iced cucumber laid on his eyelids, while Ruby performed a delicate cleansing facial.

At eight Dahlia, the housekeeper, delivered a message that Justin was held up and would not be returning till the following morning. William felt cross. He wanted company that evening, conversation, perhaps even a game of backgammon. He didn't feel like eating alone again. He looked at the housekeeper. 'Dahlia, will you join me?' he asked bluntly.

'I would be delighted,' she said courteously, and took his order for dinner.

William looked at Dahlia and wished he'd changed into a suit. Justin referred to her as Mrs Danvers whenever they discussed her. She was about thirty and exceptionally tall with a taut, muscular figure and waist-length hair combed back from her face and tied in a tight braid. 'There's nothing in the mansion that Mrs Danvers doesn't monitor,' Justin had told him. 'She rules with a rod of iron.'

William couldn't see it. She stood before him in an elegant dark turquoise dress, slit to her thigh, which reminded him of the one Sylvina had worn the night he had met her in France.

They ate together by candlelight. It was a sumptuous dinner, and they conversed easily, discussing wines, restaurants and favourite dishes. William told her about his planned weight-loss and she promised to arrange a low-calorie eating-plan so delicious he would never know it was a diet. William said he liked the idea of her controlling his food intake, and that was when the *doubles-entendres* started. He enjoyed Dahlia's titillating questions about how he liked to be controlled, and when she asked if he was too strong-minded ever to release himself into another's hands, he chuckled and said that he'd never had the opportunity to find out. Dahlia leaned across the table, drew his face towards hers and kissed his lips. She released him and sat back. 'You have the opportunity now, sir.'

Justin was eating a large slice of watermelon, his feet on the desk in William's study, watching the security monitors. He couldn't help but shake his head in admiration. Dahlia was brilliant. He flicked on a second monitor, which showed William being led up the stairs like a puppy by her. He flicked on a third monitor, which showed William's empty suite, then Dahlia and William entering.

Justin reached for the phone and dialled an internal number. 'Ruby,' he said quietly. 'Wake up, Ruby, and get ready. She's cracked it.' He giggled down the line. 'And even before coffee was served.'

'Okay,' came the soft reply, and the phone went dead.

In her small but immaculate room in the north servants' wing, Ruby selected oils, masks, handcuffs, a leather-thonged whip and various other items she knew Dahlia sometimes used. She took her time, humming tunelessly as she placed them in a wide basket. She was still dressed in her white masseuse's overall and white sneakers, naked underneath.

Meanwhile Justin slotted a tape into the video-recorder and clicked it on. He waited until he was sure the machine was recording then returned to the security monitor where Dahlia sat astride William's naked body, his face blindfolded with iced cloths.

Now Ruby entered the room, unheard and unseen by William. Justin checked the headphones to ensure that the microphone was picking up the sound. William might have forgotten the initial reason for the island's redevelopment, but Justin hadn't. He had worked towards it with relish and the length of time taken just made this moment even sweeter. Surely William wouldn't say no to the plan after he'd seen the video of this! When the show was over, Justin would have earned enough money never to have to work again. He and Laura would live the life they had dreamed of. He had always believed that everything he did was for his beloved Laura. Just thinking of her, saying her name, made his body prickle. He was missing her, and couldn't wait to see her again and tell her that the game was moving into action. All they needed were the players. They would arrive and be treated like royalty, unaware that cameras were filming every second of their intimate moments. Justin had arranged for these intimacies to go well beyond the boundaries of flirtation: the guests would be seduced by the luxurious surroundings, and drawn into a false sense of security, just like William.

The staff were not ordinary domestics, far from it. They were giving William a taste of their real calling in life and they had no limits. The victims would happily pay a fortune to keep out of the press. It would, Justin mused to himself, be a lucrative blackmail weapon. William *has* to agree. There were endless possibilities, and soon Laura would become a major player.

Justin closed his eyes and remembered Laura standing up on the high rocks near their villa in the South of France. She had been holding what appeared to be a perfectly almond-shaped piece of green glass. She had laughed softly, that husky, whispering laugh. He had never heard such a sound on anyone else's lips, and as always it touched him. He could see her in his mind as clearly as if she was standing next to him. He remembered the way she held up the glass to the light, transparent, delicate and frighteningly fragile.

'I have a frozen piece of the sea, Justin,' she cooed. 'Look, doesn't it remind you of me?' Then she turned away from him and that sweet, delicate laugh he loved so dearly was swept away with the wind and swallowed up by the sea below. She held the glass in the palm of her hand. The light glittering off it made it appear like a green eye. 'You look at it and it seems smooth,' she whispered, stroking it. Then she turned it over, drew one slender finger across it and blood came to the surface. It formed a single droplet, which she pressed against Justin's lips, then licked off the residue herself.

'Don't break your promise, Justin, we have a right to draw blood. We have waited so long. We need to make it happen, and make it happen soon.' Justin was sure that, after this evening, at long last he had in his grasp the one person they wanted to bleed to death.

CHAPTER 9

IT WAS after eleven when William finished his breakfast. He had been apprehensive about seeing Dahlia, but when he went into the kitchens she hardly acknowledged his presence. She had been reprimanding a delivery service about certain supplies that were due to be collected from the mainland. She behaved as if the previous evening's events had not occurred. 'Excuse me, Sir William,' she said, cupping the receiver in her hand, 'I won't be a moment. The fruit I ordered hasn't arrived.'

He gave her a rueful smile, and asked if Justin was back. At that moment the man himself breezed in. 'You want a spin in the Sunseeker?' he asked.

William followed him. Dahlia was still immersed in her phone call.

Sammy was waiting with the boat already uncovered and the engines ticking. William and Justin climbed aboard as Dahlia ran towards them, out of breath. 'Can you pick up the groceries, Justin? They'll be ready for collection.'

'Fine,' Justin yelled as he gave the signal for Sammy to move off.

William staggered backwards as the boat surged forward. Justin took off his sunglasses, and slipped them into his pocket. 'I'd remove your hat and shades. The wind'll whip them off. We're going to open her up today. She can do sixty-eight knots, you know.'

William lowered himself deeper into one of the leather seats and did as Justin advised. The boat's engines were so loud it made conversation impossible, but Justin tried nevertheless, shouting for William to look at the small navigational computer by the wheel, and then at all the various dials and speedometers. The wind billowed his shirt and ruffled his hair. Justin laughed with the sheer exhilaration of speed, then turned to William. 'You want to take the wheel?' he shouted.

'Better not,' William bellowed, then changed his mind. 'Okay, show me what to do.'

He made his way to Sammy's side, where the force of the wind was eased by the shelter of the windscreen. Justin stood right behind him, and at first he helped him steer, shouting instructions into William's ear.

William felt like a schoolboy, bellowing at the top of his voice, 'This is marvellous. *I love it.*'

Justin took over the wheel as they came in to dock at Wickam's Cay on Tortola. The marina was crammed with yachts and cruisers of all shapes and sizes. Navigating a path between the buoys and moored boats, he pulled in as close to the delivery warehouses as he could get. As he manoeuvred into the marked collection zone, Sammy jumped out to catch the mooring ropes.

He and Justin tied up the boat and started off towards the warehouses. Turning back to check that William was following, Justin saw him staring into space. 'William!' he called. 'Do you want to meet us up at the Harbour Bar? We'll be about an hour.'

'Oh, right, fine, see you there.'

William watched them for a moment, then patted his head. The sun was burning his scalp so he climbed back into the boat and retrieved his crushed Panama.

The Harbour Bar was a crude place with a straw roof and one long wooden counter with rows of bottles stacked on shelves behind it. An old-fashioned Coke dispenser stood on one side next to an ice-maker. On the other was a row of pinball machines. Formica-topped tables spilled out on to a small, shaded veranda. The bar regularly caught fire, so the walls were brown and discoloured; paint peeled from the doors, which were never closed. At night fairy-lights decorated the railings, curling round the posts that held up the roof. There was no air-conditioning, but two large fans spun in a slow, hypnotic cycle, more effectively whipping up dust than circulating cool air. The PA blasted out home-made tape recordings of local bands, mixed with a variety of pop, rock and disco. The mindlessness of the continual music was all part of the scene at the Harbour Bar, which was one of the main meeting places for anyone using the harbour.

Other more sophisticated bars and hotels, with ele-gant palm-filled air-conditioned saloons and waiters stood further along the marina. But none did the thriving business of the Harbour Bar, which was con-stantly packed. At night, the smell of ganja was strong and local bands played live. A small platform had been built just outside so that people could dance. Now it was peak season and the bar was heaving. White girls on holiday flirted with young black guys who hit on them for money. The local hookers led a carefree existence, their eyes roaming for rich pickings as they sat drinking Coke at the bar. William attracted no more than a perfunctory gaze before they returned to their conversations while he ordered a lager and lime. He felt hot and uncomfortable, his shorts chafing his thighs, and he could feel mosquito bites erupting. By the time Justin strolled up the steps of the bar's veranda, he had consumed two more lagers.

'Get you another?' Justin called, but he shook his head and watched as Justin sauntered to the bar. The hookers slapped his hand and the barman was already fixing him a mixture of fresh orange and lemon juice with crushed ice. Justin stopped at two other tables, chatting and laughing, before he joined William. 'We're all stocked up. We can leave any time.'

William's shirt was dripping with sweat and he took himself off to the shack at the back of the bar, which served as a lavatory. He splashed tepid water from a chipped basin over his face, but it didn't cool him. He was looking forward to getting back into the boat for the air. His chest felt constricted and he could hardly breathe.

He and Justin walked the short distance to where the boat was moored at the harbour, passing charter yachts and gin palaces. One yacht, in the most prominent position with a wide wooden gangplank, had numerous white-T-shirted crew setting out a dining area under a canopy.

More crew were carrying on crates of fruit and drinks

past the four people at the foot of the gangplank. The women wore skimpy, buttock-revealing shorts and bikini tops, their bronzed bodies gleaming. A blonde had a white baseball cap pulled low over her eyes, the other wore a wide-brimmed straw hat with a scarf knotted around the rim, flowing down her tanned back, over her sarong and matching bikini top. William identified them as English. One of the men, in a moth-eaten straw hat, was lighting a cigar. William recognized him instantly. Henry, Lord Bellingham was probably the same age as William, but looked at least fifteen years younger. The woven embroidered bracelet on his wrist gave him a hint of the hippie.

Bellingham oozed social confidence. He was the type of man who immediately made William feel inferior, the type that William had once wanted to emulate. Instead of succeeding, though, he had become the butt of their jibes. The Bellinghams of this world were involved in far worse scandals than poor William ever had been, but they never came to light: friends in the right places made sure of that.

'Do you know Sir William, Lord Bellingham?' Justin asked casually, as William joined them.

Bellingham gave him no more than a cursory glance. 'I believe so.' He turned away. 'Annabella, darling, we should make moves,' he said. He gave William another glance as he strode up the gangplank.

Justin turned to the women. 'Lady Annabella Bellingham and Countess Maria de Coveney, Sir William Benedict.'

They gave aloof smiles and Lady Annabella shook William's hand, which was hot and wet. She withdrew hers quickly. 'Do be on time,' she barked to Justin. 'We've got so much security to deal with – it's a real headache.'

Justin bowed over her hand and kissed it. She laughed and tapped his cheek. 'Oh, you sexy boy.'

She started up the gangplank. The Countess, at least, acknowledged William, before following. Now the second man shook Justin's hand before turning to William. 'I'm Gabriel, Frederick Capri's brother. I believe you know him?'

William nodded. He couldn't think of anything to say as he'd only met him fleetingly at the villa in France. 'Justin, I'll see you on the boat,' he said flatly, and walked away.

As he left the group, there was a burst of laughter behind him. William blushed angrily.

It was another ten minutes before Justin joined him.

'Let's go!' he said, hurling the ropes to Sammy and jumping aboard. He patted William's knee. 'You seem a bit out of sorts,' he said kindly.

'I'm bloody hot and just want to get the hell out of here.'

Justin gestured to Sammy, who opened up the engines and they started to move out, weaving their way between the moorings and passing the Bellingham yacht. There were now eight people sitting on it under the canopy, laughing and drinking. One young boy with blond hair was sitting with his legs over the side. He waved to Justin.

'So pretty, isn't he?' Justin mused. 'That's Oliver Bellingham. He's not allowed off the boat – just been kicked out of school for dealing drugs. The other guests on board—'

188

'I'm not interested,' said William curtly, refusing to look towards the group, who were now all watching the powerboat draw away.

Justin settled into the seat next to Sammy. 'Open her up! Jog a martini out of Annabella's hand!' The engines throbbed, all six kicked in, the bow lifted out of the water and the boat sped out of the harbour.

By the time they reached the island William was frozen stiff. It took an hour and a half, and the pounding of the engines had given him a throbbing headache. By the time they got there, William was shivering. An hour later he had a temperature of a hundred and two.

Dahlia took great care of him. She arranged for trays of tasty food, tea, lemon drinks and iced fruit to be brought up to his room. Some time later Justin caught her as she carried down a tray. 'What the fuck is wrong with him?' he asked.

'Heatstroke, but he thinks it's malaria. His temperature is quite high.'

'How long is he going to be up there?'

'Maybe a day or so. He's not eating too well, and he's sleeping a lot. He'll be fine.'

'I bloody hope so.'

William remained in bed for three days. His linen was changed and he was washed and shaved like an invalid. He was rather tickled when he discovered he had lost fifteen pounds.

On the fourth day, at William's request, Justin arranged for Kurt to give him a gentle workout in the gym. After three gym sessions, the loss of fifteen pounds, daily massage and three more self-tanning treatments, William began to feel rejuvenated. He discussed his diet with Dahlia, and eventually sent a message to Justin that he would like to have lunch with him. It consisted of salad, chicken breast, an array of apple, carrot and vegetable juices and a row of vitamin pills.

'My! We're on a health regime, I see,' said Justin, as he sat down.

'You can order anything you want,' William said, picking at his chicken. 'I just want to lose at least another ten pounds. Kurt's getting me into shape.'

'Well, that's wonderful.' Justin could just about manage some enthusiasm.

'How do you want to be paid?' William was pouring more apple juice.

'I'm sorry?' Justin leaned forward.

'Well, you can have a cheque, but it's quite a sum, and for tax reasons I wondered if you had some offshore bank account. If you like, I can set one up for you.'

'Cheque,' Justin said quickly, then frowned. Maybe he should have a think about his tax situation. He rarely, if ever, paid any. The truth was that what came in went directly out again.

'Cheque it is, but it might be useful to have a word with my accountant. It's up to you.'

Justin could hardly believe it: he was paying him off, getting rid of him. He had to get William to agree to the plan, and fast.

'You're very quiet,' William said, smiling.

'Just thinking about what you said. I've never been all that good with money, you know. If I have it I spend it. But this is quite a tidy sum.'

'Well deserved, though.' William was smiling again. Justin found this new, cheerful William a little unnerving. 'Have to say, I had some doubts . . . I mean, more than doubts. After all, you overspent the original budget by four million, and to be honest I was none too pleased. But the more I've taken in your work, the more I see it was necessary. I have never, until now, had any interest in any of my homes, but this one I like.'

'We aim to please.' Justin helped himself to salad.

'I wanted you to help me out on another little area,' William said, 'if you have the time, that is.' He gestured down at himself. 'I see how dreadful I look. How deadly my taste has been.' He looked up at Justin. 'I know it's silly, but I want to wear clothes that make me feel good. When I shopped with Sylvina, she made me buy what other people thought was good – you know what I mean? Like my ex-wives – they togged me out too and, to be honest, I want a . . .' he gave a boyish shrug '. . . younger look.'

'We can get you some local summer gear. You don't want anything too . . .'

'Safari?' William said, and sniggered.

By mid-afternoon, the gardeners and the boat-boys had been handed plastic bags filled with discarded clothes to burn. Needless to say, they were thrilled, knowing they could resell them on Tortola, or even across the strait on Puerto Rico.

While William went for a workout in the gym with Kurt, Justin started sorting out a costume for the Bellinghams' summer dance. The British loved dressing up – the more outlandishly the better. It was as if they were trying to revert to childhood. He'd been working away for an hour when there was a knock at the door.

It was William. 'I was wondering whether you wanted to watch some videos with me tonight?'

'Any other time,' Justin said, wrapping some pale blue silk around his fist and pulling it into a shape. 'I'm going over to the Bellinghams' and I've got to fathom out some kind of costume.' He plonked the turban on his head.

'You were invited?' William said, jealous.

'Yes. The son invited me, Oliver. They invite a select mob and dress up. Prizes and games. Awful, really. But quite good for me, you know, drumming up business.'

He was lying. He never used social events to ply his trade.

'They didn't ask me,' William said, disgruntled.

Justin spun round and winked. 'Come with me?' he said, holding up a bolt of pink shot silk and silver-threaded organza.

'But they know who I am. It would be hell.' William stood watching Justin wafting blue and pink dyed ostrich plumes, ready to pin them to the turban.

'Far too unacceptable for their sort,' Justin lisped, as he pranced in front of a long mirror. 'We could have some fun together.' He wafted the plume at William. 'Come as my secret partner. Everyone wears masks. Nobody need know who you are.'

William leaped back. 'No bloody way! You're not getting me done up like one of those boys.'

Justin gave a lascivious grin. 'I doubt, William dearest, that anyone could mistake you for one of my little friends.' He swished a swathe of gold lamé into the air, and draped it over William. 'How about if I dress you up as King Tut, and I'll be your servant?'

'No way!' William had never been to a fancy-dress do, even as a child. He wasn't about to make a fool of himself now.

Two hours later, he was dressed in a flowing gold lamé kaftan, with a matching turban and four huge white plumes pinned to it with a gold brooch. Justin was tinting William's face with burnt cork, mixed with some boot polish. It took ages to dry, but gradually his face became bronzed, his lips were pinked, and his eyelashes darkened with mascara.

'Take a look,' Justin said, stepping back to admire his work.

'I don't know about this,' William said, secretly enjoying himself. Justin pushed bracelets and rings onto his stained brown hands, and hung big gold hoops from his ears. William reviewed himself in the mirror, while Justin finished his own costume. When they stood side by side they looked fabulous, and when Justin sprayed a heavy perfume over them, William started to get quite excited.

'I've never gatecrashed anything, you know,' he said, preening.

'Tonight's the night, then! Come along, Your Majesty, let's knock 'em dead.'

It was after ten when Justin and William descended to the jetty where the cruiser stood ready to transport them to the Bellinghams' estate. Four boat-boys, in turbans and sarongs, carried large fans to welcome the pair aboard. Fairy-lights were strung from stern to bow. Music blasted out of the stereo as the cruiser pulled out to sea. In the cabin, buckets of champagne and plates of caviar were laid out, where William, now in the spirit of the evening, sat relaxing on silk cushions.

The Bellinghams' jetty was ablaze with lights, flickering torches and flowers. William and Justin could hear the band as they approached. The sea was calm. Rows of bobbing yachts and cruisers were moored by servants. There were loud cheers as the King and his servant disembarked. William surveyed the array of costumes from behind his disguise. There were women dressed as cats, trapeze artists, semi-naked servant girls, Tarzans and Janes in skimpy strips of leopardskin, pirates and princes in multi-coloured lamé.

The heavy smell of incense and marijuana filled the billowing marquee, and tables were laden with fruit, lobsters and exotic dishes. Butlers in masks and loincloths carried around trays of elaborate cocktails laced with vodka, gin or rum. The centrepiece was a champagne fountain surrounded by ice sculptures.

As William surveyed the room, he recognized Meryl Delaware, draped over a dark-skinned boy who appeared to be no more than twenty. There were pop stars, models and actors whose faces he vaguely knew. Sections of the marquee were cordoned off by flowing drapes. William peeped behind them. Couples were copulating on low couches, others snorting from bowls of cocaine. In another section of the marquee sat a fortune-teller – average party material, thought William, except that she was stark naked apart from a glittering G-string and a long blonde wig that tumbled over her breasts. Nearby, leather-masked men with leather-studded cocks strapped to their legs, strutted between women dressed in PVC corsets, wielding whips. Other men were crawling on all fours licking the women's black patent stilettos.

'And those bastards whipped up all that shit about me!' said William to Justin.

'Over a couple of bloody visits from call-girls.'

No one asked who William was, and after about half an hour he started to relax, enjoying his anonymity. He moved from one group to another until he stumbled across Lord Bellingham. Sitting cross-legged on a large cushion, with a backgammon board in front of him and four other people around him, he was wearing a kaftan and turban and smoking a large cigar. It was obvious to William that he was stoned. William watched him for a moment, then moved back, passing two women in a passionate, semi-naked embrace on the grass. He felt himself flush under his cork.

'I want to slide under your robes, Your Majesty.' A woman wearing nothing but a PVC loincloth stood at his side and tried to slither under his gold kaftan. William sprang back, clutching the cloth around him. 'No, thank you,' he stuttered, and scurried away.

William went in search of Justin. The last time he had seen him he was heading out of the tent with Bellingham's son, Oliver, who was so drunk he could hardly stand. William wandered about, stopping to watch the cabaret of exotic dancers, then the local rock star, who jumped up on stage to sing with the band. Those with enough energy were still dancing, but most were scattered around in groups, talking and giggling as the drugs kicked in. Cocaine bowls were constantly topped up and there was an endless supply of thick joints.

Eventually, drunk and exhausted, William hitched up

his kaftan and sat on a low couch beneath a clutch of palm trees away from the main action. His head was throbbing so violently he couldn't raise it more than a fraction and when he did, he felt nauseous.

'Pull your frock down, old boy.' It was Justin. 'Look I've got something to do, then I'll be back.'

'Have they spiked the drinks?' William asked, squinting up at Justin.

'Probably.'

'Dear God, I feel terrible. You'll have to help me back to the boat.'

'Just stay here, I won't be long.'

The party was winding down. William lay immobile, hoping to ease his aching head. Two women had sat down on a lounger on the other side of the palm trees, unaware of his presence.

'Ghastly man,' one said to the other. William could hear the clink of glass.

'The Bellinghams saw him on the quay the other day with that boy Justin.'

They were talking about him! William lay still, listening. Bellingham and his cronies joined them.

'The stupid bugger got hammered because he was so desperate to be accepted. It always happens with his kind – they get caught with their pants around their ankles.'

One disembodied voice recalled William's engagement to the Countess Lubrinsky. This created hoots of laughter and a few lurid anecdotes about Sylvina's past. Then William heard a voice he recognized. It was the hideous Meryl Delaware, desperate to ingratiate herself with Bellingham. She claimed she had it on good authority that William had paid Countess Lubrinsky to broadcast their engagement in the hope that he would be accepted by the Royal Family. But the closest he had got to them was walking past the Royal Enclosure at Ascot. 'He's more than pitiful,' said Meryl. 'He's a laughing stock.'

'Paying a trashy countess to say she loved him and was prepared to marry him! He's pathetic.'

Suddenly, a voice William didn't recognize entered the conversation. 'You're not still discussing that awful man. Just keep the money-to-burn lowlife at arm's length. I suspect he's a poofter like his crony, that sicko Maynard.'

Suddenly there were shouts that the fireworks were due to start and the group heaved their tired bodies towards the quay side without glancing back at the prone figure a few feet away from them. Bellingham, however, had recognized William. Before he left he turned and said, 'That'll teach you to gatecrash, you jumped-up parvenu.'

A few seconds later Justin was back. He helped William along the harbour to the boat. William felt the screeching rockets and fizzing fireworks reverberating in his head, smashing through his thoughts: Pathetic! Pitiful! A buffoon!

At noon the next day, William woke up with the worst hangover he had ever experienced. He had breakfast alone. Just after two, when paracetamol had eased the throbbing between his ears and ice packs had soothed his swollen eyes, he went to Justin's bungalow on the lower path beneath the main house. There was no sign of him and, worse, William was shocked to see a line of packed suitcases on the bed and wardrobes and drawers emptied. With a sinking feeling in the pit of his stomach, he went to find him. He discovered Justin down by the jetty.

'Afternoon,' Justin said brightly. 'I'd given up on seeing you today, but I'm glad I have as I didn't want to leave without saying goodbye.'

'You're going?' William said.

'Yes. I need to get back to France. I'm on my way to Paris.'

William pursed his lips. He wasn't sure how to say it, or even what he wanted to say. He just knew that he didn't want Justin to go.

'You feeling all right?' Justin asked.

'No, I'm not. Come up to the house, have a drink with me.'

Justin glanced at his wristwatch. 'I really wanted to get the late tide.'

'I would like to talk to you,' William said.

Justin had expected this to happen.

William was sitting at his desk when Justin came in. 'What about my makeover?' he said petulantly.

'Well, I've left you a list of designers; suggested who you should contact. You can hire people to do this kind of thing, you know.'

'I want you,' William said.

Justin sighed. 'Well, that's all very well, but I have a living to make and I have things to do. Especially high on the agenda is seeing my sister.'

'If it's money you want you can have it.'

'Look, if someone fucks me over I fuck them back. You can't let people get away with humiliating you. I've prepared everything here for you to pay the bastards back. But I'm tired of your indecision. Either you want revenge or you don't.'

Justin left the room and went to the control room. The time was perfect now, he was sure of it.

William walked in as he was putting a tape into the VCR.

'William, take a look at this. You never even knew it was happening, but think what I could do with it.' William stood, aghast, watching the video of himself with Dahlia and Ruby, tied to the bed, being oiled and massaged, moaning with pleasure.

'Shocked?' Justin asked, smiling. 'You ever been taken that far before?' He was enjoying himself.

'No,' William said hoarsely. 'Did you drug me?'

'You did that all under your own steam! Impressive, wouldn't you say?'

'It's disgusting.'

Justin laughed gleefully. 'Rubbish, it was done in the privacy of your own bedroom.' He stopped the tape. 'Stop whipping yourself with guilt, Willy-boy. Like I said, get even. You've got all the trappings right here on Island Exotics. All you need is your guest-list – then we can line 'em up and shoot 'em down. One by one.'

Justin waited. Had he overplayed his hand?

'No more prevarication, Justin, I'll do it. But I need you to tell me what to do.'

Which, of course, was exactly what Justin had planned. 'Fine, and since you seem so concerned that your "guests" won't show if they know *you're* their host, I think there's no need to make your ownership of the island public. You could be some mysterious tycoon.'

' "Some mysterious tycoon." You love to play games, don't you, Justin?'

William remained silent for a long time.

'Tell me, what makes *you* so eager to play out this charade?' William asked eventually, his eyes sharp as flints. 'What's in this for you?'

Justin licked his lips, averting his eyes. His mind raced. He played his hand to perfection.

'Andrew Maynard. I lost a friend and it hurt to see him vilified and abused. That's why I care about you. I knew what you meant to him.'

'I think I meant to him the same thing I mean to you. A meal ticket,' William said.

'Wrong on two counts. I've already earned enough from you, and you'll no doubt reward me for assisting you in getting some satisfaction. Also, Andrew only spoke of you with admiration and respect.'

'Mmm,' William said.

'Make them eat shit like you were forced to. Don't back down or you'll regret it till the day you die. And then, when it's over, you can settle down to enjoy your life on the most exclusive private island known to man, once again renowned as the charming, debonair tycoon, Sir William Benedict.'

William contemplated the idea for a moment, then stretched out his hand. 'Very well, we'll have a go at it. I must be mad, but yes, why not? You're on. Let's get the bastards. Just so long as you know I'm the ring-master.'

'Absolutely. It's your trap, William, not mine. I'll

just do whatever you say . . . I have a few conditions, though,' he said softly.

William gestured for him to continue.

'I think we should get Laura here.'

'Why?'

'Well, you may need her. She's very beautiful. I guarantee no man could refuse Laura.'

'Would she agree?' William asked.

'She might. It's up to you. I think you need a hostess – you know, to welcome everyone . . .'

William nodded.

'No point in her coming here directly – the season's almost over and we don't want to rush into anything. We must have a perfect time of year: Christmas is the best time in the Caribbean.'

'God, that's a while away,' William said, sighing.

'Well, we're not quite ready yet. We've a few finishing touches to make – decoration, press releases . . . and Laura will need to be primed.'

'I'll come to Paris with you.' William said.

'That's a good idea. While we're there I'll start the press frenzy,' said Justin, 'while you think hard about who you want on that list. That should be fun.' He paused. 'Talking of press, I've been looking at your little problem. I think I have identified your main *agent provocateur*. One group of publications seems to have led the way in attacking you: News Syndicate International. It so happens that those papers and magazines are all owned by Humphrey Matlock. He's still on the list, isn't he?'

William nodded, his lips tight. 'Yes, well, he was. I got invited to his place for some charity fête, but I never bothered to go.' He sighed. 'Truth was, the Sylvina

201

thing blew it all up in my face again and I couldn't face anyone.'

'So he should be a priority.' Justin stared at William, who was now deep in thought. He could be so irritating. 'Hear what I said?'

William nodded. He was listening, but his thoughts were miles away as he calculated how much money Matlock must have made out of his misery. 'Yes, he's top of my list,' he said softly.

CHAPTER 10

WILLIAM AND Justin installed themselves in adjoining suites at the Ritz in Paris. From there, the two made sojourns to boutiques and back-street stores, William following his style instructor like a lamb.

His diet and fitness regime began next day with an early-morning swim, then running up and down the shallow end until his legs felt like jelly. Next they went into the gym. They did weights one day, stretching and abdominal exercises the next. For the first six days William ate a soup concocted by the hotel chef to Justin's specific instructions. It had been originally conceived for heart patients awaiting surgery, to enable them to lose weight quickly but safely.

William lost weight rapidly. He felt fitter and more energetic than he had in years. Daily massages and sun-bed treatments were interspersed with shopping expeditions, and William enjoyed watching his size drop. His excitement was contagious – even Justin had to admire his protégé's determination.

Ten days after they had left the island, Justin and William were having their usual early-morning juice and fruit while reading the English newspapers. Justin noticed an article in *The Times* and muttered something to himself. Then he said nonchalantly, 'Bellingham's son died. His funeral is today.'

William reached over and peered at the article.

'OD'd on the night of the party,' Justin went on, spooning strawberries into his mouth.

William was shocked. 'I'm sorry. How do you know that? It doesn't say so here.'

'He was found dead in the grounds after the party,' Justin said. 'He was a drug-addict, and a raving queen.'

He tried to change the subject to the day's itinerary, but William said, 'Curious that not a breath of scandal has touched Bellingham over this. Can you imagine if it had been my son? It would have been all over the—'

'Come on,' said Justin, glancing at his watch. 'No point in dwelling on the past. We've got to make a move.'

'Where are we going?' William said truculently.

'To get your hair cut.'

'My hair?' Instinctively he stroked it. 'It's looking good. I've never worn it this long before. What's the matter with it?'

'Pass,' said Justin, as he got up and left the room.

William caught up with him. 'It's just, well, I don't know if you'd noticed, but I've got a bald patch at the back.'

'No, really?'

'Yes, I have. Don't you think this sort of covers it a bit?'

Justin grinned. 'When you're swimming, the water drags your hair forwards and all you can see is that bald spot. So don't hide it. It makes you seem vulnerable when you don't need to be.'

204

'You're not going to make me wear a rug, are you?' William stuttered.

Justin laughed at the thought. 'We'll see what Louis has to say. Trust me.'

Arriving at the salon, William was not convinced that he should trust his precious locks to Louis, who was wearing one of the worst wigs he had ever seen.

Louis began to cut his hair at an alarming pace. When he reached for the clippers William froze. Finally, with mock-bravado, Louis swept off William's cape, stepped back and said, '*Voilà!*'

William inspected his cropped head. He liked his drastic new look. Stubble short and bleached blond from the sun, the haircut said: 'I don't give a shit!' and to a man who always had, it was just what he needed.

That evening William was going to join Justin in the dining-room. It was the seventh day of his diet, and he could eat as much meat as he wanted. He planned to order three fillet steaks with spinach and green salad. He was wearing a pale blue suit, a white silk shirt with a high collar and no tie. He was looking good, but at the door to the restaurant he was stopped by the *maître d'*.

'You must wear a tie in here,' Monsieur,' he snapped.

'Are you telling me I can't eat here? I'm paying for two bloody suites. You should let me in in my underwear!'

The *maître d'* shrugged in his Gallic way. William was just about to demand a table when his elbow was gripped from behind. 'Stop being such a crass, English yob,' Justin said. 'Rules are rules. Forget it, life's too short.'

They ate in a small bistro, not far from the hotel. William remained in a bad mood but then, to Justin's surprise, he suddenly said, 'That bastard Matlock. The more I think about him, the more angry I feel. I've thought about it a lot. It was really as if he had some personal grudge against me, as if the man was hell-bent on destroying me. The other papers just followed his lead. But then he invited me to that garden fête, albeit courtesy of his wife.'

'So what? You were invited, weren't you?'

'Via his *wife*. I asked Michael to check it out for me. I think Matlock's got it in for me because of his wife, Angela.'

'Do you know her?'

'She used to be my secretary.'

'Your secretary?' Justin asked, his jaw open.

'Well, the name is the same. I've not seen her for years. I had a bit of a scene with her.'

He signalled for the bill. This was a different William. He was obviously angry, but there was a steely quality to him that Justin had not witnessed before.

'I intend to find out, and if it is Angela, I want her on the island too. We leave tomorrow.'

They took the Eurostar to London to make preparations and for William to check his business affairs. When Michael saw the new-look William, his jaw dropped. 'Good heavens, you look—' he stuttered.

'Yes?' William said gleefully.

'Like a different person, sir.'

'Thank you Michael. Did you check out Matlock's wife for me?'

'She's the same Angela Nicholls who used to work for you. They have a son, James. He's at Eton and—'

206

William wafted his hand – he didn't want to hear any more. Could Angela *really* have been behind the onslaught to which her husband's papers had subjected him? If so, she would pay for it. Returning to his study, he couldn't help smiling to himself.

The two men stayed in London just three days while William attended numerous quickly arranged board meetings. His games company had been accused of plagiarism by a German toy manufacturer: William's company had ripped off their cat-and-mouse mechanical toy, they said.

'It's a fox and hens, nothing *like* a cat and mouse! Refuse to back down. We'll counter-sue if necessary. Did you check out the manufacturers as I asked? Who are they, anyway?'

His team passed him a detailed dossier. To William's fury, he saw that the action had been taken against him by the factory he had attempted to acquire from Baron von Garten, which was now owned by William's biggest competitor. The team had determined that the original cat-and-mouse product had been designed by one of William's former employees, who had been headhunted by the rival firm, who in their turn had illegally registered the toy's patent in their name: it had already existed when the designer worked for William, which could be proved because William owned the original designs. He'd sue and he knew he would win. And he would get another stab at the Baron, who was a shareholder in the company and had paid a fortune to market the toy. William was buzzing with energy at the thought of the battle ahead.

*

Over a breakfast meeting, William showed his lawyers the drawings and proposals the Germans had used for their own gain; they had used the scandal that had erupted around William to escape their agreement to sell on a contractual nicety. Baron von Garten had reneged on the deal, retained William's goodwill down-payment, then gone on to sell to his closest competitors. Since Geffin's Toys had opened they had made vast profits and all their toys would be under review: William was sure it wasn't just one item they had ripped off. His lawyers gained the right to assess all the present Geffin's Toys on the market and to compare them with any from William's design departments.

William's researchers then discovered that Baron von Garten owned rather more than a 'small' portion of the business; he had fifty per cent. This discovery pleased William even more because, by retaining a fifty per cent shareholding in Geffin's, the Baron had opened himself up to being liable for all the legal costs and fines involved in actions brought against them for plagiarism. William was going to come down hard and heavy on 'Geffin's Toys'.

William could not keep the smile off his face as he gave orders for his legal team to sue the backside off Geffin's. They were to keep him informed of every move, even though he would not be staying in London. The new Sir William was like a hurricane, so it was with some relief that his London staff saw him depart.

William and Justin boarded his private jet for Nice. Justin had finished preparing a press-pack for the 'Billionaire's Paradise Island Home' and delivering copies

208

to the most prestigious and influential magazines: *Country Life*, *Tatler*, *Vogue* and *Hello!*. Like conspiratorial teenagers, they sat side by side on the plane, reviewing William's invitation hit-list.

'My ex-wife Katherine, and her cousin Cedric. I hate that bastard, he's always ripped me off. Humphrey Matlock and his dear wife, Angela.'

'Who are all these people?' Justin queried.

'The journalists,' William said.

'For God's sake, you have the organ-grinder, Matlock. You don't need his monkeys. Cross them off.'

'You're sure he and his family will be easy to get over there?'

'Leave that to me,' Justin said softly. Then he went to the lavatory. He needed to be alone: he could hardly contain his excitement.

His hand stroked the worn old wallet in the breast pocket of his jacket. It had belonged to his father, the monogram faded now with years of use. It rarely contained folded notes – Justin preferred to stash those in the back pocket of his jeans. It held something more precious than money: a newspaper article, folded over and over, the creases brown with age. He eased it out and opened it. He knew every line, every word by heart, but this was the first time he had read it with a smile on his face.

'Gotcha!' he hissed. 'Humphrey fucking Matlock! Gotcha!'

CHAPTER 11

THE VILLA was hidden in darkness, but the car headlights lit the main veranda. Justin jumped out and ran inside, leaving William and the driver to remove the suitcases from the boot. The lights came on in the gardens, throwing the villa into focus, and the driver stood open-mouthed as the magical garden came to life with fountains and shaded lights over the rock pools and flowers. Justin returned to help with the cases.

Suddenly Marta was running towards them. She flung herself at Justin and kissed him frantically, held him at arm's length then kissed him again.

'Is she here?' Justin whispered, and Marta nodded.

After unpacking, William found his way to the dining room. The table was beautifully laid, with candles, bowls of salad, and every conceivable cold cut. He heaped a plate, poured some chilled Chablis and sat down. After a few moments, Justin joined him and helped himself to food and wine.

'She asleep?' William asked, his mouth full.

'Yes.'

'So I won't get to meet her tonight then?'

'Maybe, maybe not.'

Laura did not make an appearance. It was after two in the morning when they both decided to go to bed. 'You want to see her?' Justin whispered. 'Come with me . . .'

Laura was lying on her side, naked, one arm stretched out, the hand cupped as if begging to be touched. One slender leg crossed over, the other leaving her hip rising like a wing. Her breasts were partly hidden by her other hand, which rested against them almost in an attitude of piety. Her silken blonde hair splayed across the pillow and fell over her shoulder like gossamer. Even in the flickering candlelight, the beauty of her sleeping face was heart-stopping. She had high sweeping cheekbones, fine arched brows and the lashes resting on her cheeks were dark. Her nose was straight, in perfect symmetry with her cheeks, and her wide pink lips were parted. She was almost too beautiful to be real.

'What do you think?' whispered Justin.

'She's perfect,' was all William could say.

'She is the bait, William.'

William went to his suite, changed and slid between the cool cotton sheets. He was aware of a strange sensation of fear in the pit of his stomach. He had no notion of why he felt afraid. He had spent enough time with Justin to think that he knew him . . . but did he? At some point he fell asleep, so he did not hear the soft moan or the conversation that went on for hours. He didn't hear a sound from above as brother and sister lay entwined like lovers, their perfect bodies catching the light of the candles: he so bronzed, eyes deep and tortured, she with the paleness of lilies that belied a terrible darkness.

*

211

'Morning,' William said to Marta, who was setting the breakfast table. She was hardly able to give him a pleasant look, never mind a 'good morning' in return. 'Lovely day,' he said. He had just received a call from his lawyers that two more toys were being inspected, and the chink-chink of the money it would cost the Baron was music to his ears.

Marta moved closer to him. 'Get away from this place,' she said tersely. Her expression said more, but she stopped abruptly when Justin appeared and swept her into his arms.

'Who is the love of your life?' Justin asked, kissing her cheeks.

'You both are,' she said.

William thought she seemed near to tears as she hurried out of the room, but he put it to the back of his mind. He beamed at Justin. 'Just spoken to my legal boffins, I'm going to squeeze Baron von Garten's balls so tightly. It's gonna cost him millions.'

'You ever think of anything else but accruing dosh, old man?'

'I do now. The dosh, as you call it, has nothing to do with my good humour. It's getting that stuck-up son-of-a-bitch.'

'That's good,' Justin said, and now he smiled. 'Like I've always said, pay-back is the best feeling you can have. You'll more than pay him back. You'll hit his reputation as well as his pocket, right?'

'Right,' said William, grinning.

Laura did not come down to breakfast that morning, but William saw Marta carrying a tray up to her room.

He was going up to the roof for a swim. Perhaps Justin would be up there. He was. Peering over his dark glasses as William approached, Justin held out the copy of *Vogue* that he had been reading. 'Have a look at page forty,' he suggested.

William sat down next to him and picked up the magazine. Flicking through the pages, he stopped at the spread of his bedroom on the island. 'Good God!' he said. He read aloud, ' "This extraordinary bedroom suite, with its canopied bed festooned with exquisite fabrics, its tasselled curtains and gorgeous rugs, like an Empire period fantasy in French opulence, announces the secret owner to be a man of taste and immense wealth. No doubt the fortunate guests will be universally famous, beautiful and strictly millionaires." ' William dropped the magazine. 'My name isn't here, is it?'

''Course not,' laughed Justin. 'Don't want to put them off.'

William read on, ' "Everything in this room, from the wallpaper to the doorknobs, is handmade, its grandeur counterpointed by its elegance and restraint. It is a room to inspire, and indulge a man's dreams. Only a high-flyer could come to rest in a bed that would have suited the Sun King himself." Did you write it, Justin?'

'Don't be ridiculous, it's that slag Meryl Delaware. I gave her the photos and the specifications. Now she's wild to see the place for herself. She believes it's owned by a mystery consortium of reclusive millionaires or royalty.'

'Maybe it wouldn't be such a bad thing to tell them whose island it is soon. I mean, we've got them all wondering now, and that thing with Sylvina has put me back on the social map.'

213

Justin had to admit that William was right, but he had grown bored with this exchange and was moving inside.

'Justin!' called William. 'Look!'

He was pointing towards the wooded area below them in the gardens. He stepped back in shock as Justin sprang on to the balcony rail and proceeded to climb down the front of the house, clinging to the ivy. 'Laura! *Laura!*' he shouted, as he ran towards the woods.

William shaded his eyes to watch Justin tear across the gardens. In a long white dress and a wide-brimmed picture hat, Laura waited among the trees. Justin caught her in his arms and swung her round, her feet off the ground, her arms around his neck.

William made his way down the stairs and out through the big french windows, then strolled through the paved Japanese gardens, past the fountains, ferns and palm trees. 'Justin?' he called, but there was silence. He headed into the forest of tall pines. 'Hello, where are you?' he called.

'Hello.' It was a woman's voice.

William turned to face her. She was standing in deep shadows between two massive fir trees, her hands resting on their bark. She was barefoot, and her dress was transparent so the light shone through.

'Laura?' said William shyly.

'You must be William.' Her voice was light with a hoarse quality.

'I saw you from the balcony,' he said, rather lamely.

As he moved closer, William noticed that she had threaded daisies between her toes. He felt like a schoolboy. 'Justin has told me a lot about you,' he said

214

hesitantly, wishing he could think of something more interesting to say.

'Did he?' she said. He still could not see her face clearly: her long hair fell like a curtain, obscuring her profile.

'It's cold out of the sun,' he said, looking upwards.

'It's nice and cool. Don't you find it refreshing?' She lifted one hand and brushed her hair off her face.

William was mesmerized by her incredible blue eyes. They were deep like her brother's, but so pale and weirdly expressionless, that it seemed as if her thoughts were trapped miles away.

He felt awkward, and his body was covered in goose pimples. 'I find it chilly,' he said.

She cocked her head to one side. 'Chilly? *C'est quoi*, chilly?' Her accent was quite strong, unlike Justin's.

Suddenly she moved towards him and slipped her arm through his. William's heart lurched. Her perfume smelt familiar, of lilies. He realized she was very tall.

'I'm hungry,' she said, and her voice had no trace of an accent at all.

'How odd,' William said. 'One moment you sound French and the next you speak perfect English.'

She laughed. 'I was brought up in England, so if I wish I am English. But I can also be French.' She wrinkled her nose. 'I think, for you, I should always be English.'

'Yes . . . but you are a very good actress,' he mused, then asked, 'Have you ever been on the stage?'

'Oh, no, I would hate to be constantly portraying other people. I'd lose myself. I have a hard time holding on to who I am anyway. Does that happen to you?'

'I've never thought about it, but I suppose so. When I am in a good mood, I feel like I have more energy to deal with people, but when I'm in a bad mood, I feel inadequate and then I wish I could be my other self. Does that make sense?'

'Of course, because sometimes it is hard to be confident. Do you envy people who are always confident?'

'You mean like Justin?'

She looked up into his eyes. 'Justin is not always confident. He may appear to be so, but I know sometimes he goes to a place of deep despair.'

William was interested, he had never considered that Justin might be prone to depression. 'Sometimes he feels very lonely, so he hides. We are very alike.'

'You feel lonely?'

She hesitated a moment, then shook her head. Her voice was soft and hardly audible. 'I am alone if I am not with Justin.'

Her eyes brimmed with tears and he wanted to hold her, protect her, wrap his arms around her frail beauty. Instead he coughed and changed the subject. 'Er, I'm hungry too. Shall we make our way back to the villa?'

As they broke from the darkness into the splendour of the gardens, he said, 'It's wonderful, isn't it? Everything so alive, growing . . .'

'Mmm,' she said lightly, then, almost as an afterthought, added, 'Everything but me.'

It was a disquieting remark, which played on William's mind.

They walked in silence for a while. Then, wanting to make conversation, he said, 'I've grown very fond of your brother.'

She smiled, 'I adore him, I could not live without him.'

'He speaks well of you.'

'He loves me too much – but then I love *him* too much. Sometimes it leaves no room for anyone else. It has always been that way.'

'Do you work?' William changed the subject.

She frowned. 'Has he not told you about me?'

'How do you mean?'

She gave a soft laugh. 'He obviously hasn't, or you wouldn't ask. It's just that I have a frail constitution. I get very nervous of people. It's silly, but I get agitated very easily and then . . . I get sick, just a nervous condition, but Justin looks after me, and Marta too. She's like a mother, we love her.'

Her voice was soft, musical, and there was a childlike innocence about her that took his breath away. William recalled Andrew Maynard's description of her, and could understand why the young man had been so drawn to these two creatures. The more time William spent with them, the more he, too, fell under their spell.

'Lunch is served,' bellowed Justin, from the first-floor balcony, and the moment was broken.

Laura picked at the food with her fingers. Often brother and sister ate from each other's plates, sometimes popping morsels into each other's mouths. The conversation revolved around the island: Justin described it all to her in minute detail, and told her how hard he had worked since she last saw it. Then he showed her the magazine articles. Laura watched him intently, and at one point she reached over and used her napkin to wipe the side of his mouth. Marta served coffee, and hot water and lemon to Laura who had refused wine, leaving William and Justin to consume a bottle each. Afterwards Justin jumped up and said he would be waiting for William in fifteen minutes to go water-skiing, and Laura disappeared. Marta materialized and proceeded to stack a large tray with all the plates and glasses.

William pushed back his chair and stood up. 'This morning, Marta, at breakfast, you were about to say something but stopped when Justin came in.'

'You must have been mistaken.'

'I distinctly heard you say something about—'

'I didn't say anything.'

As she went out with the tray, William held open the door for her. 'Laura is very beautiful,' he said softly, and he saw the look of sadness in Marta's face. 'A rare thing. A very delicate, fragile woman.'

William went to his room to change for the beach, then set off to find Justin. He was waiting in the garden. 'What did you think of her, then?' he whispered, his face close to William's.

'She's gorgeous.'

'Perfection. Lovely firm natural tits, big pink nipples, and her pussy is like a silk purse.'

William pulled away from him. 'For Christ's sake, Justin, she's your sister!'

'Oh, God,' Justin sneered, 'don't be such a prude. She's an experienced woman. She knows what's going to be needed of her. Like I said, she's going to be the bait. You telling me any man would turn her down?

She may not be every man's trip, but let me tell you, if they fuck her, they always go back for more. Laura is an adulteress with more tricks than—'

'Stop it!'

'What's the matter?'

'I don't think you should talk about her in that way.'

'You see? She's got you hooked.' He laughed. 'Imagine fucking her, William. See the swan turn into a demon. She'll have every man on that island, every woman and child eating out of the palm of her tiny innocent hand. And she can bite, you know, and draw blood like no other woman.'

William refused to listen. He hated Justin when he talked like a pimp. But he was angry with himself too – because he couldn't stop thinking of her asleep, naked, her perfect thighs, her breasts, and it made him feel ashamed.

'Maybe you should try out the goods, huh?' Justin said, hopping into a jeep parked outside.

'Why don't you shut your foul mouth before I put my fist in it?'

Justin started up the engine as William got in. 'Anything you say. You're holding the purse strings. I don't suppose she's told you how much she wants yet, has she?' William refused to answer. 'Well, you can discuss it tonight, but her services don't come cheap.'

'Services?' William was appalled.

'She'll charge a lot more than those Mayfair whores you got hammered for screwing. Laura isn't a cheap hooker, she's a courtesan. If you get Matlock, he'll bring his wife and his son. If you leave them alone with Laura she'll have each one of them.'

'Really?' William said flatly. He was sure now that

Justin was joking, but refused to join in with his sick humour.

Justin smiled to himself. He'd never met a man who hadn't wanted to protect Laura on first meeting. Tonight William would witness the other side of Laura – the temptress or maybe the seductress. She had numerous different personalities and Justin loved every one of them. He admonished himself, though, for his reckless conversation: sometimes he forgot that his straitlaced friend did not think as he did. He must not do anything that might make William scuttle away from the trap, which was now in place.

When they got back from the afternoon's waterskiing, William rested until almost nine. He was so tired he hardly felt like dressing for dinner. As he sat morosely by his dressing-table, Justin came in, wearing a white suit and a black T-shirt.

'Every bone aches. I'm not hungry, I am totally exhausted,' William said.

'Just get dressed. I've a little something to give you a boost.'

William went to his wardrobe, selected a cream linen suit, then saw that Justin had chopped out four lines of cocaine on a small hand mirror. 'I don't do drugs,' he barked.

'Just this once,' cooed Justin. 'It'll give you some energy. We don't want you falling asleep half-way through dinner. Go on, everyone should try it once.'

William hummed and hawed, then accepted the rolled banknote and snorted. His eyes watered and he coughed, but Justin pointed to the next line. 'That's enough,' William said.

'Do the other line and stop stalling.'

'Justin, I have never used drugs. I abhor them,' he said, but he bent his head to do the other line as he spoke. 'I really don't approve of this,' he justified himself, blinking back tears. 'And I don't feel anything but a runny nose,' he said, sniffing.

'Believe me, you'll be needing this tonight. Let's go down,' Justin said.

William sniffed again. He wondered why Justin thought he'd be needing the cocaine. As he started down the staircase, it hit him like a thunderbolt. His head cleared and his body felt weightless. He felt incredibly fit and alert, almost jumping down the last few stairs. 'You know, I bet any money if I went back on the skis tomorrow I'd be able to stay up. We can do it first thing before breakfast.' William crouched on the stairs with his hands held out in front of him, as if he was waterskiing.

Justin turned and looked at him, then gave that wonderful, slow smile. 'You should trust your friend. He's always going to take care of you. Now we'll have a little caviar, some iced champagne, and party.'

'Fine by me,' William said, with an inane grin.

What William had not been expecting downstairs, though, was dinner guests. 'What the hell are they doing here?' he muttered.

'Don't fret, old boy, this is all part of the plan. I've arranged a small *soirée* so that you can drop the news that it's *your* island everyone's been getting excited about.'

'We never discussed this.' William was anxious.

'Trust me. Now is the right time. That Sylvina thing has made you look all squeaky clean. Go ahead, give it a go. You'll enjoy it.'

Before he could argue, one of the guests, in the shape of the blowsy Meryl Delaware, almost threw him sideways. She was aiming for Justin, but he sidestepped her and she stumbled into William.

'Miss Delaware,' he said, thankful for the wall behind him.

'Oh, good evening. Sir William Benedict, isn't it?'

'Generally speaking,' he said, and she looked almost puzzled.

'You look very different. Is it your hair?'

'Maybe the lack of it,' he said, with a charming smile, as she backed away and bumped into Terence Hampton.

William looked around. Rent-a-crowd, he thought. He helped himself to a glass of champagne, and drank it down as if it was water. He had such a thirst! He wasn't in the least bit self-conscious or worried that no one was approaching him. Instead, he was enjoying surveying the room, and quickly realized that Laura was absent. Marta was moving quietly around, collecting used glasses and half-empty dishes of caviar, the remnants swimming in melting ice. As she passed William he asked if Laura was joining them.

'I believe so, Sir William,' she answered, and reached out to catch a glass that Princess Constantina had inadvertently knocked off a bookcase.

'I was so sorry to hear about your break-up with Countess Lubrinsky.' Meryl had had to resort to talking to William.

'I'm still broken-hearted,' he said, smiling. 'As you can see. Inconsolable.' He dipped into some caviar. He was enjoying himself and decided that this was the right moment. 'Actually, I've been recovering on my island in the Caribbean.'

'The Caribbean?' Meryl's mind was whirring.

'Yes, I think you wrote an article about it. "Billionaire's Paradise Island Home",' he quoted.

He laughed inwardly when her jaw dropped.

'Tragic about Lord Bellingham's son, wasn't it?'

Meryl blinked her mascara-caked eyelashes and nodded. Rivulets of lipstick gathered in the crevices around her mouth, giving it the appearance of a tight pink arsehole. 'I was in the Caribbean when it happened,' she said, adopting a sorrowful expression.

'So was I,' said William. 'My island is next door to theirs.'

'*Really?*'

'I noticed you at the party, too.'

'Party?' she said guardedly.

'I'd say it was one of the most decadent evenings of my entire life.'

Her hands were trembling. 'My dear,' she whispered, 'a little word of advice. Don't discuss that evening. It's best forgotten. I left early. I had a dreadful migraine.'

'I remember you being there well,' he persisted. 'Life and soul of the party as I recall.'

Meryl pursed her lips. 'I suggest you forget it.' She glared over his shoulder and caught Terence Hampton's eye. 'Ah, Terence, dahling! Are you my chauffeur for this evening?' She rolled her eyes towards William. He did not miss it. 'We should really be thinking about leaving.'

'I only just got here,' he moaned, but Meryl grabbed him and bundled him away.

William strolled out onto the balcony. Princess Constantina stood with her back to the open doors, having a heated discussion with Count Capri. 'Well, it was drugs as well,' she was saying, 'but he'd been abused and tied up. That's what I was told. You know Lord B, he'd never let that out. It was bad enough that the boy was always in a drugged stupor.'

William was eavesdropping and didn't care if he was caught. Tonight he didn't hover or hide his new slim-line figure, but leaned confidently against the balcony viewing the Eurotrash. He would have happily remained so, if Laura hadn't appeared. She was wearing a long gold satin gown that draped her breasts, while the skirt was cut on the bias and swung around her body as she walked. Her pale skin shimmered and her hair had been drawn back tightly against her head, one long plait hanging down the centre of her back. She wore no jewellery at her ears or throat, but a gold bracelet hung low on her slender wrist. 'Ladies and gentlemen,' she announced, 'I do apologize but we are expected at dinner, so if you will excuse us . . .' She stood poised in the doorway. Frederick Capri gaped. 'Who's *that*?' he squawked.

In the drive below the cars started revving up to take the guests to dinner. A Rolls and a large open SL Mercedes were preparing to leave. The room emptied fast, leaving William and Marta alone.

'Well, that was all very . . .' He tailed off and shrugged as the cars disappeared up the drive.

'Typical Justin,' Marta said. 'He bumps into someone and the next minute he has that wretched group here. Laura hates it. She won't have any part of it. He's such a bad boy. Dinner has been ready for over an hour.'

William made his way to the south veranda, where dinner was being served. As he approached, he heard a loud crash.

'That was a stupid thing to do,' Justin shouted.

'No. *You* are stupid. Why did you let those wretched people in here? They are freeloaders, gossips. I hate the *filthy bastards*!'

There was another crash and the ominous sound of tinkling glass. 'That's seven years' bad luck, you soft cow.'

'I don't care. You have those people in here and you'll have more than bad luck. They are trash, Justin, and that fat bitch Delaware is the worst of them all. You could see her scrawling her filthy little articles in her head as she talked to you.'

'Well, you'll be all right – you hardly showed your face,' Justin snapped.

'You know why? If we go through with this, the fewer people see me the better.'

William coughed and stepped into view. Broken glass and china littered the long table, which had been so elegantly laid.

Justin waved at William. 'She's throwing a tantrum. Are you hungry? If you can find a space between the broken crockery we'll get Marta to dish up. I'm starving.'

Suddenly Laura seemed to calm down, and took a seat opposite William. 'Careful you don't cut yourself. Justin'll clear up.' She picked up a napkin. 'So, William, did you enjoy these ghastly clingers-on?' She pronounced the word 'ghastly' with a wonderfully accented lilt.

'No,' he said. 'I loathe them. Especially Meryl Delaware.'

'William, we all loathe them,' said Justin. 'They would turn up at a public lavatory if they thought there was a free drink in it.' He gathered the broken crockery into a napkin. 'But Meryl is very useful. How do you think we've had such a terrific press about the island? You could feed her dog-shit and, with the right price tag, she'd make it smell like roses.' He walked into the house.

William had almost reverted to his usual self-conscious self. The cocaine had worn off, his nose was running and his head ached. Laura poured him some wine. 'Justin has told me what those horrible people did to you. I am so sorry. But we'll get back at them. It'll be fun . . . Well, it will be for you. *They* won't think so,' she said, and crumbled a bread roll. 'If you would like me to help, I am available. But I don't want to be paid in cash.'

William said nothing, watching her. She was one of the most perfect creatures he had ever met and in the glow of the flickering candles she seemed like an exotic bird. A long finger traced the rim of a glass, and William watched as she dipped her forefinger into the wine, lifted it, and caught the drop on her tongue. 'According to Justin, you are going to hire me. But I need to hear it from you. If you do want me to help you, then I must make arrangements.' He leaned forward and she moved her hand across the table to touch his lips. 'Don't interrupt.'

'I'm sorry.' She was like a different woman: colder, more sophisticated, as if the childlike quality he had found so appealing had been a figment of his imagination. There was no trace of any French accent. She was speaking like a well-educated upper-class débutante.

'Justin suggested that I should be your woman, but not in the ridiculous way you were engaged to Sylvina. It's public knowledge in Europe that she prefers women. Ours should be a more loving match. It's usual, is it not, for British men to like younger girls? Perhaps it is that they fall in love with what they could not acquire before they had amassed a fortune.'

William smiled. It was so true. As a young man he could never have hoped to date a woman as beautiful as Laura. Not even with his fortune had he ever attracted a woman like her.

'What about this? We met in Paris, and you fell in love with me. You are desperate to propose. Would you find that acceptable?'

Had Justin arranged the candles so they formed that Madonna halo?

'Falling in love with you would be any man's reaction. You look so beautiful, Laura, you take my breath away. I doubt if anyone would ever believe that I could be fortunate enough.'

She giggled seductively. 'But you do have a fortune, William, and I mean to please you. But tell me, what do you think about what I've just said? Do you think it's a good idea? Or do you have another plan?'

'I'm not sure how much Justin has told you. To be perfectly honest, I don't know all the details myself,' he said, pouring more wine. Truth was, he didn't want to get into the sordid 'hidden' cameras, the plan to catch his enemies engaged in compromising sexual activities. And Laura frightened the life out of him.

Laura continued, staring into space, 'Justin has explained the details.' It was as if she was reading his mind and he flushed. 'Justin suggested that I compromise each of your guests. I am to have a sexual relationship with all of them . . . or use whatever or whoever is necessary.'

William was sweating. It sounded so unlikely that he wanted to say it had been some kind of fantasy.

Laura moved closer to him. She lifted his arms away from the chair and sat on his lap. Taking his right hand, she wrapped it around her waist. Resting against him, her face close to his, she was silent. She lowered her hand and began to rub him lightly. Her body heat warmed him and he felt his loins stirring. He could hardly breathe. She held his face between her hands and kissed his lips, so softly. 'I don't want money,' she said, and now her lips brushed his ear.

She stopped stroking him and eased away to perch on the edge of the table.

'I will play your game.' She laughed. 'I think the men will be easy. The women will be more difficult to seduce, especially if they have never had a lesbian relationship.'

'Women?' he said, flushing deep red.

'Yes, of course. The wives and sons will be there, and I think one of your guests has a daughter, does he not – Lord Cedric?'

'Yes, but—'

She cupped his face in her hands and kissed him, her

gown sliding aside to reveal that she was naked beneath it. 'I don't want any money,' she repeated, and slid away, returning to her seat, with the grace of a dancer. Languidly she picked up a champagne glass and sipped, then ran her tongue round her lips. 'Payment will be . . .' she paused, teasing '. . . a diamond for each conquest.'

'Depends on the carat,' he heard himself reply, trying to be nonchalant and failing.

'You want to try the goods?' She smiled, showing her small, white, even teeth. Then she yawned, stretched her arms above her head, and was gone.

William wasn't clear about what went on around him after that. At some stage Marta brought him some coffee and a cigar. Justin had disappeared. After a while he decided to go to bed. He showered and lay down, but he was not ready to sleep. He considered reading, but in the end he turned out the lights and remained wide awake, staring at the ceiling. The Egyptian cotton sheets felt good against his skin – he had only taken to sleeping naked since meeting Justin. He did not hear her enter, but knew she was in the room by the strong smell of lilies. He also knew she was moving slowly round the bed, but he was too afraid to move. Then he felt the mattress dip to his right.

'Give me your arm,' she whispered, and he lifted it a fraction. She bound his wrist with a silk band, then fastened it to the bedpost. 'Now the other.' Her voice was barely audible. Next she drew the sheet away from him, tossed it aside, and forced his legs apart, tying his ankles to the foot of the bed. William lay spreadeagled, unable to move. He kept his eyes tightly shut, afraid to open them. She sat astride his chest and he winced at his impotency. His mind was aroused but his body was not answering.

'I'm sorry, I can't do this with you. Please,' he mumbled.

First she licked each nipple till he felt goose pimples break out across his body, then his neck and ears. He wanted to feel her mouth on his, but she suddenly bit into his ear-lobe, which hurt. He nearly cried out, but she covered his mouth first with her hand, then she stuffed something into it. It felt hard, a roll of leather or plastic. He bit into it, as she drew blood from his ear and began to bite down on the vein in his neck. He felt as if he was being suffocated. Her hands felt strong, masculine, and they massaged and rubbed, twisted and pinched until he was on fire, heaving for breath. Then she inched down towards his now swollen cock. Easing him into her, she leaned forward across his chest, pressing her hands against his throat, so that what little breath he had was cut short. His gasps were painful, his head thundering as she rode him, strangling him, slapping and kicking at him, until he exploded with such intensity, such agonizing pleasure that he blacked out.

Later that night, William woke with a start and looked at the clock; it was three a.m. He thought he must have dreamed the sex, and Laura, but the bands still hung loosely around his wrists and ankles, although Laura had cut him free. He dragged himself from the bed and stumbled into the shower, rubbing his body hard, to bring the blood to the surface of his skin to stop bruises forming. He returned to bed, so tired he could hardly be bothered to wrap the sheet around himself.

Just as he felt sleep descending, she slipped into bed beside him. She snuggled up to him like a child and her kisses were soft and sweet. She whispered to him that he was special, that he was a king, a prince. He was the love she had dreamed of finding, he made her happy. He had never felt such a powerful emotion: a consuming need to protect and provide for the child-woman he held in his arms.

'That must never happen again, Laura.'

'What mustn't?'

'What we did earlier. I don't ever want that to happen again.'

'Why not? Don't you like me?'

'It's because I like you too much, I respect you too much. I'm not a stupid man, I know it was to prove something to me and you succeeded. But I can't use you, even if I desire you. It's wrong.'

He was holding Laura in the crook of his arm when the naked Justin slipped in beside him and hooked his arm around them both.

'She's good, isn't she?' Justin said into the darkness.

Laura reached across William to kiss Justin. Then she flopped back. 'That was just a free sample,' she said to William. 'What carat would you rate me?' Her voice was singsong, a little girlish. 'I want a big whopper each time. You promised me, William, that's right, isn't it?'

'Yep,' said William, out of his depth.

He was unable to think straight, aghast at the proximity of Justin's nakedness.

Justin, who had hooked a long leg over William's, said, 'Listen, old boy, tomorrow we're waterskiing again, so I suggest you get some kip.' He brushed William's face with his hand then kissed him sweetly on the cheek like a young boy. 'Come on, Diamond Lil, bedtime. Get your beauty sleep.'

She jumped up and Justin, with his sister's ease and grace, got up too. Naked, they walked out, arms around each other, leaving William alone.

William patted his pillow afraid of all the demons inside him. He needed to step aside and look from a distance at what had taken place. He found he couldn't do it. What was he thinking of? It had got out of hand, this talk of Matlock and vendettas, and his ex-girlfriend Angela. He would put a stop to it first thing in the morning because he was afraid. Suddenly he thought that the paradise trap might be intended for him.

As sleep enveloped him, his fears turned into nightmares. When he'd read Andrew Maynard's secret diaries, he had envied his exploration of his sexuality. He remembered the blanked-out sections. Had Justin taken Maynard that step further, the step that William had half contemplated?

He knew without doubt that Justin had drawn the naïve Andrew Maynard into an erotic world that had eventually obsessed him, ultimately killed him. Yet that night he had experienced such powerful emotion, not just for Laura but for Justin as well and, no matter how he had protested, she had made love to him and it was as if she had opened a closed door in his mind or in his soul. Whatever had happened had not been merely an erotic excursion but some kind of baptism.

William forced himself to remember the night, on the island, with Dahlia and Ruby. He could see Justin laughing as he watched the video. He sat up quickly, his breath caught in his chest. Had they filmed him this evening? The aim of the game was to capture his guests in pornographic situations, but what if the intention all along had been to entrap William himself? Might this be an elaborate blackmail scam, into which he had unwittingly played? Fear consumed him, and then it subsided. He realized *he* was the one controlling the game; he had instigated it. From now on he would take control, not just of Laura and Justin but of his life. He knew he was the stronger; he knew he had *become* stronger. And he also knew that he had been taken on a journey. Far from destroying him, it had made him become a man. Tomorrow he would make it clear there was to be no further sexual intercourse between himself and Laura. That was the only way of knowing he was in control. He felt easier, and his eyes were heavy. He slept with the perfume of lilies, unable not to recall what it had felt like to have both their bodies entwined with his own.

CHAPTER 12

A<small>T NINE</small> William was served breakfast by Marta. He felt refreshed and alert, and ready to take control. He asked if Justin and Laura were still sleeping.

Marta looked surprised. 'Goodness, no, they were up and out to the market at seven,' she said. 'They always like to buy their vegetables fresh from the vendors rather than the big supermarkets. They'll have gone down to St Tropez to the fishmonger first.'

'How long will they be?'

'Maybe a couple more hours.' She walked out, then paused in the doorway. 'She is a child you know, sir. I blame Justin. He's been so domineering all her life, she looks to him for everything.'

'What about their parents?' William asked.

'They died when the children were small.'

'Marta,' he said sharply, 'tell me more. I need to know.'

'They are orphans. They were educated in England, and then they returned to France. This was their childhood home. Justin bought it a few years back.'

'How long have you worked for them?'

'Since they were in their teens.'

'Have they always lived together?'

'After England, I believe so. Money used to be very short at times, but Justin always found some way to provide. I think they've had difficult times, especially with Laura being the way she is . . .'

'And what way is that?' he asked not looking at her face.

'I think you know, sir.' He detected a tone of disapproval. 'She was the reason I stayed, even when money was short. I love both of them as if they were my own.'

'Educated in England?' William mused. 'Any idea where?'

Marta hesitated. 'Their mother was French, their father English. Their father's sister took care of them.' The telephone rang, and Marta seemed relieved to escape. He was perplexed and wanted to ask her more about Laura but Marta returned to the room in a hurry. 'It's your secretary. He said it's urgent.'

'Charlie has been expelled from school,' Michael stuttered. He had been accused of dealing in drugs. William called Katherine, his son's mother. She took ten minutes to come to the phone. 'William?' It was his ex-wife's nasal voice. 'Where are you?' When he told her she groaned. 'I think you should make an effort to get here as soon as possible.'

'Is he addicted?' William asked.

'He's not spoken to me. His housemaster called and I went down. He got in with a bad crowd.'

'Others have been expelled?'

'No, they were local boys . . . I don't really know. They found stuff in his room and his locker. He was caught in a seedy club and arrested.'

235

'Jesus!'

'I sent Daddy's lawyer to get him bailed, and now I can't find Charlie. I've called everyone I can think of. You're his father, for God's sake! Come and sort him out, and Sabrina too.'

'Sabrina?'

'Your daughter, in case you've forgotten. You have to go to her school parents' day. I sent all the information to Michael. I can't go and, as you've never been to one, I thought perhaps you should. I've not had time to think of anyone but Charlie. Cedric went into a frenzy.'

'What the hell has your cousin got to do with it?'

'He's more of a father to Charlie than you ever were. I'd just like you to try and talk to Charlie. Our worry is the press'll get hold of it. Anything linked to you seems to get us all on the front page.'

That was rich, coming from her, William thought. Katherine sold the story of her 'terrible life' with him to the press for a tidy sum. 'I'll get the next plane out,' he said. 'I'll contact you as soon as I'm home. Leave Charlie's address with Michael, if you trace him, and I'll see Sabrina at the parents' day thing. But—' Before William could add that his ex-wife had never wanted him to be at any school social even in the past, she had hung up.

Justin charged down the stairs with William's note. 'The bloody idiot's gone back to London,' he shouted. 'Marta!'

She appeared, drying her hands on a towel. 'He got a call from his secretary and arranged to leave immediately. But he left most of his clothes here. I think he intends to come back.'

Justin read the note again, pacing up and down the hall.

'It'll be all right, Justin,' Laura said, trying to soothe him.

'What would you know about anything.'

'Don't speak to me like I'm stupid!'

Justin wheeled round and grabbed her arm. 'Can't you get this through your thick skull? We've lost the big fish. He's off the hook. He's backing out, Laura, everything we've planned has been a waste of time. My God! When I think of the time I've wasted on that buffoon.'

Laura ran upstairs and locked herself in her bedroom, trying to ignore the thuds, shouts and crashes from below. She tried to calm herself with the thought of the diamonds William had promised her. Her fascination for them had been sparked off when she was given her mother's engagement ring. Now she took out the little Moroccan box in which she kept her collection. Each diamond was stored individually in a black velvet bag. In a notebook she had stuck cuttings from old De Beers diamond mine catalogues, which listed the carat, cut and cutter, and the estimated value of each stone. She liked to line up the diamonds on a piece of black velvet and knew every stone by touch alone. She liked their coldness and to watch them sparkle in the light. If she ever had to leave in a hurry all she would take with her were her darlings, the diamonds. Laura knew she was secure while she had them. No one knew about them, not even Justin. It was the only secret she had ever kept from him.

As Laura came out of her reverie, she realized that the house was quiet. She tiptoed to the door to listen, and could hear Justin crying. He was sitting hunched at the bottom of the stairs. Laura went to sit beside him and slipped an arm around his shoulder. 'Well, that was short and sweet,' she said softly.

He sniffed and wiped his face with the palm of his hand. 'It's just that I was so looking forward to it all, you know. I've been planning it for eighteen months, longer.' Laura stroked her brother's hair. 'I wish I'd killed that bastard Matlock when I was a kid. They couldn't have done much about it then,' he said quietly.

'You should sleep,' she said, easing away from him.

Justin drew her back and held her tightly. 'I can't move right now. Don't leave me.'

'I'll stay with you, always. Come on, now, let me take you to bed. You must sleep.' She helped him stand, then took him into his own room. A single bed stood beneath the window and tucked into it was a ragged doll. He allowed her to turn back the covers, tuck him in and stay as he curled into a tight ball clutching the doll. She sang to him until he slept, then sat with him stroking his hair.

No one saw Justin like this but Laura and, once or twice, Marta had witnessed his regression into child-like fear. When Justin was like this, he lost his bravado, his energy, and his confidence in who he was. Sometimes he lay curled up for days before he found himself again. This time, though, he joined her in the garden that afternoon. 'I'm being a ridiculous queen.' He laughed. 'I'll phone him. Maybe it's nothing to do with us. And even if it is we'll get him back.'

'Of course we will, my darling. You just needed to rest.'

He knelt down beside her. 'Thank you for taking care of me,' he whispered.

'Thank *you* for taking care of *me*,' she said, and they kissed and walked arm in arm back to the villa as they discussed their next plan of action.

William answered the phone personally, anxious for news of his son's whereabouts. It was a while before he could piece together what Justin was saying.

'I'm going to start sending out the invitations, William. They need to go out while the mags are showing the place off, and now that Meryl knows it's your place, it'll be all over the—'

William closed his eyes. 'Justin, right now I can't think about anything but my son. He's in trouble.'

'What's the matter with him?' Justin said impatiently.

William sighed. 'Justin, Charlie is my son and right now I can't think about entertaining a group of people in the Caribbean. Sometimes I really don't understand your obsession.'

'My obsession?' Justin's voice was strained. 'Fuck you!'

'Now don't get like that—'

'I am beginning to loathe the sound of your voice. I've been your friend, William, probably the best friend you ever had.'

The phone went dead, and almost immediately rang again. It was Katherine. 'Panic over. He's home,' she said.

'Thank God for that. Do you want me to come over and talk to him?'

'Could you check out clinics and things? We should think about sending him somewhere where they know how to handle these things.'

'Right, I'll get on to it and be with you tomorrow.'

The long gravel drive crunched beneath the tyres as William's car approached the large old manor house in Buckinghamshire. It had five acres of garden, a large paddock and a swimming-pool. As he drew up outside the front porch, two Labradors with muddy paws growled and padded off. William had never liked dogs.

His ex-wife was even paler than he remembered and age had not been kind to her. Her hair was tied back in a bun at the nape of her neck, and wisps of hair hung around her face. She was wearing a pink twinset, a tweed skirt and Gucci loafers. His emerald and diamond engagement ring was still on the third finger of her left hand.

'He's in the bath. He was filthy,' Katherine said, pouring herself a large sherry and offering the bottle to William. He shook his head, and wondered why she was drinking so early in the day. 'I can't get any sense out of him.' She paused. 'You look odd. What on earth have you been doing to yourself? It's your hair, you look awful. The Bellinghams have been on the phone,' she went on. 'They understand what I'm going through. Oliver was on some drug or other when he committed suicide. Lord B was saying that Ollie went to a rehab place in Cornwall. I asked him to talk to

Charlie, give him all the grisly details, try to scare him into straightening out.'

'I'll pay,' he said, with a resigned sigh.

'Of course you will.' She got up to refill her glass. 'It's already in the headlines. Have you seen it? "Terrible Tycoon's son in drugs raid." The press have been phoning here. Have they contacted you?'

'No,' he said warily.

'He's got to go before a magistrate. He was selling the stuff. No doubt the press will be in court.'

'Probably,' he said quietly. Then he asked, 'Why did you talk to the papers, give them that load of bullshit about me?'

'You deserved everything they threw at you!' She turned on him, her thin lips set in a tight line. 'I had them hanging round the house for days and it was the only way I could get rid of them. If you think I liked having my name, my children's name, dragged through the gutter press then you're very much mistaken.' She was on a roll. 'And if you think that this problem with Charlie isn't anything to do with your shenanigans, then you're wrong. It all stems from you and that wretched Maynard. Is it any wonder he's gone off the rails?' William didn't rise to the bait. 'I have never been so humiliated. I couldn't even walk into the village. And it looks like you haven't learned your lesson. You look like mutton dressed as lamb. That haircut!'

He felt his temper rising, but kept his mouth shut. 'You were a laughing stock and we all had to pay for your antics. Then flaunting yourself with that lesbian! You have no idea what harm you caused my family.'

'Katherine, you were paid handsomely for your

241

contribution to my downfall. Lucky for you, I didn't go right down. The business stayed firm so I was still around to pay your bills.'

'Oh, yes!' she screamed. 'Money! That's all you ever thought about. Money and sex.'

At that moment Charlie appeared, a half-smile on his lips. 'Ah, happy families. I'd forgotten how it used to be!'

William watched the thin, pale-faced boy saunter into the room and sit on the arm of the settee, his skinny legs protruding from a towelling bathrobe. 'Katherine, I'd like to talk to Charlie alone.'

She flounced out, slamming the door behind her.

Charlie dug into his pocket, took out a pack of cigarettes and lit one, his hands shaking.

'So you've cocked up,' William said quietly. 'You were caught selling drugs, you are to go before a magistrate and you could end up in prison.'

'Doubt it. It was only a few tabs and I'm a first offender, under age and all that. They'll let me off with a fine and a few months' probation.'

His upper-class drawl grated on William. 'What are you on?'

'What am I on?' Cigarette smoke drifted from his lips. 'What are you offering?'

'I'm your father. Show some respect, Charlie.'

'That's terrific coming from you Pa. Any woofters slashed their wrists over you recently?'

William took a deep breath and held on to his temper. 'I'll pay for you to go to a rehab centre. If you don't agree, then you get no money and neither will your mother nor your sister. I'll force them to take me to court and I'll drag the lot of you through the press.'

'I don't give a shit about your money.'

'You're throwing your life away if you give in to drugs. It's stupid, and you are not stupid.'

Charlie patted his pocket for another cigarette.

'So will you go to a clinic?'

'Yep.'

For a brief moment William wanted to hug his son, but he couldn't make the move. Charlie lit the cigarette with nicotine-stained fingers. He was close to tears but trying hard not to show it. As William moved to the door he said, 'You were never around when we needed you, or when I needed you. But in some ways I understood it was Mother's doing. She loathes you. Even at Christmas she hated it when you sent us presents. Sometimes she wouldn't let us open them.'

William hadn't expected this and he wasn't sure how to handle it.

'Oliver died. Did you know him?' Charlie said suddenly. And started to cry. 'He was my best friend.' He wiped his cheeks with the back of his hand.

'He was older than you, though, wasn't he?' William asked.

'Yeah, but we sort of hit it off. In fact I got a letter from him after I was told he'd killed himself. It didn't make any sense to me. I mean, he was arranging for us to go sailing together when he got back from the Caribbean and he had this girlfriend he was really keen on. I asked the Bellinghams about him at the memorial service, but they said it wasn't the right place. Then when I went round to their place they didn't want to talk about him. It's like he never existed.' He was looking down at his lap. 'Do you know someone called Justin?'

243

'Justin?'

'Yes, Ollie said he'd met this fantastic guy out there, Justin Chalmers. In his letter he mentioned him, said I'd get on with him too.'

'Yes, I know Justin very well.'

William sat down on the arm of the settee still wanting to put his arm around his forlorn son, but it hung limply at his side.

'Ollie was really good about getting the other bastards off me when all that filth came out in the press. I had a really bad time. It just went on and on, especially with that chap Maynard being a pervert.'

'Charlie, most of it was lies, you know.'

'Then why didn't you do something about it? Why didn't you sue them?'

'Whatever I did seemed to make it worse, so I buried my head in the sand. Reckoned if I kept quiet it would all go away, people would forget.'

'They nicknamed you Willy Wanker at school. They used to pin up pictures of you and write things on them. I hated it – and I hated you more than you could believe. I used to pray you'd die, pray you weren't my father.'

William stood up. 'Charlie, I'll make a deal with you. You really focus on getting straight, then come out to the Caribbean. Come and see the island. Get to know me. I have never stopped loving you – and you're right, I should have kicked ass about those press articles. But at the time, I just didn't have the . . .' He tailed off. He was silent for a while, then said, 'Sometimes, Charlie, we don't always do the right thing. But I want your respect more than anything else in the world. I want you to be proud to say, "That's my father."'

Charlie stood up and went to the fireplace. He kicked

at the grate, his shoulders hunched. 'Okay, it's a deal. Thanks.'

William went over to him, pulled him close and hugged him. 'Got a lot of catching up to do, lot of straightening out, but we'll do it.'

He could smell Pears soap on his son's hair and neck and remembered that Katherine had always liked it. It took him back to when he had bathed his son as a baby. It was a clear, sweet memory, the feel of his son's head beneath his hand. He cradled Charlie to his chest, and then did something he never had before. He cupped his son's face between his hands and kissed him. 'Everything will work out. We'll do it together, all right? Let me back into your life, Charlie. Let me show you I love you.'

Charlie suddenly put his arms round William's waist and held him tightly. Then he said, 'I'd like to meet this Justin.'

William felt uneasy, he didn't know why, but he smiled. 'Yes, why not? He's made a good job of rebuilding my villa on the island.'

'Yes, I know, I've seen the pictures. It was in the papers this morning. Everyone's talking about it. I'd like to come over.'

William was impressed at how quickly Meryl's gossip machine had swung into action, but he only said, 'Good, then that's something to set your sights on.'

On the drive back to London, William felt elated. He'd got through to his son for the first time ever. As he left he'd kissed Katherine on both cheeks and told her she was still an attractive woman.

245

Katherine had flushed, becoming almost girlish, which amazed William. Just by using some of Justin's phrases and a little of his manner, he was making more of an impact than ever before. He began to realize how much he had changed and how he owed it all to Justin. He saw it as a good omen that Charlie had mentioned Justin, although whether or not Justin represented a good example for his son was another thing; he doubted it. The first thing he did when he returned home was call Justin. There was no reply, so he went to bed, but he woke three times and made three further calls. He still received no reply.

William was preoccupied with business for a further three days as a costly legal case was looming: the German company had refused to accept they did not own the patent on the fox-and-hens toy. William's lawyers pointed out to him that it would not be a good idea to bring up the reason von Garten had withdrawn from his original deal, as the story would no doubt resurface in the press.

'I no longer care what is printed about me, and I'm going to kick a few arses!' William thundered.

'But it won't be cost-effective, William,' came the reply.

'Sometimes the cost of proving you can't be shat on is worth it,' he snapped, and hung up. Therefore he was not party to the conversation that ensued between his lawyers and business advisers.

As he put the phone down, the man to whom William had been speaking said, exasperatedly, 'We sue, no discussions. He wants us to hit hard and heavy no matter the cost. He also appears to be on another planet. Either that or he's losing his marbles . . . .'

One of the young assistants spoke up nervously: 'Perhaps Sir William has a point. Rumours are rife that Geffin's may go public. A contact in Germany sent us some information about a Max von Garten, the Baron's son. Apparently, Max von Garten has recently bought shares in Geffin's Toys. You can bet that the purchase has been made on behalf of his father. The Baron must know the company is going to float; I'd say he's got hold of information that has not yet gone public. He already has a fifty per cent share in the company, and now he has used his son to buy up even more, based on this inside information. Well, that's illegal share trading! All we have to do is prove that he knew the company was going on the market *before* he bought the shares, and we can nail him for rogue trading as well as copyright. Double whammy!'

The senior men looked at each other, then began to sift through the mounds of paperwork already accrued on the case. They read and reread it. The trouble-shooters William had hired had dug deep and dirty. They even had transcripts of private phone calls, not to mention private bank accounts.

'Sir William's right,' said one of the seniors. 'This'll take more time but it will be worth it. We'll have proof of insider share trading and that von Garten's company have stolen – four patents, is it now?'

'Five,' said the eager young man. 'And their share price has gone through the roof. Sir William's been monitoring them for months. It just goes to show that his designs were worth stealing.'

The team were a little uneasy at the methods used to

acquire some of the damning material, but it became obvious that Sir William and his business acumen had run rings round them as always. An elderly man, Douglas Alexander, who had worked with William for many years, tapped the table with his pen. 'It seems to me that Sir William has some personal grievance against Baron von Garten. Do we know whether anything might crawl out of the woodwork, so to speak?'

He was reminded that von Garten had sold his factory to William's strongest competitor and had poached his employees. Maybe that was reason enough for him to be hell-bent on hitting the von Garten company hard.

'But Sir William has never been vindictive. I hope there is no ulterior motive as this case will make headlines.' Douglas closed his files. 'I have also been asked by Sir William to look into the financial situation with regard to Cedric Hangerford, particularly in regard to substantial loans Sir William wishes to be repaid. If that is not possible, we are to file bankruptcy orders. Again, this is rather a delicate matter as Lord Cedric is his ex-wife's cousin, so I suggest we are polite in our dealings with him. In the past we have corresponded with him on this matter but got little response. This time, Sir William appears to want him pressured.'

William was looking forward to seeing his daughter. He wanted to get closer to her, as he had with Charlie. He was driving down the motorway on the way to Parents' Day when Douglas Alexander called him on his mobile. What he had to say made William feel even better: Douglas felt now that they could nail von Garten to the proverbial mast.

'I don't suppose there's anything personal in this, is there, William?' he asked.

'It's just business, Douglas. You've known me long enough by now, surely?'

'Indeed I have. But it'll create a fuss and, after what you've been subjected to already by the media, I wondered whether you wanted to open yourself up to any further trouble.'

William's lips tightened. 'If you are referring to the scandal surrounding Andrew Maynard surfacing again . . .'

'Of course not.'

'Good.'

William hung up. He had not thought of Andrew Maynard for some time. Now he did, and he felt more than saddened. His suicide had made him weep, but had not really grieved him. In many ways his sadness now was that he had not, for inexplicable reasons, ever formed a closer friendship with Maynard. The truth was, he had wanted Maynard to like him. He had wanted to be his friend the way he had so wanted to be Peter Jenkins' friend! Peter Jenkins, William muttered, shaking his head at himself. Dear God, why was he suddenly recalling Peter Jenkins, the freckled-face kid that sat next to him at grammar school? He remembered his overlong, curling eye lashes that made his tawny eyes look like a cat's. Poor little Jenkins who had such a bad stammer he was bullied and constantly the butt of daily jokes. Jenkins had kissed him once. Suddenly, unexpectedly, he had kissed William's neck and the shock of his small, wet lips had sent waves through William's young, pubescent body. Only now did William ask himself why Jenkins had kissed him. Perhaps he just wanted to be his friend and this was the only way he knew of expressing it. Jenkins knew that William was often bullied too. Perhaps he thought that if they became best friends, they would at least have each other. But for some reason, the kiss had only annoyed William and he had ignored Jenkins after that. He had so wanted to be close to Peter, so why had he rejected him? Shortly afterwards, Peter Jenkins was killed on a level crossing on his way home from school. William couldn't recall what had happened next, even now, but he could remember how he had felt, seated next to Peter Jenkins' empty desk, because he had felt the same way after Andrew Maynard's suicide.

William had to pull the car over and park on the hard shoulder of the motorway. He had never gone into Andrew's death this way, never asked himself so many questions. He was now even questioning why he had believed that Maynard was worth the vast sums of money he had paid out. But deep down he knew he was. He recalled how he felt on the last afternoon he had seen him. He remembered his suit with the emerald-green satin lining, and he remembered his attractive smile. His eyelashes were as long as little Jenkins', but dark like his eyes. That afternoon he had known Maynard was in some kind of emotional turmoil. That was why he had asked him for dinner. If he had accepted, if that dinner had taken place, would he still be alive? Or would William have avoided probing into his private life or taking their relationship one step further?

He turned on the radio and felt a strange feeling of

relief, as if opening the memories and facing them was yet another step in his progress towards understanding himself. Then he continued driving to his daughter's school, looking forward to seeing her and hoping to have the same success with her as he felt he had started with Charlie.

'Sir William Benedict,' said Sabrina's school secretary, rather loudly, 'would you like to come through?'

'Thank you,' he said, and followed her to the head-mistress's study.

'Sir William Benedict to see you, Mrs Harper-Nathan.'

They shook hands and he sat.

'I am so pleased you were able to join us today. We have great hopes for Sabrina. She's certainly Oxbridge material.'

He leaned forward. 'I'm very aware of how difficult it must have been for her, for all my family, during my recent troubles. But everything has settled down now and I am grateful for the way you and your staff have protected my daughter. In gratitude I would like you to accept a small donation towards the building fund.' He withdrew an envelope from his pocket and passed it to Miss Harper-Nathan. She glanced at the cheque for a second, then did a double-take. 'This is really most generous, Sir William,' she spluttered. 'A quarter of a million pounds. Thank you so very much.'

William rose. 'It's been a pleasure,' he said, and shook hands with her. The secretary told him that his daughter was waiting for him in room Four Omega. She would take him there.

He found Sabrina sitting half-way down the room facing the blackboard with a book open in front of her. She didn't look up when William came in.

'Sabrina?' he said quietly, and closed the door. She didn't speak, so he walked further in and sat on the edge of the teacher's desk. 'Is this your classroom?'

'We move around,' she said.

He sighed, and stuffed his hands into his pockets. 'Well, I didn't think this was going to be easy, but you might make some effort to be pleasant. I've driven a long way.'

'What do you want me to do? Clap?'

He laughed. 'I got a call from Charlie. He's at a rehab place in Wales. Has he written to you?'

'No.'

'I'll leave his address, then you can write to him. He needs all the support he can get.' He shifted his weight. 'I'm sorry your mother couldn't come with me. She had a doctor's appointment, but she sends her love.'

'Playing happy families, are you?' She looked up and glared at him.

'It's about time, isn't it? Sabrina?'

'You think you can just pick up being Daddy? What a farce! You make me sick. I didn't want to see you. They forced me. They all make me sick, two-faced bitches! You should have seen the way they whispered about you.'

'They seem to think you're very clever. You've had impressive exam results.' She chewed her nails and kicked the side of her desk. He continued, 'Especially your computer studies. I'm pleased about that. Maybe one day you'll take over the firm. There's plenty of opportunities for you to think about. According to Mrs

252

Harper-Nathan you're top of the league, Oxford or Cambridge. I'd have given my eye-teeth to go to either.' Sabrina said nothing. 'Why don't we try to be friends?'

'You may be able to buy Charlie, because he's as thick as two short planks. You might even be able to buy off Mother. She's in need of cash right now – that'll be the only reason she's even talking to you. She hates you, and Charlie's only being nice for what he can get out of you. And I've got a life of my own . . . a secret life. There'll be no Oxford or Cambridge.'

'All right,' said William. 'That's fine. But I want you to know that if you ever need me, I'll be there for you. I always have been, you know, not just financially. It was impossible for me to be a good father when your mother refused to let me see you.'

'Bullshit.' Sabrina picked up her book, snapped it shut and walked to the door. 'You're in for a big surprise soon, Daddy-oh.' And with that she strode out.

As William drove back to London fog was drawing in. The drive was murderous and he was angry with himself. He realized he'd allowed Katherine to turn his children against him. She had forbidden him to keep in touch with them and had poisoned them against him.

It was just after midnight when he arrived home. He was about to head straight upstairs to bed, but heard the soft murmur of voices. He wondered if it might be Michael, or perhaps his valet. But then he heard music, some dreadful rap beat. He switched on the hall light, and saw a leather valise in the hall, a sports bag and a tennis racket. Puzzled, he headed towards the drawing room. When he opened the door, he was surprised to come face to face with Charlie, who was dancing around the room, a cigarette hanging from his lips. 'Oh, hi, Dad!' he said nonchalantly. 'We wondered when you'd get back.'

William turned to see Justin sitting on the sofa with a glass of champagne in his hand. 'Hope you don't mind, but Charlie let me in.' Justin stood and wrapped his arms around William's shoulders. 'I missed you,' he said, and kissed him on both cheeks.

William was at a loss for words. Charlie poured him a glass of champagne and handed it to him. William rounded on him. 'I only spoke to you this afternoon, for God's sake. What are you doing here? Why aren't you at the clinic?'

Charlie looked evasive. 'Oh, we get weekend leave, Dad, didn't I tell you? It's a fantastic coincidence that Justin's here.'

William accepted the chilled champagne. Justin gave William a covert look and almost mimicked Charlie's voice. 'Thanks, Dad.' William raised his glass but felt a deep undercurrent. What was going on? Having Justin turn up out of the blue with Charlie felt ominous.

'When do we leave for the island, Dad?' said Charlie.

William downed his drink in one. 'I'll think about it in the morning after a good night's sleep. Go to bed, Charlie. It's late, and I want to talk to Justin.'

Charlie groaned, but his father hadn't made a fuss about his departure from the clinic and he was grateful for that so he trudged off. That is, he hadn't made a fuss yet – but he would when he discovered that Charlie had lied about the weekend leave.

William stood at the bottom of the stairs watching

Charlie disappear. He called goodnight, then turned his attention to Justin and indicated the study. 'What's going on?' he asked.

Justin raised his eyebrows. 'What on earth do you think is going on? I missed you so I came over. You called enough times, I thought you'd be pleased to see me.' He laid his hand on William's arm.

William shook it off. 'Cut the crap. What do you want?'

'Oh!' squealed Justin. 'Mr Tough Guy.'

'Is it money you're after?'

Justin sat down beside him, and pulled out a large file from his case. 'Look, the trap is set.' He tossed a wad of newspaper cuttings about the island on to William's lap. 'It's finished, all set up. It's up to you now. If you need my help you can have it. If not I'll be off.'

William started to look over the cuttings. Suddenly the phone rang. 'Who the hell . . .?' William lifted the receiver. 'Yup?'

It was Mrs Harper-Nathan. 'Thank goodness you're there, Sir William. I've been trying to get hold of Lady Benedict but there's no reply.' William wished she'd get to the point. 'Sir William, I'm afraid your daughter has gone missing.'

'But I only saw her this afternoon.'

'Well, she did leave a note, but she's packed her case and left. We were rather hoping she might have come to you.'

'What does the note say?' There was an embarrassed pause. 'Well?' asked William.

'Well,' said Mrs Harper-Nathan, 'it seems she has eloped with the school caretaker's son. She says in the note that she's pregnant by him. I've spoken to the caretaker. He thinks his son is staying in a squat in Notting Hill Gate, above a pub. The Six Bells, I think he said.' There was a short silence. 'I'm so sorry, Sir William.'

'The boy's name?'

'Jacob Mkomazi.'

'Fax me that note. And, Mrs Harper-Nathan, no police, no press.' He hung up.

'Bad news?' Justin asked.

William gave a gesture of despair and went into Michael's office. Justin trailed after him, and by the time the fax had come through, William had told him about Sabrina. 'It's one bloody thing after another,' he muttered, passing the fax for Justin to read. 'First my son, now my daughter. Dear God, if the press get hold of either story they'll have a field day.'

Justin was pulling on his jacket. 'Look, William, you may be knackered, you certainly look it, and I know there's trouble, but the best way of dealing with trouble is action. OK?' He was holding the door open. 'I'll drive you wherever you want to go.'

Justin and William sped off in William's sports car to Notting Hill Gate. They cruised the streets until William spotted the Ten Bells. 'That must be it,' he shouted.

Justin swerved into the kerb. It was pouring with rain. William got out; crossed the pavement and pushed open the graffiti-covered side-door. The dank, carpetless hall smelt of urine and stale food, overridden by the powerful smell of ganja, which made William's head reel. There were several doors, and the sound of a jazz trumpet mingled with televisions and muted voices, then, eerily, a loud, cackling laugh.

256

He knocked at one door and received no reply. Looking down the dingy hall he saw that there was a basement, and another apartment further along. He decided to listen at each flat, rather than knocking. On the third floor, he heard Sabrina laugh, a joyful sound, so unlike the bitter, hard little girl he had encountered that afternoon.

He rapped lightly and waited. The door inched open and a tall, handsome boy with shoulder-length dreadlocks looked down at him. 'Yeah?'

'I'm Sabrina's father,' William said. The boy gave a half-smile before he turned back to the room.

'Tell him to go fuck himself!' came Sabrina's high-pitched voice.

The boy turned back to William and his beautiful, dark, slanting eyes twinkled. 'Guess she don't want to see you, sir.'

'Don't call him "sir", Jacob. You don't ever have to call anyone sir, and especially not him. Shut the door.'

Jacob turned to William. 'She don't want to see you.'

He was about to shut the door when William stuck out his hand. 'Listen, Jacob. I want to see my daughter, and I want to talk to her. It'll take a few minutes then I'll walk away. She need never see me again if that's what she wants.'

Jacob hesitated, then swung the door open.

Sabrina was lying on a moth-eaten couch, with a portable TV set balanced at one end amongst cans of Coke, packets of crisps and a bowl of apples. The room was untidy and dirty. Even the bed in one corner had not been made. Jacob gestured to a dilapidated wing-back armchair, the stuffing and springs bulging out,

257

barely concealed by a big wool rug that had been thrown over it. Two guitars and a set of conga drums were stashed beside it.

'Sit down,' Jacob said, hitching up his jeans. He wore an old miner's shirt with a knitted sweater over it, dirty sneakers and no socks. 'You want some coffee?' he asked.

'Yes, please,' William said, easing himself into the chair, afraid it would collapse under him.

'You want a milkshake, Sabby?'

'Okay.' She had not even looked at her father.

'Be two minutes.' Jacob opened her purse and took out some money.

'I'm sorry, I didn't think you'd have to go out for it,' William said, but the door closed. Then he turned to his daughter. 'You're pregnant?' he said.

'I'm not going back to school. Never, never, never. OK?'

William looked at the guitars and asked if Jacob played in a band. She shrugged her shoulders. 'Right now he's cleaning tables in a bar,' she said defiantly.

'You need money?' he asked.

'Oh, for Christ's sake, it didn't take you long to get around to that, did it? Listen, I don't need a cent from you, I've got my trust fund.'

'And the fairies made that up for you, did they? Well, you can't get your hands on that till you're twenty-one. That's quite a few years to wait. If you're having a baby, you're gonna need more space than one room.'

She was unsure how to take what he had said. He hadn't been angry – in fact he seemed to have accepted her situation.

'Are you going to get married?' he asked.

She laughed humourlessly. 'Yeah, all in white with four bridesmaids.'

'Do you love him, or are you just doing this to get back at me?' He moved closer.

She nodded as tears spilled down her cheeks. 'Please go away,' she whispered.

'I will, but we need to talk about maternity bills, hospitals . . .'

'For fuck's sake don't tell me to get a nanny! I had my fill of those. This baby is all mine. At last, something of my own that no one can take away from me. We're going to bring it up, me and Jacob.'

William reached for her hand, but she pulled it away. Again she asked him to leave, but this time without anger. He stood up and laid his hand on her head. 'I love you. If you ever need me, I'll be there. Take care of yourself, Sabrina, and I hope you'll be a lot happier with Jacob than I ever was with your mother. I'll call her and tell her you're looking well and happy.'

William sat on the stairs waiting for Jacob to return. He came in carrying a cardboard tray with their coffees and the milkshake.

'Hi,' William said, trying to appear relaxed.

'Hi. She's into these milkshakes and crisps.'

'You're lucky. With her mother it was *pâté de foie gras* and champagne. Sit down, Jacob.'

Jacob squashed down beside him, his long legs stretched out as he passed over the coffee.

'You are going to marry my daughter?' William asked, removing the lid and dripping coffee over his raincoat.

'Yep, when we got some cash. Right now we're having to be real careful. She's half-way. We've got to take care of the baby.'

'You love her?' asked William, sipping the strong coffee.

Jacob's dark eyes bored into William's. 'No, I'm after her trust fund, man!'

'No need for sarcasm. Anyway, you're going to have a long wait. She's only sixteen, and she can't touch it until she's—'

'Twenty-one. Yeah, I know.'

'You work in a bar?' William asked, and sipped the coffee.

'Yeah. Sorry I'm not no accountant.'

'Jacob, I don't give a fuck what you are just so long as you're going to take care of my daughter. Listen to what I have to say.'

'I'm all ears.' Jacob drained his coffee and crushed the cup in one hand.

'You needn't tell Sabrina, if you don't want to, but I'm going to open a bank account in your name. All I ask is for you to take care of her and contact me when she's in labour. I'd like to see the baby. After all, it'll be my grandchild.'

'No thanks, no bank account. I'll take care of her 'cos I'm crazy about her and we'll get along fine.'

William stood up and looked down into Jacob's face. 'Don't turn it down. Everyone needs a break. It won't be millions, just enough to get you started in some kind of job, whatever you want. Get a decent place to bring up your kids. I may not have been a decent father, but . . .'

'Money's no object, huh?'

William leaned over him. 'I earned every cent I've ever made. If you love her you'll take what I'm offering, because if you don't you'll not stand a chance of making it work between you. It's a game for her right now, but she's scared shitless.'

Jacob bowed his head as William took out a visiting card. 'Ask to speak to Michael. He'll have all the details.'

Jacob held the card loosely in his hand before he stood up to face his soon-to-be father-in-law. 'Thank you.' William reached out and hugged him.

When William reached the car he saw that Justin was asleep, his head resting against the car window and his mouth slightly open. He looked like a small boy. William tapped on the window and Justin's eyes sprang open. There was a moment, it came and went so fast, but for that second, as Justin stirred, he seemed terror-struck: his hands flailed and he covered his face as if protecting himself from a beating.

'Sorry,' William found himself apologizing, 'do you want me to drive?'

'No, get in. Did it all go okay?'

'Yep, but I don't want to talk about it. All I can think of is getting some shut-eye.'

Justin grinned as he started the engine. 'Right, home it is.'

When they got home William directed Justin to a spare bedroom and was thankful that Justin said that they'd talk in the morning. But when he leaned close and kissed his cheek, it was perhaps the best moment of William's wretched day.

CHAPTER 13

WILLIAM STARED out of the window. The heavy rain and dark grey skies made visibility so poor that he couldn't even see the end of his walled garden. It had been lashing down all night and, with the trauma of yesterday, sleep had been impossible. When Michael arrived at nine William gave him strict instructions that if any press phoned he was to say he knew nothing and that William was out of the country. He was explaining that Charlie and Justin were both still asleep upstairs, when Charlie strolled in. 'Hi there, Dad.'

'I need to speak to you for a few minutes, Charlie.' They went into the drawing-room. 'I *will* take you to the island and I'm very glad that you've met Justin but—'

Charlie groaned. 'I knew there'd be a but.'

'But you've really got to get straightened out first. Now, you'll have to go back to this clinic and don't give me this bullshit about weekend leave. It's mid-week. Do you think I'm stupid?'

'The place is full of wankers.'

'You liked them last week.'

'Yeah, but I've never been into all that therapy stuff

262

and the group-leaders are full of shit. They were addicts themselves and all they ever talk about is their old scene.'

Justin was standing in the doorway. 'There's a great place you'd really like in Minnesota,' he said. 'It's where all the superstars go. I'm sure your dad can pull a few strings.'

William spun round. Justin was grinning at Charlie.

'Minnesota, America? Wow! Yeah, I'd give that a go. Yeah, that's cool, I've heard of that place,' Charlie said enthusiastically.

'So that's that settled,' Justin concluded. 'Now, for God's sake, can we have some breakfast?'

William gripped Justin's elbow and drew him aside. 'Stay clear of my son, Justin. Do you understand me? You stay away from him.'

'Yes, sir. Now can we have breakfast?'

By three thirty Michael had arranged a five-month stay for Charlie in the high-powered American clinic, the finest rehabilitation clinic in the world. As Justin had said, a queue of movie stars and ex-presidents' wives were waiting to be dried out and the cure rate was amazing. Charlie was frightened. It had all happened so quickly, but he agreed to leave England immediately.

The three arrived at Heathrow in good time for Charlie's flight. Justin and William waved him through the gate, then walked back to the car-park.

'Justin, if you'd like me to drop you off somewhere . . . I've been trying to contact my ex-wife all day to give her the news about the kids, but I can't rouse her. As we're on the motorway here, it wouldn't take me long to whizz up to her place. But I don't want to bore you.'

Justin put his arm round William's shoulder. 'What else would I do? Sit in front of the TV?' He clicked the remote control to open the car. 'Think of me as your chauffeur today. We can chat, listen to music. It's a good system you've got here.' Justin sat in the driver's seat and buckled up. 'So, William, fire away with the directions and off we go.'

It was dark when the car rolled up the drive of Katherine's Buckinghamshire home, splashed through the pot-holes, and drew up outside the porch.

'You wait here, I won't be long,' said William, and climbed out of the car. In the semi-darkness the house looked run-down. William noticed broken panes of glass in the stained-glass door. 'Katherine?' he called, as he opened it. 'Katherine.'

He made his way first to the kitchen, which was a shambolic mess of dirty cutlery and blackened, greasy pans. 'Katherine!' he called again, as he walked towards the drawing room.

The door was ajar, the room a mess, the fire burned out in the grate. He was worried.

He made his way slowly up the creaking staircase. Even though he presumed she would be in the old master bedroom, he glanced into his children's rooms. Charlie's was still full of cricket bats and skateboards. Sabrina's was papered with Spice Girls posters and there was an array of Barbie dolls. The spare room was dusty, unused and cold. He realized that the whole house was damp, and when he felt one of the radiators on the landing, it was cold. He sighed. The stupid woman hadn't turned on the heating – in this weather. The master bedroom door was ajar and he could hear the soft sounds of a radio turned down low. Again he called his wife's name.

She lay on her side, with a cashmere shawl draped around her shoulders. An empty sherry bottle lay on the floor beside the bed and a half-full one sat on the bedside cabinet amongst numerous sticky glasses. As he drew nearer William knew, from her grey complexion, that she was dead. The lamp gave a soft pink light through the frilly lampshade over her peaceful face. The remains of the sleeping tablets she had taken were spilled over the rose-pink satin-covered duvet. William checked her pulse, but her wrist was cold. Her eyes, half open, were glazed in an expressionless stare. A white envelope was propped against a silver racing trophy on the mantelpiece. William ran his finger beneath the flap, which opened easily. 'To whoever reads this: I am very tired, and not very well. So I have decided to go without bothering anyone, in particular my husband. I have made a mess of a lot of things, so forgive me. That's all really. Katherine.'

The next morning Michael arrived. He, too, was shocked at the state of the house, but said nothing. He offered his condolences and began to sift through the papers and outstanding bills littering Katherine's bureau.

'I'll have to get Charlie back, and he'll have only just arrived,' said William. 'Damn her timing. And Sabrina. I'll go round this afternoon, when I'm through here.'

'You'd better have a look at this, sir,' Michael said, passing over a thick file of accounts. 'They were in the locked drawer at the bottom of the bureau.'

William looked down at the files. 'Jesus! I don't believe it!' he said, under his breath, turning over page after page. Then he tossed the papers aside. 'We're leaving now.'

He went outside and leaped into the car.

'What's going down?' asked Justin, as William switched on the engine and drove away.

'Katherine has robbed the kids' trust funds, and most of the money I ploughed into them went into her fucking cousin Cedric's stables. I mean, it's one thing that she got herself into debt to the tune of two million, but she's been keeping that bastard going with my children's money!' He was shouting.

'William,' Justin said calmly, 'you have the island. Everything is in place. We'll get the son-of-a-bitch,' he said firmly. 'Remember, you have only to say the word and we start the Paradise Trap.'

'For Chrissake, shut up about it!'

Justin knew he had to keep his mouth shut. Often old Willy surprised him: he had quite a temper on him.

The funeral arrangements were taken over by Katherine's depleted family. The service was conducted in the private chapel of what had once been the Hangerford ancestral home, long since sold to the National Trust to cover debts. The coffin was bedecked with floral tributes and the chapel almost full. Even Lord Bellingham and his wife were there. Just before Katherine was carried up the aisle, Sabrina made her entrance. She was wearing a floppy straw hat with a large poppy attached, clogs and a long print dress with a big black overcoat on top. She clutched Jacob's hand, who, William was sure, was wearing exactly the same clothes as when he had seen him. The pair walked down the aisle with their heads held high.

The luncheon afterwards was tedious and rather embarrassing. The old hall, opened for the occasion, was freezing. The food was appalling and the wine no more than plonk.

'Great nosh,' said Cedric, piling his plate high. At one time he had been handsome; now he looked seedy, over-weight and nervous. William watched as he smothered butter over his roll, crunched into it and spat bread-crumbs as he spoke. 'Shame about Katherine, what?'

'Poor woman was driven into a corner, wouldn't you say, Cedric?'

Cedric looked up, a smear of mayonnaise on his chin. 'So you admit it?' he said. William was taken aback. 'Oh, yes, you and your shady life,' spluttered Cedric. 'It was always clear to us she'd made a mistake marrying you. Marrying money's all very well, but . . .' He dived down to the table and spooned more potato salad on to his paper plate. 'Mind you, funny that with all your millions you couldn't keep her in the manner to which she was accustomed. Pity you couldn't have been more like me. I'm very protective of my wife and young Clarissa.'

William looked him in the eye. 'It's just other peo-ple's families you steal from? Is that it, Cedric?' The other man returned his stare, wide-eyed. 'Maybe you haven't actually calculated just how much you sponged off Katherine, but in case you are not aware of it, I have it all in black and white.'

'You feeling all right?' Cedric enquired. 'Maybe all those high jinks addled your brain.'

'I could take it to the police, of course. To fund your bloody stables and to support her gambling, Katherine embezzled her own kids' trust funds.'

'Not a police matter, you'll find. She was family.'

'Family? You piece of shit. I've seen the letters she wrote, begging you to repay her because she was scared she'd get into trouble. She was stealing money I'd provided for my children's future.'

Cedric shrugged. 'Well, you've plenty more.' He pointed his white plastic fork at William. 'Matter of fact, I was going to ask you whether you'd like to invest in a little filly I've got my eye on.'

William threw back his head and laughed. The man's gall was beyond belief. 'You ever heard the expression "pay-back time"? I instructed my lawyers to contact you about returning loans dating back to—'

'Pay-back? I don't know what you're getting at, old boy.' Cedric was concentrating on recharging his fork with a dollop of Coronation Chicken.

'You are in financial shit, Cedric. By pay-back I mean cough up what you owe. And another meaning of that expression is to do with getting you back for being a thieving two-faced bastard!' William strode across the hall and, nodding at his children and Jacob, indicated that he was leaving. He waited at the door while they all made their excuses.

Cedric's daughter, Clarissa, sidled up to William. 'Uncle William,' she simpered, 'I'm coming up to my last term at school, and I was wondering whether you could find me a place in your office or whatever it is . . .' She gave him a winsome smile.

'What are your qualifications?' he said.

'Oh, I haven't any. I just need something to tide me over for a while.'

'Or somewhere to sit and file your nails while you get paid for it?' said William.

Clarissa giggled. 'Well . . . Daddy said you wouldn't mind.'

'Did he indeed? Well, dear, get some qualifications. If a job comes up and you're better than the other applicants, I'll think about it.'

Clarissa stared and reddened. 'Daddy and Mummy were right. You *are* a pig.'

William strode out to the car and climbed in, breathing deeply to regain calm.

He was exhausted that night but, yet again, couldn't sleep. It had been one hell of a day. Cedric and his wretched daughter's remarks at the funeral had put the tin lid on it. What had he got to lose? Justin had gone back to Paris, but the more William tossed and turned, the more he thought about him and about all the vicious backstabbing. His mind drifted back to the day he had discovered Maynard's body, and all that had happened since then. He would like to put them all through the same torment they had inflicted on him. Then it dawned on him that that was exactly what Justin had described. My God! He'd like to see that bastard Cedric caught on camera with more than his pants down. Only now did William see the funny side of it. He reached for the phone, but then realized the time. He lay back on his pillows and laughed.

*

As though by divine intuition, Justin phoned the following morning. His timing was perfect, as always. 'I'm on the four o'clock train,' he yelled down the Gare du Nord pay-phone. 'I'll be with you in a few hours.'

'I'll pick you up at Waterloo.'

'Let's get the invitations out today,' William said as they drove away from the station.

Justin laughed. 'Sure, why not?'

William leaned forward and opened the glove compartment. 'I've made out a new list, short and sweet.'

Justin unfolded it. He glanced down it, then closed his eyes in relief. Humphrey Matlock's name was at the top of the list, followed by the Hangerford family. Then came Baron and Baroness von Garten, Meryl Delaware and a few others he hadn't heard of.

Justin looked at William and shook his head. 'Too many. Do you really need to bother with that wretched Delaware woman? She's a raddled old cow, not worth the effort.'

'She was one of the gossipmongers sniffing around poor Maynard. I'd like to see her squirm.'

'Fair enough, but just get her sacked. She's not worth any more trouble than that.'

'Scratch her off, then.'

'The von Gartens have a son.' Justin giggled. 'Maybe invite him along. He'll be company for Matlock's boy.' Justin stared out of the window. 'No drug clinic for him, not like your poor Charlie. This kid's a real golden boy. Athletics, tennis, does the lot.'

'Invite him, then,' said William, recalling the boy's shares in his father's company.

'Good, it'll look better. The kids can have a holiday of a lifetime . . . whilst your Charlie's in a rehab clinic and your daughter . . .' Justin had to think this one out carefully, get the balance right. He wanted to rub it in, but he didn't want to go too far. 'I'd say your public humiliation made Sabrina throw away her career. Son-in-law's perhaps acceptable, but—'

'I don't mind that she's with Jacob,' William snapped, flushing.

'But you have to care that she's only seventeen, for Christ's sake. She's a clever kid, isn't she?'

'Yes,' William said. His lips tightened and his anger against his dead wife resurfaced. It wasn't just the divorce, the refusal to allow him access to his children, it was so much more, culminating in the loss of their respect and love, not to mention their trust funds. 'Yes, we include their kids,' he said coldly.

Justin smiled. He and Laura would quite enjoy the boys for starters, especially Matlock's son.

'So, it's Matlock, his wife Angela and son, Baron von Garten, his wife and son, and the Hangerfords. Nine is a nice easy number to control. You don't want to get too ambitious.'

They drove in silence for a moment before William laughed. 'I'm looking forward to seeing them all arrive on the island. Let's just hope they accept.'

'They will,' Justin said, and even placed a fifty-pound bet on who would reply first.

But William shook his head. 'No, I won't play around, not any more, Justin. This is too important. If we don't hear within a week or so, we'll get Michael to make a personal call on my behalf. Fuck it, I'll make the calls myself, better that way.'

'If you have to,' Justin said, and suggested that, if need be, William could renew his friendship with Angela Matlock, just to ensure an acceptance. 'After all, it's a very special Paradise—'

'Trap,' William said.

First to reply was the 'horse thief', as Justin had nick-named Cedric. He was soon followed by Baron and Baroness von Garten's acceptance, but the Matlocks did not reply, and William, to Justin's frustration, flatly refused to make personal contact with Angela. 'You just remember who's running the bloody show,' he said. 'I do not want to contact Angela fucking Matlock. You get him there, or get that bloody Sylvina to help. Just get Matlock on to the island.'

'If you want Matlock, you shall have him.'

The truth was, Justin was at a loss as to how to handle Matlock's lack of interest. He never replied to an invitation and he was impossible to get to. He was an obsessively private man whose only interest apart from making money was fishing.

Strangely enough it was an article published in one of his own newspapers that gave them Humphrey Matlock. Meryl Delaware lunched with Justin at the Ivy and Justin leaked to her there, in confidential tones, the names of the guests who were to stay at the spectacular island. On pain of death, she must not mention Sir William Benedict's name, he said. Neither should she mention that the Prime Minister and his wife had been invited. So was . . . Justin leaned close to her ear, and whispered.

'No, that can't be true. Are you kidding? But he's Matlock's biggest rival. Are you sure?'

Justin grinned and rubbed together finger and thumb. 'Money, my darling. He's switching parties, so rumour has it, and with wealth like that . . .'

Meryl Delaware had a scoop she had to handle carefully. But that blond boy couldn't be trusted and printing even the smallest hint about the 'Big White Chief' might have dire repercussions for her waning career. At five she decided to call his PR woman, who she detested but lunched with. Perhaps now all those lunch bills she had met would start to pay off . . .

Elaine Dunn's crisp voice was eventually on the line. 'Sorry to keep you waiting, Meryl, but the Chief's in today. What can I do for you?'

Meryl dragged on her cigarette. 'Actually Elaine darling, it's about your *numero uno*. I've heard a rumour and I just wanted you to verify it.'

'Well, you know, Meryl, if there's anything—'

'It's just an enquiry, Elaine. I don't want to know who he's shafting! It's just – can you tell me if it's true that he's a guest with the Prime Minister on Sir William Benedict's island this Christmas?'

There was a pause then Elaine's voice lowered. 'I don't think so. I know he received an invitation but I'm sure he turned it down. For God's sake don't print that.'

'Oh, I won't, of course I won't. I just wanted to check out the truth of the story. Both Matlock and his *bête noire* have been invited, you see. Do you know anything at all?'

'No more than I've just told you and now I really have to go – we must have lunch.'

'Yes, we must,' Meryl said, as the phone went dead. She drained her glass and lit another cigarette. 'Lying little shit.' She thought of Justin. Still, she'd had a free lunch.

Elaine, however, wrote a memo and passed it to Matlock's private secretary: the note said she had it on reliable information that the Prime Minister was to join a party on the most exclusive Caribbean island for Christmas. The other guest rumoured also to have been invited was Matlock's biggest competitor.

Meryl Delaware had played right into Justin's hands: there was no way Matlock would walk away from an invitation of this calibre. But she had slightly overplayed her relationship with Elaine. After Elaine discovered that Matlock had accepted the invitation, she was warned that he wanted his privacy guarded and required the source of the rumour about his vacation. Elaine was asked to speak to him personally. 'The woman really is a bit of a lush nowadays, sir. I have no idea how she came to know about the guest lists, but I'll make sure it's never printed.'

'That has already been taken care of, but thank you for your diligence. It is greatly appreciated.'

Elaine sighed with relief. Matlock never appeared to acknowledge Meryl Delaware, or Elaine's indiscretion in speaking with her, but the cryptic message that went round to all editors and magazines was that Matlock's organization no longer required the services of gossip-columnist Meryl Delaware.

*

Later that evening, as Justin made arrangements for their departure to the island, William was in his study, sifting through documents that required his signature. He was pleased to note that the case against the Baron was now moving forward swiftly. Perhaps that was why the stuck-up bastard had accepted the invitation.

Then his mood swung to a darker place. He had found an envelope from the Metropolitan Police. It contained a short note of sympathy and enclosed Andrew Maynard's suicide note in a plastic cover. William sat staring at the waterstained note with the blurred writing. Then he opened a drawer and searched through it until he found an old memo from Maynard. He compared the two pieces of writing. Obviously the police must have checked that it was authentic but to William something was wrong. He took into consideration that Maynard must have been drunk and drugged, so perhaps his scrawling, looped hand would appear different.

Dear William
    I have no ambition left, just heartbreak and terrible longing.
    I am sorry,
        Andrew

William delved around in his desk and withdrew more letters. In one, written to him on thin airmail paper, Andrew had signed off 'Longing to return to work'. It was the word 'longing' that did not match the suicide note. The letter 'L' was looped on the note but Maynard's Ls were straighter. He chewed his lip.

The office door banged open and Justin appeared.

275

'Right, we're all set. We leave early in the morning, first flight out.'

William looked up, covering his papers.

'Did you hear what I just said?'

'Yes, yes, just clearing my desk, join you in a moment.'

Justin closed the door and William sat for a few moments longer. He knew that Justin had been the main beneficiary in Andrew's will, but that had been a mere few thousand. *What was he thinking of?* He gathered up his papers, replaced them in the drawer and joined Justin in the drawing room.

CHAPTER 14

WILLIAM WAS holding his 'script', making final notes as Justin joined him after his morning swim.

'Morning,' Justin said cheerily.

'Morning. I've been rethinking a few moves.'

Justin held out his hand for the thick pile of carefully typed notes.

'Can't afford any mistakes,' William said. 'We've only got two more days. So let's start from the top. I don't think I should be on the jetty to greet everyone.'

Justin raised an eyebrow. 'Why not?'

'Angela might just freak; who knows how she's going to feel at seeing me again. She might persuade Matlock to do a U-turn off the island.' Justin nodded. 'So, you make up some excuse, say I've been delayed. It'll be more dramatic and I'll make a good entrance *after* they get nice and relaxed . . . What do you think?'

Justin nodded. It irritated him that William was making this last-minute adjustment but he had to admit it made sense. 'Anything else?'

'Yes.' There was a heavy pause. 'Partly to protect myself . . .' William began and paused. 'When things get under way, perhaps I should find some excuse to leave the island. This will obviously protect me from any repercussions, should there be any.'

Justin couldn't have asked for an easier way to make sure William was out of the way when the game commenced. Nevertheless, he sighed and studied William with a concerned look. 'I don't know about that. It sounds as if you're backing out.'

'Think about it, Justin. I get called away – we'll make up some emergency. I travel to London for a few days and what goes on here has nothing to do with me because I wasn't here. And it'll leave Laura alone. It's a far better idea than me staying.'

'You're right,' Justin said. 'You're a wily old codger, aren't you?'

William shrugged. His plan meant that whatever Justin and Laura got up to his hands would be clean. He hadn't liked the ruse about the Prime Minister being a guest and was worried it might cause problems.

'But you'll be here for their arrival. You don't want to miss that, do you?' Justin asked.

''Course not. I'll hide in one of the beach houses and make a grand entrance. In fact, you could say I got called away again to check on security for the rest of the guests.'

'My, my, you've thought of everything, haven't you?' Justin said, with a grin.

William was thoroughly enjoying himself. He loved the script sessions, which invariably involved discussions with the staff, who had been briefed one by one: Dahlia would co-ordinate the 'girls' who, on the surface, were attentive servants, their other attributes to be offered quietly at the right moment. The handsome Kurt had been primed to prepare workouts and 'special extras'.

The massage rooms, sauna, steam room and the gym were all filmed continuously, as was every other area of the island. Every sexual predilection could be catered for and recorded.

Opening night was near, the cast waiting in the wings, but the man still nominally deemed the ringmaster remained supremely unaware that Justin was pulling the strings. It was obvious to all except himself that William Benedict was dancing to Justin's tune. Nevertheless, all the staff were instructed to maintain the pretence that William ran the island, and due to his rearranging sections of the plans, there was no reason for him to believe otherwise.

Justin lowered the binoculars. He was standing precariously close to the cliff edge he had nicknamed Suicide Point because of the sheer drop down to the rocks below. He could hear the plane but it was hidden by clouds. He looked down, without trepidation, at the swirling, foaming water below, battering against the lethal, jagged rocks.

'Here we go,' he said. 'William, time for you to hide.'

William's stomach churned. So many months and all this preparation. He crossed his fingers. 'Good luck,' he said.

'You know the agenda, William. Wait till the coast is clear, then into the seaplane. A launch is waiting for you just beyond the two rocks.'

'Roger and out,' said William, saluting.

Through the clouds, the seaplane suddenly emerged, much lower. 'I'll wireless you when we need the love scene!' Justin yelled after William, who laughed as he headed for his prepared hiding place.

Justin trained his binoculars on the seaplane. It dropped lower and lower, and then, like an osprey, hovered before swooping down to the waves. It made a smooth landing on the water, then motored slowly towards the jetty. Justin made his way down there, training the binoculars on the disembarking passengers. Baron and Baroness von Garten were already on the quayside, looking around with astonishment. Even with their nonchalant disregard for the trappings of vast wealth, they were unable to hide their surprise. 'You ain't seen nothin' yet,' murmured Justin.

He looked down at his list and ticked them off in the column headed 'Arrivals'.

Klaus von Garten was six feet tall, wearing white shorts and leather thonged sandals, his Gucci shades pushed back on his forehead. His statuesque wife Christina stood beside him. At forty-four, she was still the envy of many women: the surgery to her face and neck had ensured she was unblemished by age, and enhanced her Germanic high cheekbones and full lips. She was beautiful, intelligent, bilingual and had great social graces. She oozed class.

Next to alight from the plane was a rather handsome boy of about eighteen, whom Justin recognized as the Baron's son, Max. He had a lovely, rangy adolescent body with long, slender arms and legs and strawberry-blond silky hair. Behind him came another boy. Justin double-checked with the profile in his folder: James Matlock. Smaller in stature than Max and already tanned a deep golden brown, Justin could tell that, although James was around the same age as Max, he was far more worldly. He was athletic, with strong muscular legs, a tight torso, and even his worn shorts and T-shirt had a groovy 'I'm cool' look, unlike the beige chinos and white shirt worn by Max. Justin knew he would enjoy breaking them in.

Next came Cedric, Lord Hangerford, fat, puce and sweating, just as William had described him. He was followed by his fatter wife, Daphne, and their daughter Clarissa. Then came another woman, mousy, plump and nondescript. Her face was pleasant enough and she obviously took care of herself: her pale skin was barely wrinkled, even though she was in her late forties if not early fifties. Her blonde hair, probably natural, was cut into a simple style, neither elegant nor flattering. So this was William's ex-girlfriend, the 'pretty, sweet' Angela, Matlock's wife.

Justin's heart beat fast as a man emerged from the hatch behind her. It could only be Humphrey Matlock. He double-checked with the folder. The man looked bigger and heavier in the flesh. He was at least six foot two and his black hair, greying at the temples, was thick and glistened with hair oil. He wore dark glasses, had a cigar clamped between his teeth and wore a light alpaca suit and open-necked shirt. Bingo! They were all here.

Dahlia stood in front of a line of boys ready to take the luggage. Justin giggled with pride. She was a stunner, Dahlia, tanned to a dark gold, wearing a demure YSL black dress, neat black ballet slippers, her dark hair coiled severely at the nape of her neck. Justin observed the way the Baroness ran her eyes over Dahlia, struggling to ascertain who she was. Since when had a housekeeper looked like this and worn such elegant clothes?

'Welcome,' Dahlia said, 'to the Paradise. I am Sir William's housekeeper.'

Buggies were waiting to drive them up to the house, leaving the luggage to follow with the boys. The sun beat down and they fanned themselves as they drove the long way round to take in the wondrous gardens, eventually pulling up at the main entrance. There Justin stood in the doorway.

'Hi there, folks,' he said, grinning at the Baron and Baroness.

'He seems at home,' said the Baron to his wife, as they passed into the hall.

'According to the magazine clippings we were sent, he designed the place. Remember how much we liked his villa in France? Met him at one of Sylvina Lubrinsky's dinner parties.'

The Baron raised his eyebrows. He had not wanted to accept the invitation, especially after insulting William and even more so after his withdrawal from their business transactions, but his wife had insisted. They were in financial trouble and perhaps a new deal could be negotiated with William.

The next buggy held the Hangerfords and close behind them came Matlock and Angela. They were discussing the gardens. The Matlocks were avid gardeners – or, at least, avidly capable of instructing their gardening staff. Neither of them had ever seen such opulence, though, quite so many rare blooms in such profusion.

Dahlia arrived in the foyer in time to introduce them to their personal maids. Ruby for the Baron and Baroness, Kiki for their son Max, Nina for James Matlock, Ella for the Hangerfords, and Dahlia herself for the

Matlocks. The curvaceous Ruby, with her wide brown eyes and long hair, wore a simple white linen tunic, white shoes. Kiki was darker, almost six feet tall with beaded hair that sparkled around her head. Her sister Nina was stockier, with the muscular build of an athlete. Ella was the shortest, with a square, masculine body, wide shoulders and strong hands, whose strength she demonstrated by picking up a large carry-on bag belonging to Daphne Hangerford. 'This way, please,' she announced, her voice deep.

Last but not least was Kurt, in white shorts and tight T-shirt. He was the type to make any teenage girl swoon. Any adult woman with any sense would bypass him fast.

The Baron and Baroness passed covert looks to each other as they were led to guest suite three. Ruby opened the massive oak doors to reveal inside a male servant awaiting their orders, a tray of iced drinks already laid out on their private veranda. The Baron accepted a glass of chilled vintage Krug champagne, while his wife poked around, noting the fridge stocked with caviar and chilled wines, and fresh fruit piled on iced platters. She grabbed one of the magazines left for her perusal then saw the folder titled 'The Paradise'. It gave details of the facilities: the gymnasium, masseurs, the beauty treatments, the cinema, beautifully drawn maps of the island, which highlighted the sporting facilities and the beaches and coves. She carried it to her husband on the veranda and sat next to him.

Sipping his Krug, the Baron could hardly take it in. No hotel or private residence he knew could match the island's outrageous luxury.

'Well!' she said softly. 'Sir William certainly knows how to put on a good show. The place feels more like a hotel than a private residence.'

'You complaining?' said the Baron, irritated by her need always to find fault. But for once she wasn't and by now they had both been silenced by the stunning view.

Their son Max had been allocated one of the bungalows and he loved it. Initially he had not wanted to join them on holiday, hardly relishing the thought of being hemmed in on an island with them both. He had spent little time with his parents during his childhood: he had been sent away to school at an early age and his holidays had been spent in the care of nannies as his parents jetted around the world. But when he had come into adolescence, they had suddenly wanted to have him constantly at their side. His mother found him especially useful, using him as her walker when she was invited to a function that his father would not attend. At these events she monitored what he wore, to whom he spoke, what he ate and drank, and never gave him an opportunity to move from her side, a protective diamond-studded wrist resting firmly on his shoulder at all times. She would laugh and tease him about being the man in her life, and God help him if he so much as glanced in the direction of any young female his own age: his mother would immediately run through the girl's social background and her unsuitability. As a result, Max was naïve and shy at eighteen, having only a fleeting knowledge of the opposite sex.

Suddenly James Matlock jumped over from his veranda next door and strolled into Max's bungalow suite. 'It's fucking mind-blowing,' he said, looking around. Max flushed as James opened the fridge. 'We can get really pissed,' he exclaimed, and laughed.

The boys had met on one or two occasions before, and had sat next to each other on the plane; Max had been reduced to tongue-tied shyness, as James talked about the girls he hoped to get his hands on. Unlike Max he was well experienced, and enjoyed broadcasting the fact in a loud whisper.

'I've got my own maid,' Max said, nodding to the bedroom to indicate to James to mind his language.

'So have I,' James said, winking. 'You want to do a tour?' he asked, going back out on to the veranda.

Max followed. 'Okay. But perhaps I should see my parents first.'

James shrugged, he had no intention of getting a lecture from his old man. He climbed back to his own quarters.

Max found himself alone with Kiki, who passed him a menu. 'All you have to do, sir, is request the time and state where you'd like to eat – the beach, sun deck, here in your room, wherever – and your order will be brought to you. Dinner is served in the dining room from seven thirty until ten.' Max smiled shyly, wondering if he should tip her. 'May I suggest, sir, I put some sun block on you, especially on your shoulders? It's very dangerous to go without at this time of the day.'

Max hesitated, but Kiki gestured for him to go into the bedroom where she had already set up a padded massage-table covered in soft white towels with a tray of oils.

*

In the adjoining suite James was already lying on his veranda while Nina rubbed sun-oil over his back and shoulders. He had a hard-on, feeling her strong hands smoothing on the sweet, perfumed oil, her big breasts sweeping over his back. He reckoned this was going to be the best holiday of his life. Nina leaned in close, letting her breasts slide up his arm. 'If you need any extras, sir, you only have to ask,' she said.

'Extras?' he repeated dumbly.

'Intimate massages. I am here to see that you are totally satisfied.'

This was a cocky little sonofabitch, Nina thought, and she could see his crotch swelling as she moved her hands expertly over his beautiful young body. She was rather glad she'd been allocated a boy rather than one of the older men. She liked breaking in young guys, but she reckoned this one was no virgin.

'Oh, yeah, that's great,' James said closing his eyes. Nina bent low and whispered into his ear, 'I can also provide any substances you require.'

His eyes sprang open just as the top button of her stretched white tunic released itself. His already swollen cock was upright now, like a gun primed to shoot.

Matlock was lying on the vast bed, wearing just a short cotton dressing-gown. Unlike his wife, he paid little attention to the elegant suite. She crossed the room now to open the floor-to-ceiling Gothic windows. With the touch of a button, the electric blinds glided back into virtually hidden alcoves to reveal the large patio. It was partly shaded with tropical plants and a striped awning around a private dining area, leaving the other

286

side bathed in bright sunlight. Two sun-loungers were laid out and a chilled bottle of champagne with two glasses stood in the shade on a small marble table.

'Nothing has been overlooked,' Angela said softly.

'What?' her husband enquired, tossing aside the brochure. It made him feel as if he was supposed to put in a bid for the place. 'What was that?' he barked to his wife.

'One's every need is catered for,' she said, shading her eyes to look down to the glistening water then upwards to the cliffs. Matlock came to stand beside her and saw James way below walking with Max. 'He's really going to enjoy himself,' she said.

'We all are, darling. That invitation was heaven-sent. It's so rare for us all to be together. I'm glad I changed my mind about coming – it would have been a shame to miss all this, and I'm sure there's some great fishing to be had, deep sea. I'd love to try my hand at that.'

'Yes, I'm sure.' Angela's calm exterior belied the fact that she had had to take extra Valium to prepare herself to face William.

Matlock changed the subject. He didn't want to give her the real reason for changing his mind: two weeks with the Prime Minister and his biggest competitor had been too good an opportunity to miss. 'Apparently there's a damned good library and gymnasium. Must say that is one hell of a pool,' he said.

There was a knock on the door. Angela went to open it. It was Dahlia. 'Just checking you have everything you want,' she said.

'A cup of tea,' yelled Matlock. 'Good old English tea.'

'Everything's lovely. I was just going to take a

shower.' Angela nodded to Dahlia. 'Thank you so much for unpacking. It's something I always loathe doing.'

'Would you care for a massage?' Dahlia asked. 'I am a fully trained masseuse, ma'am, reflexology and therapeutic herbal massage.'

'Another time, perhaps.' Angela was unable to meet Dahlia's direct gaze: for some reason she couldn't identify the maid unnerved her.

'Very well. I'll order tea. Would fifteen minutes leave enough time for your shower?'

'Oh, good heavens, yes. Thank you.'

Dahlia closed the door and left. Angela looked out onto the veranda, but her husband was already snoring. She had wanted to ask him when they were to meet William, but decided against it. They would confront each other at dinner.

The Baroness, wearing a white bikini, her hair tied up in a flowered scarf, lay with her eyes closed in the jacuzzi. She loved the feel of the herb-scented water as it massaged her body. She had a second glass of champagne at her elbow and one of the white-coated servants had unobtrusively placed a small platter of canapés beside her. She sighed. This really was perfection.

'You should see the gymnasium,' her husband said, perching on the side of the jacuzzi. 'It's better equipped than any place I have ever been to, and the instructor seems pleasant. He's from Berlin.'

'Really?' she said, eyes closed.

'I'm going to work out while I'm here,' said the Baron, accepting a glass of champagne from the same hovering servant. 'According to Kurt, I could still lose some weight. When you get to my age, it gets harder to lose those few extra pounds.'

He accepted a fresh platter of canapés and, despite his talk on weight-loss, began to eat them.

'Where's Max?' his wife asked, yawning.

'I have no idea. He went off with the Matlocks' son, James. He's a good-looking boy, isn't he?'

His wife's eyes opened and she squinted up at him quizzically. 'A word of warning: be careful.'

'For God's sake, I only said James was good-looking.'

'I know you and your good-looking boys.'

'But he's Max's friend.'

'Hasn't stopped you before, has it? But this time just remember whose son he is. Those two are so prudish, and if you cross him he'll crucify you on the front page of so many newspapers.' She sighed with impatience. 'He did it to William Benedict and look what happened to him!'

'Judging from this place, that scandal didn't hurt him.'

'Perhaps not, but tread carefully. He must have a hidden agenda. Why else would he ask us here? Maybe he wants to do business again. Let's hope so.'

They had shelled out thousands to pay the press to keep his homosexual dalliances private and his wife had protected him for years. The Baron's face tightened as she continued languidly, 'I'm surprised he wasn't waiting to greet us with a sledgehammer, considering the way you backed out of that deal.'

'All's fair in love and business deals,' he snapped.

'I'm sure it is. I just wish you had a little of his success. I presume that was why you accepted the invitation, in the hope of getting into bed with him, so to speak.'

'For God's sake don't start. Don't you think that maybe, just maybe, he wants to get into bed with me? In a business capacity, obviously.' He made no mention to her of the legal case he was fighting with Benedict. His lawyers had suggested that this trip might be a good opportunity to discuss it, perhaps in an informal way.

'I say! This is all rather lovely, isn't it?' Angela Matlock was wearing a large-brimmed sun-hat, a pale lemon dress and flat white sandals. She carried a straw basket with her cross stitch sticking out of it. 'It's a little too hot for me in the sun. I'll sit in the shade. I can't go too far, Humphrey's sleeping. He hates it if I'm not close when he wakes.'

In the control room, his feet up on the console, Justin spoke into the mike.

'William?'

'Yup,' came the crackly reply.

'You in position?'

'Yup, I'm in the charter-boat. We're just inside the two rocks.'

'Then this is your call for onstage,' he said.

'Roger!' said William.

'Roger yourself!' replied Justin, then hesitated. 'Hang on, what are you wearing?'

'What you and Dahlia put out for me.'

He was about to describe his clothes when Justin cut him off with 'Break a leg.'

*

290

The Baroness stepped out of the jacuzzi, selected a robe from the pool-side table and put it on. She looked around and then decided to sit at the far end of the pool, beneath a yellow striped awning near Angela Matlock.

'Who else is expected?' she asked Angela. 'Have you any idea?'

'I'm not sure, but the place is big enough to accommodate goodness knows how many. Have you see William Benedict yet?'

'No, I presume he'll be at dinner, though,' mused the Baroness. 'Does Justin Chalmers count as a guest? Or is he staff?'

Angela pointed towards the sea. 'It looks as though someone is arriving,' she said, reaching for her glasses.

The Baron strolled over to join them. 'Boat coming in,' he said.

William stepped out of the cabin and looked up at the island. Dahlia was on the quay waiting, her hand held out to guide him down the ramp. They saw him kiss her cheeks.

'Oh, my God! Is that his latest? His housekeeper!' the Baroness said sarcastically, then leaned forward.

Angela shrivelled into her cross stitch. With every fibre of her body she wanted to see him, but she refused to look.

Matlock woke with a start when he heard the powerful engines of the boat at the dock. He was sweating like a pig and had spent too much time in the sun. He swore, wrapped a towel around himself and stood up in time to see William step into the waiting buggy and head for the house. He sat like a king, tanned and relaxed, smiling: a happy man.

In the control-room, Justin was applauding. 'Bloody Oscar-winning stuff,' he said, into the mike. 'I'll see you after dinner. Just do as instructed, then meet up at the westerly cove. Now I've got to set some tapes recording . . .'

'My God, he looks like something out of a movie. How many servants has the man got, for heaven's sake?' asked the Baron, downing the rest of his champagne. 'Certainly splashing his money around, as if he was printing it himself.'

They all laughed. Within moments, they were joined by Cedric Hangerford, who'd been monitoring William's arrival from his own veranda. 'Typical of that jumped-up parvenu,' said Cedric.

At that moment, Humphrey Matlock appeared. 'I see our host has arrived. Rather like Anthony Steele in one of those sixties movies.' He laughed.

Angela couldn't help thinking that William looked rather good. Then she remembered how much he had hurt her, ignored her, treated her like a nobody. Seeing him again had unsettled her. She reached out and patted her husband's arm. 'You look very hot, darling,' she said.

'A few lengths will cool me down,' he replied, turned and dived into the pool with a tremendous splash.

Angela watched her husband swimming up and down and recalled her first meeting with him. At first she'd found him loud-mouthed and frightening, but she'd soon discovered his deep-seated insecurities. It was a touching evening when he told her that he longed to better himself. He knew he was going to be successful and he wanted, or needed, someone like her to smooth off his rough edges. 'Excuse me,' he had said, 'if I'm a bit unrefined. I don't have your high-society connections.'

She'd laughed and told him the truth: her family was middle class with social aspirations. They'd saved every penny they had to send her to Roedean, so that she would meet all the right 'gels'. But despite that, Angela was still a greengrocer's daughter. Her elongated vowels and Sloane style were cultivated. She'd told him how frightened she was of love. She said she had been in love before, but she'd been hurt. Twice. Later that evening Humphrey told her all about his childhood, told her things he had never mentioned to another living soul. It was as if they had found sanctuary with each other. Six months later they married.

In many ways, Matlock was like William. He had the same insecurities and the same need to be educated in the social graces. But, unlike William, Matlock had married Angela. Perhaps deep down, though, Angela always knew that for her Humphrey Matlock was second best. As the years progressed, she learned to put up with his moods, his aggression and his terrifying temper. He grew more and more successful and Angela felt the need to hide herself in his shadow. She knew about his mistresses, nothing ever escaped her, but she felt this was a cross she had to bear. She doted on her son, but at times she couldn't help seeing he was a mirror image of his father.

Sinking deep into depression, Angela's hatred of William resurfaced. She was a woman who appeared to have everything, but in truth had nothing. She had a wretched, loveless marriage, for which she blamed William. He had taken her youth and love, and had humiliated her twice. She had waited many years to repay him. She had badly wanted to hurt him and she had used her husband to do so. It was reading about Andrew Maynard's death that had set it off. She urged her husband to dig deep, to ruin William, even hurt him through his own family. When he questioned her obsession, she murmured only that he owed her: she had turned a blind eye to his own philandering. Matlock had laughed and then, of course, had obliged.

CHAPTER 15

THE NEXT DAY dawned with a cloudless azure sky and just enough breeze to blow away the humidity. The guests explored the island, swam, rode the jet-skis, played tennis, worked out in the gym. Now they gathered on the veranda overlooking the jetty for tea. Plates of sandwiches, pastries, muffins and fruit were placed in the shaded buffet area, with every conceivable variety of tea: Assam, Formosa Oolong, Orange Pekoe, Earl Grey, and herbal. They chattered excitedly, sharing their day's discoveries, all relaxed and enjoying the food. They turned as a powerful speedboat appeared on the horizon, heading for the island's jetty, the boys running hot-foot to welcome the new arrival.

The guests shaded their eyes against the sun to stare.

'Here comes someone else,' Cedric Hangerford stated unnecessarily, as the boat's engines were cut. To Matlock's disappointment, only one figure could be seen, and it was that of a woman.

Laura remained in the stern of the boat, her eyes shaded by dark glasses, an ice blue chiffon scarf draped around her head, matching her Chanel shift. The staff hurried to remove her Louis Vuitton suitcases, but she remained a serene figure. Extending one slender hand to a waiting boy, she stepped from the boat in a fluid movement, like a dancer. As if in slow motion, she unravelled her trailing scarf and her white-blonde hair swirled around her shoulders as perfectly as if she had been in a shampoo advertisement. Laura was not tanned: her skin was translucent, pale, like that of some exotic ice maiden.

Max let out a long sigh of admiration. 'My God, she's so beautiful . . . like a mirage.'

The Baroness gasped and turned to her husband. 'Isn't that . . . it is, isn't it?'

'What?' said the Baron, buttering a scone.

'Laura. It's Laura Chalmers.'

The Baron looked up, butter trickling down his chin.

'Justin's sister, remember? We met her once at Grimaud.'

'Ghastly temper,' the Baron said, holding his empty teacup for Kiki to refill. 'You remember Christa, that evening when she appeared like a Hollywood Oscar in that gold lamé dress?'

'There's Benedict again,' shouted Hangerford, grabbing the binoculars.

William was walking casually down the jetty, and they saw the beautiful woman turn, and then, to their astonishment, fall into his embrace. To even further amazement, they watched the couple kiss.

'Bloody hell, she's young enough to be his daughter,' spluttered Hangerford. 'The dirty old sod. After all that scandal, I think I'd have shot myself if I was him. But look at him!'

They all expected Laura and William to join them for tea, but by five thirty, they had not made an appearance, so they drifted off to their various suites to digest the day and rest before dinner.

Dinner was well attended that night. The Baron and Baroness were seated at a table for four with Cedric and Daphne Hangerford. The Matlocks were at an adjoining table with their son James. Max and Clarissa sat at a table by the open balcony doors. The main dining table, which could seat twenty, remained empty, save for two Mexican silver candlesticks that stood in the centre. A mellow light threw shadows around the wall, enhancing the oil paintings and tapestries and making the suit of armour shimmer. The room could just as easily have been in England, Austria or Russia; the ambience was theatrical.

The guests, including the younger ones, had all dressed up, the women in long gowns and the men in dark suits, except the Baron, who wore a white dinner-jacket with a white bow tie. A boy sat in a corner, quietly strumming bossa novas on his guitar. The waiters moved around quietly and efficiently. The wine flowed and the level of conversation lifted as each group relaxed and enjoyed their dinner. Nobody could fault the food, except the Baroness, who only took one spoonful of her avocado and lime soup.

The diners had all but forgotten their host when the door opened and he walked in. Momentarily the room fell silent. Then an animated conversation began again. William led Laura to her table like a lover. She did not acknowledge anyone and sat with her back to the room.

William fussed over her, making sure her chair was in the right position. She wore a delicate gown of silver chiffon, which fell loosely from a halter neck and swirled like gossamer. Her blonde hair was braided down her back and tied with a fine silver ribbon. Her shoes were silver, with a spiked heel and a band of silver leather around the ankle.

The adults were impressed, but disguised it by continuing to talk. The younger guests stared openly. William was wearing a white dinner-jacket, with a black, tight-collared shirt and well-cut black trousers. Now, at last, he turned to his guests. Moving around with an elegant confidence, he shook hands with them all, apologizing for not having been there to greet them but explaining he had had pressing business meetings. He came last to Angela and Matlock.

'Angela, what a long time it has been. I can't tell you how delighted I am that you accepted my invitation.'

Angela's cheeks flushed as his hand reached for hers. When he kissed her fingertips, she had trouble breathing and had to gulp before she was able to speak. 'You look better than ever,' she said nervously.

'Thank you. And this must be your husband. I don't believe we've actually met. I am delighted that you and your family are here. I do hope you enjoy my island.'

Matlock's voice boomed, 'It's a paradise, wonderful place. This is my son James. James! Say good evening to your host. William Benedict, James Matlock.'

But James could not stop looking across the room at the wonderful naked back opposite him. He drank in the woman's every move as she picked up a glass – filled, James presumed, with the champagne his parents were guzzling – and sipped it.

'James, dear, do stop staring,' Angela said softly.

'Nice to meet you, sir,' James said eventually, and William smiled warmly as his eyes, like James's, turned back to Laura.

Then William rejoined Laura and took her hand to help her rise. 'One of the main reasons I invited you all here, and we are hoping more guests will join us shortly, is because I wanted to introduce to you the love of my life. She is soon to be my wife: Laura.'

Laura gave a dazzling but demure smile, as William paraded her from table to table. She rested an arm around William's back as she walked. On her hand glistened a diamond ring that made the Baroness gasp. William raised his glass. 'A toast to my darling. She has made me the happiest man alive. To Laura.'

They all lifted their glasses, and Laura cupped his face between her hands and kissed him, before turning back to implore them gently, 'Please, continue eating, we've interrupted your dinner long enough. Come and sit down, darling.'

Clarissa Hangerford also kept her eyes on Laura, but with a look of envy. She had been getting on well with both James and Max and had been secretly hoping for a fling with one, if not both of them, though Justin of course would be preferable to both. But seeing this gorgeous creature had shattered all her confidence. She had blonde hair too, but of quite a different type: it didn't shine like Laura's, and swimming had made it frizzy and dry. Clarissa had also caught the sun, and was blotchy, red and sore. The gown Laura was wearing was any young girl's dream, and Clarissa wondered how on earth it stayed up with just a tiny strap around her neck. It made her own white cotton dress seem dowdy.

She looked down at herself and noticed that it was already crumpled, with a nasty crease running around the waist. She immediately hated her thick-soled, trendy platform shoes, which she was sure made her feet look enormous.

Clarissa's dinner companion, Max, had already decided he was in love with Laura, but believed her to be beyond his reach. He had returned to his hamburger and French fries. His parents rarely, if ever, allowed him to eat such fatty foods and his mother would not have a bottle of ketchup in the house. He ate with rare relish. Clarissa munched fried chicken and salad, but delved constantly into Max's chips.

Max appeared not to notice, his eyes glued to Laura's exquisite back. 'Is she a movie star?' he whispered to Clarissa.

'I dunno. If she is, I've never seen her in anything and didn't your oh-so-elegant mother tell you it's rude to stare with your mouth open?' Then, unable to contain herself, 'How old do you think she is?' she whispered.

'No idea,' said Max, as he moved his wine glass to the left, to enable the waiter to refill it. He glanced at his parents to see if they were monitoring him, but they were deep in conversation. As he turned back to the table, he saw James cast him a rueful look and tap his glass of mineral water. Unlike the Baron, his father watched over him like a hawk, and as he'd been caught drunk recently, he had to be on his best behaviour . . .

Laura was served a green salad, followed by a Dover sole. Max watched the way she held her cutlery and wished he could feed her morsel by morsel. James was still staring too and his mother had to kick him beneath the table as his father asked him about his exam results for a second time.

He was stoned. Knowing he would not be allowed to drink, he had rolled a spliff before coming down to dinner. At first he had not felt the effects, but now, confronted by his father's burning red face, he did.

'I'm sorry, Dad, what did you say?'

'We must discuss your last exam results, James, because if you need extra tuition we should arrange it before you return next term.'

'Oh, well, yes, but you know part of my problem was being on the rowing team. It meant I had to do so much practice in the mornings and evenings it didn't leave all that much time for cramming for the exams.'

'I thought it was tennis,' Matlock said, wiping his mouth with his napkin.

'Yeah, well, I'm in the first team for that as well,' James lied. He hadn't played for months and the rowing team had dumped him.

Matlock sighed and looked at his wife as she toyed with her food.

'Don't you like it?'

'It's delicious. I'm just not very hungry.'

Matlock looked across at the intimate couple, and leaned closer to his wife. 'Making a damned fool of himself with the girl. What did he say her name was?' he whispered, too loudly.

'Keep your voice down,' she hissed.

'Do you always have to tell me what I should or shouldn't do, for Christ's sake? They can't hear me.'

'I'm sorry, I've got a headache.'

'Yes, a permanent one,' he snarled, and she cringed into her seat.

The desert trolley was wheeled in, laden with sweets so tempting that even the Baroness could not resist. As the boy with the guitar began to sing softly, Laura kissed William lovingly and slipped out of the room.

'Will you all excuse us?' asked William, as he drew back his chair and followed her.

As soon as they left, the dining-room broke into loud conversation, like the tidal wave after a dam has broken.

'Well, where on earth did he find that little filly?' Hangerford wondered aloud.

Matlock was more concerned with when the PM was expected, not to mention the other guests he had been told would be joining them. But no one appeared to know and the abundance of such exquisite food became the focus of all their attention.

'How's my princess?' whispered Justin, as his sister hugged him tightly, giggling.

'You should have seen their faces. We were so good, weren't we, Willy?'

William kissed her cheek. He felt like a conspiratorial child. 'I am having a good time. What a pompous, fat-arsed man that Matlock is . . . and I did such an elegant eye-to-eye with his wife. To think I almost married her. Dear God!'

Justin looked at Laura then back at William. 'It's phase two now. Time to make yourself scarce.'

'Oh, no! Can't you give me another day?'

'No. Don't start messing around with the schedule, it was all agreed. You can't back out of it now. And, anyway, you decided it, William.'

'But I don't want to miss the fun.'

'You won't, and as it's all recorded you'll have it for posterity. If you're here it'll hold things up.' William sighed. 'Make yourself scarce, you old bugger. It was your idea, so get your arse out of here and let the fun and games begin. Besides, it'll keep them waiting for the extra guests who aren't going to appear,' said Justin, pushing William through a door.

Before disappearing, William turned and blew a camp kiss. 'Knock 'em for six,' he said, and was gone. But just to make sure he didn't change his mind, Justin kept the monitor running, watching as he made his way out through the back corridors.

'I'll not start on the younger ones,' said Laura quietly. 'They'll be too easy. I think I'll go for his lordship first. Then I'll work my way to Angela. Is that OK?'

'Save the pig Matlock until last. Make him beg,' said Justin quietly, his eyes on the screen. William was in one of the golf carts being driven down to the jetty where the boys were waiting to take him off the island.

'Of course he has to be last. I'm not stupid.'

Justin switched the monitor screen to the main hallway. 'Here they come. Go into the lounge and be waiting.' He left her side to welcome the guests as they drifted up the stairs into the drawing room for coffee and liqueurs. As they entered the light, airy room, their bellies full, tired from the day in the sun and the sumptuous dinner, they were surprised to see Laura, who looked ravishingly fresh. Justin made a show of serving coffee alongside the servants, but was watching Laura as the men moved closer, like bees to honey.

Max looked into her eyes then immediately dropped his gaze, even though she said no more than how pleased she was that he had come to the island. She eased away from Max and moved on to James, then to Clarissa. When she shook Cedric Hangerford's hand, he held hers far too long. He only let go when his wife interrupted them to admire Laura's gown. The Baron and Baroness mentioned that they had met before. Laura smiled sweetly but made no attempt to recall when or where. The Baroness examined the woman who made her pale into insignificance. She was adept at fast appraisals, and wondered which designer had created such a delicate dress. She reached out and took Laura's left hand. 'What a beautiful engagement ring. So simple. I always think diamonds look best with platinum. Who designed it for you?'

'William. It's sweet, isn't it?'

Sweet it was not. It had to be worth a few hundred thousand pounds.

'Lady Matlock, this is my sister, Laura,' Justin announced, ushering her away from the Baroness. Angela smiled but did not take Laura's hand. She turned to her husband. 'Darling,' she said, in turmoil. The girl's eyes were magnetic with the colour of the sea, her lily perfume like clean air.

Humphrey Matlock, cutting a slice of cheese, turned round. He wiped his hand on a napkin. 'You have stunned us into silence yet again, like an angel passing over.' He kissed her hand.

She allowed it to remain against his lips just a fraction longer than necessary. 'Thank you,' she said softly, and watched as he returned to his cheese.

Then Justin slipped his arms around her shoulders. 'But this poor darling is going to be all alone for a few days,' he announced.

Everyone turned their attention to the brother and sister.

'My fiancé has been called away. He's expecting other guests so he's gone to the mainland. Something to do with security,' Laura said lightly, before Justin assured them their host would not be away for more than a few days. Then he led her out of the room. Again, as soon as they disappeared, a hubbub of conversation broke out as they wondered who the guests might be – the island already seemed entirely secure.

'I heard it was the Prime Minister,' Matlock said flippantly, and they looked from one to the other.

Angela's lips tightened. She knew now why he had insisted they accept the invitation, even though he had been aware of what torment it would cause her. 'You never said anything before about the Prime Minister,' she said softly.

'Only just found out,' he lied, and made no mention that he had been told his main competitor was also expected. Still, it meant that he had a couple of days to enjoy himself and not think about business. He began eagerly enquiring about fishing.

Justin unhooked Laura's dress and she stepped out of it, kicking off her sandals. He fetched a robe and put it around her shoulders. Then she sat at the dressing-table while he unplaited her hair and began to brush it.

'So?' he asked.

She half turned and lifted her hand. 'Kiss it,' she said. He did so and she laughed. 'Now give me your hand. You be me and I'll be Matlock.'

Justin held it out to her. She lifted it to her lips,

brushing them against his fingers, then darted her tongue between two.

'He did that?'

She nodded, and turned back to the mirror. 'It's going to be easier than we dreamed. I will have him crawling, begging for it. And you know what'll make him crazy? I think he'll find out that his son has been there before him.'

Justin flopped on the bed and laughed. He loved to hear her talk dirty. 'Shall I fuck him too?' he asked.

'James? Why not?' she said, creaming her face.

'What about William's ex? The strait-laced Angela,' Justin asked. He didn't relish the idea of screwing her. 'God, that man had lousy taste.'

'You take her first. I think she's got to be given something, maybe half a tab.' Laura plucked a tissue to wipe over her face.

Justin rolled on to his stomach and told her what the maids had said to him, that despite her frumpy look, her lingerie was lacy, flimsy and sexy.

Laura got up and lay on top of him, nuzzling his neck. 'The Baron and Baroness seem tedious. Do we need to bother with them?'

'He'd roll over for a monkey,' smirked Justin, 'as long as it had its mouth taped up so it couldn't give away his secret.' He turned on to his back.

Laura remained on top of him, feeling him erect beneath her.

'What about Clarissa?' he said.

'She's wet just looking at you. The skinny boy Max isn't a push-over, though. And he's got the hots for the Hangerford girl. He looked as if he'd never had an erection before, never mind fucked anyone.'

306

Laura sat up and moved away from the bed. Justin yawned; he was really tired. He stretched, and his jeans slipped down to reveal his tight, flat belly. No man had ever made Laura feel so aroused. She sighed and reached over to unzip his pants. 'This'll make you sleep.' She knelt down between his legs, taking him in her mouth.

'We have to be careful,' he said, eyes closed, loving the feel of her mouth around him. She sucked harder, clawing his thighs and twisting his testicles. The pain made him gasp and with a moan he climaxed into her mouth.

'That was a quickie,' she said, wiping her lips with a tissue. Usually it took much longer.

'It's been a while.' He zipped up his trousers. 'And I've had a hard-on all evening thinking about you.'

She went into the bathroom and started to clean her teeth. Justin lolled at the door. 'Willy must be on the flight by now,' he said. 'You know, I've become fond of him.'

'Oh, no.' Laura sighed. 'Don't tell me you've fucked him. I told you not to.'

'I haven't, and I like him. He's good company. Sure he can lash out a bit, but considering all the tedious family situations he's had to go through, he's impressed me.'

'I like him too,' she said softly, then laughed. 'He kisses like a teenager. He was so nervous of taking me in his arms, even if it was just for show.'

'He means us no harm, Laura, I know that. Sometimes I think he's the only man I've ever trusted.'

'Are you in love with him?' she asked, her voice soft and afraid.

'Hell, no, I mean . . . it's more that I love him like
. . .' He thought about it for a moment. '. . . I don't
know.'

'Love him like a brother, perhaps?' She stared at
Justin in the mirror.

His brow was furrowed in a deep frown and he
shook his head slowly. 'No, not like that. Maybe it's
because I've never known anyone for such a length of
time. I dunno. It's a new one on me, but the old codger
grows on you.'

He stood behind her and slipped his arms around
her, hugging her close. He had a vulnerable side, and it
was the side she cared for most of all. 'I miss you so
much when you're away from me. I love you, Laura,'
he whispered.

'I know, I know. Now go on. Go to bed.' She
cupped his face between her hands and kissed his lips.
'We only have two weeks, then it'll all be over and we'll
be free.'

'You won't leave me?' he said anxiously.

'No, of course I won't. Will you leave me?'

'Not even with all the diamonds Willy's going to
give you?' Justin insisted.

'We'll be together, Justin, I promise. We'll live in
our villa, just you and me, and no more nightmares.
We'll have paid Matlock back and we'll be free. It'll all
be over.'

'Yes,' he said, then kissed her lightly before he left
the room.

This was the side of Justin that William had rarely
seen. Hardly anyone had ever seen it, apart from Marta
and Laura. This was not the vicious, twisted Justin, or
the over-confident, witty, talented Justin. This was the

child who hid in the darkest recess of his adult mind, when Laura became the stronger of the two.

Next morning, Justin and Laura went to the control room to survey the guests at play. Justin's mood had lifted, and he was chuckling at the film footage.

'Well, I'd better start work,' she said. 'If I have to begin with Cedric Hangerford, you'd better stand by. I doubt if it'll take long. His kind never do. Where is he?'

Justin flicked on a monitor and pointed at the screen. 'As arranged. He's midway through a workout with Kurt in the gym. He's got a massage booked immediately after with Kiki.'

'Tell Kurt,' Laura said softly, 'to suggest to his lordship that he has a sauna. Justin? Did you hear me?'

'That's not on the list.'

'No, I know. I've just had a good idea. I'll work him over in the sauna. So arrange it.' Then she leaned towards him, and whispered further instructions.

'Sauna it is, my darling. And just remember, Big Brother is watching you.' He picked up the intercom phone. He adored Laura: sometimes her mind was even more warped than his. She was right, though: they needed to move fast on William's tedious guests, get rid of them as soon as possible, leaving Matlock for the plucking.

Kurt replaced the receiver.

'I've arranged a sauna for you,' Kurt said to Hangerford, now flat on his back, arms splayed at his sides.

'Christ, I don't think I can get up,' he said.

Kurt put out his hand and hauled him to his feet. 'I'll take you through, sir. I'd keep to the lower bunks,' he added, 'it's hotter and better for your skin.'

They went in and Kurt laid out a towel for Hangerford, who flopped down with an exhausted sigh of relief. Then he passed him a bottle of chilled water. 'Drink as much as possible,' he said encouragingly, and waited a moment as he watched Cedric gulping it down.

Laura lay on the top shelf of the sauna, naked apart from a small white towel across her thighs, her body glistening. When the door opened she didn't move a muscle, but remained still with her eyes closed. Hangerford sighed again, as soft relaxing sounds drifted into the sauna, the noise of waves and whales over the sighing ocean.

Hangerford did not notice that the sauna was already occupied, until one perfect white hand swung down from the bunk above. Then Laura sighed, and yawned as if just waking. She dropped her towel, which brushed his shoulder, and he half sat up, wondering who was above him. As the sighs grew louder, he realized it was a woman, and that she was masturbating. His body flushed with anticipation. Laura began to mew like a kitten and then she moaned. Hangerford could feel the tremor of the bench above him and he was now fondling himself. As she became more and more vocal in her arousal, so did he. His body felt as if it was on fire.

Laura swung her hips and legs down over the side of the upper bunk, and gripped the slats with her hands to keep from dropping to the ground. Cedric raised himself on one elbow. She thrust herself into his face.

310

He put his head between her legs and began licking and sucking, grunting. She pushed her hips forward and wrapped her legs around his shoulders. He was virtually buried inside her when the sauna's incredible heat enveloped him. His brain felt as if it was about to explode. He tried to draw his head away from her legs. He was gasping and unable to get his breath, but the more he panted, the dizzier he felt. He couldn't breathe and his heart felt as if it was about to explode. Darkness descended and he passed out.

Laura shoved him away from her, picked up her towel, and opened the sauna door. As it closed behind her she turned up the temperature and walked into the shower. By the time she felt cleansed, her skin tingling from her body scrub, she reckoned Hangerford might need assistance. As she passed the sauna, she lowered the temperature and headed for the changing cubicles. Justin joined her. 'Get him out quickly,' she said.

Justin and Kurt carried Hangerford out of the sauna and into the shower. They remained with him as he spluttered and shrieked from the ice-water jets. From her changing cubicle, Laura saw Dahlia walking towards the sauna with Clarissa. With a white towel clutched to her naked body, she told Dahlia that she could never take more than a few minutes in a sauna. Dahlia laid the towel along the top bunk and assisted Clarissa up the ladder; then she lowered the heat, threw some pine essence on to the coals and closed the door. Laura left the changing rooms with Dahlia.

Hangerford was resting, another glass of water in his hand. He wished Kurt would stop hovering around him. He insisted he was perfectly recovered and, in fact, felt remarkably fit. Just thinking about getting back into the sauna gave him an erection. It had been the most exciting sexual encounter he had ever experienced.

The moment Kurt left him, he went straight back inside. His heart was thudding in his chest, yet he felt focused, full of energy and sexual drive. He closed the door and dropped his towel, proudly revealing his bloated penis. He walked to the bunk he had used before, lay down and stretched his hands up to fondle beautiful firm breasts. His hands roamed over the young body and he grew more excited as he masturbated the woman, pressing his fingers between her legs. Feeling her opening he could no longer contain himself. 'Come down, I want to finish where I left off. I want to fuck you.'

Clarissa raised herself on her elbow. She could hardly catch her breath. *'Daddy!'* she gasped, leaning down to behold not Justin, as she had hoped, but her father.

Hangerford charged out like a crazed bull.

In the control room, Justin sat smoking a cigar, the camera still focused on the terrified face of Clarissa. Beautiful! The film would splice together perfectly. He also knew that his lordship would believe that his head had been between his daughter's legs. He giggled. William was going to love it. Imagine releasing this to the *Racing News*! Better still the Jockey Club. Hangerford had certainly had quite a ride even if he hadn't finished the race!

CHAPTER 16

WILLIAM SAT in the Harbour Bar with a large Scotch and water. After leaving the island he had arrived at Tortola only to discover that his flight had been cancelled due to technical problems. Overnight, a heavy mist had fallen and the next flight had been postponed until conditions improved. He wondered how things were going back at the island. He would have liked to call Justin, but knew that that would be childish. Although he himself had instigated his departure, he now had reservations. But he told himself it made sense and, besides, he knew everything would be caught on video.

Lost in his thoughts, he was surprised by a nudge on his shoulder. It was Lady Bellingham. 'Are you stranded too?' she asked. 'I'm trying to see some friends off. They've gone to do some last-minute souvenir hunting so I thought I'd come in for a drink. It's such a bore this hanging around.'

William was unsure whether he should offer to buy her a drink. This was, after all, the longest conversation they had ever had. Boredom must have forced her to approach him.

'Do you mind?' She indicated the empty chair at his

table. 'It's always tricky, a woman alone having a drink in a bar,' she said, sitting.

William ordered a gin and tonic and they fell into an awkward silence. He was trying to think of something to say when Lady Bellingham remarked, 'I hear that your son Charlie has gone into rehab. An old school-friend of Oliver's is in Minnesota too, and he wrote to us.'

'Fingers crossed, he seems to be doing well.'

Another lengthy silence prevailed as she sipped her drink. Then she rattled the ice cubes around her glass nervously. 'Oliver didn't have a chance,' she said, look-ing down into the glass. 'His body was pumped full of ecstasy, heroin, crack – you name it.' She bit her lower lip. 'I don't know where he got it. I know there's lots of pot around, I take it myself. But we wouldn't let him have the hard stuff, and we kept him under pretty tight surveillance.'

William recalled the party on the night their son had died. He hadn't noticed much 'surveillance'. Lord Bel-lingham had been stoned out of his head, along with most of the guests.

A tear rolled down her cheek and dropped off her chin. 'I'm sorry, so sorry to mention it. Let's change the subject.' William passed her a handkerchief. 'I thought you'd sold up, or were about to,' she said, wiping her face. 'I've read so much about your place. We're thinking of leaving. You must give me the name of your estate agents. They're doing a grand job of promoting your island.'

'Journalists,' he said, 'always get the wrong end of the stick. I'm not selling, quite the contrary, I love the

314

place.' The silence was descending again, but he found something more to say. 'As a matter of fact I've lent my place to Justin Chalmers and his sister Laura while I do some work in London. I'll just be gone a few days.'

She put her head quizzically to one side. 'Justin Chalmers?' she said, and seemed perplexed.

'Designer,' said William. 'Did the place up for me.'

'Is that the Justin Oliver knew?' she asked.

William nodded. 'Charlie talks about Oliver. He was very upset.'

Lady Bellingham put her hand on William's, blinking back the tears. 'I can't talk about it, I'm afraid. If I do I'll start weeping. It's been quite horrible, the whole business and, er . . .' She swallowed rapidly.

An announcement came over the crackly PA that the weather conditions were clearing and the airport would soon be functioning normally.

'Oh, Lord,' cried Lady Bellingham, rising. 'Must find my chums or they'll be stuck here! Or, worse, I will!' She drained her gin and tonic, then gave a brittle smile. 'Nice talking to you, Sir William. You really must come and join us for dinner some time.'

William was surprised that she had stooped so low as to converse with him, let alone invite him to dine. He, too, downed his drink and walked out on to the quay to get a taxi to drive him the five miles to the airport.

In the lounge, he opened his laptop to discover a welter of e-mails from Michael, requesting he contact London immediately. But he had no time to place a call: the flight was already boarding. The messages worried him. What could be so urgent? Perhaps something had happened to Charlie. He never gave a moment's thought to the idea that it might just be business: his concern was for his son. At last he was taking on the role of father.

As the flight took off from Tortola, the paradise island was silent: most of the resident guests slept late, apart from Max. He wanted to watch the sun rise and had walked to the highest point of the island with a camera.

Max was in the agony of a schoolboy crush on Clarissa, who had played cards with him and James late into the night after they had arrived. The following day she had not come out of her room and when at last he saw her she averted her face and refused to speak to him. Why?

He walked on briskly because the early morning was still dark and the air chilly. He wondered if he was ever going to lose his virginity. With James around, he doubted if he'd get a look in here. He didn't particularly like James: he was so competitive and aggressive. He seemed constantly to have to prove himself, whereas Max was more passive. As inexperienced in worldly and sexual matters as he was, he maintained an adult calm and perspective – which was about to be shattered.

Laura was sitting with her hands clasped around her knees, perched close to the edge of the jagged rock, her hair blowing around her. Max emerged from the woods fifteen yards or so from her and was taken aback when he saw her. Although he was so close, he didn't know whether she had heard him or not. He took a step further forward, but she gave no indication that she knew she was not alone.

'Miss Chalmers,' he stuttered, and her back arched

like a cat's. 'It's Max,' he added softly, and wondered if perhaps he should turn back but she beckoned him to join her. Max stepped closer, a little afraid as she was so close to the cliff-edge, but she patted the space beside her for him to sit. He hesitated, edging closer, then got to his knees for safety and crawled up to her.

'You know, if you watch the sun rise close to some-one, you are bound together for ever by its rays.' Her voice was a soft whisper. Max could think of no answer. He was close enough now to feel the warmth of her body beside him. They remained silent, waiting, as the amber glow spread before them.

'Here it comes, wait, wait . . . It's coming any second now,' she gasped. He held his breath and she reached out for his hand. 'No one but us will ever have this moment . . . no one but us.'

She tilted her head to catch the rays as they grew stronger, before the golden globe appeared in front of them, bathing them both in its brilliance. But Max had eyes only for the woman beside him. For him, the sun was a pale star beside her, this magical mirage, her blonde hair shimmering like a halo.

Nothing could have prepared him for this moment, nothing in his wildest dreams. She eased her body down to lie on the warming rock, holding out her arms for him to lie beside her. Without a word, he obeyed.

The kiss took his breath away. It was sweet, but it was hungry, and he felt such a surge of emotion that his body shook. She stroked his face, planting delicate kisses on his cheek and neck, her lips tracing his ears, till he felt such ecstasy he let out a moan. Max would never have considered approaching this girl-woman, he was far too shy. But, wrapped in her arms, it was as if he had always known her. He wanted the moment never to end. But it did, as abruptly as it had begun.

'I must go back,' she announced suddenly, and rolled away from him. She was up and running before he could reach out to stop her. All he could do was watch her disappear from his sight. Then he started to cry. He didn't know why: it had just been too much for him.

Max saw her fleetingly again that morning, first at breakfast then down by the jetty. He flushed deeply every time she passed within touching range, afraid she would discover he was following her. His legs shook and his heart beat so rapidly he felt sick. But he thought he had managed to appear in control of himself. After lunch they spoke again. Laura had dropped a hair slide as she passed him on her way to the pool. At first Max had simply wanted to keep it as a reminder of her, but then he plucked up courage to approach her. Just the touch of her fingers against his hand, as she thanked him, rendered him incapable of saying a word. She did not refer to the sunrise and he could not bring himself to mention it. She was, after all, Sir William Benedict's fiancée. He even questioned whether it had happened at all. But he knew it had, and now, speechless before her, it was all that filled his mind.

'You have beautiful clear eyes,' she said softly. He wanted to say something poetic in return, but she walked on.

There were four or five more fleeting meetings that day. At last he stuttered that he had hoped she didn't feel he was stalking her. She leaned closer. 'I'm sorry, what did you say?'

'Nothing,' he replied, as his breath caught in his chest.

To his astonishment and consuming delight, she suggested they walk a while. They went down to the jetty, and twice her shoulder brushed against his. There was one glorious moment when she asked him to hold her hand as she slipped off one of her sandals to shake out the sand. Her closeness made him break out in a sweat and her hand felt cool and soft, like silk.

Over the next few nights, Max could not sleep. All he could think of was Laura, but she did not appear again to greet the sunrise. The dining-room meals became the focus of his day because he knew he would see her there. He tried hard to not make his adoration obvious, but he could hardly contain himself, glancing clumsily in her direction. He started to make elaborate plans for accidentally meeting her and what he would say. But, try as he might, he could never pin down her whereabouts. She never dined at the same time in the evenings, never swam or walked at any specific time. He spent hours hovering round the places he hoped she might be, sometimes sitting in the dining-room for hours. Mostly she didn't appear to notice him.

The meeting that changed everything was when she asked him to help her open a sunshade. They were on the lower beach. He fixed it, then fetched an armful of towels and laid them out along a sun-bed. Laura was wearing a white cotton kaftan, and at certain angles the sunlight shone straight through it to outline her body like a soft shadow. He wanted to kneel at her feet, to kiss each toe, to tell her he was her slave. At one point their eyes met and he was sure she was going to say something to him. With an encouraging smile, she patted the towel beside her. But as she lay back against the cushions, his mother appeared. 'Hello, darling. Get me some towels, would you? And move a bed into the sun for me. Is there a bar down here? I'm so thirsty.'

Max fetched and carried for his mother, who kept up a constant embarrassing chatter about why he wasn't swimming or waterskiing. 'Take your shirt off, darling, you need some sun. You back hasn't broken out in spots again, has it?'

He wanted to die and he shook his head, trying to make the Baroness change the subject, but it got worse as she continued her conversation to Laura with her eyes closed. 'Poor boy, he's got such delicate skin. But, then, they all have acne at that age, don't they? It's ever since he started shaving. At least his face has cleared up. He used to get terrible boils and—'

'Mother!' hissed Max, his face crimson.

Laura got up suddenly, and excused himself, saying she had forgotten her book.

'Are you coming back?' Max asked. He had sounded so desperate and what made it worse was she didn't look at him, just continued walking towards the path.

'Not very friendly, is she?' his mother said, plastering herself in oil.

Before Max could hurry after Laura she insisted he did her back. He hated doing this. She took off her bikini top and lay face-down on the towels for him to spread the oil over her.

'She's really rather rude,' the Baroness continued.

'There's her book under the sun-lounger,' Max said, with delight. His mother looked up as he bent down to retrieve it. It was a volume of children's poems. He wanted to kiss it. 'I'll take it to her.'

'Oh, don't bother, darling, leave it. I'll take it back to the house.'

But Max was already hurrying after Laura. Out of sight of his mother, he opened the book. He could hardly believe his eyes when he saw that a note was tucked into the first page with his name on it. At first he was sure it was a joke, but why would she do that? Then he wanted to weep when he understood that she had suggested they meet by the waterfall. It had to be real.

Max waited for more than an hour past the appointed time. He had almost given up when she came into sight. His heart lurched. The note had said lunch-time, which he had taken as twelve, but she clearly thought lunch was at two. Laura was welcome to take lunch at whatever time she pleased.

Max stepped behind the rushing curtain of water to hide as she approached. She wore a wide straw hat, the same long, white kaftan, and she had threaded flowers through her toes.

'Max,' she said softly, 'I know you're here.' She removed the hat and her hair tumbled down. Slowly, she began to raise her skirt, lifting it to her knees, then her thighs. Hardly able to breathe, Max watched as the white robe inched slowly up her body. Beneath it, she was naked. Like a nymph, she stepped into the cascade of water, holding out her arms to catch the stream, her head tilted back and the water rushing off her. 'Take off your clothes and come and join me. Don't be shy. No one will see us here.'

Max hastily tore off his clothes and walked towards her into the clear, thundering water. Slowly her hand reached out for him. She drew him into the recess cut into the rock behind the screen of spray, and cupped his face in her hands to look into his wide, fearful eyes. 'It's all right,' she whispered.

His fear evaporated as their bodies inched closer. 'I love you,' he said, aching to kiss her.

His look of adoration frightened Laura: he reminded her of Justin as a boy. She searched his face, trying to fathom whether he was lying to her, but she saw there only innocence.

To her surprise, when their lips touched she was not thinking of anything or anyone but him. The experience confused her, and she broke away. Then her eyes concentrated on his lips, which she kissed again, as if to make sure the moment between them was real. After kissing him three times she broke away. Max was overcome with emotion and began to cry. She licked his tears as they mingled with the mist from the waterfall, and thought she too might weep. It puzzled her. This was a job, but it felt like something else. She had teased the boy for days, drawing him behind her like a puppy. She had meant to arouse him, play with him then withdraw. But something inexplicable had stopped her. She had never felt this for anyone except Justin. Was that why his kisses felt so nice? They were like Justin's, but they weren't. The feel of them made her want to continue kissing, but she wanted to kiss him as a boy, not as a man.

It was Max who changed the tone. Max became a man then, kissed her strongly and searchingly. Laura allowed herself to be drawn to lie beside him on the cool, mossy earth, his hand clasping hers. She clung to him as if she was afraid to let go.

'I love you,' Max repeated, and she began to sob. She had never known such a powerful, explosive feeling in the pit of her belly. He whispered to her, 'I don't know if I'm dreaming this, if I am mad, or even if it's real. I'm scared to close my eyes and lose you.'

'Ssh!' she said, cradling him in her arms, his head resting against her breasts. She loved his caring gentleness. She liked the way he had put his shirt beneath her head when they lay down, worried that the ground was damp. He didn't paw her or force her hand down to touch him. Their roles had been reversed so unexpectedly and without any calculation on her part. She loved the smell and touch of his lean, young body. He was clean and untouched.

When he asked if she could feel his heart leaping, he endeared himself to her more.

'Do you want to make love to me?' she asked.

Max admitted that he was afraid his inexperience would make her ridicule him.

She held him closer. She felt protective, almost motherly towards him. 'I promise I would never tease you. You will be the best lover I have ever known.' She meant it as a joke, but he gripped her tightly.

She wanted to weep as his kisses on her neck made her thighs ache, and the even sweeter kisses on her lips made her want him to make love to her. But his fingers threaded through hers and rubbed her ring finger. Feeling the solitaire diamond, he released her. 'We mustn't do this, it's wrong, it's . . .'

Laura sighed, and held up her hand. The diamond glittered. 'Don't you ever do anything wrong, Max?' she asked.

'Everyone does, but if you were to make love to me, with me, I couldn't bear to see you with another man.'

She let her hand drop to one side and he caught her fingers, pressing on the diamond with his thumb. 'When are you getting married?'

She closed her eyes.

'Do you love him?'

Again she sighed. 'It's none of your business.'

He sprang to his feet and fetched his jeans, unembarrassed now by his nakedness.

She propped herself on her elbow. 'Where are you going?'

'I can't stay. I can't be with you like this.'

'Why not?'

He zipped his fly, then looked around for his trainers. He sat on the edge of a rock as he slipped on one, then the other. He left the laces untied and looked over; she still lay on his shirt. Suddenly he felt strong, his mind clear.

'We should go,' he said, and moved towards her to pick up his shirt. The whore in Laura had abandoned her, slunk off to hide, unable to deal with the purity of emotion. She couldn't speak. She let him ease away his shirt from behind her. But he didn't put it on: instead, he draped it round her shoulders, as if to hide her breasts. She let him remove the diamond ring from her finger. He placed it carefully on the edge of a rock. 'I want you to marry me.'

She accepted his proposal, but he had no ring. 'Give

me your wedding finger,' he said. She held it out tentatively. He took it and bit it until he drew blood. She touched it with the tip of her finger then licked it.

'That will be our ring,' he breathed. 'Bite me now.'

She bit harder and longer into his finger. It hurt like hell but he wouldn't stop her. Eventually, she drew his head on to her lap. He was unsure what to do, so she told him how to use his tongue. Soon she was begging him to enter her, and as he came into her, she did what she always did: averted her face. Max noticed and withdrew. 'What did I do wrong?' he asked.

'Tell me you love me,' she said.

Max caught her hand and raised it to his lips. 'Right now, if you asked me to, I'd die for you, Laura, and I will kill anyone who takes you away from me. I want you to tell him.'

'Well, I can't straight away. He's had to return to London.'

'When he gets back?'

'Yes . . . yes, I will.'

'Promise me.'

'Yes, if you promise to keep this a secret until I have told him.' She leaned over him. 'This is odd for me . . .' She hesitated, then kissed his lips.

'What is?' he asked.

'I feel such love for you. It is the first time I have felt like this for anyone.'

'You've never made love to another man?' he asked, sitting up.

'I meant I have loved only one man before you, but he doesn't count. Tell me again.'

'I love you,' he said simply.

She laughed, hugging him, not wanting to let him go. 'And I you.'

Justin was furious. For one thing, Laura was not working up to speed: she had disappeared for the whole afternoon. For another he had not been able to capture on film anything that had taken place between her and Max because they had hidden behind the waterfall. Enraged, he confronted her. 'You are so stupid at times. You know where all the microphones are! What the hell did you take him up there for? You must have known I couldn't record you.'

'Maybe I didn't want you to see or hear me with him,' Laura said.

'*What?*'

'Nothing,' she said, looking at her watch. 'I should go. I don't want to keep Angela waiting.'

Justin pretended to pay attention to the dials on the console in front of him. 'How are you going to work on her?' he asked.

'Dahlia is helping,' Laura replied.

'In what way?' he snapped.

Laura ran her fingers through her hair. 'Angela and I share a predilection for lace lingerie, I'm told. Now, thanks to Dahlia "mixing things up in the wash", she has a few pairs of my panties.'

'Well, don't fucking take her up to the waterfall to do it. Did you by the way?' he asked moodily.

'Did I what?' she said, opening the door.

'Screw him?'

'Not yet,' and she closed the door. She felt disturbed about lying to Justin, so to calm her nerves she slipped off the solitaire diamond and felt Max's toothmarks on her finger. It kept him constantly in her mind. A secret.

Angela heard the light tap on her door and removed the ice-pack from her head. 'Who is it?' she asked.

Laura remained silent.

Angela opened the door.

'Apparently, and I don't want to get her into any trouble which is why I came myself,' said Laura, 'Dahlia mixed some of my lingerie with yours.' She held out a small parcel. 'You have mine, I believe.'

'Oh,' Angelia said, and opened the wrapping. She seemed embarrassed as she admitted that the panties and brassière were indeed hers. She went to her wardrobe and opened a drawer to find Laura's. Laura followed her and stood close . . . too close.

Angela moved away. 'You're wearing a lovely perfume,' she said, intent on searching the open drawer.

'Thank you,' Laura said, then leaned close to Angela, who was wearing some kind of gardenia cologne. 'Yours is nice too.'

Angela withdrew Laura's panties from the drawer. 'Oh, they are lovely, and . . .' She took out a brassière and a gossamer-thin silk slip.

'I have them made to my designs,' Laura said, as she laid them on the bed, pressing tissue paper flat to wrap them. 'I love packing,' she said, and went on to explain how a nanny had taught her how to fold garments so they never creased. Eventually Laura looked up from her packing. She indicated the cross stitch Angela had left on the arm of the chair. 'What lovely work,' she said.

'Thank you,' Angela replied, then added hesitantly, 'would you like me to teach you how to do it?'

'Oh, that would be wonderful!'

Angela walked over to an armchair and picked up her bag. She took out some silks then found a small design of a rose. Laura perched on a chair arm. 'Oh, thank you,' she said, as Angela showed her the soft colours, from pink to oyster.

'I think these would be perfect for that rose.' Angela laid out the silks in a row.

'What delicate shades. And the stalk?'

'I'm sorry?'

'The stalk, the leaves and the thorns?' Laura looked into Angela's nervous hazel eyes.

'Oh, yes. Well, I have some greens, but not so many shades to choose from.' Laura leaned in close, her bare arms touching Angela's as the other woman threaded a needle. 'Now, it is imperative you make a good knot. It's so tedious if it works loose.' Angela was rather enjoying the beautiful girl's avid attention. 'Now, I'd begin with the outer, lower petal first. It's very simple and quite therapeutic, but there's an art in getting the stitches even. One tighter than the others leaps out conspicuously.'

Laura was genuinely interested. She had hardly held a needle before, and was so inept that Angela giggled. 'There's no need to be quite so rigid. Hold the needle lightly between your first finger and thumb.'

Laura jabbed in the needle and withdrew it so sharply she dug it into Angela's arm. 'I'm so sorry,' she leaped to her feet with concern as Angela rubbed the place where a pinprick of blood appeared. 'Oh, my goodness me,' Laura said, moving Angela's hand away. 'I'm so sorry.' She kissed the tiny speck of blood, then licked Angela's arm with her tongue.

'It's fine, really, it doesn't hurt,' Angela said, the flush of heat between her legs making her cheeks flame.

But Laura did not pull away. Instead she moved closer. 'I want you so much.'

Angela gasped and, shakily, said that Laura should leave. But Laura did not move away. She slid one arm around Angela, and opened her blouse. Angela felt as if her legs would buckle beneath her.

'I want you to dress in my underwear,' Laura whispered, as she licked Angela's neck, then flicked her tongue into an ear. By now, her hand was working a breast free of its lace, her fingers rubbing the nipple. She knew when she felt the nipple harden that it would be even easier than she had anticipated. 'You have the most incredible breasts.' She nuzzled Angela, then traced Angela's mouth with her fingertips, slipping one into her mouth. Angela began to suck as Laura drew the blouse away from the waistband of her skirt.

'Oh, yes, oh, yes,' Angela murmured, and began to drag her blouse free, to throw it to one side as Laura inched her skirt lower. 'Lock the door,' Angela gasped.

But Laura had drawn her skirt to her ankles and was on her knees, her tongue tracing the band of Angela's lace panties. She brought Angela down on to the floor, and couldn't resist glancing at the tiny red blinking dot in the corner of the room.

She tilted Angela's chin up. 'Surprising what a little prick can lead to!'

They both smiled, and Laura glanced again at the

camera lens, laughing because she knew that every moment had been filmed.

'I chatted to William Benedict this morning,' Annabella Bellingham said to her husband, as they drove back from Heathrow airport. Her husband barely looked up from his paper: it was enough for him that he had had to meet his wife. Conversation was surely beyond the call of duty. 'He seems rather nice, really. Not at all the sleazy character the newspapers had us think. We talked about that fellow Justin, the designer.'

'Wasn't he a friend of Oliver's?'

'That's right. Justin Chalmers.'

'Chalmers,' her husband repeated. Bellingham recalled Justin's face. He didn't know the boy terribly well, but now, somewhere in the fog of his mind, a bell was ringing.

His wife was powdering her nose. 'You remember him, you invited him to the party. Well, he's throwing some sort of bash over at Benedict's island while he's away.' She peered at herself in the tiny mirror. Just mentioning the party where Oliver had died had made her heart sink again and she steeled herself not to cry as she had just finished her make-up.

Annabella snapped shut her compact. 'Justin Chalmers is staying there with his sister, Laura.'

Her husband banged his hand down on the open newspaper. 'Justin and Laura! That's it, Justin and Laura. But Chalmers wasn't their name was it? What were they called?' He clenched his eyes in thought. 'Moorcroft, that's it. Child A and Child B, as they were known in the press. Justin and Laura Moorcroft. I knew I recognized them.'

'What are you talking about?'

Bellingham explained that while he was going through his drawers to find the relevant paperwork required for the shipment of Oliver's body back to England, he had come across some old files and documents belonging to his father.

'I don't understand what this has to do with the Chalmerses.'

'Wait, and I'll tell you. You know Father hoarded everything and that I'd always meant to clear out his desk but never got around to it? Well, I was tossing stuff into the wastepaper basket, when I found this file among a stack of others. It was headed "The Moorcroft Case".'

'The Moorcroft case?'

'Yes, I just said so, didn't I? I flicked through and caught sight of some photographs of a couple of children. I knew they looked familiar, but I couldn't put my finger on who they were.'

Bellingham pressed the intercom to speak to the chauffeur, turning to his wife as he did so. 'Did Benedict say where he was heading?'

'No, but he was on the same flight,' she said, as her husband barked at the driver to pass him his mobile phone.

'Do you know what you dial for Directory Enquiries?' he asked his wife.

'Ask the operator.' Sometimes the way her husband switched subjects infuriated Annabella. It was as if anything she had to say was immaterial. But she was taken aback when she heard him ask for Sir William Benedict's number. She sighed: he wouldn't be listed. She was right, but after numerous calls to friends, Bellingham succeeded. He had to talk to Benedict, urgently.

Angela walked on to the veranda for afternoon tea. The Baron and Baroness were arguing but stopped abruptly as they saw her approach.

'Oh, I'm gasping for a cup,' she said, sitting down primly, cross stitch bag at her side.

'Have you had a pleasant afternoon?' the Baron asked, as his wife poured tea.

Angela gave a girlish giggle. 'Yes, I have, as a matter of fact.' She was hoping Laura would join them, but next to arrive were Daphne and Clarissa Hangerford.

'Was that your husband I saw earlier?' the Baroness asked Daphne. 'On an outgoing boat?'

Daphne nodded. 'It's always the same. He just can't settle. He was worried about a horse or something. I didn't really understand. He just went all silent. To be honest, he's been impossible to deal with the past few days. And this morning, he sprang out of bed, determined to go home. That nice Justin has been so helpful arranging his flight. He asked if we wanted to go as well, but we've only just arrived.' She shrugged. 'So that's that.'

'Sod bloody Daddy,' said Clarissa. Her mother glanced at her. She had been in a terrible mood recently, and no matter how many times she'd asked why, Clarissa had refused to answer her.

Clarissa could not stop thinking about her father and every time she did she wanted to scream. She had washed herself over and over. Now she wanted to hit out and hurt someone, preferably him. Now the bastard had slunk off, afraid to face her. He was a perverted sexual deviant. He had fondled his own daughter's body as if she was a whore, then run away. 'Where's Max?' Clarissa asked, in a strained voice.

'I think he went waterskiing, didn't he?' Angela turned in the direction of the Baroness and smiled at James as he joined them.

'He is,' James said moodily, sitting beside his mother.

'I thought you were supposed to go out fishing with your father?' she tapped James's hand.

'Yes, well, he left without me.'

'Who left whom?' Justin said, strolling in.

'Dad,' James informed him. Justin had noticed, with interest, how keen James had been to talk to him. He seemed just as intrigued by Justin as he had been by Laura, if not more so. Justin decided to play on this.

'We came back hours ago,' he corrected James, and sat down beside him, allowing one muscular thigh to rest suggestively against him. 'Anyone seen Laura?' he asked noncommittally. Angela blushed. 'What about a trip to Tortola this evening?' he suggested. 'Spot of dancing?' James promptly said yes, as did Clarissa. Justin rubbed the back of James's neck. 'Good. Down at the jetty about six. We have to leave early for the tides.' He stood up abruptly and walked out.

When he left, they all fell silent. Only Daphne Hangerford had food on her mind; everyone else was thinking of sex. Daphne was delighted to be able to enjoy the rest of her stay without Cedric's nocturnal importuning. She had not the slightest notion that his last dalliance had involved her only child.

There was an hour to go before the boat left for the disco. Clarissa stood in front of the mirror. Her foul mood was lingering but not all consuming. Sometimes she felt as if two people were chattering away in her brain, one threatening to beat up her father and kick him in the balls, the other crying, reaching out for comfort, because she felt used, dirty and unbalanced. She'd tried on practically everything in her suitcase, but nothing pleased her. She went to the veranda and peered out, trying to see if anyone was on the jetty. She didn't want them to go without her.

'Hi, I was coming round to get you.' It was Justin. He was standing below her veranda.

'I'm on my way,' she said, giving him a coy smile and trying to keep her dress held up; it was unzipped at the back.

'You look as though you could do with a hand,' said Justin, climbing adroitly up the front of the veranda. 'Turn round,' he ordered, frogmarching her back into the room. Clarissa felt the zip being pulled but not up as she had expected. The dress fell round her ankles. 'Mmmm,' said Justin. 'Fancy a quick one?'

'What?' she said, startled.

'Drink,' he said laughing, drawing her closer and massaging her breast. He eased his body on to the bed and slowly unzipped his fly. 'Come here,' he said softly.

She had wanted him from day one. She had almost given up imagining that she stood a chance. There was a moment of fear when she remembered her father's sweating hands on her body, but this felt different, this was what she had been dreaming about. Justin was beautiful, with a perfect body. Clarissa edged closer and opened her mouth.

Justin kept an eye on his watch. To hurry things along he gripped her head and twisted his hands in her hair to force her to increase the rhythm. Clarissa gasped as he pushed himself deeper into her mouth. Mission completed, the little red dot capturing every second, he sprang away from the bed.

'My turn now,' she said, in what she thought was a sexy tone.

'Another time, sweetheart. We don't want to miss the tide.'

She sat on the crumpled bed as Justin left, slamming the door behind him. For a moment she was that little girl who wanted to cry and be comforted. Then she stood up, angry and bitter. Her father had treated her like a whore, and now Justin had too. She began to dress, telling herself she hated men: they were all bastards.

When he arrived in London, William was jet-lagged. He felt bloated and tired. Right away he had been forced to settle the sale of Katherine's house, and had gone straight there from the airport. The urgent e-mails from Michael had concerned the lawsuit against the von Gartens. He was required to make statements. His lawyers had become frustrated by the lack of contact, especially as William had been driving them to get things moving fast.

And there had been a new development: he discovered that lawyers representing Baron von Garten had

had the audacity to ask whether he had any interest still in purchasing the same factory that had been sold to his rival. No doubt this was the reason why the Baron had accepted the invitation to the island! Further enquiries, and illegal investigations into the Baron's financial situation had revealed that his own companies were now in deficit, and he was short of cash. The Baron's main asset was the shares he owned in the company that he had sold to William's competitors, but even they were feeling the pinch because four of their biggest selling items could now be proved to have first been patented by William's company.

The wheels were turning rapidly and in William's favour; he was delighted. He was even more buoyant when his lawyers, having received no contact from Hangerford, filed a backruptcy order. Cedric Hangerford's entire business was being sifted through by the men from the Inland Revenue and also by VAT officers. They were buzzing around his property like flies. While Hangerford was away, he had left his lawyers with power of attorney and his stable manager in charge of business dealings. Had he been there himself, no doubt he would have barred the door.

Now back in London, his business affairs in order, William decided to check up on Charlie at the clinic. He had to hold the line for over fifteen minutes as Charlie was tracked down and then, to his irritation, his son said he couldn't talk for long. He shared a few monosyllabic exchanges with Charlie then hung up. His conversation with Sabrina was equally tedious, but at least he was making sure his children were taken care of. He was just about to replace the receiver, when Sabrina asked if he had heard about Uncle Cedric. He was immediately on his guard: he had made no mention to his daughter that her aunt and uncle were on his island with Clarissa.

'It was in *The Times*. He's been made bankrupt. There was even a photograph. It was all over the racing papers too, even on Channel Four's racing programme. He looked terrible on TV,' Sabrina continued, as William digested the fact that Cedric was in London. He must have left the island shortly after William.

After he had said goodbye to Sabrina he placed a call to the island. He had a long wait before he was put through, and then was frustrated to be told by Dahlia that neither Justin nor Laura was around as they had gone to a night-club. He asked Dahlia to make sure Justin called him as soon as possible.

The phone rang in Michael's office.

'Sir William Benedict's residence . . . One moment, please.' Michael caught William heading for the stairs in the hall. 'Sir, it's Lord Bellingham.'

William frowned. 'Hello . . .' He perched on the edge of the desk, fiddling with the change in his pocket. 'Justin Chalmers, yes, that's correct . . .' He listened then stood up. 'Yes, he redesigned my . . .' His face darkened. 'Laura, that's right.'

'My father, Lord Chief Justice Bellingham, reviewed their case,' said Henry Bellingham. 'He often discussed it, long after they'd been forgotten about.'

He told William as much as he remembered of what he'd read in his father's file. William's hair stood on end. 'I had another look through the file,' continued Bellingham. 'Chalmers was their aunt's name. They must have taken that name after it all blew over. Moor-croft was their original name.' William sucked in his breath. 'Well, thank you for telling me, I appreciate it.' He hung up and drummed his fingers on the desk. 'Get my plane ready, Michael. I have to go to Nice immediately, and I'll need a car standing by. I'll drive myself.'

'But aren't you returning to the island?'

'No, Michael. I said Nice, as in France. Now!'

William found the driveway to Justin's villa even more beautiful than it had been before. There were so many different flowers, and the hidden lights gave a fairy-tale feel to the long lane. Marta was waiting on the steps and gave him a cautious welcome, surprised by his sudden arrival. As she showed him into the bedroom he had occupied before, William was struck by a strange feeling of comfort. The villa somehow felt more like home than any of his London houses or apartments.

He showered and changed before joining Marta in the kitchen, where she was baking bread.

'We need to talk, Marta,' he said gently. She busied herself, avoiding his gaze. 'Marta, we have things to discuss. Justin does not know I'm here.' She opened the oven to remove a loaf. 'I love Justin and Laura, and whatever we say now is not intended to be a betrayal. To be honest, I've grown closer to them than I am to my own children.'

She sat down opposite him, a little uncomfortable. 'I love them too,' she said.

'Tell me about them, from the beginning, or from when you first became a part of their lives,' he said.

338

Marta sensed his concern and intuitively knew that something was wrong. 'May I ask why?'

William hesitated and then explained his situation; his reasons for being there and his growing friendship with Justin. But not until he began to elaborate on the island and the payback game did Marta become attentive.

She chewed her lower lip and sighed. 'The children had an aunt Frances who lived at Mole Cottage in a village near Aylesbury. I had known her since we were schoolchildren. When she discovered that my husband had died and I was in financial difficulties, she asked if I would become her companion. I accepted.' William wondered where this was going to lead, but did not interrupt. 'Frances had lost contact with her brother, Martin, whom she described as a malicious boy. Martin Moorcroft was married to a frivolous Frenchwoman, Madeleine. A great beauty and a socialite. I never met her.' Again Marta fell silent, twisting her hands. 'Martin had two children, Justin and Laura.' She plucked at her skirt. 'He was a man who should never have had children.'

'I don't understand.' William leaned forward.

Marta shifted her weight and her cheeks flushed. Then she spoke quickly. 'He was arrested for molesting a little girl when he was still young himself. He was a paedophile, a masochistic, a horrible man, who married a woman with equally disgusting tendencies. The pair, it seemed, were well matched.'

William looked directly at Marta. 'Were Laura and Justin . . .'

Marta had tears in her eyes. 'From a very early age.

They were immersed in a living nightmare. And who could they turn to? How could they know that theirs was not a normal childhood?'

William waited, but this time Marta paused for a considerable time. 'What in God's name happened, Marta?'

She was openly crying now, delving into her apron pocket for her handkerchief. 'A child can only take so much.'

'So what happened?'

'Come with me,' said Marta, and led him through the giant oak door to the wine cellar.

'Are you taking your medication?' asked Justin.

'Of course,' replied Laura. 'There's no need to get snappy. I'm doing everything we arranged. What's the matter with you?'

He caught her in his arms. 'You aren't being silly with Max, are you? I want them to go soon and they'll take him with them.'

'Can't he stay?'

He pushed her away. 'For God's sake, you know why he can't. We've discussed it.' He changed the subject, pointing to film footage of the Baron with the boat-boys. 'When he wasn't screwing them he was pawing Karl in the gymnasium. The Baroness just ignores it.'

'Two such awful parents,' said Laura quietly, 'have made such a sweet child.'

'Oh, God, I don't believe I heard you say that. Sweet child!'

'He's a nice boy, with beautiful manners. He's also

well educated. At least you can have an intelligent conversation with him.'

'Really?' Justin teased. 'Well, perhaps you should make sure you have these intelligent conversations within range of the microphones because so far he's the only one you keep skirting around.'

'I do not.'

'Yes, you do, and I'm sick of it. The rules are clear. You get every single one of them, Laura. That's what you're being paid for. Now, I've got to call William and give him a progress report. What do you want me to tell him? That you think that little prick is a sweet boy?'

'I want to speak to him when he calls,' she said.

'Now you're really annoying me,' snapped Justin. 'So go. Go on, get out.'

Laura wandered to the door then turned back to him. 'Don't get nasty with me, Justin, you know how it upsets me.'

He forced a smile and told her he loved her, but she had gone before he could kiss her and make up. He knew he had been brusque with her, and part of him excused it because he was getting closer to their pay-back. Only one of the guests mattered to Justin, the main man, and he couldn't care less about the others. He didn't want anything to go wrong so he was being over-cautious with Matlock. But although he tried to remain calm, tension was building in him. And he could not admit that he was jealous of that kid Max. It infuriated him.

The wine cellar, unlike the rest of the house, had not been renovated, but remained almost as it had been

341

when Justin and Laura were children. Marta lit some candles.

'They must not be hurt,' said Marta. 'They are still children, especially Laura. She is the most fragile. She cannot be without Justin, she is dependent on him. Without him she would be locked up again.'

'Laura?' asked William, perched on a dusty barrel in the dark. The damp cellar chilled him. 'Has she been locked up in the past, then?'

Marta was rooting about behind a rack of red burgundies. 'Most of her life,' she whispered, and pulled out a dusty cardboard box. Inside was a black leather photograph album filled with newspaper cuttings. She passed it to William and sat silently beside him, letting him read.

The headlines were beyond belief: 'Killer Angels', 'Deadly Babes', 'Devil Children Let Loose'. On and on went the hideous clippings, describing what William now knew to be two tragic children.

'They killed both their parents?' he asked. Marta nodded. 'And the police were called by the nanny?'

'That's right,' said Marta, pointing to a photo of her. 'They stabbed her and pushed her into the pool, but by some superhuman effort she dragged herself out and crawled down to the village where she raised the alarm.'

William wondered why the police hadn't picked up on Justin's background when Maynard died. He had been the main beneficiary of Maynard's will, after all. Then he remembered that children's criminal records are only kept for a few years. As they grew up, the pair must have been given a clean slate and allowed to go free. Furthermore, the children had adopted a new name, Chalmers. Provided they were never caught again, the police would be none the wiser.

'What happened to the nanny in the end?' asked William.

'She died in a car accident, I think. I recall Justin reading something to me a few years back now – well, actually to Laura. I don't remember all the details, just that he was cutting out the article. I think I asked him who she was and . . .' Marta frowned. 'Is this important?'

'Yes, very.'

'Well, that's it, really. He was reading the newspaper and cutting it out. He said she had been their nanny. That's all.' Marta turned a few pages, then paused. She pointed to a clipping. 'This is about her funeral in London.'

'Camilla Maynard.' William's stomach churned. 'Did she have a brother, cousin, any relative called Andrew?'

He had a vision of the dead man floating in the overflowing bathtub, the water pink. He felt the sweat trickle down his back as he recalled Maynard talking about a much older sister who had died in a car accident. It had to be a coincidence, he thought, but he shuddered as he now saw the story's chilling logic.

'Answer me. It's very important, Marta. Have you ever heard Justin mention Andrew Maynard? In connection with this nanny, perhaps?'

'I don't think so.'

'But you must have met him, surely. He stayed here at the villa – a tall, dark-haired man. A young English politician.'

Marta hesitated, and nodded slowly.

'Ah yes, I did meet him, I mean, I served him his meals once or twice. But really, I hardly spoke to him.'

'But he came here frequently. You must know more.'

'Well, Justin explained that he wanted to be alone with him as much as possible, so I sometimes went on vacation when he came. Sometimes I went to see Laura. She was booked into clinics, you know, when she relapsed. She's very fragile . . . physically as well as mentally.'

William asked her to continue her story of their childhood.

'French law decreed that they couldn't be locked up or tried there. They were too young. They were sent instead to a specialist psychiatric unit for disturbed children in England and my friend, Frances, took them into her home, as I told you. All was fine, until a budding young journalist wanted a scoop to kick off his career. He pressed on and on, determined to get his story. It became clear that they could not attend school, could not live in an ordinary home without people throwing bricks through the window. The stress of being hounded made them both become difficult. I don't know exactly what went on. All I do know for sure is that they were taken away, separated.' She showed William a garish paperback book. 'Their case was then taken up by the British courts.'

'Lord Chief Justice Bellingham,' muttered William under his breath. The pieces of the jigsaw were slowly fitting together.

'Justin was sent to borstal, Laura to a psychiatric hospital. The author probably didn't even know what he had done. He wrote about their separation as if he had made some successful coup, but he ruined their lives.'

William glanced down at the cover, emblazoned with a picture of two pretty children wielding an axe that dripped blood. *Angels or Devils?* It was by Humphrey Matlock.

The book smelt of the dank, musty cellar. It contained further pictures: Laura's frightened face as a small child being carried by a police officer, Laura's face at a barred window, Laura in a garden aged twelve. There were more snatched photographs that had obviously been taken from some distance by the spying journalist, each one slightly blurred.

One photograph in particular made William want to weep: Laura in a car with raindrops trickling down the window, waving, a sweet smile on her angelic face. Then came pictures of Justin, who, unlike his sister, showed no sign of terror on his boyish face. He glared out from one photograph after another. There was one of him in a blaze of anger, hurling something towards the camera. There were a few photographs of the children together, hand in hand in sombre school uniforms. In the last section, there were pictures of their parents. William tried hard to imagine exactly what these two inhuman creatures could have been like. Their father's eyes seemed pale and washed-out. His close-cropped hair and tidy beard made him look like D. H. Lawrence. Hard as he tried, William could not detect cruelty in their appearance. The last picture showed their mother holding Laura on her knee, her husband standing behind her chair with his hand resting on his small son's shoulders. They looked like a normal happy family.

William read the book from cover to cover. It was, he hated to admit, well written and engrossing. He was intrigued when he read a quote from a nanny, who had obviously refused to give her name, which described the way the children had made sexual advances towards her and attempted to kill her. She was quoted as saying: 'I knew from the first day I began caring for them that these were not normal children. They were too well behaved. Their manner was formal, and they seemed to be constantly entwined, at times speaking as one. The boy was over-protective of his sister. They even slept together. I saw them feed each other like birds. Yet, on the surface they looked like angels. I soon discovered a terrible, dark side to them. They frightened me. They were truly evil. Maybe they became that way because of whatever they had been subjected to by their parents. But I will never forget the nightmare I became embroiled in, and all I want now is to forget I ever met them. But it is hard to forget the sight of Laura and Justin, with their father's blood dripping from their hands. It has haunted me.'

With that comment hanging in his mind, William closed his eyes. He felt leaden. He, too, had become embroiled in their lives, but he believed them to be far more dangerous as adults. It gradually dawned on him that he had been used. He now knew that the charade into which he had been drawn had been set up for one reason alone. William chastized himself for his blindness. How could he have allowed this to go on? His weakness and vanity gave him the answer. He had so wanted to get back at people and he had believed the lies he had been told because he wanted to. If he had applied just a modicum of his intellect, he would surely have been suspicious. He bowed his head, ashamed. He knew deep down in his heart that he had uncovered the truth. All along he had been suspicious about Maynard's death and particularly the suicide note. Had Justin murdered him and written the note?

He recalled how Justin had gone through his hit-list, leaving only four main targets. No matter which way he looked at the overall picture, it was so sick it beggared belief. He recalled asking Justin whether or not he should invite his victims' children, and he had replied that William's own son and daughter had suffered at the hands of the press, so why not? He felt the ground opening up beneath him; dear God, had Oliver Bellingham been a part of it too? He was Lord Chief Justice Bellingham's grandson after all. Had Justin's revenge been planned to hurt even the younger, innocent generation? His blood ran cold. On the island there were three kids: James Matlock, Clarissa Hangerford and Max von Garten. Was Justin directing his madness against them? Hadn't he said that they deserved to be punished?

William paced up and down erratically, as his mind jumped backwards and forwards. He had *agreed*, he had encouraged Justin! The sins of the fathers . . . Dear God! What monster had he released in his name? The fear that Justin would hurt the women and their children escalated in him. But surely even Justin wouldn't do that, would he? But Oliver Bellingham was dead . . .

CHAPTER 17

Max had been waiting almost an hour at Suicide Point and was about to give up when he saw her running, her skirt held high in her hands and her wonderful hair flying loose like a silver wave. His heart leaped with joy as he held out his arms. She threw herself into them and hugged him tightly. 'Oh, I have missed you so much, but I just couldn't get away to see you. We have to be so careful.' They embraced and then she eased him forward.

'Laura, take care, we're very close to the edge,' Max said.

She laughed at him. 'Don't be afraid. Are you scared to look down?'

'Terrified,' he said, holding her hand tightly.

They linked arms and, from a safe distance, looked over the edge to the swirling water thrashing the rocks below.

'Would you jump if I asked you to?' she asked.

'No, because it would mean I had to leave you.'

'Would you jump if I was dead?'

He drew her close. 'Don't say things like that, even as a joke.'

'I'm sorry.' She wrapped her arms around his neck and kissed him.

Justin saw them embracing like lovers and his face tightened with jealousy but he couldn't look away. He called her name. Laura drew away from Max and listened.

'It's Justin,' Max said, pointing, and they looked along the narrow pathway to where he stood.

'We're going to Tortola tonight. Are you coming?'

Max looked at Laura, who hesitated. 'I can't,' she said, then smiled at Max. 'You go. It'll be fun.'

'I want to be with you,' Max said.

'I can't, I have to . . . see someone. It's arranged.'

'Is it Justin?' asked Max. 'You don't want to come because of him?'

Justin was jumping the rocky surface, getting closer. 'Yes, yes. We must keep our love secret. Trust me. I don't want William to hear any rumours about us, not until I've told him face to face.'

Justin was beside him. He hooked his arm around Max. 'You coming?'

'Er, yes, why not?'

'Run along, then. Go get your glad rags on. You've got about twenty minutes to get that fluff off your chin.'

Max looked at Laura, but she averted her eyes and he had no option but to leave them. He hated the way Justin had spoken to him, as if he was a twelve-year-old.

As soon as Max was out of earshot, Laura punched her brother. 'You needn't have done that,' she said.

'I did! Sneaking off to places you know I can't film or record. I'd say you were doing it to make me jealous.'

'Don't be silly.'

'I'm not being silly. We don't have much time and we have an agenda to keep. Next minute William's gonna be back, before we've done the dirty deed. Or deeds.'

'I'm on schedule. Haven't you seen the videos from this afternoon?'

'Not yet.'

'I've done the deed with Angela Matlock so I'm getting the job done. Are you?'

'I'm sorry,' said Justin, pulling Laura towards him. 'It's just this Max thing. I don't want you distracted, and you are.'

'I'm fond of Max and I don't see what's wrong with that. And with him it's fun. It's always horrible with everyone else. I notice you seem to enjoy teasing the Matlocks' son.'

'So you've fallen for him?'

'I have not. He's young, he's naïve, and sometimes it's nice to get screwed without a hidden agenda,' she lied.

Justin lifted her hair away from her face and kissed her neck.

'No, Justin, not here.' She had never rejected him before.

'I want you.'

She felt like weeping: lie was beginning to follow lie. 'I want you too, but please not here. Someone might see.'

Justin nuzzled and kissed her cheek. 'You're right. It's me who's dumb. It's just that seeing you screwing everyone else keeps turning me on.'

'Never bothered you before.' She was calming down

now, more in control. 'You get into such bad tempers, don't you?'

'Maybe because I know we're about to reach the big climax, and I don't want anything to distract us. We're so close, Laura, so close. I just want everyone gone, off the island so we can be together. But we can't until it's done.'

He turned away from her, his eyes brimming with tears, and she could barely hear what he was saying. 'I get scared. I know I couldn't do it on my own, not without you. I've always needed you.'

She linked her arm with his. She could never resist him when he was like this, vulnerable. 'If anyone's around I'm not going inside your room with you.'

'There's no one,' he whispered, but he knew there was. He knew the lovesick boy was watching them.

As they were heading for Justin's bungalow, James looked out of his window. Although he didn't spot Laura and Justin, he saw Max approaching, pushed open the shutters and shouted to him, 'Hey, Max, you coming with us?'

Max whipped around, startled. He wanted to follow Laura and Justin. 'Bit tired. Listen, I've got to go.'

Max tried to walk on, but James was still talking to him. 'You were waterskiing with Justin again today, weren't you?'

'Yes, I was. Listen, James, I really have to go.'

'Where to?'

Max sighed with impatience. 'For Christ's sake, James, I'm gonna see my parents.'

James hesitated, then said, 'Is he coming on to you?'

'What?' Max was confused.

'You heard. Is Justin hitting on you?' James's face was flushed.

'You're talking like an idiot, James. Why? Has he been coming on to you?'

James shouted, 'You calling me a poof?'

'Jesus Christ, James, what's the matter with you?'

James leaped from his veranda and swung a punch at Max, who staggered and fell. Before he could get to his feet, James kicked him in the groin. 'Stay away from him, you hear me? Just stay away from Justin.' He went back into his own room and straight for the cocaine. He didn't bother to chop a line, but stuck his nose over the vial and snorted till his eyes smarted and ran with tears.

Justin's attentiveness to James had gone unnoticed by the others, although he had made sure he constantly brushed against the younger boy as he helped him up into the ski-boat from the water, or to put on his sub-aqua gear. At times, he casually laid an arm across James's shoulders. James was quicker on the uptake than Justin had expected, an easier fish to bait than his father would be. The truth, of course, was that Justin was not at all interested in James.

Justin was sure that James was bisexual and had had more than a few experiences beyond schoolboys' hot kisses. It would have been fun breaking Matlock's son in to some sex games, but he doubted the boy would need much encouragement, which took all the enjoyment out of it for himself. What Justin had not

352

contemplated, though, was that James would become obsessed with him, as Oliver Bellingham had. Perhaps he would die like him too.

Max wiped his bloody nose on his sleeve and took his time getting back on his feet. His balls felt like they were on fire. He rubbed his crotch then headed to his own room, grabbed some ice, wrapped it in a napkin and held it over his face. James was obviously as high as a kite.

'That Justin is a prick,' he muttered, then flopped back on to the bed. He decided he had to talk to Laura. He didn't want to go to the nightclub.

James ran to Justin's bungalow and kicked open the front door, shouting his head off. Hurriedly Laura drew the sheet across her bare breasts, but before Justin could get out of bed, the bedroom door burst open and James barged in. Laura flipped the sheet over her head; she didn't need this, didn't need anyone seeing her being intimate with Justin, let alone naked in bed beside him.

'You lost something?' Justin said casually, leaning back on the pillows and reaching for his cigarettes. 'Don't tell me you've run out of the four grams I gave you last night?'

James shifted his weight from one foot to the other then pointed to the bed. 'I know who's there. I know you've been playing us off against each other and I don't like it. You're a piece of shit.' His face was red with fury.

Justin tossed his lighter on to the bedside table. 'Get out of here, James, before I lose my temper.'

James stuck out his bottom lip like a spoilt child. 'No, I won't.' He dived round the bed and snatched off the sheet. When he saw Laura he stumbled backwards. Confused, he looked from her to Justin, who was smiling, the smoke drifting from his nostrils. 'What's she doing here?' he said. 'She's your sister!'

Justin inhaled deeply and his eyes narrowed. He glanced at Laura, as if to give her a signal. She caught it and, even though she was furious, she controlled herself, stretching her arms above her head, finally dropping the sheet to reveal her breasts.

'Come here,' Justin said to James, the cigarette stuck in the corner of his mouth. James hesitated but then, as if he was hypnotized, walked slowly towards Justin and stood a foot away from the bed.

'Closer,' Justin said, tilting his head so that the cigarette smoke drifted into his eyes.

'No,' James whispered.

Justin reached out and hooked one finger into the leg of James's shorts. 'Naughty boy, come here.' He drew James towards him and began to undo his zip. As he did so he glanced at the bedside clock. 'We don't have long. We're going dancing tonight, aren't we?'

'Yes,' James croaked.

'Mmm, Laura, I think I might need some assistance here.'

James closed his eyes and his legs trembled, but he couldn't move as Laura crawled over the bed towards him. Justin stubbed out his cigarette, eased off the boy's T-shirt and began to pour oil into his hand. Laura drew the frightened boy to lie between them.

*

Max looked at his bruised eye in the bathroom mirror. The ice had reduced the swelling so he rinsed his face with cold water and patted it dry. He put on a clean shirt and light trousers, and slipped his feet into rubber flip-flops. Returning to the bathroom he caught his reflection in the mirror. His blond hair was silvery now from the sun, his pale skin tanned a light golden brown. He was struck at first by his resemblance to his mother, and then became rather pleased by the change in his appearance. He could see the effects of his love affair, as strong as the effect of the sun on his slender body. He would have been embarrassed to admit it, but he suddenly realized that he was, as his mother called him, 'a beautiful boy'.

James lay face down on Justin's bed, sobbing into a pillow. He had crossed a line in his life that he had always known was there, but was too afraid to face. He was still weeping as Justin came out of the bathroom, showered and changed. He looked at James, annoyed to see him still lying there. 'You'd better get yourself together. We're leaving in five minutes.'

James rolled over painfully. 'Come on.' Justin hauled him upright. 'Get down to the jetty. I'll see you there.'

James stumbled out of the room. Across his back were deep red welts, and in some places the skin was broken, leaving small beads of blood.

Laura came out of the bathroom, buttoning her blouse. She was angry. 'I said that was risky, but you wouldn't listen to me. What if he starts talking about us?'

'Don't be a fool. You really think that Master Matlock is going to rush to Mummy!'

'Or Daddy,' she said coldly.

'No way is he going to spill the beans on us. I'll make sure of it by the end of tonight.' He left for the boat, and Laura returned to her room. She looked out of her window and could see Clarissa and Justin boarding the speedboat. She wanted to see Max, and be alone with him without Justin monitoring them. She had an agenda, worked out by Justin, but she would follow her own now too. She dialled Max's number.

He sounded so pleased to hear from her that her spirits lifted. They agreed to meet by the waterfall.

'We need to talk,' he said.

'Yes, I think we do,' she said softly, and hung up.

Max flopped back on to the bed. 'She wants me,' he said aloud. 'Laura Chalmers, my beautiful goddess, wants me.' He was unaware that James had overheard him from his adjacent veranda, and had realized he'd been wrong about Max and Justin.

Laura was shaking with nerves, but had almost made up her mind. She was unsure if she had the strength to do it. It would be up to Max to persuade her. Laura was forming a plan to leave the island and Justin. He had said he doubted that he could handle Matlock on his own, and she was sure he couldn't. She was not intending to back out of the murder, though: she just had to make it happen faster than planned. It was imperative to get the Baron and Baroness off the island, leaving Max with her. She knew Justin could easily handle Clarissa and James, and Daphne, that fat, foolish woman, wasn't the problem. Laura's problem was Justin. She had got away with lying to him already. Now she planned on doing much more, because she knew she had to escape him.

'Yes, yes,' she whispered, and told herself that she had made the right decision, unaware that she was pacing up and down the room. If Marta or Justin had seen her doing this, the rapid footsteps, the urgent instructions, repeated to herself more vehemently each time, they would have been worried. Marta always knew this was the first danger sign. The second was when Laura made brushing strokes down her thigh. On these occasions, Marta acted fast, and doubled Laura's medication. But Marta was a long way away. This time Laura was on her own.

CHAPTER 18

WILLIAM CAUGHT the night flight back to London. He phoned Michael from the villa, asked him to check out Camilla Maynard and arrange a flight to the Caribbean. He intended to leave immediately after his arrival in England.

Michael didn't phone back until William was in the limousine coming into London from Heathrow. He confirmed that Camilla had been Andrew Maynard's sister. Had Justin known from the beginning and used William from the moment he had visited that awful mews cottage in London? He was sure now that Justin had forged the suicide note.

When he got back Michael was waiting for him, although it was after ten. 'Get me Charlie on the line,' William shouted at him, dropping his bag and making for his study.

By the time he was at his desk, the call was put through. William snatched up the receiver. 'Charlie? The letter,' shouted William down the line. 'The one you told me about, from Oliver Bellingham. Have you still got it?'

'Oh, it's somewhere in my stuff,' he drawled. 'But, Dad, let me tell you about—'

'No time,' shouted William. 'Is the letter in the stuff you left here?'

'The big black canvas bag. No! Maybe the duffel bag or in the small gym bag. It's somewhere amongst my gear. What's the problem?'

'Can I read it?' William pressed on.

'Why?'

'It's a matter of life and death,' said William.

'Oh, yeah right, sure, man. I mean it's personal but, like, go ahead.'

William gripped the receiver. 'I love you, son,' he said, 'but I'm in a great hurry. I'll speak to you later, OK?'

William took another deep breath and ran upstairs to the room where Charlie had left his bags. Furiously he rummaged through odd shoes and dirty shorts, until he spotted a gym bag that was full of exercise books, loose pages from *Biker* and music magazines. There were bundles of letters from Katherine to Charlie at school. At last, in a worn and well-thumbed air-mail envelope, he found the letter from Oliver Bellingham. The large sloped handwriting began 'Hello, Wanker!' Next to the greeting, Oliver had drawn a grinning cartoon face. In the first few paragraphs, he described life on Tortola, the surfing and the clubs. He also mentioned that keeping straight was tough on the island, where everything was accessible in vast quantities, especially the ganja. There was another grinning cartoon face. There was some reference to his girlfriend and a lot of dots and dashes after her name, and then an underlined passage about receiving a letter from her so that it appeared 'all was not lost'. This was underlined three times. Oliver mentioned the forthcoming 'wrinklies party'. He was quite looking forward to it because he had met this bloke called Justin in the Harbour Bar. 'He's a really great guy. Very handsome – blond, taller than me and quite a bit older. I've been with him on and off most days and nights.' He wrote that he'd invited Justin to his folks' party – his parents didn't really want him to come, but he didn't care. Justin had promised to bring some gear so it would be a behind-the-bushes job.

A young boy's infatuation with a handsome older man had led to his death. William knew Justin and his sister had been killers as children, but he was also certain they had not stopped killing. He was sure that between them they had murdered both Andrew Maynard and Oliver Bellingham. God knew how many others there had been, perhaps even Maynard's sister. William was determined to find out. The other thought that dawned on him, but oddly did not frighten him, was that perhaps he, too, was earmarked as a victim.

He traced an aunt of Maynard's, his only living relative, as far as William could tell. He did not make excuses as to why he had called out of the blue but came straight to the point. 'This is William Benedict, an old friend of your nephew's.'

'I know who you are. I've read all about you in the press. Why are you calling?'

'I think it is possible Andrew was murdered.'

'Really? Whatever makes you think that? Are you sure you want to open this all up again? I'd hate to have the press coming down here.'

'I'll make sure they don't.'

'I doubt that you of all people would be able to do that. I'm old and I don't want to get involved in any scandal.'

'Please, could you tell me how his sister died.'

'What's she got to do with this?'

'Perhaps nothing, but do you know how she died?'

'A car crash. She was planning to visit me here in Brighton when she died. Her brakes failed on the motorway. I don't know the technical details. It happened years ago, I think it was in March 1992.'

'Did you ever meet someone called Justin Chalmers?'

'I don't think so. Unless . . . Is he the young man who . . .' She trailed off, and William held his breath. 'No, I'm sure I don't know that name. All I do know is that shortly before Camilla's death she met a couple. I thought it was a bit strange because they didn't come to her funeral. They were apparently the last people to see her. If I remember correctly they met her somewhere in London.'

'Did she describe them?'

'No, but I think they were foreign. European, possibly French. I think they had offered her work as nanny to their children. She used to work in France . . .'

'Thank you,' William said, desperate to hang up but forced to hold on out of civility.

William was certain the couple had been Justin and Laura, just as he was sure that they were preparing to kill Humphrey Matlock. He felt powerless to stop them. As for the staff, could he trust them? They had been hired by Justin. He groaned. The last thing he wanted was to involve the police, even though he knew he should. He felt Matlock was probably safe while there were plenty of other people on the island. He knew that neither Justin nor Laura had any personal grievance against the Hangerford family or the Baron – surely they would not harm them? But William was not due to return for three more days. Could he make it in time to stop the madness or had he unwittingly become a party to murder?

The voice of sanity told William to contact the police immediately. But insanity was taking over. Or perhaps it was his own survival instinct. Perhaps he had sensed all along that something was amiss and it was this part of his brain that that had arranged for him to leave them on the island to their own endgame. God Almighty, he mused, I played right into Justin's hands. If he was to contact the police, he would be forced to incriminate himself: he would have to explain how he had come to this conclusion. In any case, how could he possibly explain the situation to anyone? No one would believe him. And he would be humiliated by the press again if they got so much as a whisper of this. He'd probably be arrested as an accomplice, or done up in a strait-jacket.

'Get hold of the goddamn reins, William,' he muttered to himself. 'Stand up and sort this mess out.' It was now imperative he return to the island, but he knew he had to do it without ringing alarm-bells for either Justin or Laura. He closed his eyes, trying to think like Justin. Who could he trust to have a boat standing by to pick him up? He had to arrive without their knowledge.

'Money, you old fool, buys you anyone and anything,' Justin's voice rasped in his ear.

William decided that Dahlia should be the one and only person to know he was returning ahead of schedule and to keep it secret.

*

Max waited almost an hour. When Laura didn't appear, he thought at first he must have misheard the meeting-place. Could it have been Suicide Point? He was sure she had said the waterfall. He returned to his bungalow and called her from there. The phone rang and rang, but there was no reply. He tried Justin's bungalow, but again there was no reply. Max returned to the cliff-tops, making a round trip from one of their secret meeting-places to another. Still no sign of Laura. He returned a second time to his bungalow. He had been waiting for her for almost two hours.

Laura could hear the phone. She was lying on the floor, stiff and cold. Slowly she forced herself to rise and unsteadily made her way into the bathroom to bathe her face. It was another fifteen minutes before she could function fully. Her mind was woolly and she'd bruised her hip when she fell, but she had no recollection of what had taken place. All she knew was that it had happened many times before, when Marta had been at hand to take care of her. Laura examined her body for the telltale marks, but just as she was about to reach for her medication, the phone rang again.

'Laura? It's Max. I've been frantic.'

'William called and I had to be up at the main house. I've got a migraine.'

'I'm back in my bungalow. Do you want to come here or . . .'

Laura was tired. She knew she needed to sleep. But instead she agreed to meet Max, afraid that if she didn't he would turn up on her doorstep.

'Five minutes.'

363

'No, two,' he demanded, and said he would be outside waiting.

During the long walk to the cliffs Laura felt exhausted. Max rested his arm on her shoulder, and she ached to lie down and sleep, but gradually the cool breeze off the ocean cleared her head.

'Feeling better?' Max asked, concerned.

'Mmm, yes, I'm fine.'

'Good.' He kissed her neck, then held up her hair. 'How did you do this?' He touched the purple marks.

'I fell against the cabinet in the bathroom coming out of the shower. It's nothing.' As if to prove it she began to run as they arrived at the end of the path leading to the open cliff-top. Max watched her spinning and turning, her hair billowing out, her arms raised above her head like a dancer's. She was so fragile, he was afraid the wind would scoop her up and blow her away. She danced to the mossy area where the edge of the cliff dropped to the sheer rocks below, and flopped down. Max joined her. He had picked a posy of blue flowers, and tucked them into her hair by her ear.

'Let me lean against you, as if you were my rock,' she said.

Max swivelled around, and felt her body heat as she leaned her back against his.

'Wouldn't it be nice if life was always this perfect?' she said.

'It would, but it never is. Tell me about Justin,' he said, and felt her spine stiffen.

'You see that little black cloud high in the sky, over there to the right?' She pointed upwards. 'That's Justin. He makes the sun go in sometimes, but then you see it peep out again. Justin has always made me believe that he controls the sun.'

Laura found it easier to tell Max what she had to say without looking at him. Even though she skirted around the horror of her childhood, explaining that the fire that killed her mother was an accident and the attack against her father had been in self-defence, it still sounded like a nightmare. For the first time in her life, Laura was telling someone who was not a psychiatrist about her past. She told him about the long years in homes, about the electrocution therapy, the drugs that left her with no memory for about five years. She admitted that her relationship with Justin must be difficult for an outsider to understand. 'We only had each other, so we must seem unnaturally close.' Laura pressed herself into him. 'He is very dominating and I allow him to be so. If it had not been for him, I might never have been released from the home and allowed to return to France. I owe Justin . . . I owe him everything. And I was content for him to be the most important person in my life until . . .'

'Until?' Max asked softly.

'You,' she said simply.

'Do you love me, Laura?' he asked, holding his breath.

'You are open and trusting and . . .'

'You didn't answer my question.'

He turned towards her and she looked into his face. 'Yes,' she said.

He took her hand and kissed the palm then drew her close to rest against him.

'I know I'm young and inexperienced, just a kid, but

365

I also know I love you, Laura. I want to make up for all those hideous years and make you happy.'

'You do,' she whispered, loving the feel of his arms around her.

'I want to be with you. Will you leave and come with me?' he asked.

'I don't know. That's impossible, isn't it? Besides, Justin would never let me go.'

'Then don't tell him, just leave. We could leave right now. Will you come with me?'

'Yes,' she said. 'Yes, of course I will.'

'When?'

'As soon as possible, but—' She broke off and took a deep breath as the little black cloud covered the sun, like an omen. 'We're just being foolish. Justin would find me, no matter where you took me. And I don't think your parents would approve. You're much too young.'

Max stood up and drew her to stand in front of him. 'I am not. I have a trust fund, so money is no problem. I knew I loved you from the moment I saw you. My parents will have to know, but so will William.'

'When he calls I'll tell him.'

'No, Laura, you can call him. Besides, I thought you'd spoken to him this afternoon.'

'No, no, I didn't. I had such a migraine,' she lied.

Max put his hands on his hips. 'You told me it came on after you spoke to him. Don't treat me like some idiot. I'm serious. I love you. I want to get out of this place. I want you to get away from your brother.'

'Justin will go to any lengths to stop me leaving with you.'

'Then we'll escape without his knowing. We could

go right now, while he's off the island.' He caught her face between his hands and kissed her.

'Believe me, Justin must not find out.' Her voice caught in her throat.

'You sound as if you're scared of him. Are you using him as an excuse? I don't mind telling him. I'm not afraid of him.'

'Oh, Max, I'm scared he'll make me feel so guilty I won't be able to leave. And I do want to, I really do.'

'Well, I'm not scared. We can go and tell my parents, now, then wait for him and confront him.'

'No, we can't do that. He'll turn you against me and make you hate me. Justin has a powerful hold over me. You have no idea how much it took for me to come to you today. Justin is already jealous of you, he already suspects I care for you, that he is no longer the centre of my universe.'

'How much does he know?' Max asked.

'Enough.' She traced his jaw-line with a finger. 'He only has to look at me to know. I find it hard not to smile when you're close to me. In fact, when you're anywhere near I want to look at you, touch you.'

He clasped her to him again. She was saying words that filled him with passion: words he had only dreamed of hearing. Nothing had ever sounded so sweet.

Suddenly Laura pushed him from her. She felt somehow as if she was flying. 'Wait! I have a plan. The mail-boat docks at our quayside at about six in the evening. We can leave on it.'

'Tonight?' Max tingled, either with fear or excitement.

'No. It comes every other day. It's due tomorrow. Maybe we'll be able to leave then. If not, we have to wait just two more days. We can stay over on Tortola and catch a plane first thing the following morning.' She paced up and down, making brushing motions with her hand, a determined expression on her face. 'We'll stay apart until then, and the night we leave we must be careful not to give a clue to anyone, especially not Justin. You pack your bags, I'll pack mine, and we can leave them hidden close to the jetty. We'll meet up at Suicide Point. Say that you're taking a walk, so that no one suspects. I'll come via the lower path, you take the long route round. No one will be able to see either of us from the house on those routes, and from up there we can see the mail-boat coming in.'

'But if it always comes at six, why don't we just hide down there?'

'It's never on time, and we'll have to wait until Justin has collected the mail. He always takes the crew some beer and chats for a while before he brings the mail and the newspapers up to the house. When he's gone they sit and drink their beer on the boat. That'll give us time to get on board and leave the island without Justin seeing us or anyone suspecting anything.'

Max was so overcome that he didn't notice the deviousness of her plan, or that she had been able to make it so quickly. All he could think about was that she was agreeing to be with him. 'Until then, we keep apart, ignore each other. We must not give ourselves away.' Laura was excited, her face glowing, sure she had not overlooked anything. The fact that he was little more than a child and she an adult woman, fifteen years older than him, was unimportant. They were two people infatuated with each other, holding their world in their arms.

'Whatever you say. I'll be waiting.'

They kissed and parted, then ran back into each other's arms and kissed again, neither wanting to let the other go. Eventually Laura made him turn his back and ran until her lungs felt as if they would burst, her hair flying, her skirt caught in her hands above her thighs.

'We'll get married!' he shouted after her, and his voice caught the wind and echoed. But she didn't hear. He could see her figure darting and jumping, ducking beneath overhanging trees, and then she was gone.

Laura ran full tilt into Humphrey Matlock and lost her balance. He had to catch her or she would have slipped over, dangerously near to the cliff edge.

'Dear God, you're crazy. It's slippery here,' he said, still holding her arm. She gasped her thanks. Her cheeks were flushed, her eyes danced. She rested against him to regain her balance and catch her breath. 'I was looking for James,' he said.

'He's gone to Tortola for the evening.'

'Ah, well,' he said, towering above her. His black hair was tousled from the wind and his face was even more tanned after another day's fishing. 'Are you going back to the house?' he asked, and she nodded, walking backwards a few feet in front of him.

'Did you catch anything?' she asked flippantly.

'You mean apart from you?' He smiled. His teeth were large and slightly stained from the cigars he smoked. She could smell brandy on his breath. 'I didn't have a good day, but tomorrow we're planning to go further afield, start at the crack of dawn. I've not enjoyed myself so much in as long as I can remember.'

Matlock went on chatting to her, indicating with his hands the size of the fish he had lost, describing the dolphins and how close they had swum to the boat. Then he stopped and sniffed. 'God, smell the air, it's so fresh. But that perfume, it's all over the island.'

'It's lilies, Justin has them shipped in.' She spoke softly, glancing coyly at him. He looked down into her upturned, exquisite face. She gazed into his dark eyes as he lifted his hand and hooked one finger into the opening of her dress. He drew her a fraction closer. She felt his rough finger run along the lace of her brassière, then he withdrew his hand, afraid that he had gone too far.

'So you do want me,' she said softly.

Hoarsely he grunted, 'Yes.'

'Maybe one day we'll do something about it.' She turned and ran on, leaving him standing there with a huge hard-on, unfulfilled and feeling idiotic.

'Did you have a good day, darling?' Angela asked, as he turned on the shower.

'No.' He began to strip off his clothes. 'Caught bugger all.'

Angela looked at her watch. It was already almost eight. 'You were out a long time.'

'James didn't show up. I went to have a talk to him, but he's gone off to some disco. About all he's interested in doing.' He stepped out of his tracksuit. 'You do anything?' he asked, not really interested.

'I had a pleasant day.' She smiled. 'Would you like to order dinner before your shower?'

He glowered and said she could order for him, so

she walked out of the bathroom. She hated to see him naked. There was something so monstrous about him: with his deep-tanned face and arms and the hideous vest marks over his torso where his skin was still alabaster white. He was grotesque.

She ordered *filet mignon* for them both, a chilled tomato and lime soup and fruit. Then she called Daphne Hangerford to see if she would join them but received no reply, so she tried the Baroness instead.

'Have you heard?' drawled the Baroness, excitedly. 'Cedric Hangerford has gone bankrupt. The stud farm has gone, plus their two homes. It was all over *The Times*! That's why he ran off from here with his tail between his legs. He must have known!'

'How awful,' said Angela.

'Mmm, isn't it?' The Baroness hung up, wishing she had someone else to gossip with, and Angela realized that she hadn't mentioned dinner arrangements. Oh, well.

She was looking through her wardrobe, undecided as to what to wear, when Dahlia tapped on the door. Angela opened the door in her robe and Dahlia presented her with a small tissue-wrapped parcel tied with a pink ribbon. 'I was asked to make sure you received this before dinner,' she said.

'Thank you,' Angela said softly, and her heart fluttered. She couldn't wait to rip it open, sure of what it would be. And it was. A pair of Laura's panties and a little note asking her to wear them to dinner, as it would make her feel close. As a postscript she added that she longed for their next cross-stitch session.

*

371

Daphne Hangerford, her hair newly cut and tinted in what would have been a rather flattering style for someone twenty years younger, sat polishing her nails. The manicures had made a world of different to her hands but she had put on a considerable amount of weight over the holiday. Right now she didn't care; her brain wouldn't function and she was confused.

She had placed call after call to her husband, her lawyers, her trainers and the stables but she couldn't get through. She was distraught and even more so when she opened her purse and discovered she had only a small amount of money left. She had a cheque book but she couldn't use that and her credit cards were all heavily in the red. She was sure Clarissa didn't have any money with her. However, she had their return tickets for London and decided she was going to leave as soon as possible. Her panic spiralled out of control when she couldn't get hold of her daughter. When the phone rang she grabbed it but it was only the kitchen staff wanting her order for dinner.

She demanded to speak to someone about leaving immediately, and after a short while Dahlia knocked on the door. 'I have to get off this bloody island. I have to leave,' Daphne screamed.

'Certainly, Lady Hangerford. Would you care for your maid to pack your cases? You will be able to get the launch first thing in the morning – it leaves at seven fifteen. Will your daughter be accompanying you?'

'Clarissa? Yes, of course.'

'I will make arrangements to transport you to the airport, and if you wish I can also arrange for a limousine to collect you at Heathrow.'

Suddenly the panic subsided, and Daphne deflated

like a pricked balloon. 'Thank you, that is most kind. I can't seem to work the phones. I have to call my husband.'

'By all means. Would you care for me to get through for you?'

Daphne clasped her hands in relief.

'It may take a little while – connections have been problematic lately.' She listened, then asked to speak to Lord Hangerford and passed Daphne the receiver.

Daphne's hands were sweating, but she waited until Dahlia had left the room before she spoke into the phone. She could just hear a distant, 'Hello? Hello? Who's speaking, hello?'

'Is that you?' she barked.

'Yes.' His voice was slurred.

She eased herself into a chair, sweat trickling between the rolls of fat on her belly. 'What's going on? I've seen the papers. Is that why you left? And how dare you not tell me, you bastard!'

'Yes, it's true,' he stammered. 'But you know the media – someone must have tipped them off. I couldn't tell you. I just had to get away and give myself time to think.'

'But the money situation?'

He broke down sobbing.

'What about William? Couldn't he help us?' shouted Daphne. She was shaking with nerves. Hangerford began a tirade against William. 'There's more, Piggy!' He used her pet nickname, which she hated: it always spelled trouble when he used it.

'What else could there be?' she said flatly.

'I'm leaving you.'

'What?'

'I said, I'm leaving you.' Then he told her about Judith, the twenty-six-year-old stable girl with whom he had been having an affair. He didn't mention that Judith had a private income, and that although it wouldn't keep him in the style to which he was accustomed, it was better than joining the dole queue and meant he would have a roof over his head.

By the time their conversation had ground to a sickening halt, Daphne Hangerford was in a semi-stupor. She eased her bulk slowly from the wicker chair, opened the fridge and took out a bottle of gin and another of tonic water. She'd never been a great drinker and she was reminded of Katherine Benedict. She remembered the last conversation they had had. Katherine had been sitting surrounded by her dogs. She had been drinking heavily. 'I am sorry to have to ask you this, Daphne, but I need you to repay some of the money I lent Cedric. I'm in a rather difficult position. I've had to use my children's trust funds to tide me over and . . .' This reminded Daphne that Clarissa also had a trust fund. It was still intact and her husband didn't know about it. She giggled. It had been her secret; hers and her beloved father's. He had seen his son-in-law carve his way through his daughter's inheritance, so he made sure his granddaughter's future was secure. There was a few hundred thousand, if not more, that she could get her hands on. Daphne Hangerford raised her glass and vowed that her husband would see her in court if he tried to get his hands on one penny. 'Thank God for you, Daddy!'

*

The Baroness had just showered when Laura tapped at the door of her suite. 'Who is it?' she called.

'Laura.'

The Baroness opened the door and her towel slipped to reveal her breasts. 'Oh, sorry, come in.' She made only a half-hearted attempt to cover herself.

'Are you alone?' Laura asked, closing the door.

'Yes. God knows where my husband is.'

Laura sat down on the enormous sofa loaded with cushions. 'I think you know perfectly well where your husband is.' She smiled sweetly.

'What do you mean by that?'

Laura opened her bag, removed a video cassette and held it between her thumb and forefinger. 'See for yourself.'

The Baroness sat opposite Laura on a low seat, her legs wide apart, knowing she was leaving nothing to the imagination. 'So what is this video, darling? Not of you, is it?'

'It's nothing to do with me, but you'll thank me for passing it on to you. There are two seats reserved on a plane tomorrow morning. The launch will have to leave rather early so that you don't miss the flight. I'll get your maid to help you pack, unless you'd prefer not to use Ruby.'

She slipped the tape into the VCR, then sat back and crossed her legs. 'I wouldn't mention this to the other guests. Just make sure you and your husband leave tomorrow.'

The tape whirred into action. On the screen the Baron, naked, walked into shot, his erection leading the way.

'Or the film will be shown to all the guests in a specially announced screening tomorrow night,' Laura added.

The Baroness was speechless as she watched her husband cavorting with a couple of the boat-boys. 'I'm in love with Max,' said Laura. 'He's asked me to marry him and I have accepted.' She looked at a small flower in the curtains behind the Baroness, her wide eyes clear and focused.

The Baroness was glued to the screen. She had always known of her husband's antics, but seeing him perform had silenced her.

Laura pressed on: 'We want to be left alone, to lead our own lives.'

The Baroness stood up suddenly. 'You lay one finger on my son,' she screamed, 'and I'll scratch your eyes out.'

Laura continued, 'It's not only the Baron on tape. Shall I fast-forward? I notice you have been spending a lot of time with Kurt.' She looked the Baroness in the eye. 'Well, I see I have no need to elaborate. Why not sit and view it for yourself? Think about whether you'd like Humphrey Matlock to get hold of it.' Laura straightened her skirt and stood up. She smiled. 'See you at dinner.'

Left alone in her suite the Baroness played the video through. It was still running when her husband returned. 'Beautiful evening,' he said, as he came in.

'You are in for one big shock,' said the Baroness. 'Sit down and get yourself a stiff drink. And while you sit and watch that video, I'll be packing – without a servant, because it appears you have fucked every single one of them.'

The Baron sat in a stupor, staring at himself on the screen. He was mortified. Then his wife was back. 'Oh, by the way,' she said, 'Max is staying on here, with that two-faced whore.'

'Who?' said the Baron, cowering.

'Laura Chalmers has her claws into Max. She said they're going to get married.'

'But he's only eighteen,' he stuttered.

'You think I don't know that?' Tears of fury streamed down her face.

The Baron's shoulders slumped and he started to cry. His wife screamed, 'Get showered and changed. We're dining at nine thirty and we don't let so much as a hint of this show, do you hear me?'

He nodded, and with a sick feeling in the pit of his stomach he turned to watch the video. He felt ashamed. The boys, he realized, were younger than his son. Then the screen went blank. A new scene: the Baroness entered the sauna. Kurt was lying on the top bunk. He eased himself down and began to rub oil over her chest. They were joined by Dahlia. The baron watched in horror. His wife would blame him for driving her into the sex games, but he was too humiliated to argue with her.

Matlock, swathed in a towel robe left undone to reveal his naked body, carried his gin onto the veranda, a cigar clamped between his teeth. 'You ordered dinner?' he looked to his wife, as he slumped on to a cushioned *chaise-longue*.

'Yes.' Angela passed him a bowl of prawn and oyster canapés.

'Odd that Benedict's still not shown. I'd say the Prime Minister's not coming either.'

'I doubt it. He's at some European summit. It's in *The Times*.'

Matlock clicked his fingers. She put down her cross stitch and went to retrieve the newspaper. She hated the way he did that. He was so uncouth at times it made her skin crawl.

Matlock roared with laughter as he read of Lord Hangerford's downfall and held out his glass to be re-filled. 'Probably why Benedict's not shown up. They're related, aren't they?'

Angela poured his drink and returned to her seat. 'By marriage only. Hangerford was his second wife's brother.' She began selecting silks.

'Ah, yes, I forgot you knew so much about them.' He snorted as he turned the pages.

'I find it hard to believe that you would forget that I went out with William Benedict.'

He lowered the newspaper. She didn't meet his eyes, but continued to sort through her silks.

'Slip of the tongue. Of course I haven't. All the same, when you think about it, it's odd that we should be here accepting his hospitality.'

'This was your idea,' she said primly, her lips tight.

'So it was, and I'm glad I did accept. Even if the PM doesn't show, I'm having a good holiday.'

Angela concentrated on threading her needle. Now she understood why Humphrey had come here. It had been too good an opportunity to refuse, no matter what she might feel about facing William. Her husband, she mused, would be able to commit murder and blank it from his self-obsessed mind, just as he had her pitiful threats of divorce. Months ago she had claimed that she could expose Humphrey's indiscretions: they would make headlines. Usually it was an employee who caught his eye, and no one ever lasted longer than a few months, but his callousness hurt her. Finding a credit-card slip from Aspreys for a diamond bracelet that had not been for her had been the last straw. 'I want a divorce,' she had said.

'Don't be stupid.' He had held his hand out for the credit-card slip. She saw him wince as he realized what it was.

'I'm not being stupid. How many women have you played around with? This time I mean it, I MEAN IT.'

Matlock stood up and reached for her, drawing her close. 'Let me make it up to you. What do you want from me? I'll do anything to please you and stop all this nonsense about divorce.'

She had wriggled away from him, still angry, then turned on him again. 'I've been made to look a fool once too often. If you want to make it up to me then ruin William Benedict. It's your choice, because I won't be persuaded to forget about this.'

Matlock had sighed and picked up the paper. The story of Andrew Maynard's suicide had only just been leaked and there would be a lot more to come. Perhaps his wife had hit on something newsworthy in Sir William's indiscretions. And if there weren't any to be exposed, Matlock and his cheque book would invent them. 'Deal,' he said, and lit a cigar. 'I never realized how much he hurt you.'

She did not add that if she had married William, as

she had so desperately wanted, she would not have been tied to a man she detested. 'Just ruin him anyway you can,' she spat out.

He had been as good as his word, had perhaps gone even further than Angela had intended, but she had read of William's disgrace with relish.

'Penny for 'em,' Matlock said now, holding out his empty glass again.

'I was just wondering how late James was going to be.'

Matlock swung his legs off the *chaise-longue*. 'I'm going to have words with that little sod. You spoil him, lazy good-for-nothing.'

'He's with all the youngsters at a disco,' she said, pouring his gin, slicing lemon and scooping up the ice.

'He's missed out on some fantastic hours on that boat.' Matlock had been the first up and the last to return ever since he had arrived, fishing from early morning until dusk. 'You make sure he comes out with me tomorrow,' he said, deep in the article about Hangerford again, hardly able to contain his delight. He checked the journalist's name and wondered who'd leaked the scoop. It was certainly a good one. 'I must call the office tomorrow,' he muttered, tossing the newspaper aside. The photograph of Cedric was on the front page and he chuckled.

Something somewhere was lurking in Matlock's brain, making dull connections, but he didn't have the energy to gather together the train of subconscious thought and link the 'scoop', the 'journalist' and the 'story' that had made his career, so long ago.

*

380

As the guests on the island prepared for dinner, their offspring, apart from Max, arrived in Tortola. Justin ushered James and Clarissa ahead of him into the dark, dingy back bar of the Coca-Baba club. They were early and the place was only half full, so he suggested they sit at the bar and order some drinks. He felt irritable and tired, and when James leaned close and asked if he needed a hit, he shook his head. He watched James head for the lavatory then ordered a round of rum punches.

Clarissa slid up next to him. 'You were so horrible to me,' she said, pouting.

'Was I?' Justin turned away and lit a cigarette, as she went on to complain about the way he had treated her. It had made her feel terrible.

'You know, sometimes, Clarissa, a man needs to shoot his load. You just struck lucky. Think nothing of it. I don't.'

'You hateful shit,' she said, returning to her stool.

Justin looked around the club, which was slowly filling up with kids on vacation with their parents – the 'Brit Pack', as the locals nicknamed them. James returned from the toilets. He was so high he almost missed his seat and went flying into Justin. When he eventually sat down, he ordered more drinks. 'Pity Max isn't here,' he said.

'Yeah, life and soul of the party is Max,' Justin said flatly. 'Good-looking, and getting more so every day. His body's filling out like his dick.'

James seethed. 'Yeah, well, we all know where he wants to stick it.'

Justin laughed. 'Jealous?'

'I didn't mean you. Max is panting after your sister.'

Justin's jaw tightened.

James leaned closer to him. 'I think she's cute too. I may even try and fuck her again myself. She's easy meat, I'd say.'

Justin hooked his foot under James's stool and tugged hard. The stool slid sideways and James fell awkwardly to the floor, where Justin kicked him hard in the groin. 'Never talk like that about my sister. Now get up, sit up and shut up.'

Clarissa giggled as James heaved himself to his feet and picked up the stool. She was obviously intending to get blotto before the night was over. She was going to show the repellent Justin Chalmers that he couldn't hurt her with his snide remarks.

Laura slipped into William's study to check that the tapes were in order. Satisfied that everything was working and ready to go, she was about to leave when she saw one of the intercom lights flashing. She crossed to it. It was the jetty phone. Then she noticed the light blink on Dahlia's line, which made her worry. She wondered if perhaps the weather had turned bad: sometimes it was too rough to make the trip across. She pressed the speaker button, which enabled her to listen in on any call made anywhere on the island.

'He'll be on the first plane, so be waiting. It is imperative you say nothing, especially to Justin or Laura. Sir's orders.'

Laura gasped. 'Sir' had to be William. Why was he returning before time, and why was his arrival to be kept a secret?

*

Max was finding it difficult to stop smiling. He was seated at his parent's table and rose to greet them as they arrived. 'Hi, I thought I'd sit with you this evening as everyone else on my usual table's gone clubbing.'

'How nice,' his mother said, as he held out her chair.

'You look stunning,' he said, kissing her cheek.

'Thank you.' She sat with rigid shoulders. 'Your father will join us shortly. As usual he's taking his time dressing.'

'Would you care for a glass of champagne?' Max asked, and his mother nodded. He signalled to the waiter, who crossed to them and poured two glasses. Max looked around the room. 'We're the first down,' he said, trying to make conversation.

'How observant of you!' She lifted her glass, wanting to throw its contents into his silly, boyish face. Max half rose again as the Matlocks came in.

'Are we all dining together?' Matlock said loudly, looking at the table set for eight.

'I believe so,' the Baroness said, forcing a smile, then looked at Angela, who clung to her husband's arm. 'You look quite lovely, Angela, adorable dress. Very flattering colour, lemon.'

'Where's your better half?' asked Matlock.

'He'll be joining us. We've had some troublesome news from Berlin, and I'm afraid we're forced to cut short the holiday. We're leaving early in the morning.'

Max looked astonished. 'You never told me. Does this mean I have to go with you?'

'No, dear. You can stay on. You're enjoying yourself, aren't you?'

'Yes, I am,' he said, with relief.

Daphne Hangerford shuffled in with the Baron. She

was leaning against him and clearly quite drunk. 'Don't get up, please.' She plonked herself into a seat and shook out her napkin. 'This'll be my last night. Clarissa and I have . . .' she hesitated '. . . a few problems.'

The Baroness almost gave herself whiplash she turned so quickly. 'What did you say?'

Daphne broke open her bread roll, scattering crumbs over the table. 'Just personal things. I have to leave.'

'If it's the report in *The Times*, we've all read it.'

Daphne gulped some water, but before she could reply the Baroness leaned closer. 'We're leaving too, we're so bored here. We've got tickets booked, but we're not broadcasting it, and if I were you, I wouldn't say too much. Don't want to appear ungrateful, do we?'

'We're missing one,' Matlock said, nodding to the empty seat at the head of the table. 'Ah, no, she's here.' He looked with admiration towards the door where Laura stood. She was wearing a white sequinned gown that floated around her like stardust, tied in a halter-neck with a white satin ribbon. She crossed to her usual table and signalled to the waiter to bring iced water.

'Won't you join us?' Matlock asked, leaning back in his chair.

Laura turned and smiled. 'Thank you, but I'm rather tired and will retire shortly.'

'Nevertheless we'd like you to at least spend a few moments with us.' Matlock had stood up and was holding out his hand to her. She hesitated before allowing him to guide her to the empty seat next to him.

'Thank you,' she said coyly, smiling at everyone apart from Max, who had flushed. Matlock asked her if she would care for a glass of champagne. Just like his wife, he had eyes only for Laura.

'No champagne, thank you.'

The lights lowered, leaving the room candlelit. The young guitarist entered and began to strum unobtrusively in the corner.

The atmosphere seemed affable, but tense undercurrents were building and Laura was at the eye of the storm. Matlock wanted to fuck her, Max was in love with her, as was Angela, and the von Gartens loathed her. They thought her nothing but a cheap, blackmailing whore. Daphne Hangerford, too drunk to be aware of the immediate situation, was the only person who didn't want either to strangle Laura or make love to her.

Laura behaved as if she was privileged to sit with them, keeping her eyes down and maintaining a sweet, shy smile. Matlock eased his thigh to rest against hers beneath the table.

The big fish was hooked, but his demise was endangering her secret plan with Max. She knew she could not leave the island before the final showdown with Matlock, but time was running out. When Justin discovered everyone was leaving he would be furious, and especially with her for acting without consulting him. She wondered fearfully if she dare carry out the revenge alone. No, she knew she couldn't.

'That was a long sigh,' Matlock whispered. She gave him a tiny, intimate smile and he leaned closer again. 'A penny for 'em.'

'Oh, my thoughts cost more than pennies,' she said softly, her mind jumping. Having orchestrated the imminent departure of the Baron and Baroness, along with Daphne Hangerford and Clarissa, Laura knew that the Matlocks and Max would be the only guests left, and Sir William would turn up at the most inopportune moment.

Laura felt Matlock's leg pressing harder against hers, then his hand fumbling with her skirt. She made the decision. If Justin didn't return on time as they had agreed, she would carry it out alone. She was determined that nothing would stop her running away with Max.

She glanced across the table. They were trying hard not to look at each other, but intuitively Max turned round. His eyes glowed, and she forced herself not to react. Beneath the table, she unzipped Matlock's trousers and began to fondle him, but now she felt disgusted at herself. How could she do this to a man she hated whilst the boy she loved was sitting right opposite her? She concentrated her mind on the plan and drew comfort from the thought that all this was part of a greater scheme.

The plan was for Laura to make Matlock desire her to such an extent that he would agree to meet on the quayside. They would board one of the boats and Justin would be waiting.

CHAPTER 19

BY MIDNIGHT, the Coca-Baba club was so crowded that there was hardly any space on the dance floor. Customers perched on the veranda railings and hovered around the rickety steps while the local ragga band pounded away at the microphones, which seemed constantly on distort. The loudspeakers added a high-pitched feedback that almost assisted the vocals and backups. The air was dense with cigarette and ganja smoke, and it was as hot and damp as a sauna. Perfumes mixed with body odour as the dancers writhed to the music. Flickering ultraviolet lights added to the surreal atmosphere: teeth became whiter than white, white clothes glowed with a strange phosphorescence, black skin disappeared leaving only eyeballs and teeth glinting from darkened corners as wraps, joints and folded dollar bills were passed.

Justin sat outside on the roof of a parked car. He had another tepid bottle of beer in his hand and had been eager to leave over an hour ago. Clarissa had danced with anyone who'd have her. She was being passed from partner to partner, necking and clinging to each one as though they were long-lost lovers. Justin watched her, bored. Her eyes occasionally darted him a frenetic glare of hatred. She was proving, if not to him then to herself, that she was sexy and sought-after, which indeed she was. Locally, white meat, especially with money, was referred to as a 'honey pot'. James had become moodier as the evening progressed. He had snorted cocaine, then complained to Justin that it was baby powder or, worse, laced with borax: his nose was dripping and painful.

Justin decided it was time to go home. The tide was in their favour and the water appeared quite calm. Enough, he thought, was enough. His charges were wrecked. He drained his beer, tossed aside the bottle and pushed his way into the heaving mass. Clarissa angrily faced him out: she was not ready to leave. Justin gripped her wrist and dragged her to the steps. 'Get off me,' she screeched. 'I've lost my watch!'

'Shut the fuck up! You want a pack on to us? If you lost your watch, then forget it. Maybe somebody took it in payment for screwing you up the arse in the john.'

She tried to hit him but he ducked. She fell forward and began to vomit.

Justin hauled her away from the onlookers towards the wasteground at the side of the club. There he found James. He was lying face down, his shirt torn, his pants round his ankles.

Justin hauled him to his feet. Get your pants up, man. We're out of here.'

'I was just taking a piss,' James slurred.

Justin signalled for the boys waiting on the speedboat to help him get the pair on to the deck.

'Why did you bring us here?' Clarissa wailed. She continued to snivel about her watch, until she realized her gold necklace was also missing, which brought on a fresh onslaught of tears.

'Think yourself lucky you've not lost a lot more. Stop bleating, and have a good shower when you get in. You're probably lousy with crabs.'

Clarissa gasped and shuddered. 'I didn't let them touch me,' she moaned. But she had, and had lost count of how many.

Justin ignored her. He had noticed James was white-faced, his lips blue. He still seemed unable to focus. 'You okay? James?'

James swung his head round. 'Yeah, man . . . I'm cool.'

The return trip to the island was a long, slow haul. When they arrived at the island, Justin strode off towards his bungalow. He wanted to shower and get the stench of vomit out of his nostrils. As he passed Max's room he crept up to the half-open shutter. The lights were on but, although the sheet had been pulled back, the bed was empty. Justin listened, but heard only the sound of crickets, so he moved on. Where could Max be at this hour?

Laura's suite was in darkness, shutters closed, door locked. He walked on to his own room where the lights were blazing. 'You're late,' said Laura, as he came in, closing the door.

'I couldn't get them to leave the club. I got back as soon as I could.' He began to peel off his clothes. 'Don't come near me, I stink.' He stepped out of his trousers.

'We have to talk,' Laura said.

'Not right now. I need a shower.' He disappeared into the bathroom.

389

Laura sat drumming her fingers on the bedside table. She had it all worked out. By the time he had left the bathroom Justin was more relaxed. He flopped down on the bed and Laura stroked his damp hair.

'Okay. How did it go with Matlock? You made progress?'

'Yes, he's all over me like a rash. But I don't know whether I can go through with it. The man disgusts me. I don't know that I want to give him the pleasure of fucking me.'

'Well, there's no need, is there? I mean, I think I've done a pretty good job of getting him into the fishing anyway. He'll be dying to get out there tomorrow, and I'll just tell the boat-boys that I'm going to take him out alone.'

For a moment Laura was hurt. She had wanted to be there for the grand finale. Then she realized that perhaps with Justin absent she would have a chance to get her things together for her escape with Max.

Justin saw her look and interpreted it as disappointment. 'Don't worry, my princess. I'll just get him drugged up on the boat then bring him back to the harbour. Keep an eye open for me and we'll finish him down there. I should be back around twelve thirty.'

She took a deep breath. 'Now, just listen and don't interrupt. I've had to push things along a few notches. Tomorrow the Baron and Baroness leave, along with Daphne Hangerford and Clarissa.'

'What?'

'They might have become a problem, and we don't care about them anyway.'

There was something about her tone, her confidence, that alerted him. 'What did you do?'

'Oh!' She shrugged. 'I let them see themselves on the video. They're packed and ready.'

'Is Max going with them?'

'Of course.'

He giggled. 'So that leaves just . . .'

'Matlock, his wife and son,' Laura said softly.

He caught her hand. 'What is it? What's wrong?'

Laura withdrew her hand. 'I think William's coming back.'

'Well, we know he is. It *is* his island.'

She faced him angrily. 'He might be here tomorrow.'

Justin's face drained of colour.

Clarissa walked slowly with the wretched James. He kept stumbling, and had to lean heavily against her. 'What on earth have you shovelled up tonight?' she asked, almost buckling under the weight of his arm around her shoulders.

'Not enough,' he muttered.

'For God's sake, I can't prop you up. We'll have to get one of those golf carts.' She looked around but didn't know where they were kept. She wished she'd asked the boat-boys to help them. 'That bloody Justin just pissed off,' she said, wondering whether or not to leave James where he was and find someone to help.

'He's a shit,' James mumbled, then started to cry, sinking to his knees. 'I'm so messed up,' he sobbed.

Clarissa sighed and caught sight of Max not far ahead of them. 'Max?' she called.

Max had been unable to sleep. He'd read and watched a movie before deciding to walk around the island. 'My God, look at the state of him,' he said.

James was now lying flat on the pathway.

'He's done some drugs, God knows what,' Clarissa said, as they tried to haul him to his feet. 'Help me get him to his room, will you?' Max hooked an arm around him and hauled him upright. The three staggered to James's room. As they reached the door, Clarissa let go of his arm. 'I'm going to bed,' she announced, and walked on.

Max was furious. 'We can't just leave him. He could choke or something.'

'Stick him under the shower, then. I've had enough of him.'

Max stripped off James's clothes and was appalled at the marks all over his body. There were bloody scratches, bites, dark bruises and raw red welts across his back. 'James, who's done this to you?'

James lifted his head, his eyes drooping. He tried to say something but he passed out. Somehow Max dragged him into the shower and turned on the cold tap, soaking himself in the process. Then he returned to the bedroom to brew some coffee and fetch some pyjamas. When he returned to the shower James was still unconscious, but his face was deathly pale and the skin round his mouth was turning blue. Max called Dahlia, who said she would send Kurt.

Laura moved off the bed and began to pace up and down. 'It's got to be him. Why would she say we mustn't be told? And who else could it be anyway? Just to make sure, I asked Dahlia if she had heard from him. She acted a bit cagey and said nothing had been confirmed, that he was possibly coming home but she wasn't sure.'

Justin stood by the shutters. 'She said that? Are you sure?'

'Why would I make it up?' Laura snapped. 'Now you know why I had to move things so fast. I wouldn't have done it if it hadn't been an emergency, not without you.'

'Well, well! Speak of the devil,' he said softly. He walked over to the door and opened it. 'Dahlia! What on earth are you doing up at this hour?'

'It's young James Matlock. He's unconscious. Kurt is with him. He says we must get a doctor.'

'Kurt's a trained nurse,' Justin said.

'A nurse is not a doctor,' said Dahlia, 'and the boy doesn't look good. I've just come from his room.'

'Shit!' Justin dropped his towel and went back into the room to grab a tracksuit. 'Come in for a minute,' he called to Dahlia. As he dressed he asked her if William was arriving ahead of schedule. She was evasive, until he snatched her arm. 'Listen to me, bitch,' he hissed. 'You're here on a massive salary, courtesy of me, so don't fuck me around. Is he coming or is he not?'

She nodded. 'He asked me to tell no one, made me swear not to.'

'Your loyalties are to him now, are they?'

She shifted her weight. 'I didn't mean to do anything wrong, Justin.'

He stared at her. 'I'll let this one go, but don't think I won't remember it. You'd be back in that whorehouse, and your kids along with you, if it weren't for me. Now, get out of my sight.'

Dahlia slipped out, terrified.

Justin's face was taut with anger. Then he said, 'I'd better go and see that dumb piece of shit.'

Laura asked if he would like her with him, but he told her to go to bed, she must be exhausted after having to sort so much out by herself earlier. He spoke with the venomous camp lisp she hated.

As the door closed behind him, she sighed with relief. She was sure he had not detected her lie or, more important, suspected anything about Max, and that he had no idea of her intentions. She took a small suitcase, opened it on her bed, and packed the few garments she felt were absolutely necessary. Her heart beat rapidly. She was excited and her hand trembled as she crossed back and forth to her wardrobe, laying out clothes beside the case. Suddenly she felt dizzy and her head throbbed, but she sucked in her breath and didn't stop. Her pace quickened and her hand began to brush at her skirt.

James was now in blue pyjamas. His face above the tight, white sheet was pale and his lips still blue, but his breathing was regular.

Max was in the room with Kurt, who had a medical kit-bag.

'You should leave this to me,' Kurt said. Max chewed his lip. 'Go on, son, you've done more than enough. I'll look after him now.'

Max hurried off and, passing Laura's room, paused: the lights were on. He went up her path and peered into the bedroom between the partly closed shutters. She was undressing, the room lit by candles. Max wanted to call out to her but he couldn't say a word.

He was mesmerized. She was naked now, brushing her hair, her eyes half closed. Suddenly he heard footsteps and ducked down as Justin hurried past. He remained hidden, listening, afraid Justin would discover him.

By the time he straightened up, the candles had been extinguished and Laura's room was in darkness.

If he had been a moment earlier, he would have seen a different Laura, shaking convulsively as she took out her pills. She managed to swallow them, then took deep breaths to calm herself and picked up her hairbrush. With her eyes closed she whispered, 'I'm all right, Laura's all right, Laura's all right.'

James was now lying face down as Kurt dabbed his cuts with antiseptic.

'You shouldn't leave him on his stomach,' Justin said, as he entered.

Kurt shrugged. 'These sores need attention.'

Justin lifted James's eyelid. Only the white of his eye was visible. 'Shit! He's really out of it,' he muttered.

'He needs a doctor, man, the sooner the better.'

Kurt laid compresses over James's back and ran a roll of surgical tape across them to hold them firm, then gently turned him over. Then he said they should take the boy straight to hospital.

'That won't be necessary,' Justin snapped.

'Justin, he's real sick. Look at him! Christ only knows what he's taken.'

'I'll make the decisions. Now get the hell out.'

As the door closed behind Kurt, Justin propped up James on his pillows and snapped open a bottle of poppers. He broke one and held it under his nose.

James heaved, gave a spluttering cough and his eyes fluttered open.

'Breathe in, James, there's a good boy, nice deep breaths. Gonna give you another.'

Max walked in. 'Should you be doing that?'

Justin whipped round. 'It's just to bring him round. We've spoken to a doctor and he's on his way.'

'Should I fetch his parents?' asked Max, concerned.

'No, he's coming to and I don't want them to know the state he got himself into. You just piss off back to your room, there's a good chap. You and your folks are leaving early tomorrow morning.'

Max hesitated. 'Actually, I'm staying on.'

Justin straightened up. 'Really? You're having such a good time, are you?'

'Yes, I am.'

Suddenly James began to cough, chest heaving. Justin sat him up further, shoving pillows behind him. 'Good boy, that's it. Come on. Deep breaths, now.' Justin turned to Max. 'Shut the door as you leave.'

Again Max hesitated, then left. Justin split open yet another amyl nitrate capsule and pressed it beneath James's nose. The boy gasped as his heart-rate soared. His arms flailed and his eyes rolled back. Justin felt his pulse, sat for a while then ran from the room.

James was carried on to the speedboat. Kurt did not say anything as he helped the boys make him comfortable. Justin told Kurt to stay with James while he was in the hospital and to report back.

'You not coming?' Kurt asked.

'No. Tell the boys to return after they've dropped you off.'

'Okay, but don't you think his parents should be told? Maybe they'll want to be with him.'

Justin told them to get moving. It was now almost five, and at any moment the house would begin its morning rituals.

Kurt watched Justin as the powerful boat's engine churned up the water. He'd always known there was some scam going on – that much had been obvious from the amount of money he was being paid and that he'd been hand-picked by Justin. But Kurt was worried that whatever heinous scheme Justin was part of, he was drawing him into it. He decided he'd not risk staying on. Just as soon as he'd sorted James out, he'd go pack his belongings and leave the island. Perhaps Justin intended murdering Sir William.

Her mother had to shake Clarissa awake. She sat bolt upright. 'What? What is it?' When she saw her mother, she flopped back. 'Christ you nearly gave me heart-failure, Mother. What are you doing here?'

'We're leaving.'

Clarissa turned to see the time. 'It's only five fifteen!'

'We're getting the launch to Tortola. There's a flight out at nine and I want to be on it.'

Clarissa sat up. 'Well, I don't, I'm staying.'

'No, you are not. You are coming with me.' Daphne started to sob. 'We're flat broke. The houses are gone, stables, everything. That bastard spent every cent I had. He's borrowed from every one we know and now he's moved in with that bitch from the stables. I wish to

God I'd never set foot in this God-forsaken place. I hate it! It's like a prison.' Daphne stood up. 'Call for someone to help you pack. Don't forget your passport, and if you have any money we'll need it, because I've only got forty pounds to my name.'

'I've no cash at all.' Clarissa sat back on the bed. 'What's the point of going back?'

'We have to. To see what we can salvage. Right now we don't even have a roof over our heads.'

'I see,' Clarissa said softly.

'It would have been nice if you and James had hit it off. The Matlocks have more money than they know what to do with.'

'I wouldn't get involved with that poof,' Clarissa said, searching her make-up bag unsuccessfully for some paracetamol. She had a splitting headache and her body ached all over. She gave her mother a hooded look. Did she really want to go all the way back to London and face her father?

'I'm not leaving,' she said firmly.

'You are,' her mother said, equally firmly. Then she took a deep breath. 'If you want your trust fund intact, you'll not waste a second. I've always known your father's a bastard, but it turns out he's also an accomplished thief. He took every cent Katherine Benedict possessed, including her kids' trust funds.'

'Can he get his hands on my money, Ma?' asked Clarissa.

Daphne looked hard at her daughter and was shocked at what she saw. It was like looking at a stranger: there was no shy, deferential look in her eyes, no innocence left. Here was not a girl who had blossomed into a woman, but a seedy, slovenly girl, brazenly standing with her dressing gown undone, unembarrassed by her nakedness.

'Because if he even tries, I'll have him fucking arrested,' Clarissa continued, as she padded into her bathroom and reached for the paracetamol on the shelf above the basin.

'What has happened to you, Clarissa? I hardly know you any more,' Daphne said.

'Well maybe being almost fucked by my own father had some effect.'

Clarissa took two pills and swallowed them in one gulp.

'You're lying!' her mother said. As much as she loathed her husband, she could not believe what she was hearing.

'I'm not. Ask my father what happened here in the sauna. He groped me. *You* only want me to go back so you can get your hands on my money. Well, it's all mine, Ma, and I need it. You won't get a penny!'

Daphne slapped her daughter's face so hard that Clarissa fell off the chair with a howl. 'If you don't stop acting like some cheap tart and get packed, you might not have any money left.'

Daphne swept out, banging the door behind her. She stopped to catch her breath, and the heady scent of the ubiquitous lilies made her feel sick. How she hated this place!

The Baroness was standing in the hall, her luggage packed and ready to be taken down to the jetty. She looked as immaculate as ever. Her husband, though, seemed nervous and jaded.

Daphne Hangerford was waiting for her cases to be brought down. She didn't want to return to her suite, or to be alone. 'Do you mind if I give you some advice?' she said to the Baroness. 'Don't let your son stay on. Make him leave with you. This is a terrible place.'

The Baroness gave her husband a furtive look then turned away. 'He's old enough to make his own decisions.'

Daphne shrugged her plump shoulders, and saw Clarissa appear, followed by one of the house-boys with her bags. At this moment, a maid approached the Baron with a fax that had just arrived for him. He opened it and froze. Benedict's lawyers were taking him to court. His own team had tried to delay the action, but there was now an even more serious charge of insider dealing. It was suggested he return as soon as possible. He was about to lose everything he owned and the news had been leaked to the European press. Any day now it would hit the British papers.

Angela Matlock came down the stairs to say good-bye, puzzled by what appeared to be a mass exodus. She kissed everyone and asked if Max was staying: she wanted company for James.

'Yes, he is,' the Baroness said.

'I was on my way to James's room,' Angela went on. 'His father is just leaving for another fishing trip and wants James to join him.'

Clarissa grinned. 'I doubt if he'll make it. It was quite a late night.'

Humphrey Matlock was already aboard the fishing-boat and waved to the departing guests from the deck. He had paid little attention to what his wife had said and thought that they, like him, must be embarking on some day-trip. It was a clear, brilliant day, and although it was only seven in the morning, the sun was already beating down. He had hoped James would join him, but there was no sign of his son.

Justin strolled towards him. 'Have you seen James?' Matlock asked.

Justin rolled his eyes. 'He's still in his pit. Rather the worse for wear after the disco, I'm afraid,' he said, jumping aboard. 'Come on, cast off. I'm crewing for you today. The regulars have demanded a day off. I suspect they've got hangovers too.'

Matlock untied a mooring line, disappointed. 'Wretched boy. Spoiled, pampered idiot. I wash my hands of him.'

Justin signalled to the boat-boy to start the engines. 'We're going into deep water this morning and if you get a big catch,' he laughed, splaying his hands out, 'I'll help you reel it in!'

Matlock pointed to the jetty. 'Looks like a mass exodus. Sightseeing, are they?'

'Yes, and hitting the tourist shops.'

'Thank God I'm not roped into that.'

'Yes. We'll have much more fun . . . fishing.'

Angela headed for her son's room. She paused, gazing down at the jetty as everyone climbed aboard the cruiser. Then she went on her way to James. She pushed open the door to his room. It was in immaculate order. The maids had cleaned it and changed the linen.

'James?' she called. This was so unlike her son. His

own room at home, even with maids, was in constant turmoil. Angela opened the wardrobe. His clothes were all neatly pressed and on their individual hangers. Even the drawers were tidy. She turned guiltily as Max tapped and peered in from outside. He was a little out of breath as he had run back from the jetty to see his parents off. He had been disappointed to discover he had missed them, and was more than a little confused as to why his mother had not even called into his suite.

'Hi,' he said shyly.

'Hello, Max. I just dropped in to see James.'

'Is he feeling better?'

'Better?' she said, puzzled.

Max came further into the room and he, too, looked around in surprise. 'Well, I saw him last night and—'

'And?' she said quickly. 'Had he been drinking?'

'A bit. He wasn't feeling too good.'

'Then where is he?' she said, now showing her worry.

'I have no idea, but he came home late. They went clubbing.'

Angela gave a soft laugh. 'Of course, he'll be with his father. He was going on a special fishing trip this morning.'

'Oh, that may be it,' Max said, but he doubted it. He excused himself and left, checking the time. It was not too long to wait. He decided he would go for a walk – anything to take his mind off Laura.

Dahlia looked up with surprise as Laura walked into the laundry room. 'Have you heard how he is?' she asked.

'Who?' Laura asked, as she crossed to where her clothes were drying.

'They took James Matlock to hospital,' Dahlia said, watching her intently.

'Justin didn't tell me.'

Dahlia continued folding towels. Laura seemed unconcerned by the news and, to Dahlia's surprise, gathered all her lingerie into a basket.

'Where is my tissue paper, Dahlia?'

'I had it ironed. It's in that drawer.' She pointed.

Laura placed it carefully on top of her basket. 'You're not planning on leaving, are you?' Dahlia asked.

'No, I'm not.' Laura was about to walk out, but then she turned. Her eyes were chilling. 'When do you expect Sir William?'

Dahlia licked her lips. 'Perhaps some time today.'

Laura gave an odd, secretive smile. 'Good.' And she was gone.

Dahlia found Kurt in the gym, working out alone. 'You have any news about James Matlock?'

'They took him into intensive care and said they'd keep Justin informed of his progress. I think he'll be okay . . . Didn't look too good, though.'

'What drugs had he taken?' Dahlia asked, placing pristine white towels in the racks.

'Christ only knows, and in that club they sell shit. They've been handing round Ecstasy tabs like they were M&Ms.'

'His parents haven't been told,' Dahlia said, with a hint of disapproval. Her bleeper went off. 'I've got to go. See you later.'

'You won't, I'm quitting,' said Kurt. 'Be gone by this afternoon.'

'Why?'

'I don't know exactly what's going on here but something is, and it's not smelling good to me. You know Justin's given all the boys two days off, plus the kitchen staff? I reckon whatever's going to happen will happen soon.'

Dahlia hurried out. She began to feel the same trepidation as Kurt, but she had kids – she needed her wage packet. Her bleeper went off and she hurried back to the laundry room.

Dahlia closed the laundry-room door, went to the phone and called William. He was at the airport. If he had been there an hour earlier he would have passed his erstwhile guests, but now the airport was virtually empty. 'I need to be picked up,' he said. 'Is everything all right over there?'

Dahlia took a nervous look around. She knew Justin was out, but was worried that Laura might walk in and catch her. William listened as Dahlia listed those who had left. He asked about Humphrey Matlock. 'Out fishing, sir.'

She hesitated before she told him about James.

William told her he would go straight to the hospital and check on James. 'Where's his mother?' he asked. When William discovered that she had not been told, he bellowed down the phone so loud that Dahlia had to hold the receiver away from her ear. She then told him that half of the staff had been given two days off, including some of the boat-boys and several of the kitchen and domestic staff. 'On whose orders?'

'Justin's,' she said. Then, after another lengthy pause

404

and feeling even guiltier, she hinted that something odd was going on but she was not quite sure what. 'I may be wrong, but I think Laura is planning to leave.'

'Is Justin going too?' William interrupted. 'Where is he now?'

'Oh, I think he's out with Sir Humphrey on the fishing-boat.' Dahlia listened as William barked instructions down the line, repeated that she must carry out everything he told her to do, without question.

William slapped off his mobile, and remained standing with the phone for a few moments. Then he did what he should have done earlier: he called the coastguard.

CHAPTER 20

AT AROUND nine, Dahlia found Angela Matlock sitting by the pool in the shade. As usual she was working on her cross stitch. 'Excuse me interrupting you, madam, but I have an urgent message for you. Your son is in hospital on Tortola. He's very sick.'

'What?' Angela stood up and her cross stitch fell to the ground.

'I have arranged for you to be taken there directly,' Dahlia said.

Angela's face drained of colour. 'Has anyone told my husband?'

'He's still out on the fishing-boat, madam. I'm afraid I can't contact him from here. We have tried their radio, but it appears to be switched off.'

Matlock had a cigar clamped between his teeth. It was still early, but he had a glass of iced Pernod which he lifted in a toast to Justin. 'This is one of the best times I've had in years,' he said expansively, then gave a deep rumbling laugh. 'No bloody women on board for starters!' He drank thirstily. 'No son either.' He refilled his glass. 'I don't know what to do about him. He's had every opportunity handed to him on a plate: the best education money can buy, a doting mother, and myself obviously. I'm fond of the lad, but you know . . . I hope this will go no further.'

Justin lit a cigarette. 'That's what fishing trips are for. Male bonding they call it, don't they?' He tilted his head to look up to the sky, and squinted against the glare of the sun.

'What do you make of James? You can be honest.'

Justin shrugged his shoulders. 'He's handsome, friendly, good at sport and yet . . . He seemed to be searching for the right expression.

'Weak,' Matlock said, and sat down heavily.

They sat side by side, Matlock in contemplation, Justin in reverie.

'Tell me about yourself, Matlock said, helping himself to yet more Pernod. He had been drinking it like lemonade, and up till now it had apparently had little or no effect on him.

Justin stretched out his arms and crossed his legs. 'Well, it's quite a long story. I was born in France . . .'

You hardly have any trace of an accent,' Matlock said, his attention waning as he stared at the ocean. 'Looks like it might get rough.'

'I was educated, if one could call it that, in England.'

'Where?' Matlock still wasn't interested.

Justin paused a fraction. 'A children's detention centre.'

Matlock stopped in the act of raising his glass to his lips. 'A young offenders' institution?'

'Yes. I was sent there at the age of fourteen.'

Matlock was taken aback, but tried not to show it. 'Drugs was it?'

'No.' Justin was enjoying himself, and took his time. He said he had not committed any petty crime and had been only ten years old when he committed it.

'Ten? Good God! What on earth could you have done at that age for them to put you away?'

'Murder. The murder of my parents, to be exact. You may recall the case. My father's name was Martin Moorcroft, my mother Madeleine. I was Child B.'

Matlock had thought he had recognized Justin and Laura when he first saw them together at the island, but had not thought about it again. Until now.

'I do remember something . . .' His mind was spinning but he hid his confusion by drinking, then searching for a cigar.

'My sister, Child A, came to England with me after the murders,' Justin continued. 'We were there as wards of my father's sister, a widow, Frances Chalmers.'

Matlock clipped the end of the cigar. He couldn't look at Justin because the truth was dawning on him. 'We were both accused of the murders,' Justin continued, in a conversational way, as if he was discussing nothing more serious than the weather. 'There was also a third murder, the body found in the swimming-pool, but it had decomposed. It had been one of our first nannies, a horrid woman. Everyone thought she had just upped and packed her bags but she hadn't.' He giggled.

'Then there was Camilla Maynard. She came out to look after us much later. You must remember her. Her brother was Andrew Maynard MP. He committed suicide. Well, his sister Camilla had talked to all the journalists about us. Doesn't ring any bells?' Matlock took out his lighter, and put it to his cigar. He sucked in too strongly and the smoke burnt his lungs. 'My mother died in a fire.' Justin was studying the curling blue cigar smoke.

'Your sister?' Matlock asked, his voice sounding thick.

'Child A was only eight, and they couldn't find a place in prison for her. She was far too young. According to French law, we both were. Instead we were sent to a specialist psychiatric unit in England by the French government.' Justin's eyes bored into Matlock's forehead. 'My sister was always highly strung, very dependent on me. Well, we had never been apart and were very close. After a few sweet years of care in the hands of the psychiatric unit and our dear aunt, the whole thing blew up again. She was taken to a hospital for the criminally insane eventually. I think she was twelve or thirteen when they shipped her off there. She was manic, or so they said. She was moved from one place to another. Not a lot of places could accommodate a little girl like that. She was always on some drug or other and she was hardly recognizable because of it. Her name was Laura.' Justin's eyes were like slits.

'I think I do recall something about the case now,' Matlock said, the sweat dripping from his forehead in beads.

'You should. It made the headlines for months. Do you recall Lord Chief Justice Bellingham? He handled the case in England. His grandson was over here with his parents, Lord and Lady Bellingham, recently. Now, they threw some good parties. At the last one, poor old Oliver OD'd and choked on his own vomit. Sad, really.

He was such a nice kid, about your son's age, and the amount of drugs young James consumes I'm surprised he's not overdosed. Or maybe he has, for all we know.'

'What have my son and this boy Oliver to do with you?'

Justin looked skyward. 'Ah, well, the sins of the fathers and all that. Anyway, before the nightmare began, we were both happily living with our aunt.' Matlock bowed his head. 'You remember the case now I bet,' Justin said softly. 'We made your career, didn't we? You, your alarmist articles and your bestseller. Of course you remember Camilla Maynard. You interviewed her, didn't you? Yes, of course you did! Oh, did I tell you she died in a car accident? Her brakes failed. Bang! Straight across the dual carriageway she went, into oncoming cars. Hers exploded, I think. Awful to watch anyway.'

Justin sighed, leaning back. 'After that novel of yours and all your headlines about us being devil children they didn't dare leave us free. We had to be punished. We had to be publically tried for our crimes. *You* tried us, Matlock. Your filthy articles and your seedy book tried us. You wouldn't leave us alone because we made your stinking fucking headlines. We made your career, didn't we? You are responsible, for Laura's sickness, for the hell she went through in that asylum, for my wasted years at borstal. You are responsible.'

Matlock could not move. He wanted to get up, move away from Justin and his quiet chit-chat voice, but he couldn't. 'Would you like to know about our mother, Madeleine Moorcroft? She was part Argentinian, an olive-skinned woman with large luminous eyes and a hooked nose. She was not plain – ugly, yes, but

410

some people find an ugly woman attractive, don't they? You used some photographs of her in your book, but they never did her justice.'

The movement of the boat was making Matlock feel queasy. 'How long before we drop anchor?' he asked, desperate to change the subject.

Justin stood up, shaded his eyes and looked around. 'Be a while yet. You wanted a big fish! Ever caught a shark?' he asked.

'Not as yet.'

Justin laughed. 'Nor me, but I will today.' His face took on a strange, twisted smile. 'Let me tell you what my mother used to force me to do.' Matlock didn't want to hear, but there was something about the way Justin moved closer, invading his space. He almost brushed against him, but then Justin removed his glass. 'I'll just top you up. It's quite a long story and it's one I want you to hear.'

'I think I've had enough.' Matlock said.

'No, you have not, not by a long shot!' And Justin filled his glass with Pernod and dropped in ice, which rattled against the glass as he handed it back. 'My mother enjoyed pain. She was a masochistic bitch, a woman who became sexually aroused by giving birth. She described the pain as exquisite, said it felt like her insides were being ripped out.'

Matlock felt his skin crawl. 'I don't want to hear this.'

'You have no option. You see, you're now my prisoner.' Justin chuckled. 'You're going to listen to every word I say because I have waited years for this moment.' Matlock rose to his feet but Justin pushed him back roughly. '*Sit*. Sit down and listen.' He was speaking as

411

if to a naughty child. 'I shall begin at the beginning. The first time, she woke me in the middle of the night and carried me into her bedroom, where my father was waiting. I wasn't afraid. They were my mummy and daddy. They loved me. I loved them. They said we would play loving games.'

'Please, I don't want to hear any more,' Matlock slurred.

'I've only just begun,' Justin said.

Matlock held up one hand. 'Listen to me. Perhaps you've harboured some kind of deep-seated hatred against me, understandable from what you've said, but I was just a youngster, and I was paid to allow some other writer to do that book. I had nothing to do with it, believe me. I suppose if I had, you and your sister's faces would have been imprinted on my mind. It's what they call a ghost-writer, do you understand? I didn't write that book.'

Justin watched Matlock as he drank. He knew he had to be lying, not that it mattered. If it hadn't been for him they would never have been hounded. 'Did you coin the phrase "Devil's Children"?'

Matlock drank again. 'I don't recall.'

Justin repeated the phrase, then leaned close and touched the man's knee. 'Maybe it was a fitting description. Maybe it wasn't.'

'Listen, son, if this is about money—' Matlock's head cracked back against the combing as Justin punched him in his face.

'I'm not your son, and this isn't about money. Don't you understand what this is about? This is about me confronting you, my devil. There is no way off this boat, no way you can make it back to the island without

412

me. You are my prisoner, and by the time this is over, you will understand what fear means, understand that you must be punished for what you did to Child A and Child B, like everyone else who hurt them. You are going to die.'

Matlock wasn't sweating any more, he felt icy cold. Justin's face became a blur. 'Dear God, you'll never get away with this.' He tried to stand, but fell back into his seat.

Justin laughed, picked up the empty glass and tossed it overboard. He turned back to stare at the frightened man. This was the culmination of years of secret planning. In some ways it had been Matlock who had helped him to survive all along; without doubt, the idea of destroying him had given Laura the focus she needed to keep her sanity. He had promised they would play this scene together, rehearsed it so often between them. But she had always balked at the killing, and Matlock was the prize that Justin had lived his life hunting.

William had to wait a considerable time before he eventually got through to Dahlia. She confirmed that she had carried out his instructions to the letter, but still had not heard from Matlock or Justin. William placed a second call to the coastguard. They had sent out a launch. William felt relieved enough to leave it in their hands and he hurried to the hospital.

James was on oxygen and a glucose drip, and was linked up to a heart monitor. At this stage they were unable to ascertain if he had suffered any permanent damage. His temperature was stable and a dialysis machine was standing by in case his kidneys failed. His pale face was like a sleeping child's, his arms out straight, like a soldier's, resting on the white sheet. The air-conditioning ensured the room was cool and a ceiling fan turned overhead, making a soft grating sound. Could Justin have had something to do with this? Could he have engineered it? He turned as the door opened, and a nurse ushered Angela in. 'I want to take him home,' she whispered.

'He mustn't be moved,' said the nurse. 'He's still unconscious. We're doing all we can.'

Then Angela saw William. He drew up a chair for her to sit beside the bed. She was twisting a tissue round and round in her hands. 'I asked them to contact my husband,' she said to the nurse. Then she looked pleadingly to William. 'Can you make sure he gets here as soon as possible?'

'Yes, it's being taken care of right now. He'll be here, I'm sure, Angela.'

When the nurse had gone, she said, 'He is so like you, my husband. The only difference is he married me, while you betrayed me.' She threw the torn tissue into the bin. 'You seemed to gain such pleasure from hurting me. You are the most destructive, heartless man.'

'I don't think this is the right place to discuss—'

'No? Funny how there never is a right time, is there?' William shifted his weight from one foot to the other as she stood up and faced him. 'I loved you, you said you loved me. You made me believe you had every intention of marrying me, but within two weeks of making promises, *two weeks*, you took up with that whore! You replaced me in your affections and in my job! I'd had that job for years. You left me when I was ill. You took everything away from me.'

William wished the ground would open up and swallow him. 'It was a long time ago.' He could not believe she was launching such a venomous attack at him while her son lay in a coma beside her. 'You must have hated me,' he said lamely.

'Hated you?' She gave a bitter laugh. 'I tried to kill myself. All I could think about was dying. You almost killed me. I was broke and mentally sick, my mother was suffering from Alzheimer's and I had no one.' She gave a shrill laugh then looked at him. 'But life has a funny way of dealing the cards. My husband's mother was in the hospital too, and that was how we met. Like I said, he reminded me of you – not in looks, just manner. I didn't marry him for that reason. I married him because I thought I loved him. I never did. I tried to make him be like you but he wasn't and then to be used by him with his other women . . . One day I decided that, no matter how long it took, I would have my pound of flesh because I blamed you for my being married to him. I wanted to cause you pain, William, as much as you had caused me.' Her eyes, usually so submissive, blazed. 'Well, I paid you back, William Benedict. You couldn't have had the slightest idea where I was, let alone that I could have been instrumental in . . .'

'It must have been tough harbouring such deep resentment for so many years.'

She was silent for a few moments, then plucked a clean tissue from the box. He could not take his eyes off her hands as they shredded it. 'I never slept a single night without thinking about you. In the end it became second nature, like a ritual.'

'Sleeping cruelty,' he said softly.

'You deserved all you got. Maybe you always were a queer. Maybe that's why you doted on that boy Maynard. You certainly made a big fool of yourself over him.'

William understood it all now. Suddenly he didn't feel any anger towards Angela any more, only sympathy and guilt. Guilt because he had cared for her, and never loved her.

'To begin with my husband always wanted to please me, but gradually I saw through him; I was just a useful appendage. I was afraid he would leave me and take James. It wasn't till I discovered how to control him that I got the upper hand. He was terrified that someone would turn the tables on him. If I divorced him and threatened to feed dirt about him to his competitors he would have been devastated. And believe you me there was plenty of dirt. If you think your little forays with prostitutes made headlines, you should have seen what my beloved husband got up to! He didn't write the articles about you himself, of course, he's above all that now. My husband's only interested in circulation – or money. Rather like you. As I said before, you two are very similar.'

'And you fed him all the inside information about my life to create one scandal after another? My wives, my children?'

'Correct.' She smirked. 'I had always followed your career, William, and your marriages. For God's sake, you even invited me to your first wedding. Can you imagine what that did to me?'

He wanted to explain why he had never loved her or any other woman, but there was no point now.

She looked at the boy in the bed. 'Perhaps now I

will have to pay for it.' She was silent again for a moment. 'Why are we here? I didn't want to come, nor did Humphrey. But he changed his mind. Did you organize this? Did you find out it was me?' she asked softly. She turned to him. 'Did you want me here to hurt me again? Well, if my son is the price, you've won the game. But I don't understand. I believed you never gave me a second thought.'

'I never did,' William said quietly. He hesitated before he continued. 'What do you know about Laura Chalmers?' he asked. 'And her brother, Justin Chalmers?'

'Nothing! Why should I?'

William hooked the back of the spare chair and drew it to the bed to sit next to her. 'Has your husband ever discussed either of them with you?'

'He's never even mentioned them. Neither of us ever met them before we came here. Why do you ask?'

Before she could respond, James began to moan. As they leaned over him, he opened his eyes.

'Oh, thank God, thank God,' Angela wept.

William rang for a nurse, then looked back at the weeping mother caressing her son's face. 'I'm here, darling. Mummy's here, my love. You are going to be all right, I'm here.'

James shut his eyes again. 'I know you are, I've been listening to you two. I just didn't have the strength to tell you to shut the fuck up! I've got to play cricket and I must find my pads,' he said feverishly, trying to sit up.

The heart monitor began bleeping at an alarming rate, and a doctor and nurse hurried in. Angela looked terrified and the doctor asked her to leave, but she hovered at her son's bedside.

'Is he going to be all right?' she gasped, and repeated the question over and over as she sat beside William in the corridor outside James's room.

Half an hour later the doctor came out. He said they had given James something to calm him down, and he would sleep for a few hours. Angela went back to his bedside.

'We found not only cocaine in his body but also heroin and Ecstasy,' the doctor said to William. 'I've had three other Ecstasy cases in the last month. One didn't recover, one had irreversible brain damage, the other's back with his family, showing little or no side-effects. Earlier this year we had a young boy dead on arrival.'

'Oliver Bellingham?' William asked.

The doctor gave a brief nod. His other patients had been local kids, and William felt the man's undercurrent of anger.

'Do the police know who's dealing it?' asked William, with a sick feeling in the pit of his stomach.

The doctor was already moving off. 'If your son recovers, I suggest you ask him who he bought the tablets from. Nothing I say makes the slightest difference to the police. Perhaps they'll listen to someone with your wealth!'

William did not correct the doctor with regard to James. Perhaps if he had known he was not related, he would not have been so forthcoming.

'He thought you were his father,' Angela said, bitterly shaking her head. 'How incongruous. If you knew how I longed to be pregnant by you, longed for your child, then prayed that you would marry me. Now here we are praying for my son to live. But he's not yours. I want my husband here, William. Please try to find him – at least do that for me.'

He walked outside, hoping to God the police would get to Matlock in time – not for Angela or for James, but to save Justin from committing another murder. He called the island, only to be told the fishing boat had not yet returned. William wanted to walk away from the wretched Angela, and he worried about Justin, but he went back into the hospital to sit with her. It was the least he could do.

Matlock's big hands were clasped around his knees. They had been anchored for a while, and the boat was rocking gently. 'Please, I'm begging you, turn back,' he said quietly to Justin.

'We can't turn back, Matlock, because I haven't finished,' he replied.

Matlock tried to stand up. To his horror he couldn't. His legs felt like lead, his head throbbed and he started to panic.

'Fix you another?' Justin held up a clean glass.

Matlock looked up, and his vision blurred. 'What the hell have you given me?' His voice was thick.

'What they used to pump into Laura. Largactyl it's called. Just so you know what it feels like. Remember, she was only a little girl.' Justin delved into his pockets and took out one newspaper cutting after another, waving them in front of Matlock's face. 'How much did they pay you for these? Or did they pay you more to write a good headline? How much did you earn for "Devil's Children"?' he screamed.

Sweat dripped down Matlock's back as he fought to

keep his eyes open. His tongue felt as though it was swelling and filling his mouth. His ears were ringing and buzzing, his heart thudding, and he had lost control of his limbs. It was a living nightmare.

'And the book. *Killer Angels!*' Justin prodded Matlock's chest with it. 'I'm going to make you eat every word you say you never wrote. *Liar!*'

He gripped Matlock's jaw, prised open his mouth and stuffed in newspaper cuttings and pages of the book. Matlock was trying to breathe. He felt as if he was dying.

A siren was wailing, growing louder, closer.

Justin looked down at Matlock. The man looked like a rag doll; in his dead eyes he saw the reflection of his own face, a devil's mask of rage.

Justin had his hand on the lever to pull up the anchor when the coastguard's launch came alongside. A man was yelling through a megaphone: 'Prepare to board!'

'No!' Justin screamed, dragging at the lever.

Then he realized he wouldn't be able to stop them. He moved back to Matlock. 'It isn't over. You hear me? It isn't over.'

Matlock tried to stand, but slumped back on the deck. He tried again, clawing at the sides of the boat.

'You got a Humphrey Matlock on board?' the officer shouted.

'Yeah, what's up?' Justin called back.

'We got an emergency. He's wanted back on Tortola. We're coming aboard.'

'He's drunk!'

Matlock clung to the railing and tried to steady himself. He swayed towards the officer's voice, but the boat rocked and he lurched to the side, toppled over and fell into the dangerous water between the boats.

Seconds later, he surfaced, his arms held out for help. But the swell dragged him under. He surfaced again and was thrown back towards the launch. His head cracked open and blood streamed down his face.

Justin uncoiled a rope from one of the capstans and threw it into the water a good six feet from the struggling man. The officers also threw ropes and life-belts, but Matlock was still grappling with the water. Justin pulled off his shirt, shouted directions for the coastguard to move away, then dived into the sea. He swam underwater for a few seconds, resurfaced, then took a deep breath and went under again. He found Matlock easily. The man's eyes were open, his legs hardly moving, arms splayed wide. He was sinking and a small stream of bubbles drifted from his mouth. Justin swam beneath him, took hold of his foot and dragged him down. Then he surfaced, gasping for breath.

'I got him,' he shouted, holding up one hand for the rope. He caught it, took a breath and went down again. He found Matlock and held him down until the last faint stream of bubbles ceased. Then he looped the rope beneath Matlock's arms, swam up and signalled for the men to pull.

Gradually Matlock's body inched out of the water. His head lolled on his chest. The officers hauled him to the deck and tried to resuscitate him. One gave him the kiss of life, but something was blocking Matlock's airway. The coastguard stuck his fingers down the man's throat and pulled out a sodden piece of newspaper. It was an article with the headline 'Devil's Children'.

CHAPTER 21

WILLIAM HAD sent out one of the orderlies for some coffee and sandwiches, which he now looked at with distaste. Angela, however, sipped her coffee, rocking backwards and forwards on her seat.

'What did you hope to gain by getting us over here?' she asked. William said nothing. 'Oh, come along, there must have been some ulterior motive, knowing you.'

'It was your husband I wanted,' William replied wearily.

'Good God, why?' she asked.

'I wanted to humiliate him, make him a social outcast, like he did to me.'

'Really? And how were you going to do that?'

'Catch him in the act, with his trousers down, photograph him.' He told her about the hidden cameras and the way the island had been set up. 'Laura and Justin agreed to give me explicit footage of your husband, the Baron and Baroness, the Hangerfords, every guest in fact, including their children.' He sighed and stood up. 'I know it all sounds petty, but for a while I was unbalanced. It seemed everyone was against me and I contemplated suicide. Everything in my life had turned sour, and you'll be amused to know that even making money had lost its appeal. I have never known such loneliness.'

Angela put down her cup. All she could think of was her lovemaking with Laura. 'You have all the rooms fitted out with hidden cameras?' she said.

'Yes.' William flushed. 'Only now I see it wasn't really set up for me at all.'

Angela tried to make sense of what he had just said, but all she could think of was the video of her. What would her husband say when he found out? 'Were you going to blackmail us?' she asked.

'It had nothing to do with money. I simply wanted everyone who had made me feel like a worthless piece of shit to know what it felt like. If I chose to, I would be able to make headlines in every paper, especially with your husband being who he is. Can you imagine what his competitors would have done to get their hands on a single photograph? They would have had a field-day with it.' William took a deep breath. 'Now I know that what was really going on was a lot more devious and dangerous than anything I could have dreamed up.'

'What do you mean?' Her chest felt tight.

'It's Laura and Justin Chalmers. This is their revenge.'

Angela was now very scared. 'Why should they want revenge?'

William took out his wallet and passed her some newspaper cuttings. 'Because of these. Read them for yourself. Most importantly, see the name of the young journalist. Your husband built his reputation on the exposure of those two poor kids.'

Angela began reading, then looked at William. 'This

423

can't be the reason, for God's sake! These are years old. And if Humphrey had anything to do with this, don't you think he would have remembered them?'

'He obviously didn't. As you said, it was a very long time ago, more than twenty years. Why should someone like him remember? They were probably just a step up the ladder. He must have hurt a lot more on his way to the top.'

'Like you,' she snapped, and he turned on her, his face pale with anger.

Before he could reply, a nurse tapped lightly on the door and peered in. 'May I speak with you for a moment, Sir William?' she said, and held the door ajar.

William got up and walked out. In the hospital corridor she told him to call the coastguard station immediately.

Laura was growing impatient. There was still no word from Justin and it was now after two. She had been down to the jetty three times. She knew Matlock would be drugged by now and that Justin should be returning for the final part of the game. She was worried that, if they left it any longer, she and Max would not get away. She had forced herself not to go to him, but had occupied herself with her packing, her obsessive method of laying a sheet of tissue paper between each garment, tucking it into sleeves and around collars. Now her case was ready. They would soon be together.

At four, she saw the fishing boat return and hurried down to the quayside. Justin stepped off the boat alone. 'Where is he?'

Justin hooked his arm around her. 'You want the good news or the bad?'

'What happened, Justin? Don't play games with me. You said twelve thirty. I've been waiting and waiting,' she said.

Justin withdrew his arm. 'What the hell has got into you lately, huh? You're so impatient.'

'I'm sorry, but I've been here all by myself.'

'William's back,' Justin said flatly.

'Where's Matlock?'

'Probably on his way to see William.' Justin laughed, reached into one of the cool boxes near the edge of the quay and opened a can of Coke. 'I just wish I'd had a camera because it was worth seeing. But at the same time there was nothing I could do. William contacted the goddamned coastguards to take Matlock off the boat to go and see his son in the hospital.' Justin gulped the Coke and burped. 'Well, dear Sir Humphrey will be in hospital now, close to his beloved son. You should have seen it – he was all bloated and green in the face—'

'Is he dead?'

'Yes, and I'm sorry. I know what it meant for you to be in at the kill but it just couldn't be helped. I had to do it myself.'

'So, it's over,' she said softly. She hugged her slender body and snorted with laughter.

'Yes, he's gone. They're all gone, all the bad people, darling, all gone.'

Laura gave a soft sob, and spread her arms wide. 'I feel like I could fly now it's all over.'

'I guess it is, bar the diamonds,' he said, moving close to her and rubbing her neck.

Laura looked at her watch. Four fifteen: only two hours to go before she could escape. She had never felt so in control of herself. 'When is William going to show up?'

His hand felt warm and comforting but Laura winced as he gripped her tightly. 'I dunno – but I'm starving.' You want to grab a bite to eat with me?' He nuzzled her and kissed her softly, but laid his hand firmly on her neck.

'No, I'll stay here.'

She inched away from him but Justin drew her closer. This time he kissed her mouth, then broke away and withdrew his hand. 'We'll leave this place soon and go back to the villa. I've missed Marta, missed our home.'

'Me too,' she said. Justin was all hands, touching her, needing her. He wouldn't leave her alone. He cupped her face and kissed her lips again. She felt as if she was suffocating.

'We'll be able to live easy now. I'm sorry about you not being there, but maybe it's for the best – it looked accidental. And with old Willy back, you know what a fuss-pot he is . . . Still, he'll have some exhilarating home movies to watch.'

She held him tightly. 'I love you, Justin, I always will.'

He stepped away from her and looked at her. The way she had said 'I love you' hadn't sounded right. It was as if she had been saying it for the last time. 'And I love you, Laura, and only you, always. We'll always be together, won't we?'

She nodded. 'Nothing will ever come between us. Whatever happens.'

His eyes narrowed. He could feel how tense she was, and his concern deepened. 'Maybe you should lie down. Have you been taking your medicine? I mean, do you think you need it?'

'I'm fine, just . . .' She plucked at her skirt. 'Maybe you're right. I'll go and lie down. Join you later.'

Angela had been given a sedative, but was adamant she would accompany William to identify her husband's body. He suggested that to keep the media at bay they tell no one until the body was ready to be flown back to England. There would be an inquest and the usual documentation to deal with, all of which William promised to handle. At first he was shaken when he heard of Matlock's death, then afraid to ask for details: he was so sure he had been murdered. When the police told him it was an accident, he was relieved. When they said Justin had risked his life trying to save Matlock, he was puzzled, but then even more relieved because he must have been wrong about him . . . and he hoped desperately that he had been.

William's speedboat arrived at Tortola stacked with the Matlocks' cases and a neatly packed envelope containing their passports and money from the private safe in their suite. Angela's jewels were in a small leather case, guarded by one of the boat-boys who handed it separately to William. He arranged for all the luggage to be delivered to the hotel he had booked for Angela. When he slumped into the boat to return to the island, he was in need of a shower, a change of clothes and a good night's sleep. But he doubted if he'd be getting any sleep for a while. He knew he was going to have to face both Justin and Laura.

Justin strolled into Laura's room, where he found her lying on the bed.

' "Why so pale and wan, fond lover?" ' he quoted, throwing himself on the bed beside her. 'It's odd, isn't it? Now that we've done it, somehow it's unsatisfying.'

Laura sighed, and Justin rolled on top of her, tickling her. She tried to move away from him.

'Diamonds, diamonds, diamonds . . .' he said, with a wide grin. He pulled her close and tickled her again. She couldn't stop him; it was the way it had been ever since they were children. He began mimicking Matlock's death scene, plunging off the bed on to the floor, swimming on the carpet. He mimed coming up for air, clinging to the sheet as if it was the edge of the boat, wailing as he fell back.

They laughed until they were exhausted, then lay wrapped in each other's arms. She started to cry and he rocked her back and forth as if she was a baby, making soft sounds to calm her. Then he started to sing. He loved it when she sang with him.

Max had put away the windsurfer, and now strolled to his room to fetch his case. There was an hour to go. He wandered round the house. It was strangely quiet when no one was about.

'Justin?' he called. He stood in the large empty hall, and his eyed drifted to a door he'd frequently seen

Justin disappear through. The office, he supposed. 'Justin?' he called again. No reply.

He entered some sort of control room – it was full of switches and a great panel like you saw in documentaries about rock-stars. Amused, Max sat at the main desk and pressed a button. A monitor overhead flickered and came on. Max discovered he was watching some porn film. But the girl looked familiar. The man had his back to camera and she was sucking him off. God, it couldn't be? It was! Clarissa Hangerford and Justin!

Max didn't like being a voyeur. He stabbed at another button; the VCR stopped, and the monitor flicked to what looked like security mode. The screen showed the front hall. Max pressed the button again. His parent's bedroom! Again. The sauna! This was fun. He wondered whether his own room was included. The dining room, the swimming-pool, the jetty, another bedroom, and another, and another. He flicked again, then flicked back. The last bedroom had people in it: Laura and Justin lying on a big double bed.

'We did it,' said Justin, throwing his head back against the pillow. 'We got every single one of those motherfuckers.' He turned to face his sister. 'Tonight, Laura, we'll dance. I want you to wear that gold dress.'

Laura smiled. She had a faraway look. Max knew it was because she would not be dancing with Justin that night but in his own arms speeding away from this place for ever. 'It was fun killing him, sweet one, I wish you could have seen how cleverly I did it. I pulled him down into the water, and they all thought I was trying to save him. Really I should get an Oscar.'

Laura faced her brother. First he'd mimed it all, now

he seemed to want to go over every detail again. 'Justin,' said Laura, 'you're not kidding me, are you? He is dead, isn't he?'

'Would I lie to you?'

She stroked his head. 'You lie to everyone else. Maybe you would. You know how much it means to me, and now with Angela and James not here, he might just have gone to join them.'

Max leaned in close to the screen. His heart was beating rapidly.

Justin nodded sombrely. 'Would I lie to you? Jesus, how can you even think for a second I would lie about something as important as this? For Christ's sake, he's dead, and the others are ruined.' He wrapped Laura tighter in his arms. 'Oh, sweetness, I've missed lying in bed with you, holding you in my arms. Believe me, I never lie to you, you are the centre of my universe.' He leaned on his elbow, tracing her face with one finger. 'Just as you'd never lie to me. Right?'

She gave a small smile, as he moved his index finger across her perfect lips.

'But I've been jealous of Max. I admit it. For some stupid reason I thought that maybe you really did care for him. I'm glad I was mistaken.' said Justin. 'I understand it now. Max was just part of the scam, wasn't he? He never meant anything else to you?'

Laura shook her head. 'Of course not,' she said, her lips only an inch away from her brother's. 'The only man I have ever loved is you.'

They kissed, at first almost innocently, then the kiss became deeper and more prolonged.

Max gasped. His breath felt as if it had been squeezed

from his lungs and his heart felt as though it was jumping out of his chest. He ran out of the office, out of the house, out into the oncoming dusk. His body felt as if it was on fire. He hurt inside so much that he couldn't get the sight of Justin with Laura out of his mind.

William's stomach churned as the boat crashed over a wave; the sea always got rougher as they headed inshore towards the island. He stretched, then stood up in the boat to admire his paradise as they approached. This evening it looked glorious, with the sun sinking into the horizon and all the outside lights twinkling, making the island appear like a magical mirage. He moved closer to the rails and took deep gulping breaths. It made him feel better: all the anxiety and emotional strain of the day were blown out of him. He was glad to be coming home, and once he'd said that word in his mind, he knew it *was* his home. This was where he wanted to be more than anywhere else.

He had a future he wanted to live his own way, without any interference or guilt. He knew now that it was linked to Justin, because none of what he saw or felt would have existed without him. Now he acknowledged the effect this man, this wild crazy boy, had over him. Never before had he craved to see someone, or felt his belly churn with anticipation at the prospect of being close to somebody. His heart fluttered and he laughed. He would never have believed it was true.

He could hear Justin's laugh, see his face in a multitude of expressions. They overlapped and juggled for space in his mind until he felt weak and had to sit down. Like a lovesick boy, he ached to see Justin, no matter what had happened in the past.

But as the boat drew closer to the jetty his confidence began to waver, leaving him with a terrible dread that Justin might not want to remain his friend. After all, hadn't Justin used him as he had used everyone else? Suddenly he was afraid he would lose Justin. He was unsure whether he could deal with such a loss: Justin was closer to him than anyone else, and no matter what he had done, William would have to confront him with all he had discovered. He fell into contemplation of how he would approach him: he knew he had to be told the truth, no matter what.

When Laura couldn't find Max in his room she was worried. Then she remembered they'd agreed to meet at Suicide Point. She reprimanded herself for being so stupid. She had made the arrangements, after all. She checked her case, stashed behind some ferns, before starting along the winding path up to the point. She'd thought Justin was never going to leave her room. But he'd suddenly heard a boat coming in, and rushed out. It was either William or the mail-boat arriving, he'd called. She waited ten minutes before she dared leave.

Laura ran, panting, to the peak, the highest point on the island. As she turned the last blind corner to climb higher she caught a glimpse of Max in the distance, standing with his back to her, facing the sea. He was barefoot, wearing dark trousers and a white shirt, billowing in the wind. His hands were on his hips and he was standing so still he might have been a statue. Laura began to run, but as she drew closer she froze.

It wasn't Max, it was Justin. She stared at him for a moment, frightened. Where was Max? *What had he done to Max?* She clenched her fists and forced herself to continue towards Justin, who stared out to sea, watching William's speedboat approach the island.

'Where is he?' She was only a few feet behind him.

Justin tensed. He said nothing.

She came closer and her voice was shrill: 'Where is he? What have you done to him? If you've hurt him, I'll . . .' She was close enough now. One hard shove and he would topple over Suicide Point into the crashing sea below.

'He's not coming, Laura,' Justin said.

She raised both hands to push him over but Justin grabbed her wrists. 'He's on the jetty, ready to leave. He's going alone.'

He still held her wrists as her body relaxed and the anger subsided. She shook her head, smiling. 'Oh, no, not this time. I don't believe you. He's waiting for me.'

He grabbed her and held her in his arms so she could hardly breathe. He guided her to the cliff's edge, and forced her to look down towards the jetty. Max was standing with his suitcase beside him. She eased away from him, and stepped closer to the edge. Justin dragged her back.

'What have you told him?' Laura screeched. Justin threw her to the ground and bent down to her. She kicked him between his legs and he howled in agony. 'You bastard, what did you tell him? He loves me.' Laura clawed at the grass. Her eyes were demented and her face twisted with uncontrollable rage. 'You had to spoil it. I knew you would if you found out because you were always jealous, jealous that I had a chance to be free of you. I hate you! I hate you!' she hissed, and with that she came for him, scratching and snarling like a savage.

Then she began to sob. 'I never told him anything. I wouldn't have done that to you.' She could taste the blood in her mouth and gasped, taking deep breaths. She was calming down, bringing her anger under control.

Justin watched her fearfully. The rage quietened, but he could still see it swirling inside her. Her wild eyes belied the smile on her lips.

'You never told him anything, did you, about us?' Laura pleaded.

'I swear on our graves.'

Laura knew he was telling the truth. When they were children they had dug their graves ready for them to lie side by side. They had often laughed about how they would have to dig them deeper and wider if they were to fit into them as adults. His sad, vulnerable face made her open her arms to him and cradle him against her breasts.

Justin was crying. He was so afraid for her when she was like this, when her eyes frightened him. When Laura hid her fury she was very dangerous. He had to stop her seeing Max. He sobbed out, 'I will never leave you, I will always be here for you.'

'Ssh, ssh,' she whispered, kissing his head and rocking him. 'We have to leave each other some day, Justin,' she said. She felt as if her heart would burst open and bleed. Max was not going to get away from her, but she knew that if Justin suspected anything he would never let her go. 'Haven't you ever wanted to be free of me?'

Justin shook his head and slumped to the ground.

She crouched down beside him. 'Oh, yes, you have. Come on, Justin, you can admit it to me. You have wanted to be free of me, haven't you?'

'Sometimes,' he admitted.

'You know, if you could find someone to love and be loved by, I wouldn't stop you or try and spoil it. You do know that, don't you?'

He gave her a sidelong look. This was a route they had never travelled down before. He could not see her eyes or her expression: her hair fell like a curtain across her face. 'Okay, Laura, *would* you feel the same way about me? You know, if I found someone?' His heart pounded. Could he leave her and not feel guilty? Justin took her hand and threaded his fingers through hers. Her hair still hid her face and she made no reply. The pain inside him was like razors slicing into him. A terrible sense of loss consumed him. 'Laura? Is it over now?'

Laura stood up and brushed her skirt down, then took a deep breath. 'I have to go to Max.'

He closed his eyes. 'Let him go, Laura. Let him go.'

She looked down at him. 'No, I won't. It's you I'm letting go, Justin. It's time.'

He had found her hidden suitcase, and knew now she had lied. It hurt him so much.

'We love each other,' she said firmly. 'Not the same way as you and me, that will always be special, our secret. But I have made a decision and you can't stop me. He can take care of me now.'

435

'No, he can't,' Justin said, his voice breaking.

'Yes, he can. He has a big trust fund and we'll find a little house, perhaps close to the villa in France.'

'I think he went into the control room,' he said softly. But she was talking rapidly to herself, making plans as she brushed down her skirt.

'We could hire you to make our house special.' She cupped his face between her hands. 'This will all be perfect, you'll see. I had better go now, I don't want to miss the boat.'

Justin stared at her as tears rolled down his cheeks. Her eyes were empty. She was already somewhere out of his reach, so he let her go. He watched her walking to her case, brushing aside the ferns, picking it up then turning to wave to him. He couldn't stop her, not this time.

William stepped on to the jetty and was surprised to see Max there, sitting on his case. He rose to greet William. 'Would it be possible to be taken to Tortola, sir?' he asked.

William looked back at the boat-boys. They had made the crossing so many times that day and they looked worn out. 'I'd prefer it if you waited for the mail-boat,' he said. 'It should be along at about six. It'll be a longer trip but my boys are tired out.'

Max checked his wristwatch. It was just past six o'clock.

William raised an eyebrow. 'It'll be here, give or take half an hour. It depends on the tides, and how many deliveries they have to do.' He headed for one of the golf carts then glanced back.

Max was shading his eyes and looking out to sea. He called out, 'I can see it!'

Goodbye, then, have a safe journey home,' William shouted and continued towards the golf cart.

The mail-boat crew agreed to take Max aboard, but said they would need a half-hour break. Max returned to sit on his suitcase. He didn't want to go near the house again. All he wanted was to leave. The more he thought about Laura, the more thankful he was he'd found out. It had been a stupid fantasy. He could not have married Laura. He would never have been able to finish his studies or been able to provide for her. It was just one of those stupid holiday things.

The longer he brooded, the more he reverted to the boy who had stepped off the launch on his arrival. He cried a little, and wiped away the tears with the back of his hand. She was a cheap whore, a slut. Thank God he'd walked into that office. Thank God he'd switched on the tapes.

Laura hurried down to the jetty. When she saw William in the golf cart heading towards the house, she paused, remembering the diamonds. That didn't matter, she'd contact him after she and Max were married: they might need the diamonds to help buy a little house. William wouldn't cheat her. She kept walking, talking rapidly to herself, making her plans.

She didn't realize she was stumbling, almost falling. She felt slightly dizzy. She was so intent on seeing Max that she was unaware of the signals, and blamed the way she was feeling on the weight of her suitcase. She tossed it aside: she didn't want to miss the boat.

Suddenly her legs almost buckled beneath her as the darkness crept upwards. Then came the fear, making its way up her legs to her thighs. Soon it would be dragging at her intestines. Laura gasped for breath as she crawled back to her suitcase. She fumbled with the clasp and got it open to find her medicine box. At any moment now she would be incapable of helping herself. As she opened the box, spilling tablets on the ground, the horror seized her. She tried to stand but her body jerked backwards and she fell heavily on the floor, cracking her head against the paving. Blood seeped into her hair, but she couldn't feel the pain, and she thrashed around, slithering across the stone-flagged path, twisting and turning, spittle at the corners of her mouth.

Not a quarter of a mile away, Max walked along the narrow gang plank to jump down on to the deck of the mail-boat. He watched the boys haul in the planks, the engines started up, and the boat eased away from the jetty. He saw Justin running like a man possessed along a narrow path, saw him bend out of sight. The next moment he was carrying Laura in his arms. Max turned away, not wanting to see them, not wanting to remember what he had seen. He only wanted to forget, but it would take a long time.

Justin pushed open the bungalow door and laid his sister on the bed, praying that it was over, that it would not take hold again. But just as she seemed peaceful, it began again in such force that her body seemed to lift itself up, as if hurled by unseen hands. In a panic he rummaged for her medicine box and realized it was back down the path in her suitcase. He ran out of the bungalow.

Justin's breath heaved in his chest. He'd picked up the pills and the medicine box, shoved them in the case and dragged it back up. Now he opened the box, took out a thick wedge of rubber and stood over her. He calculated how long it had been going on, and tried to hold her down, but her strength was awesome.

'What the hell are you doing?' William shouted from the doorway.

'She's having a fit. It's been going on for a long time. It'll kill her. Help me get this into her mouth – she's biting her tongue. She'll choke herself.'

William could not believe the strength of the fragile woman. At last Justin gripped her head long enough to prise open her mouth, and used a platinum spatula to force her teeth apart. Blood trickled from her mouth where she had bitten through her tongue, but at last he was able to insert the wedge. He stepped away from her, then filled a syringe and injected her with a sedative.

'Get away from her. There's nothing we can do except hope it'll be over soon.'

They stood watching Laura as she continued having spasms and slithered across the floor like an eel. Slowly the fit subsided and she lay twitching and snorting. Her body was black and blue where she had slammed against the furniture and the wound to her head bled freely.

As soon as she was calm enough, Justin lifted her and carried her to the bed.

William fetched wet towels to wipe the blood from

her head, then watched as Justin dressed her in a satin nightie. He tucked the sheet tightly around her and took the wedge out of her mouth. She was still now, in a deep sleep. William was moved by the tenderness Justin showed her.

At last Justin turned to him. 'I'm so glad to see you, Willy.'

'And I'm glad to see you, Justin. I've missed you.'

Only then did he see the scratch marks on Justin's face, the bruises on his neck. 'Dear God, don't tell me she did that to you?' William said, shocked.

Justin shook his head. 'No, I fell. It looks a lot worse than it is.'

William made him sit down, got some disinfectant and bathed the cuts. Some were so deep they bled profusely. Justin remained silent throughout.

Tears slid down Justin's cheeks, which William wiped away. He did not know why it happened, but suddenly he took Justin's face in his hands and kissed him on the cleaned wounds and his neck, but was afraid to move to the lips he wanted more than anything to touch with his.

Justin clung to him as though he never wanted to let go, and the kiss, when it came, was instigated by him. For William it was shocking but also the ultimate pleasure of his life. The embrace took him to a world of love he had believed was beyond his reach. He was filled with desire and hope. This was where he knew Andrew Maynard had been; this was the love he had written about. A shining peace swept through every fibre of his body.

'I'm so glad you're here, Willy,' Justin murmured.

'Me too.' William hesitated before he spoke again.

'I've missed you Justin. I've also been so afraid, but it's all going to be all right now. I'm here for you both. It's all going to be all right, I'm sure.'

'Is it, Willy?' Justin said. 'Promise? I bet you daren't! There's so much you don't know about me and Laura. We're not good people, Willy. I'm not a good person.'

'Justin, trust me, I know everything about you and Laura now, and it doesn't make any difference to me. Marta told me. She loves you and . . . and no one will ever hurt either of you again. I'll see to that.'

He went to the door, overwhelmed by his emotions, but he knew it was not quite over yet: he had to know more. 'I'll arrange for Dahlia to sit with her and we'll get Marta over here.' He faced Justin. 'I have to eat. Would you join me?'

Justin followed him. 'I'm so glad to be with you, Willy. I don't think this time I could have coped. I've been on my own for so long, and I'm tired. Laura needs to be taken care of, she always has. These fits get worse. I've been told that each time it happens, her brain is damaged a little and it terrifies me.'

William put his arm around Justin's shoulders. To his delight, Justin caught his hand and threaded his fingers through it.

'You're not on your own, Justin, not any more. You've got me, and I'll get Laura the best medical attention money can buy. She's my responsibility now.'

'Why?' Justin asked.

'I love you both, that's why.'

Justin appeared to accept his answer and they strolled on into the house.

*

William fingered the stem of his glass. He had to choose his words carefully. They had both bathed and changed, and now sat across the table from each other. Yet again, he had a feeling of peace and calm, as if his life at long last had come into focus.

'I have never been what I would call a happy man,' he began. 'There has been little joy in my life. But suddenly I realized . . . you have given me that. It hasn't been plain sailing, but I look forward to seeing you more than anyone. And when I began to think you were . . .' he sipped the champagne '. . . planning murder, it was not that you were about to commit a crime that concerned me, it was the thought that I might not see you again. I realized you had become a very important part of my life. But I need to be told the truth, all of it, so that, if need be, I can protect you both. You must tell me everything. I want the facts, no matter what they are.'

'Maybe you won't like me if you know it all, Willy. You might have taken on more than you bargained for.'

'Try me. I'm offering you this island as your home, a place to stay for ever. What is your alternative? Where else will you go?'

Justin shrugged. 'Oh, back to the villa, get some more design commissions. This place will do me a lot of good as far as that goes.'

'And Laura will go with you?'

'Yep, that's the game plan. I'll earn enough to look after her, and she loves the villa.'

'Isn't that where you both suffered so much? Isn't that the very place she shouldn't return to – or you for that matter? It's there, no matter how you disguise it with waterfalls and flowers, that it all happened to you both.'

'I guess it is, but I've never let us think about it. What it looked like then, and what it now is . . . It's different. It's home.'

'This could also be your home, and you could work from here. You love it here, don't you?'

'Yes, you know I do, but . . .'

'I would like to make it my home, live here with you both.' William sat back, twisting the stem of his glass. When he looked up, Justin was staring at him and his body was rigid. Twice he started to say something and then stopped.

William tried to ease the tension. He poured more champagne. 'I read Andrew Maynard's diaries, and I was envious of his joy at finding love. He wrote of being so happy that it had changed his life. In many ways, you have changed mine, Justin.'

Justin's eyes flicked to the dark ocean. 'Ask me if I killed him, Willy. That's what you really want to know. All this bullshit about being envious, just cut it out.'

'Andrew committed suicide,' William stated.

'Did he?'

William gripped the stem of his glass.

'I wrote the note, Willy, let it sink into the bath-water so the writing would be hard to read. I've always been expert at copying signatures. I also wrote the yellow sticker to make sure you would be called . . .'

'I don't believe you. How could you know that the housekeeper would call me and that I would remove Andrew's diaries?'

443

Justin leaned back in his chair. 'Because you were in love with him. Maybe you weren't even aware of it. Andrew sussed that you were. Even if it wasn't love, you must have desired him in some way. You certainly saw him often enough.'

William stared at the tablecloth. 'I admired him, I trusted him, I believed that he would have a great future—'

Justin leaned across the table and grabbed his hand. 'You want me to be truthful – why don't you start playing the game straight as well? You didn't lay out all that cash just to be his paymaster. *What did you want out of it?*'

William flushed as he said angrily that he had wanted Maynard's success, nothing more. 'I admired him, yes. Truth was, I bathed in his glory, and I got my knighthood through him, but . . .'

'But?' Justin asked softly, and William couldn't meet his eyes. He told Justin about a little kid who had sat next to him at school, a stammering boy with long eyelashes who had kissed him and had been killed on a level crossing.

'Andrew reminded me of Peter Jenkins, that was his name. Maybe there is something latent in me. I doubt if I could face up to it, but I often wondered why I was so distressed about him. But with Maynard I only wanted him to succeed. I wanted him to be my son. I had little or no relationship with Charlie then.'

'Did you doubt your feelings or did you just not dare show Andrew what you really felt about him?'

William stared hard at him. 'I don't want to answer that, and we're supposed to be talking about you, not me.'

444

'But it all has to be ironed out, don't you think? Lean forward, Willy.'

William did so, and Justin kissed his lips.

'Are you afraid to love me?' Justin asked, and rocked back in his chair. 'You keep on saying how much you love me and Laura, but let's take just me. Are you afraid to lie naked next to me, Willy, afraid to let me make love to you?'

'Yes, I am, and that's not why we're here. I have offered—'

'To take care of me and Laura. But you want me to tell you all my secrets yet refuse to tell me yours, or admit them. I'm not your son. I'm not Charlie. I'm Justin. To what depth does your love want to go?'

'I won't answer that. I'm just confused, and I need to know – did you kill Andrew?'

Justin kicked his chair back and walked to the window. 'Yes. He had to die because he was becoming dangerous. He found out about my background. He was always delving into drawers and trying to find out more and more about me and Laura. Then he found out about his fucking sister and—'

'She died in a car accident,' William said, hardly audible.

'I know. I fixed her brakes. I even followed her along the motorway and saw her car veer across the lanes. Camilla Maynard gave exclusive interviews to Humphrey Matlock. She was part of it. By the way, I held Matlock under the water until he drowned. What do you say about that? I mean, surely you don't need to ask me why? You said you knew why. You said you knew everything. Well, now you do, and what do you think of me?'

William pushed back his chair and crossed to Justin. He held out his arms and Justin's bravado evaporated. Like a small boy, he went to William and clung to him, sobs shaking his body. William held him tightly, soothing him, letting him weep until he was silent.

The thoughts that zigzagged through William's mind made it difficult for him to remain calm. What Justin had said was shocking, yet he had suspected it all along, suspected and been afraid of it since he had talked to Marta at the villa. But it did not feel as if he was holding a killer in his arms, only a wounded boy whose suffering had obsessed him.

'You're the only friend I have ever had in my life,' Justin whispered. He rested his head against William's shoulder. 'Sometimes I feel like I am insane. But the need to hurt those who tortured me and Laura would never go away. I had to do it, William, otherwise I would have gone crazy, like Laura.'

William led him back to the table and sat him down. He patted his shoulder, then used a napkin to wipe his tears. 'How much a part of it is Laura?'

'Oh, nothing but the planning. We planned everything together. We're not just brother and sister. We're lovers. We could only ever trust each other, you see? Can you understand what we became to each other? We were each other's parents. We were all we dared to love because everyone else seemed intent on destroying us, and the more pain we experienced, the more we were drawn together. Only by being so close could we protect each other.'

William returned to his seat. His mind was in turmoil as he tried to assimilate the terrible things Justin had just told him. But he knew he must now allow Justin to see how affected he was by the truth.

Justin drained his champagne. 'You're confusing me,' he said softly. In the candlelight his face was astonishingly beautiful, his high cheekbones shadowed, his jaw-line chiselled and his eyes glittering like azure stones.

William turned away on the pretext of pouring more champagne. 'I'm sorry, I didn't intend to . . . er, confuse you. I'm trying to be as honest as I can. You've helped change my life. Now I want to help you straighten out yours. After what you've told me . . .'

'What if it's too late?' Justin said.

'It's never too late. Look at what you did for me. And I'm not just referring to making me lose my gut. It's what you did for me up here,' William said, tapping his head.

'But what if my confessions repel you, frighten you? You may betray me out of fear.'

William kept his gaze steady. 'I will never betray you, Justin, and I mean it. This island will be a safe place. Do you understand what I'm saying? No one can get to you, or harm you or Laura. I will protect you both.'

'Does that mean you can forgive me and forget what I have done?'

William watched as a multitude of emotions played across Justin's handsome face. 'No one is aware of what you have done. Unless they are told or the police reinvestigate Maynard's suicide, they probably never will be.'

'Unless you tell them. You see what I've just done? I've put my life in your hands.'

'I have promised that I will protect you.'

'Why? What makes you want to do that? Or, for that matter, what will stop me killing you? Now that I know you know, and you are the only one apart fom Laura who does, what do you think will stop me killing you?'

William met Justin's eyes, and this time he didn't look away. 'Because I love you, and you have made a difference to my life. I am prepared to—'

'Be my lover?'

'*No!* Stop that! I am offering to be . . . like a father to you.'

'My father is dead,' Justin said. Suddenly he stood up and his chair fell behind him. 'Just give me Laura's diamonds, the ones you promised, and we'll both leave. I don't want to hear any more crap from you. You've had too much to drink.'

William stood up too. 'The diamonds are under your sister's pillow.' He noticed this freaked Justin. He continued, 'I've also destroyed the tapes. You will never be able to use them against anyone.'

'Oh, I see. So you want to destroy me next,' Justin snarled.

'No, I don't. You've not been listening to what I've been saying. I'm offering—'

'What the fuck do you want from me? What do you expect me to say to you? Do you want to keep me here like some fucking plaything? What's happened, Willy? You still afraid to come out of your closet? Why don't you admit it now? Go on, look at me. Tell me you want me to fuck you. Do you think that's what I want? You? With your wispy hair and flaccid belly? I don't want you near me, you repel me, and this bullshit about protecting me is all for one reason. You want my body just like that prick Maynard did.'

William hit him hard across the face. Justin stumbled to one side then laughed and started to give William a slow handclap. Then he glared and became the waspish, lisping man Laura and William hated. 'Well, well, how the worm turns!'

'What did I say that was so bad, Justin?' William was not going to be drawn into a shouting match.

Justin pushed his face forward so that he was almost nose to nose with William. 'You wiped my precious tapes. I needed them. You're a liar and a two-faced bastard. And you, Willy-boy, are not my father. If you were you'd have a knife stuck in your chest. As it is, if you keep me prisoner on this island you'll never be safe. I'll hurl your body off Suicide Point. Just another accident.'

'You wouldn't do that to me.'

'You want to bet?'

Justin turned and walked out, knocking aside the waiter as he carried in their tray. The dishes crashed to the floor but Justin did not turn back. William sat up and shook out his napkin, anything to stop his running after Justin. He had just seen the madness in him, the killer, and it scared him. Whatever he had dreamed up about being a fatherly figure to that wild creature was insanity, and he knew it. But he did not want to back away. He had come to see Justin and to explain himself. But explain what? The reality was that he was in love with Justin. He wanted that love reciprocated, and for a moment when they had embraced, he had felt sure that it was. But instead of telling Justin this he had offered to be a substitute father, and Justin had snarled in his face. And he *did* want to lie naked beside him, to make love to him. He wouldn't let Justin's rejection alter the fact that he was still the most important person in his life, and he would stand by what he had offered: his protection.

William forced himself to eat his dinner. Each mouthful was hard to swallow, but he was not going to chase after Justin. He needed to cool off. They had to talk again.

Dahlia put her finger to her lips and pointed to the bed. Laura was propped up with pillows. Her hair had been combed and tied with a ribbon, and there was a plaster across the cut on her head. However, her eyes were clear and bright and her cheeks slightly flushed. She looked like a little girl. A square of black velvet lay across the white sheet. It was covered with sparkling diamonds.

'She's had a sedative,' Dahlia whispered, gesturing for William to move to her side. 'She doesn't seem to know where she is.' Dahlia showed William the tablets, vials and hypodermic needles in Laura's medicine box. 'Justin was here. He told me she sometimes reverts back to childhood. It takes time for her to readjust, he said. He also said—' She faltered.

'Said what?'

'That in the past she had electro-convulsive therapy if she remained in her own world. But it was a last resort.'

William nodded then asked her to make him some

450

coffee. As she left, he took her seat by the bed. 'How are you feeling, Laura?' he said softly.

She turned and gave him a sweet smile. He was uncertain whether she knew who he was: there was a deadness in her eyes. She blinked slowly at him, then turned her attention back to the sparkling stones.

'They are diamonds,' she said slowly, as she began moving them from one side of the black velvet to the other. 'One for Lord Cedric, one for his wife, one for Clarissa, one for James, one for the Baron, one for the Baroness, this big one for Matlock, and this one for Angela.' She counted them again, moving them back to the other side of the velvet, her brow furrowed.

Dahlia returned with a tray. 'She's been doing that for quite a while. She remembers who was here, so she can't be that bad,' she said.

They both turned as Laura spoke. 'One missing! There's no diamond for Max. Max should be the biggest.' She turned to William. 'Are you jealous, like my brother, because I love Max? I'm going away with him.' She busied herself again, smoothing the black velvet.

William leaned forward. 'I must have miscounted, Laura, I'm sorry. You'll have another tomorrow, the biggest one of all. And then Marta's coming to look after you,' he said.

'Thank you,' she said.

'Do you like being here?' he asked. She made no reply. 'If you want to stay on the island for ever, I will always take care of you, Laura.'

'Thank you,' she said.

He turned to Dahlia. 'Is that true, about Max?'

'They were planning to elope, but I think the boy changed his mind.'

'Thank you,' said Laura, to nobody.

Dahlia stood behind William and put her hand on his shoulder. 'I have never heard anyone say those words so sweetly, or so sadly. When Justin said he was leaving, that was all she said to him. She looked up, smiled just as she did now and said, "Thank you."'

William gasped. 'Justin said he was leaving? But he can't have! The mail-boat went ages ago.'

Dahlia nodded. 'I know, but it stops off at all the islands. Fifteen minutes ago he said he was taking the speedboat with one of the boys to catch it up.'

William left the room and ran panic-stricken to the jetty. The speedboat was just returning. There was no sign of Justin. His heart sank. He called to one of the boys swabbing down the decks on the cruiser. 'Have you seen Justin?'

'He left, sir. I took him to the mail-boat. He went aboard at Mustique. He and the young man, Max, left for Tortola together.'

William felt as if his panic would spiral out of control. He shouted orders for the crew to come immediately to the dock and get the speedboat ready.

'But, sir,' said the boy, 'look at the sky! There's going to be a storm.'

'Just do it!' he shouted.

He had to sit down, his legs were shaking so much. Why had he said it all? He had forced Justin to run away. Then he thought of what Justin might do to Max. He knew he had to get to the mail-boat – had to reach Justin before he killed Max.

452

CHAPTER 22

THE STORM that had been threatening made a spectacular entrance with a terrifying crack of electricity. Lightning lit up the sky and the ocean, before everything was plunged into darkness again. A second later, a shorter bolt flashed, heralding the thunderclap that followed, and showing Justin in silhouette on the deck, as he waved farewell to the speedboat crew. Max was already worried about the storm and was sure Justin had come after him. He moved closer to one of the men on board, expecting some kind of argument to break out. But Justin never even looked at him.

The mail-boat rolled on the choppy waves, but the crew seemed unconcerned. Max constantly looked skyward in trepidation. He wasn't sure which was worse: Justin being on board frightened the life out of him, but the crew regaling him with stories of real 'horror storms' they had survived made him tremble. They had been at sea more than three-quarters of an hour after delivering the mail to the islands, and it was coming up to eight o'clock. The sky was already pitch black when the rain started. Thankfully it was not heavy. One old man smiled at Max, said the worst was over, but it didn't make him feel any better.

Justin sat hunched at the stern. He had ignored Max from the moment he had come aboard. He knew the boy was constantly looking at him, knew he was afraid of him, but he wasn't interested, not yet. He had no desire even to speak to him. His face was set in an expressionless stare looking out to sea. He had taken money and his passport, but wasn't sure what he intended to do after he had completed his new mission. He was a little ashamed of having taken off in the way he had, but William had unwittingly touched a raw nerve that had made him act on impulse . . . he had felt the terror rise, the memories of his anguish. Only Laura had dried his tears. Then came the shame he felt when they had taken tiny Laura into their room, not him. He had covered his ears when he heard her calling for him. Later that first night, he had crawled in beside her, bathed her tiny bruised body. Then they had clung to each other, night after night, waiting with fear for their bedroom door to creak open.

'Come with Mummy, Laura.'

'Come to Daddy, Justin.'

They had been subjected to such perversion, such pain, and threatened with more if they whispered to a soul what had happened to them. The devil would eat them alive if they ever told anyone about their mummy and daddy's games. They were special secrets, and they would die if they ever told them. They would be buried alive – and to make sure they understood, they had been forced to watch the burial of their pets, forced to watch the earth cover a tiny canary's feathered chest, a pet spaniel tied by his paws. They had waited to dig him up and seen the maggots and bugs filling his mouth, his ears and his eyes. They reburied him, more afraid than ever. So they kept the hideous secret until Laura lit the candle and held the flame to her mother's sheets. Then they had another secret to hide, and another, and another . . .

Justin had had no option but to get away. He had been afraid of what he might do to William. Seeing Laura regress yet again had not helped: it had made him feel wretched, even though he had seen it many times. He knew she had come out of them before. Sometimes it had taken days, months, but Justin was certain that, whatever happened to him, William would care for Laura. He had never entrusted her to anyone but himself and Marta, but knowing their old nurse would soon be arriving had made his leaving easier to bear. He blamed Max for Laura's collapse, and now he would make him pay. He would be the last, he swore to himself. After Max there would be no more.

Like a dark shadow, the island disappeared from view. How he had loved it, built it with such dedication and care. Never before had he been so content or happy in a place. He knew every flowering bush, every tree and every cove. He would have liked to spend the rest of his life there because it was his paradise. In his heart, it had become his the moment he had stepped ashore for the first time. That was where he could find peace, forget the horrors that tormented him. Now he was leaving it and he didn't know or care where he was going to. He would not let his mind drift back to William, who loved the island as much as Justin. If only William had been honest, if only he could just have offered to love and nothing more, but he hadn't. Instead he had used the hated word 'father', which had cut through Justin's heart and turned him back to the madness that lurked just beneath his beautiful exterior.

William had touched a raw nerve in the hope of gaining some understanding. How could he know he had pressed the button that made Justin want to kill? He turned to face Max, and their eyes locked.

'They say the storm's passing over,' Max said, as justification for speaking to Justin. Their proximity had given him the confidence that no harm would come to him, but he saw Justin flinch. 'How much longer do you think it's going to last?' he asked.

'As long as it takes, Max.' Justin's voice was low, and his eyes bored into the boy's fearful face. He wondered if it would appear too much of a coincidence if Max were to drown like Matlock. But the crew were everywhere. He would have to think of some other way, but he felt so tired.

He watched Max slither back to the shelter of the little cabin. Maybe the storm would toss the boy overboard without any assistance from him: it was not blowing over by any means. The rain had only just started to fall and would come down much heavier. The distant booms of thunder would soon return seaward.

Max hovered close to the cabin door, and was told to go below deck. But he preferred to cling to the guard rail. 'It seems to be getting rougher,' he said, and was frightened by the seamen's looks as they dragged on their rain capes and hooked safety harnesses to their belts.

'You go below when we tell you, son,' one man shouted.

'Isn't the storm over?' Max shouted.

'No,' came the reply.

Justin focused on the mounting angry waves. He wondered how long it would take to drown and be really free. How would it feel?

William wore a cape and sou'wester. The rain dripped off him as the speedboat cut through the swell. They had made radio contact and discovered the route the mail-boat would now be taking. William planned to overtake it. He hoped he had not misjudged the journey. He had no intention of trying to get aboard mid-way, sure that Max would be safe until they had landed. He just hoped to God he would get there in time.

The storm was at its zenith when William landed on Tortola. He stood at the quayside waiting for the first sighting of the mail-boat. He knew he had overtaken it, but worried now that perhaps it had anchored in one of the inlets until the storm blew over. It was almost ten o'clock. He bought a bottle of brandy from the Harbour Bar. He felt stiff and cold. It had been the longest day and night of his life. Nothing he had ever been through had made him so emotionally drained yet so positive. He was there for Justin and he hoped to God that Max had come to no harm.

*

457

Max clung to the sides of the cabin as the boat thudded and rolled, the waves crashing over the deck. He was now wearing a cape and a safety harness hooked to the guard rail. He had gone below for a moment, but had started to vomit so had returned to the deck. Tears of fright mingled with the relentless rain; he could see nothing but blackness. The crew had started pumping out the bilges – they had taken in a lot of water. Using a rope and hook to edge along the railings of the deck, one of the crew made his way to the stern. He was shouting for Justin. There was no reply. He called again, screaming against the wind.

Then, to his horror, Max saw him, balanced like a trapeze artist outside the rails, arms raised, face tilted back.

'Justin! Justin!' Max's voice, too, was lost in the howling gale.

Justin remained upright for a few seconds. Then the boat banged against a twenty-foot wave and Justin sailed into the air, as if he was flying. His body lifted above the boat then dropped into the churning sea.

'Man overboard!' the cry went up.

'Justin! *Justin!*' screeched Max.

The crew risked their lives in leaning over the edge of the boat to find him in the swirling water, and the skipper turned on a searchlight, but there was nothing. Only the deafening howl of the wind, and the thundering waves. They searched for over an hour, before the skipper accepted that he was dead.

At midnight William saw the old mail-boat cruising into the harbour. The coastguards had been informed of a man overboard, but had been unable to launch a rescue craft. When the old boat dropped anchor, there was no mistaking the despair of the crew over the recent loss. William searched for Max. He was sobbing, but safe, being helped down the gangplank on to the jetty. His relief was short-lived however— 'Where's Justin?' he called, running towards Max.

Max's teeth were chattering, his whole body shaking, as he stammered. 'Overboard!'

William sagged. He didn't want to hear this. It couldn't be true.

The sun rose, an amber globe that turned into a deep crimson ball and seemed to come up from the sea-bed to send shimmering rays across the now quiet waters. William was on his way back to the island. All the way he scanned the ocean with his binoculars. As they passed the two jagged rocks, he looked up at Suicide Point, hoping to see Justin, but no one was there.

The coastguards had been searching, and reported that no body had been found. With the storm at its height when he went overboard, he might have been swept for miles down the coast. They continued their search, in small coves and inlets, but they knew there was no hope of finding him alive after twenty-four hours.

William left the boat and went up to the house for breakfast. He had not eaten for hours, and he wolfed down the food, though he tasted nothing. As the perfect day took hold news spread round the island. William saw huddles of gardeners whispering. One man, older than the others, was squatting on his heels, sobbing loudly. The boat-boys sat side by side, their legs dangling over the jetty, arms around each other. They had loved him too. Everyone here had loved Justin. He was there in every blade of grass, in every secret path, even in the air, perfumed by the blooms he had chosen.

As William was about to enter Laura's room, Dahlia appeared and drew him aside, inching the door shut behind her. They walked a short distance before she spoke. 'I can't believe it,' she said.

'Have you told Laura?' William asked.

She shook her head. 'On the night of the storm, she woke up. It was about ten o'clock. She seemed frantic. Then . . .' Dahlia started to sob. Eventually she blew her nose and her face puckered. 'She turned to me and said, "Justin has gone now. He's never coming back." I tried to calm her and said everything was all right, but she said, "No, Dahlia, Justin isn't ever coming back." How did she know?' William could say nothing to comfort her. As she gradually became calmer, she wiped her eyes. 'I said I would sit with her, and she thanked me. She didn't cry, Sir William, it was the most heart-breaking thing I have ever experienced. She said she didn't need me as he was with her, Justin was taking care of her.'

William entered the room and looked down at Laura. He was as memerized by her as he had been from the first moment he saw her portrait in his bedroom. Her silken hair was loose around her shoulders, her eyes were clear, the helpless look had gone. Her face, devoid of make-up, had a luminous quality.

'Hello, Laura.' His voice was a hoarse croak.

'Hello, Willy,' she said, patting the bed for him to sit beside her and reaching for his hand.

He was unsure of what to say. 'How did you know?' he asked.

'That he'd gone? Well, how could I not?' Her voice didn't waver. 'We have always read each other's minds. Since we were children.'

'I loved him,' William said, head bent.

'I know you did. He couldn't believe you meant it. You see, Justin always believed he could control everyone. But when you grew to love him, he didn't know how to handle it and then . . . you said something to him. You killed him,' she said.

William gasped. 'No – no! I never wanted him to leave.'

'Ssh.' She put a finger to his lips. 'You couldn't have understood. You told him you wanted to be like a father to him. Isn't that what you said?'

'But – but I . . .'

She lay back on her pillows. 'Our Father who art in Heaven . . . If he had stayed, Justin would have had to kill you, Willy, because a father figure represented evil to him. A father would control him, punish him, as our father did. You see, whenever we needed the strength to . . .' she couldn't bring herself to say 'murder' '. . . we would just remember our father and what he did to us. Then we could do whatever we wanted. It made it all right.'

William bowed his head. His eyes brimmed with tears.

'But he would never have *wanted* to hurt you, Willy, not you. He knew you would take care of me so it meant he was free. I have been a burden to him, I know that.'

William could say nothing.

'He didn't hurt Max, though, did he?' She smiled.

'No. Max is back in London now.'

Her face twisted and then she unfurled her fingers. 'Good. No harm done. And with no one finding Justin, he can't be buried, can he?' she asked, puzzled.

'I can arrange a memorial service.' William gulped.

'No, this island is memory enough. And he's here, William, he won't ever leave. I don't want any service, he only loved me, you and this island.'

Laura drew him into her arms as if he was a child.

'Marta will be here today,' he said.

'Marta will like it here. She will take good care of us.'

William's heart leaped as she said 'us'. 'Will you stay on?'

'I would like to stay here always,' she said, without any hesitation.

'I will never let you down, Laura. Please believe that, without him, you are now the most important person in my life.'

'Thank you,' she said.

Marta arrived late in the afternoon. William was waiting for her and held her tightly as she cried. He gestured for the boys to carry her luggage to the waiting golf cart, and hooked his arm through hers. Later she sat with William on the veranda, sipping a glass of chilled champagne. 'You can feel him here,' she said, 'in the plants, on the breeze.'

William nodded: he believed it. In some ways it had eased his grief. Marta's eyes filled with tears, and when she patted her pocket for a handkerchief, William handed her his.

'Thank you,' she said, and dabbed her eyes. She asked if he had noticed how often Laura said that phrase.

'I have. It's very endearing.'

Marta folded and refolded the handkerchief on her lap. 'It isn't. It's heartbreaking. If you were to rape her or to brand her with a red-hot iron, she would thank you.' Marta sighed. 'They were both forced to say it after whatever they had been subjected to. Justin used to say it as much as Laura. Once he stole some money from my purse, just some loose change, but I was angry. I smacked his hand and he looked at me and said, "Thank you." When he brought Laura home from the asylum, I used to watch him looking at her as she repeated over and over: "Thank you, thank you for the pain."'

'I am in such pain now, Marta,' he said bleakly.

'You are not to blame,' she said kindly.

'I am, Marta. I said I wanted to be a father to him. I know now it was the worst thing I could have said to him and, anyway, it was a lie. I was incapable of admitting to him, and to myself, that I wanted him to be . . .' he swallowed, unable to admit even now that he had wanted Justin in every way a man can love another man. He was still ashamed to acknowledge his feelings.

'You don't need to say any more, I understand. Remember I used to see you together, see the way he looked at you, and you at him?'

He leaned over and kissed her cheek. 'Marta, I will

protect Laura with my life. No one is ever going to hurt her again.'

Marta was frightened: he had to have an ulterior motive. William saw her anxiety and understood.

'I want only to care for her,' said William. 'Justin changed my life. I intend to come back here to live, because he is here. Here I'll be close to him.'

William's life took on a different perspective in the period after Justin's death. The coverage of Matlock's funeral was on the front page of every newspaper, and in all the television news broadcasts. Angela gave the performance of her life as the grieving widow, dressed by Valentino. At long last she was the focus of everyone's attention. James remained in a child-like state, dependent upon his mother, most of the time unaware of where he was, or that his father was dead. Max returned to the dominant arms of his mother as she searched for a suitable, rich wife for him. They rarely, if ever, saw the Baron whose downfall had been written up in the press world-wide. They now lived totally separate lives.

The Hangerfords divorced and Daphne was obliged to live in more meagre circumstances. The lack of money, however, meant that she lost more weight than she had ever done before and she felt considerably happier with herself. Clarissa discovered that her father had also plundered her trust fund and she conceded to finding work as a nanny.

William returned to London when Sabrina went into labour, producing robust twin grandsons. Considering her new 'free' lifestyle, she was appallingly conventional:

she had a Harley Street consultant and a private room at the Portland Clinic. Jacob remained steadfastly at her side, only rushing in and out to tell the pacing William that everything was going to be fine. When William held the babies he felt a tremendous rush of emotion. 'They'll love to play on my island,' he said to Jacob.

Charlie seemed to have got his life on some kind of path. He had formed a 'steady attachment' to a wisp of a girl, who made wheat-free pies and bread, and wanted to open a 'health-food café'. William discussed with him where it might lead, but could feel no deep, emotional bond with his son. He knew he should be ashamed of this, but his children had been brought up by Katherine and he had spent so little time with them. He set aside large trust funds for Sabrina, Charlie and his grand-children, even though he initially balked at the idea of making their future lives financially secure. Although William now accepted he would never be close to either his son or his daughter, he cared for them deeply. They were getting on with their lives, and he felt no guilt at cutting loose from them. He would always be there for Charlie and Sabrina, if they needed him, but he doubted it would be for more than money. He also drew up a new will, leaving vast sums to charitable foundations, particularly organizations against child abuse.

To his employees he became a calmer figure. One by one his companies were restructured to enable him to have as little to do with them as possible. Rumours spread that he had some incurable illness, and was preparing for death. Nothing could have been further from the truth, of course: he was preparing to live his life and to enjoy it to the utmost. But William had ceased to worry about what other people said. He knew that what you feel inside is more important than anything anyone else thinks.

While in England, William put in order his financial affairs, to leave him free to relocate to the island. He wrote to Laura every week without fail, and telephoned every two or three days. He hired an art teacher for her as she had begun painting, and he was delighted when she said she had been learning to sail. He became paternal, even over-protective, towards her, warning her not to go too far out when she swam, to use sun cream and always to wear a lifejacket. He loved to hear her giggle and call him an old fusspot. Laura became the child he had never been allowed to enjoy.

Marta gave him bulletins on Laura's progress, and she, too, sounded pleased to hear from him, saying how much they missed him. She listed the new plants she had put into the flower-beds and worried about over-spending: she was now keeping the household accounts. William enjoyed these lengthy discussions with Marta, who always asked his advice, even on the smallest matter. He liked her consideration, but above all he loved her honesty. Only half the staff had been retained on the island, and Dahlia had brought her son over to live with her. She and Marta had become friends and ran William's island home with an attention to detail that ensured it was always immaculate and ready for his arrival.

Over the course of a year, William saw his work come to fruition. He had handed over to others the day-to-day running of his business affairs. He had sold off many of his homes, and shares in his major US and Japanese companies. The last to go was his London house.

*

William was overjoyed to return to his paradise island and Laura. As the launch neared the jagged rocks, he saw her, way up on the cliff edge, waiting for him. His heart pounded: she was waving a big yellow towel to make sure he saw her. He watched her run down the path to be on the jetty as the boat came into the harbour. Laura was fit and filled with energy – she was a different woman. She ran towards him, arms wide. William picked her up and twirled her around. She clung to him, kissing his cheeks.

'Welcome home.' She held his hand, dancing alongside him as they headed for the golf cart, hopped aboard and drove him herself. She was full of a new confidence, pointing out all the plants and shrubs Marta had told him about.

As they reached the house, Marta came running down the wide stone steps. She hugged him, then both women insisted he inspect everything they had been doing to make the house into his home. After that he had to view Laura's paintings. Many were of himself, copied from photographs. His heart lifted so high it was flying.

Then Laura tugged at his hand, wanting him to go into his suite. 'But keep your eyes shut,' she said. He stumbled and she steadied him.

'Stop now,' she said, 'but keep your eyes closed.' She and Marta moved away from him. 'You can open your eyes now, Willy,' she said breathlessly.

Straight in front of him, in place of the painting of herself, Laura had hung a new picture. She had commissioned a well-known artist, recommended to her by her painting teacher, to execute a full-length portrait of Justin, barefoot, wearing torn jeans and white T-shirt.

His blond hair was bleached by the sun, and his skin deeply tanned. The artist had caught the way he tilted his head before his face creased into his wonderful smile.

'It's for you from me,' said Laura, searching his face for a reaction. She whispered in his ear that she had used her diamonds to pay for it.

William stood in front of the painting, his heart pounding. Laura had seen his dream. It was a dream he had often had since Justin had died, that one day Justin would return, that one day when William was heading back to the island he would see him waving from the high point and would watch him run to greet him as Laura had that day. Now William could walk into his bedroom knowing that Justin would always be there. It was painful, but the pain would be his reminder not only of what he had lost but of what he had gained. Slowly William smiled and his eyes filled with tears. All he could say in a soft, painful whisper was, 'Thank you.'

The island between islands by the sun and the sky deepened. The suns had eaten? the was a blur the road below his feet ground and he would not... "you met me," said Laura, look here for a moment. She whatever to but far than she not... been damned to pretend...

When stood in front of the patience, his head began. Laura had seen his dream. It was a thought he had often and since luxury had shot out one... the most would argue, that one day when William was a day under the island he would see him saying from the chair alone and would waited in chains into that... Laura had that day, New William would with saw the... saying enjoying that him around about to... It was cursed, but his pain would be too scorned. And only so that he had not but of what he had gained. Slowly William waited and movies to filled pictures. All he could say at event, pulled in more up? thank you.